# CUSTODY

## "BLOOD IS THICKER THAN WATER"

BASED ON A TRUE STORY

# DANIAL KENNETH MASON

Copyright © 2022 by Danial Kenneth Mason

Hardcover: 978-1-958381-58-8
Paperback: 978-1-958381-57-1
eBook: 978-1-958381-59-5
Library of Congress Control Number: 2022911386

All rights reserved. No part of this publication may be reproduced, distributed, or transmitted in any form or by any electronic or mechanical means, without the prior written permission of the publisher, except in the case of brief quotations embodied in critical reviews and certain other noncommercial uses permitted by copyright law.

This is a work of nonfiction.

SWEETSPIRE LITERATURE
——— MANAGEMENT ———

If you have a dream, then pursue that dream.
Life is like a circle and seasons come and go
and what you cannot achieve today
there is always tomorrow.

When you think all is lost, never give up.
Hope, have faith, and believe in what you can achieve.

—Danial K. Mason

# TABLE OF CONTENTS

# PREFACE

In the 1970s in Australia, United Kingdom, and New Zealand, a group was formed named Families Need Fathers (FNF). This was a registered charitable social care organization that provided information, advice, and support to parents whose children's relationship with them is under threat during or after divorce or separation, or who have become alienated or estranged from their children. This was due to the fact, as the research had shown, one-third of children from separated parents have no contact with their father. The organization is chiefly concerned with maintaining a child's relationship with both parents during and after family breakdown.

The law in New Zealand at the time favored the mother of the children as it clearly stated that a child or children under five automatically goes with the mother; in many cases, the father does not even get access to their children. The court and welfare system favored the mother despite what she may have or have not done.

In cases of domestic violence, when the father of the children is abusive toward his spouse/ partner or the children, then that is another issue, and the father in these cases should lose all his rights to protect his partner and the children. In these cases, FNF provides relief, assistance, guidance, and support to those parents.

In New Zealand, Families Need Fathers (FNF) group was founded in the 1970s. It is a registered charitable social care organization that provided information, advice, and support to parents, particularly fathers, whose children's relationship with them is under threat during or after divorce or separation or have become alienated or estranged from their children.

FNF also advocates for stronger court actions when a custodial parent defies court orders, requiring them to allow their children a relationship with the other parent. The goal is that children of divorce and separation should not lose the love and care of one of their parents.

FNF and other groups advocated for shared parenting, more time for children with their noncustodial parent, and stronger court actions when a custodial parent defies court orders, requiring them to allow their children a relationship with the other parent. The organization's goal is that children of divorce or separation should not lose the love and care of one of their parents.

This is very significant to the story you are about to read as this relates to a mother who dearly loved her son, a father fighting for his rights to have custody, and one little boy, three and a half years of age, torn between his mother and father when his mother left the family home and was the center of a hotly disputed custody battle.

My name is Danial Mason. I was born in Australia in 1944 in a town that was built in the gold rush era in the 1850s, a place called Bendigo, and this story starts in Australia. I was part of a very large family—ten boys and three girls—and I was the second youngest child. I have blond hair like my mother and elder sister, and the rest are like Dad with black hair.

I was called Smiley by many, but mainly at school, I was called Snowy as I had blond hair. We were what you called a not-so-well-off family, and my mum was something else. We went through very hard times when we lost our father. I was then seven years old. Noel was the youngest; he was four years old.

I decided to take on a journey at the age of twenty-one to venture out into the world, and the destination was New Zealand and the year 1966. I had no idea what was in store for me over the next ten years that took me to 1976 into a courtroom in Auckland, and I was embroiled in what was said at the time, *"This is a hotly disputed application for custody."* This remark reflected onto the unusual custody case, at that time recorded as being the longest custody case held in New Zealand with an unusual, overwhelmed verdict.

The novel *Custody* is nonfiction and is based on factual events set against me being the father and my quest to have the custody of my only son *Oliver*. One may say this was out of sheer revenge against the boy's mother, not a fight for justice. This clearly was based on an unfair legal system at the time to favor the mother, and as the law stated, any child under the age of five years automatically is awarded to the mother.

This ruling was a harsh and bitter one and set by the Child Welfare Justice System, and then I, being the father, set out to challenge this. This was a monumental challenge, and I faced many difficulties to find a lawyer who would represent me, let alone set out to try and win the case. The lawyer itself was a defining part of this extraordinary court case and how it all unfolded.

The story covers many incidents and events leading up to the court hearing. Some you will find hard to believe, but the mother left the family home and left her son behind and shifted in with her lover. Did the court have pity on her being the mother, or was this her undoing?

# THE STORY BRIEF

This is a story based on actual events. It became a bitter battle between the father, *Daniel Mason*, and his wife Claire over custody of their only son, Oliver.

First and foremost, this story is about the father's endeavors to keep custody of his son. Claire, his wife and the mother of his son, left the family home when Oliver was three and a half years of age. She had an adulterous love affair. She embarked upon defamatory evidence that she put in her submissions prior to any court case as she claimed that the father was a very violent person. He assaulted her and portrayed him as a potential murderer. Her many accusations were supported by her lover and her family.

A major point was, was her lover the best person to be the father figure in the child's life? As you will find out, her lover did have a shady past.

The father of the child *operated* a movie business and screened the latest movies to various clubs in and around Auckland, and also at his home where he had a very large home cinema. This raised many concerns that became a central part in statements proceeding the court case and was a contentious issue throughout the court hearing. These allegations were very damaging as they claimed he had shown blue movies. They also claimed he showed adult movies when his son was present and that he had him up at all hours when he should have been in bed. There were many allegations that he held drunken parties; then there were the questions relating to the Child Welfare Department as it was suggested by her lawyer that they assisted in his application for custody, which was farther from the truth. Then there were allegations against the kindergarten, then the issue about Claire's father being involved in domestic violence and his drinking. It was said at the time at the hearing by the judge, "I am very conscious of what the lawyer for the mother has said that one needs the wisdom of Solomon in a case as this.

The story covers the father's fight for justice to keep his son, Oliver, from being caught up in the trauma between his father and his mother. This resulted in bitter dispute along with arguments— the hurtful experience of a very fierce and intense court hearing for the custody of one little boy, Oliver. Despite the father's efforts to protect his son, the mother was very vindictive and created incidents, which also involved her family in particular her mother.

The racist slur by her brother and sister-in-law regarding the Māori children that Oliver played with was seen as racist and a slur against Māoris.

This story is all about justice, and in doing so, it is to give fathers the courage to challenge the welfare and court system to obtain custody or to have access of their children. Men are continuously wrongly accused, inasmuch of not being supported within the child welfare system or within the family courts. This often results to their children being taken away from them, the custody of the children awarded to the mother, and access denied to the fathers, and far too often, the mothers do fabricate stories that do influence the courts as well as the welfare system and lawyers and backed by injustice laws in favor of the mother.

It is also important to mention that in many cases, many fathers lose all credibility because of domestic violence and child abuse, and this always should be condemned by the courts and welfare and deal with them accordingly, and they do lose their rights to their children.

*The story and the court case the father was faced with was a huge dilemma* that he could not find a legal representative to take on his case, despite many efforts to find one to represent him. Then something extraordinary happened when he had a premonition to go to church on a particular Sunday, and at the service, there was a guest speaker who spoke about single mothers and the welfare system. He thought at this point that this was the reason why he went to church this particular day. After the service, the minister of the church introduced him to the guest speaker, who then heard the father's story and the difficulty he had and what he experienced finding a solicitor to take on his case.

Then what took place next was quite remarkable as the guest speaker arranged a meeting with a prominent barrister, a woman who was conversant in the family law and custody matters where she held a distinction in this field, and after hearing his story, she then took up his case. This was a blessing and a game changer for him.

He found that he was well supported by the church and lady lawyer; and as this unfolded, there were many issues, rights, and wrongs on both sides, although it came very apparent that the mother loved her son even though she walked out of the family home. It also became noticeably clear that she was a vindictive person along with her family as well as her lover—based on the lies and the exaggerated accounts of incidents, which were many and supported her in her endeavours so she can regain custody.

You will find this story as it unfolds as a compelling one when a high-profile lawyer defends a father in an unusual custody case never been held before in New Zealand—her professional manner and the understanding of her client, how she took on the case and presented the crucial evidence during the court case when all odds were against the father.

The presiding judge gave a lengthy judgment, and he had a challenging task to make his decision on evidence that was fabricated and damning toward the father, portraying him as a violent and potential murderer and that he also abused his wife.

This story is written by the accused, Daniel Mason, and outlines and deals with various incidents in detail prior to the court case as well given in evidence to support the mother's application for custody of the boy. It was also noted by the judge, and I quote, "I am satisfied that the father of the boy is aggressive when roused. I am also satisfied that there have been deliberate attempts to arouse him and to provoke him so that the mother's case could be better advanced in court."

It was also stated and should not be overlooked that the father of the boy was not totally exonerated. Inasmuch, the mother entered a world of lies and deceit and created violent scenes, as did her own family, and created incidents that neither took place nor were substituted or provided with credible witnesses to such events. This resulted to the father overreacting to many situations. What was the final outcome of the custody case? Did the court hold to the law where a mother

is awarded custody of a child under five? Did the mother get custody or the father? It was without question that "the welfare of the child is paramount," and the final decision was made on what was best for the child moving forward.

It is a well-established fact that a very large majority of separated people go through varying amounts of stress; this is regardless of if you're the one who was left or the leaver. In this case, there was a large and strong pull toward the marriage that Danial Mason cannot deny. As time went on, the situation worsened after the breakup, then at times anger and resentment made him detest his estranged wife. He found himself at times very alone as his family was back in Australia, unaware of the situation. He found himself in a very uncomfortable and, in fact, a lonely situation. Then again, he felt that if he was the one who broke up the marriage, then he may have done things differently. The person who was the most loved and dearest to him was his son, Oliver. It was his mission in life to make sure that his son remains with him.

Oliver's mother had different ideas, and her desire was not to give up her son. The anger she demonstrated and her fighting for the custody along with her family and her lover plunged into destructive behaviors and nonstop activity; and in many opinions, she became delusional and lost all sense of what was really taking place.

Danial Mason then became the enemy, and she spent every waking hour wrapped up in the past and what he was doing. She and her family became very hostile toward Danial. Danial was extremely lucky and fortunate that he had many friends who supported him along the way. Then of course, his religious beliefs and the guidance the church gave him helped in so many ways.

The ironic part of this story is that Mrs. Mason made Danial out to be the guilty one. He also was not quite sure if Claire may have had a split personality. Her claims to police and lies, including bizarre behavior, became a feature of her sometimes hard-to-believe allegations toward Danial—such as bizarre claims of him wanting to kill his son. Then one of her closest friends she knew from childhood came face-to-face with her in one incident. Many of Danial's friends became hostile enemies. Her accounts of things did become quite bizarre. Her secret love affair that went undetected added to the conflict that unfolded.

Anger and resentment finally made Danial detest his wife, Claire, whom he once dearly loved. He had hopes for her to come to her senses—this was not to be. He had no doubt that he played no part in the marriage breakup. This was despite her lies and deceit, her love affair, and her not taking full responsibility for her actions. Danial looked at his marriage to Claire as a legally binding and bonding relationship; and this, he found, was hard and difficult to give up. The shared intimacy and the shared parenting of their only son, Oliver, made this very upsetting. Her leaving the matrimonial home was devastating for Danial and very hard to comprehend and was upsetting. As it was, there was no turning back, and he came to the final conclusion it had to be.

*Footnote:*

*The interest or belief by anyone concerned about the ultimate impact of court proceedings and choices on a child's best interests makes this a must-read book. All this should be considered by a wide range of readers interested in child custody matters.*

# 1

# AUSTRALIA (1946–1966)

*My Story Starts in Australia in 1944*

It was in November just before the Second World War ended. It was a hot stinking day well over one hundred degrees when I came into the world, as recalled by my mother as she told me many years later having me nearly killed her. My father did not go to war. As it was said, at the time the war broke out when men were enlisted, my father was told he was too much of a liability to go to war as he had too many children. In fact, I was number twelve. Noel came a few years later, and that made up thirteen children. I was named Danial Kenneth Mason, after my father.

We lived in a very small house. It had two bedrooms, a small kitchen, a small lounge, and a bathroom. I am not sure how we all fit into such a small house, but we did.

For some reason, Mother did favor me in many ways, and it did show some resentment from the younger brothers. Father was very strict, and if visitors came, we all had to go outside. There was one time when a couple of the older brothers got into trouble. Dad would hitch them up on the old peach tree down the back of the yard and let them dangle by their braces. I was called Danny most of the time, and because I had blond hair, this changed to Snowy and sometimes Smiley as I always had a big smile.

Bendigo, where I was born and raised, had a lot of history—a city built on the foundations  of the gold era in the Victoria Gold Rush during the 1850s. It was once the richest place on earth because of the gold. People came from all over the world, in particular the Chinese as they have formed a great part of Bendigo's history and continue to the present day.

In 1908, Sidney Myer and his brother Elcon opened the first Myer store in Pall Mall, Bendigo. The brothers opened a second Bendigo store in 1911. Sidney Myer bought adjoining properties on Melbourne's Bourke Street and opened the Myer Emporium. In 1915, this then became their head office. The original Myer Store remains today.

After the war, Bendigo flourished and showed steady growth and opportunities, even though it was the post-war. Many families struggled to make a living while others progressed and met the challenges of the '40s and '50s. It was this period, and early childhood and upbringing, that played a very import part of my determination later in my life due to coming from a poor family.

My father worked day and night to provide for us. He had a market garden, a large property near Pyramid Hill; the block we called it. This was some fifty miles from Bendigo, and on this property, Dad grew lots of vegetables that supplied the local market. We had a dog called Bluey. He was a blue healer, and he was a very smart dog, and what Bluey did was remarkable. It is still hard to fathom how he knew his way home from the block. Bluey was always with Dad when he worked in the market garden.

As I recall on this day, I was outside playing out front, and Bluey turned up. I ran inside and yelled Bluey had come home without Dad. This was very odd as the block was many miles away, in fact around fifty, and then we all felt something was wrong. One of my elder brothers, George, went to the block, and he found Dad lying facedown in the paddock. It was apparent and a shock to George that Dad had passed away. It was only for Bluey coming home to Bendigo that alarmed us that something was wrong.

I was just seven years old at the time, and my father died at the age of forty-five. This was tragic and had a significant impact on the whole family and a huge burden for my mother to survive and look after thirteen children.

My mother was now left with thirteen children to bring up. The youngest, Noel, was only three years old, and the eldest was Boy, only eighteen years of age. It was extremely hard to imagine how my mother managed to look after us all on her own. Not long after Dad died, my mother struggled and worked endlessly to provide for the family, which drew the attention of the Child Welfare Department as she was confronted by them seeking to take all the younger children away and we to become wards of the state.

On this day, two welfare officers arrived at the house, stood at the front door, and told my mother that they will take all the young ones away as she cannot or could not manage all these children on her own—inasmuch that the young ones will become "wards of the state." My mother, in response to the two welfare officers who stood at the door, courageously picked up a broom that was resting at the front door and boldly told them in a nice and polite way that no way were they were taking any of her children. Defiantly she raised the broom at them and chased them out on to the street and shouted that they will never take her children away from her.

The overall incident (I remember it very well at that time as I was standing right beside her when they came to the front door) apparently was the way it was then. They—the system—did things in those days, and it was well known that the welfare could and would take children away without the consent of the parent/s.

It was well documented at that period that the Welfare Department took the indigenous children away from their parents as well as noncolored children, inasmuch as the Welfare Department took custody of children or a child from young girls who had children that the department felt that they could not support or who do not have support from the girl's parents.

This structure of receivership and custody over children did come into force when a parent or parents abused or neglected their children, as on many a case along with alcohol- and drug-related issues. It was unfortunate that in my mother's case, the welfare was trying to seize the children. It was none of the other cases listed, but through the misfortune of losing her husband tragically, with the task of being a great mother and provider for her children, as that was all that mattered to her, and all she wanted was her children, which was overlooked by the welfare system.

The Baptist church played a significant role in my mother's life. She was raised as a Baptist, she had strict beliefs, and she attended church every Sunday and made sure that all the children attended Sunday school and took part in the morning service—nicely dressed and well presented with a bonus that she gave us a penny for the plate, even though it may have been my mother's last penny. My mum was much loved by the church and well respected.

The gossip, which one could call rumors, spread around quickly about the welfare officers coming to our house. The minister at the Baptist church at the time heard about it, and so did most of the congregation. With my mother being a very staunch member of the church, the minister and members of the church decided to prevent Mother from losing her children. It was arranged that all the young children would go and stay at different church members' homes—an ideal arrangement until Mother got back on her feet, so to speak, and she could cope looking after us again without being stressed and bullied by the authorities.

All of us young ones were billeted out to good homes. We were all loved and cared for. It's worth noting that Welfare did come back to the house and, by this time, found that we were all settled in the various homes and being in the care of loving families. The minister of the church and the mayor at the time, along with church members, said there was absolutely nothing they (the authorities) could do about it, and the Welfare was duly notified by the church minister and the mayor of Bendigo.

I along with my brothers and sisters spent around six months away from our home. We all did get visits from Mum at the various homes we were all staying in. Each Sunday we would all catch up at Sunday school when Mum came to the church service. It was like a family reunion each week. My mum was a treasure, and how she handled all of us, as I look back, she made sure we were all well fed, clothed, and often and on most cases, she went without a lot of things herself.

The family I was privileged to stay with was a young newly married couple, and looking back on it now, I did give them a hard time. And being so young, just losing my father, and very unsettled as well as missing my mother and the rest from the family, I did cry a lot. But as time went on, I settled down as they were great people I stayed with. How grateful we were that the Baptist church rallied together to keep us all together as a family. The love and affection the minister and the parishioners did for our family was instilled in me throughout my life. There are so many bad things you hear about people, and this enshrined in me there are still very good people in this world who do lend a helping hand, particularly when people are in need, as I found out so early in my life.

My early life was not like a bed of roses. It was tough, but I would not change it for anything. I often envied kids who played sport with their dads, went camping, fishing; and when they talked about their dads, I missed that part of my life. Some of our older brothers did take me to the movies, or we played games.

We as a family always went to the annual *Sunday School Picnic*, allotted annually on the *Melbourne Cup Day*, a great church gathering, which took train rides on the huge steam train to a chosen location, but that was different from having your father around.

When growing up, I did see the event of television in 1956. It was September 16 and Channel 9, and Bruce Gyngell was the first person seen in-vision, introducing *This Is Television*. One of my older brothers, Milton, was a genius. He loved electronics, and he built his own television set, and we did see the 1956 Summer Olympic Games in Melbourne in November that year. As I was a bit of a larrikin growing up and loved playing tricks on people in a fun manner, when the Olympic torch toured around Australia, I was then twelve years of age, and I dressed up in white shorts and T-shirt and made a replica of the Olympic torch, and I ran down the main street with the torch with a large flame coming out of the top. The streets were crowded. As I ran down with the torch, people applauded as they thought it was the real thing. I heard someone in the crowd yell out, "It's Danial Mason!" It was a lot of fun until I was escorted off the road by a policeman who was not amused by my prank, and he said to me, "You did fool us all."

At the age of fifteen, I had to leave school. Things were difficult for my mum, and she could not afford for me to continue with school. I remember the day very well as it was my fifteenth birthday. Mum said to me, "Take this letter and give it to your teacher." I went off to school and handed my mother's note to the teacher.

The teacher read the letter and said, "Daniel, your mother cannot keep you at school any longer, and she wants you to leave today." The teacher was taken aback a little by the letter and could only reply, "I am sorry, Daniel, that I had to tell you this."

My only response was that I never said a word to the teacher and was emotionally upset. I went to my locker in tears, packed all the books and other gadgets I had, and stuffed them into my schoolbag. I went home all upset and said to Mum, "It's my birthday, and I had to leave school today."

Mum put her arms around me and said, "I know you will do well, but I just cannot afford to keep you at school any longer."

To me, the whole bizarre affair was a reality shock, and I thought, *Welcome to the big wide world. What unfolds, unfolds.*

The next day I looked for a job, and the first place I went to was an exceptionally large variety store, which was situated in the main street of the town. I went to the main office and asked if they needed any workers. I was taken quickly to have an interview with the manager. I was so nervous, and after the interview, he said that I could I start the next day. He also said, "Your brother John also works here." I said yes, and he did not know I had applied here for a job. I wanted to do this on my own. "Good for you," he replied.

I started work at the variety store the next day, and I was put in the storeroom, this being my brother's department. My pay was three shillings and sixpence for a whole forty hours per week. I thought I was in heaven having money to spend; I did give Mum most of it and kept what was left over for myself.

In the late '50s and into the '60s, self-serve grocery chains opened around Australia with threats of overtaking the small grocery shops. With the new threat of the supermarket, a new self-serve supermarket was opening in the town and looking for staff, as this was now the new era in grocery. I decided that I needed to move on, and having worked at the variety store for well over twelve months. I applied for a job, and I started there as an apprentice grocer.

I worked in the grocery business for over four years, and during this period, I met James, and we had a lot in common and got on rather well. We became great mates, and we spent a lot of time after work to go to football as oddly enough, we found out we both barracked for the same team. In 1964, we went with others from work to see the Beatles concert at Festival Hall in Melbourne. It was just hysteria, and the screaming was so loud, you could not hear them sing. At least we were there, and as years rolled on, the Beatles created history as their music and hysteria made them famous worldwide.

At the age of eighteen, I became assistant manager and then relieving manager and travelled around Victoria working at New World Grocery Stores operated by G. J. Coles. I left school at an early age, which made me a different person, and at the time, I did not understand many things. With the thought there would be no tomorrow, I did not have the education that I wanted or even needed. However, I made up for it by sheer determination, a willingness to learn, and I strived to do better by working hard and showed enthusiasm and took on any job given to me, where I found it was my success, and I did not need an advanced education. My willingness to work hard and learn was my success.

## *1962: Vietnam War*

In 1962, the Vietnam War had broken out, sending almost sixty thousand Australians, including ground troops and air force and navy personnel, to Vietnam where 521 died because of the war and over three thousand were wounded. By the end of the year, it had committed two hundred thousand troops to the conflict. In that year, compulsory national service for twenty-year-old males was introduced under the National Service Act of 1964. I had just turned twenty-one and was in the lottery draw, which was called the Vietnam Lottery for Service. The selection of conscripts was made by a sortation, which, in governance, sortition is also known as selection by lottery. This was the selection process of political officials as random samples from a larger pool of candidates or what they called a lottery draw based on date of birth. All conscripts were then obligated to give two years' continuous full-time service, followed by a further three years on the active reserve list. In 1966, the Australian Task Force was committed to Vietnam, and on *March 8, 1966,* it was announced that the Australian Battalion in South Vietnam will be replaced by a larger task force under Australian command consisting of 4,500 men.

I was very fortunate I missed out on the lottery draw by two days that was carried out in March in 1966, and I was not conscripted; but one of my best mates, Alex, whom I grew up with, did get conscripted, and he was one of the ones who did not come home. One of my best mates, David, who lived three doors down from where I lived, joined the air force. As history tells us, many Australians lost their lives, and there was a lot of controversy that surrounded the Vietnam War, and plenty of protests were held around Australia.

## *1964: The Beatles Tour Australia*

It was June 14, 1964, when the Beatles came to Melbourne, and they stayed at the Southern Cross Hotel in Bourke Street, Melbourne. It was estimated around one million people were outside of the hotel and filled the whole street, and they made their famous appearances on the balcony of the hotel and later at the Melbourne city hall. I was there with James and friends to witness this, and then three days later, we all went to the Beatles concert. This was a memorable occasion. The concert was held on June 17, 1964. The noise during the concert was electric, and you could not hear them sing. The girls were screaming and fainting; it was unbelievable to see. One thing was that I was there to witness such an iconic event.

*The Concert as Reported in the Newspapers.*

It was an iconic performance from the Festival Hall. It was the thick of Beatlemania. The band graced the country for thirteen incredible performances. The lineup consisted of John, Paul, George, and fill-in drummer Jimmie Nicol—Ringo missed the tour due to illness.

<h1 style="text-align:center">2</h1>

# THE NEXT CHAPTER IN MY LIFE

We arrived in New Zealand Airport, and it was around eight thirty, not long since dark. We picked up our luggage from the baggage hall. I turned to James. "Right. Let's ring that hotel and check out our reservations." We quickly located the airport's phone booths, and I called the hotel where we had booked before coming over, and we planned to stay for the night. And rather disappointing and frustrating, I found out they did not hold our booking, and the only option that we had do was to find somewhere else to stay. I said to James, "This is a great start to our venture."

Not knowing our next move, or for that matter where we would stay for the night, sleeping in the airport's lounge was an option. I noticed large tourist posters showing major tourist sites and another large sign, "Visitors' Kiosk." Under the heading was written "New Zealand Government Tourist Bureau." We wandered over to the visitors' kiosk where a woman of Māori heritage met us. I explained to her that the hotel did not hold our booking, and we had nowhere to sleep for the night. She beamed with enthusiasm. "No worries. We'll just have to find somewhere for you two boys." Very efficient, well-organized, very lovely manner, and helpful, she smartly called around to various hotels and hostels and very quickly found a hotel in the city. She had the right approach, and we got a good introduction to a new country. She was very pleasant and welcomed us both to New Zealand. This was the first time I met a Māori and was very impressed, and she gave me a slip of paper with the address on it and said the hotel was expecting us. She turned and picked up a phone. "You boys hang on for a minute. You'll need a cab to get you to that hotel." We waited no more than several minutes; she put the phone down and said, "There's a cab waiting for you outside in the taxi rank, just outside our main exit door."

We sat back in the cab, relaxed, as now things did not seem all that bad. The Māori taxi driver was a very chatty fellow, and he asked, "Where you boys from?"

We told him we were from Melbourne.

He laughed. "Maybe I will see Melbourne sometime?" He pulled up in front of the hotel right in the city center. I paid the driver and thanked him. He smiled, and then he asked me if I could pay him in Australian dollars as *Australian currency* was worth more in New Zealand. I said that I am sorry because I exchanged my money at the airport. After I paid him for the fare, he said, "You guys have an enjoyable time, and welcome to New Zealand."

The first night was a bit ordinary. It was a low-budget hotel, not that flashy, but will get us through to the next day as our next move was to find a flat or unit where we could stay.

The next day we went to a local estate agent in Auckland, where we were told that there was a shortage of flats and units. The cost was, at that point, over the top, and knowing that we had to find somewhere to stay, the agent said, "We have a listing of a boardinghouse in *Herne Bay* very close to the city, and it has some vacancies. I am sure it will be suitable for you and your friend. You would have your own room, but share the bathroom, kitchen, and lounge."

I said to him "Yes, it sounds ideal. We will take that." I agreed as we had to have a place to stay. We hurried out to Herne Bay in a taxi with our luggage and arrived at the boardinghouse in Mascot Avenue, which had a great view across the harbor. We were greeted by the landlord, and he was a *"Pom,"* a rather tall person, and he had strict rules. He said, "No parties, no girls allowed, and pay your rent on time. Keep the kitchen clean and your room. There is cleaning stuff in the cupboard and a vacuum cleaner, and I will do a weekly inspection."

The place was very old and a bit dumpy, and we had no option but to take it. Jimmy and I paid the landlord four weeks in advance, so with that, we moved in and quickly settled in. Later that day, we met up with the others who stayed at the boardinghouse as this was a very large boardinghouse with many rooms. All the boarders congregated in the communal lounge. Most of the people staying there were on working holidays like we were, except one who was a permanent, and he was hard at times to understand.

The next important thing to do was to find some work, as we did come over with limited cash as we were told there was plenty of work in New Zealand. I had exceptionally good references from my church and employer back home in Australia along with character references as they were important if you were looking for work.

The following day, it was a Tuesday. I went to one of the large department stores, and my interview went very well; and with my experience in retail and management and the employment manager really liking my references, I started the next day. This was great as at least I could start earning some money. And that day as well, James got a job in a downtown hotel as he had particularly valuable experience in working in hotels as a barman, apart from his supermarket experience.

We both decided to have a beer and celebrate, so we headed off to Ponsonby, an inner-city suburb of Auckland located two kilometers west of the Auckland CBD, all just a ten-minute drive from the city center. We went into a local pub called the Glue Pot, which was close on the way back to our boardinghouse.

On entering the pub, we realized that it was full of smoke and very noisy, and I noticed it was full of islanders and Māoris, and we were the only whites in the place. I looked at Jimmy and said that I was not sure if we should stay here or not. Immediately as I said this, a big Māori guy came up to us.

He was at least six foot six, and he said to me, "Bro, where you boys from?" We replied, "From Melbourne, Australia."

He said he'd never been to Melbourne but had been to Sydney. He asked, "How long you boys been here?"

We said, "A couple of days."

He then invited us over to his table, and he said to meet his brothers, as he called them. We had a few beers with them, and I found that the Māori people were lovely and friendly. They told stories about the All Blacks as rugby was like a religion to them. We did not stay much longer than we expected.

Well, after leaving the pub, I said to Jimmy, "The people here are very friendly and amazing and made us very welcome." I learned this area was predominantly islanders and not so many Māoris lived in this area.

We did visit that pub a few times, and each time they remembered us from the first time. It was convenient as the trolley bus stopped right outside, and we used to get off there and then walk from the pub to our boardinghouse.

I started work the next day at the department store, and I was placed in their food court. This suited me down to the ground as it was exceedingly small, like a mini supermarket. I found the store staff exceptionally good, and I soon fit into my job. The manager said that next year, New Zealand will be changing over to decimal currency, and it would be an immense help as I had just experienced this changeover in Australia.

I agreed and said, "I can be of great assistance as it went very smoothly as long as you have the right training for staff well before the event."

The store department manager, Mr. Sheldon, agreed with me, and he said I could call him Peter, and we did get on very well.

I celebrated my twenty-second birthday during my first week in New Zealand. Peter, along with Jimmy, and I invited a few others from work to get more acquainted with them, and we all went out to dinner.

Peter suggested a nice restaurant in Auckland we could go to dine and have a few drinks. We all had a good time, and I made sure it was not a late night because of work the next day. As time moved on, Jimmy and I settled into Auckland, and we had good jobs, which paid well. We were living in the suburb of Herne Bay where I eventually became a member of the local Presbyterian Church. On Christmas Day, James and I went to the *Christmas Day Service*, and we were invited to Christmas dinner with one of the church leaders, a *Mrs. Fields*, and both of us went there, and we had a lovely Christmas dinner and spent the rest of the day at her house. She worked as a receptionist/nurse at a *doctor's surgery*. Dr. Henderson was also an elder at the church.

Mrs. Fields was a widower, and we became particularly good friends. She helped me in many ways in my early days in New Zealand. She was a devout Christian, and she had lost her husband due to a serious illness, and she also liked the company of other people, and often she invited us to her place.

It was through Mrs. Fields that I learnt a lot about New Zealand, and it was through her that I became a Sunday school teacher at the church. I think having a connection also with the church did help me in many ways as this enabled me to meet a lot of new people of all ages, from the young and old, and helped me settle into the country much easier.

The department store where I was working was closed over Christmas, and I had the normal Christmas period holiday and would start back on January 2. In this period, Jimmy did not waste time in finding a girlfriend, as he met her at the hotel where he was working. And on New Year's Eve, Jimmy and his girlfriend and I all went to downtown Auckland to ring in the New Year of 1967. My first two months in New Zealand was great, meeting people and landing an excellent job, and I became very settled in many ways.

When I was in Australia working in supermarkets, I had an uncanny knack for picking out shoplifters and catching them. Most times it was because of their unusual behavior. Now while I was at the store for just a short time, I noticed different staff going to the in-store post office sometimes on a daily basis. To me, this looked very suspicious. I mentioned this to my manager, and he said, "We will look into this," so a store detective was alerted. Within a week, the loophole was closed down as some staff were sending parcels out without paying for the goods. The issue was also the store has a post office right opposite the food hall and was easy for staff to steal stock and send this out to relatives and friends. The post office staff would not think of this as out of the ordinary as they thought it was customer purchases. I know this finding was appreciated by the management, and they never told anyone who the source was who detected this. The store detective was not doing his job.

# 3

# 1967—THE YEAR I MET CLAIRE

Well, another year had gone, and who knows what this year would bring. I started back at the department store, and it was good to get back earning some money again. The following Sunday was January 7, and New Zealand held the Formula One car race, so I went along with Jimmy James. We headed on a bus to Pukekohe, which was down south of Auckland. I was very interested in Formula One car racing and thought this was also a good way to see some more of New Zealand. Going down on the bus, I could not get over how plush and green everything was. We arrived around 10:00 a.m. and soon found a good advantage spot to see the race, and as I recall, the race had nineteen starters, and it was a great day with plenty of crashes. Jackie Stewart won the race, and our Australian Jack Brabham crashed out, and it was not far from where we were watching the race. On the way back, there was a fatal car crash at a railway crossing, which held up the traffic for miles, and we arrived back in Auckland some three hours later than anticipated.

Well, my hopes and dreams to venture on from New Zealand, as what we both planned, may not be on the agenda anymore. It was this year when I met Claire. I never would have dreamt that I would meet a girl and stay in New Zealand. Our plans to go to Canada was not even mentioned as Jimmy found himself a nice girl and was now content to stay on in New Zealand.

I loved my work in the department store and made friends with many. I found most people I met easy to get along with, and the people at the church, in particular Mrs. Fields, was like a mother figure to me. There were many times, being away from home in Australia, I had my moments, and after chatting with her, things seemed a lot better. Most Sundays after church, she would have us over for either lunch or dinner. I offered to bring something, but she insisted we don't as she appreciated our company.

It is strange how things seem to fall into place as I settled back into work after the Christmas and New Year break. The work I was doing was well recognized by the management, particularly Peter, whom I did get on very well with. He told me that training for decimal currency conversion was starting soon, and he said with my experience, I should be part of the team. So in early February, I was selected to work with the management team in the main office on the staff decimal currency conversion training.

So fate happened as this was where I met Claire. I did often see this young girl around the store and thought I would love to meet her; she was very attractive, and I used to see her glide past, and she was wearing a pink smock, and so did other women who worked in the office. So I then guessed right—she was one of the office staff.

The day I started in the head office, I did get a chance to say hello to her. She was working at her desk, and I introduced myself to her. She said, "I know who you are as you have only been here a few months, and I do your pay-up each week."

I said, "I would love to meet up with you some time, and we may have a coffee after work." She said to me, "I will think about that."

Oh, I thought I may have a chance here, so I did see her often in the office. We said hello to each other. On this day I was in the staff canteen; I went there most days as the food there was exceptionally good and only then one pound per meal as this was subsidized by the company. This day I was in the queue buying my lunch, and Claire was in front of me. I leaned over and said quietly, "Do you want to share a table with me?"

Claire replied in her soft voice, "Yes, I would like that." Claire waited for me until I got my lunch, and I picked out a table for us both. We sat down, and Claire spoke in a very quiet voice, and we chatted over lunch, mainly about where I came from and what I was doing in New Zealand and if I planned to stay.

I said, "Depends, I suppose. This is a great country, and the people here are very friendly, and I just love the Māori culture." We seemed to hit it off, and over the next few weeks, we did.

We met regularly for lunch at the staff canteen. I eventually got the courage to ask Claire out. I suggested to Claire we could see a movie or dinner.

Claire replied, "Yes, I would love to. Before you take me out, you will have to meet my parents first."

I was a bit taken back by this. *Oh well*, I thought, *if that is what a man has to do to take her out, so be it.* I said this was fine by me. I was not sure how old Claire was, and one day at the canteen, she told me that she would turn eighteen soon.

Claire told me, "My father is very protective of me. My mother is too, but not like my father." With that, I arranged to meet her parents on the following Saturday afternoon as they lived on the North Shore. I had to board a bus that went over the Harbour Bridge. I could have taken the ferry, but I decided the bus would be quicker.

I finally arrived at Claire's place. Their house was on the main highway Ocean Road, and luckily, it was not far from the bus stop. I walked up the pathway, and I knocked on the door. In a few minutes, the door opened, and a stubby man stood there. He seemed rather youngish-looking, and he said, "You're Daniel?" I said yes, and he shook my hand and said, "I am Kevin. Please come in."

Then Claire appeared at the door, and she said, "I see you already have met my dad." With that, she introduced me to her mother, Rose; then there was her older brother, James; and the younger brother, John.

On first appearance, I thought, *What a lovely family.*

Rose, her mother, said, "Claire has told us a lot about you."

I was invited to have lunch with them. Rose fussed over me and made sure I had plenty to eat. After lunch, we all ventured into the lounge room, and Kevin, Claire's father, said, "You plan to take Claire out?"

I said, "Yes, if you are okay with that."

He replied, "Yes. You seem like a pretty decent fellow."

It was arranged then, so I said I would take Claire out to dinner as seeing it was our first date, so to speak; and if Claire agreed going to a restaurant, then that was what we would do.

Kevin said, "I will bring Claire into the city around 7:00 p.m., and we can meet in Hobson Street."

I said, "I will then bring her home."

Kevin said in a stern voice, "Make sure it's not too late as she is only seventeen, you know." Claire yelled out, "Yeah, Dad, I will be eighteen soon."

We all chatted for a while, and Kevin told me about his work where he was a supervisor in a food processing plant, and Rose worked in a clothing factory a few days a week. James was a builder and an exceptionally good football player, and John was still at school as he was ten years of age, the youngest of the family. Well, that was the family I had met, and this family becomes a major part of the story that unfolds.

Rose said to me, "When you bring Claire home tonight, you can stay here as we have a spare room."

I said, "Thank you. I will take you up on the offer." I then added, "I will get a cab from the city to make sure I get her home on time."

Rose said, "Do not take much of her father as his bark is worse than his bite," and she laughed. I did observe her father was watching the races and had a big bottle of pint-sized beer.

It was around 3:00 p.m. when I left Claire's place, and I caught the bus back into the city. Kevin did offer to take me, but I said, "No. It's okay. I will catch the bus." At this point, I did not have a car, so I had to rely on buses and taxis.

When I arrived back in the city and caught the trolley bus back that stops at the end of my street, it was getting very late in the afternoon and not much time to get ready. I had a shower, and I put on my best suit. Around six thirty, I caught the trolley bus back into the city and arrived around 7:00 p.m. where Claire's father, Kevin, was dropping her off in Wyndham Street near the hotel. I was there only a few minutes when Kevin pulled into a parking bay, and Claire got out of the car. I thanked her dad and said to Claire she looked so lovely. Claire suggested the hotel in Wyndam Street. Claire said they have good food there, and her family had been there many times before. I said this was good enough for me.

We walked to the entrance, and the bouncer at the front door said I was too young to go in. He then said, "Your girl can," and I was taken aback by this.

I said to the bouncer, "I am twenty-two years of age," and he then asked for ID, but I did not have a license or any ID to show him.

He said, "Sorry, you cannot come in," so we had to leave the hotel. I thought, *This is a great start for our first date.*

Claire said, "I know a good restaurant, but we would have to grab a cab as it's in Khyber Pass." I hailed a cab, and we shortly arrived at the restaurant. It was the El Matador, and it looked impressive. As we did not have a reservation, however, we were lucky they had a table for two left. It was said to us Saturday nights are usually hard to get into the restaurants unless you book. Lucky for us, there was a cancellation. We were shown to our table by the waiter and seated, and I said to Claire, "Wow, what a restaurant."

The waiter then asked what we would like to drink. I was shown the wine list, and Claire picked out a bottle of sparkling wine.

"This wine," she said, "is from a very famous winery, Corbans. It is just out of Auckland, in the region they call the Henderson Valley."

The waiter told us it was a good choice. I did agree it was good wine, and so did Claire. We had prawn cocktail first and followed by their prime steak. I was told by Claire their steaks were renowned for excellence. The steak was marinated and melted in your mouth. We enjoyed a great meal, and I said to Claire the food was really something, and we must come back here again.

Claire said, laughing, "You're getting ahead of yourself. Yeah." She smiled. "We must come back again."

Our first date was a very memorable night.

We then caught a taxi from the restaurant and returned to Claire's place on the North Shore around 11:30 p.m. Kevin, her dad, was still up, and the rest of the family were in bed. Kevin, I found, was a very heavy drinker, and he was very intoxicated when we returned. Kevin asked me to have a beer with him, and as Claire and I already had a few glasses of wine at the restaurant, I said to Kevin, "Just one," as I did not want to offend him.

Claire said, "I will make coffee while you're having a beer with my dad."

I chatted for a while with Kevin, and he called it a night. Claire took me to the room where I was to bunk down for the night, and she told me this was John's room. I thanked her for a good night and gave her a good night kiss and said, "I will catch up with you in the morning."

There was a pair of PJs that Rose left out for me, and I changed and slipped into the PJs. I jumped into the bed and went to sleep, thinking what a catch I had in Claire.

During the night, I was in a very deep sleep. I suddenly woke up screaming in pain, and there was Claire's younger brother, John. He had a wooden stick and was hitting me and screaming at me. Claire and her mother rushed in, and Rose grabbed the stick from John. It was what they called a copper stick used mainly in the laundry. It was a solid wooden stick, and it bloody hurt! I was bleeding heavily as I had a head wound, and my arms were badly bruised as well. This was because I had stretched out my arms in front of me, trying to protect myself.

Rose came running into the room and screamed at John and said, "Why did you do that?" John did not reply and ran back to James's bedroom where he was sleeping. Claire was terribly upset about what had happened and stayed with me for a while. Rose cleaned the wound and put a bandage around my head. It did not require stiches as it just grazed the skin that caused all the bleeding. Rose said repeatedly, "I do not know why John did this. I am so sorry."

I looked at the clock in the lounge room. I could see from where I was sitting it was 3:00 a.m. I finally did get a few hours' sleep, and next morning, Claire was still visibly upset over this incident as well as Rose. Kevin was unaware as he slept right through the whole commotion. Rose made a lovely breakfast for me as she cooked up bacon and eggs, one of my favorites, and brewed coffee.

Rose said, "I do hope you're okay, and please don't think bad of us."

"No," I said, "things happen." I was trying to be diplomatic. I tried to smooth things over by saying, "I think John was upset that I was in his room and on his bed. I can understand that."

When Kevin finally got up just before I left, he offered me a ride back to the city. I said, "No, it's fine." I also had in my mind his drinking to all hours that maybe he was still rather intoxicated, and I did not want to take such a chance. I said, "It's okay as I will catch a bus back to the city."

I thanked Rose for the lovely breakfast and for allowing me to stay for the night. I said jokingly to both Rose and Kevin, "I hope to see you all again soon. I suppose it is up to Claire."

Claire walked me to the bus stop, and she said, "I cannot understand why John did this to you." I said to Claire, "Look, what has happened, we just have to put it all behind us."

Claire then said to me repeatedly, "I hope this does not stop you from seeing me again." I replied, "Claire, no, it won't."

We embraced each other.

Claire gave me a big kiss as the bus was approaching and said, "I am so happy meeting you."

I said to Claire, "I am very happy too, as you're such a lovely person. I will see you at work tomorrow."

I know when I left Claire, she was still very upset about what happened, and as the bus was leaving, she stood at the bus stop for a while as the bus was disappearing down the road and threw me a kiss.

I pondered on the way back to the city on the bus. I thought what happened with John was like out of a horror movie, and it reminded me about Alfred Hitchcock's movie *Psycho*. I wondered what I had gotten myself into with this family; however, this did not deter me from seeing Claire. Next day I was working with the staff for the decimal currency conversion, and Claire came up to me and gave me a nudge and asked, "Are you okay?"

I replied, "Fine, how about you? We had a great time Saturday night, I hope we can do this again soon."

She replied, "Why not we meet for lunch?"

I got the feeling Claire liked me as I sure liked her, and I was not sure how this would pan out for us, but I arranged to take her out again the following weekend.

It was Claire's eighteenth birthday, and I went with their family to the hotel where I was not allowed in. Kevin paid for the meal and drinks. I did offer, but he refused. He said, "Son, this is on me."

We had a very good night, and I gave Claire a designer watch for her birthday, and she just loved it.

Working in the head office also allowed me to see Claire every day. The training for the changeover to decimal currency was on July 7, 1967, and this day went very smoothly. I was thanked by the management for my assistance.

Throughout the rest of the year, I spent a lot of time with Claire, and in the meantime, Jimmy, my good friend who came to New Zealand with me, decided he wanted to go back to Australia. He left New Zealand and went on to Sydney, and him leaving left me paying for the room we shared. On my own, it became unaffordable.

I then decided to look for another place that may be a lot more affordable. As fate happened, I discussed this with Claire, and she told me about her grandmother. She told me that her Gran was her mother's mother. Her grandmother lost her husband last year. She said her grandfather was a good man, and her grandmother sadly missed him.

Her grandmother had a spare room in her house. The house was a small dwelling, and she lived in an outer suburb of Auckland, which was about twenty minutes from the city. Claire took me over to meet her grandmother. She was such a lovely lady. She said to me to call her Gran, so I did. We got on very well, and Gran said I can move in as a boarder as she had a spare room that I can have, and I did not have to pay any rent to her except help with the food bill.

This just seemed too good to be true! I shifted in later that week as I had little luggage. It was an easy shift, and over the remainder of the year, we spent increased time together, and on weekends, Claire stayed at her grandmother's place.

*Buying My Own Car*

It was costing a lot of money in taxis and buses, and now that I was earning a very good wage, I decided that I needed a car. I was banking at ANZ Mount Roskill branch, and I arranged to meet the bank manager to see if I could get a loan for a deposit on a car. As I was banking at the branch, he could see what I was earning, and he said he would give me a loan.

So with that, I went out and picked out a secondhand car from a dealer in Mount Roskill as I now had enough for the deposit, and the bank loaned me the rest. The car I purchased was a Holden sedan, and it was in very good condition. I did bring with me to New Zealand an international license issued from Australia, and I used that instead of obtaining a New Zealand license as I thought my international license would suffice.

How wrong I was. One day I was driving along the road in Point Chevalier, and the lights changed yellow as I approached. There was a truck alongside of my car, and he drove through the yellow light like I did, and by the time we crossed the intersection, the traffic lights turned to red. Then suddenly, a cop came up behind me with his lights blazing and his siren blaring. I stopped the car, and the cop got out of his car and said I went through a red light.

I said, "No, Officer, I did not. When I entered the intersection, it did change yellow. I thought it would be very dangerous to stop, so I continued on. What about the truck that was alongside me? He went through the same time as me."

The cop said, "I am not interested in the truck." He was a bit on the nasty side, and he said abruptly, "Where is your license?"

I showed him my international license, and he said, "How long have you been in New Zealand?" I said, "A few months."

The police officer said, "This international license is for a brief period only. Sir, is this your car?" "Yes, it certainly is," I told him.

Then in a rough voice, he said as he stood over me like a giant (he was at least six feet eight inches), "How do I know it's yours?"

"I have the papers in the glove box, and it's all in my name, plus the car passed the warrant of fitness." I showed him the papers.

The cop said, "Its obvious you're working here and intend to stay. You need to obtain a New Zealand driving license. I am giving you an infringement notice, and you will be summoned to go to court. In the meantime, you can drive with your international license, but I will keep a check on you and make sure you get the New Zealand driver's license." The police officer gave me the ticket. I said, "Thank you" as I drove off. I thought it was best to be nice to him, even though he was on the grumpy side.

A few months later, I did get a summons in the mail to attend a driver refresher course in Auckland, and it stated if I do not attend, then I will have to face court. With that, I had no option. I went along to this driver refresher course. It was held by the traffic road police, and the officer who conducted the course said at the opening address, "A number of you here tonight are here voluntarily or by summons."

As it turned out, I was summoned to go as I held an international driver's license, and seeing I had overstayed the permit, I had to attend these sessions. After two sessions, the officer in charge asked why I was made to come here. I explained what happened, and he said to me, "Okay, you're released from these meetings. Please apply for your New Zealand license."

Lucky for me, I did not get a fine but just a warning, and shortly after did I obtain my New Zealand driver's license.

Later in the year, New Zealand introduced the end of the six o'clock swill bar closing times as this was extended to 10:00 p.m. It was on October 9, 1967. This of course followed Australia as Australia did bring this in the previous year.

New Zealand's 6:00 p.m. closing for pubs had been introduced as a wartime measure in 1917 and made permanent the following year. The term "six o'clock swill" means the practice of drinking as much beer as possible before closing time. Several generations of Kiwi men as well as Australian grew up in a binge-drinking culture.

This night, I went along with a few guys from work, and we all went to a downtown pub to be there. When six o'clock came, it was like mayhem. I experienced this in Australia the year before. There was shouting and much excitement, and the pub owner gave everyone a free beer. It was an occasion to remember. I was not a big beer drinker myself as my mates would drink, say, three to my one.

It was in October that year Claire decided to leave the variety store. Claire landed herself a very good job at an accountant's office in the city as an accounts machine operator. This office was only a few blocks from the store where Claire and I worked. I did arrange to have lunch together most days, and we met at a nearby café. I did miss my lunches at the store canteen as they were so good and inexpensive.

The year did finish on a high note as I spent Christmas with Claire's family. I did call home to speak to Mum and some of my brothers and sisters who were home at the time. Meeting Claire was the highlight of the year. She was a lovely girl, and I really enjoyed her company.

I wondered what next year will bring, as it seems at this point that the travel to other places is out of the question. With Jimmy gone back to Australia and having now a girlfriend and an excellent job, this made me very settled. I always thought Australians as very friendly people, and no one can beat that. I think New Zealand must come a close second.

It was early in the year when the then manager of the food store left. I was promoted to manager of the food department, and this gave me extra money each week, which was exceptionally good, and this helped me pay the car off more quickly.

As the year progressed, I spent a lot more time with Claire's family, and a lot of things happened. I also started to see another side of Claire's family. The father, as I was convinced, he did drink quite excessively.

Sometimes when I was not having lunch with Claire, I would go and have a counter meal at one of the pubs in downtown Auckland with some of the guys I work with. On this day as we headed down Queen Street, I spotted a sleek white convertible, and there were young girls screaming and running down the street, and they crowded around this white convertible.

I asked, "Who is that?"

"Oh, that is John Rowles. He is a very famous singer in New Zealand."

"Oh yes, I have heard his songs on the radio. I reckon he sounds like Tom Jones."

We had trouble walking past as the crowd got bigger, and people came from everywhere.

I said, "Well, that's the price you pay to be famous." He had a brother also who was a good singer. His name was Lou Rowles, but not as good as his brother John, I thought.

It was on April 9 this year that a massive disaster happened in New Zealand. when I was watching TV, the show was interrupted by a news flash, and it said the Union Steam Ship Company's 8948- ton roll-on-roll-off passenger ferry the *Wahine*, the largest ship of its kind in the world that was completed two years earlier, left Lyttleton on the South Island of New Zealand at 8:40 p.m. on the evening of April 9. There were 734 passengers and crew on board. Storm warnings had been issued, but rough seas were nothing new in Cook Strait. As it turned out, the *Wahine* was about to sail into one of the worst storms ever recorded in New Zealand. The ship reached Cook Strait as tropical cyclone Giselle swept south and collided with a southerly front. The combination of warm tropical air and chilly air dragged up from Antarctica produced exceptionally violent turbulence. They said would-be rescuers stood helplessly on the beach at Seatoun as the *Wahine* succumbed to Hurricane Giselle. They said this was one of the worst storms recorded in New Zealand history and was, at that time, the deadliest modern maritime disaster and would ultimately claim fifty-three lives.

It was a sad day for New Zealand. Everyone next day at work were all talking about it.

## Change of Work

It was midway through the year, and I had a few days off. I went into a supermarket in New Lynn as this was not far from Gran's house, and I picked out a few items in the store. At the checkout, a voice said, "It's not Daniel, is it?"

I looked up, and I said yes. To my surprise, the checkout girl was Patricia, and she worked in one of the stores I managed in Australia. "Well," I said, "fancy seeing you here! How long have you been here?"

"Oh," she said, "a couple of years as I married a Kiwi." "Great!" I said. Patricia asked, "What are you doing here?"

I said, "I came here on a working holiday and have met a lovely girl and decided to stay here. I am working in a department store in the food department in the city. I have just finished my annual leave and will go back next week."

Patricia said, "I am due to having a break soon. Why don't we meet up at the coffee lounge just across from here? We can have a chat as it is good seeing you again."

On my way over to the coffee shop, I said to myself, *What a coincidence meeting up with Patricia!*

I was her boss for a while when I was relieving manager in the grocery store back in Melbourne. I wandered over to the coffee lounge, and shortly after, Patricia arrived. She sat down, and we

chatted over old times. Then she told me the food company Foodrite was looking for managers as they were very short on staff. Patricia said, "Why don't you apply as they pay very well, and with your experience, you should consider it?"

I said, "I will think about that as it does sound exceptionally good. It does sound promising."

Patricia said, "I must go back to work." She wrote on a napkin the name of Mr. Jackson and his phone number, and she told me to call him.

I thanked her very much and said, "It was great seeing you again, and yes, I will follow up and call this Mr. Jackson."

I did call him that week and had an interview the following Monday, and soon, I was given a trainee manager's position on the North Shore of Auckland, Takapuna.

I left the department store two weeks later. I had to undertake training as trainee manager for a period of three months at the Takapuna store on the north shore. Well, after three weeks, I was called into the office on Friday night by the manager and was told that as of Monday, I had to report to the store at Henderson. "You will be met by Mr. Jackson at 8:00 a.m. at the store, and as of Monday, you will be appointed by Mr. Jackson to be the manager of the New Lynn store."

I met Mr. Jackson at the supermarket at 8:00 a.m. the following Monday, and he introduced me to the staff. As I already knew Patricia, this made my transition to the role as manager easier. I soon settled into the job. The staff was very good. Patricia looked after the front end of the store and the checkout girls. I had a store man who I was not that impressed with, and I fired him for stealing when I was only a few weeks into the job.

The fruit and veg manager, Frank, was a Pom, and we got on very well together. We would often sit in my office, and we discussed the share market. He put me on to a broker, and I traded shares for a while, and I did make some extra money out of this as I got very good inside information.

In the job as manager, I had to undertake store displays and produce creative ideas. One display had my photo with the display in the grocery magazine as I built a giant castle made of Kellogg's Corn Flakes. The rep was so impressed, he took a photo, and that ended up in the grocery magazine. In my capacity as the manager of the supermarket, I met many representatives as well as sales managers. One in particular was the sales manager from Crest Foods. He came in regularly, and he always asked me to come and join them as he said they wanted people like me who were creative.

He said, "I would give you a job."

I thanked him for the offer, and I said I would think about it.

Then there was the Nabisco sales manager named Bert, and we got on very well. He had a holiday home up the coast, and often, Claire and I would go there. He would pick us up on the weekends if we were free and take us to his holiday home up north at Healesville, and boy, did he drive like there was no tomorrow. He was also a renowned speed car driver, and he often gave me free passes to go to the speedway at Western Springs in Auckland on Saturday nights to see him race. Often he used to take me to lunch, and we went up the hills. I had the usual crayfish mornay. It was a whole lobster, and it was something out of this world. I did go to Bert's place several times as his wife Becky was a lovely person, and she always made you feel welcome.

In many ways, I came up with innovative ideas, so I asked the store sign writer, a very young talented woman, and I got her to cut out circles on bright red cardboard with the prices of the items on them. The items were advertised as "Red Hot Specials" in the local newspaper, and this was a great success. The management at head office were very happy, and they adopted this throughout their stores.

The end-of-year results came in incredibly good after the annual stocktaking was done, and the store improved well over 50 percent on last year's figures, and I was told that before I came, the store was running at a loss.

As I spent a lot of time with Claire's family, I found that her father, Kevin, was a very aggressive person on many occasions and did drink quite heavily, despite many denials to this fact. It was said by many that incidents did take place, but despite his tirades, there were also many good times I had with the family. Not all was on the downside as we all went along to many sporting fixtures when James played his football.

There was one occasion that I often chuckle about. Kevin and James like myself loved horses, and we had a bet or two. This Friday night in particular, we were all at the family home, and there was John and Claire and myself. James came in with his girlfriend, Fiona. Fiona was a very attractive girl. She had a beautiful complexion, and she looked as if she was part Māori.

I said to Claire, "Fiona is such a lovely person. James is a lucky guy." Claire agreed.

James said, "I have a horse that will be racing tomorrow at a country meeting, and it's a cert he will win!"

I said to James, "There is no certainty in horse racing."

Well, James, with a smirk on his face, convinced us to all put in $10 each, and he said we take a win and place trifecta and running double. He then told us the horse's name was Mr. ZigBee. We all went along with this. James had the betting guide, and I looked up the horse and said, "James, this is 100 to 1."

James chuckled and said, "Don't worry, it's all under control I will put on the bets for all of us in the morning."

So the next day, I listened to the race on the radio, and the odds were well over 100/1. The race caller said when he went through the starting list, the horse Mr. ZigBee was the outsider of the field at 110 to 1, and the caller said there was no hope for this one.

The race started, and I heard the race caller say, "Mr. ZigBee, the outsider of the field, has bolted out of the gates and is now well out in front."

It was an eleven-hundred-meter race and was a short distance to the turn and then down the straight to the finish line

The caller got excited at the turn as he yelled our Mr. ZigBee was more than a dozen lengths ahead of the other horses. "He has flown to the finishing post!" He said all the others had no hope at all in catching up to him, and Mr. ZigBee won by well over eight lengths.

He went on to say, "This is a boilover! I have never seen anything like this for a horse that has never won a race before!"

With that, Mr. ZigBee paid over $120 for the win for one dollar. This again stunned the race caller.

Later that day, we all met up, and James gave us all just over $600 each for our stake of $10, as we not only won the win and place, but also the trifecta as it paid over $3,000. This was a lot of money in those days. I do think James put more money on this as he was jumping for joy in excitement—in fact, I would say over the moon as one would expect over such a result. Looking back, this was one of the happier moments the family had for many a long time.

The following week, I looked up the races, and Mr. ZigBee was not listed in any race. I met up with James a week later and asked when Mr. ZigBee was going to race again, and he replied with a big grin, "Never."

"Why?" I asked.

He told me Mr. ZigBee lost all his hair. "He had enough dope in him to kill an elephant," James said, "and to my knowledge, he will never race again."

To this day, James never told me where he got the information from.

Claire and I often visited her Uncle Stan and Aunt Julia, mainly on weekends, and on one occasion, they invited Claire and me to a cabaret night, which was her uncle's work function. It was held in a venue at the waterfront in Auckland.

On this particular night, the compare was a TV celebrity, a comedian and a very good singer. After we had finished our meal, the music started, and they asked everyone to get up and dance. With that, Claire and I got up with Uncle Stan and Aunt Julia, and we were dancing away. Then halfway through the song, the music stopped, and the compare said, "Ladies and gentlemen, tonight we have a celebrity in our midst. It is the one and only Danny Kaye!"

Then suddenly, a spotlight was on me. I could have shrunk into a ball and rolled away. Funnily enough though, I was always told I did look like Danny Kaye in my younger days. People started applauding, and the music restarted. I was so embarrassed as people were coming up to me, shaking hands with me, and they said, "Welcome to New Zealand!"

I said to Claire, "Let's get out of here."

Claire said, "No, just go along with it as it is fun and will make our night very interesting." And so it did.

Uncle Stan said, "Yes, the compare is right as you do look like Danny Kaye."

As the night wore on, I did go along with it. At the end of the evening, we were just leaving, and the compare came up to me and said, "I am sorry that I may have embarrassed you, but you do look so much like Danny Kaye." He patted me on the back and added, "I am sure it made your night, and you took it in good spirit."

I said, "Yes, but the funny thing was so many people really believed it."

***

I asked Claire if she would like to go with me to Australia to meet my family. This was in December. Claire's parents did allow her to go, and we left a few days before Christmas. The family did take to Claire, and we stayed at my brother Michael's place in Bendigo with his wife Anne. Michael was one of my older brothers.

Mum and my elder sister May and her husband took a shine to Claire and said how quietly spoken she was. They took us to a few trips around Victoria to show Claire around. Claire did not like the heat as it was right in the middle of summer, and there were many days. It was over 100 degrees in the old scale.

I suppose Claire not seeing a kangaroo or a koala bear before was exciting for her. Then when at one time we stopped the car to show Claire a tiger snake that was on the road, she just screamed. We said it won't hurt you unless you disturb it. It then slid off into the grass.

The family loved Claire and thought what a nice girl she was. The trip back home to Australia went off very well and ended that year on a high note. On New Year, we went down to the fountain in Bendigo where the celebrations were. There were hundreds of people, and at midnight, the crowd went wild. Some took their clothes off and jumped naked into the fountain. The police were there, and they stood back and enjoyed the time like everyone else.

We arrived back in New Zealand the second week of January, just in time to go to work. It was now 1969, and now I had been here for over two years. I suppose the old saying, "Love changes everything," is true. I did stay connected with Mrs. Fields and the church. Claire did go every now and then with me, but she was not that way inclined. Claire liked going to the speedway at Western Springs Stadium on Saturday nights, and often, we took her young brother John along.

I liked going to the cinema as it was always a passion of mine growing up, and I would often take Claire to the movies, and on many occasions, I did take John to the Saturday afternoon matinee shows when there was a good western screening.

# 4

# THE ENGAGEMENT

I soon settled back into my routine. Claire and I had been dating now for some time since early 1967. She has now met my family, and over the past two years, I have grown madly in love with her. I thought it was time I popped the question to her.

This night I arranged to take her to a very expensive restaurant on the waterfront, and on this occasion, I ordered a bottle of champagne. Unbeknown to Claire, I slipped the engagement ring in her glass. As the waiter poured the wine, he noticed what I had done and gave me a wink and smile. I handed Claire her glass of wine, and I got on one knee and said, "Claire McDonald, would you marry me?"

With that, Claire took the ring from her glass of wine, and she said, "Yes, yes! I want to marry you!"

People around us clapped and congratulated us. This was one night I cherished as Claire was now going to be my wife.

Her parents were very happy, and so too were her two brothers. We did have a quiet engagement and a small party held at Gran's place. I announced that we planned to get married February next year. Her longtime girlfriend Jasmine and her husband Trevor were at the party, and Claire asked her if she would be her bridesmaid, and she said she would love to. Both Claire along with Gran were incredibly happy.

Kevin was not saying too much. He was more interested in his bottle of beer he was drinking.

I said to Claire, "I will ask my brother Noel to be my best man." And I then added that I would like Claire's brother James to be one of my groomsmen. And with that, Claire then asked Fiona to be her bridesmaid along with Jasmine. She replied that she would love to.

Claire's Uncle Stan proposed a toast to us, and I was asked to give a speech as I was used to speaking at various functions and work presentations. So I did this with ease, and I thanked Uncle Stan for his kind words. I said, "I am so lucky to have a girl like Claire in my life as she has made me so happy, and I look forward to the day we can get married."

The night went off without a hitch, and Kevin, despite his drinking, behaved himself.

I called my mother and told her the good news, and she said she would come over for the wedding. I asked if Noel, who was my younger brother, could come over with her as I wanted him to be my best man as the wedding was being planned for February next year. I did receive a call from Noel that day, and he was delighted to be my best man and would make arrangements to come over a week before the wedding.

I said, "I will make arrangements for you and Mum where to stay." I knew one place they would not be staying—Rose and Kevin's place.

I then mentioned this to Gran and said, "My mother and younger brother Noel are coming over for the wedding, and I have to arrange somewhere for them to stay."

Gran said they could stay at her place.

I said, "That would be great as this would be ideal for all of us being all together." I did thank Gran very much, and I was sure Mum would get on well with Gran.

Claire and I decided to take her parents out to dinner to celebrate our engagement at the same hotel where I was refused entry because I did not have my ID with me. I was ready this time but was not asked to show my ID. I thought, *What a shame.*

This night was for Claire's parents, and her parents enjoyed the night out. It was like we were one happy family. We filled them in with our arrangements and told them that my mother and brother Noel were coming over and told them what we had arranged. Everyone seemed incredibly happy with our plans.

Gran organized the local hall to have the reception for us, and Claire's parents and Gran said they would pay for this. We then arranged the day with the pastor Rev. Anderson at the Presbyterian Church in Auckland where I was now a parishioner there. I decided to change churches as this was closer for me, and now Claire wanting to get married there was extra special as it was known as one of the best churches in Auckland due to is majestic structure.

It was decided we would get married on February 7, 1970, at 2:00 p.m. I was overjoyed with the fact that I was going to marry such a lovely girl, and my mum and my younger brother Noel would be over here for the wedding.

As the year rolled on, I did avoid as much as I could going over to Claire's place, and she did spend more time at Gran's place. I fully understood why as her father did create plenty of problems for the family, and she just wanted to spend time away from the drama. No doubt she loved her parents, and I respected that; however, on the other hand, I could not dismiss a lot of dramas he had created, mainly due to his drinking, which could not be disputed. Claire was, I am sure, afraid of her father, although she was reluctant to discuss this.

I came from an exceptionally large family in Australia, and we respected each other and was never involved in family violence. To see this take place in Claire's family was very disturbing. It is commonly thought that family disturbance and violence is related to alcohol abuse. This is not entirely true, although alcohol can be a trigger. In Claire's father's case, he tends to have difficulty with controlling his alcohol consumption. He resorts to violence when angered or frustrated, and if he abuses his family, he needs to recognize that he has two or more separate problems. The other point is when the police are called, he quickly sobers up.

Claire's mother Rose never charged him but instead defended him. Kevin had a problem, and this was never addressed, and he could continue time after time. When he was not drinking, he was a genuinely nice person, and I did get on well with him. Kevin's drinking did come up in court proceedings, which was denied by his family. A later chapter outlines what I am on about.

I understand that "blood is thicker than water," but complete denial and lying about incidents that took place only serves one purpose in this story that it suits their own agenda.

The story is not all about Kevin and his tirades, but it played a significant part in the proceedings that followed. You can choose your friends, but relatives, you're stuck with them. One of my uncles told me when I was young that loyal friends are exceedingly rare. You can count these on one hand. These words have always stuck with me.

I was extremely fortunate through my journey in New Zealand. I did meet some lovely people, and yes, some became loyal friends. This next chapter outlines Claire's father and domestic violence. In this world, it's unfortunate domestic violence is an issue, and New Zealand is no exception. Victims should be able to live fulfilled lives free from fear of violence. In Claire's family, they turned

a blind eye to all this, which was a shame as this should have been dealt with by the authorities.

# 5

# FAMILY VIOLENCE

It is now established that Claire's father has an issue with alcohol, and I do think it is rather important to mention various incidents that took place, despite many references made particularly in the court case that he did not drink heavily or was a violent person often when he consumed too much alcohol. On the other hand, when he was not drinking, he was such a different person and good to get along with.

One incident was when Kevin was driving home from his work's Christmas break party. He crashed his car into several other cars on the northern highway. I was told later he was heavily intoxicated. It was the year that breath tests came in, and Kevin would have been well over the limit. I was never told he lost his license, and this incident was kept well under the radar, and the outcome never was disclosed.

I witnessed firsthand many of his alcohol-fueled incidents. I can also understand why Claire spent more time at Gran's place than in her own home. One episode happened during the winter months, and it was a wet winter evening. I found winters in New Zealand very cold indeed and always seemed much colder than I experienced in Australia. This night, I was invited to Claire's place for dinner. It was a Friday night, and as always, Rose put on an exceptionally good meal as she loved cooking and always cooked more than required. Kevin for some reason got very agitated as he had been drinking, and he started smashing things. He threw the television set through the lounge window. This resulted in the family having to go over to Gran's until the next day when things calmed down.

Then there was the time I planned to take John, the young brother of Claire, to the movies in the city. Kevin was to bring him over to Gran's place, and then I would drive both Claire and John into the city. Well, Kevin came down Gran's street, and near Gran's place, Kevin lost control and hit a power pole. The result was John was hurt and had a bad head wound. Claire and I did take John to the hospital where he was under observation, and they had to stich up the cut on his forehead where he hit his head on the dashboard.

We found out later Kevin had been drinking and should not have been driving. It was James who came to the rescue that day and took his father home and arranged the car to be towed away before police were involved.

The worst one I witnessed was when James's girlfriend Fiona was living with Claire's parents when they shifted into a new home in Ōtāhuhu. This night we were all there.—John, James and Fiona, Claire and myself, along with her parents. This night Kevin had few too many drinks, and he argued with James. He chased him into the bedroom. The father was screaming at James, and he struck James in the throat. James fell unconscious to the floor. I managed to drag James outside, and Claire called an ambulance. James was in a serious condition.

On the way to the hospital, I had to hold the oxygen mask on James at the back of the ambulance. Fiona was very upset, as well as myself and Claire. Rose arrived shortly after we arrived at the hospital. James stayed in overnight. I along with Fiona, Claire, and Rose stayed there all night. This is one night you would not forget...or would you? I am sure this one night you would not forget in a lifetime.

James was released from the hospital the next day; his mother Rose told the hospital he tripped in the bedroom and hit his head on the bedpost.

This incident was a horrible experience, and again I stress how could one forget such a night? This incident of domestic violence could have killed James, and don't forget what he went through. And yet they denied this as this came up in the court hearing. It was astounding that out of all the people, his fiancée at the time, Fiona, forgot such an incident. However, this suited their narrative that the father was not a violent person and that he was not a heavy drinker.

## *Joining Crest Foods*

While working in the supermarket and in my capacity as manager, I met up with many salesmen and supervisors and area managers. Two in particular stood out. One was from a Nabisco cereal company. His name was Bert, and he had a lovely wife named Becky and two young boys. I spent many a weekend with them with Claire at their beach house up north of Auckland. And then there was the area manager for Crest Foods, Jonathon King.

What took place was a game changer for me. I was approached many times during the year by Jonathon as he often said to me to come and see him at his office. "I can offer you a very good job." I did feel at this time I needed a change, and I finally followed this up when he came into the store and said to me this day that he had a vacancy in the merchandising department. "With your experience, it would be ideal."

With that, I arranged a meeting the following Monday with Jonathon, and I accepted the position. Then I gave three weeks' notice to be fair to the company. They were not happy with me leaving, and they offered me a substantial pay increase, but I declined.

I started with Crest Foods a few weeks later, and I was put on the merchandising team. I had to undertake display work in supermarkets within the Auckland region, and I was part of a very large team.

I settled quickly into my new job. This was a great company to work for. I received an exceptionally good salary package—far more than what I was getting to manage the supermarket. Also I had an expense account along with a company car. I sold my car I had put into my home savings account I set up with ANZ as I thought a New Zealand and Australian bank suited me better. It was great having a company car as I was allowed weekend usage, and the other benefit was I did not have to pay for petrol or running costs of the vehicle.

Yes, it was a game changer, not because it provided me with a company car or an exceptionally good salary; the fact that I was working with an international company and the experience I gained from working in sales and marketing and the freedom and support I was given by the company were defining factors in my fight for custody later on.

I must mention on a sad note, before I left the supermarket, my good friend from Nabisco, Bert, had passed away. His wife Becky came into the store and told me he had passed away a couple of weeks ago. He died suddenly.

I said to her, "Why did you not call and tell me? I would have gone to the funeral." She said, "I am so sorry, but as this was so sudden, I just did not think."

This was sad news as I along with Claire did spend some good times together with him and his lovely wife and his boys. He was such a go-getter and full of life. Becky was left with two lovely young boys. Later, I heard that they all relocated to the South Island, and I lost contact.

I quickly got to know many more people and made friends with some work colleagues, such as Greg Doherty, David Thomas, and Donald Monroe. All became particularly good friends, and we spent time after work to either dine out or go to each other's place for an evening. As I did not have a house at this point, I felt I could not invite them as Gran's place was so small. With that, I was limited by just going to their respective places, or we all went to various restaurants to dine.

One of my favorites was the Matador Restaurant. This was where Claire and I went on our first date. Sometimes we went to some of the clubs around Auckland. The night scene was very good, and there were lots of places to go.

One night, we all went to the Royal International Hotel, and this was very crowded, full to capacity. A fight broke out, and there were glasses thrown all over the place. A few dozen people joined in the brawl, and as we were all close to this, we made a beeline to the exit, and we had to push and shove our way out. As I was leaving, I noticed the bouncers joined in, and the bar staff jumped over the counter to try and stop this. We got out unscathed; lucky for all of us as this was ugly indeed.

It was just after six months with the company when the merchandising supervisor left Auckland to take up a new position with the company in Wellington. Jonathon called me into his office on the Friday afternoon before we had our weekly meeting with all the representatives, and I was offered the job as supervisor of the merchandising team. This meant that I was to become the boss of several of what I called mates that I was working with. I said to Jonathon, "Surely Greg has been here longer than I and also many others."

He said back to me, "I like your sentiment. However, your expertise and experience in merchandising is second to none, and the job is yours. It will come with a much larger pay and a lot more responsibility and freedom."

I now had to plan for the team to undertake all the display work. With that, he called in all the reps and told them of my promotion. To my amazement, they all accepted this, though I thought others should have gotten this before me. So now I was in charge of the team.

It was the following week when the company announced they were embarking on new product launches and a heavy TV advertising campaign. It was my job to go around to all the major outlets and presell the products and organize display space, which I was very successful in doing. My major food outlet was Food Town as they had outlets right across Auckland as well as Woolworths and Shoprite stores.

It was very important and critical to ensure the company's products were properly displayed and had to have the best prime shelf positions. This was an ongoing issue as other companies had the same idea;

however, as Crest Foods was the market leaders, this did give us the competitive edge. Me along with my team made sure we had the best front-end display space when our products were advertised on TV or as store specials. My job was to allocate each representative what stores they would work in each week. The company Crest Foods—you could not wish for a better company to work for.

The regional manager Jonathon often had a barbecue at his place. He lived on the North Shore at Takapuna, and this night he served up the most delicious steak I have ever eaten. The flavor alone was great, and the tenderness? It just kind of melted in your mouth. He told me that he had them marinated since yesterday in bourbon and some spices.

I said, "I will remember that and try it next time when I have a barbecue."

On this night, he congratulated me on my engagement to Claire, and I then explained to him that the wedding was early next year and well after our annual Christmas and New Year holiday break, in which the whole company closed for this period. So I asked if I could have a few weeks off for the wedding.

He said, "Course you can," and jokingly added, "Long as I am invited to the wedding."

I said, "Yes, plus most of the boys and their partners will be invited." I told him my mum was coming over as well as my younger brother. When I told him I was one of ten boys in the family and there were three girls, he nearly fell off his chair.

"Your parents must have been busy, no doubt no TV in those days," he said jokingly. Jonathon did not hesitate to allow me to have the time off; he also said I could still use the company car while on leave.

A lot of things happened while working at Crest Foods. Without digressing from the story at hand, it is one you must be so mindful of when you hire people, especially when they are given   a company car as all representatives of the company were provided with. It's not a given—it's a privilege. If you lose your license, you lose your job.

Now this young guy was interviewed and employed by Jonathon. His name was James Mahony, and he was put in my team. He seemed a very nice young fellow, and I did notice he did drink a lot. Most Fridays we all went to a local pub, and drinks were provided by the company. This night I was home at Gran's place, and the phone rang. It was Jonathon, and he said that he had just gotten a phone call from Greg. He said that James had hit a power pole, and the company car was wrapped around the pole—a write off, I believe.

I asked how was James and was told he was in hospital, but he was okay. But the worst was that I found out he was drunk. This next bit shocked us all. We found out he was an unlicensed driver. I said, "Shit, how did he get a job with us?" One of the employment questions was, "Do you have a current license?" I said, "This means the insurance company will not pay out on the loss of the company car."

Consequently, James did lose his job, naturally, but Jonathon had one hell of an explaining to do as he hired James. One of the major account reps who recommended him was also reprimanded as no checks were done on James. Lucky for me I did not employ him in the first place. I said to Jonathon, "In the future, all staff to be employed as representatives must have a current driving license and a clean record."

With that, all future recruitments for my merchandising team became my responsibility.

The year ended on a high note as we were now preparing for our wedding, and this is where the next part of the story takes me into a different direction and a to roller-coaster ride of drama, deceit, and an experience that one never saw that was extremely hard to believe and understand. My love for Claire was something I cherished dearly, and with her now soon to be my wife was something I was longing for.

I have a saying: "Life is what you make it." And yes, you have days when things go wrong, but when things go awfully bad, you wonder, "What in hell I did to deserve all this?"

Christmas would come and go, and I would settle into the New Year and was now looking forward to the next chapter in my life that would start with our wedding.

It was coming up to Christmas, and the company held a Christmas break party at the German Hofbräuhaus Restaurant in Auckland. We had a wild night. Claire and I had a wonderful time with plenty of dancing, singing, and of course, the beer drinking. I did not drink too much as I knew I had to drive back home.

The year ended on a high note as we were now preparing for our wedding, where the next part of the story would take me into a different direction and to a roller-coaster ride of drama, deceit, and an experience that one never saw that was extremely hard to believe and understand. My love for Claire was something I cherished dearly, and her being my wife soon was something I was longing for.

I have a saying: "Life is what you make it." And yes you have days when things go wrong, but when things go awfully bad, you wonder, *What in hell did I do to deserve all this?*

Christmas came and went, and I settled into the New Year and was now looking forward to the next chapter in my life that would start with our wedding.

*Mother and Brother Arrive in New Zealand*

My mother and brother Noel arrived early February a couple of weeks before the wedding. They came on a direct flight from Melbourne. Claire came with me to the airport at Mangere to pick them up. The flight from Melbourne was on time, and it did take a while to go through customs. When they came out, Mother was radiant as ever. We hugged and kissed and said it's been a while since we last saw each other. Noel gave me a big brotherly hug and shook my hand and said, "Hello, brother." He was a great brother, and I was so pleased to see them both.

Mum gave Claire a big hug and kiss, and so did Noel. I said, "This is a lovely reunion. Claire will be joining our family in a few weeks' time, and she will be Mrs. Mason."

Claire chuckled and said, "Yes, I will be very soon."

With that we drove Mother and Noel to Gran's place in Green Bay, which took some thirty minutes from the airport.

We arrived at Gran's place at around 10:30 p.m., and I introduced Mum and Noel to Gran. She made them very welcome. She prepared some supper for them, and we all chatted for an hour or two. As it was getting late, we all retired for the night.

Next day, I took Noel and James to get a fitting for our suits as Noel was my best man, and James, Claire's older brother, was my groomsman. After the fitting, we went and had coffee and chatted for a while.

I said to James, "I hope your father behaves himself at the wedding." James said, "I hope so."

Noel looked a bit puzzled at that remark, and I said to him, "I will explain later."

With that, we all left the café. We headed back to James's parents place to drop him off. I thanked James for coming today, and then I drove back to Gran's place. On driving back, Noel asked, "What is wrong with Claire's father?"

I said, "It is a long story. However, the short of it is her father put James in the hospital when he had too much to drink, and James is very cautious of his father, which I do not blame him at all. Let's just hope he is alright at the wedding. I think we should leave it at that."

As I did have time off work for the wedding (in fact, one month), and as I had things all planned and in place, the next evening, we had the rehearsal at the church, and all went well.

I said to Mother and Noel, "While you both are here and have come all this way, you should see a bit of New Zealand. With that, I have planned a few days to do some sightseeing. First I will take you to Rotorua, this is full of Māori culture." I turned to Mother. "There you will see a Māori in a grass skirt. It's a great place and lots to see."

I asked Gran to come along with us. She replied, "I would love to come with you all." Claire said she will not go as she had plenty to do to prepare for the wedding.

Next day, off we went and left Auckland, and we went through Hamilton. I said to Mother, "This city is like Bendigo as the population is about the same, I think."

Then we drove on to Rotorua. This was one of New Zealand's top tourist destinations. We all booked in a lovely hotel.

Mother commented going into Rotorua, "What a smell! It smells like rotten egg gas, and look at all the steam coming out of the road."

When we pulled up at the hotel, there was a small lake opposite the hotel, which was bubbling, and little spurts of steam puffed up into the air. I said to Mother, "You will get used to it as it is a sulfur smell."

She replied, "Yes, it is like rotten egg smell."

We went that afternoon and visited the Māori village. This was so impressive. We had an incredibly famous Māori guide to show us around. They called her Guide Rangi. She took us all around and told us stories about the village, and we then visited the hot pools and geysers. She told us we had to be careful we did not slip in. There was one point she stopped and said, "This stream is where they catch the fish." Opposite there was a hot stream, and she joked, "We catch fish on one side and then cook the fish in the hot stream."

This was an amazing place, and Guide Rangi and the Māori people were so friendly, and I just loved their culture. In the evening, I arranged that we all go to a Māori concert as well as they will put on a *hangi*. This is where they cooked the food in the ground. The food was just out of this world. We had plenty to eat, and then we settled into the Māori concert. The music and dancing was great as well as the stories told. It was a night to remember.

I said to my mother, "This is great, isn't it? Not like what we have in our own country as we should have our indigenous brothers and sisters doing something like this."

I found the Māori people as loving and friendly, and they welcomed us everywhere we went. We had a very memorable night.

Next day we all went to Huka Falls near Taupo, and you could see Mount Ruapehu in the distance and smoke coming from it. This was an active volcano. We all then hopped on a Jet boat ride, and we could hear the Huka Falls well before we could see them. We were told it's the sound of nearly a quarter of a million liters of water per second erupting from a natural gorge and thundering into the Waikato River, we were told by the tour guide. He also said this incredible waterfall is the most visited natural attraction in New Zealand. It was hard to steer your gaze away from the endless mesmerizing torrent.

The jet ride was something else. The speed and the thumping of the water and going so close to the rocky cliff edges was frightening. I thought one slip, and we would be all goners. I was hoping Mother and Gran did not panic or freak out, but they enjoyed it better than us young ones.

After we went so close to Huka Falls and the exhilarating boat ride, we all ventured on to Lake Taupo. This was at the heart of New Zealand's central volcanic plateau, where sits the largest freshwater lake in Australasia, Lake Taupo. This shining expanse of water, moving between aquamarine blue and jade green, is crystal clear to a depth of thirteen meters. It is home to one of the best wild trout fisheries in the world, more than thirty species of water birds, and several types of native fish and native koura (crayfish).

Lake Taupo was a magnificent lake, and we all loved seeing it. I wished Claire was here to enjoy this experience with us.

The following day, I drove back to Auckland, and we arrived back around 8:00 p.m., and as we had not eaten yet, Claire prepared a meal for us all. We told Claire what a wonderful trip we had. Claire told us she had a good day and had her final fitting on her wedding dress as well as her two bridesmaids, Fiona (James's wife) and Jasmine (her long-standing girlfriend).

It was a few days before the big day, and Claire said she was concerned about James and her father not being on good terms. I said to Claire, "You cannot blame James as your father did nearly kill him."

Claire said, "Yes, but I also hope it does not spoil our day."

"I am sure your father will not spoil your day. I have also spoken to James, and he is okay with it all. You just must settle yourself, and I am sure it is going to be a momentous day for us both."

Before the wedding, we had to have a place to live in after we got married as it was not right to live with Gran as we just wanted a place of our own. We found a unit in Mount Eden. This was very close to the city, and it was fully furnished, in fact. It had three bedrooms and was fully equipped, and this suited us both.

# 6

# THE WEDDING

The day had finally arrived. Our wedding was well organized, and I was so happy that my mother and my younger brother Noel was over here to share this day with me. The service was held at the Presbyterian Church in Auckland. I was really nervous, and Noel said to me, "Stop shaking, it's going to be all fine."

The church bells rang out, then I knew Claire had arrived. She came down the aisle with her father, and she looked magnificent, and so did her bridesmaids. She came alongside of me, and through her veil, she gave me a lovely smile. She took hold of my hand and gave it a tight squeeze. It was a short service, and after the service, we signed the registry, and the marriage certificate was given to us by the minister, Reverend Anderson.

We went outside the church, and there was plenty of people gathered and many onlookers. We were greeted with plenty of hugs and kisses, and we headed to the Auckland Domain for photographs. I said to Claire how wonderful she looked and how happy I was and lucky to marry a girl like her.

After we left the Domain, we then arrived at the reception, which was held in the local community hall. Rose and Gran organized all this, and we had some fifty guests at the reception. I had most of my workmates attending the wedding, including my boss. The reception went very well, and Kevin did have a few drinks. Rose kept him in check, and this was to everyone's

surprise as a number of us were concerned if Kevin would play up.

Kevin delivered his speech and welcomed me into the family. Uncle Stan proposed the toast to the bride and groom. I responded, and then Noel welcomed Claire to the family on behalf of Mother as she did not want to speak and asked Noel to do that. He did a good job with his speech and thanked the bridesmaids, and he then proposed a toast to them. He actually fancied one of them; this was Claire's good friend Jasmine.

The night was getting late. We had stayed for a few dances as well as the bridal waltz, which was a tradition, and they sang "Auld Lang Syne" before we departed on our honeymoon.

As we were leaving, Rose pulled me aside and said, "You take care of my little girl, and make sure you have protection."

I was taken aback by what she said, but I replied, "Do not worry, Mother dear. I will look after her as you wish."

Her comment for sure was unbelievable. Claire often said to me about her mother preaching to her about sex and relationships and how she should be a virgin whenever she got married. Often she reminded me of this when we were dating, and she always wanted to be a virgin when she got married. I respected that. Also, I knew this was instilled into her by her mother's belief of no sex before marriage, but me being a randy old bugger myself, I found this very frustrating indeed. Many times it could have happened, but Claire always did say no when we got to the point we could have had sex. I always honored her wish to maintain her virginity. I was brought up to respect women and not to take advantage of them. It was often said sex before marriage is an effective way to see if you're compatible or not or have any issues. It's best to sort this out before marriage. In my case, as it turned out, there is some truth in having sex before marriage.

I arranged James and Fiona to take my mother and Noel back to Gran's place. I said to them on leaving, "I will see you both when we return from our honeymoon from up north in about a week's time, just before you leave to go back to Australia."

I booked a lovely place at Helensville; this was up north from Auckland. We would leave early the next day as we planned that night to stay at the Royal International Hotel in Auckland. In the car going to the hotel, I told Claire what her mother said to me, and I thought what a nosy old woman she is.

Claire replied, "We are married now, and we make our own life together from now on." "Yes," I agreed. I thought this was heartening to hear as I thought she was tied to her mother's apron strings. We arrived at the Hotel International that I had earlier booked well before the service along with my brother Noel. When I picked up the key for the room, I also paid for the accommodation as I was not sure how late we would get back to the hotel.

We finally arrived in our room. It being the first night as a married couple, I said to Claire how lovely she looked. We embraced each other, and we hugged and kissed. I said, "I will run the spa for us so we can relax in this for a while as you need to relax. It has been hectic for you."

The spa bath filled up with plenty of bubbles. We undressed, and I opened the bottle of bubbly. We sipped our champagne, and we cuddled together in the spa. I said to Claire that this was going to be a joyous night for us both. We stayed in the spa for a while and finished our bubbly. I looked at Claire's naked body, and she just looked stunning. I felt at that point what a lucky guy I was having a lovely person like Claire as my wife.

We both changed into our night attire, and I gave Claire a lovely nightwear set. Claire was delighted with her nightwear, and I had a surprise for her and gave her a lovely gold necklace. As we both were very tired, we did not have sex at all. I put it down to having a big day. We both snuggled up to each other and fell quickly to sleep.

We did sleep in as the checkout time was 11:00 a.m. We hurriedly got into the shower together, got dressed and we left Auckland on Sunday morning, around 11:30 a.m., and headed to Helensville, north of Auckland. It was a few hours' drive. I had made reservations in a holiday unit.

We arrived there early in the afternoon. We were rather tired as it had been a hectic couple of days. On arrival, I organized to have dinner in our room. We watched TV for most of the afternoon. We had dinner that evening, and Claire changed into her lovely nightwear that I gave her. I said to Claire how lovely she looked in it and how she seemed to glow. I told Claire how much I loved her and how lucky I was to marry a girl like her. She said to me how lucky she was also having me for a husband.

Our first night on our honeymoon became a disaster, and it was frustrating, to say the least. After waiting for so long to make love to the one you just married, we found that we could not have intercourse. Claire was very distressed and just cried and cried. I tried to comfort her the best way I could. We did try again, and I found I could not penetrate into her. Claire was so distressed. I said, "I do not want to hurt you. Let's discuss this in the morning." Claire was so upset that I held her until she went to sleep.

I was not sure what the problems was. Claire called her mother, and Claire broke down and cried and told her mother that something was not right with her. That day we decided to head back to Auckland, we went straight to our unit in Green Bay.

Between us, we understood there would be many questions being asked from her parents and my mother and brother, so we decided to tell them Claire was not well, and now she had to see a doctor, and I arranged this the following day. Claire did confide with her mother, but as far as I know, this is as far as it went. This was a dramatic experience for us both, and not knowing what the problem was made it more stressful for us.

We did go and see our GP and did our best we could to explain our situation. I felt a bit embarrassed, and so did Claire. He did examine Claire and said this was far way out of his expertise.

He said he would make an urgent referral for Claire to a see a gynaecologist. The doctor said, "It's not a good start to your marriage," and Claire and I agreed.

The doctor managed to get an appointment the following week. Usually appointments to see specialists take months. The GP said to us to look positive. "I am sure it can be remedied. You're very young," he said to Claire, and he wished us both the best.

I said to Claire on leaving, "I am sure the doctor knew what the problem was, but he left this to the specialist to discuss this with us."

I along with Claire spent a few days with my mother and brother Noel before they left the following Sunday back to Melbourne. I never told them what the problem with Claire was, maybe it was because of sheer embarrassment. I told them Claire had a medical issue, and she would be okay, it was nothing serious. What else could I say? I did call them later that night to see if they arrived back home safe and sound. John, one of my older brothers, picked them up at the airport in Melbourne and drove them back to Bendigo.

The next day, Monday, I took Claire to see the gynaecologist. He was extremely nice to Claire, and she explained what her problem was. He also had the referral from our own doctor. He examined her thoroughly, and then he explained the problem, which he said was serious. He told Claire she has what is called vaginal agenesis. It is a birth defect that affects few women (1 out of 5,000).

"But unless it is fixed, in your case, it has made you having sex impossible for you both, and if you both want to have a baby, at this point it's impossible," he explained. "It occurs when the vagina does not develop fully. Some girls may have a shorter vagina, or a remnant of one, or lack of one altogether. It is common to have other issues in the reproductive tract, such as an abscess or small uterus. This is not a good start to your marriage, however, it can be fixed, but it may take months of treatment." The doctor looked at Claire. "You will require an operation, which is needed. I will arrange this next week for you, knowing you have just gotten married. After the operation, I will see you in around three weeks after the surgery and again around three months after. After the operation, you will have to start using a dilator daily. No sex at all during this treatment stage."

After we left the doctor's, I said to Claire, "You must stay strong.

With that, Claire went into hospital the following week. The operation, we were told, was a success and would not require additional surgery. Claire after three weeks started the treatment as this gave her body time to heal. Claire went through months of treatment, which lasted over six months. Claire had to use the dilator. To me, it looked like a penis made of glass. This was to enlarge her vagina. The doctor told us under no circumstances should there be intercourse as we could damage what has been done, so he told me on uncertain terms to be patient, and I was.

This brings in again the argument about having sex before marriage, and I fully understand that it is frowned upon to have sex before marriage by many religious bodies and parents protecting their daughters. This was instilled in Claire's upbringing, and I did honor that, but on the flip side, if only we did have sex before we got married, this could have been avoided and fixed as the specialist said when a girl is younger and the condition is found out earlier, it is much easier to fix. However when a girl is fully developed, it is much more serious.

I felt this was a very traumatic experience for Claire and a trying time for me also. I did feel so sorry for her as this was not a great start to our marriage. I am sure the trauma did take its toll on her. It really affected her as she became really depressed.

Much later in the year since we got married and finally after months of treatment, Claire was given the all clear that we could finally have intercourse, and the specialist told us we both had to be gentle and not to rush having sex, to do it gradually. We did that, and it was like for the first time, we got hit by a flock of birds.

Yes, things became normal, and Claire and I settled down as the trauma over the last year was very emotional. I have no doubt this played a very big part in Claire's psychological well-being and what was yet to come. When you love someone and see a change in that person, it is very worrying.

***

It was June 2, 1970, when the news of the tragic death of Bruce McLaren at the age of thirty- two was a big loss to the Formula One racing fans. I did see him racing at Pukekohe F1 racetrack along with Jack Brabham. He was a great Formula One driver, and he famously was New Zealand's top racing driver. He was also the designer of Bruce McLaren's racing cars. He died while testing one of his Can-Am series cars on the Goodwood circuit near Chichester, England. Bruce McLaren had become the youngest Grand Prix winner in 1959, with victory in the United States during his Formula One career. He won four races and placed in the top 3 twenty-seven times. He was runner up in the Formula One World Championship in 1960. His abilities as an analyst, engineer, and manager contributed much to his success of the cars that still bear his name today. The McLaren racing team Bruce established in 1963 was one of the most successful in Formula One Championships along with driving stars like Jack Brabham, Alain Prost, and Ayrton Senna.

Later on in the month, it was just after Claire's birthday, and I remember this very well as we were watching the news as I like to do each night, and this night, it was all about the Crewe murders, which shocked New Zealand. It was all about husband and wife Harvey and Jeannette Crewe, who were found to be missing from their bloodstained farmhouse at Pukekawa, Lower Waikato, on June 22, 1970, by Jeannette's father, who had been asked to look in on them by an alarmed neighbor because they had not answered the telephone for days. The Crewes' eighteen-month-old daughter Rochelle was found distraught in her cot.

At the time, no one had been charged for this, but later, a prime suspect, neighbor Arthur Allan Thomas, was being interviewed and later charged.

Claire decided she wanted to go back to her work at the accountant's firm. I felt this would be good for her and to get her mind off things. I was very concerned for her well-being as she was very depressed, and her doctor gave her medication to help her. I supported her and gave her all the love and attention she needed. My work with Crest Foods was not hindered in any way, and I was so grateful to my boss with the time off I was given.

He said good staff get rewarded for efforts they put in. "You give 101 percent, and you go the extra mile, and the team of guys you work with have the greatest respect for you." I thought about what Jonathon, my boss, said. It goes to anyone who gives their best effort in what work they undertake. I give all my team of guys the work to carry out and the trust that they undertake this; if the trust is broken, then that is a different matter I would deal with.

There was this incident that was due to one of the Senior sales staff, Mike. He was the major accounts manager, which means he should have had more sense. This day I had phone calls at the office that the displays at Food Town supermarkets were not done, and the reps had not turned up. I thought this was odd and very strange indeed. I then headed out over to Panmure to see If I could locate any of the boys.

For some uncanny reason, I went down this side road to take a shortcut into Panmure, and I noticed five station wagons parked in front of this newly built home. The wagons had all the display materials in the back. I walked into the house, and there were five of my team in shorts and tops painting the house inside. I blew my stack and said, "What the bloody hell are you all doing here?"

Well, they said, "It was Mike who got us here as he said he would cover for us."

I said, "Mike is not your boss. Now get out of here, get yourself dressed, and get back to Food Town and do the displays you're scheduled to do."

As they were all leaving, Mike turned up. I said, "What are you doing with my boys, getting them to paint this house?"

He said, "I have to have it finished this week as I have sold it." I said, "Pay some painters, and do not use my staff."

He pleaded with me to not to dob him in. Stupid me, I did not dob him in, and I got my staff together after work that day as they had to work later to get all the scheduled work done. I said, "You have broken my trust, and I put you all on notice. One more slip-up, and I will have you out of here. Furthermore, I am in charge of the team, not Mike, so bear that in mind."

Did they learn their lesson? Who knows, but it was a week or so later when Australia was playing New Zealand at Eden Park in the first cricket Test match, and Mike and few of the boys decided to go to the cricket game this day. Unknown to them, Jonathon, the area manager, was also at the game. He was invited through one of our major account customers, which was not uncommon for him to go to such functions.

Anyway, next morning, all the ones who went to the cricket match was called into the office, and Jonathon asked them where each one was yesterday. They all gave different answers. Then he told them they were seen at the cricket match, and he warned them that this was not acceptable and told them like I did that they were on notice. The company was tolerant in lots of things, but if you step out of line, then this became a different matter.

My good friends Greg, Donald, and Grant were not involved in this, thank goodness. It was obvious that Mike had influence over some of the boys. I called him the king pin.

There was also a big fraud in the company, and everyone was under suspicion as it involved many company representatives. It involved stock and coupon fraud as the company as a promotional tool sent out to households coupons where they can have, say 10¢ or 20¢ of their purchases when they buy the products on the coupon. The fraud came in where the company found out that reps were giving the stores a credit on their order, or they can get a check from the rep. The reps did this on their expense accounts and can claim back, but what they did was put the coupons on the stores' order sheets, and these coupons had to be sent to the head office.

The king pin, as he was known, got the reps to hand the coupons to him, and he gave them cash for half the value, and he kept the rest.

He was getting away with this as he had the biggest accounts and was not easily detected.

Instead of the sales reps sending the coupons into head office, he got the reps to hand the coupons to him and he gave them cash for one-half value, and he kept the rest, how did he try and get away from this, it was due to the fact he had the biggest accounts and was not detected.

I was advised about this by an unknown informant, and head office in Wellington was notified, and he was finally caught. He was asked this particular day to come into the office, and he was asked for his car keys. They searched his car where they found checkbooks with all the reps' names he exchanged coupons with. This implicated reps from other regions, and the sales force at the time was halved.

Mike the King Pin was not charged but lost his job. One other point was on his salary, he bought his wife a brand-new car, a rest house, and another house. This went on for who knows. It was suggested by some to have lasted at least two years. I was lucky that no one from my team was involved.

As a matter of interest, I loved my sports—Formula One, cricket, soccer, and rugby. Rugby was like a religion in New Zealand, and this year, there was controversial as to the issue of rugby contact with South Africa that dogged New Zealand throughout the year. It was told prior to 1970 that Māori players were excluded from All Black sides touring South Africa because of that country's unwritten (and later written) policies of racial segregation. In 1970, more than,000 New Zealanders signed a petition opposing that year's tour. This became one of the largest petitions in New Zealand history.

Māori players were selected for All Blacks tour to visit South Africa—would you believe it?—as "honorary whites." This caused an outrage, and most people felt this was no improvement and condemned the NZ Rugby for agreeing to such terms. Others argued that sports and politics should remain separate. The All Blacks lost the series 3–1 after being defeated 20–17 in the final test.

Well, Christmas this year, we spent Christmas Day at our unit in Mount Roskill seeing it was our first year being a married couple. Gran visited along with James and Fiona, Rose and Kevin, and John. I put on a big Christmas dinner, which started with a seafood cocktail, then the main course was roast lamb, chicken, and turkey with all the trimmings such as roast kumara, which was what I called the Māori potato, along with roast potatoes, pumpkin and carrots, and steamed vegetables. Then we finished off with the traditional plum pudding my mum always made, which was handed down from her mother.

We had a great day. I had a few drinks. I did provide some wines, and Kevin brought along a few beers. This was a harmonious occasion, one that was the best, except of course our wedding day. This topped off the year for us as Claire went through a lot of turmoil, and to see her have a wonderful time was well worth it.

It was a tough year for us both and did strain the marriage a great deal as we did not get off to a good start. As the story unfolds, I have no doubt the health issues affected Claire in so many ways, and now being her husband, I had to support her in in every way I possibly can. She did have her mother for support; however, I still shed some blame on Claire's mother's upbringing along with her father's tirades. Maybe she just wanted to get away from it all and start a new life. Her mother played a dominant role in her strict upbringing, and you will find out she also contributed to a lot of her daughter's involvement in incidents and so-called allegations about me. It was once said to me if you live in a glass house, you do not throw stones.

People say blood is thicker than water when they mean that their loyalty to their family is greater than their loyalty to anyone else. Families have their problems and jealousies, but blood is thicker than water despite what can lie ahead or the consequences. They believe one side and not another. Putting all that aside, for the time being, 1970 was a memorable year—the wedding, Claire's health issues, my mother and brother in New Zealand, the loss of Bruce McLaren the F1 driver, and the Crewe murders.

Now 1971 was just around the corner, and what lay ahead was the big question. Surely things will get better…or will they? Time will tell.

# 7

# THE PREGNANCY

The year 1971 did start on a very good note as it was New Year's Day, and James and I went to Ellerslie Racecourse when the Auckland Cup was run. Claire did not go as she said she would stay with Fiona at her parents' place. At the races, before the main race and before the cup was run, we were in the huge queue waiting to put our bets on. I said to James, "I have a good feeling about the horse Artifice. It is at good odds." I put some dollars on the horse, and then we watched the race. Artifice won the race, and this topped off the day as we both had a very good time. Between us, we backed a few winners, including the winner of the Cup. The best part was we came back home with a few more dollars than we went out with.

In 1970, the Crewe murders happened. This was big news around New Zealand and the world, and now Waikato farmer Arthur Allan Thomas was found guilty of the murder of his neighbors, Jeanette and Harvey Crewe, the previous year. Following an appeal, he was convicted for a second time in 1973. A campaign led in part by Pat Booth of *The Auckland Star* attempted to overturn Thomas's conviction. After forensic scientist Dr. Jim Sprott asserted that a cartridge case crucial to the conviction had been planted at the scene by police, Thomas was eventually pardoned in December 1979. No one else has been arrested for the murders. Arthur Thomas was awarded compensation for wrongful arrest and awarded one million dollars. He now lives in Queensland, Australia.

It was in early May when Claire found out she was pregnant; we were both overjoyed over this news, and the baby was due early next year in January. When James and Fiona came around home that day, we told them our good news. They were so happy for us. We then had to tell Claire's parents as they soon will be grandparents, so I said, "Let us all celebrate this good news," and with that they invited us to dinner. We had a few drinks, and we stayed for a while and ventured home. I called my mother in Australia and told her the news and said, "You're going to be a grandmother again." My mother in Australia already had twelve grandchildren at that time. She was delighted for us both. Then of course we went and told Gran as now she will be a great-grandmother, and she, like the rest, was so overjoyed with the news.

On most days, I would meet Claire for lunch, and on this particular day, I remember very well as it was on May 4, and I was in Queen Street, downtown Auckland, waiting for Claire to show up. I did see hundreds of people in Queen Street, and this was quite unusual during the week. I wondered what all the crowd and commotion was about. There was lots of shouting on loud speakers, banners waving, and as it turned out, it was the anti-Vietnam war protest, and the protesters were disrupting the civic reception held to mark the return of 161 Battery RNZA and 4 Troop from their deployment in South Vietnam.

I was watching the parade just a short distance from the Auckland Town Hall, and things looked peaceful; that is, until the troops marching reached the Auckland Town Hall. This then turned into mayhem as in front of the town hall, firecrackers and red paint bombs symbolizing the bloodshed in Vietnam were thrown on the road. Paint-covered protesters sat on the road, disrupting the parade, and soon after, the police moved in. There was a confrontation with protesters, which became very ugly until they were removed by police.

I thought the protest was uncalled for as I had good friends who fought in Vietnam. I know many people did disagree with the war that involved New Zealand, Australia, USA, and other countries.

Claire finally caught up with me as she had trouble getting to me as the crowds were excessively big. We got away from the crowds and found a quiet place to have lunch. The Vietnam War was a major issue in New Zealand, likewise in Australia and USA, and this led to later that year, New Zealand's prime minister, Mr. Holyoake, announced in August that New Zealand's combat forces would be withdrawn from South Vietnam by or about the end of the year 1971.

We had a visit from James and Fiona. They had just gotten engaged, and the wedding was set for mid next year. I did get on very well with James and Fiona, and we would go out with them, usually to a restaurant, or we all went to a dance in which we all had an enjoyable time. James was a builder by trade, and he was in the process of building a house in a new housing estate in south Auckland and should be ready around the time they got married next year.

I now had to set my sights on getting our own home as knowing now that I was going to be a father, and I would take up more responsibility for the family. I discussed with Claire that I want to do extra work at nights. It was not that we needed the money as I got a very good salary from my day job. I wanted to make sure I can provide a house for Claire and our baby due early next year. Claire agreed. I was given a cleaning contact from one of the office staff at Crest Foods as her husband operated a very large cleaning business. It was centered mainly around business offices and at night. I contacted her husband, and he gave me some work four nights a week and for around three to four hours. I had only three offices to clean. One was an accountant's office, and the other two were legal practices. All three were allocated to me.

The work was extremely easy, such as take out the rubbish (like empty the bins at each desk), dust, vacuum, and clean the toilet area. I spent around one hour at each office. They were always closed. I had the keys to get into each office, and I had to sign in and sign out for each office. All together, they were relatively new and very easy to clean.

This is where I met Merle Jones. Merle worked in the accountancy firm. She was much older than me, and she was very well spoken and polite. We often chatted while I was working, and one night, her fiancé came in to take her home. Merle introduced me to him. His name was Max Dubbeld. He said, "Merle has told me a lot about you." Then he asked in a nice way, "Why are you doing this extra work?"

I said to him, "I am saving to buy a house."

He replied, "Yes, it's not easy these days. I also understand you're a supervisor with a large international firm."

"Yes, I am," I replied.

Over the following months, I did get to know Merle and Max very well, and they became very good friends. They told me they were getting married soon, and they invited Claire and me to their wedding. It was a splendid day, and this was the only time that Claire met Merle and Max, now Mr. and Mrs. Dubbeld.

After they got married and they settled into their new home, Max invited us when he came into the office to pick up Merle. He invited Claire and me to dinner on Saturday night.

I replied, "Yes, I would love to, and I am sure Claire will too."

The Saturday night came, and I was ready to leave. Claire said she was not well enough to go. I said, "I will call them and say you are not well, and I will cancel tonight."

Claire was very insistent I should go and to just tell them she was not feeling well. With that, I did go. I called Claire a few times to see if she was okay. I felt really guilty leaving her on her own, but she said she did not mind at all.

The friendship I had with Merle and Max was, in a way, a blessing, and I had a few dinner nights with them. Strangely enough, Claire did not go for whatever reason. They also had an exceptionally good circle of friends, and we used to have a card night playing canasta. They often called me the canasta king as I won most times, all in great fun.

My work at Crest Foods in my capacity of being a supervisor was very significant as I had a lot of free time and had a very good team of guys. I formed a very good relationship with them at work as well as after work. There was Greg Doherty and his wife, Addison. They had a home in Green Lane, which was similar to Remuera. Claire had met them several times before, and we were invited to their place for dinner. This particular Saturday night and to my surprise, Claire said she would go with me. We had a good night. Greg did all the cooking, and he served up a great meal. We had a few wines, and we chatted and listened to some classical music.

On many occasions, we went to Greg and Addison's place. Greg would also invite other workmates along, like Donald Monroe, and there was David Thomas; he was single and joined the group often.

I did find having new friends apart from Claire's family circle was important, and as it turned out later on, that made a significant difference to me as all my family were in Australia, and at times I felt very isolated. I so much enjoyed having people around whom I could relate to, as Claire's family did have many problems, and I found breaking away from that circle and making new friends did make me more settled, I suppose, whereas Claire was the opposite and did not fit in like I did.

## Fiona Stayed at Our Place

At the time we were still living in Mount Eden in our three-bedroom unit, As I recall this was the start of many dramas to come. As mentioned before, Kevin, Claire's father, was often involved in domestic disputes, and there was much denial that he was well known for his drinking, despite what some of the family and others thought. Fiona was right in the mix of things and was caught up with a confrontation with Kevin.

This particular night, there was a dispute that took place at the McDonald household. Fiona was staying there before her wedding with James as her family lived on the South Island, so she had no family to go to. On this night, James came around to our place with Fiona, and she was very upset and crying. Claire put her arm around her to comfort her. Then James told us that his father had an argument, a fight of some sort. He said his dad had been drinking and was very argumentative. He asked if Fiona could stay with us for a while, at least until the wedding as this was set down for March next year.

Claire and I both agreed that she could move in as we had two spare rooms. One, of course, was for our new baby. So with that, she moved in for a while. I did not press Fiona what the situation was as she was too upset. James seemed to be still on good terms with his father from the time his father put him in hospital. However, Fiona only stayed about six to eight weeks. She was great company for Claire when I was working nights in the city doing my cleaning work.

The reason why Fiona only stayed a short while was because Claire was going through a very tough pregnancy as she developed toxemia. The doctor said it's a condition in pregnancy also known as preeclampsia and often caused in a sharp rise in blood pressure and can result in oedema, like swelling of the hands, feet, and face. He also said preeclampsia can be a sign of serious problems.

The doctor was right as Claire literally blew up like a balloon. Her face, hands, feet—in fact, all over, she just swelled up. Claire did disobey the doctor as he said to her, "You must give up your work." But Claire insisted on working. This then resulted in Claire being hospitalized well before the birth. This was late October. She was not happy about this and that she had to give up work. Now under strict doctor's advice, she would have to stay in the hospital until the baby was born.

If she did not, she could lose the baby. In fact, it got so serious that she could also die. This was a frightening thought.

By Claire now going to the hospital, Fiona had to shift back to the McDonalds' home as it was not proper, they said, if she stayed in the unit with me. Fiona reluctantly left as she said she did not know what was in store for her back at the McDonald household. I really liked Fiona, but unfortunately, as time went, Rose highly particularly influenced her. Fiona did tell me a few times that Rose was an interfering bitch. So when Fiona went back to the McDonalds, I know she was reluctant to go as she was so settled in staying at our place.

In the meantime, the doctors and nurses were very concerned about Claire's well-being as she was very emotional and stressed. At one point, I was told by the nursing staff she threatened to jump out of the hospital window, and she was put on twenty-four-hour watch, and they had to have her well sedated. The doctor told me her state of mind and condition was not good for the baby or indeed herself. This was a grave concern for me, and I went to the hospital and spent many hours there between work and at nights. This was now late October, and the baby was due in January next year, which felt a long way away.

It was sad to see how unhappy and how unwell Claire was. She had no choice but to stay put in the hospital. If only she did what was asked of her from the beginning, things could have been much different.

I felt I needed a break, and it was the first Tuesday in November. James said, "Let's have a bet on the Melbourne Cup."

The Kiwis, I found, was all for the Melbourne Cup, and like the Aussies across the ditch, they loved to have a bet on the race. I went to the local tab, and we put a few dollars on Gala Supreme. Then we both went back to my unit to watch the race and have a beer or two as I was not a big drinker and just loved one or two to be sociable. I was lucky to see the race run live on New Zealand TV as this was the first sporting event to be broadcast live via satellite in this country following the opening of the Warkworth satellite station earlier in the year.

We watched the race. It was 5:20 p.m. here in New Zealand and 3:20 p.m. in Australia. It was a long race, over two miles. Gala Supreme won the race easily, and I did not have a huge amount on it, just $10 each way, and I got back around $150 as the odds were around 12–1.

Later that day, I went back to the hospital after the cup was run, and Claire was in a very emotional state. The doctors and nurses were all concerned for her well-being as well as the baby's. Claire remained in the hospital well over six weeks now, and it was the second week in December when the doctor decided that they were going to induce Claire. He told me her life and the baby's were in danger.

I said to the doctor, "Why are you not considering doing a caesarean?"

He said emphatically no. The doctor went on to say the priority now is the mother. I said, "What about the baby?"

He said abruptly, "Again, the mother is my priority, and at this stage, she must come first." Then the doctor told me the baby may survive. "I will do all I can for both. I am calling in a pediatrician as well to attend the birth."

I was emotionally upset and very confused by all what the doctor told me. If her life and the baby's life were both at risk, then why not do a caesarean? Who was I to judge as he was the doctor caring for Claire.

# 8

# THE BIRTH OF OUR SON OLIVER

I stayed all Saturday during the day as well as all night. I had no sleep. Early Sunday morning, I was literally kicked out of the hospital by the doctor attending Claire. He said, "Go and get some sleep, and I will call you when the baby is delivered."

I said, "Why, cannot I be there at the birth?"

He said, "No, there are too many complications."

With that, I left the hospital and went to Claire's parents' place, and I broke down and told them what was happening. They wanted to go up, and I said, "No visitors are allowed."

Rose said bluntly, "I am the mother, they will let me in."

I said, "Please no, they said they will call me here as I gave them your phone number." I managed to get a few hours' sleep, and it was well after 5:00 p.m. when the hospital called and said, "You can come up now as your wife has just delivered a little boy."

I asked, "How are they doing?"

The nurse replied, "Okay at this point."

I was not sure of the hesitation, but I raced up to the hospital. I was allowed into the delivery room where Claire was sitting up and having a cup of tea. I gave her a big hug and kiss and asked, "Where is the baby?"

Claire said, "They have taken him away as he is very ill."

The doctor came in and told us the next twenty-four hours was critical for our little baby boy. "You must be prepared as he may not make it."

I asked the nurse who was attending Claire, "Is our baby that critically ill?" She said, "Afraid so. He is so small, around 4 lb., 7 oz."

I asked the nurse, "Can I see him?"

They said not yet as the pediatrician was still with him. We waited for several hours, and they put Claire back in her room. A nurse soon came in and said, "You can go down now to see your son. We have him in the preemie ward." The nurse put Claire in a wheelchair, and we had to put on gowns and masks, and the nurse taking us down said, "This is where we look after all the preemie babies and the ones that are critically ill."

We entered the room, and there were around twelve other babies in either cots or humid cribs. The nurse walked us over to where our son was. He was in a humid crib, and he had so many wires on him, and he looked so tiny. The name tag on the outside read Baby Neville, 4 lb. 7 oz.

"The doctor will be in shortly to discuss with you about your son."

They left us alone, and I said to Claire, "He is yellow all over and so tiny. I just hope and pray he makes it."

Another nurse came in and said to us, "Your boy was around six weeks premature, and he had developed jaundice due to the toxic poison in his mother's system. If he gets over the next twenty-four hours, he will make it. Sorry to say that, but it is important you understand the critical condition your son is in."

Shortly after, the doctor came in and told us again, "Your baby boy is in a critical condition, and the next forty-eight hours will tell us if he will come out of this alright. He has breathing difficulties as well as his jaundice due to the toxic poison he gained from his mother during the pregnancy."

I said to the doctor, "Yes, I understand, but the nurse told us also she said the next twenty-four hours is vital, and if he gets past this, he should be okay."

The doctor was adamant that the next forty-eight hours was my timeline. "I am the doctor in charge," he said in a stern voice. "And in the meantime, we will do all we can for your baby."

The next forty-eight hours was a waiting game, very strenuous. We could only watch and wait. We spent most of the forty-eight hours with our son. We took turns to have some sleep, quick naps. At this stage, we had not named our baby boy as we waited for the doctor's report and our boy's progress.

The forty-eight hours had come and gone, and we waited for the doctor to come and advise us what was the status and condition of our baby. The doctor came and told us, "Your baby is finally out of the critical stage. He still will be monitored, and possibly in a week or two, you may be able to hold him. The next problem we are facing is his weight. We want him to gain as much weight as possible to allow him to go home. In fact, he will be here for quite a while."

With that, the nurse told Claire she should be allowed home in about a week's time as Claire was still very sick from the toxemia.

I said to Claire, "We have not given our son a name yet." Her parents wanted our son to be called Kevin. I put my foot down and said, "No way will my son will be named Kevin." I convinced Claire to call our son Oliver and the second name Kevin to keep the peace. This was agreed upon. I said to Claire, "It's our baby, not theirs, and we do not have to go along with what they say all the time." Claire was allowed to come home a week later. We did spend every day at the hospital after she came home. Then Christmas Day came, and we went up to see Oliver. The nurse told us he was slightly improving. We said we would have loved him to be home for Christmas; however, this was not to be. It was a very emotional time for us. We got to his humid crib, and there was a lovely blue Christmas stocking on it. It read "Merry Christmas, baby Oliver, from the nursing staff." in it was a pair of booties, and we thanked them very much. The nurses were great and loved Oliver and really looked after him. The nursing staff and doctors did a wonderful job and were so dedicated to their work, and Claire and I were very thankful and blessed.

We still were not allowed to pick him up or give him a cuddle. We were only allowed to touch him through what I called the portholes on the side of the humid crib. Oliver had mittens on his hands to stop him scratching himself. We were waiting for the day we could hold him.

The major concern by the nurses and doctors was that Oliver was not gaining any weight, and the nurses nicknamed him the one-ounce kid. We did see the doctor that day and asked when could Oliver come home.

The doctor said, "He has to reach a good weight before he is allowed home. The jaundice is gone and his breathing much better, but he is not putting on much weight." The doctor laughed when he heard from the nurses they called him the one-ounce kid.

We decided to make a change, and we shifted into a brand-new unit in blockhouse bay as this was in a lovely area and was also furnished and was less expensive than the one we were living in at Mount Eden, and we were there for only a short time, as you will see.

## Oliver Comes Home

It was late January when baby Oliver finally was allowed home. He was in the hospital for over six weeks after he was born. No doubt he was a very critical and sick baby, and we are very lucky to have him, which was a blessing. It was a trying time for us all.

We were very thankful for the doctors and nurses as they did such a wonderful job. The care they gave Oliver was something I am ever thankful for and blessed. The nurses said to me that they were very happy to see him go home, but they will miss him as well.

There is no doubt in my mind that the trauma that Claire had gone through from when we were first married and now the difficulty of having the baby, I am sure this played a significant part in her well-being and also psychologically. I knew Claire was not well, and I had to do all I could to help her. I was reassured as Claire had her mother and Fiona to give her as much help as possible. We just recently shifted into the unit in Blockhouse Bay when Oliver came home. We were so happy and pleased. I set up the bassinet in our bedroom; however, we had a very bad experience in the unit we rented, as this night, we heard what seemed to be a grinding sound. It went on for a long time. I finally got up, and the noise was coming from the laundry. Under the laundry sink, there was a small cupboard, and when I opened the door, out sprang a huge rat! Without exaggerating, it was the size of a large cat. Its teeth were so large, its mouth wide open, and it started attacking me. I screamed out to Claire to get a hammer or something heavy as I was getting attacked by a huge rat. Claire threw in a hammer, and I closed the door as Claire did not want to let the rat inside the unit. I managed after a long while to kill the rat. Boy, did it take some hitting. Lucky it did not bite me or tore my PJs in places.

I boarded up the hole in the cupboard, tossed the rat into the rubbish bin, and cleaned up the laundry with lots of disinfectant as there was lots of blood everywhere. It made me feel unclean. After I cleaned up, I went to Claire, and she was beside herself sobbing. She said, "We must move out of here!" She was hysterical, so I had to calm her down as it was around two in the morning.

I said, "You get some sleep, and we will deal with this in the morning. Look, it's okay now. I have boarded up the hole the rat made, and it's safe anyway. Please go back to bed, and we will discuss this in the morning."

With that, Claire did settle down and went back to sleep.

Early next morning, I was outside of the unit talking to one of our neighbors, who by the way was a pilot for Air New Zealand. I told him what happened during the night. He then said that the creek running at the back of the units was infested with rats. I then took him over and showed him the huge rat I killed that I shoved in the rubbish bin. I said it took a lot of beating.

"Wow," he said, "it's the size of a small dog. It's huge!"

We both agreed we had never seen a rat that size. He then walked me down and showed me the creek. This was full of rubbish, no doubt a health hazard. As we walked back to the units, he said to me, "Having a baby or any child here is not good."

I said, "Claire wants to look for another place, and I have to agree with her despite just shifting into the unit."

He replied, "That is a very good idea, and what I have now seen has made me very uneasy as well. I also have a small family, and I think a move out of here is the right way to go."

Claire got up still very upset and said, "Let's go over to my parents' place."

So after we had breakfast, I drove Claire and Oliver over to her parents' place. Claire, still upset, blurted out to her mother about the ordeal with the rat.

Her mother said, "Is Oliver okay?"

"Yes, he is okay. The rat did not go near him."

Her mother just doted over Oliver and was really concerned about where we were living. The traumatic experience about the rat was like we were in a horror movie.

Now what took place next, I still to this day do not know how this became about. Claire's mother got us into a newly built unit that was owned by the government housing commission. It was in Buckland Road, South Auckland, and it was close to shops and other amenities such as doctors and chemist. There was also a corner store they called a dairy. The plan was that we stay in that place until we got our own house.

The downside, in my opinion, was it was very close to where Claire's parents lived.

How we got this place is the part that I was very puzzled about as to get a place from the housing commission can take months or years in many instances. I am not sure what story Rose and Claire came up with and was never told the true story. I was never consulted, and for the sake of peace, I went along with it. My guess of the story was that Claire had nowhere to live and had a sick baby, and she was a single mother. All this including the incident with the rat as well could be the only explanation I could think of as to why Claire got a unit in one week. I did ask Rose how this came about, and she told me the less said, the better. I left it at that.

We shifted into this housing unit the following week. I also noticed the payments for the unit were in Claire's name and not joint names. From that, my suspicions were right, that they told the housing commission she was a single mother. Again, I did question this with Rose, and she said, "Look, you all have a lovely new unit close to everything, and think of this: you all have a lovely place until you get your own home."

I did agree with her on this score as my plan was to have our own home, and this can be now the stepping-stone to do just that.

Claire settled down and really loved the unit, and baby Oliver was doing well.

## *Oliver's On-Going Sickness*

We settled into the new unit, and we had Oliver home with us now for a few months. My concern was that he was not doing so well. I said to Claire, "We must take Oliver back to the pediatrician we had at the hospital."

Claire was not happy about this as for some reason, she had a thing about hospitals. With that, I called the pediatrician at the hospital and explained to him that Oliver was always being sick and bringing up his food. He told us to bring him in straight away. With that, Claire was not happy with this, but I insisted, so we put Oliver into his baby carrier, and we arrived at the Mater Hospital. Oliver was examined, and the doctor said to us that he had to go back into hospital as he was

a very sick baby as he keeps throwing up all the time and not putting on any weight since he left the hospital some weeks ago. He had to be put into the hospital.

Claire was crying. "I do not want my baby back in the hospital!"

The doctor said, "I am sorry. you do not have a choice as if you don't, you most likely will lose him."

So it was arranged that day to put Oliver in at the Karitane Hospital in Auckland as they cared for new babies who were not thriving at home.

This distressed Claire to no end. Heartbreaking as it was, I knew it was the right thing to do. Oliver was put on a drip feed and, in a few days, was looking much better. He was there for at least three weeks and was doing very well. The drip feed came off as he started putting on weight, and he started back on bottle feeds. As you may recall, Claire could not breastfeed because of her toxic condition. I went up every day and every opportunity I had and stayed for a many hours. Claire stayed there all day, and most days, Rose stayed with her for company.

There is always a twist in the story as Claire and her mother Rose were so possessive but overreacted as to what they did next. A virus or what you call a bug spread through the hospital and did cause some babies to die, and there were many babies with acute dysentery and vomiting. This, no doubt, was a concern for us both having Oliver in there. However, the hospital doctors and nurses reassured us that Oliver was in no danger as they had all the babies that were not affected in isolation. Knowing Claire was incredibly stressed about this, I tried to reassure her and Rose that Oliver was safe where he was.

I suppose nothing would surprise you. What Claire and her mother will do about the situation and what happened next is beyond belief. I was at work and in the local supermarkets, and it came over the intercom, "If Mr. Mason is in the store, can he come to the main office?"

I hurriedly went to the office, and they said, "You have a urgent phone call." It was lucky that had a schedule of my days work at Crest Foods, so it was easy to track me down. The message from my office said I had to ring urgently the hospital where Oliver was. I used the supermarket's phone and called the hospital. I did fear the worst as I thought something had happened to Oliver. My heart was pounding as I was transferred to the doctor, the pediatrician at the hospital.

He was blunt with me and said, "What are you people doing?" He then told me that my wife and her mother were at the hospital and discharged our baby boy and have taken him home. He went on to say he was not happy, and he began shouting at me down the phone. "You people need to face facts of life! Your wife's actions are so irresponsible when your boy is doing so well!" He swore at me and said, "As far as I am concerned, you find another doctor as I am not going to take any responsibility for this stupidity your wife has done." He went on to say, "The important thing now is the welfare of your son. You now have to deal with that."

I replied, "I am so sorry for this. I had no idea or knowledge of what they had done. I have always tried my best for Oliver, and now this. I am so sorry."

With that, the doctor hung up the phone on me. I could understand how he felt as this shocked me as well.

I came off the phone and was so upset, I was visibly shaking. I knew Oliver could not get better care where Oliver was as they specialized in sick babies, and the nurses loved Oliver and took really good care of him. And now having him discharged by Claire and her mother was totally irresponsible, as the doctor said. I was outraged and very upset. I phoned the office and told them I had an emergency and had to go home. I quickly explained Oliver had been discharged from the hospital by his mother, and she should not have done that.

I drove back home in haste. Luckily the supermarket I was working in was only fifteen minutes away. When I pulled up the house, Kevin's car was in the driveway. I quickly went inside, and there was Claire and Rose and Kevin in the lounge room, and Oliver was in his mother's arms asleep. I said to Claire in a raised voice, "What have you bloody well done! Have you lost your marbles? And for you, Rose, I thought you would have more sense as you're always the doting grandmother!" I was very angry and upset and looked at Kevin. He was just sitting there saying nothing. I then explained I received a call at work from the doctor who was looking after Oliver, and he told me Oliver was a very sick child and needs to be in the hospital. "And you went there and discharged him? How bloody stupid! For God's sake, where are your bloody senses? The hospital had Oliver in an isolation ward. You two have both overreacted. The doctor said on the phone that he is finished with us, and we now have to find another doctor, thanks to you lot, and he gave me a dressing down over the phone. This should have been you, not me! And you're the one with your mother that discharged him." I shouted directly at Claire, "You are not thinking rationally, and now you have put our son in danger!"

Oliver woke up and started crying. I went over and picked him up and cuddled him, and tears were running down my cheeks. Claire knew I was angry with her, and she said, "We decided that because of the virus at the hospital that Oliver is better with us at home."

I said, "Who are we to judge? He is a very sick child, and he should be back in the hospital!" "Me and Mum thought that it was best for Oliver to get him out."

I said angrily, "Don't I get a say in this? Surely you could have called me at work and told me." I then told Rose in no certain terms, "Butt out of all this as it's our baby, and what you both have done is totally irresponsible." I then told Rose and Kevin, "It's best if you left as you have done enough damage for one day."

With that, both Rose and Kevin stormed out of our unit. As they went,they shouted back at me, "We did it for Oliver, not you!"

I closed the front door and said, "Claire, as harsh as it may seem, the fact is that Oliver is an extremely sick baby. You have known this from birth, and we nearly lost him. Do you want to go through all this again? Hospitals are for sick people, and they are for a reason to get better and to be well cared for 24-7. You need to take some responsibility." With that I went and prepared dinner. Claire went up to the bedroom with Oliver.

I am afraid this was not the end of the matter as Oliver was still not doing too well. What he gained at the hospital was now back to where he was when he first went in. We had troubles coping with Oliver over the next few months. He was gaining very little weight. I did all the night feeds as Claire was so tired, she never woke up. When I gave Oliver his bottle during the night, I did have a very good setup as when he woke up crying, I had a piece of string tied to my big toe, and it was attached to his cot we had in the bedroom. I would pull that back and forth, which settled him until I had his bottle ready for his night feed. I had a Birko, which was a food warmer, and had the bottle already in the Birko. As soon as the bottle was ready, I would feed him. This would happen usually every two to three hours each night. Going off to work next day was always challenging. We had Oliver in our room for safety precautions. Also knowing how sick he was, I did not want to take any more chances.

My concern was that I knew Oliver was not getting any better, and he was throwing up more than he can hold down. I felt this was a major issue. We did go to a doctor that Claire's mother went to, and he did prescribe different medications; however, in my opinion, Oliver was not improving. Claire took Oliver for a check-up at the baby center, and the nurse said, "Oliver is not gaining weight still. You need to go back to your doctor. With his continual vomiting, Oliver has an outlining issue, and this needs to be looked at by a doctor who specializes in sick babies." And of course, Claire did not mention Oliver was discharged from the Karitane Baby Hospital.

Now, I had to take a different approach and take matters into my own hand on this as the situation was not getting any better. Oliver kept throwing up, and the problem keeping anything down was a big concern as this was going on far too long now. After hearing what Claire told me what the nurse said at the baby center made me more concerned. At times I think Claire did not have a clue when it came to Oliver, and this made me more anxious.

I did go to church regularly whereas Claire did not. I phoned Mrs. Fields, a dear lady friend I met in the church in Ponsonby. She was good to me, particularly when I first arrived in New Zealand. She worked in Dr. Henderson's clinic. I told her of my concerns about Oliver, and she said, "I will discuss this with Dr. Henderson and see if he can fit Oliver in as he has a very good history and reputation with sick children." Dr Henderson was also an elder of the church and is well respected.

She arranged the appointment for the next day for Oliver to see the doctor. I felt rather confident knowing he specialized in children's illnesses. He may by the grace of God, an answered prayer.

I told Claire that night when I got home from work. I said, "I have the day off tomorrow, and we will all go and see Dr. Henderson." I explained to Claire, "He also specializes in sick children and is very good with baby's health issues. You will like him as he is a very good man."

Next day we arrived at the doctor's clinic with Oliver, and Mrs. Fields greeted us. She gave me a big hug, and I introduced Claire to her. She said to Claire, "Nice to meet you as I have heard so much about you. Call me Fran." I never called Mrs. Fields by her first name as I always respected my elders. She then said, "The doctor will see you soon. It's really good to see you again, Danial. We missed you coming to our church as I know you shifted from the area, and you went to another near your place, which is understandable." She turned to look at Oliver. "This is your little one?" "Yes," I replied, "this is our little bundle of joy, Oliver. Unfortunately, he is not well and not a

happy little fellow." Oliver had a nice blue cap on his head, and he smiled at Fran. She said, "He is a lovely little boy."

Dr. Henderson came through the doorway and said, "Good to see you, Daniel. And this is your wife Claire we have heard so much about?"

We went into his room and sat down. Dr. Henderson asked what the problems with Oliver were. I told him the story as best I could from when he was born and to the issues we were having now, like Oliver being sick daily, which was our major concern.

Dr. Henderson examined Oliver all over. Oliver was only nine months old but still very tiny. He said, "Apart from what you tell me, he is pretty healthy. I will prescribe a very old medication for Oliver. The chemist will have to make this up for you. It will be in a small bottle, and you give him a few drops prior to have him being fed. It's Phenergan, and it will make him drowsy. Also I will put him on a special baby formula, and this will also help." He gave us a prescription for the medication as well as a prescription to take to the hospital to get this special baby formula. The doctor also said to keep him off any milk for the time being.

We both thanked the doctor very much and said goodbye to Fran and thanked her. We left the doctor's with a glimmer of hope. This time we may be on the right path as it's been a very hectic twelve months or more with Claire during her pregnancy and Oliver being so ill. It has been a major concern as well very stressful for us both, and noticeably to Claire as she has her own health issues to deal with. She also has deteriorated in many ways, physically and mentally.

Oliver started his treatment, and it sure made him drowsy as he would roll back his eyes while having his bottle and go to sleep. The medication and baby formula worked; it stopped his vomiting, and he held down his formula the doctor prescribed. After a few weeks, we did see signs Oliver was getting better. He was not crying as much, and he held down his food we gave him like custards and mashed vegetables as well as his baby formula. Oliver was putting on weight, and he seemed more settled. The special baby formula from the hospital did make a huge difference. This came in a carton of six cans. We did get this subsidized, but it still cost us a lot. I felt the cost was immaterial as it was more important that we get Oliver better.

Claire would often let her parents have Oliver, and when I came home from work and found Oliver was not at home but was at her mother's place, this annoyed me. I looked forward to coming home from work to see Oliver as when I did come home, his face always lit up and smiled at me. I made my point angrily at Claire and said, "I do not mind your parents seeing Oliver as they are his grandparents, but Oliver is our baby, and you're just as bad by letting him go there all the time." This was not overreacting as the issue was that Claire could not cope. I suggested, "Your Mother can come here and stay with you during the day until I come home. I think that is reasonable, don't you think?"

Claire remained silent.

I added, "The other point is your father. If he goes off his rocker when Oliver is there and harms him, I won't forgive you."

On most days when I came home from work, I had to fix the dinner. I opted to bathe Oliver and put him to bed. Claire in a strange way seemed in another world. She was depressed and not happy. I did all I could to help her as I did understand what she had gone through. The other issue was her parents as they did interfere a lot, and this annoyed me as I did all I could toward Claire and Oliver's well-being. I know her parents meant well, but as we know Oliver being as sick as he was, we should not be told every day how we handle Oliver. I said to Claire, "We have to stand on our own two feet, and we do what is best for Oliver. I suppose your parents do mean well, but you're the mother of Oliver, and it's your responsibility, not your parents. Letting your parents take him home all the time should stop. I don't mind occasionally to give you a rest, but he is still a baby. Get you mother to come here during the day."

Claire reluctantly agreed. She was not happy. I did feel I had to put my foot down. Rose did start coming around during the day and helping Claire out, and Claire seemed much happier. I know she needed the support, and she appreciated my concerns but never told me.

In the middle of the year, James married Fiona. It was a lovely wedding, and this went off without a hitch. Claire was the matron of honor. I met Fiona's parents for the first time, and they were such lovely people. Her mother was like Fiona. Later in the year, we were told they were expecting their first child. We often visited their house, which was newly built.

Both Claire and I along with Oliver were at Fiona and James's place to have dinner, and then Rose and Kevin turned up. The relationship with James and his father was obviously very strained, but they were in speaking terms. James told me he would not forgive his father for what he had done to him as he nearly killed him. Then James pulled me aside and said, "Claire is not coping well with Oliver."

"Yes," I said, "I do understand what she has been through. She is very emotional and irrational, and I have to do a lot to keep the peace in, which I do not mind as this is my responsibility, but she cannot rely on her mother all the time."

James nodded in agreement. He said, "Claire should come here during the day as Fiona would love to have Claire around with Oliver."

Claire did take up James's offer, and I noticed a more relaxed Claire. There was also a huge difference in Oliver as he was not being sick anymore and gaining a lot of weight, and when Claire took Oliver to the baby center, the nurse told Claire that he was doing so well and was in very good health. When she came home and told me this, it was pleasing to hear.

The year 1972 seemed to fly past quickly despite all the drama. This was election year in New Zealand, and I for many reasons supported the Labour Party. I think mainly because Claire's parents were all staunch Labour voters, and so were many of the people I worked with. This particular year, the Labour Party had a very strong leader, a very big man named Norman Kirk. He spoke well and had plenty ideas for New Zealand, and the people loved him.

Before the election, I did get to know some of the candidates in the electorate I was living in. I met them through my work, and they asked me would I assist them on election day, which was on December 8. They gave me a task to pick up the elderly people so they can cast their to vote and then take them home again, and when the voting closed, they asked me to stay on when the counting started to be a scrutineer. This was to overseer the counting and eliminate if any mistakes were made on the ballot papers.

Well, later that night, I finally got home. As the result was not known at the polling booth I was at, I turned on the television, and Norman Kirk won the election. Yes, it was a big win for Big Norm as he did win the election by a landslide. The politician I was helping also romped in, and later, he became the treasurer. The Sunday papers reported the Labour Party went into the general election with the slogan "It's time."

It seemed the people of New Zealand had grown tired of the National Party. The Labour party was led by the increasingly very popular Norman Kirk. He had become known as Big Norm (because of his stature). Their slogan was "It's time," and time it was. Labour won fifty-five seats to National's thirty-two.

Shortly after taking office, Kirk announced New Zealand's diplomatic recognition of communist China and the withdrawal of New Zealand training teams from Vietnam, ending our involvement in this controversial war.

I had Oliver back to the Dr. Henderson for a checkup and was greeted by Fran. She said, "Is your boy doing well as he looks well." He gave her a big smile. Dr. Henderson called us in, and after he examined Oliver, he said, "He is doing well," and we also explained the sickness has stopped.

We left the clinic and headed back home, and I said to Claire, "You should be happy now that Oliver is doing well. It has been a long journey for you, and now you must start looking after yourself as your health is so important."

She agreed.

## Oliver's First Birthday

Oliver turned one, and this was a big occasion and a happy one for all of us as he got through his first year. This was a very difficult and also a very trying time for him as well as us parents. I looked back on the past year and was ever so thankful by the grace of God that he had come through such a terrible time.

I arranged his birthday party at our unit, and we invited the grandparents along with Fiona and James and Claire's young brother John. Then there was Jasmine and her husband and their two children, as well as Greg and Allison along with Dylan and Emily and their children.

I am sure Oliver did not know what was going on as everyone made a big fuss over him, and he got lots of presents. As it was a nice summer day, we had a barbecue outside, and after we then lit the candles on the cake, and we all sang "Happy Birthday." This was a joyous occasion, possibly one of the best with all the family and friends together. Yes, it was a great occasion, one that was memorable. Claire was so happy as well, and I was hoping this was the turning point for her.

A few weeks later, it was Christmas Day, and I am sure Oliver did not know what all the fuss was about. He got many clothes and toys from us. Not to be outdone, the grandparents brought him a rocking horse and lots of clothes and some toys, and his uncle James and aunty Fiona gave him lots as well. I prepared the dinner, and we had roast lamb and turkey along with all the trimmings. I also made my mother's recipe of the traditional plum pudding. This recipe is over one hundred years old and was handed down from her grandmother.

This was an exceptionally good occasion, the last one we all had as a family together. I said to Claire, "How about we take Oliver over to Australia for Christmas, and Mum and the others and the rest of the family can see Oliver."

She agreed, and I made the booking to fly out on December 23, a couple of days before Christmas.

We told Rose and Kevin, and they were not pleased with our decision. I finished work a week before we planned to leave, so it was all set. I phoned Mother and told her we were coming over.

# 9

# OLIVER'S FIRST VISIT TO AUSTRALIA

It was December 23 when we landed at the new international airport at Tullamarine. This was opened in 1970. It replaced Essendon Airport. When we arrived, I could not believe the size of the airport. It was just sheer luxury.

We finally got through customs, and there was my mother with my brother Lawrence and Serena to meet us and take us back to Bendigo. My plan was to stay at my mother's place. This was a very old house, over one hundred years old. Claire was not happy at all staying in this house. When we arrived, it was just a few days before Christmas Day, and we spent Christmas Day at my brother Lawrence's place. Mother was also there. Mother just loved Oliver.

We all had a very good day, and then shortly after, it was New Year's Eve to celebrate. We all got together at my eldest sister's place. The next day, New Year's Day, my brother Brad and his wife invited us all to a barbecue at their in place in Kangaroo Flat just outside of Bendigo, and we faced another calamity as there was a record-setting heat wave around Australia, not just for days, but for weeks. Temperatures regularly eclipsed 45 degrees Celsius (113 degrees Fahrenheit) in multiple locations across Australia. Where we stayed in central Victoria, we were coping with this very heat wave badly. It was very unfortunate that we came over at such a tough time. The heat wave and being over 40 degrees nearly every day affected us all. In fact, you could fry an egg on the roadway; the asphalt was melting on the roads. This affected Oliver, and he got extremely sick, and we had trouble settling him.

On New Year's Day, Claire said she would stay at my sister Leslie's place where they had good air-conditioning. I went to the barbecue, and most of our family was there. In fact, it was too damn hot to stay outside, so we all ventured inside, but we had an enjoyable day.

When we first arrived, Claire and I were staying at my mother's house, but it did not have air- conditioning as the house we lived in was very old and did not have the amenities Claire would have liked. She insisted we go back to New Zealand. This upset my mother very much as Mother wanted us to stay all the time at her place, and I can understand that.

My older brother John was three years older than me. He and his wife Mary said we can stay at their place as they had air-conditioning and a spare room. It was just out of the main city center as John still worked at Woolworths.

They made us very welcome. They had two children, Kath (who was two years old) and Mathew (who was four years of age). Oliver was very settled there, and the children spent a lot of time playing with him. However, the issue was Claire as she did not help the situation at all. Claire just wanted to go back to New Zealand.

I did call the airlines, and they said they are all booked out as it was the peak holiday period. I told Claire that she just had to battle it out—stay indoors and keep out of the heat. We were invited to my eldest sister's place Leslie and her husband Keith. They had two children, Thomas and Pauline, and we stayed there most of the day. My sister Leslie loved Oliver and really made a big fuss of him. That day Oliver got extremely sick, and my sister organized a doctor to see Oliver. My sister Leslie drove us to the doctor's clinic. His name was Dr. Mathews. We did not wait long, and we were taken into his room. Leslie introduced us to the doctor, and he examined Oliver.

He said Oliver was badly dehydrated and should be in the hospital. Claire said abruptly, "No way! He is not going to any hospital."

The doctor looked at her and said, "I will give you a script to get medication for him and a solution of electrolytes to help with the dehydration. You keep your boy in an air-conditioned place and keep him cool. A tepid bath is a good way to cool him down. Again, please keep up the fluids. He has to have plenty of fluids to replenish his system. If he brings it up, do it again. What I gave you will settle him down, and in a few days he should improve."

The doctor said in a stern voice directly to Claire, "If Oliver gets any worse, he will be put into the hospital. Do you understand?"

I said to my sister, "If I had my way, he would be in the hospital."

As we were leaving, she said to me, "Is Claire that stupid and going against a doctor's advice?"

I said, "Yes, that is what she is like. Let's get him back to your place, then you can take me to get his prescriptions, then I will explain a few things to you."

With that we dropped Claire and Oliver back at my sister's place, and Keith said he will look after Oliver with Claire while we were away. Keith was a teacher and very good with people. He loved his cigars, and he was a great guy.

I explained on the way to the chemist to my sister Leslie that Claire had a thing about hospitals, the issues we faced over the past twelve months, and in my opinion, Oliver would have been better a day or two in the hospital as they would give him a drip feed as he was not holding food or fluid down. I told her also about Claire's pregnancy and nearly losing Oliver.

Leslie replied, "That does explain a lot."

After I got the prescription medicine, we went back to my sister's place, stayed a while, and then went back to my brother Lawrence's place.

The day finally came, and we were leaving to go back to New Zealand. I said our goodbyes to the family, and Mother, Lawrence, and his wife Serena drove us to the airport. At the airport, Mother said to me, "Have a safe trip, and look after Oliver. He is such a dear little boy."

Mother gave Claire and I a big hug and kiss and a kiss for Oliver. She was upset by us not staying at her place, but I am sure she understood.

Claire did not make a big impression with the family, I must say. My brother Lawrence said, "She just spoilt your trip over here. She is not right in the head the way she carried on."

I agreed that yes, it was not a good holiday, and Claire did carry on too much, I am sorry to say. It now has entered my mind that I have a huge problem to keep all this together. Oliver was such a beautiful little boy and needed me around to make sure things were kept in order. His health issues were not going away, and Claire needed all the help she could get.

We all settled back from our trip to Australia. Looking back on the trip, with Claire wanting to come home early, and as I had explained that I had no way to get a flight back to New Zealand as this was the peak holiday period and all flights were all booked out, her attitude and not wanting to work in with my family did dampen the mood and made it very difficult to go anywhere. Some of my family commented to me she seemed a bit neurotic and very irrational. At that point I was blind to that fact that she was very irrational.

Coming back to New Zealand to a much cooler climate, I must confess Claire and Oliver were much more settled. The heat wave we experienced was severe, and having temperatures in the old scale over 100 degrees day in and day out was exceedingly difficult, and both Claire and Oliver did not take to the heat at all.

It was 1973 when we settled back in New Zealand. I found out that travel between Australia and New Zealand's travel arrangements allowed citizens of Australia and New Zealand to travel freely between the two countries without a passport. Then I heard the news that Prime Minister Kirk cancelled the proposed All Blacks rugby team Springbok Tour, and there was a lot of mail waiting for us when we returned. One was from the prime minister's office, and we received an invitation to attend a dinner to celebrate the victory of the election, and Prime Minister Kirk wanted to thank the people who volunteered to help in their campaign.

We both attended this dinner, and it was a great night. Meeting the prime minister personally, I felt it was a great honor, and he personally thanked me for my contribution.

New Zealand was not immune to lives lost in car accidents, just like Australia and most other countries. Lives were lost mainly due to drunk driving. Kevin was in this category. The incident with his son John in the car while intoxicated put John in the hospital and could have ended more tragically. This was a stark reminder of Claire's father and the danger he puts not only himself in but also his family.

This year in New Zealand, it was the introduction of blood and breath alcohol limits for drivers. The stats showed in 1960 that 374 New Zealanders lost their lives in road accidents. By 1969, the number of fatalities had increased by almost two hundred per year, with cars becoming more powerful. There were calls for an increase to the open-road speed limit of 50 mph (80 km/h). This was raised to 55 mph (88 km/h) in 1962 and to 60 mph (96 km/h) in 1969. While speed was one factor contributing to the ever-increasing road toll, drunk driving was another. In this year, blood alcohol limits and breath-testing procedures were introduced to tackle the latter problem. Breathalyzers helped identify drivers with more than 100 mg of alcohol per 100 ml of blood in their systems.

A funny side to this was we were invited to a friend's party early in the year not long after the introduction of roadside breath tests. There were a few cops at the party, and they brought with them a box of the balloons you blow into to see if you are over the limit. I tried one and was okay. Some others were well over and were advised not to drive home and get someone else to.

That year the Munich Summer Olympics were on, and all of New Zealand were stunned to learn that there was a terrorist attack in which eleven members of the Israeli team were killed. It did cast a shadow over the games. A few days earlier, the New Zealand rowing team won gold. "God Defend New Zealand" played at an Olympic medal ceremony on its own for the first time (it had been played in 1952 when Yvette

Williams won the long jump, after "God Save the Queen"). That year, New Zealand's population reached 2,929,686, and Australia had a population of 13,244,162. It was an interesting year, and going back to Australia was a bit unsettling, but soon we settled back. New Zealand was my new home, and now having a family to look after made this even more enjoyable. My focus was on Claire's well-being as she had gone through a very traumatic time. Oliver got over most of his illnesses and was much more settled. My ambition at this point was to get our own home, and my efforts were undermined in many ways, and the way Claire remarked on my lack of attention to her and Oliver was far from the truth. I am not looking for credit, but I did all the night feeds and made sure they were both well cared for, and to hear this from Claire was very disappointing indeed.

In life, we are all not perfect; we all have our faults and letdowns in life, but we must strive to do better and help each other through the good times and the not-so-good times.

# 10

# THE MOVIE BUSINESS

This is a very important part of this story as it became a big issue leading up to and during the court proceedings that unfolded—my love of the cinema and going to the movies. Like most kids growing up, I just loved going along every Saturday to the matinee shows. There was always long queues and anxious kids waiting to get in. The show usually started with a cartoon and then the shows such as Tom Mix, *Zorro, The Phantom,* and many others. These usually ended in a way you had to come back the following week to see what happened. These shows were packed with screaming kids, and we all loved the cowboys and Indian movies. We used to cheer and yell at the heroes.

If a Hopalong Cassidy movie was on, I was nearly first in line, and I did have the privilege to meet him personally when I was ten years of age. His real name was William Boyd, and he toured Australia in 1954, and he also brought his horse Topper with him. How I met Hoppy, as we kids called him, was he came to Bendigo in a Wild West show. I was standing out in front of this big tent. He came out, and he was standing on a platform. A large crowd gathered, then Hoppy looked at me and said, "Son, would you like to come up here and help me out?"

I just could not believe he picked me out. I was so excited. I quickly climbed up to the platform. I was gobsmacked, thinking, *Is this real?* I looked at him in awe. He had guns in his holster. He had on his famous outfit. He asked me to hold an egg and for me to place this into a bag that he was holding. Suddenly the egg somehow disappeared. He then did a few more tricks to draw in the crowd. After that he then asked me to be part of his show to be his assistant. I was shaking with excitement.

My hero took me into the huge big tent. The show started some fifteen minutes later, and quickly the tent was full of people. Hoppy then asked me to hold pieces of paper. He brought out his whip, and he cut these in half. He did lots of tricks. After the show, he gave me a signed photo (unfortunately, over the years this was sadly lost). I then ran home to tell Mum and the others and showed them the signed photo.

I was what you called an entrepreneur  in many ways and loved doing creative things and  was well recognized by all I worked for. Like any business, you need to do some research and development. I then went about undertaking some research on the various clubs such as the sporting leagues as well as the working man's clubs. I found that they already had entertainment, such as live shows and bingo nights. My idea was to screen movies at these venues. I then went around and approached the various clubs. This idea was met with enthusiasm. They said to come back with a price and come up with a list of lots of movies I could show. They also said all entertainment in these venues was scheduled with agents. They then put me in touch with the booking agency that scheduled most of the entertainment for the clubs. Her name was Mrs. Perry.

I then phoned her and set up a meeting. This day I arrived at her office in the heart of the city, her office was full of posters of artists, books, and papers everywhere. I looked at the mess when I walked in. Her office desk was cluttered so much, I was sure she had not a clue what was on it.

I introduced myself, and she said to call her Barbara. I then told her my plan and said, "I already have researched this with the various clubs, and they are very interested in showing movies at their respective venues."

Barbara said, "Can you get hold of the latest movies?" I said yes.

She then said, "Get the available list and then drop this into my office. It's a great innovative idea and a first." She would do the bookings for me and be my agent. Her commission was also very good at 15%.

As I was leaving, she said to me again, "Danial, they must be current movies," and I agreed. I suppose this was putting the cart before the horse as now I must get the latest movies.

I was very confident the film distributors would go along with my plan. I then set up a meeting with the film distributors in Auckland. I found out who was in charge of the hiring and schedules. I then contacted a Mr. Johnson and made an appointment to see him. I introduced myself, and he said to call him Brian.

As it was nearly lunchtime, I said, "Why don't we have a chat over lunch?" We then went to the Royal International Hotel, and I discussed my plan to show movies at the various clubs. I told him the success of this will be the capability of getting the latest movies.

Brian said to me that seeing the clubs were private clubs by membership, he could not see any issue hiring the movies. He said, "See me Friday, and we can go through the list."

I could not wait until we met up again on Friday later that week. He gave me a list, and these movies were currently being screened at the city cinemas, so my plan was to beat the suburban theaters to screen movies as soon as they are finished at the city cinemas. Brian said he would help me and said each Monday, the new list comes out, and it takes usually a few days before the suburban cinemas book the movies. He then said, "Come in on each Monday, and you can do the bookings for the movies you want. This way you will be first in and then able to schedule your screenings."

I just could not believe my luck, and now I had the go-ahead. At the time I was still living in Buckland Road, and I spoke to my good friend Dylan Watson, who also was a close neighbor. I told him of my plan. He said if I set this up, he would love to work with me. I also said to him I would need projectionists to work on nights as I could not do this all the time as I will have to spend time at home. "We can do alternate nights. Also I will train you so you will be a full-on projectionist."

Dylan was excited with this as he said, "I can see the latest movies as well as get paid."

I had previously discussed this with Claire, and she seemed reasonably happy with the idea. Although I am sure she did not fully understand what it was all about, she asked where was all the money coming from, and she said, "Do not dare touch our home loan account." This was a  bit ironic as she did not put one cent into that account as this came from my wages as well as my part-time work doing the office cleaning a few nights a week.

I said to her, "If I set this up, it will help us to buy our own home." I explained to her, "I will need to get a loan, and as promised, I will not touch our home loan account. The movie business will take care of that."

I then quickly established a Pty Ltd company called Movie Hire Services. This then enabled me to get equipment and other things I needed at wholesale rates. Now with all this set up and in place, the next step was to source the equipment I needed. I met the distributor for EIKI Projectors and picked out the latest state-of-the-art projectors, costed out the sound system and the screens required, and then went to the bank with confidence that the bank manager would give me the loan as I did get on well with him. I put together a detailed business plan that showed him the actual costs along with expected revenue and profit before tax. He said to me my business plan was well put together, and he loved the concept.

He said to me, "This can turn into a lucrative business," and he gave me a loan of $2,000. He said, "You have savings from the part-time cleaning work you're doing as well as your work with Crest Foods."

The bank manager went on to say that I was in an exceptionally good financial position, and our home loan account was looking extremely healthy. I said to him I promised Claire that I would not touch the home loan account.

He said, "Wise decision. You seem to be a very entrepreneurial person. Good luck with your new venture."

I thanked him very much.

The bank manager put the funds of $2,000 straight away into my checking account. This was more than enough to set the business up.

I went back to the distributors of EIKI and paid for the two EIKI projectors along with accessories to screen cinemascope and spare reels and rewinders and sound system. Dylan helped me to design and construct the large movie screen as this was 10 feet high by 20 feet wide. This was constructed so that it was portable, and I had the frame designed that it fit neatly and could be put up quickly and dismantled quickly.

I was all set to go. Next thing now was getting the movie list from Brian at the distributors. He gave me the list when each one was available after they had finished in the city cinemas, and as my plan was that I had to get in before the suburban cinemas, this is gave me a competitive advantage and was well received by the clubs as they got to screen the latest movies to their members.

Each week I gave my agent Barbara the list, she was excited as she said, "These movies are now showing in the city cinemas."

I said, "Yes, and I hire these before they go to the suburban theaters."

She was extremely impressed. The bookings came in, and this was really something as I had to schedule shows that were every second night at the various venues. The first movie was *American Graffiti*, and we showed this at every club, and it went down very well. Movies like *The Exorcist*, *Papillon*, *Serpico*, James Bond's *Live and Let Die*, and the big hit *The Sting* with Paul Newman and Robert Redford. This was followed by many other top movies as this was a first for New Zealand sports and working and returned servicemen's clubs showing the latest movies for their members. I showed movies on average three to four times a week, and between Dylan and myself, we rotated the work. We had an assistant when either Dylan or I had a night off as we had to be fair to our partners as we could not operate the movie nights on our own. Claire's younger brother John helped on these nights.

Despite criticism later by Claire, it was a very profitable business, and I did pay people well. The income derived from showing the movies showed a very handsome profit after all costs were taken such as wages, commission to the agent, and the loan repayment. I put in extra funds from this business into our home loan account as this will secure the deposit required and have enough funds to furnish our new home as well as to have all the grounds done as the movie business was doing very well.

## Community Service

I received a phone call one night and was asked to attend a meeting at the shopping center by the management. I was very curious what would the center management want with me. The meeting was scheduled for 10:00 a.m. the following day.

When I arrived at the meeting, there were two police officers. They introduced me to them as well a local councillor. I thought to myself, *What the heck is going on here? Surely I have not done anything wrong.*

Then they spelt out the issues they were having with the kids on Friday nights, and I thought to myself, *What has all this to do with me?*

The manager of the shopping center asked me if I would be interested in showing movies on Friday nights at the hall across the road from the center.

You see, as you know, New Zealand has late Friday night shopping as all shops are closed Saturdays and Sundays. The local shopping center here has a big issue on Friday nights. This is because the large crowds of kids of all ages were mingling around and upsetting the Friday night shoppers. Then there was an upsurge of fights among the kids, mainly teenagers, and a lot of shoplifting took place.

The manager said, "If you would be willing to show movies on Friday nights, we will promote the movies throughout the center, and the traders are all behind this. We will pay you for this, whatever your costs are."

I could not believe what I was hearing. I replied, "Yes, I will do that. You pay for the hall and have a community club that can run a canteen, and they can put the profits back to the community. They could help at the door as well."

The people in the room raised their eyebrows and had smiles on their faces.

I then said, I will charge the kids 50¢ to cover my costs, parents free, and by this you do not have to pay me anything as I will do this as a community service."

They all stood up at the meeting, shook hands with me, and said how grateful they are and will work with me on this project as all this was agreed upon.

It was two weeks later that I ran the first show. I put on a western movie, and only forty children turned up along with a few parents. I then thought of doing a quick survey and found most of the kids were either of Māori or Island origin, and they loved kung fu movies.

The following week, the shopping center advertised that the movie this week was Bruce Lee's *Enter the Dragon*. The word had gotten around as well, and when Dylan and I turned up an hour before the screening, there were kids lining up outside the hall. I said, "This is amazing."

We had over two hundred kids who came along that night. Each week after that, the hall was packed. It was a roaring success.

We had regular visits from the police and council to see how it was all going. The canteen was run by a local charity, and they did very well out of this as they sold plenty before the show and at the interval.

I was told because of the Friday night movies, the crime rate had dropped as well as the fighting, and the store owners as well as shoppers were happy with hardly any kids roaming around and causing trouble.

The price I charged the kids was more than enough to cover expenses. Also the film distributors gave me a half-price deal seeing it was what I called a community service.

*The Complaint*

The next issue I had to deal with was a complaint put into the local council by the local cinema operator. This was taken up at the local council meeting. My Friday night shows was the complaint. As I had the backing of the council in the first place, plus it was the council's community hall used, it was said at the meeting by the councillor that I had a license to operate to screen the movies, and this was also a community service. This also had the backing of the police plus the town center. Collectively, they all endorsed this.

The cinema operator at the council meeting was outraged and was far from happy, and he stormed out of the meeting. He was not satisfied with this, so next, he then took his complaint up with the film distributors in his efforts to stop me. As I was well informed from the council meeting and what took place at the council meeting, I called Brian at the film distributors and advised him of what took place.

The local cinema operator, when he arrived in Brian's office, claimed I was running an illegal operation with my movie company and running these movies at the community center and various clubs. Seeing Brian was well advised of the council meeting, he told the cinema operator he was told I had a license and had their backing, and he also told him this has the backing of the local council and the police. "I am sorry, but unfortunately, you cannot do much about this."

He dropped all the complaints, and I was allowed to continue.

The success of these movie nights was well recognized and was appreciated by the store operators in the shopping center. They would come up to me in the street and tell me what a difference this has made on Friday nights. Overall, the fights and crime rate had dropped. The ironic thing was I never had a license from the distributors; I just had an agreement. If that constitutes a license, I am not sure, but that never came for me to provide the proof if I had a license or not. The support of the distributors, maybe because it was the private screenings I was doing at the various clubs, I was not sure. The movie business I operated was a first, and I am sure it did hurt a few local cinemas. The word got out to one of the local rugby league clubs, and they asked me to show movies

to the kids after the game on Saturday afternoons. They had a very good hall that could pack in a hundred or so kids. Most of the children were Māori or Island heritage, and they told me they liked kung fu movies, so again I screened *Enter the Dragon* with Bruce Lee, and this brought the house down. It was hard to hear the movie as they screamed and shouted so much.

On most Saturdays, over one hundred kids watched the movies while the parents partied on after the game. Oliver attended some of these shows on Saturday afternoons, and he just loved being with all these kids of all ages enjoying themselves.

I found my movie business was high in demand. It was exhausting at times. My ambition and plan was to buy our own home. My mother always told me hard work never killed anyone. If you want to succeed in life, you have to work hard. That was my way also.

I have no doubts the movie business and what I set out to achieve was not treated as one would expect it should have, as later on it became a major issue. The extra income I made by operating the movie business at times was more than my day job brought in. The business did help me with the deposit for the new house more than Claire ever gave me credit for. This was her way of trying to justify her downfall, and later when it suited her, she and her family made various issues and did become very contentious.

# 11

# 1974—THE YEAR OF INCIDENTS

Oliver was now three years of age and growing up quickly. This year, many incidents took place. It was not only a concern for me but also Oliver as many involved him. My aim was this year to buy our own home and hoping this will appease Claire. Or was she the loving, faithful wife she made out to be? Was this year the start of the demise of the marriage? Now looking back, yes, it was.

The unit we lived in was brand-new and had a lovely backyard ideal for Oliver, and it was fenced off so he could not get out onto the main road. Across the road was a shopping strip, and right across the road was the dairy corner store, chemist, a doctor's clinic, and a small grocer's shop. This was handy to have all this nearly at your doorstep. The plan was to stay in the government housing unit until we bought our own home. The corner-store dairy, as they call it in New Zealand, is what we call in Australia a milk bar. This dairy was run by Simon and his wife Patricia, and I became good friends with them.

At the back of the unit were a Samoan Island family, and they often would chat over the fence with us. This day of what I can remember, it was rather a hot day, and I was digging a vegetable patch. My neighbor at the back said, "Hey, boy, do you want to try my home brew? I have a cold one in the fridge."

I said, "Okay, I will have one." I did this not to offend him.

He came out with two glasses in hand and opened up the bottle. He poured me a drink and handed it to me. I took a sip, and boy, was it potent. I did drink what was in the glass, and he said, "Boy, let us finish off the bottle." The second glass I do not remember as what I was told later was that I fell over backward in the new garden and had to be taken inside and put to bed. I did not wake up until the next morning. Boy, did I have a headache. I never, ever had another one of his home brew again. I am not sure what he had in it, but it was potent.

Another day Oliver was outside with us in the backyard playing, and we had a rug spread out so he can sit on it. Suddenly he just went limp and stopped breathing. He was unconscious! I said, "Quick, Claire, get in the car as it's quicker to get him to the hospital as it is not far from us."

He was going blue, and I sped up the car, and I had my lights flashing. Claire shook Oliver over and over again, and he did start breathing but was still out cold. I ran through two sets of red lights, arrived at the hospital, and drove straight to where ambulances are parked. Claire ran in with Oliver in her arms. I quickly parked the car and hastily went into the emergency department. Claire was talking to a nurse.

They took Oliver from Claire, and they went into a cubicle. They put Oliver on oxygen, and the doctor came, and they gave him an injection. The doctor was not sure what happened to Oliver. They checked for bites as they said he may have been bitten by a bee or wasp, but they could not find anything.

After a short while, Oliver came to, and the hospital ran a few tests. They could not explain what happened. They wanted to keep him overnight to keep an eye on him, but Claire said no; she wanted to take him home. This was a frightening experience.

The next day, we took him to our own doctor, and he also ran some tests, and it was all a mystery. They put it down to heat stress and dehydration. I would have preferred Oliver to stay overnight at the hospital as they may have found out what did happen.

This brought back memories when Oliver was only a few months old and in the Karitane Hospital, and Claire and her mother took him out of the hospital when he was still extremely ill. I am not sure if this is being overprotective or only plain irresponsible on both of their parts. Despite my disapproval, they did what they felt was best in Oliver's interest.

I always had a continual battle with Claire and her mother over Oliver's care. They possibly mean well, but it was to the detriment of Oliver's well-being.

## The Sleeping Pills

After having Oliver, Claire, in many ways, she changed. Often she was depressed, and she found it hard to handle things. Her mother helped her out a lot, as did Fiona. Despite what Claire has said in her statements that I was never around and implied I did not do much at all, this was far from the truth. I actually did all the night feeds when Oliver was a baby, and I did most of the cooking and helped out with the housework. This brings me to this incident and was mentioned in the custody court hearing. Her version and mine were poles apart, and as to her version of what really took place, it was just another of her hiding the facts...or was this a sign she needed help?

It was a midweek night, and I came home from work around 5:00 p.m. Dinner was not prepared. As always, Oliver was pleased to see me, and his eyes always lit up when I came home. There was always lots of hugs and kisses.

Claire, on the other hand, was very quiet this night. I asked her how the day went, and she just shrugged her shoulders and said alright. I went ahead and cooked up a meal. I decided on a chicken dinner with lots of vegetables as I was a stickler for having steamed vegetables. I put Oliver in his high chair, and Oliver had his favorite bowl, and I mashed all his food for him. He was at the stage where he was feeding himself. At times a lot missed his mouth and went on his bib.

We finished dinner, and I helped Claire clean up and do the dishes. I said to Claire that I would be leaving around seven thirty after Oliver went to bed as I had a screening tonight at the leagues club, and Dylan would be here soon to collect the gear.

I did ask her again if she was all right as she did seem a bit quiet. She replied, "I am okay, a bit tired."

I put Oliver to bed as he loved me tucking him in for the night. I gave Claire a big hug and kiss and said, "See you in a few hours."

Dylan arrived at the house, and we packed the wagon up with the gear, and off we went. We both arrived at the club just before 8:00 p.m. The show was to start at eight thirty. As both Dylan and I had this down pat, it did not take long to set up. The room where we showed the movies was nearly full when we arrived. It was good for the members as they could have a beer or wine while watching the movie.

We started on time and showed *The Godfather.* This finished just after 11:00 p.m. As we always have an interval to allow the members to get refreshments or go to the bathroom, we packed up and left the venue around eleven thirty and arrived back at my placed just before midnight.

Dylan always stayed to help me put all the equipment away. We unloaded the wagon. I took out the front door key, and for some reason, I could not open the door. I said to Dylan, "This  is strange. It seems I am locked out. Let's go around the back door as I should be able to get in through that door."

With that, Dylan and I went around the back of the house. I tried the back door and could not open that either. I could see the hall light was still on, but all the windows were closed. I could see through the venetian blinds as they were slightly opened. I looked into the main bedroom as this was situated at the rear of the house. I could see Claire in bed, and you could slightly hear moaning. Was she snoring or in a deep sleep?

I knocked on the window very loudly and was calling out to Claire, "I cannot get into the house!"

No response.

I said to Dylan with concern, "She looks like she is sick." Dylan said, "We better knock the door down."

The back door also had a safety chain on it, so I said to Dylan, "I have a jemmy in the back shed."

So we had to jemmy the door open, then we had to break the safety chain. The noise was so loud, you would have thought that would wake anyone up, but not so. When both of us went inside and turned the light on in the bedroom, we noticed Claire sprawled across the bed. I shook her a bit and said, "Claire, wake up."

She did not stir.

Then Dylan called out loudly, "Look at this on the floor!" It was an open bottle. It was a small bottle and contained many tablets. Dylan asked what was in it as I picked the bottle up.

I replied, "Look at the label. It is Valium tablets."

Dylan then asked, "How many were in the bottle? It seemed quite a few."

I replied, "Yes, looks like to me she has taken an overdose. Look, let's see if we can awaken her." I tried not to panic, but I knew we had a serious situation on our hands here.

Dylan said, "I will go home and get Addison." His wife was a registered nurse, and she could help us here. Dylan then flew out of the house as he lived only a few doors down the street. It would not take him long.

It seemed liked eternity till he came back as he explained, "I had to get my wife out of bed."

In the meantime, after a lot of shaking and shouting, Claire started to arouse. Then Addison came in, and she was in her nightwear. As she was a nurse, she would be able to advise me what to do. I was panicking, which did not help the situation.

Addison said, "Seeing she is coming around, we can give her some coffee and may have to put her in the shower."

I said, "Whatever it takes."

Allison in the meantime called the local hospital. She explained what the situation was, and they said seeing she has been aroused and her speech was slurred gave them the indication she was over the worst. "If she worsens, then you must call 111 and call an ambulance and bring her in."

Allison and I got Claire into the shower, and this did bring her around. She became very erratic and called us a few names and told us to bugger off and leave her alone. We put her back into bed, and she went straight off to sleep. Allison said her vital signs seemed okay. "Keep an eye on her, and call me if you need me."

Dylan and Allison left. I checked on Oliver, and he slept right through all the commotion. I stayed home the next day. I got Oliver up and gave him his breakfast. Claire came out around 10:00 a.m. She did not say much; in fact, she did not have a clue what happened last night. She was still very drowsy.

I asked, "Why did you take so many tablets last night? Also, you locked me out."

She denied locking me out. After she had some breakfast, she went back to the bedroom and spent most of the day in bed. Later that day, I did organize a doctor's appointment for the next day. She went on her own as I looked after Oliver. She did not tell me what the doctor said. In short, she said for me to mind my own business.

I knew Claire was not herself, and there was another reason, I was sure, behind all this, as I found out later. I did think at this point, Claire had many issues she was dealing with, and this was a big part of her well-being. I did love Claire and Oliver very much and cared for them both. This episode with Claire was profoundly serious, and this was the start of many incidents that did take place. It is what I described in this story the beginning of a slippery slope, despite all my efforts to keep it all together, this was not to be. In life, you make decisions or do things that can have future consequences, and if you lie or are not true to yourself or your partner or your child, then what happens on the course you embark on not only affects you but all people around you, then you must take full responsibility of your actions.

Was this the case with Claire? Let us see.

## *Claire Home Late*

When we were still living in the unit in Buck Road a lot did take place similar to the episode when Claire took the sleeping tablets and the supposed overdose. All this was categorically denied. She claimed that she did not take too many; however, between myself along with Dylan and his wife, we knew differently.

Claire decided she wanted to start work again, and she found work for a few hours at night at the local car dealership. She was employed to do their accountancy work, so I was told. I was not working that night as Dylan and John, Claire's young brother, screened the movie *Blazing Saddles* at the working man's club. Dylan arrived back well after 11:00 p.m., after he dropped John off at Claire's parents' place.

I helped him unpack the gear as all this went into our spare bedroom. I said to Dylan, "Claire is not home yet. She is usually here around 11:15 p.m."

Dylan said to me, "She may have been held up." Dylan stayed for a while, and over a coffee, we chatted how well the show went. Dylan left just after midnight, and I waited for Claire as it came well past midnight. This was very unusual for her. I called Rose and said when she answered the phone, "I'm sorry to call you so late, but have you seen Claire tonight?" I then explained she was not home from work yet.

Rose said she had not seen her for a few days. "Why," she asked, "is Claire working at nights?"

I said, "This is what she wanted. You know Claire, she makes her mind up on things, and that is that."

Rose said, "I hope she has not had an accident."

I agreed. I said to Rose, "I already called her work and no answer. I will call again when she comes home."

Rose said, "I am worried about that woman as she has been acting strange lately."

*Hallelujah,* I said to myself. Her doting mother of all things now thinks something is wrong with Claire. She would not accept Claire taking sleeping pills. I then said to Rose, "Go to bed, I will call you." With that I ended the call and placed the phone back in its cradle.

I went to Oliver' room and checked on him. He was fast asleep hugging his Cookie Bear as he absolutely loved sleeping with his Cookie Bear.

This was one night to remember as it was the beginning of the end of the marriage. At this point, I was not quite clear what really was taking place. I trusted Claire and did all I could to take care of her and made sure Oliver was also okay. Oliver was the bright light in my life.

Shortly after I spoke to Rose, I heard a car pull up in the driveway. *Oh great,* I thought. *Claire is home.*

However, it was Rose and Kevin. The front door was not locked, and they came straight in. It was very obvious they were very concerned. Rose went into Oliver's room and said to me, "He is such a sweet boy." She looked at me a moment and continued. "What is going on with you and Claire? And why does she work these stupid hours?" Rose blasted at me.

I said, "Keep your voice down. I am not sure why, we do live well within our means, and we also financially sound. Claire keeps all the money she earns at this part-time job. She often says it may come in handy one day." This often made me wonder if she had an ulterior motive or a plan on which she is working.

Shortly after, a car pulled up on the front lawn, and I looked out the window. It was Claire. I said to Rose, "She has some explaining to do coming home at this ungodly hour." I looked at the clock; it was well past 1:30 a.m.

Rose flew out of the front doorway and screamed at Claire and told her how stupid she was coming home at this late hour. I could not get a word in, and Dylan, who lived a few doors down, heard the commotion and came up. It was at this point that Rose hit Claire across the face. I quickly grabbed Rose and said that was uncalled for and pulled her off Claire.

We all went inside, and I said to Dylan, "You go, and I will speak to you in the morning." Rose was still at Claire. She pulled Claire's handbag from her, and out fell two wineglasses. Rose lashed out at her again, yelling at her.

I said, "Please be quiet, you will wake Oliver up. This is going nowhere."

Rose yelled again, "Where have you been? All of us have been worried sick that you may have been in an accident as you were not home at your usual time." She was screaming at Claire. "Look at the time! It's nearly 2:00 a.m. Daniel called us earlier to see if you were at our place as you were not home, also because how late it was. We got very concerned and decided to come over."

Rose was very agitated and upset. I tried to get a word in, but I could not get a word in either way. I suggested that Rose and Kevin leave, and I said I will sort this out with Claire. "I will call you in the morning."

Suddenly, Oliver came in crying. "What is all the noise, Daddy?" he looked at his mother and said, "Why are you crying, Mummy?"

I then said quickly to Rose, "Seeing he is awake, can you take Oliver back to your place, and I will pick him up in the morning?"

Oliver gave me a big hug and kiss. Oliver took Cookie Bear with him. He left without saying goodbye to his mother. This was very noticeable. When Rose and Kevin left, it was well past 2:00 a.m.

When they left, Claire would not give me an explanation straightaway as she was on the defensive. I said to her, "What if I did the same to you, how would you feel?" Claire just shook her head. "It's obvious you have been drinking. But with who?" This was the big question.

She replied, "With some friends at work."

"Then why didn't you call me and tell me what you're doing?" I asked. "Surely you owe me that much. What are you hiding?"

She replied, "It's none of your business."

I screamed out, "What none of my bloody business? You're my wife, for god's sake, and you have been out till all hours of the night, and it's none of my business?! You're a bloody joke! You need to wake up to yourself. Oliver along with you are my family. I try and do everything for you and Oliver. Soon we will be applying for the home loan as we can then look at what house we are going to buy. Isn't this what you want?"

She replied, sobbing, "Yes!"

I replied, "Then you have a strange way of showing it."

Claire went off to bed. I was so confused and upset. I thought that there was more to this than what Claire was letting on. I slept on the couch that night, and I did get a few hours' sleep. I did check in on Claire, and she was still asleep. I took the day off work, and being supervisor, I suppose it gave me some leeway. I was very lucky I was employed by a very understanding company.

I had a cup of coffee and then went around to Claire's parents' place around nine o'clock to pick Oliver up. When I arrived, Rose said Oliver was still asleep. Rose said, "I need to have a word with you." She took me into their lounge room.

Oliver must have heard me come in; he gave me a big hug and kiss. I said to Oliver, "You go into the lounge with Grandpa while I have a chat with Nanna."

Oliver nodded and went back out.

I said to Rose, "Oliver is such a delightful little boy, and because he is so young, he cannot understand what is going on."

Rose said she has had suspicions for a while that Claire was having an affair. "I am sure it is this Craig bloke. He works with her, and I think he is her boss or supervisor." She went on to say, "Claire has been talking about this Craig guy."

I said to Rose, "If this is the case, I am the last to know as I always trusted Claire and never expected this from her. I will have it out with Claire and see what she has got to say."

With that I took Oliver home, and we both spent the day playing with his train set as well as taking him down to the children's playground. It was good spending the day with Oliver, and he asked me, "Is Mummy sick?"

I said, "She is tired working so late at night."

It is difficult to tell or explain to a three-year-old that his mother and father are having issues. When we got back from the park, Claire was up, and Oliver said he was tired. I put him down for an afternoon nap. I went back into the lounge, and I said to Claire, "Can I make you a coffee? We need to talk as you have some explaining to do." I made a cup of coffee for each of us, and we sat in the lounge.

I spoke to Claire very quietly and did not raise my voice at all. I came straight out with it. "Last night, you were with Craig, I believe?"

"Yes," she said, "but it is not what you think. We did have a few drinks after work, and time got away from us as we were chatting. I can talk to him."

I said, "You can talk to me."

"Oh," she said, "it's different with Craig. He is very understanding. Anyway, you're so wrapped up in the movie business and no time for us."

I said, "That is nonsense. I cook most of the meals, also I bathe Oliver, and I do provide for you both. The movie business is bringing in a lot of money, and soon we can get our home loan. Isn't that what you want?"

Claire teared up and said to me that she was sorry about what happened last night and that it won't happen again.

I said, "What about Craig?"

"Oh," she said, "he is just a work friend. You do not have to worry about him."

I took Claire at her word and arranged a nice dinner for us all. Oliver was happy to see his mother not crying, and he gave her a big hug and kiss. I have noticed when Claire is upset or crying, Oliver just clams up. He avoids her, which is very noticeable.

It was December, and it was Oliver's third birthday. We gave him a lovely party, and we had friends and family there. For some reason, I felt Claire was not herself and was preoccupied. I was unsure if Claire was having an affair with Craig as at times things felt normal, although her feelings toward me did change. I felt the relationship was strained. I asked Claire again what has changed. She replied, "Nothing at all. I am still here, aren't I?" She told me again she was not having an affair with Craig, that they were just good friends, and she considered him as someone she can talk to.

I said, "Claire, I know and understand I am not always here for you and Oliver. I do work hard to get us where we are today."

She just said again, "It's different with Craig."

I said, "I am not sure what you mean by that." I then said no more to keep the peace and avoid any arguments.

It was a Saturday night, and as I had a free night, Claire and I along with Oliver went to Dylan's house, and we stayed for dinner and had a wine or two. We were discussing what movies we should get to show at the clubs. I always had an advance list of the availability of the movies being released. Suddenly we heard screaming and shouting out on the main road. It sounded like someone being murdered!

We rushed outside, and up the road, there was a naked woman in the middle of the road swinging a small axe—a tommyhawk, I guess— and in the front of the house there was a man yelling at her to stop. He yelled, "Jessy, stop this, stop this!" He went to start his panel van, which was in a driveway.

Next thing you know, this woman mad in rage started smashing the windows of the panel van. She actually broke nearly every window and also hit what we assumed was her husband with the tommyhawk. He was hurt badly, and shortly after, the police arrived and took her away.

We all went back outside, and we finished our schedule of movies and left to go home. I said to Claire, "Well, that was a sight to see. I hope the guy is okay as he was hurt badly."

I was talking to Dylan the next day, and he told me the crazy woman came back later in the morning. Simon at the local corner store told Dylan she was drunk, and it was her husband whom she bashed up and hurt badly.

*Drive-In Movie*

I always came up with different ideas, and this day I said to Dylan, "You have a big backyard and easy access to it. For fun's sake, why don't we show a movie in your backyard, and we can drive our cars in and watch the movie from the car? This can be a first to have a drive-in outdoor theater."

Dylan loved it and jumped at the idea. So we planned the night as it was summer, and should be a fine and a warm night. Dylan's backyard was so large. We put around twelve cars plus seating for more people. The word did get out with neighbors and friends, and they all wanted to come along to this night.

On the night, Dylan and I set up the big mobile screen, projectors, and sound system. The sound system was set up around his backyard so everyone could hear. The movie screened that night was *Battle of the Bulge*, a great war movie. Although released in 1965, we thought it was such a good film, and most had not seen this before.

On this night, Claire invited Craig, and Craig turned up in his car, and he was with his daughter Cindy. I said to Craig, "Where is your wife?"

"Oh," he said, "she has other arrangements."

I had to be stationed with Dylan at the projectors and the controls for the sound system. The movie started, and I said to Dylan, "Where is Claire?"

He said, "Oh, she is in the front seat over there."

I said, "That is Craig's car. Craig was her manager or supervisor where she worked part-time at the car dealership."

Dylan said, "Who else is in the car with them?" "That is his daughter Cindy," I replied.

Dylan said, "I did see him earlier and wondered where he came from. This Craig guy, he is very red-faced and looks a bit creepy."

I said to Dylan, "Yes, I agree."

A funny thing happened during the movie. When the tanks in the movie rolled over the top of the hill and started firing, the wind came up and blew the screen down. It was like the tanks firing in the movie did this. Everyone broke into laughter. Dylan and I put it the screen up again and secured this with more rope. This was to ensure we can finish the movie.

It was a very good fun night. I noticed Claire made a fuss over Craig's daughter. During the intermission we served supper, and there were savories and sandwiches and tea and coffee provided. A lot of people asked who was that person Claire was sitting with in the car over there. I shrugged this off and said he was just a friend of the family.

This was obvious to many as to why Claire was with Craig and his daughter. Some said, "Surely, she is not having an affair with this guy?"

I said, "I certainly hope not."

I was unsure if Claire was having an affair with Craig as at times things felt normal, although the relationship was still very strained. I challenged her about Craig, and she told me that she was not having an affair with him. She was so convincing that I took her at her word.

The episode of the sleeping pills and the night she came home late after being with Craig and her mother slapping her came up in submissions and was mentioned in the court hearing, but again the full story did not come out, funny that. It was strange that I was portrayed as the villain. Claire was the innocent victim in all this, or was one person named Craig Kelly misleading her?

Over the coming weeks, Claire seemed more distant. She did come home on time, but she had no interest in what I did or at times Oliver. She did take Oliver to her parents' place more often.

I told her we can start looking soon for a house to buy, and I said, "Let's look into the new estate where James and Fiona are living as there are lots in the street nearly being completed."

She said, "We will go on the weekend when there will be an open house."

That weekend, we picked out a house. It was nearing completion as this would be ready around March next year. I put a deposit on the house and then went to the bank to apply for a home loan, and having a good relationship with the bank including the manager, I had the loan approved. Claire was so happy about this and was more than delighted that finally we can have our own home. The next chapter happened just after Oliver's third birthday, and this did astonish many how Claire blatantly went on a trip and how she deceived me along with the lies she told to cover her well-planned trip. To be a good liar, you also need to have a good memory. She portrayed me as the aggressor and the villain. I then wondered how much can you do and try and get away with it and fool people? I think Claire took me for a dumb fool, and she must have felt in her own way she can get away with her deceit and lies. This took place while we were still living in Buck Road,

and we had been married for four years now.

I thought things looked a lot brighter for us, and Claire loved the prospect of having a new home. I did all I could to hold on to the marriage as I always loved Claire, and we had a beautiful three-year-old boy. This next story did get a mention when asked if she went away with Craig. The astonishing things is she selected a house with me in Clee Crescent, a lovely three-bedroom home with a large lounge and kitchen and dining area.

What Claire did next was hard to imagine and left me bewildered.

# 12

# CLAIRE'S SECRET TRIP TO WELLINGTON

You could not make this stuff up. This is my recollection of how this unfolded. Claire said she wanted a break for a few days and wanted to go to Wellington with her girlfriend Jasmine as she would go with her for company. Jasmine was her bridesmaid at our wedding. They were longtime friends as they both grew up together. Claire also asked to take Oliver with her as she said she arranged a ticket for him.

Well, I thought this was well planned, and anyway, I also felt this would do her good. I said I would take them to the airport at Mangere, but Claire insisted she would take her car and leave this at the airport as Claire said she was not sure what time they will be coming back, and she did not want to bother me. Oliver was so excited that he will be going on a big airplane again, so on the Friday afternoon, they both left. I never thought any more about this again until the next day. I said to Claire, "Call me when you get to Wellington," and she said she would, but for some reason better known to Claire, she did not call me. The next day I went down to the local[ix] shops on Saturday morning. It just happened that I met Jasmine's husband Trevor, who was also in the same store doing some shopping. After saying hi to him, I said to Trevor, "How are the girls going?"

He looked rather puzzled at what I just said. "What do you mean?" he asked.

I then I explained that Claire said she was going away for the weekend to Wellington with Jasmine. "Claire has also taken Oliver with her."

Trevor said, "No, that's not right, as for one, Jasmine has not seen Claire for several months. I am sorry, but it seems you may have a problem with Claire. This is not right and also bringing Jasmine into it. I can tell you Jasmine won't be happy with that."

Wow, what a situation for me. This was a big blow for me. Later that day, I went around and spoke to Jasmine, and she told me that Claire seemed very unhappy, and she was seeing this Craig guy. "Also her mother Rose had called me often and confided in me as we have been very close friends since we were kids living in the same street."

"Yes, I know. I did not know Rose has been calling you," I said to her. "I am sorry you have been dragged into this mess."

Jasmine was such a lovely person and understanding, and she also said to me, "If Claire leaves you and Oliver, I will have no more to do with her, I can assure you of that."

Jasmine and Trevor said to me on leaving, "You take care of yourself, and look after Oliver as he is a beautiful little boy. You make sure no harm comes to him, and you both are welcome anytime."

I said to both Trevor and Jasmine, "I appreciate your support, and I will let you know what happens when Claire gets back."

After I left speaking to Jasmine and Trevor, I was very upset and thought, *How could she betray me like this?* Her lies and deceit is not what a normal person would do. I could not wait until Claire returned. In the meantime, I did mention this to her parents.

Later on Monday afternoon, Claire came home with Oliver, and I confronted her and said, "How did the trip to Wellington go?"

"Oh," she said, "we had a great time."

I said, "What about Jasmine? Did she have a good time too?"

"Oh yeah," Claire replied. "We all had a great time looking around Wellington."

I then said to Claire, "You're a bloody liar and a cheat. I know you were with Craig." Then I told her I was at the local shops and met Trevor as he was in the same store where I was in.

Claire snapped back at me and said, "I know who Trevor is!" I was sure Claire knew what was coming as she was very defensive.

I said to Claire that I asked Trevor how the girls were going as I had not heard from Claire since she left on Friday afternoon on the flight to Wellington. "Trevor looked at me stupidly and said, 'Jasmine is home with the kids.'"

Claire went very pale as she knew she had been caught out, and this time her cheating has been caught out.

I was terribly upset as one can imagine. Having someone you love do this to you is unforgivable. I screamed at her and called her a bloody liar and a cheat. Claire just looked at me. She had a shocked look on her face and did not deny it at all. Claire became very emotional and burst out crying and went up to the bedroom.

Oliver said, "What is wrong with Mummy?"

I said, "She is a bit upset and not feeling well." I knew then the focus must be on Oliver, being so young and having this drama around him. I took him into the lounge and gave him one of his favorite icy poles and put the TV on to his favorite cartoon channel. I said to Oliver, "Mummy will be okay. She is not feeling well, and I will get your dinner soon." Oliver was such a good kid. He seemed to understand a lot at his age.

I made dinner for us all, but Claire did not come out of her room. While Oliver and I were eating our dinner, Oliver said, "Why is mummy with Craig? Mummy told me not to tell you." Oliver then said a strange thing. "I do not like Craig as he put me into a cupboard. I was there for a long time." Oliver said when he opened the door of the cupboard, Craig and Mummy were in bed together.

I explained to Oliver, "Do not worry yourself about this as they are simply good friends." I had to pass this off somehow to Oliver as he was just an innocent child. This made me so angry inside, I just had to hold back.

I gave Oliver his bath as he loved his bath time, and I made sure there was plenty of bubbles in it, along with his yellow duck and the toy submarine I gave him for Christmas. I dried him off and put his PJs on, and he gave me a big hug, and he said, "I love you, Daddy."

This brought a tear to my eye, and I said, "I love you too." I went and put Oliver to bed, and I said, "I will be back in a minute, and I will read you a story." I went into the bedroom and said to Claire, "I have bathed Oliver, and he is in bed. Do you want to say good night to him?"

She just looked at me and said, "No, just leave me alone."

I read a story to Oliver; it was *Jack and the Beanstalk*. I only got through a couple of pages, and he was fast asleep. It had been a big day for him. I gave him a gentle kiss and said, "Love you."

What followed left me dumbfounded. I went then to the bedroom to speak to Claire, and she was sprawled across the bed crying. Her face was bright red, tears running down her face. Claire told me she was with Craig, and it was due to work. "We had to drive two cars to Wellington and bring one back."

I said, "Where did you stay?"

"We stayed in motels going down, and on way back, I had a room on my own with Oliver. Craig had his room."

"Oh, I suppose you expect me to believe all this? Why did you not say so in the beginning?" Claire replied, "You would not have approved."

I said to Claire, "You're a bloody fool. Did you really think you would get away with this? Your lies and having an affair with a married man? What about his family? You are prepared to break up two families for your own selfish desires? This shows me you don't care a shit about me or Oliver!"

There was silence.

I then said quietly, "I have prepared dinner for you."

Claire replied, "I don't want any dinner. I just want to be left alone."

I left the bedroom, and I felt so annoyed, betrayed, and disappointed. "What a selfish bitch," I muttered under my breath as

I restrained myself and held back my anger and hurt with Claire. *It is Oliver I must keep safe.*

It was around 8:30 p.m., and I was watching TV in the lounge when Rose and Kevin turned up, and they asked where Claire was.

I said, "In the bedroom. She has told me she went to Wellington with Craig."

Her parents went up to the bedroom, and there was a lot of yelling and screaming. I went up and said, "Please, can you quiet things down? Oliver is in bed asleep."

It was obvious to me her parents disagreed with her behavior.

I heard Rose say, "You have a good husband and a lovely little boy, and you're going to destroy all this? What is wrong with you?"

Kevin started shouting at her and told her to wake up to herself. I asked again, "Please keep the noise down."

Then Oliver appeared at the doorway. He was holding his Cookie Bear he loved so much. Oliver said, "Why is Mummy crying and Nanna and Granddad here shouting?"

I said, "Oliver, Mummy is not feeling well, and she is okay." I took him to his room and stayed with him till he went to sleep.

Later, Claire's parents said they are leaving. I walked them outside to their car. Rose said, "I am not sure what to say. I do not know what has gotten into her." I said, "I will see you tomorrow, or I will call you."

Rose said, "Please try and put some sense into Claire's head." I said, "I will do my best."

They left. I could see they were very upset with their daughter. I did have a long discussion with Claire, and she assured me that she was not having an affair. To prove her point, she would leave her job at the dealership.

Things did settle down, and Claire said she was not seeing Craig anymore, and now not working at the dealership was a step in the right direction. Then she started work at an accountant's office in the city, and this settled things down. I did take her at her word.

Remember and the old saying "Love is blind"? Yes, I was blind to the fact she was doing all this behind my back. I suppose she got herself in a tangled web and could not find a way out of it. Christmas came and went, as well as New Year's Eve. We did not do too much as Claire was not her usual self, and I was not sure what the problem was or problems were. She just bottled these

up inside of her.

It was a few months away when we shifted into our new home. Will this be the beginning of the revival of our marriage, or will this be just the first stage of failure?

Over the next few months, we were busy choosing what we needed for the new home. We were allowed to choose the various color schemes for the rooms, fittings, and appliances, and then of course the furniture. All the pathways will be done after we shift in, and I planned to have a large garage installed.

All this made Claire more contented, and she really put in an effort toward the new home. My aim in life was to provide a place where we can call home and live together as a family. My efforts to provide this was by doing several jobs and running the movie business, and I did accomplish this.

# 13

# OUR NEW HOME

The house was ready in March. The day finally came, and we shifted into our new home in Clee Crescent. I was so happy that now we had a place that we can call home. I knew Claire was unsettled in many ways, and I was hoping this would settle her down.

The shift from Buckland Road went smoothly, and James and my good friend Dylan helped with this. Dylan said to me, "I hope Claire settles down."

I replied, "I hope so too."

Oliver was so happy. He ran in and said, "Where is my room?"

Between all of us, we set up his room with his new bed along with his toys, a small wardrobe to put all his clothes in, and a toy box for him. I looked at Oliver, and he was beaming and looked so happy. I put my arm around Claire and said, "This is great, isn't it? We now have our own home."

"Yes," she said. "It's really good." She had a tear in her eye and walked off.

Looking over the past couple of years, Claire was not the same the person I married. I put this down to the drama when we first got married—the pregnancy and continuing illnesses and her depression and Oliver being so sick, along with fact we could have lost him at birth.

Then there were family issues involving her father. I am sure it did take its toll on Claire as it did to me.

When you have a crisis like what we have gone through, you have to pick yourself up and cope the best way you can. Claire had plenty of help from her mother and also Fiona, but she found things difficult. Having our own home, I was hoping things would change for the better.

I did work very hard to get this house. The movie business played a big part along with my part-time work I did, let alone my day job with Crest Foods. Claire contributed in a small way, but she kept most of her wages to herself, and she did have a separate bank account from mine. The movie hire business had a separate account, and we had a joint account set up mainly due to the house loan.

Submissions made about the movie business by Claire were unfounded as I had sufficient funds to pay the deposit, furnish the house out, and we both went out together and picked out all that we required. This was paid from my own checking account. Claire was in her element choosing things for the house, and she seemed so happy.

Oliver settled into the new home, and he was just beaming and settled in. It was not long when he made new friends, and over the back, there was a Māori family. They came over and introduced themselves and welcomed us to the neighborhood.

There was a lot to do around the house, such as the paths and garden and driveway, so after a week or so after we shifted in, I arranged a concrete party. Claire got her friend Craig Kelly from her previous work at the service station, and he brought his brother-in-law Greg Sanders along as well. I had some of my mates from work along with Dylan. Claire's brother James also pitched in. We put down the driveway and pathway to the front of the house all in one day. The first load of concrete arrived at 7:30 a.m., so it was an early start for everyone. For lunch we had a barbecue and plenty of refreshments. The work was all finished by three in the afternoon. I put on a few drinks for everyone, and they all left around four in the afternoon.

*The Home Cinema*

My plan was to set up a cinema, so I discussed this with Claire, and surprisingly, she did agree on me having the double garage built, and then have this converted into a home cinema. She did ask, "How are you going to pay for all this?"

I then showed her my bank statement from the movie business and the income generated from it. I said, "This is what I earned from the clubs." Showing this, I assured her that I had all this covered. She remarked on how much I earned from the business.

I did get the garage built; it was 40 × 40. I had made friends with various businesses that supplied carpet and seating, and because of having a registered company, I purchased all the supplies and equipment at trade prices. This also included the bar supplies and the confectionary such as chips and peanuts and soft drinks, all from the wholesalers.

Dylan helped me set up the home cinema. The screen was nearly forty feet long and six feet wide. I got Merle's husband Max to set up the surround sound system. The cinema had a nice carpet on the floor and seating for forty people. James organized the carpenter to build the projection room, including a canteen that also was the bar.

After this was all completed, I arranged for the opening night to give this a test run. We had Dylan and Emily, Greg and Allison and Henry, Elizabeth, James, and Fiona along with their baby Josie, and Claire's young brother John. Merle and her husband could not come as they had another engagement.

We had a good night, and everything went without a hitch. The movie shown was *American Graffiti*. This was a great movie, and the music in it fit the times. I still held many movie nights in my home cinema as this was my pet hobby. I held these regularly for friends and neighbors. I charged them a small amount to cover the hire costs of the films, and this was a third of the price they would pay at the theater to see the latest movies. They just loved it and always asked when the next one was on.

I then screened *The Towering Inferno*. This was a blockbuster, and I had this booked at all the clubs as well. To show this in my home cinema, as I could only fit forty in at a time, I had to run this over a couple of nights. I held many movie nights in my home theater, and they were the latest movies available. To cover costs of the rental, I charged everyone $2 and had a bar, and to keep this legal, I did this on a ticket system, and they did buy these tickets prior to the movie. They could sit in a nice comfortable chair and have a drink and watch the movie. Most times they started usually around 8:00 p.m. as I would have to put Oliver to bed around 7:30 p.m., and I made sure he was okay. It was strange how the word got around as most people would come from my place of work and their friends. On these nights, I had one parent who opted to stay in the house to look after the children. This at times were a dozen or more.

I was planning to set up a cinema club. This was to be on the same line as the one operated out of Queen Street in the city. I was going to call this Club 51, and I needed at least fifty people to make this viable as they would get free entry, but pay for drinks and eats. I was planning an open night for this, and I sent out a flyer to people who came to the movies. I got little response, so I did not proceed with the club.

Most preferred to come along when I have a good movie, and this was what was done, and they were happy to pay $2 a movie. Actually this suited me as the movies shown were already paid for the hire charges. This meant what money I collected was sheer profit. Also the drinks and snacks on top was a bonus as well. Where else can you see the latest movie and have a drink? This is what attracted everyone. I did use a ticket system as this was to get over the law about selling liquor.

In hindsight, a lot was illegal, but for some reason, I did get away with it all. People enjoyed this. There were also the Saturday afternoon shows, and I had sometimes a hundred kids packed in, and where they all came from, I was not sure. The parents around loved it, and I charged the kids $1, and the amount they spent on lollies and soft drinks was incredible. I loved what I was doing, and it did give people a lot of enjoyment, and that is all what matters.

Oliver just loved these afternoon shows as he was in his element sitting will the kids at his place. The Māori kid next door, Peter, helped each time I ran these movies, and he collected the money at the door for me, and I let him and his little brother and sister in for free.

This next chapter will leave you speechless as now we have been in the house for some six weeks. I was blessed to have a child like Oliver; he is the love of my life, and you do all you can to ensure the happiness of the child. What happened next will leave you wondering why wait until you move into a new house, giving the impression all is well, and then it is not. Was this planned?

# 14

# THE BREAKUP

Despite all my efforts in providing a home for Claire and Oliver, plus the undeniable love I have for them both, I am sure you will find that what happened next was not hard to believe. It is what I called at the time an act of bastardy and betrayal or whatever you may like to call it.

As you recall, we shifted in early March into this new home, and I felt Claire was well settled. Oliver loved his new room decked out with toys, and his bed had a cowboy cover on it. I have no doubt we as a family were reasonably well off, and we did not have any financial strain to complain about. Claire gave up her work at night. Having material things and wealth is not the same as having love and health and happiness. I was blindsided by Claire and how wrong I was as Claire decided to leave.

Claire leaving was bad enough; the most upsetting part was that she was in the new house for around six weeks. It begs belief why she wanted a new house in the first place. She helped me pick out the furniture and fittings and agreed on many things, and now she tells me she wants to leave? This was like someone hit me with a hammer right in the guts. Maybe her plan was to kick me out and move in with her lover. I have no doubt this breakup was orchestrated by this bastard Craig Kelly.

As to Oliver, if she thinks he is going to leave with her, then she is mistaken. Her plan may be to get going and come back later to get him,

I was not sure. Oliver stays with me, and I will make it perfectly clear if she wants to leave, she can, but not with Oliver.

I felt strongly at the time that I was in my rights to hold on to my son. I provided a home for Claire and Oliver, and it was her having an affair not me. I had provided for her and stood by her and gave her my undying love, and now she just wanted to throw all this away for what I call a sleazebag? If for one moment you think that is harsh, wait until you hear what others say, how stupid and blind I have been. I am standing up for what I believe is right—Oliver stays with me in his own home.

Over time, I was not sure what was the final reason for Claire to leave. I had no doubt that Craig Kelly was the main reason behind this. I also found out later that Craig had just left his wife and set up a place in Henderson, which was a suburb west of Auckland. I also found the affair with Claire was going on for well over twelve months, despite all the stories and lies told by Claire, her convincing tales and telling me she no longer was seeing Craig. All this was bullshit, and what a fool I was in believing her. I was blindsided and was later blamed for the breakup and that I did not look after her or Oliver. This was just to justify her deceit and lies and what she told her parents and others. She created situations to suit her own agenda.

Now I will go back to the weekend when Claire left. That Saturday, we were invited to attend a wedding from one of my workmates, and Claire was happy to go along. I took Oliver to stay at his grandparents on the Saturday morning. Also it was arranged to pick him up later on Sunday afternoon.

We arrived at the church for the wedding ceremony well before 2:00 p.m., and I spoke to Greg and Addison, and I said, "How about we all sit together?" Claire stood back and did not say too much. When we sat down in the church, Claire sat next to Addison, and I sat next to Greg.

Greg whispered to me, "What is wrong with Claire? She does not seem happy." I said, "I am not sure, but she seems preoccupied."

The service took around forty-five minutes, and the reception was set for 6:00 p.m. later that day. After the service, a few of us went to a hotel and had a few drinks. It was around 5:45 p.m., and we arrived at the reception. Refreshments were handed out on arrival.

The bride and groom arrived, and we were all seated at the reception, which was held at the Royal International Hotel. Claire suddenly said, "I need to speak to you, but not here. Let's go outside."

I said, "Sure."

Claire had a face like she just swallowed a whole lemon, a very sad and sour face. I knew there was something on her mind. We went outside, and she came straight out and said she has decided to leave me.

I said, "You've got to be joking. Is this a sick joke? Why tell me now when we are out at a wedding and out to enjoy ourselves? I bet you're going with Craig. You're a selfish bitch!"

She replied that she wanted to have a break.

I said, "Let's discuss this later. We better get back in." With that, I was terribly upset and did not enjoy the rest of the night. I told Greg what was going on, and he could not believe it, I said to Greg that I somehow knew at the back of my mind she was not faithful to me. What she told me actually hit home, and it was a hard pill to swallow.

After the wedding dinner, people got up and danced, and Claire and I were on the table by ourselves. I let Claire have it and said, "If you leave, Oliver stays with me." I made that very clear. I did not threaten her in any way, but I said, "Oliver belongs in the home I provided for you and him."

Claire said, "I do not intend to take him with me." "Well, you better not," I said angrily.

I just felt so lousy. I was not enjoying myself. Claire left to go to the restroom, and I did tell some of my closet friends who were also there at the wedding that Claire said she was leaving me. I became very emotional, and I said to Greg, "I am going outside to get some fresh air." I did have a couple of drinks, but not too much to drink.

I went outside, and Greg followed me. He said, "What are you going to do?"

I said, "I am not sure, but I will tell you this: that Oliver stays with me. Damn it, I am going home. Stuff her, she can find her own way home." With that I drove home.

Greg called me later that night when he got home to see if I was okay, and he said that Craig came, and Claire left with him.

I said, "The rotten mongrel. He has played a major part in Claire leaving."

I was in Oliver's room when Claire came home well after midnight. I told her what a deceitful and hurtful bitch she was, and I yelled at her and said, "You leave tomorrow! Don't bother coming back, and you leave Oliver with me! He is my son, and he deserves better. You're a disgrace!" I again screamed at her. My emotions boiled over. I went out to the lounge and poured myself a bourbon. I was so upset and felt all my world had just gone out the window.

Yes, now my major concern was Oliver. It was obvious Claire had made her mind up despite all my efforts to make her stay. I felt so betrayed. My next important step was looking after Oliver. Early the next morning, I told her parents, "Claire said she is leaving today, and she told me that she is going to live with Craig. I tried my best to keep her here, I pleaded with her. All this pleading did not help. I said to her in no circumstances would Oliver go with her. I have some work to do today and cannot change this, and as soon as I am finished, I will pick Oliver up later in the day around four or five."

Rose said to me, "I am so sorry. I am disgusted with Claire, and I do not know what to say. She better not come here, or I will let her have it."

I knew then Rose was dead set against Claire for leaving, and I was hoping they would keep Oliver at their place until I get there later in the day.

Just after lunch, I left the house to pick up Dylan, then we went off to do the movie at the local leagues club. This finished around 4:00 p.m. We packed up all our gear and headed back to my place. Dylan said he would go back with me to my place to unpack the gear, and after that I can take him back to his place.

On the way to pick up Oliver, we were driving down our street when Dylan called out, "There goes Claire across the vacant blocks of land." This was where they were building new houses. He yelled out, "She has a suitcase and is carrying a couple of bags!"

I stopped the car, and I did see her for myself. Dylan said, "Are you going to stop her?"

I said, "No, let her go."

We watched as she went on to the main road. With that I spun the car around and headed around to the main road, and there was Claire hopping into the car with Craig.

I said to Dylan, "What a stupid fool going off with that son of a bitch." I then quickly went back to my place and offloaded all the gear, dropped Dylan off at his place, and then went to Rose and Kevin's to pick up Oliver. This was around 5:00 p.m.

Rose was preparing dinner. I then told them what had happened, and they said, "You better stay here for dinner."

This I did. We had a long chat about Claire, and her mother said, "Let Oliver stay here tonight, and we will work something out."

I said, "Okay, and I will drop some clean clothes around later. I will take the day off tomorrow as I am too upset."

Rose said to me, "Claire is a bitch to do what she has done and break up the family home."

I could not disagree. Claire's parents spelt it out repeatedly that they were against Claire leaving. I said to them, "It is all over with Claire. She had made her decisions, and my concern is Oliver now." And with that I picked up Oliver. He gave me big hugs and kisses, and this lit my day up and made me feel a lot better.

Oliver is now three and a half years of age and at an age that he does need stability. It is hard to tell if he is affected in any way as he is such a wonderful little boy and so loving that he makes life worth living.

The rest of this story is all about my fight for justice to keep my son. The matters relating to the breakup that involved Oliver played out in the custody hearing, and it is significant to note that Oliver stayed three days a week at his Aunty Fiona's, and he came back to me each night, and the weekend he was with me. Rose the grandmother, as she worked three days a week, had Oliver for two days a week, whereas I also had Oliver stay at his grandparents those two nights, and she had him during the day. It was later found out that Claire went to see Oliver at her parents' place. The time Oliver spent at his grandparents when Claire first left was around six weeks. The claims made by Rose were incredibly significant, as you will read in her statements and evidence she gave at the hearing.

The old saying "Blood is thicker than water"—how true this is.

One other significant fact is that Claire maintained I threatened her, and she used this against me, which, in fact, was far from the truth. She left on her own accord. I was not home when she left, and to say I stopped her taking Oliver with her was also a lie as Oliver was at her parents' place.

## *Meeting Craig Kelly's Wife*

There is a lot now to digest and cover. I went and picked up Oliver at his grandparents. I did call work that morning and just called in sick. I had my work covered by Greg as I told him Claire had gone. I arrived at Oliver's grandparents' and took him back home. I was still in a very bad state and emotionally upset.

That night, I called my boss and told him what had happened. I was thinking it was best if I left my job. He came around to the house that night on his way from work, and we chatted, and he told me, "Stick it out. We will help you the best way we can." He wanted me to take a week off, and he would cover for me. What a true gentleman he was and a great boss. It is these things that inspire you, and you know you have backup. The company was amazing to work for. I never ever worked for such an organization that looked after its staff like they did for me.

We had a beer together, and I thanked him for his support. On leaving, he said, "Oliver is just the image of you. He is your responsibility now. Take care. Call me anytime if you need a chat."

I thanked him, and when he left, I just welled up, and I was very emotional and had to bring myself together for Oliver's sake. I did not want him to see me upset.

Early the next day on Tuesday morning, it was around eight thirty when the phone rang, and the voice at the other end said, "Are you Danial Mason?"

I said, "Yes, who is this?"

The woman on the end of the phone said, "I am Craig Kelly's wife, Cheryl. I would like meet up with you to discuss a few things with you, but not over the phone. Can we meet personally? I believe your wife is with my husband."

With that I arranged to meet Cheryl at a coffee lounge in downtown Auckland.

I was not sure what she looked like, and as I walked in to the coffee lounge, this woman came up to me and said, "You're Danial?"

I said, "Yes, and you're Cheryl?" She nodded.

We sat down ordered some coffee. I asked Cheryl, "Do you want something to eat?" She said, "No, I am fine."

I was very curious at this stage what Cheryl was going to tell me. Cheryl opened up and told me that Craig had been unfaithful before, and she was glad he has gone, but she said sorry it was my wife. "There is a lot on the side of Craig that you should be aware of."

This made me more curious.

After a long chat, she said, "You must give this man a call. His name is Brian Smythe." She wrote his name and contact details on a piece of paper she took out from her purse. She said, "It would be in your best interest to call him and you meet up. I won't say any more than that."

Cheryl was such a charming person. She was well dressed, spoke lovely, and was very attractive. She also told me that her daughter was very upset with her father leaving. She said, "It was my daughter Cindy who told me about your wife."

I said, "Yes, that would be right, as your daughter was with your husband one night when we showed the movie *Battle of the Bulge* at my friend Dylan's place, and I did notice Claire made a fuss of her. Claire sat with your husband and your daughter that night."

Cheryl said, "She is only thirteen, not good for the child. Craig has not been a good father for some couple of years now." She then wished me all the best, and we shook hands, and we departed. That was the last time we spoke or saw each other again.

I thought this was bizarre, meeting up with Craig's wife, and her husband was shacked up with my wife. This is what happens when people have affairs. It is the people they leave behind and does affect so many people. In Cheryl's case, she was glad to get rid of him. What a great testimony for Claire.

I quickly followed up on the contact that Cheryl gave me. I called Brian Smythe and explained who I was and told him, "Cheryl Kelly said I should speak to you regarding Craig as she said you would enlighten me on a few things about Craig, as she said it may be useful to me later on. I was curious what this was all about."

I arranged with Brian to meet the next day, and we met up at 3:00 p.m. at the café in the shopping center. I was so grateful having the week off as I needed this to sort myself out.

*Meeting Brian Smythe*

I did meet up with Brian at the café at 3:00 p.m. as agreed, and when I walked in, this rather tall man strode up to me and said, "Daniel? I am Brian. I found a table for us over in the corner so we can speak privately." We ordered some coffee, and he said, "What I will tell you, under  no circumstances are you to mention my name or where you got this information from, do you understand this?"

I said yes. This made me more curious, and I was wondering what he was going to tell me and why so secretive.

"First," he said, "Craig is not a good person, he is a sleazebag."

"Wow," I said to Brian, "my sentiments as well. I know you really should not hate people, but I really despise him."

Brian said, "I believe you have a young son, and as far as I am concerned, Craig should not be associated with him in any way." He then went on to say that Craig was working with young boys and girls, transporting them to school and other activities.

I said, "Like a bus driver?"

"Yeah," he said, "something like that. It was reported that Craig got one of the young girls pregnant, and she, I believe, was either seventeen or eighteen years old at the time, and he did have an affair with this girl for a few months."

I said, "While he was still was with Cheryl?" "No, he left his wife for a short time, I believe." "What a rotten so and so!"

Brian then said, "She was a very attractive Māori girl, and it was also reported Craig sent her to the South Island."

I said, "Was this to make sure she was well out of the way?" Brian said, "I believe so."

I then said to Brian, "Are you sure about this?"

He said, "Yes, as I was working with him at the time, and it was common knowledge." I said, "Did Cheryl know about this?"

He said yes.

"So is this is why she wanted you to speak to me? Why was he not charged?"

Brian said he was lucky as it was all swept under the carpet to protect the school. "But mind you, Craig lost his job."

I said to Brian, "He lost his job again? What a coincidence. There is a pattern here about this character."

He said, "Cheryl had enough from him as over the past couple of years, he has hardly been home at night or comes home late."

"Yeah," I said, "I have found out that the affair with between Claire and Craig has gone on for a long time, well over twelve months I believe."

Brian expressed to me, "You make sure that Craig does not have anything to do with the upbringing of your son." He could not have been more adamant about this. We chatted for some time. Brian then gave me his address and said, "We must keep in touch."

I invited him to a movie night the next time I had one, when things settled down. He thought this was a very good idea. I thanked him very much, and we left after we shook hands. Brian and I became particularly good friends as time went on.

Hearing what Brian told me gave me more good reasons why I must make sure that Oliver stays with me. This whole scenario with Craig was a major concern and, more importantly, what Claire had gotten herself into.

Word got around about Claire and Craig, and some of the people I made acquaintances with did not have anything more to do with me. This happens often in a breakup of marriages. No one wants to take sides but wants to keep clear, maybe to protect their own marriage or just do not want to get involved. I understood this and appreciate them not getting involved. It's very hard, I suppose, when people who you know very well, do like the both of you, then do not want to take sides. This I can fully understand. However, on the other hand, I found I had plenty of support from various people I got to know through work and other activities such as the community work I was doing. Jonathon said, "Your case is vastly different to mine as I applied for legal guardianship, and this was granted uncontested."

I said to Jonathon, "This is incredibly sad about your wife."

Jonathon said, "The girls do go and see their mother as I do also. One day she may come home, but highly unlikely. You must fight for the rights to bring up your own child, and if and when the time comes and if you need my support, I will support you. I know what Craig is like, and he is not the right person to have around your son."

I was surprised to hear that the stolen radios implicated Craig's brother-in-law, and it was also mentioned I informed the police, which was not true. I myself think Craig and his brother-in-law were involved somehow, and I also think Jonathon was the one who reported this to the police. He never told me, but I had my own view on all this as when I did ask him, he had a smirk on his face, which said it all.

## Change of Plans

For the first six weeks since Claire left, I did have the odd phone call from her. I also felt it very strange that Claire did not ask to see Oliver. It was by a sheer slip of the tongue when one afternoon, I was at James and Fiona's place picking up Oliver on my way home from work, that I found out by Fiona that Claire had been seeing Oliver at her mother's place, which they never told me or discussed this at all. They often told me they had not seen or heard from her.

I was incredibly angry about this. This was a betrayal of my trust by her parents. I was now uncertain her parents might hand over Oliver to his mother. Fiona said I had to hold my tongue as the last thing she wanted was to have Rose against her; however, she told me to be aware of this. I do understand that Claire should see Oliver as when it is said and done, she is his mother, but doing this behind my back is very deceitful. So now this puts things in a distinct perspective.

The arrangement between myself, Fiona, and Rose was wildly disputed as to what was organized as a daily routine for Oliver. The facts were that I had hardly heard from Claire in the early stages after she left our home, but she claimed in a lot of her statements and court evidence that she called every night and came around to see Oliver. It was sheer nonsense, in fact a damn lie. It was my opinion and others that she made up stories as she went along to suit her own agenda and made out she was the loving, caring mother for Oliver. Then the statements and accounts by Rose and her role looking after Oliver was also questionable as she worked three days a week, and on those days, Fiona looked after Oliver, and I picked him up after work, usually between four and five each day. The other two remaining days, Rose did have him for these.

I then had Oliver with me each weekend. Rose claimed she had him totally after Claire had left. This was disputed. I know Oliver loved his grandparents along with Fiona and James, and having them a part of life was so important, and with that he seemed very settled. Love for his mother at this stage was confusing as he asked why his mummy was not home with both of us. Of course he loved his mother, and I would not detract from that.

I had to take matters into my own hands as Oliver was my main concern. My other major concern was that his mother would take him from her parents' place despite what they said earlier that they would not have any more to do with her. Now finding out she has been going around to their place for weeks has put me on my guard. On that basis, my trust has diminished somewhat. Now Oliver is not going to his grandparents during the week. I had to ensure Fiona was not implicated in this change of plans.

Of course Claire wants to see Oliver; this was not the point as she is the mother, and she should see him. It was the way it was done behind my back. It is also important Oliver does see his grandparents. Grandparents do play a significant role in a child's life. So I made sure throughout this was the case.

Then on the other hand, they also must be responsible and be up front with me rather than do things behind my back. Now I feel I cannot trust them, particularly Rose.

Rose and Kevin often called around on their way home from work. I also did take Oliver around to them on weekends. I also let them take him to a football game, which he loved.

Despite all my efforts, as time went on, things did deteriorate with the grandparents as to my challenge wanting to have custody of my son.

No doubt Claire had to find another way to see Oliver. If she approached me, I would have allowed her to see him. After I put a stop to him staying at his grandparents' during the week, she then changed tactics as she did not come around at all back to the home in the early stages of the breakup. Then she started phoning me early in the morning or late in the afternoon. She knew when I was home from work or later at night. Despite all my efforts, I could not get her to come home. For the life of me, could not understand why she went into the relationship in the first place with Craig, what I called a creep of a guy. I am not saying this because he is with my wife, but what

I have been told by his ex-wife and others was enough for me to make that observation.

Then there were outrageous claims by Claire that I did not give her enough attention and did not look after her and Oliver, which was totally untrue. I provided a house for her and looked after her in her illnesses, knowing she was not a well person. Then there was Oliver and his sickness and how we nearly lost him at birth. I gave her and my son all the love and attention a husband and father would and should provide.

Then Rose joined in and said to me it was because of the movie business. The situation now is Claire has to justify why she left to whoever will listen to her.

Her response to her parents and others made me very angry, and I said to her parents, "The movie business was very good and profitable. Without that, we would not have had the deposit or loan for this house. It also contributed to lots of items around the house and also our well-being."

Claire got the benefits from the movie business despite her objections. She also agreed with it as I explained the money was covered in the first place. She was happy to see all the money coming in. She has a short memory. In fact, it also paid for the garage and all the fittings for the home cinema as well as the concreting.

Claire also forgets where the money came from as it did not grow on trees. "I worked hard," I said to Rose. "Claire did not contribute to any of this. I have the bank records to prove this.I let her keep her own pay. She did buy the groceries and clothes for Oliver, and that was about it." Rose did say to me, "Yes, I do agree you were a good provider, and you took care of them both."

I responded by saying, "Yes, and for what? She ups and leaves."

It was a few weeks since I stopped Oliver going to his grandparents during the week. I am sure they did not figure out why and that Fiona told me about Claire going around to their place. This night I assumed they were on their way home from work, and they called in. Kevin in his usual manner was rather aggressive toward me and asked why I had stopped Oliver staying at their place during the week. Oliver was in his room playing, and I said to them, "Please keep it down as I do not want Oliver upset."

Rose said to me, "Don't you trust us or something?"

I said, "No, it is not like that. I am his father, and it is my responsibility to look after him. I do appreciate your help."

Rose asked angrily, "Then why does he stay with Fiona now all week?"

I said, "That is my choice." Things got a bit heated, and I said, "I know Claire has been going around to your place when you have him, and you have lied to me and covered this up."

Rose flew off the handle and said, "Who told you that?"

I said, "I have a friend who lives just around the street from your place, and he told me. You also know him as well."

Rose then said, "We did not want to tell you as it would upset you."

I said, "How can I trust you when you do this as for weeks? You told me you have not seen Claire."

With that, Oliver came into the lounge. He ran over to his grandparents and gave them a big hug. They both said, "We will discuss this another time," and they left. As they were leaving, Kevin said to me, "You a bastard, and this is all your fault" as Oliver was close by. I let that slide, and they drove off in haste. I could not dare tell them Fiona told me as this would more than flare up things. The last thing I wanted was to fall out with Claire's parents, so I did go around a few nights later, and I left Oliver with Fiona. I thought I would straighten things out with her parents. Kevin was sitting in his chair as usual with his bottle of beer, and Rose was preparing the evening meal.

She said, "Where is Oliver?"

I said, "I left him with Fiona as I wanted to sort this out with you both in regard to Oliver." Kevin said to me, "You're a lousy bastard. You do not want us to have him."

I said, "That is not true at all. Oliver is now my responsibility for the time being." Kevin said, "I know you stopped Claire taking him as you threatened her."

I said, "That is not true."

He yelled at me, "Yes, it is! Claire told us." I said, "Do you believe all she tells you?" "She is our daughter!" Kevin yelled out.

"Yes, that is what she wants you all to believe. The fact was the weekend she left, Oliver was with you both. I did tell her if she leaves, Oliver stays with me, and she did agree. She had no intention at that time to take him with her. Now she comes out and tells you that I threatened her?" I raised my voice at them and replied, "If that is what you believe, then I am wasting my time discussing this with you lot."

Rose said, "Claire is our daughter, you know, and we did not agree her leaving you, but she does insist you threatened her and would harm her and Oliver."

"Oh god," I said, "I see what she is saying. Is this to justify why she left? Look, I came here tonight to sort things out with you both, and Oliver is part of your life, and I would bring him around on weekends, and you can take him to the football games as well on occasions. I am not discussing any more of this with you both. I am leaving." When I was going out the door, I said, "I think you should think about what you have said, and do not get sucked in what Claire says to you both."

I left their house, and I drove back to pick Oliver up. Fiona was home on her own as James was at football practice. I told Fiona what happened. "They have not got a clue what you told as I told them I was told by a friend of mine who lives close by, and he saw Claire going to their house. Do not worry. If they bring it up, play dumb."

I did keep to my promise and allowed Oliver to stay overnight at his grandparents on occasions. Also they did take him to football games.

The relationship with Rose and Kevin did deteriorate and was not the same going forward. Rose was very calculated in many ways. Meeting her was like butter would not melt in her mouth. She came over as a very charming and kind person, but behind this charade was a very deceitful person who was caught up with her daughter's plan to destroy my credibility to gain custody of her son.

The reason is plain obvious—they are being fed with a lot of stories from Claire and her untruths and to make me out as the aggressor and make them believe I threatened her and was going to harm Oliver. Yes, in circumstances like this, any parent would side with their daughter if it was true. The sad fact is that from the beginning, her parents sided with me. I gave them lot of access to Oliver, and they accepted what I told them as the truth. Then Claire in her very calculated way changed their minds as she was involved in many incidents and fabricated them in ways to not only get her parents on her side, but also to suit her own agenda toward her quest to gain custody of her son.

I was told this is not uncommon when there is a dispute over custody matters. I am hoping in the final analysis, the truth will prevail.

## My Confrontation with Craig Kelly

When Claire left, I was understandably upset. I was angry, and I had to confront Craig Kelly. This incident did take place within the first few weeks when Claire left, and understandably, I did take Claire leaving very hard. I learned where Craig was working after he left his previous work as this was where Claire met Craig when she worked there on a part-time basis.

It was around the second or third week after Claire left the home, and I suppose in hindsight, it was stupid of me to go to his place of work as I was still so upset, and anger welled up inside me. I stewed over her leaving all Sunday night, and I thought over and over again, *It is about time I confronted this mongrel.* I know it takes two to tango, as they say, but in my opinion, he must have played a big part on her leaving despite the fact the affair had been going on for well over twelve months. The lies Claire told me and the various times she was with Craig but telling me different stories, also after chatting with Craig's wife, it was apparent this was well planned by Craig as he left her and set up a place in Henderson. He was cocksure Claire would go with him.

I have no regrets for this as this incident was part of Craig Kelly's submission and mentioned at the hearing. His accounts of the event like most of Claire's and his were either exaggerated or just not telling the truth. Again it boils down to that it fits their narrative to try and justify their own account of things. I do agree on one thing: this incident on my part was well over the top. I did go to his place of work and might have ruffled him up a bit. Did that constitute as assault and charged by police?

Well, this is my account of how this unfolded. It was early Monday morning around 8:30 a.m. I had just dropped off Oliver to his Aunty Fiona. I then drove to where Craig was working in Panmure. I walked into his workplace, and when I walked into the showroom, he spotted me coming toward him. He went bright red like a fluorescent light. He was in a group of at least six of his workmates, obviously all having a chat before work started.

As I approached him, I grabbed him by the shirt and pushed him against the wall and said, "Where is Claire?" I did call him a rotten bastard for what he had done. The rest of the guys standing around stepped forward. I yelled at them to back off. I said, "This mongrel has taken off with my wife, and this rotten cow has also left his wife and daughter. My wife has left her son. He is only three years old, so back off. This guy is a rotten scumbag. He is not worth a piece of dirt." They all backed off and did not utter a word. I did push him hard against the wall. When I was leaving, I gave him an extra shove and walked out. I was shaking all over, and it gave me some satisfaction. I then went to work for the day.

Later that day when I got home from work, I did get a visit from the police, and they said, "A Mr. Kelly has laid an assault charge against you. He claimed I hit him and tore his shirt."

I told the police the circumstances. "He has just taken off with my wife and left me and my little boy, who is just three and a half. I did not tear or rip his shirt as it was a very cold day, and he had a pullover on. Also I did not hit him at all. I may have shoved him a bit."

The police asked me to do a statement, which I did. The following day, the police asked me to come down to the police station, which I did. They said that Craig told them that there was at least six guys who witnessed the assault. The policeman said, "We have been to his work, and we have interviewed the people who Mr. Kelly claimed witnessed the assault and that you bashed him. Well, I am not 100 percent sure what went on there as he did have a torn shirt as he showed us that. However, not one of the people whom he worked for said an assault took place."

I added, "That is strange. He had a low-neck pullover on, so how did his shirt rip?" "The police officer said, "I am not sure."

His story did not add up. So there were no witnesses to this incident, and the police did say it was obvious that an incident did take place. "Understandably you were upset, and if it was my wife who took off with another man, I possibly would have done the same." The police told me there would be no charges made on this occasion, and they told me just to be careful. I thanked the officer and left the police station.

Well, this was a very strange outcome, and Craig had no witnesses. I did push him against the wall. If that amounts to assault, I am not sure. I was lucky that his so-called workmates did not defend him. I believe the reason why is that a lot of people condemn men who run off with other people's wives or play a role in marriage breakups, particularly when children are involved. Was this the case maybe? Worth thinking about.

Craig in one of his statements claimed when I was leaving the police station, I ran into a police car, which was untrue and unfounded. If this were the case, the police would have charged me. You see the pattern here? It gets even better.

I am not a violent person, and what took place at Craig's work that day I do not for one moment regret what I did. What it does was to show people what Craig has done, and the ironic part of this was he left that place of work that week. Was he fired or just was so embarrassed by the events that took place that day?

## *Bitter Pill to Swallow*

The effects of Claire leaving me was a bitter pill to swallow, and I do confess this did get the better of me. After going to Craig's due to my anger against the man who was a part of the marriage breakup—his part, in my opinion, was the major part in the breakup—I have no doubt Claire was in a very vulnerable state as her taking of the sleeping pills was a fair indication. The problem when we were first married, her illness during her pregnancy, and nearly losing the baby, I think all played a big part as many times, despite my efforts to discuss things, she shut me out. I tried to make our marriage work, which now has come to nothing.

Craig rented a unit in outer Auckland in which he set up, and this is where Claire initially went to. It was later found out she felt this was not suitable, and she claimed it had no phone, yet she called her mother on most days and later started calling me.

They then shifted to a place in South Auckland, and through my contacts, I was given the address. Probably one would question why I went there. The answer was simple. I got some reports, particularly from her mother, that she may be on drugs. She was incoherent at times, which bothered me. Even her sister-in-law Fiona was concerned, also her brother James. The fact of the matter was I still loved her, and if there was some way I could get her back, I would, and at that point, I was ready to forgive her.

Going to their rented unit in Pakuranga was blown right out of proportion, and what was in their statements and the court hearing, various accounts in my opinion were very bizarre. You will read in the statements about this incident, and was I in the right going there?

Like any incident, there are many variations, but in most cases, they all tell the truth in various ways. This is my account of things. Oliver was three and a half years old when his mother left, and Oliver, like any young child, got sick, like colds, and he was no exception. He went down with a severe cold that turned into a chest infection. I though his mother should be well aware of this. It was a midweek night, and she had been gone now for over six weeks. Oliver not feeling well and the various information about Claire's well-being also disturbed me.

This night was a wet and cold typical winter's evening. It was around 5:00 p.m. when I arrived at their place. I was on my own, and I drove into their driveway behind Craig's car as he just pulled into the driveway. He got out of his car. I then got out of my car and said to him, "I am not here to cause trouble, but I do need to speak to Claire." We were both getting soaking wet.

Then he angrily told me to piss off and leave them alone as Claire wanted nothing more to do with me.

I yelled at him, "That is your opinion! I suppose you have her so doped up, she does not know what she wants to do anymore. Suit yourself as I am not moving until I speak to her." Then I shouted out loud, "You took my wife away, and you left your wife and kid like my wife has left us!" I looked across to the side of their unit, and I noticed a person peering around the corner of the dwelling. At that point, I did not know who he was, but I did find out later it was their landlord. He did watch all this unfold, and his account against mine was what I call stretching the truth to again suit their narrative—in other words, he backed up what Craig and Claire wanted him to say. Craig pulled a yellow raincoat from his vehicle and put this on. I was getting drenched as the rain was pelting down, and I had a suit on, and the jacket was so wet, it just flopped. I then noticed Claire come out of the unit. She looked like a cat that was dragged through a sewer. She looked

pale and drawn. I said, "Claire, I want to talk to you please."

Claire turned to Craig and said, "It's okay, go inside, and I will talk to Danial." With that, I went for cover at the front of their unit out of the rain. Claire said, "You have no right being here." I said, "Claire, would you come home with me? I would forgive you. Being with Craig is not good. Oliver has a bronchial infection, and he is at your mother's place tonight, and with you not having a phone, I thought best I come around and tell you." Claire said she would go and see Oliver later on.

I told her, "I am now going to pick him up, and he is going home with me. Come home, and you can see him."

She said, "I cannot." I asked, "Why?"

She said that she needed time to sort herself out, and she told me to leave. And with that, I did.

Claire did not come around to the home to see Oliver. The claims by Claire, Craig, and their landlord was so far from the truth as the story they told later about me coming around was that I went into their unit, and I had Oliver with me when I was at their place. In fact, Oliver was at his grandparents' that night.

The coming months were exceedingly difficult for me as I did have many doubts about Rose and Kevin as I was not sure which way they will go as at the end of the day, Claire was their Daughter and Oliver their grandson. And if it looks like Claire will get custody of Oliver, then they no doubt will side with her as blood is thicker than water.

My concerns mainly about Rose became apparent. The months rolled on, and within the first six months, there were many incidents that involved myself and Oliver. Despite all my efforts to get Claire back home, it was getting to the point it was fruitless.

No doubt she was always influenced by Craig, and she must have felt the grass is greener on the other side and he will give her a better life. This was far more from the truth. The events that took place must have had a toll on her well-being as much as it did affect me. Oliver, on the other hand, remarkably handled this most of the time, and there were times it took a dramatic effect on him. I suppose when you sum it all up, both Claire and I were pigheaded, and we both wanted what was best for Oliver. Could a lot of incidents have been avoided? Yes, I have no doubt. I always maintained I was not totally innocent, "but" the but was I being up against constant police involvement, family interference, lies, and the allegations about my care for Oliver, to the point I was the potential murderer as it was claimed.

## The Brick Incident

This incident had many variations, and many versions played out in the court case as to actual times, who saw this, and on it goes. I know when you read this, you will say, "What the hell was this man doing?"

This incident did take place a few months after Claire left. I know at times either I overreacted or made situations worse than they were. The amount of abuse I got from Claire I found was very hard to contain, along with many times placed in very vulnerable situations. This did not show me as the responsible parent that I wanted to be.

Claire for some reason started coming around at different hours at night, knowing very well that Oliver would be well in bed. It may have been the rationale behind such visits, as it was often said I kept Oliver up very late at night, and by Claire coming around, it was to catch me out as she had no reason at all to come at these late hours as she would be well aware that Oliver would be in bed asleep.

I suppose I should not make excuses; however, I was still angry and very upset, disappointed, and I did have a hatred for Craig and also very strong anger toward him. When it is all said and done, he was the one in my mind who was behind the breakup. I know it takes two to tango, but he must have made advances to Claire, and knowing his own marriage was well and truly over, he then made advances to Claire.

Despite what a lot has been said in this matter, I was trying to get Claire back, regardless of what Claire has done. The old saying "Forgive and forget" is true as I would have forgiven her. At that point, I did want her back.

This incident on this particular night, it was well after 8:00 p.m., and she came to the house, as usual unannounced, no knocking, just stormed into the house.

She demanded to see Oliver. She said her mother told her he was not well.

I said, "He is fine." This was another occasion where he had a chest infection, and I told her I had him to the doctors. I said, "Oliver has been in bed for over an hour or so now, and it is well past eight o'clock, and I do not want you to wake him please."

With that she wanted to see if he was alright.

I said, "Yes, you can go to his room, but please do not disturb him as the doctor said he needs plenty of rest." With that I then looked out the kitchen window, and there was Craig. He had parked his car in the driveway and had his lights on. I said to Claire, "What the hell is he doing here?" I was enraged.

She said, "He drove me over as I wanted to see Oliver." She started screaming at me. I then told her to get out. With that, I ran outside, and Craig took off. The street was a cul-de-sac, that is one way in and one way out. I knew he had to come around again to get out. I was waiting on the footpath for him to stop, but he drove the car straight at me as he was trying to run me over. With that, he went around again.

I did notice as the car went past that there was someone else in the car crouched down, and you could not see who it was as I am sure he did not what me to know he was there. I thought to myself, *This is planned so they can witness if anything were to go wrong.*

You could hear him roaring around the street corners. I waited for Craig to come around the bend in the street. As I was in front of the new houses on the footpath that was being built in this new housing estate, Craig came speeding down the street toward me. He mounted the footpath, and I quickly jumped out of the way. He then went around again the third time, and I waited for him to come around. I regrettably out of rage picked up a brick. This was from the stack in front one of the new houses being built. There was no sign of him slowing down; he was speeding toward me. He mounted the curb and came straight at me.

I thought, *You mongrel.* He was definitely trying to run me over. With that, I then threw the brick straight through the car windscreen. Craig then drove out of the street and back on to the roadway at high speed.

Claire screamed at me and said, "What did you bloody well do that for?! You're crazy."

I said to Claire, "Just get out of here, you have no right to come here at this time of night, and don't you dare ever bring that bastard here ever again!"

Then Claire took off on foot down the street. I was terribly upset about what took place that night. One or two people did see this across the road, but no other person was in sight.

There were many variations of this dramatic event. One was the recollection by Craig's brother in-law and James, Claire's brother, as they were both questioned on this in the court case. As far as James said, he witnessed this. Well, I say this was impossible as his house is out of sight from my house, which is at the beginning of the street. This cannot be right as from his house, there is a curved bend from the end of his house that then leads up to my house. I actually intentionally looked from his house toward my house, and you could not even see the roof, let alone any disturbance going on. Also, on that night, James was nowhere to be seen as he claimed he did see this unfold. The stories were varied and far from the truth, and I did admit I did wrong in a spat of anger. How did the court view this? One comment made by the judge as to Craig being there was "Like showing a red flag to a bull."

## The Police Raid

Well, if you thought things could not get any worse, this incident I refer to was very much planned by Claire. Her efforts to discredit me were hard to fathom out as I did not know from one day to the next what she has planned.

This particular afternoon, I came home around 4:30 p.m. from work, and I just got Oliver inside. I heard cars at some speed coming down the street. I then looked out the window, and there were two police cars come up the driveway. Out jumped at least six cops, and one was the superintendent. He met me on the back steps, and he said, "I have here a warrant to search the premises."

I said to the officer, "What is all this about?"

He said, "We have a complaint you have blue movies on the premises, and you regularly show them."

I said, "I can guess it in one go who told you this shit. You're welcome to go ahead, but you will find nothing, I can assure you."

They spent an hour or more, and to my amazement, they did not make a mess at all, which I thought would happen.

The superintendent said, "You have a great setup here."

And then Greg, the cop who lives across from me, came across. As he was still in uniform, he was told what was taking place, and he explained to the officer in charge that he attended many nights here with his family and also said I had Saturday movies for the local kids as well as the movies at the community center, which he said is approved by the police. He went on to say he had been called here when there had been a domestic disturbance and my ex-wife is involved. "She has caused a lot of trouble for Danial, and the boys have been here many times. If this complaint is by a Claire Mason or Craig Kelly, you take this like a grain of salt. If there is anything untoward as to showing blue movies, I would have known."

The police looked at my collection of Walt Disney movies and westerns I had and could not find any adult movies. The superintendent said to me he was sorry for the inconvenience. "But when we get complaints like this, we must act upon it."

It was getting late, and I had to get dinner ready for Oliver and myself. The police stayed for a while in the home cinema, and I gave them a few beers, and we chatted for a while, and then they left. I thanked Greg as he put the record straight with his superintendent, and as it turned out, I was told that it was his boss.

I was so distressed about all this. We had a late meal, and I put Oliver to bed. I sat in the lounge and watched TV for a while. I thought to myself, *When is all this shit going to end? Claire seems to make all these allegations, and nothing is said or anything done to stop her.*

Later that night, Claire called and asked, "Is everything okay?" I said, "No thanks to you, bitch."

She said, "What do you mean? Fiona called me and told me that there were several police cars at the house."

"Yes," I said, "because you made a complaint to the police that I was showing blue movies. They came here with a warrant to search the premises."

She said, "No, it was not me."

I yelled down the phone at her and said, "Stop this bloody nonsense as I know it was you as the police told me! You don't think of Oliver as he was very upset." I told her what he said to me while the police were here.

Oliver said to me, crying, "Daddy, are they going to take you away?" I said to him, "No, son, it is okay. They will be gone soon."

I said to Claire, "Just stop these allegations. You are hurting your son." I then banged the phone down in her ear.

If I thought for a moment things would get better, I was grossly mistaken. The accusations and claims about the movie business and the showing of movies in my home cinema and that Oliver was up later at night watching such movies was a contentious issue. The allegations that I showed blue movies was just another attempt to discredit me.

The setup I had at my home theater was to establish a private club, and I needed at least fifty people to join to make it worthwhile as there was the hire of the movies and running costs. The plan was to call it Club 51, and because I could not get enough people to join, I then charged everyone

$2, and they were happy to pay this as they did see the latest movies available. I made extra by selling drinks at the bar and also snacks to cover costs, so to keep this legal, I did this on a ticket system, and this required them to buy tickets prior to the movie.

Rose made a big issue of this in her submissions to the court, then the issue as to Oliver being up late at night was unfounded as I would have put Oliver to bed around 7:00 p.m., and I always made sure he was okay.

I think if you make claims you cannot back up, it creates a dangerous precedent, and in fact, when you state accounts of things you are not sure of or just hearsay, including making stuff up, and you are caught out, then this can be your downfall.

Despite all the goings-on, I was hell-bent on making sure Oliver was well cared for and was kept away from the drama that was going on. I said this a few times that Oliver, strangely enough, hardly mentioned his mother. Was he bottling this up inside him? I was not sure. Was it that he was sick a lot, and the breakup was behind this? Oliver was such a delightful loving boy. He had his little ways he showed affection toward me. One he does always make me smile. He puts his two fingers up and says, "I love you two much, Daddy." No one can dispute my love for Oliver, and he loved me, but not apparently so with Claire and her parents as they held different views that came out in the proceedings.

Marriage breakups are not easy and affects you in many ways, and the sad part is the impact on children. I know this did affect Oliver, and all my efforts to ensure he was well cared for was undermined by others.

Months passed. It was around eight months now, and I was not sure what Claire will do next as at this point, she has not tried to have custody of Oliver. I had this feeling of all the things that has taken place, something is in the wind. I just had this feeling that Claire was mounting a plan so she can gain custody. I would not underestimate her as well as her parents and not excluding Craig. My opinion on this is why did Claire not take Oliver with her initially? Yes, I demanded but not forced her to leave him with me; however, I felt and still do feel that Craig did not want him with them from the beginning.

Life is like a circle, and it does go around and around. It is like the seasons; they come and go. Life is also what you make it. I have always treated people with respect as my mother always taught us growing up to respect your elders and love all people despite their color, religion, or beliefs. These were wise words. She always said if you make a mistake or do wrong, own up and be honest. But if anyone crosses the line or makes life unbearable for me or Oliver, then this becomes a different matter.

As this story unfolds, we now enter into a more different and more dramatic drama for both Oliver and I, Claire and Craig, along with her family and others all for her and her quest to have custody of Oliver. I had no family to help or to defend me, but lucky for me, I had good, faithful, and honest people who supported me.

Then there was the issue of the Family Law and Welfare I had to contend with, which made this a one-sided affair as to the rights of the mother. The situation for me was not good, and my love for my son is what has kept me going. My fight to keep him has now begun in earnest.

# 15

# CLAIRE'S CUSTODY APPLICATION

It was always in the my back of my mind that at some point, Claire would decide she wanted Oliver. She has gone well over eight months now, and a lot of incidents had taken place. There is a lot I have not bothered to mention. This particular Saturday morning was one I was not prepared for, and Claire fired the first shot to have custody of Oliver. In hindsight, this is something I should have done earlier myself, but I did not.

It was a lovely morning, a typical warm summer day. It was early November 1974. I was doing some work outside and cleaning up alongside the driveway. I heard a car pull up at the end of the driveway. I looked up, and a well-dressed man stepped out of the car and walked up the driveway to where I was working. He asked who I was. I said to him, "Daniel Mason, why? And who are you?" He did not answer, but he dropped papers at my feet. He did not even have the courtesy to hand this to me or say who he was. He then said out loud, "Consider yourself served." Then he took off at haste down the driveway. I thought, *What an idiot.*

I then sat on the back steps of the house and started looking at the papers, Oliver was outside with me and asked, "Who was that man, Dad?"

"Oh," I replied, "it was a man from work."

Oliver said, "Why did he run away?" Oliver was very observant.

I said, "The man had to get back to work in a hurry." I then looked at the documents that were thrust upon me. This was from Claire's solicitor and was an interim custody application to be held at the Magistrates' Court. I gasped and realized it was set down in three weeks' time. At this point, I did not have a lawyer, and up to this stage, I did not even think about it, but now with her applying for interim custody, it changes everything. I was not sure at this point what the law or procedures are, and of course, with no one to represent me, all this has put my whole world in a huge spin.

I went back inside with Oliver and made myself a cup of coffee and gave Oliver a glass of made-up cordial. He said to me, "Daddy, you look sad."

I said, "No, son, I am okay." I felt at that point, how can she try and take Oliver away from me knowing very well how much I loved my son and protected him? I said, "Oliver, let's go and see Uncle James and Aunty Fiona."

Oliver said, "Come on, Dad, let's go."

I knew I had to pull myself together, and I was very upset. I put Oliver in the back seat of the car, and we went to James and Fiona's place as they lived only a few minutes way.

I walked in with Oliver, and they looked at me and said, "Is everything alright?" I said, "No. Can Oliver play in the front room?"

James set up a soccer game for him, which he loved playing, and when James came back into the room, I told them that Claire was going for custody of Oliver, and I showed them the papers that were served to me earlier today.

James said, "What are you going to do?"

I said, "I have to fight this. No way am I parting with Oliver."

James said, "You will need to find a lawyer to defend you, and this lawyer has to be one that deals in custody matters."

James was dead right. I had to find a solicitor who dealt in child custody matters.

I did stay for a while, and Oliver loved playing with his uncle. As I was leaving, Fiona came out with me, and she said she was certain Rose and Kevin were also behind this. "They told me if you keep Oliver, then they will not see him anymore, and the possibility that you will take him back to Australia."

I said, "Fiona, that is out of the question. I am happy living in New Zealand. I have a great job and business."

She put her arms around me. She said, "Be strong. Oliver is your son, and you do what you think is best for his welfare."

I said, "Thanks. Yes, I will just do that."

I drove off from their place terribly upset, and I decided then not to go and discuss this with Claire's parents and that I was not going there this weekend and taking Oliver over as I did most weekends. Later that day, I did get a phone call from Rose, and she asked if everything was alright. I said, "Yes, under the circumstances." I felt she knew something was not right, so reluctantly I told her about Claire wanting custody of Oliver and then blurted out to Rose, "No way she is going to take him away from me, never, never."

Then Rose said, "Calm down. Claire is his mother, you know, and has rights as well."

This made me wonder now which side she was on. I said, "Rose, Claire was the one who left us, and you also disagreed with her leaving. What has changed now?"

Rose said, which made me very angry, that I threatened Claire and would harm her and Oliver if she took him.

I said to her that was not true. I said to her quite bluntly, "That is what she wants you to believe. Do not get caught up with her lies and the crap she comes up with."

She then asked, "Are you bringing Oliver over today?"

"No, I am spending the rest of the weekend with Oliver. Claire is your daughter, I understand, but do not fall for the trap and believe all she says as you may go down with her."

Rose swore at me over the phone and called me a lousy bastard, and yes, she was not happy with me and hung up.

I now knew Rose and Kevin were going to be an issue. Fiona warned me, and she was right. I have no doubt they are two-faced; one minute they make out they're on my side, and in   another they make it clear they are on Claire's side. People have to be careful what they wish for, and far as Rose and Kevin go, they are the grandparents, and they have their rights to see Oliver, and I had no intention to stop this despite what they think.

It was Sunday afternoon, and I invited Greg and Addison around to have a chat and stay for dinner. Over dinner, after putting Oliver to bed, I told them about Claire's application. Greg was a good worker and teammate, and he said, "Have you called William?" He was our area manager. "No," I said. "I will later. James said to me, which was very concerning, that fathers do not get

a fair go when it comes to custody matters. He also said he knows fathers have been denied even access to their kids."

Addison then looked at me and said, "Be prepared as you have done no wrong. You love Oliver, we know, so any help you need, we will be there for you both."

I said, "Thanks for this."

Greg and Allison left around eight o'clock, and yes, I found myself that I had little time to find a lawyer who dealt in child custody matters. With that, I phoned my area manager at Crest Foods and told him my situation, and as I was due for annual leave shortly, I asked for an extra two weeks. I said, "I don't expect to be paid."

The company was very supportive of me, and I was given I months leave. How lucky I was working for such a company and having an area manager who was so supportive under the circumstances. They gave me all the time off I wanted, and I could not ask for anything more. My boss said to me I was a valued employee, and he also said that Oliver deserved a father like me and fully understood the position I was in.

I thanked him so much, and a tear came down my cheek. "I will call into the office in the morning and hand over the company car."

He said, "No, you hold on to the car as you will need it." I said to him, "Are you sure?"

He said, "Yes, Danial, I am sure."

I could not thank him enough. This raises a very valid point. Privileges are earned, and to have respect, it is not a given. You earn that respect as you go about daily life.

I have no doubt that respect is a feeling when you treat someone well for their qualities or character traits, but respect can also be a manifestation of dignity toward people. Employees and managers should respect each other as it creates an excellent work environment; in turn, this increases employees' productivity. Crest Foods is a prime example of this.

Now the challenge awaits me ahead as this is just beginning for my crusade to keep my son Oliver. Unaware of what challenges awaited me, Monday came, and I dropped off Oliver at Fiona's place, and I called into the office at Crest Foods. I thanked William very much for his kind understanding.

He shook me by the hand and said, "Danial, we will back you all the way."

I could not thank him enough. As I was walking out, Carol the receptionist said, "Danial, I have heard the news from Greg, and we all here wish you well. I am sure you will find a way. Take care!" The first challenge for me now was to find a solicitor who will represent me as all this was all new to me, and I was in unchartered waters, so to speak. This caught me well off guard. I said,

"Thanks, Carol, I will be in touch." I then headed back home to ring around to find a lawyer. Later in the morning, I made an appointment to see a solicitor in the afternoon at 1:00 p.m.,

and another I arranged around 4:00 p.m., just in case the first one did not work out. I arrived at the office of the legal firm Becker and Becker, and I had a meeting with a solicitor named Mr. Newman. He was very young, and he claimed he dealt in family law matters. Then I went about telling my story, and I showed him the papers that was served to me.

He went through them, and he then said, "Under the law, the mother does get custody of the child. As your child is under five, she will automatically be awarded custody."

I said to him, "This is nonsense. The law is an arse then."

He said to me, "The best-case scenario is you can get access rights."

I said, "You're kidding. No, I do not accept to have access rights. I want custody of my boy."

He said, "I am sorry, but that is the way it is." He went on to say that he can draft a letter for me to have access rights and for Claire to have custody.

I said, "No thanks. So you won't take my case on and we fight for custody?" He replied, "I am prepared to get you access rights."

With that I thanked him for his time and walked out. When I got outside, I was shaking and felt this was not looking good at all and thought this was a bigger challenge than I could imagine. I had another appointment at 4:00 p.m. I decided to then go to a coffee lounge in the city and have something to eat. I felt so dejected, and I was hoping the next meeting with the solicitors may be more promising.

I had over two hours to fill in, so I went to a cinema in the city and watched a movie to get my mind off things.

It was just before 4:00 p.m., and I went to my next appointment. The solicitor was a Mr. Flynn, and his law firm dealt in family law, so I was more than hopeful. Unfortunately, he was no better than the last one I went to. He was much older and said to me the best-case scenario was for me to get access.

I took exception to this and said to him, "So you're telling me fathers don't have a say in these matters?"

"Sorry," he said, "that is the law. What gives you the right to have custody of your child as your child is under five? The child should be with his mother."

I said, "I have bloody rights too. I am his father, goddamn it!" I thought, *What an attitude and a stupid thing to say!* I said, "Fathers are capable of looking after their children, just as much as a mother does. What gives the women the right to say they should have custody of the children?"

The solicitor said, "That is the law here in New Zealand, a child under five, the mother automatically gets custody."

Then I said, "The law is an arse and needs changing." I got very emotional and said, "No way am I giving up my son for you or anyone else."

He said to me, "You have to face reality. I am sorry, the law is what it is. Your wife has applied for custody, and as the law stands, you have no hope of winning such a hearing. That is the law, despite what the mother may or may not have done.

I said, "She walked out on us, surely that must account for something?"

"No," he said. "Look, the best you can do is we can represent you, we will apply for access rights."

I said, "No way am I going to agree to this. I will somehow contest this. The law is biased against fathers, and this must change. Fathers have rights too."

The lawyer said, "I am sorry, you are wasting your time. No lawyer will take your case on as your son is only three years of age and four soon."

I raised my voice and abruptly said, "Yes, but I am the father. I have rights too." The lawyer said, "Think about it and call me if you change your mind."

I said as I was walking out of his office, "You call yourself a lawyer? I though lawyers like you take on such cases."

He replied, "If there is no way that I can win, it's a waste of my time and your time and money." I thought what an attitude by this lawyer as they call themselves lawyers for custody matters. As the week progressed, I tried many other lawyers, and the answers were all the same as the lawyers told me as it was the mother's application applying for interim custody, so under the law at the time, it was 100 percent on her side, and the best I could do was apply for access rights. I felt this was utter crap, and I was very dejected, and I could not believe that lawyers were so gutless that they would not take the case on because of the law. This in my opinion stinks, and the law has to change.

I got to the point that I should defend this case myself, but I had no legal background, and seeing the application was Claire's, this made it more and more difficult for me. No way was I going to allow Oliver with his mother while she was with Craig, and with what I know about his background, he should not be near my son. All this played on my mind. Claire her erratic behaviour was also a major concern.

I called my good friend and workmate Greg and told him my dilemma of not finding a lawyer. With that he said, "Come over to dinner on Friday night, and of course, bring Oliver."

I said, "Yes, I will see you around 6:00 p.m. I felt so traumatized. I needed to discuss this with others.

Friday arrived, and I brought with me a nice bottle of local red wine. Allison greeted us at the door, and Oliver gave her a big hug and kiss. Greg was preparing the dinner, and he called out, "Go into the lounge, and I will pour you a beer."

We all chatted for a while, and we sat down to dinner. I explained to Greg and Allison what the lawyers told me. Oliver was with their children and out of earshot. I explained I felt the law was very wrong. I said, "Fathers are capable of bringing up their children if given the opportunity."

Greg and Allison were particularly good at listening, and they supported me from day one. Greg said, "There must be a way, and with your determination, I am sure you will find a way."

On leaving their place, Oliver said, "Daddy I love going to Uncle Greg and Aunty Allison's."

I said, "That is nice, Oliver, as they love you coming over." I left their place around 8:00 p.m. as it was getting well past Oliver's bedtime. On the way home, I briefly called James and Fiona and told them what was happening. They were at this point very supportive of me, and I felt them to be on my side, and I was very grateful for their support, in particular Fiona as she just adored little Oliver. James being the brother of Claire, I was not 100 percent sure of what he thought of this and his support for his sister. I said to them, "I just have to find a way somehow." They both agreed.

At home, I gave Oliver his regular bath as he always loved playing with his toys in the tub, and I dressed him for bed. I always read him a story before he nodded off, and he always gave me a big hug and kiss and tells me he loves me, and I always say, "Oliver, I love you too." One saying Oliver had that always tickled me is "Daddy, I love you too much," and he put up two fingers. Oliver was such a bright little boy, and things he does makes it more and more the reason why I just cannot part with him.

You must fight hard for what you believe in, and if there is a will, then I have to find a way. I now had to think out of the box as so many incidents had been taking place. I decided to have someone else in the house with me as I had a spare room. I heard from Greg that Jim Baxter was looking for somewhere to stay as he just was transferred from Wellington with Crest Foods. Greg thought it would be ideal for me as a backup. I agreed and said having someone else around would be a good alibi for me as to Claire's comings and goings.

Jim shifted in that weekend on the Saturday after I spent all week trying to find a lawyer. It was exhausting, to say the least, and I was so down in the dumps. I was in the lounge listening to my favorite singer Neil Diamond, and it was getting rather late. I was getting ready for bed when Jim came back from seeing his girlfriend. The phone rang, and I said, "Jim, it will be Claire again, I am sure. Can you tell her to bugger off or something?"

He did and said, "Stop ringing up here at all hours. It's well past 11:00 p.m." He then hung up on her.

Jim and I made a coffee, and I said to him, "I have no doubt that people will think that by me having my son was to get back at Claire.

If they think that way, then I am sorry as that is not the case, far from it. She left the family home, and it was her who broke up the family unit, not me. I did all I could to hold it together. It was her who had the affair, not me. I am very capable of bringing up my son. If I felt I could not cope or Claire was with someone who was of good character, then maybe it would change things or everything may be different. The fact is I love my son, and she made her choice. As far as I am concerned, she lost her rights to have custody of Oliver, and that is what I believe in and what I believe is worth fighting for."

Jim did not say too much but agreed.

For some reason, I poured this out to Jim, and we chatted on for an hour or two. I said to him, "I may have strong feelings on this, but if one partner leaves the family unit and leaves their children behind for no other reason that they are having an affair and leave to live with their lover, then it should be they lose their rights as a parent. This also applies to partners who are violent or abuse their children, they to lose their rights.

"I understand violence against women and children should not be tolerated, and the same goes for women who are violent to their partners and children. What I feel let down by all this is that I worked hard and bought a new home for us. I was never violent or abusive. I loved my wife and adore my son. Claire had an affair that went on for over twelve months.

"She then left under the influence of Craig, and damn me and Oliver as she did not consider us at all when she decided to leave. Her wanting Oliver now is beyond me, and I will find a way somehow. I will use all my might as I do not plan to give up my son."

Jim said, "Danial, it's good to get this off your chest and talk to someone." I said, "Thank you for listening and me giving you an ear bashing."

With that we called it a night.

I did get in touch with Families Need Fathers group in Auckland, and I did attend one of their meetings. The stories fathers told me were alarming, and it has become very clear to me that this is a very contentious issue. I am sure Claire has been told she has the law on her side. The many fathers that do not get custody or have access to their children is appalling, and the law somehow needs change. These men were well-to-do people; they condemned family violence, and their spouses had affairs or were abusive toward them, but the mothers got custody, and some got access and others no access at all. This was heartbreaking for them. They said that either the courts, Welfare, and their spouse gives evidence against them to the point that evidence against the father is fabricated and have friends and family to back up the mother's so-called claims. FNF group was very supportive of me and said to me, "You must fight this although the odds are against you." They hope one day things may change. They respected my rights to fight this as they said, "We have been there and did not get anywhere." Most said their cases were thrown out of court and sided with the mother. They also said to watch the Welfare people as they side with the mothers and do not support the fathers.

One father took me aside before I left the meeting and said to me, "Danial, the laws in New Zealand toward fathers' rights is appalling." He said his wife was abusive to him and his children, and she not only got custody but also stopped him seeing them. "I admire your tenacity to fight this, and the trouble is no lawyer will take on cases for fathers to fight for custody."

I said, "Yes, this is what I have found so far."

He then said, "I hope you find a way, and come here anytime to our meetings as that is what we are here for."

I thanked him and left. After listening to the fathers and their stories and the way they had been treated was very disturbing to not only hear but listen to. Some had similar issues like mine, and the fact was the families of their spouses lied and made up stories and incidents that the lawyers, courts, and the Welfare believed.

The mention of Child Welfare and what was said also concerned me as they said at the meeting that they did not get a fair report as they tend to favor the mothers.

I was glad I did go along to this meeting and to find people who did go through the same situation I now found myself in. No doubt I know that I am facing a huge battle to keep my son. It's made me well aware that I not only had to deal with the marriage breakup, but I had to deal with the lies and allegations made against me, being now called a potential murderer, that I ill-treated my wife and was abusive to her, that I threatened her when she left and made sure by my threats she did not take Oliver with her.

I came back home around 10:00 a.m. Jim looked after Oliver for me. As I walked, he said, "You look so down."

I told him about the meeting I went to and how so many fathers had the same battle I was going through. I said, "This is not looking good for me, and it has got to me. I must somehow find a way somehow. I must.

The interim custody case was now less than three weeks away, and as yet, I have not found a legal representative knowing what lay ahead, the battle before me, as it has been clearly spelt out that the law is in the mother's favour. Despite what the law is, I will fight to have custody of my son. If I was a violent person or a wife basher or mistreated my son, I would fully understand. I had to put the bitterness behind me as I was blindsided and cheated on.

My destiny was now to find that solution as time now is extremely critical. To have faith in what you believe in gives me the strength to soldier on.

# 16

# PREMONITION OR DIVINE INTERVENTION

In life, strange things happen for many reasons, and some you cannot explain. I often attended church in Auckland most Sundays, and I would take Oliver with me, although he was too young at that stage to attend Sunday school. He goes into the crèche where he can play with the other young boys and girls. However, when he turns four and goes to kindergarten, then he can go to Sunday school.

I had not been to church for a few weeks now mainly due to the up-and-coming custody hearing. The hearing was now less than two weeks away, and for some unexplained reason, I was drawn to the church. It was during the night as I slept that I had a dream, and in that dream, I met a man at church who would be able to help me. When I woke up the next morning, I had this strange feeling that I cannot describe. I said to Jim and Oliver over breakfast that we were off to church today.

Oliver said, "Good as I can play with the other kids." He seemed very delighted with this. Before we left, I told Jim about my strange dream and my premonition. It was like I was being guided. This I am sure did not make much sense to James. He may have thought I was going loopy. I know minds can play tricks on us. I was at a very low ebb and was also very down all week. I thought by attending church, it would be uplifting as well as give me some moral support. This I really badly needed.

Oliver and I arrived at the church well before the service was due to start. I took Oliver around to the crèche and settled him in, then I went around to talk to the minister Reverend John Anderson. He was an elderly gentleman. He was a very well-known and loved minister of the church. He also knew about my separation from Claire as he did at some point go to her place and spoke to her, which I was not aware of at the time. It was also Rev. Anderson who married us. He also had met Oliver on many occasions. He always told me, "What a lovely young boy you have."

I told him about the custody hearing and the difficulty finding a lawyer to represent me as the hearing was now in two weeks' time. He listened intently. I also explained how the law was on the mother's side, and the law as it stands favors them, especially when children like Oliver is under five.

He said, "I understand all this."

I said emotionally, "I do not want to lose Oliver. He is all I have. I know it will be a tough fight for me to keep Oliver. I cannot give up my son."

He put his hand on my shoulder said to me that he fully understands my situation, and he will keep me in his prayers. Then what he told me next stirred me to no end. He said, "At the service today is a guest speaker, a Mr. Dunbar, and he is involved in Family Affairs, such as custody matters, single mothers. He is also advisor to the courts in all family case matters. You need to meet this man. I will introduce you to him after the service. In the meantime, I will speak to him and briefly tell him about your situation. I am sure he would be able to help you and advise you. You are a good man, Danial, and you love your son, and you have faith and courage. I agree and understand you have a big problem. Let us all pray that you can find a solution."

I said, "Thank you, and I cannot wait to see Mr. Dunbar."

The church service was due to start. I went into the church. I found hardly a seat as it was packed. I then spotted a spare seat at the back of the church. I pondered over what the minister told me. Is the premonition to attend church today the sign or intervention that I was feeling? I sat quietly and said a prayer, and the service started with a hymn, "How Great Thou Art."

The sermon followed. I could not believe it; it was about the prodigal son. The minister and his sermons were always enlightening. He had a very good way of describing things and to bring it down to our level. At the close of his service, the closing hymn was "Onward Christian Soldiers."

After the normal greeting by the minister when everyone was leaving the service, he said to me as he shook my hand, "Daniel, I will see you shortly. Go around to the hall and have a cuppa, and I will then introduce you to Mr. Dunbar."

I was having a cup of tea when the minister said to me, "Come with me, and I will introduce you to the guest speaker, Mr. Dunbar."

He was an elderly gentleman. His address was mostly about single mothers and children's welfare and the struggle for single mothers, and hearing this, I thought, *Here we go again, favoring the mother and not a mention of fathers. They are just as important as the mother's role in families.* I felt very apprehensive.

I was then introduced to Mr. Dunbar. He said to me, "I think you have a story to tell me. With that, let's go into the vestibule, and we can speak privately." I followed Mr. Dunbar into the vestibule. I told him my story.

He was shocked to hear that no legal firm would help me, and he said to me in his experience, mothers do get custody of their children over the father, but it does not say there cannot be changes made. He said, "Danial, you do have a big challenge ahead of you. Your faith and your willingness to look after your son is commendable. The problem with family court matters is that they can become so ugly, a lot of lawyers tend to not take on such cases, which is a shame."

I did understand what Mr. Dunbar said to me.

Mr. Dunbar said, "I know a lady lawyer, in fact, she is a barrister. Her name is Ms. Chamberlain, and I will arrange you to meet her tomorrow." He wrote down her details, and he said, "Call her around 11:00 a.m., and she will be expecting your call. She is an expert in child custody matters, and I am sure she will take your case on. She also is a personal friend of mine."

With that, I could not thank him enough.

He said in closing to me, "Never give up hope or your faith. If there is a will, there is a way."

I left the church that day with Oliver, and I thought, was this the answer? I was searching to find a lawyer to take my case on. The unexplained was that I was going to meet a stranger this day, and he was going to help me. This was so surreal that it gave me goose bumps.

I then went back home and told Jim, and I said, "You would not believe what happened today." Jim was gobsmacked, and after telling him only this morning what I dreamt and was going to meet a man who can help me, it was just so hard to comprehend.

Was this the beginning that will put me on the right path to fight for my rights to have custody of my son? I am fighting for change. I hope Ms. Chamberlain takes my case on, and I cannot wait until I see her Monday.

# 17

# MEETING MS. CHAMBERLAIN

Monday morning came. I had a restless night and was still on leave from work. I got Oliver up out of bed and dressed him and made his breakfast. He wanted one of his favorites rice bubbles; he always chuckled when they made a popping sound. I told him he will stay with Aunty Fiona till Daddy comes home later in the day.

He said, "Daddy, you do not have to go to work today?" "No, Daddy is seeing a very important person today."

I dropped Oliver off at Fiona and James's place. I said to Fiona, "I have some hope today," and I told her the story about meeting Mr. Dunbar at church. "He is going to organize a lawyer for me today."

Fiona seemed very pleased. I left their place, and I went back home to prepare all the documents. I then phoned the lawyer's office around 10:00 a.m. I did get an appointment for 11:00 a.m. I could not get into the city quick enough. I soon arrived at the solicitor's office just before 11:00 a.m. It was on the fifth floor and had a great view over the city. I walked up to the receptionist. I said, "My name is Danial Mason."

She said, "Please take a seat as Mrs. Chamberlain is expecting you."

I was given a cup of tea and did not wait long. Mrs. Chamberlain came out of her office. She was a tall person, possibly in her forties. "Please come in, Danial." She spoke in a very quiet voice. "Mr. Dunbar had called me and explained your situation."

I walked into her office. I said, "What a magnificent view you have of the city."

She said, "Yes, it's good view." After a pause, she said, "Mr. Dunbar is a personal friend of mine, and he briefly told me your story."

I handed over the documents that Claire's lawyer served to me. As she was going through them, she said, "I see you go to St. David's Church."

"Yes, I do."

"Your minister is a very nice gentleman." "Yes, he is," I replied.

"Well," she said, "you do have a dilemma on your hands. Now tell me more of your story, and I'll see if I can help you or not."

I briefly told her about Claire and how she left to go with a married man. "She also claims I threatened her, and that is why she did not take the boy. In fact she says I am a potential murderer." I told her about many incidents. "As you can see by her application, she wants custody of my son. I am not prepared to give him up. I want Oliver with me. I am his father, and I am not prepared to give him up."

Mrs. Chamberlain sternly looked at me as she went through the served papers. She then remarked, "Mr. Mason, this is just over a week away. Why in God's name have you left it this late to get someone to represent you?"

I then explained to her about the solicitors I went to, and they were only interested in access arrangements. "I was so depressed and upset and did not know which way to turn, then for some unknown reason, I had this premonition to go to church yesterday, and this is when I met Mr. Dunbar, and he told me about you."

"Well, yes, he is a very decent and nice man. He has children's interest at heart. I see your case is very complex. Oliver is nearly four. He now is three years of age, and as the law is that children do go with their mother under the current law. Now it is not to say things can change. The other issue is that the application has been made by the mother of the child, and this will be very difficult for you to get interim custody."

My eyes started to well up. I said to Mrs. Chamberlain, "We have to find a way as the man who Claire is with is a no-hoper, and I do not want my son near him. I love my boy. I want him with me. Claire can have access, but he stays with me.

She replied, "I do not want to give you false hope on this. It is not easy as fathers do not get a fair hearing. You will have to face the welfare department as well at some stage, and you do have a huge mountain to climb. Your faith and your passion and the love of your son is commendable." In her very quiet voice, she said, "Mr. Mason, we have a case to present. We have only a week to go, which is not enough to prepare the case. I will be asking for an extension to allow us to prepare for this hearing."

I could have jumped out of the chair and hugged her. I said to her, "You are going to take my case on? I thank you so much!" I said to myself, *Thank God, I have someone who will represent me.* Mrs. Chamberlain could see the emotion in me as a few tears rolled down my cheeks. She said, "I will go through what you have given me. In the meantime, I will get the extension for the hearing, and I must now contact your wife's solicitor and inform them I am acting for you as well advise them we will be asking to get the extension for the hearing. I will see you on Wednesday at 11:00 a.m., and we will do a declaration of facts to support your application. No doubt we will also have one from your wife, which you will need to respond to."

I could not thank her enough, and I said, "Can you also call Mr. Dunbar and thank him as well?" I shook hands with her on leaving. I said, "You do not know how much this all means to me." Tearfully, I said, "Thank you, I am sorry if I got emotional." Yes, the emotion of the moment did get to me. Mrs. Chamberlain did see this. I felt embarrassed.

She said, "Danial, I see by your reactions what this means to you. I want you to keep out of trouble, and see you Wednesday."

I said thank you again. I left her office and went down to a coffee lounge in the city and had something to eat and drink and pondered over what had taken place. Meeting such a lovely person as Mr. Dunbar said, she is a distinguished person and well respected in the legal circles; also she knows the family law.

I then went out to the office at Crest Foods and told my boss, "The hearing will be now in a few weeks' time as my lawyer is asking for an extension, and I will come back to work up until the hearing, if you agree, as I have had so much time off. I am so grateful for what you have done."

My boss said, "You're most welcome, and this will help you to keep your mind off things."

With that I said, "I will be on deck tomorrow." I spent an hour or two with my boss to go over what needed to be done as there was a lot of catching up to do.

I finally got back to pick up Oliver at James and Fiona's place. James was not home as yet as he was at football training. Fiona already gave Oliver his dinner, which I thanked Fiona for. I briefly told her, "I now have a lawyer to represent me, and now the battle lines are drawn. If Claire thinks she has this in the bag, then she is mistaken. Now I have one of the top lawyers in Auckland representing me. I am going back to work until the hearing. Is it okay for you to look after Oliver for me? I will drop him off around eight thirty and pick him up after, say, four."

Fiona said she would love to as she knew Oliver loved her and also was no trouble to her. I thanked her as she was a godsend. I do not know what I would do without her.

I went back home and settled Oliver into bed. I said to Jim after I put Oliver to bed, "I have found the right person to represent me. It is not going to be easy, I know, but I must think positively." Jim poured me a bourbon and Coke, and we sat and chatted for a while. We put on Neil Diamond's *Hot August Night* album and listened to that until it was time to call it quits for the night. Jim said as he was heading to his room, "Funny Claire has not called tonight." "Yes," I replied, "it is a change."

# 18

# STATEMENTS MADE
# BEFORE THE HEARING

The Wednesday could not come quickly enough. I went up to Mrs. Chamberlain's office and went straight in. She told me that we now had an extension, and the hearing was now set down for the first week of December. "Today I have a few supporting documents that was served on me this morning from your wife's solicitor."

I said, "Boy, they did not waste time."

Ms. Chamberlain said, "What we must do is go through each one and respond to them. They portray you as a very violent person. This also includes responses from your wife's mother, a Ms. Rose McDonald, as well as your wife's de facto partner, Mr. Kelly."

I said, "Nothing surprises me anymore."

Ms. Chamberlain said, "Let us read your ex-wife's application, and we can make notes as we go along. First she is asking for interim custody. She also states you were married in 1970, and Oliver was born in December 1971. She is asking the court for sole guardianship of Oliver, the child of the marriage. She also wants a maintenance order in respect of the said child."

I said, "This is a bit rich as when I have had Oliver all this time, she has offered nothing to me. She has more class than my backside."

"She goes on to say she is living in a de facto relationship with a Mr. Craig Kelly." The next bit Mrs. Chamberlain commented on was quite confusing. "On one hand, she is seeking interim custody of Oliver, and then she states that her mother should have actual custody of Oliver, then she says that Danial would have access to him, and you both pay her mother maintenance for looking after him. It gets even more bizarre as she said in the event of her being granted custody, she will stop work and be a full-time mother to Oliver."

I looked at Mrs. Chamberlain and shook my head and responded, "What the heck is that all about? She made a few contradictions. Surely her lawyer should have made this clearer, one would think."

We then read on, and I said, "This next bit is what I call the denial and cannot face the fact. She walked out on me and Oliver, but she claims she wanted to take Oliver with her, and I physically prevented her from doing so. She also claims I made her life most unpleasant, then she accuses me that I made repeated threats to harm her, including Oliver and Craig Kelly, her lover."

Ms. Chamberlain remarked to me, "Danial your ex-wife is not painting a good picture of you. I think let us carry on and see what else we need to deal with here."

This next bit left me speechless as she claims that she loves Oliver very much, and she also believes that she can care for him better than I can. I would argue on that point. If that was the case, then why did she leave in the first place? Claire being his mother, I agree she does love him, however, she left us. Surely no decent mother does that. In my opinion, it was her lust for her lover she put first, then she says she is quite happy for me to have very liberal access to Oliver.

I said to Mrs. Chamberlain, "She now thinks she is better suited to look after him than I am. Her actions to date and her leaving in the manner she did must account for something. Surely her actions speak for itself."

Mrs. Chamberlain remarked to me, "Your ex-wife can say what she likes about you, but at the end of the day, a lot is hearsay and also very confusing as well as conflicting with her statements along with her making outrageous allegations about you. All this will be left up to the courts to decide who is telling the truth or not. I do agree with you, Danial, after going through her entire statement, there are a lot of anomalies and confusing statements. What we do now is answer her statements the best way we can."

I then with my lawyer put together my response, I started by saying that we did, in my opinion, have a happy relationship until she formed an association with Craig Kelly, that he was a married man and also had a young daughter. He lived then in West Auckland. It was at the time in May 1975 that Claire left the matrimonial home. This was six weeks after we shifted into our new home. She then went to live with her lover, Craig Kelly. His wife soon filed proceedings for divorce on the grounds of his adultery with Claire.

"I find that the statements as to when she decided to leave the family home and that I stopped her from taking Oliver, including that I was going to physically harm her, that is just total nonsense. I pleaded with her in many ways to stay. Her obsession with her lover was the reason why she left. Oliver was not home that day as he was with his grandparents.

"In her statement, she claims that I would not let her take Oliver, also that I threatened her. Firstly when she left that day, Oliver went to his grandparents on Saturday and was still at the grandparents' home the day she left the matrimonial home. The other point was I was working on Sunday with Dylan Watson at the leagues club in Mangere, showing a movie for the children. When I was heading back to my house, we observed Claire walking across the empty paddocks (this is where the new houses are being built). I noticed she had suitcase and a large bag. We followed her without being noticed, and she went to a car parked on the main road, and I could see it was Craig Kelly. I did not confront her and dropped off Dylan at his place, and then collected Oliver from my in-laws and back to my house, where he has been with me ever since.

"Her claims that I physically stopped her and not allow her to take Oliver is just stuff made up as Oliver was at his grandparents. I mentioned in my statement that I have looked after Oliver after she had left. As I also had work commitments, I did drop Oliver off two days a week at the grandparents, and for the remaining days, he stayed with James and Fiona until I came home from work, usually about four o'clock. I also stated I will be seeking an interim order for Oliver along with filing for divorce on the grounds of Claire's adultery with Craig Kelly. I did mention I have provided a new home, and Claire only stayed some six weeks after we shifted into the new home. Oliver has made many friends in the area, and the ones out the back of our house is a Māori family with three boys and a girl. Oliver spends a lot of time with them. I also have enrolled Oliver for kindergarten, and he will start early next year."

Mrs. Chamberlain was taking notes and listening intently to what I was saying as I know she will put this in a better way to present to the court.

I said, "My job is geared, so if I require time off, I will be given it. My area manager would support me on that. The other point I would like to make is that my ex-wife is now working from 7:00 a.m. to 3:30 p.m. and works overtime on Saturdays and Sundays, so I believe she is in no better position to have Oliver than I am. As to Craig, I am not certain about his financial commitments. It would seem impossible for her to give up work. I know Oliver is happy with me."

Ms Chamberlain said she will put together my final statement, and we will get this sworn at the Magistrates' Court in the morning. She said to come around 10:00 a.m., and we will then head up to the court.

Next day after my statement was filed at the Magistrates' Court, we then went back to Mrs. Chamberlain's office, and she said, "We now have to look at your wife's mother's, Mrs. Rose McDonald, outrageous supporting statement. At this point we will not respond to her statement as she claims you are turning your son away from her, and she also makes claims you threatened her last month. She also claims you will deny her any access to Oliver. She also claims that since your wife has left, they have looked after Oliver."

I just shook my head, and Mrs. Chamberlain said, "It is all very similar to your wife's statement, and you will get your chance to respond. Ms. McDonald also states that Oliver has no friends to play with in the street, you take him to your work doing your rounds, his toys are neglected, and some are stolen. Oliver does not show any affection to you. She also claims you threatened your wife when she was leaving."

I said to Mrs. Chamberlain, "This is all made-up rubbish, and if you read through their statements, they are all the same. It is almost word for word."

Mrs. Chamberlain replied, "Yes, I agree, a lot is hearsay, but they have made some damning evidence against you. Let us hope we get a good magistrate who will listen to your side impartially." I arranged on the Friday before the hearing to meet up with Mrs. Chamberlain to get a final briefing, and what she said just floored me as she said, "I will propose the following, and because the hearing is being held at the Magistrates' Court, I will be on your behalf lodging an injunction order to stop the interim custody case to be heard in the Magistrates' Court, as I will then be applying for a full custody hearing to be heard in the Supreme Court, and this order should allow you to remain having interim custody of Oliver. This of course will depend on if the magistrate is a good one and adheres to the letter of the law. If he does, then the magistrate should go with the application put forward."

Well, I was taken aback by this and unsure which way it will go.

Then Mrs. Chamberlain said, "You are not to disclose this to anyone, absolutely no one. Do you understand? I do not want your wife to do the same. Now go home, I will see you at the Magistrates' Court on Monday at 9:30 a.m., and the case is set down for 10:00 a.m."

I thanked Ms. Chamberlain and left her office more hopeful, and I must sweat it out for three more days and hope and pray that the magistrate will allow me to keep my son with me. Was this the beginning of something that changes everything? And was the strange feeling going to church that Sunday meant to be, and having such an astute and caring person like Ms. Chamberlain?

I spent the weekend with Oliver, and I kept away from Fiona and James. I went over to Greg and Allison's place on Saturday afternoon, and Oliver played with their two children. Greg and I played pool for a while. He asked how things are going, and I said, "Going okay. Monday is D-Day," and I left it at that.

We stayed for dinner, and over dinner, I arranged for Oliver to stay at their place Monday as  a security measure while I was at the hearing. Greg did say, "What happens if she gets custody?"

I said, "I am not going there and not thinking of that outcome."

I arrived back at our place around 8:00 p.m., and Jim was there with his girlfriend. I put Oliver to bed, and then Jim and his girlfriend and I watched TV, and we had a wine or two. The case on Monday did not come up.

The next day, I took Oliver to Takapuna Beach. We had a very good time and had lunch there. We arrived back home later on in the afternoon. We had an early dinner and put Oliver to bed, and then I settled into the lounge. I listened to Neil Diamond and Buddy Holly and had a glass of wine and went over notes I had the for the hearing the next day. Jim came home, and we chatted for a while. He asked, "How do you think you will go tomorrow?"

I said, "It is in the balance. She has made a lot of outrageous claims against me. She says I was going to harm her and Oliver. She also claims I am an extremely dangerous person. The other fact is the court system favors the mother, so now it is a matter of the court to decide. I am now in their hands.

"My solicitor is exceptionally good. She leaves nothing for chance, and I am sure she will have a plan in place. As what I have seen and read so far, Claire's lawyer is not what I call smart as he has allowed various statements that are confusing and contradictory, and I am absolutely sure my solicitor is much smarter than that."

The Sunday evening before the hearing, I could not sleep at all. I tossed and turned and thinking what worst-case scenarios or outcomes I would be facing. How would I tell Oliver, a three-year-old, if he has to go with his mother and away from me? Oliver will turn four shortly in December, and damn it, I am going to fight like hell.

In the morning, I told Oliver the best way I could without being emotional and not to upset him. I said, "Daddy is seeing a man today, hoping that you can stay with me. It may also be that you will have to go with Mummy."

There was a tear in my eye as Oliver sobbed and said, "I don't want to go with Mummy! I want to stay with you. I don't like Craig."

I said in a hopeful voice, "Everything will be alright."

Oliver put his arms around me and said, "I love you, Daddy."

At that point, I was unsure Oliver understood what was going on. He has been going through a lot, and he was the main one in this dispute who had no fault of his own.

# 19

# INTERIM CUSTODY HEARING

I was not my normal self as I had to be at the court at nine thirty. I drove over to Greg and Allison's place and dropped Oliver at their place around eight thirty. Greg was heading off to work and said, "Oliver will be okay with Allison as she is great with kids."

I then thanked Allison for looking after Oliver. She gave me a big hug and kiss and said, "Wish you well!"

Oliver came over to me and gave me a big hug, and he put his two fingers up and said, "I love you two much."

I said, "Oliver, you will be okay with Aunty Allison. Daddy will be back soon. Oliver, I love you too." I gave him an extra big hug. I said to Allison, "I am not sure how long this will be as I do not know how this will go."

Allison said, "Oliver will be here waiting for you."

"Yes, I know. One other thing I suppose we must prepare for is the worst-case scenario if—a big if—Claire gets interim custody, which is well on the cards, that I cannot dismiss."

Allison said, "Let us deal with that if that happens. Stay positive!" My mind was just in a spin when I left their place.

My drive into the city was very difficult as not only I had to contend with the peak-hour traffic on the motorway and being anxious and nervous not knowing how this will unfold today; what if, in regard to Oliver continuing staying with me or will he go to his mother. If a change took place, all this would be hard for a little boy to cope with as he has been with me all this time after Claire left, let alone I felt, at the time she left, gut wrenching. All this is very trying times and can have emotional effect on you as I did experience.

I finally found a parking area close to the courthouse. I arrived at the court around nine thirty. I had my best suit on. I did not have to wait long before my barrister, Mrs. Chamberlain, arrived. She quietly spoke to me and said, "At this point, you may not have to address the court. If you do, then follow my lead. I will present your case, and I will put forward what we discussed on Friday at our meeting."

We both were heading to the courtroom, and Claire was with Craig and her mother. I said to Mrs. Chamberlain, "That is Claire my ex-wife, next to her lover. Claire does not look well."

It was the first time Mrs. Chamberlain had seen Claire. She said, Is that the man she left you for?"

I replied, "Yes, that is him."

She shook her head and said, "Let's get ourselves into the courtroom."

I said fine. With that, we both entered the courtroom. I sat down within the allocated seating as assigned for the lawyers and who they were representing. Where we sat was facing right in the middle, directly where the magistrate would be presiding.

Mrs. Chamberlain then asked me how I was holding up. I said, "So far, so good."

Then we heard people coming in. She looked over and said, "Your ex-wife has just come in, along with your wife's male friend." She then remarked how badly dressed he was for the occasion. "A low-neck jumper, no tie, and he looks scruffy."

I looked around to them where they were sitting and said, "I do agree. This is why I am doing this for Oliver as what I know about this guy leaves me cold."

She asked about the older woman next to Claire. "Is that her mother?"

I said, "Yes, Rose McDonald." I then lowered my voice. "I just hope and pray that Claire does not get interim custody today as this would break my heart." I sat calmly as I could beside my barrister.

She leaned over to me and said, "Stay quiet and look straight at the magistrate."

This was now the decisive moment. The court commenced, and the clerk of courts read out, "The court has two applications of interim custody of Oliver Kevin Mason, one by Claire Anne Mason, the applicant, the mother of the child, and one by Danial Kenneth Mason, the respondent, the father of the said child."

Mrs. Chamberlain then got up from her chair and addressed the court. "I am representing Mr. Danial Mason on his application for interim custody of Oliver Kevin Mason. Currently, the child is in the care of his father."

This is where she dropped what I call a bombshell.

"I would like to submit to the court the application for full custody of Oliver Kevin Mason to be heard in the Supreme Court of Auckland in July next year. I also ask the court today that the boy in the center of this dispute, Oliver Kevin Mason, remains with his father as he has done so since the applicant had left the matrimonial home in May this year."

Then there was an outburst from Claire's lawyer, and he said, "I am representing the applicant and object to what Mrs. Chamberlain put to the court." He then jumped out of his chair and said, "May I address the court in this matter?" He went close to the magistrate's bench, waving the papers he had in his hand, and said loudly, "First, we are here today for my client to have interim custody of her son. Then we have not been advised of this new development. I object the validity of such an application. Furthermore, I have been informed that the mother of the child, Mrs. Claire Mason, is not well and unable to give evidence today."

Mrs. Chamberlain then interjected. She stood up out of her chair and said, "As Mr. Danial Mason has applied to the Supreme Court for a hearing set down for July next year, so I ask the court to give interim custody to Mr. Mason as the Supreme Court application must supersede the application that is now in this court today."

Claire's lawyer was still standing and yelled out, "We have had no warning of this, and no papers were served on the applicant."

Ms. Chamberlain, in her quiet and authoritative manner, said, "I now ask the court to dismiss this application presented today in preference to the Supreme Court application."

The magistrate no doubt was taken back about this application to have this heard in the Supreme Court that Mrs. Chamberlain made on my behalf. He then asked both lawyers to sit down. He then addressed Mrs. Chamberlain. He stated, "I am fully aware of the proceedings and ruling of the high court."

Then Claire's lawyer jumped out of his seat and raised an interjection. He expressed the mother's rights that she should be given interim custody as to the letter of the law. "The father should hand over the child back to the mother today."

The magistrate abruptly said, "Mr. Sherwood, sit down and stop shouting. I fully understands this new application and will address this accordingly."

This was only around twenty minutes into the hearing when the magistrate said, "I agree with the counsel for the petitioner, Mrs. Chamberlain, as the application has been submitted to the Supreme Court for a hearing set down for next year. Also, this order overrules the application put to this court today. This application is that I have to rule interim custody remains with the father and the mother to have liberal access. Also under the Guardianship Act, I make a further order to the counsel for both Mr. and Mrs. Mason to obtain a Social Welfare Report and have this report dealt with as soon as possible. I also see in Mr. Mason's application if he was successful today, he planned to take Oliver to Australia for Christmas. Seeing he is awarded interim custody, he is allowed to do so, and on his return, the said child Oliver will stay with his mother for one week." I felt like the heavens opened up on me, and I was allowed to keep Oliver.

The outcome of this interim custody hearing would have gone to the mother as under the Guardianship Act, this was automatic. This changes everything and now put me in a better position. However, it was a great move by Mrs. Chamberlain to file an application to the Supreme Court on the Friday before the hearing today. Yes, the Supreme Court application overrides the Magistrates' Court. This was an act of genius by Mrs. Chamberlain.

This was no doubt the next step toward the custody hearing to be held in the Supreme Court set down for around July next year. I remarked, "Well done!" to Ms Chamberlain. "You're just wonderful." I could not help myself and wrapped my arms around her and gave her a big hug, and a few tears rolled down my cheeks.

The magistrate was still in his chair. I looked at him and said thank you. He nodded back to me with a smile.

Today, what took place in the courtroom was in some ways a historical achievement as the law states a child under five remains with the mother. The magistrate no doubt was caught blindsided as well and had no alternative but to hand down his decision; however, this does not mean when it goes to the high court that I will get custody. This was now the beginning of a bitter dispute over one little boy, Oliver, to be played out into Supreme Court.

Mrs. Chamberlain said to me after the magistrate handed down his decision, "Danial, do not get ahead of yourself today. Yes, it was a victory. Your ex-wife and her family will now throw all they can at you."

I know what she did today. She knew and understood the law. How lucky and fortunate it was for me to get a barrister like Mrs. Chamberlain. I was so blessed. I looked back on the day I went to the church service and meeting the guest speaker Mr. Dunbar and his introduction to Mrs. Chamberlain. This was a true godsend.

This was a victory that deserved a celebration, and I asked Mrs. Chamberlain if she would come to dinner at my place tonight as I already arranged a few people to come, and seeing we had a victory today, I would ask a few more. "I know it is short notice, but it is only early afternoon, and I will have time to prepare the dinner." Mrs. Chamberlain said she would love to come.

As we were both leaving the courthouse, just before we stepped outside, we got a barrage of abuse from Claire and her mother as she called me a rotten bastard. She shouted, "You do not deserve to have Oliver!" I could see Claire was emotionally upset. I am sure they believed they had this in the bag today.

Mrs. Chamberlain said to me, "Keep walking."

And then Craig the idiot grabbed me by the arm and said, "You do not deserve to have Oliver." I said, "Get your grubby hands off me! That is your opinion. Claire should get a better lawyer.

He was way out of his depth."

"Now you see, Mrs. Chamberlain, you have firsthand knowledge what I am dealing with." Craig and Rose kept yelling abuse at me.

She pulled me aside and said, "Ignore them." With that, she walked me to the car park. "Danial, I will see you later tonight around six thirty."

I said, "Look forward to you coming."

I then climbed into my car, and Claire and Craig came from nowhere, rushed up to the car, and yelled at me, "Where is Oliver?"

I started the car up. I did not bother to answer them except to give them the finger, and I drove off. A few blocks away, I stopped the car. I just sat there, and emotions came all over me. It suddenly hit me what took place today. This was a miraculous result. No doubt it was a big shock to Claire, and I can understand how she felt. If it was me who lost, I would have felt the same.

I finally composed myself. I then drove to pick up Oliver at Greg and Allison's place. As I planned ahead to keep him away out of sight for the day, I arrived around 1:00 p.m. and walked into their house. Allison put her arms around me and said, "How did it go?"

I said with tears, "We have won today, but this is just round one. I am allowed to keep Oliver until the full hearing in the Supreme Court set down for later next year." Yes, I had tears running down my face as I told Allison what took place and how Mrs. Chamberlain took everyone by surprise. I then asked, "How is Oliver?"

Allison said, "He is having a nap. He did watch a few cartoons and fell asleep."

I said, "I am having a dinner tonight as this was planned a few weeks ago, and now it coincides with today's outcome. We can have a celebration! You and Greg and the children are welcome to come along tonight. Also you can meet my solicitor, Mrs. Chamberlain. She is an absolute gem." I could not praise her enough. Greg was still not home from work when I left as it was still early afternoon.

This was a very special day for Oliver. He asked, "Daddy, did you see the man today?"

I said, "Yes, Oliver, Daddy did." I am sure he was not aware of what took place today. All I said was, "You can stay with Daddy, and you can go and visit Mummy."

With that he just shrugged his shoulders and gave me a big grin and looked at me, as if to say, "What has changed?" He was such a bright boy for his age. I had no doubt he figured this out. I told him the best way I could in the morning, just in case he had to go with his mother. He looked at me with a tear in his eye and said to me, "Daddy, I want to stay with you." I was overwhelmed with this and knew I had to face this if he had to go with his mother, and now as it has turned out for the time being he stays with me. This has been an emotional roller-coaster ride, and I would need all my strength to take the final hurdle to gain full custody at the Supreme Court next year. Listening to the lawyers earlier on, they would not take my case on as the best-case scenario was Claire would get custody and I get access. This really played on my mind as well as the FNF group as I heard the experiences of fathers not able to get custody and, in some cases, no access at all. I think back to the twist of fate and the fact that I had, through the church, guidance and then able to get a lawyer who represented me. The minister said to me at one time, "Danial, have faith in what you want to achieve, and be positive. If there is a will, God will find a way."

How true that was as today, there was a lot of truth behind all this. The words Mr. Dunbar said, "Mrs. Chamberlain is the best when it comes to custody matters. She is a remarkable woman," I was able to find out.

I was on the way back from picking up Oliver from Greg and Allison's. I called in to see Fiona as I knew James would be still at work. I rang the doorbell, and Fiona answered the door. She said, "Come in." When I walked into the lounge room, there was Rose sitting in the lounge chair, having a cup of coffee. I looked at Rose. I said hello. She did not answer me. She had a sour look on her face.

Then I said to Fiona that I was awarded interim custody of Oliver today. She replied, "Yes, I know. Rose filled me in."

"Oh, I see." I looked at Rose. You could see she was far from happy. I then said loudly, "I will have Oliver with me until the Supreme Court hearing later next year, I think around June or July, as it does take a while to get these cases heard, and that gives us plenty of time to prepare our case." I asked Fiona and James if they would like to come to dinner as I was having a few people around.

Fiona said, "No as I have invited already James's parents to come for dinner tonight." I said, "Okay, that's fine."

I did say goodbye to Rose, but she did not reply. If looks could kill, Rose just glared at me going out. Fiona came out with me as she wanted to say hello to Oliver, who was sitting in the back seat of the car.

I said to her it was very obvious whose side Rose was on. "No doubt Claire's," I said. "At the hearing, Claire and her mother thought they had it in the bag. They were blindsided by the unbelievable move by my barrister. It stumped her lawyer as well as the presiding magistrate as they were totally unaware of what she had planned. She told me last week not to breathe a word about this to anyone."

"Now I understand," Fiona said to me. She gave Oliver a big hug and kiss, and when I was driving off, she said, "I am incredibly happy for you, good luck."

I did feel sorry for Fiona as she was a great person and incredibly supportive of me and Oliver. She was caught right in the middle.

# 20

# THE DINNER PARTY

It was not unusual for me to have guests around for dinner. This occasion so happened to coincide with the day I was awarded interim custody of Oliver. I had already arranged this night with Marlene and Max Dubbeld. There would also be David Thomas, Donald Monroe, along with Jim Baxter, who was staying at my place. We all often had a dinner together either at my place or at the Dubbelds'. This being a very special day for Oliver and I, I decided to add a few more people to celebrate this with us. I added Greg and Allison, Peter Benson, my good friend, along with Dylan and his Emily. Then there was Mrs. Chamberlain. She said she would love to come along as she said this was a milestone victory today rarely accomplished by a single father.

When I was preparing the dinner, Oliver said to me, "Daddy, is it my birthday party?"

I said, "No, Oliver, it's a few friends coming to dinner. Your birthday party is two weeks away." He looked disappointed. He really thought it was going to be his birthday party. I told him, "There will be a lot of other kids coming tonight. You can play with them and look after them for Daddy."

With that he had a big smile and said to me that he will go to his room and get some toys out so they could all play.

After, I did a quick ring around and made calls to various ones to come to dinner this evening. I know it was short notice for some, but they did not mind and said they would love to come. Then I got busy preparing the dinner. I put on the lamb to roast as this would be slow-cooked for around two and a half hours. I then got busy preparing the usual vegetables like roast potato, pumpkin, and steamed peas and beans. Because of the extra people, I added more vegetables. I also prepared a cheese and brandy fondue for starters, and I am sure this would go down well. I also made a sticky date pudding for dessert.

Around six thirty, everyone arrived, and we had a few drinks before we sat down. I introduced Mrs. Chamberlain to everyone. I made sure while Oliver was present having dinner that we did not discuss about the hearing, nor did we hardly mention this afterward. Oliver stayed up until we had finished the main course.

"Daddy, I do not want pudding. I want to go to bed." He rubbed his eyes and said, "I am tired." He then said good night to everyone. Then I took him to his room. He had a frown on his face and said to me, "Daddy, do I have to go and live with Mummy?" This was obvious it was still on his mind.

I said earlier I prepared him just in case he had to go with his mother. I then asked Oliver, "Do you want to go with Mummy?"

He replied no.

I said, "Don't worry about it. You are staying with Daddy." I put him to bed and made sure he was settled. I gave him a big special hug and kiss. I turned off his light. He called out as I was walking out of his room, "Daddy, can you leave the light on?"

I said, "Yes, I will. Good night."

This was just after eight o'clock, a bit later than usual, but not too late.

I did sneak back shortly after, and he was fast asleep. This made me realize how things could have turned out if I had to hand him over to his mother, which is the reality. I stood in the hallway for a few moments and contained myself as I became a bit emotional before going back into the dining room.

When I walked back in, Mrs Chamberlain remarked, "What a lovely, well-behaved, and well- mannered boy. It is a shame what he has been put through."

I agreed. We did have a few drinks, then after we all finished our meal, we all sat in the lounge and had coffee. Mrs. Chamberlain said she has had a big day, and she then said goodbye to everyone. I walked out with her.

"Danial," she said, "you have a lovely home. You're also a very good cook. I thank you for the lovely night. It was nice meeting some of your friends. Oliver is the spitting image of you. He is such a lovely boy. Now I can see why you are fighting to have him."

I thanked her again for what she has done for me and Oliver today.

She replied, "That's my job, and that is what you hired me for. In this game, you have to be ahead of the rest."

After she left, I told them briefly what happened at the hearing today, which I suppose was only natural. I said, "What she did today, words cannot express how professional she is. She has taken on my case personally as well." I did explain briefly about my premonition and then about the guest speaker at the church service and his introduction to Ms. Chamberlain. When they heard this from me, they were all amazed at what had taken place.

The evening wrapped up around 10:30 p.m., and they all left. Jim helped me clean up, and he said, "What a lovely group of people we had here tonight, and Mrs. Chamberlain, she was so delightful. You're a lucky man to have such a woman backing you."

I said, "There was no way I could have done this without her. Those other stupid so-called solicitors should be ashamed of themselves as they did not want to represent me. All they wanted was access rights. What a joke."

The next day, I had the expected phone call from Claire. She was ranting and raving on the phone and accused me as having a drunken party, and we all got drunk and went through many bottles of wine. She also said Oliver was up until all hours of the night.

I said to Claire, "I am not concerned what your bloody spies are telling you. It's my house, not yours anymore. Mind your damn business, and get you facts right." I hung up the phone on her. She did ring back a few minutes later. She screamed down the phone at me, yelling, "Don't you hang up on me!"

I said, "Why not?" then slammed the phone down again.

It did ring a few times more when I was leaving the house. With that, both Oliver and I went into Qantas in the city. I booked our trip to Australia. Oliver was all smiles as he said, "Daddy, we are going to Australia?"

"Yes, son. Yes, we are." I wanted to leave around the December 22, in time to have Christmas in Australia. We would come back on the second week in January. Then as arranged, Oliver would go to his mother for a week.

That same day, I then took Oliver to the kindergarten in Mangere. This was where I met Mrs. Tuohy, the head teacher. I arranged to have Oliver start at kindergarten early next year when it starts in February.

Mrs. Tuohy took Oliver by his hand and showed him around. He could see all the other children playing outside. He seemed okay with the idea of going to kindergarten. From there we both went to see Rev. Anderson at the church. When we arrived, he spotted Oliver. He said hello to him and shook his hand. I then told him the good news. He said to me, "You were in our prayers." With that, I thanked him for his support.

I said, "Can you tell Mr. Dunbar and thank him also? It's very difficult to explain, but I was drawn to the church that day when I met Mr. Dunbar. It was through him I met Mrs. Chamberlain, as she took on the case where others did not. She is an outstanding lawyer, and Mr. Dunbar told me she was the best, and yes, she was." We chatted for a while, and I said, "See you at church on Sunday." We left and headed back home.

We arrived back to the house around 4:00 p.m. Jim was home early from his work. He said, "This stupid woman keeps ringing, asking where Oliver is. I have left the phone off the hook."

I said, "Next Saturday is Oliver's fourth birthday. We will be having a lot of kids here. Should be a good day. I have arranged a clown to come to entertain the children. Oh, by the way, we booked our trip to Australia, and we leave on the twenty-second of December and back again on the fourteenth of January. I'm looking forward to this to get away from it all."

Jim said, "By the way, Mrs. Chamberlain called, I forgot to tell you." With that, I called her at her office.

She said, "Thanks for a wonderful night last night." Then she said, "I have a letter from Claire's lawyer, which was hand delivered today. She is objecting you taking Oliver to Australia for Christmas, along with another complaint. We can discuss this at a later time."

I told her that I had already booked, and we were leaving on December 22.

She said to me, Go and have a good holiday, and we will speak when you get back. I will deal with Claire's lawyer."

I asked, "What is the issue now?" As I said to Mrs. Chamberlain, this was discussed at the court that I was taking Oliver to Australia.

"Don't worry," she said, "it is just another ploy, and she cannot do anything about it. You have interim custody, and the court also agreed for you to take him out of New Zealand, so that's the end of the matter."

With that, I wished her a Merry Christmas. "I will see you when we return."

I sent her a bunch of flowers and a thank-you note for what she had done along with a Christmas greeting.

The trip to Australia for both Oliver and I will be much welcomed to enable us to get away from all the turmoil that I was embroiled in, and having Oliver caught up in all this will do him good to get away as well.

## Complaint Made by Claire

If you think Claire was going to stop her allegations, then you are so wrong. Ms. Chamberlain sent me a letter, and what the letter contained was extremely hard to explain. Claire's complaint was not justified and in fact a straight-out lie. This time she implicated Ms. Chamberlain. I have felt for some time now the stories and different accounts of incidents of what Claire has said or done or what others have done have been hard to prove or have no witness to such incidents. This complaint she made against Mrs. Chamberlain is quite extraordinary, to say the least. She claims that we harassed her outside the courthouse. In Mrs. Chamberlain's letter, which I received, was a copy of the complaint. When I read this, it was just so ludicrous. She was a straight-out liar. I was now getting more convinced the woman I married was becoming delusional or making up claims to try and justify herself as not being the innocent party. No mention of her mother or Craig who was with her that day to witness this. She also made assertions about the dinner party.

Unbeknown to her, Mrs. Chamberlain was also present that evening, along with many others. About the dinner party, in addition to her complaint, was that she was involved in an ugly scene at the courthouse. This was so bizarre, I did not bother to respond.

One other point where they got their facts wrong, this dinner party was held on a Monday night. For a lot of reasons, it was never disclosed that Ms. Chamberlain was at the dinner.

This stunned us as Ms. Chamberlain received a complaint from Claire's solicitor in reference to Claire's allegation as she claimed there was an ugly scene that developed at the court hearing on the first day of December.

She stated, "I arrived at the court with my solicitor, who went into court before me while I waited outside. I was approached by the petitioner, Mr. Mason, and his solicitor, who began to hassle me. After facing this onslaught, when my solicitor came out of the courtroom, I was terribly upset. Then my solicitor took the view that my state was such that I was unable to give evidence. Mr. Mason also told me that he was taking Oliver to Australia, that he would leave New Zealand, and I would never see him again." This was also part of her submission to the Supreme Court custody case, which was to take place the following year.

Mrs. Chamberlain called me after receiving this letter. We discussed this new allegation. I said, "This woman is delusional."

Mrs Chamberlain said, "When we both arrived at the court, your wife Claire was with her male companion along with her mother. I am not sure where she got this from. This is very odd and strange indeed."

I shook my head in disbelief.

"What I cannot understand is if this was the case, why didn't her mother, who was with her, along with Craig Kelly, put in a complaint as well?"

I replied to Ms. Chamberlain, "Now you know firsthand what lengths Claire goes to as she now has included you in this so-called allegation."

She replied, "I intend talking to her lawyer on this matter."

I just could not for the life of me understand what Claire was even thinking, implicating my solicitor. This was quite bizarre indeed.

## Cookie Bear

It was coming up to Oliver's fourth birthday. He often did see Cookie Bear on TV advertising biscuits. He always laughed when he saw Cookie Bear. As it so it happened, I knew the person who was in the Cookie Bear suit. Seeing it was Oliver's fourth birthday, I arranged for Oliver to go with me to the supermarket where Cookie Bear was entertaining the children and handing out cookies. I said to Oliver, "How would you like to meet Cookie Bear?"

He said, "Really? When?" I said, "Today!"

This was Friday afternoon. This, by the way, was where I think they got the idea I took him to my work in the supermarkets. Anyway, we arrived at the supermarket. As we walked in, so it happened Cookie Bear was walking toward us. Oliver clutched my hand. He hid behind me. I said, "Oliver, it's Cookie Bear!"

And with that, Cookie Bear said, "Hello, Oliver, it's your birthday soon, and I have a surprise for you."

He then gave Oliver a toy Cookie Bear. With that, he shook his hand. Oliver was so excited, he was speechless. On the way back home, he could not stop talking about it. These are memorable moments you have to cherish.

### Trip to Auckland Zoo

It was on a Saturday when I had Oliver with me for the weekend. I said to Oliver, "Why don't we go to the zoo today and see all the animals?"

He said, "Great, Dad, let's go!"

So we went around eleven o'clock in the morning. It was only a twenty-minute drive from our place. When we got there, I said, "Oliver, what do you want to see first?"

He said, "The elephants and the monkeys!" He ran ahead of me. I was sure I kept him in sight. He was so happy seeing all the animals. We had lunch there, and Oliver had a few ice creams and drinks as it was a warm summer day.

On the way back home, I said, "Oliver, which of the animals did you like most?" He said, "All of them, Daddy, all of them!"

"Surely you must have a favorite?"

"I liked the baboons and the meerkats." "What about the elephants?"

"Yeah," he said, "but I think the highlight was the ride on the elephant. Yes, Dad, that was great."

Then there was silence. He was in the back seat, so I looked in my rearview mirror, and he was fast asleep. He had such a big day with lots of walking, but I carried him a lot as well.

The odd thing was in all of Claire's statements, she always made out I did not spend any time with Oliver. This was far from the truth. Oliver and I have an extraordinarily strong bond. We do a lot of things together, things that Claire and her family would not even know.

Oliver also liked watching the cartoons and Walt Disney movies like *Snow White and the Seven Dwarfs* and *Pinocchio*. When I first showed him this, he cried when he thought Pinocchio was dead. Then when he turned into a boy, he clapped and clapped. I showed these to him in the home cinema on the big screen, and he just loved seeing them.

I think that Claire and her family do not give me any credit, except to say that I neglect my son, which is far from the truth.

# 21

# OLIVER'S FOURTH BIRTHDAY

Oliver's fourth birthday was not long after the interim custody hearing. I thought it was fitting to celebrate his birthday with style with a party for him. I asked all the children he played with in the neighborhood. This included the Māori children along with their parents. They lived at the house that was the back of our house facing the main road. It was important I mentioned this because there were some what I called racist remarks regarding Oliver playing with these children. More on that later.

Those invited were a large number of friends to come along, like Greg and Allison Doherty and their two children, Dylan and Emily Watson and their two children, then there was James and Fiona McDonald and their little girl, and Jasmine and Trevor Egan and their three children. Out of courtesy. I invited the grandparents. I called Rose and Kevin. I told them, "I am holding a party for Oliver, and you are most welcome to come." I thought by having them there may show them that I was not the rotten bastard that they claim me to be.

Rose said on the phone they would think about it. Well, on the day, I was very surprised they did show up. I know they came for Oliver's sake. I was glad for him as he loved his grandparents. Claire's younger brother John as well as James and Fiona with their baby daughter arrived. Then there was Don Monroe along with Jim Baxter, who at the time were both staying at my place. By inviting the Māori children along, I am sure this did not go down well with James and Fiona based on their attitude toward the Māori kids that Oliver played with. They seem to dislike them for some reason. These children were well behaved and delightful, and Oliver loved playing with them, and far as I was concerned, that was all that mattered.

When everyone had arrived, we started the party around 4:00 p.m. Oliver received a lot of lovely gifts, toys and clothes, and he was having a great time—in fact, the best I have seen him so happy for such a long time. This made it more special as a couple of weeks ago, I was unsure if he was going to be with me or his mother. By the grace of God, he is with me. I felt it was well worth it to give him this party.

During the party, Rose came up to me and said in a narky voice, "Why did you not invite Claire?"

I said bluntly, "You've got to be kidding. Having her here would spoil Oliver's day as well as other people here. Anyway, I did allow her to see him this morning for a couple of hours, and she gave him some toys and clothes for his birthday. At least she did see him on the day. I think that is fair enough, don't you think so? She cannot have it all her way, you know. I am not going to argue with you on this as I know how you feel toward me, and getting interim custody is a sore point with you, so let us enjoy the evening for Oliver." With that I walked off. Kevin just glared at me and did not say one word.

I was lucky I had Don and Jim as they helped me get things ready. As the party was held in the home cinema, we had to empty out a lot to make way for the tables and chairs, and we opened up the large garage door so people could freely move in and out. I had Dylan in the bar, and he served beer and wine for the adults and soft drinks for the children. Around 5:00 p.m., we all enjoyed a barbecue. There was a good choice of food like sausages, hamburgers, and steak along with prawns as they go well on a barbecue as we do the same back in Australia. All this was accompanied lots of salads I prepared. Fiona brought along a pavlova for dessert, and Rose brought along a trifle. James and Greg did all the cooking on the barbecue.

Jasmine brought out the birthday cake lit with four candles, and we all sang "Happy Birthday." The look on Oliver's face was priceless. He was so happy! He sat on my knee as he blew out the candles. He then gave me a big hug and went over and gave his nanna a big hug, which made her day.

I asked Oliver if he was having a good time, and he said, "Yes, Dad. Look at all the presents I got!" I was so happy for him. He was a special little boy, and with what he has endured lately, now to see him so happy was well worth the effort.

I went over to Rose and said, "Look at Oliver, he is just bubbling over and so happy."

She replied yes. She actually thanked me for putting on such a good party for him. I think Rose did see another side of me as a week or so before at Fiona's, she did not want to speak to me. When it's all said and done, we have to do what is best for Oliver, then put aside any issues.

The big surprise came around 6:00 p.m. I had Bonza the Clown arriving in a red tray truck, and he drove up the driveway. The kids just screamed with delight, and he performed for the kids for over thirty minutes. He had his tricycle with him and did his juggling act as well as blowing up balloons, and he made a dog for Oliver. He was so excited having a TV star at his party, as Bonza was well known to the kids being on TV as well as performing at shopping centers. I got to know him through my work, and he told me he would be delighted to come to Oliver's party.

Oliver could not get over having Bonza the Clown at his party, and he threw his arms around me and said, "Daddy, it has been the best day ever!"

This brought a tear to my eye.

Bonza left just after 6:30 p.m., and the kids chased him down the street. I could not have imagined how well this day went, and I felt it was all well worth it to make one little boy happy.

Addison came up to me and said, "I have been looking at Oliver. Isn't he having a great time?" "Yes, it is good to see. It is good for him to get away for a change from all the trauma he has

been subjected to."

She said, "Kevin the grandfather was noticeably quiet. He did not say much. Then Rose, she just went around telling everyone what a wonderful boy Oliver is. She also mentioned to a few it's a shame about Claire and she should have been here tonight."

Addison, when she overheard this—she was never short of words as she says things straight to the point and holds no punches—she said to Rose in a sharp voice, "No, she shouldn't have been here tonight. She made her decision to leave Oliver and Danial, and what he is doing is a great job with Oliver. He is so happy. Surely you must see that."

Rose replied back, "I suppose you're right, however, I look after him as well. His mother, you know, does love him. I thought it would be nice if she was invited."

Jasmine, who was a longtime friend of Claire's as well as the family's, chipped in and told Rose in a harsh voice, "Not after what I saw of Claire a while back. It was disgusting when Danial invited us for dinner, and we had to leave early with our children because of Claire and her tirade. We were very good friends, and now she does not want to know me. I am not taking sides with Danial. I just want to be friends with both of them. I cannot believe she left Danial for this Craig fellow based on what I have heard from others what he is like."

Rose kind of agreed with Jasmine, but she said, "Claire is still my daughter, and I was against her leaving until I heard that Danial threatened her and would harm Oliver."

Jasmine said to Rose, "Honestly, do you really believe that rubbish? Look at Oliver over there and Danial. They are a typical father and son. If you believe what Claire tells you, I am sorry, but I do not go along with that."

This was heard by many, and they all said what a great job I was doing with Oliver.

In the meantime while these heated discussions took place, Dylan and I set up the home theater as we had to clear the tables out and put the chairs back, and also set up the screen as we had the large door open to allow people to come in and out. In the evening for the adults, I put a movie on in the home cinema, *The Sting*, with Paul Newman and Robert Redford. This started around 7:30 p.m. I had Dylan to man the projectors for me while I put Oliver to bed. He was absolutely tired out. Rose came in and tucked him in and gave him a big hug and kiss. I said good night, and he gave me a big hug and kiss, and he told me how much he loved me and what a great time he had.

Rose walked out of the room with me, and she said, "He is a happy little boy." I said, "Yes, he is. Are you and Kevin staying for the movie?"

"Yes," she said, "we are."

Most of the adults stayed for the movie. We had one adult who stayed inside to look after the children. It is very significant to note that Rose, along with Kevin as well James and Fiona, all stayed for the movie. The movie started around 7:30 p.m. and finished just after 9:30 p.m.

The important part of this was that it was Oliver's fourth birthday, we had a barbecue and had a clown putting on a show for the children. Would you forget this important day?

## *The Movie* **The Sting**

Now I will get to the point as it is incredibly significant to mention. Yes, it was Oliver's fourth birthday party. It was such an important event. I found out later when people were questioned about this day and the movie *The Sting* and what night it was shown, they somehow forgot such an occasion. The claim was made that I had Oliver up for all hours one night watching movies, and the movie was *The Sting*, yet Oliver was well in bed around 8:00 p.m. Also they did not remember it was his fourth birthday party.

The whole purpose of not remembering, I was rather puzzled. I think of all the false claims and lies and different versions of events against me somehow caught up with them, and they could not remember the truth because of the so many lies they told. Jasmine told me later well after the party when she called me on the phone what she said to Rose. "I felt it was time someone told them a few facts and not to believe what they are being told, particularly from Claire."

I said, "Well done, Jasmine, for you to put her straight. This nonsense that I threatened Claire and was going to harm Oliver is outrageous. This may be their undoing as they believe this, and now her parents side with Claire. They claim I am a potential murderer and a violent person."

Jasmine said to me, "Rose calls her often as she says that she is concerned about Claire's welfare. Anyway, you and Oliver have a good trip to Australia, and we'll see you both when you're back."

I wished her and the family a Merry Christmas.

Before we left for Australia, I allowed Oliver to see his mother for a few days. This was despite her efforts trying to stop us from going. Oliver also spent a couple of days with his grandparents. I tried the best I could to show that I had no malice toward them, but under the circumstances, for Oliver's sake, I had to bite my tongue. He did love his mother and grandparents, and I could not deny that.

I have been made out as the villain in all this by them. People are not stupid. They are intelligent enough to see through this charade and to also make their own mind up. Sure, I am not perfect; like most people we all make mistakes, but to lie about things that did not happen or think it may have happened or make up stories to suit your own agenda is, in my opinion, either not right in the head or only plain cunning, thinking that if they tell enough porkies, they will be believed or get away with it. Claire's plan before the interim court case was to discredit me, but so far, it has failed. These matters will be dealt with in court. I am hoping for the court to see through what Claire and Craig and her parents and others have said regarding the contradictory statements and allegations they have made against me. I heard that the solicitor Claire had representing her was given the flick, and now she has a different lawyer. I did wonder myself why her legal counsel allowed stupid statements that were so contradictory. Let's see what the next year brings as this is the year of the Supreme Court hearing.

# 22

# CHRISTMAS IN AUSTRALIA

It was on December 22, 1975, that Jim drove us both to the airport. We all went into the overseas terminal, then I walked up to the Qantas counter and showed our tickets. I was lucky as I managed to get a window seat for Oliver. We then put our luggage through.

Jim nudged me and said, "Look who is over there."

I looked around and could not believe it. There was Claire along with her mother. Oliver spotted them and waved to his mother. I said, "Oliver, go over to your mother, and be quick as we have to go into the departure lounge as our flight has been called."

With that he went over to his mother, and she gave him a big hug. I was out of earshot, and I did not hear what was said. She was crying and so was Rose.

I then ventured over to them. I said, We have to go now." I wished them all a happy Christmas. I took Oliver by the hand, and we then headed off to the departure lounge.

I thanked Jim and said, "See you in a few weeks. I am sure it will be quiet for you as you know who won't be calling." I shook him by the hand. "Yes, you and Jessica have a good Christmas, and see you in the New Year."

The flight went well. The flight stewards on board really fussed over Oliver. They gave him coloring books and pencils. Then to his surprise, the captain came down. He said, Are you little Oliver? I heard you had a birthday recently. I have a surprise for you. Come with me."

Oliver was shy and reluctant to go.

The captain said, "You can bring your dad too."

With that, Oliver gave a big smile. We then headed off with the captain. He took Oliver into the cockpit, sat him in one of the pilots' chairs, and put a pilot's hat on him. Well, the look on Oliver's face was priceless.

I have never been in a cockpit of a plane before, and it was just amazing. They had a small window they had to look out of, and I could not believe all the instruments. The captain gave Oliver a toy airplane. I am sure this made Oliver's day. I thanked the captain very much. We then headed back to our seat. Oliver was beaming and showing his toy to people as we were going to our seats.

Then an announcement came over the intercom. "This is your captain speaking. Today we have a special guest, his name is Oliver. He has just turned four."

With that, all the crew and passengers clapped. Oliver was smiling and said, "Dad, that's for me!"

Shortly after, we had a meal, and then Oliver nodded off and slept most of the way. He woke up when we were some fifteen minutes away from landing.

It was a great flight, and we arrived in Melbourne around 8:30 p.m. We were met by my mother and my older brother Brad and his wife Margaret at the airport, and we spent most of the time between my mother's place and my elder sister Amy's and odd times with Brad and Margaret. We had Christmas dinner at Amy's, my eldest sisters place. She just adored Oliver. The family gave Oliver lots of gifts. We all had a wonderful Christmas Day.

My eldest sister Amy and her  husband Noel took us on  New Year's  Day to Maryborough  to the highland gathering. In fact, the Maryborough Highland Gathering is Australia's oldest, continuously running sports event. The district's first highland gathering was started by Scottish immigrants drawn to Central Victoria by the lure of the land or, during the 1850s, by the world's greatest ever gold rush. Each year, people come from all over the place for this special day.

We watched the highland dancing, wood chopping, and running events. There were various rides for the kids too. It was a great day out.

The following weekend, they took us to Ballarat, and we went to Sovereign Hill where Australia's history comes to life. This is a unique open-air museum, and it is just like stepping back in time. They had created a main street to the Red Hill Gully Diggings. This was where we panned for real gold, and we did find a few specks, and yes, it was ours to keep. Then there was the parade down the main street. The men were in red coats, the diggers and the women in period costume. It was a great fun day. On the way back, Oliver slept most of the way to Bendigo.

While I was back in Bendigo, I caught up with all my siblings, and they made a fuss of Oliver. I did not discuss my situation at all with them, and all they knew was I was a single dad looking after my son. I think being away from all the drama in New Zealand, I did see a different boy as he was so happy. He loved playing with all his cousins. Sadly, our holiday ended, and we headed back to New Zealand. I suppose the temptation was there to stay, but I had one big hurdle to get over this year—to obtain full custody of my son.

On the flight back, the captain came down again and spoke to Oliver. He remembered him from when we came over before Christmas. He gave Oliver a poster of the new plane, the 747B, which the captain said has only been in service for just over a month.

I said to Oliver, "Say thank you."

He shook hands with the captain and said thank you.

Well, that was the highlight of our trip going back. On our return on the due date of twelfth of January, and Oliver as arranged was to spend a week with his mother, I suggested he needed at least two days after we came back for him to settle down. I did keep my side of the bargain. I prepared his clothes, and Oliver went to his mother on January 14. He was due to come back on January 21. Claire came to pick up Oliver, and surprisingly, she seemed quite chirpy, no doubt glad to see

Oliver. She asked, "How did the trip go?" Oliver said, "It was great, Mummy."

Claire said, "You can tell me all about it when we get back to my place."

Off he went with his mother, and I sent him with a lot of new clothes I had bought in Australia. I did not hear all week how things were, as I did not want to do a Claire and ring all the time. I knew in my mind he would be well looked after.

However, when he came back from his visit from his mother, his clothes I bought in Australia were not in his case. When I approached Claire on this, she just said he hardly brought any clothes with him.

I thought, *What a bitch*. What's the point in arguing with such a spiteful person? I was glad to get him back with me. He seemed incredibly happy, and he told me he had a particularly enjoyable time with his mum.

I said, "That's good, Oliver, glad you had an enjoyable time." I then asked, "Where are your new clothes?"

"Oh, Mummy said she would keep them for when I come over next time."

I just had enough of her stupid nonsense, so what I did next time she had access, I sent Oliver with just a toothbrush along with toothpaste in his bag. Yes, you guessed it. My solicitor received a letter from her solicitor complaining I sent no clothes with him. I simply replied by saying, "You kept all the clothes I sent him over after I came back from Australia, and if you do that again, I will do the same." Funny thing is it did not happen again.

Oliver said to me, "Daddy, when I am going to her, why does Mummy take all my clothes off and puts me in a bath, then she puts all different clothes on me? When I am ready to come home, she changes me again. Nanna does the same."

I just said to Oliver, "Mummy just wants to see you nice and clean as well have nice clothes, and so does nanna."

But he said, "I go to Mummy's with nice clothes."

"Yes, I know. Do not worry, Oliver." I was not sure how to handle this as he was asking questions about his mother and nanna as to what they do when he arrives to stay on weekends or during the week. The motive may be that they think I do not bath him or have nice clean clothes. Yes, this was an issue as I found out later that Claire and her mother along with Craig claimed about his clothes. All this about clean clothes and other matters relating to Oliver's well-being, including what

he eats, who he plays with, and on it goes. This was ongoing. No doubt this was a way to try and discredit me. Did it work for them in their efforts to make their case better? Wait and see.

Mrs. Chamberlain was well aware now of what Claire and others were up to as she too had been implicated—a stupid move by Claire as now she had not only me to contend with but also my barrister.

Now the court hearing was only months away. things got even more full on with lots of incidents and allegations involving me and others.

I fully understand the law as it stands in New Zealand that for a child under five, the mother is awarded custody. My fight is to have this changed as fathers have rights too and are capable of bringing up children the same as the mother. The law's main concern is to ensure that a child's best interests are met by being protected from physical or psychological harm. In fact, it states that the welfare of the child is paramount (the highest priority). No doubt the court will consider that both parents are involved meaningfully in Oliver's life. The court will consider many factors when deciding if I get custody or Claire, and what types of arrangements are in the child's best interests. I fully understand what lies ahead, and I must also be prepared for the worst-case scenario; however, I have an incredibly good barrister, one that is articulate and very smart and knows the law inside and out, and if she can find a way, she will.

She often told me, "This will not be given to you on a silver platter. We must fight to change the law. This is a big task. My job is to prove you are the better person to take care of your son."

# 23

# SUNDAY SCHOOL AND KINDERGARTEN

As you may recall my early years when I was growing up as a child, I attended Sunday school along with my brothers and sisters at the Baptist Church. This was especially important in my upbringing. We never as children attended a preschool or kindergarten as times have changed. I now felt this would be particularly good for Oliver as he can mix with other children in an incredibly happy and safe learning environment by attending kindergarten. I did also go to church regularly, but not all Sundays. I did place Oliver into the crèche when I attended the church service.

Oliver attended Sunday school early in the year as he started this just before starting kindergarten. He enjoyed going as he often asked, "When am I going to Sunday school again?" This showed me that he enjoyed it as he told me he loved meeting up with the other boys and girls of his age. He also loved the stories the teacher told him.

Often during the church service, my mind wanders back to the day I attended the church service [ix] and having the premonition the night before to attend the church service that Sunday. I cannot fully understand why. Some would say it was a grace of God, and he was looking over both Oliver and me.

I also found going to church was so fulfilling. This gave me that strength and courage to soldier on. This day the service ended with the hymn that always stuck in my mind, "Onward Christian Soldiers." I did sing this with gusto. It brought back special memories as this hymn was the one that was sung on that day I met the guest speaker. This changed everything for the better.

After the service, as usual, the minister greeted people going out. As I was going out, he said to me, "Are you staying for a cuppa? There is someone you should see."

I said, "Yes, I will love to stay." I was curious who this person was. I picked up Oliver from his Sunday school class, and he showed me the drawing he did. His lady teacher said to me, "You have a bright little boy here."

I said, "Thank you." We wandered around to the hall. It was filled with people. Then a voice behind me spoke and said, "How are you, Danial? How is Oliver?"

I looked around, and there was Mr. Dunbar. He said he had heard from Mrs. Chamberlain that I had been awarded interim custody.

I shook him by the hand and said to him, "It is by the grace of God I had met you that Sunday, and with that you put me on to Mrs. Chamberlain. I could not speak more highly of her. She is a remarkable person, and I thank you so much."

He then knelt down and shook hands with Oliver. He said, "You have a wonderful dad. You look after him."

Oliver smiled at him. Yes, he replied he would.

Mr. Dunbar went on to say, "What you have achieved so far, many men would only dream of achieving as the law is, I am sorry to say, on the mother's side."

I said, "Mrs. Chamberlain is the one who has achieved this milestone, not me."

With that we shook hands. He said, "Danial, it is great to see you again. You take care of this little man. He is special."

Oliver said, "He is a nice man, Dad." "Yes, Oliver, he sure is."

I then drove Oliver back home, and on the way, we stopped at the corner store and bought Oliver an ice cream along with a small bag of sweets. After we left the shop and headed home, I was smiling.

Oliver said, "Daddy, what are you so happy about?"

I said, "I was so happy meeting Mr. Dunbar again today. One day you may understand." Then Oliver asked again, "Who was that man, Daddy?"

I replied, "A very good friend to both of us."

***

It was the first week in February when Oliver started kindergarten. Claire claimed she registered Oliver in kindergarten. The person she named as the teacher who booked Oliver in never worked there, despite Claire claiming she already had. This was found out to be untrue.

I made arrangements with Fiona to pick Oliver up around twelve o'clock each day, and I would drop him off each morning at eight thirty on my way to work. Without Fiona, I would not have survived each day. She was the most reliable person and backup I had. She made things possible for me.

Oliver going to kindergarten I knew would be good for him as he could mix with other children of his own age. Fiona was extremely happy to pick him up and take him home each day at midday and do this for me. She would give him lunch. Fiona and I did get on very well. I did advise the kindergarten only myself or Fiona his aunt were authorized to pick him up. Out of courtesy, I did tell the grandparent he was going to kindergarten. Rose, for some reason, was happy about this arrangement. I said, "You can still see Oliver when I bring him around to see you over the weekend."

Rose said in a narky way, "I suppose so. Why could we not have him instead of going to kindergarten?"

I said, "With you working three days a week, it would make this very hard for you. Anyway, he is better off going to kindergarten and mixing with other children."

Next, Claire called me at home the night before Oliver started kindergarten. She shouted abuse at me, yelling, "You're not capable of looking after Oliver. You should not be allowed to have him. I can stay home and look after him. I will give up my job!" She just raved on.

I politely said, "It's my decision, not yours." I reminded her that she was the one who left us for the idiot she was with. "Now I am the one who has custody of Oliver. He is in my care and also my responsibility. I will do what I think is best for him, regardless what you protest about." I said to Claire, "I do not want any more to do with you. You're the one who buggered off with Craig. You just have to wear it."

She then started again, yelling and screaming at me through the phone. Then I had to hang the phone up on her. I thought, *Good riddance.*

After I got off the phone, I walked back into the lounge. I said to Jim, "It is that crazy woman again. She now objects me sending Oliver to kindergarten. She claims she had already booked him in." This was another lie as Mrs. Touhy has been there for five years, and she is the only one who registers each child.

I was very upset over these phone calls, and I said, "Damn if I do, damn if I don't. I cannot do anything right in her eyes."

Jim said, "The fact is you have custody for the time being, and you have to do what is best for Oliver. She just has to start accepting that."

I agreed.

One would surely agree that a small child at the age of four going to kindergarten would benefit the child in preeducation and mixing with other children, but in Claire's case and also her mother's, they bitterly objected him going to kindergarten.

The difficulty, I found, was trying to juggle work as well as my part-time business and also devoting my time to Oliver, then putting up with the crap all the time from Claire. It was at times incredibly stressful.

So the day arrived; it was Oliver's first day at kindergarten. I had him up early and gave him his breakfast. I made sure all his clothes were ironed and he was well dressed. I put him in nice shorts, a lovely

T-shirt, and new shoes with his white socks. He looked like a million dollars. He was all set to go to kindergarten.

I explained to him where he was going. I told him, "You met the lady last year at the kindergarten, a Mrs. Touhy. She showed you around, remember?"

"Yes, Dad, I do."

"There are many play things and also lots of other boys and girls you can meet and play with."

He seemed a bit unsure. I hoped Claire or Rose did not get in his ear as earlier on, he was all for this, and now, he seemed unsure. With that, I said, "Let's go, my boy."

We shortly arrived at the kindergarten as this was only a four- to five-minute drive from where we lived. I took him by the hand as I got him out of the car. He did not want to go in. He started yelling and screaming as we both stepped inside the gateway. Mrs. Tuohy was greeting all the newcomers and their parents. She heard Oliver yelling at me, "I hate you!" He yelled this again. "I hate you!"

She came up to Oliver and said, "Hello, Oliver. Come with me and meet the other boys and girls." She then took him by the hand. She said to me, "Go, I will look after him."

Oliver was still crying and screaming when Mrs Tuohy took him inside. I said to myself, *What have I done leaving him so upset?* This upset me so much. I got back into my car, and I could not control myself with emotion. Tears were falling down my cheeks. I said, "I have to pull myself together." I thought, *What are we doing to this little boy?*

These emotional episodes went on for a few days. This day, one mother said to me, "He will get over it. My little girl did the same to me. Now she cannot keep away from the place."

I said, "That is reassuring."

Mrs. Tuohy knew I was very distressed about leaving Oliver in such a state. She took me aside this day and said to me, "Go outside when I take Oliver in. Just wait a few minutes, then come in through the side door. Sneak quietly and go into my office as I want you to see something."

I did what she said, and what I did see was Oliver playing and laughing with the other children. She came into her office. "You see, soon as he comes in each morning, he stops crying straight away, and he starts playing with the other children. Please do not feel bad as he is fine. A lot of children do this when they first come here. Your little boy is no different."

I said, "By seeing this, I do feel relieved as this was playing on my mind and was also very upsetting." I then agreed with Mrs. Tuohy as I am sure all parents go through similar events when children go to kindergarten or school for first time. My boy Oliver is no different than any other child of his age.

Fiona also told me when she picks him up, he is so excited to see her. He tells her what he has done at kindergarten. I did collect him sometimes a few days a week. This was to give Fiona a break as she has a small girl to look after. I experienced the same as Fiona when I picked him up. He was so happy as he told me what he did for the morning. I would take him home for lunch, and then I would take him for a drive. Some days I would take him to the beach where he would play in the sand while I was doing my paperwork. Usually this was once a week. Me picking him up during the week was another contentious issue, as you will find out later on. This again was without any foundation.

I did see a change with Oliver after a week or so as he settled well into kindergarten. He could not wait to go each day. The change in Oliver was very noticeable, and he was back to a happy little boy growing up.

There is a lesson here for all of us, that we must go by our instincts and ensure our child is well cared for. We do what is best for our child, regardless of what others may think. Right from the start, I well knew that Claire and her parents, mainly Rose, were not in favor of Oliver now going to kindergarten. Many allegations and remarks will be highlighted as this story unfolds. It was claimed he was being bashed up at kindergarten, that I send him off to kindergarten with dirty clothes. There was Craig as he claims he goes past several day a week past the kindergarten while he is doing his job delivering to stores in the area, and he remarked on the clothes that Oliver was wearing. This seemed to me a bit over the top as most of the time they are in the classrooms and spend only a short time each day outside, so I took this on like a grain of salt. There is no doubt they will come up with anything to justify why he should not be going to kindergarten or why should Oliver be in my care.

Then there was another episode about kindergarten that was blown was out of proportion. It had something to do with Mother's Day. The teachers got the children to make Mother's Day cards. Oliver made several ones: for Fiona, one for his nanna, and one for his mother, and one other, which I will explain later. The issue was twofold. First off, Claire said she did not get a Mother's Day card from Oliver, as she claimed the teachers told Oliver he did not have a mother. When I heard this and told Ms. Tuohy, she was extremely upset about these allegations. She was not sure about the Mother's Day cards as all children made cards that day. As far as a teacher saying to Oliver he has no mother, it is just not right.

Then they produced the story and alleged that Oliver was being bashed up. This was just sheer fabrication, in fact, so ridiculous. When all this came out, it was until that point I never discussed with Ms. Tuohy or any of the staff I was a single parent. This never came up.

The other Mother's Day card, yes, this was simply great, as it told me what Oliver really thinks. He handed me a card, and it said simply, "Happy Mother's Day, Dad." He gave me a big hug. I never did tell Claire about this as I knew it would upset her, and this was just kept between Oliver and me. This also told me he was happy with me despite what Claire and her family have said and want you to believe. It is noticeably clear that they cannot come to terms to the fact that Oliver is in my care. They go out of their way to discredit me, and they do not want to give me any credit for such a lovely boy he is and also that he does love me.

## *Appointed President of the Mothers Club*

Oliver had been at the kindergarten now for a couple of weeks and now has settled well into it. As always each morning, rain, hail, or shine, Mrs. Tuohy the head teacher was always at the front gate to see all the children in and also to make sure they are all okay. On this morning, she called me into her office. *Oh*, I thought, *something may have gone wrong with Oliver.*

She explained to me about the Mothers Club, what they do as a club. She said, "We cannot get fathers to come along. Would you come along to our meeting tonight? I know it's short notice, however, would you consider to come along to this meeting? The meeting starts at seven thirty and usually takes an hour or so."

With that I said I would love to. I had to arrange with Fiona to look after Oliver as I explained to Fiona that Mrs. Tuohy asked me if I would attend the Mothers Club meeting.

Fiona chuckled and said, "A Mothers Club meeting?"

"Yes," I said. "They have problems getting fathers to go to these meetings." She agreed to look after Oliver so I could go to the meeting that evening.

I went sheepishly along to the Mothers Club meeting. I was not sure what to expect. I was given a nice warm welcome. Then the president said that I was a single father, and my little boy recently has been coming to the kindergarten.

I looked around. Yes, no other father was in sight. I got many smiles from the mothers as I looked around the room. Then it was said by the president that it was the night of the AGM, and all positions will be vacant. I thought it may have been a reason why I had to come here tonight, or was this a stitch up? I was not sure.

As the night progressed, the positions were all filled except the president as they had to find a new president. The outgoing president said it would be nice if more fathers could attend these meetings. I thought yes, maybe it was the stigma that it was a mothers' club. I am sure that made them hesitant.

The meeting progressed well, and nominations for president were asked, and no one responded. Then Mrs. Tuohy said, "I nominate Daniel Mason to be president." She asked me if I would consider being president of their Mothers Club. She said this may encourage more fathers to attend meetings. As I was nominated by Mrs. Tuohy, someone else seconded the motion. This was carried unanimously. I was then appointed as their president.

I did not have any time to put together a speech as I was asked to address the meeting. I said, "Well, this is a surprise. Coming here tonight, I did not think I would be voted in as your president." I looked at Mrs. Tuohy, and I gave her a smile. "I am honored to be appointed as your president of the kindergarten committee. It is very obvious to me as looking around, no fathers are here tonight. I do understand you have a problem getting fathers to attend your meetings. If you want more fathers to attend, you will need to change a few things, such as renaming the Mothers Club to a Parents' Club. This way I feel the fathers would be more inclined and also feel more comfortable to attend your meetings. A good example was tonight, I dropped my little boy off at his aunt's place as I told her, 'I am off to a mothers' club meeting.' She laughed and said, 'You're going to a mothers' club meeting?' 'Yes,' I said. You see, this is the stigma attached to the name Mothers Club.

"When I was asked to attend tonight by Mrs. Tuohy. I was very apprehensive knowing it was a Mothers Club. Saying that tonight, as your new president, I would like to put a motion that the Mothers Club be changed to the Parents Club. This way we all can work toward getting more fathers here."

They all agreed and said, "What a great idea!"

I was given a very nice applause, and the mothers were delighted as the motion was seconded and moved unanimously. The meeting finished on a high note. I chatted with a lot of the mothers after the meeting, having a cup of coffee along with some cake and biscuits that the mothers brought along.

Mrs. Tuohy said she was so happy. "I know this was mean of me to dump this on you," she said. "I know you are the right person we need at this kindergarten. You're well respected." Before leaving, she said, "I have some puppies at home. Would you like Oliver to have one?"

I said, "I am sure he would like one."

So she arranged to have a baby dachshund, just eight weeks old, to be picked up the following day.

I left the meeting and went and picked up Oliver from James and Fiona's place, and I told them what took place at the meeting. "And now I am president, and it's now changed to the Parents Club."

I took Oliver home and tucked him into bed and told Oliver, "Mrs. Tuohy is going to bring a puppy into kindy tomorrow, and you can bring him home."

Oliver's eyes lit up and said, "Dad, what do we call him?"

I said, "Let's think about this, and we bring him home tomorrow. We will give him a name." I read Oliver a story, but as usual, it did not get far into the story as he was soon fast asleep.

I watched TV for a while and pondered over my role being president of a mother's club. How ironic! But my plan was to get more fathers involved as well as to raise more funds into the kindergarten as they were short on many materials plus equipment.

The next day, Mrs. Tuohy greeted me with a big smile. She said, "Thank you, Mr. President, for what you did last night accepting the role as president. It's now official. I have put together a newsletter already. From now on it's the Parents Club. It's also advising the parents who the president is along with the new committee. Now come and bring Oliver with you."

There was in a box a lovely dachshund puppy. He was so small.

Mrs. Tuohy said to Oliver, "This is your puppy to look after. You can take him home today."

Oliver picked the puppy up and cuddled him and had a big smile on his face. Oliver said, "He looks like a fox." Oliver knew what a fox looked like as I showed him many pictures of animals. He remembered what a fox looked like.

I said to Oliver, "Why don't we call him Foxy as he does look like a fox?"

That night we set up a place in the garage where he can sleep and be safe during the day. Being president of the Parents Club was an extremely rewarding role, one I took with pride as

my time I was president. I did work hard for the kindergarten. They were so kind to me and Oliver. The kindergarten was lacking in funds, so my plan was to change all that and undertake a lot of fundraising activities, plus get more fathers involved like building new play equipment and getting them to help when we run trivia and movie nights.

It was never disclosed that I was president of the Parents Club of the kindergarten where Oliver attended to Claire and her family. I know Fiona knew, but this was never brought up by Claire. Mrs.

Chamberlain was aware that I was appointed president of the Parents Club, and she said any report that would be given by the kindergarten to the up-and-coming court hearing had to be objective, unbiased, not to favor me personally. This all made sense to me.

During my year of being president, I organized many activities and raised a lot of money, and all funds raised was put into new equipment and materials for the kindergarten. I got to know a lot of mothers. After time, we had nearly as many fathers as mothers attending meetings. This was a complete turnaround for the kindergarten. The enthusiasm was shown by the parents being actively involved at working bees and attendance at the various functions that was held, including movie nights held in my home cinema. I charged everyone who attended $2, and all the funds went back to the kindergarten, and I paid for the film hire. I believe this was taken up by many other kindergartens and schools throughout New Zealand.

We also held a few bingo nights. This also raised much required funds. My year of being president was a rewarding experience, and to have the Mothers Club name changed to the Parents Club was a meaningful change that I believe was taken up by other kindergartens and also schools throughout New Zealand.

## Wise Words from My Solicitor

You have to give credit when its due. I have already said how I came across Mrs. Chamberlain through the church. She was a very religious person, was soft-spoken, and was dedicated to her work. She was articulate in every sense of the word, and she believed in people's rights and, in my case, my rights to obtain custody of my boy Oliver. She was firm but immensely strict and on many occasions put me in my place. She always said to me from the beginning when we met, "Due to the law as it stands, it will be difficult for you to have custody. Possibly the best-case scenario is for you to have liberal access." However, in saying that, she also said, "Laws can be changed, and I believe you have a very good case to make this change."

The best indication so far was being awarded interim custody as this was a step in the right direction, no doubt. However, this did not mean I would get full custody.

She said to me on many, many occasions, "You do have a mountain to climb." In her way of saying things, she said also that mountains can be conquered, and this is what I intend to do. She also instilled in me the seriousness of the situation I will be facing. "You now have been given interim custody. Now the hard part is the Supreme Court hearing. Let's hope that you get an understanding judge. You must keep away from any trouble your ex is causing for you to react to various situations."

The more I did see Mrs. Chamberlain, I came to the conclusion that this is her battle as well. It speaks for itself as the time and effort that she put into this was more than outstanding, more than anyone could imagine. She was my rock and inspiration. I was so damn blessed to have her on my side.

Then she drilled into me definitely no girlfriends, no relationships. In a stern voice, she said, "Do you understand me?"

I said, "Yes, I do."

Then the mention of Jessica Phillips came up, as I have been cited as her lover by Claire and others. They had also hired a private detective.

I said, "No, she goes with Jim, not me. When we were told a private detective was snooping around, she did come around for a while, but I have not seen her for some time. Jim still sees her, I believe."

Mrs. Chamberlain did meet Oliver a few times when I brought him in to have sessions with her, and also when she came to dinner one evening. She even remarked on how well I kept the place and also what a good cook I was. I always prided myself when I cooked meals. When Claire was with me, I did most of the cooking.

She often remarked to me what a beautiful boy Oliver is, and he is the spitting image of me. "No doubt who the father is," she chuckled. I often remark to people the continuous work she put into the case is beyond what anyone can ask for. The meetings and phone calls were endless, and never once did she not take my calls or refuse to have a meeting at her office. She was always there for me. I feel so indebted to her. She completely understood the continuous barrage I got from Claire along with others. This did consume me day and night. I had to keep myself together for Oliver's sake but also my own well-being.

She said, "Go along to the court and pick up the booklet on family law as this may help you understand the situation better."

On her advice, I did go and purchase the booklet. I read up on the family law procedures. This did give me a better understanding. Now I understood that the upcoming court hearing was for sure not in my favor; it was mainly because of the fact Oliver will be only just four years of age going on five by the time the case will be heard at the Supreme Court.

I pointed out all this to Mrs. Chamberlain when I read through the booklet, and she said, "Let us work on that." She also said, "I fully understand what the law is. That is why I wanted you to get a hold of the booklet so you may have a better understanding as this case of yours is overly complicated."

I did say Oliver being with me for so long and his mother leaving him for her lover surely must count for something.

She replied, "Yes, they are all valid points. There are several things that may not go your way. That is they claim you're abusive, you threatened her, and you are a potential murderer, you neglect your son, on it goes. Now what we have to do is to discredit what they have to say. One last point, remember the law as it stands that the mother obtains custody of their children. That is the law, and somehow, we have to change this law. That is my job. I do not want to give you false hope. Claire, I am sure, has been told all this, and the more they can make claims against you rightly or wrongly goes in her favor. Please try and don't let them get the better of you as that is their plan."

In the Supreme Court, this is where the custody will be dealt with. The law clearly stated that with a child under five years of age, custody will be awarded to the mother of the said child or children. However, here there is another clause that says, "The welfare of the child is paramount." This was incredibly significant to me as I felt that the welfare of Oliver should remain with me because I have provided a home, and he has been with me all his life. By the time of the Supreme Court case, he would have been with me for around fifteen months since Claire left the family home. The added fact and I think is more important is that his mother left him.

Well, so much for keeping out of trouble. The months leading up to the court case, things accelerated. At times I was not sure. I even wanted to give up work as things got too much, but my boss told me no, he did not want to lose me, in which I was grateful to him. I think under the circumstances, a lot of employers would have dismissed me.

The following part of this story is focused on many incidents that took place. It was like *Ripley's Believe It or Not!* as most of these incidents are just so outrageous, very hard to comprehend, and leaves you wondering who is telling the truth or what was behind these incidents and allegations. It is worth mentioning again who is telling the truth or telling porkies or just plain making things up. Claire saying things that did not actually happen, she no doubt, in my opinion along with others, had a hidden agenda. It was no secret she wanted to obtain custody of Oliver at all costs, regardless of who she hurts on the way, including her son. This became the same with her family, and the change of attitude toward me diminished.

As the date was now set down for the Supreme Court hearing, the Child Welfare Department in South Auckland had delayed this. They were supposed to have their report ready by midyear, and the court case was to be around July. However, now this was set down for October due to this delay. This was now only several months away.

Leading up to the hearing, there were many incidents that took place and were part of the evidence presented in court. It was no doubt in many of these incidents, they were designed to make Claire's evidence and claims she made much better. The incidents that took place were ever constant. If it wasn't so real, I am sure no one would have believed them. Some earlier incidents were very hard to explain and to prove.

This I found very difficult to live with. When you're continually harassed, spied on, spat on, as well as having police involved, I found it was extremely difficult trying to defend yourself when lies and allegations were made against you. This then becomes a huge effect on your well-being, more especially Oliver. He was a great kid, and to see him go through so much drama between myself, Claire, and her family, it was very disturbing. This came abundantly clear as the saying "Blood is thicker than water" comes into play.

From the statements provided by Claire and her family and of course Craig, it became apparently clear by all that these incidents were to show that I was not the proper person to have custody of my son. I do not for a minute say I was totally innocent. I got embroiled in various disputes and incidents, and I also did do things that I should not have, but what actions I did take were not seen as helpful by my lawyer, Mrs. Chamberlain, or the judge presiding over the custody hearing. After Claire left the family home in May 1975, later on I had two people staying at my home. One was Jim Baxter, and he was working for Crest

Foods in Wellington, and I had met him several times at conferences. He was the industrial chemist at the time for the company. He then left the company and came to Auckland and was waiting to commence work at another company in Auckland that dealt in cosmetics, and I offered him to stay at my place until he got his own place.

The reason he stayed on was to provide witness to events.

The other person was Donald Monroe. He started work at Crest Foods as a sales representative, and he was originally from America. He only stayed for a short while until he found his own place. I found that by having both Jim and Donald, it was very reassuring as they became valuable witnesses to some of the many incidents and tirades from Claire when she came to the house on many occasions, not forgetting the continuous phone calls and the various allegations about the movies and supposedly drunken parties and keeping Oliver up until all hours of the night, that he was up watching movies, including adult movies.

I was awakened also to the fact that Claire had taken documents from the house and other possessions such as an iron, and would you believe, that became a big issue in the court hearing? Some papers taken became evidence in court, and these papers were in the phone console drawer, and they went missing. She also took evidence regarding Jessica Phillips. Yes, this became part of her evidence. We were woken up to her antics. I made sure every time she came to the house, she was watched and did not take any more of my personal papers or belongings.

Oliver was the victim here as we had on one hand me, the father, who wanted to keep him and a mother who wanted the same; however, what was concerning in all this was the way that the mother has created many incidents. Her family was once on good terms with me, but all this diminished over time. This came abundantly clear as the saying "Blood is thicker than water" is spelt out.

After Claire left the family home in May 1975, I had two people staying at my home one was Jim Baxter, at the time we met he was working for Crest Foods in Wellington, I had met him several times at conferences, he was the Industrial chemist at the time, he then left the

Company he then came to Auckland, was waiting to commence work at another company in Auckland that dealt in cosmetics, I offered him to stay at my place until he got his own place. The reason he stayed on was to provide witness to events. The other person was Donald Monroe, he started work at Crest Foods as a Sales Representative, he was originally from America, he only stayed for a short while until he found his own place, I found by having both Jim and Donald was very reassuring as they became valuable witnesses to some of the many incidents including tirades along with heaps of continuous phone calls from Claire, as well when she came to the house on many occasions not knocking just barge straight in, then the various allegations about the movies and supposably drunken parties, keeping Oliver up until all hours of the night as he was up watching movies, including adult movies.

I was awaken also to the fact that Claire had taken documents from the house and other possessions such as an iron and would you believe that became a big issue in the court hearing, some papers taken became evidence in court and these papers were in the phone console drawer, they went missing, yes this became part of her evidence, She also took information as to Jessica Phillips. we were woken up to her antics I made sure every time she came to the house she was watched, she did not take any more of my personal papers or belongings.

I was allowing Claire to have access to Oliver. This was a directive from the court when I was awarded interim custody as I was to give adequate access to Claire. However, it was apparent that the fortnightly visits were very distressing for Oliver. I am sure he did not fully understand what was happening. He would come back home from the visit he had with his mother and at times was very aggressive toward me, and he was not the happy little boy I loved and knew. After a day or two, he settled down again. This was also noted at the kindergarten where on Mondays, he was noticeably quiet and would not interact with other children. This again usually lasted for a day or two. The point being was it was obvious the times with his mother were very unsettling for him. I was not sure what took place or said when he was with his mother.

Oliver never said much what he did on these weekends. I and others did see what this was doing to him on his return from his mother. I know what it was doing to me as to the stress of it all. We grown-ups, to a point, can handle such stress as well as the emotional side of things that takes place when parents split up. The sad part is that it is the children who do suffer the most. It was not Oliver's doing that his parents

split up. Children are more vulnerable and do suffer, despite efforts you make to lessen this.

One of the key issues and was overly concerning was the rubbish they told Oliver about me, and they told him what an awful person I was. Oliver would come back from his mother's, and he would tell me these things. For example, how would a four-year-old boy know what the word *bastard* means, let alone say it. On this occasion, when Oliver came back from his mother's, he called me a bastard. I was horrified. He also said he hated me. I was outraged for a moment. I slapped little Oliver. I said, "Stop it, stop it! This made me so sad. I grabbed hold of him, hugged him, kissed him. "I am so sorry, Oliver!" He cried and I cried. I said, "I do not know what Mummy and Craig are telling you, but your daddy loves you so much."

Oliver told me, "Nanna and Grandpa were at Mummy's place. They said all those things." I said to Oliver, "Do not listen to what they say."

With that he put his arms around me, crying, and said, "Daddy, sorry," and he said he loved me. This was a very emotional time for both of us. This played on my mind. How can a four-year-old boy know the word *bastard*? I told him it was not right to say those words, and he said, "Grandpa does." It just shows what type of people I was dealing with. The poison they were telling him was disgraceful. This pains me to no end.

***

This day I was working at the local shopping center at one of the supermarkets, organizing displays with my team. I came across Kevin. He looked at me and called me a rotten bastard. He yelled at me, saying that I took Oliver away from his mother, and with that he spat in my face.

I wiped my face and said to him, "You're just a lowlife, you telling my son I am a bastard. You should be ashamed of yourself."

Kevin walked off. I stood there for a while and composed myself. I headed to the washroom. Later on when I had finished work at the store, I headed to my car. Kevin approached me again

in the car park. I quickly said, "If you come near me again and spit on me, I will drop you on the ground. You're the one who should be called the bastard as to what you have put your family through, telling your grandson I am a bastard, and you put your son James in hospital. John you also threatened and also had a go at Fiona, James's wife. You're the lowlife, not me! People like you should be locked up." I said all this loudly so that others could hear as plenty of people were around as well as some of my workmates. I thought if he attacks me here, there would be plenty of witnesses. He stormed off without saying another word. My workmates came up to me to ask if I was okay. I said, "Yes, let us finish for the day."

I suppose the truth hurts. I was quite upset over this incident, and I thought to myself, *What an arrogant person, and spitting in someone's face is even more disgusting.* I went and picked up Oliver at Fiona's place. I was to pick him up around 4:00 p.m. I arrived a lot later, James was not home yet, and I told Fiona what Kevin did at the shopping center. I said, "What a pig. Also over the weekend, he told Oliver to call me a bastard."

She said to me, "That is disgraceful. They are all for Claire now as they all say you're the one that is violent and threatened Claire and also you would harm Oliver."

I said, "Do you really believe this?" Fiona, I find, is always truthful, and her being the in-law makes it difficult for her.

She said to me, "They do lie about things and make matters worse than they are. You have to be careful as to what you say as James gets upset with all this going on."

I said, "I am sorry you're dragged into all this, and I do appreciate what you do for Oliver as he loves coming here. I do not know what to do if you were not able to help me." With that I thanked her, and Oliver gave Fiona a big hug.

I then took Oliver home. I do not know what to expect next, but what they put a four-year-old up to is just unbelievable and the lengths they will go to.

Oliver may come out at times to say things to gain attention, but to say things about his father that are not true was to hopefully turn my son away from me.

Many times Oliver would come out and say things, but I never ever said anything about his mother to him.

One night, Oliver was in the hallway where we had the phone. He was talking on the phone. I said, "Oliver, who are you talking to?"

He said, "Nanna."

I took the phone from him and said, "Is this you, Rose?" "Oh yes," she said. "I showed Oliver how to ring me."

I then said to Oliver, "Say good night to Nanna as it's bedtime."

With that he said good night. When Oliver got off the phone, I said, "Did Nanna teach you how to call her?"

"Yes, Daddy."

The strange this was this did not happen again. When it is said and done, she was still his grandmother; a bitch she may be in my world, but to Oliver, it was his grandmother, and I respected that.

With that, Claire came on the phone. I said to her, "What the bloody hell are you doing to Oliver and asking him to run away to meet you at James and Fiona's place?"

Claire responded by saying, "Oliver said he wanted to stay with me."

I said, "That is what you believe. You're enticing him. Are you that stupid and narrow-minded? If Oliver went off with you, then I would call the police and have you arrested. That would be a change, wouldn't it?"

She said to me, "He is my boy too."

"Yes, he is." I got angry and also very aggressive with her as I said, "I just have had a gutful of your endless issues and incidents. Also, what you are doing is hurting Oliver. This must stop. You are not thinking correctly. I am the one who has custody. You can be charged for taking him. For god's sake, you need to stop this nonsense. You're just confusing Oliver. You are filling his head with ideas, then asking him to run away. He is four years old. Tell me how would he know to put his pajamas along with other clothes into a bag? You're the one telling him all this. I am telling you now, you stop this lot, or I will stop your access. Also remember, it was me who recommended that you have access in the first place, not the court. I will discuss this with my lawyer!"

With that Claire hung up the phone.

This incident was a prime example of what I am dealing with. It is just sheer madness. I never said anything bad to Oliver against his mother, so why is she doing this to our little boy is beyond belief.

I gave Oliver his dinner. I knew he was very upset and confused, so after dinner, I gave him a bath, then put him to bed. I started to read a story to him. He dropped off quickly to sleep. I looked at Oliver when I was leaving the room, and I thought to myself, *He is such a beautiful little boy, and he is right smack bang in the middle of an ugly dispute.* Seeing Oliver being hurt in this custody battle really gets to me. There was no clear answer to this. I was trying my hardest to keep Oliver distanced from this spiteful and bitter dispute. I had a very bad night.

The following day, Oliver seemed okay when I woke him up. I then dressed him, and we had breakfast. Oliver loved his porridge most days and his rice bubbles on other days. I then drove him to kindergarten. He seemed very settled and happy to go in. I told Ms. Tuohy what had happened, and she said she would keep an eye on him. Ms. Tuohy, for some reason, just adored Oliver. He was one of the youngest there. She often said he was such a bright and alert child.

After I dropped Oliver off and I knew James was at work, I called in to see Fiona. I did get on very well with her. She was someone I could trust. She told me that Claire planned that with Oliver so she can say Oliver ran away from me. I said, "So she can claim custody of him. She stops at nothing." I then said to Fiona, "Look, in the meantime, I will pick up Oliver from kindergarten today. I will take him to the shopping center, and we can have lunch there as I have some reports to do, then I will take him home."

Midday I went in to pick up Oliver from the kindergarten. Mrs. Tuohy said, "I need to speak to you. Let Oliver play for a while as I want to show something to you." First she said, "Oliver seemed very upset today, not his usual self." She then showed me a drawing he had done today. The drawing was someone looking out of a window. It had children on the street playing and on bikes. Mind you, it was very sketchy and used stick figures.

"Then I asked Oliver, 'What is this, Oliver?' 'Oh,' he said, 'this is at Mummy's place as I am not allowed to go outside and play. I watch the kids on bikes from the window.'" He also said to her, "They say bad things about my dad."

Mrs. Tuohy continued. "He cried a bit, and he also told me his grandpa said his dad is a bad man. I told him, 'Your dad is an exceptionally good dad. He loves you and also looks after you well."

With that I took Oliver to lunch, then we went home. I left my paperwork for later, and we played with his train set, and he soon brightened up.

What Ms. Tuohy told me just added to the turmoil I was in. I phoned Ms. Chamberlain and asked her to advise on this, and she said she will take this up with Claire's solicitor. "If this continues, we may have to stop access for a while. Just keep calm," she said, "and do not do anything stupid." This was extremely hard to contain as now the custody hearing was getting closer. Then there became increasingly more incidents involving Claire, Craig, and her family. Then there was the welfare I had to deal with. It became apparent I was not in a very good position to remain having custody of Oliver. Mrs. Chamberlain told me that the allegations and incidents that have taken place is a calculated attempt to discredit me. "It will be up to the court to determine what is the truth, what is fabricated and hearsay. Your wife has set you up good and proper, and will the court agree with her and her family, or your side? That is what we need to focus on."

## The Private Detective

I had a feeling that I was being watched. There was a lovely Māori family where their house was at the rear of my place. There was a small wire fence that divided the two properties, one you can easily jump over. The front of their house faced the main road. They were a lovely family. I got on very well with them, and so did Oliver. He played a lot with their children.

It was a Sunday afternoon when their eldest boy, Peter, came running in. He said, "Mum wants to see you quick, you must go."

I said, "Look after Oliver for me. You stay here and play with him on his train set as he would like that." I ran to the back fence and jumped over. Mrs. Palau was waiting for me. She said,"I had to tell you as I am sure your house is being spied on. I know you are having lots of issues with your ex-wife. There is a man, I am sure he is watching your house with binoculars. He is parked right next to the phone box."

I said, "I left Oliver with Peter."

She said, "He will be okay, Peter is a very sensible boy."

I quickly went back inside our house. I said to Peter, "Take Oliver around the front of the house, then around the back where you cannot be seen by whoever the person is on the main road. Take him to your mum. I will be back soon to get Oliver."

I quickly jumped over the their back fence, making sure I was not sighted. I then went down the street along the vacant blocks. I then was in full view of a car parked on the wrong side of the road with its window down. The person was looking through his binoculars. I then made sure I was well past the view of the phone booth. I then doubled back and crossed the road. I sneaked up and went behind the car parked alongside the phone booth. I quickly went right up to the driver's window, grabbed the person by his arm, and said, "What are you bloody playing at, spying on me?" I then grabbed the binoculars he had around his neck and yanked the cord very hard. With that, the binoculars snapped off. I then threw them onto the road. I grabbed him by the neck. "You're a slimy son of a bitch, stop spying on me." Then I recognized who he was. I said to him, "You are that scumbag of a private detective that was caught stealing from the department store where I was working at."

He then argued with me. He said, "That is rubbish."

"Yeah?" I said. "I was working at that store as the manager. Yes, also you were charged. You're no better than the ones who hired you. I know now who you are. You tell the ones who hired you to back off. If I catch you here again or catch you snooping around our house as I know you have been, I will take matters into my own hands. Now get out of here!"

He yelled at me, "You will pay for this! And he took off at high speed down the road.

The binoculars were all broken in. I kicked the pieces into the gutter off the road. I went back home, and Peter and his younger brother and sister were all playing with Oliver at their place. Mrs. Palau said to me, "That car lately is often parked near the phone box."

I said, "If he comes back again, send Peter over, and I will deal with it."

It was great to have such good neighbors. I am not sure what the private detective was up to as if it seemed it was to see if Jessica was at our place. He would have been sorry as this day, Jim Baxter was with her. From where the phone box is situated on the main road and between the houses, he had a clear view of the house. Now I am fully aware I had a private detective on my trail. It seems they will stop at nothing.

Jim came home later with Jessica. I told them what happened. Jim said, "Sometimes at night, I am sure I have heard someone walking around the house. I did look but could not see anyone. I did not want to worry you as you had too many issues you are dealing with."

On queue, Claire rang. I answered the phone and said to her, "Get your lousy private detective to stop spying on me. If I see him near the house or the phone booth again, I will take matters into my own hands and deal with him. So will Jim."

Claire said, "I do not know what you're talking about."

I said, "Do not take me for a fool as I know it is you involved." Again I hung up the phone on her. I did find out later by Jessica that the private detective was hired by Claire and Craig, as her ex-husband told her that she was being watched. Because she comes to my home, I was now accused of having an affair with her. She had not been living with her husband for a long time now, and also he was applying for a divorce. I am sure the plan with Claire was to implicate me.

I was right on this as this allegation of an affair with Jessica came true a few days before the custody court case. Was this the final attempt to try to involve me with adultery? Claire would not stop at anything, and if she can find a way to better her case, she will. This all became so surreal, and my life was like an Alfred Hitchcock movie full of drama and suspense.

## Car Accident

The reason this incident is mentioned is that certain parties made statements that I had lost my driving license along with many speeding fines. The fact of the matter is I never lost my license; however, earlier on when I first arrived in New Zealand, I was driving on an international license, and this was changed to a New Zealand license. I did have two infringements for going over the speed limit. These offenses was were minor as they were recorded just over 5 km on one and 10 km on another over the limit. I got a small fine on both occasions. It was also alleged that I went over a rail crossing when the signals were flashing. This was not true as I never ever drove over any rail crossing. Then there was this accident, which, in my mind, things could not get any worse.

This particular morning, I had just dropped off Oliver at kindergarten. It was around 8:30 a.m., and lots of children were going to school. I went to the corner store to buy the daily newspaper. I spoke briefly to Simon, and he asked how things were going. I responded, "Just the same old, never a dull moment. Cheers, see you soon."

I then drove off from the corner store. I was driving at a very slow speed. On both sides of the street on the footpath, there were children going to school. Then suddenly, I caught a glimpse of a little girl who ran onto the road right in front of my car. I did see who I presumed was her big sister just cross the road. She had left the gate open. This little girl ran after her, and she then went right under my car. I heard a thump. I went cold. I thought I may have killed her.

As luck had it, I was only doing a very low speed, possibly 20 mph. I stopped the car, flew out, and I looked under the car. She was not moving. A lot of people gathered around. I yelled out, "Someone help me get this little girl out from under my car!"

With that her mother ran out of the house hysterical. I with some bystanders pulled her out. She was unconscious but breathing. I thought, *Thank god for that.* I said to her mother, "How old is she?"

She told me, "Just three years old."

Within a few minutes, the police arrived along with the ambulance. I was in a state of shock and was trembling.

I said to the mother, "I am so sorry, but your little girl ran right out of your house as the gate was left open. She then followed her older sister, I assumed it was her sister. The little girl went straight onto the road in front me. It happened so quickly, I had no time to pull up."

I got no answer from the mother as she was in a state of shock. The girl was put into the ambulance and taken to the hospital along with her mother.

The police did take a statement from me. I explained she ran after her older sister that just crossed the road. She left the front gate open. Then her older sister came over. She told the police what happened. I said to the police, "I should go to the hospital to see how the little girl is."

They said, "No, keep away. Let us deal with this."

Simon from the corner store took me into his shop as I was in a bad state, and I stayed there for a while. After a couple of cups of coffee, I went to work about two hours late. I did report the accident to my boss, just in case there were some repercussions, but nothing more was raised on this, and it played on my mind for a long time.

Later that day, the police called me and said the girl was doing okay and no broken bones or major injuries. "It was lucky you were not travelling fast as the outcome may have been more serious. This is the end of the matter. I do hope you are okay."

I thought, *What more can go wrong?* This little girl was just a bit younger than Oliver. This was a stark reminder as slow speeds in built-up areas can save lives, near schools, including shops and playgrounds, as little children do not know the dangers of crossing roads, as I found out the hard way.

At this point, I was at an extremely low ebb. I had to pull myself together and get into a better frame of mind. Later in the day, I went to the church and sat down with the minister. We chatted for a while, and he said a prayer for me.

It was time to pick up Oliver, and after going to the church and pouring out all my troubles, it soon lifted me up again. In life when you think all is lost, you need someone to talk to. Yes, I had my friends. I think the minister put it all in perspective for me. He did say, "If there is a will, there is a way. Keep up your faith." Wise words.

# 24

# MORE INCIDENTS, ALLEGATIONS, AND LIES

Now as the court case was now fast approaching, so too were the many incidents that took place. The tempo did accelerate. There were many incidents. I could not describe them all as this would take up volumes of writing. However, the ones I am going to mention were all part of the court hearing.

This was of course the Department of Child Welfare. I felt they were very biased. One of the key principles I maintained was that "the child's welfare is the paramount consideration." I may add all considerations other than what is considered to be in the child's best interest, in my opinion, are secondary as there was the delays to the court case by the Child Welfare in getting their report to the court early in the year. This in my opinion was seen to prejudice the welfare of Oliver. The case was originally scheduled for June, and now it was set down for October 1976.

This delay played a significant part as I was not sure Oliver would stay with me or go with his mother. This uncertainty did play a big part in Oliver's well-being along with mine as well. The court was critical of the Department of Social Welfare for such delay. The final outcome is in the balance and now depends on whether or not the court considers making an order to the father or the mother. That is the only way to serve the child's best interest, which I can say I honestly maintained. Then there was the issue of the law at the time, which states a child under five stays with its mother. This was the key issue that hung over our head. I am sure Claire's legal team were well aware of this and will be a major part of their defense.

The issue now moving forward for me was to deal with the ongoing incidents and allegations. A lot of these were highly motivated and orchestrated by Claire and her mother and continued right up till the eve of the hearing.

The submissions made by Claire, her mother, and along with others were damaging to my application to gain custody of my son. I had no family living in New Zealand. This was exceedingly difficult for me; however, I did have lots of people, good honest people who, on their own fruition, supported me, like the church. This was very important. A lot was now in the balance.

The following stories were months out from the hearing, well organized and very calculated, some you will find hard to believe. I had to live with the fact that one day I may have to let go as Oliver might go with his mother, but I am adamant this was out of the question as my fight is to have sole custody. She can have access, which I would not object to, despite all her allegations she made against me.

*The Crest Ball*

It was midyear, and I was not going to the ball as I did not have a partner. Then my boss at Crest Foods said to me that his wife had a girlfriend, a single mother named Anne. He said, "Why don't we see if we can arrange you to take her as your partner to the ball?"

I said, "Okay, but I have to be sure she is not seen as a girlfriend. You know what Claire would do is try and put this on me as a girlfriend."

With that his wife arranged to meet this lady named Anne. She was tall and very attractive. I asked her if she would like to go to the ball with me, and she said she would love to, so this was settled.

The night of the ball, I went and picked her up. I forgot to take the tickets with me, so I went back to my place to pick them up. Anne came in with me. Jim told me that Oliver's grandmother phoned and asked, "Could Danial drop over a pair of pajamas for Oliver? He was sick, and I do not have a clean pair for him."

With that I drove over to the grandparents' place. I had Anne with me. When I got to their place, I took the PJs in to Rose, and Oliver gave me a big hug. I said, "Daddy will pick you up in the morning."

With that, Rose walked me outside. She spotted Anne in the car, and she then assumed it was my girlfriend. I said, "No, this is a friend of my boss's wife, and seeing I had no partner to go to the ball with, they arranged this for me, that's all. She is not my girlfriend."

So off we went to the ballroom, which was on the waterfront. I met up with the guys from work. I introduced Anne and said she was my partner for the evening. I asked Anne what she would like to drink.

She said, "A nice Riesling would be fine."

I went up to the bar to get our drinks. Then Mr. Saunders approached me. He had a bit one too many. He said to me about his brother-in-law Craig, about how I have been harassing them. He asked me stop calling his place.

I said, "Are you sure you have the right person?" I did get the drinks and started to walk off. He then grabbed me by the arm, and he blurted out loudly, "You won't be dealing with Craig, you will be dealing with me."

I said, "Is that a threat?" He replied, "Bet yah it is."

Then I said, "Lay your grubby hands off me and bugger off." I then walked over to Anne. She said, "What was all that about?"

"Oh, it's nothing really. He is the brother-in-law of the guy who is shacked up with my wife. Anyway, let's not talk about that. We are here to enjoy ourselves."

The guys from work said they heard a lot of what he said, "Do you want us to say something?" "No," I said. "He is very intoxicated, let it go."

Despite the altercation I had, we all did have a good night. The food was great, and the dancing superb. We left around 1:00 a.m. I drove to Anne's place. I pulled up in her driveway. We chatted for a very long time. She told me about herself. She had a very aggressive husband, and he lived in Wellington. She said she came to Auckland to get away from him. She had two children, a boy aged six and a girl aged ten.

I explained that I was going for custody of my boy, who was nearly four. She invited me in, but I declined. I gave her a good night kiss. I thanked her for such a lovely evening, and that was really it. I was not interested in having a girlfriend at this stage. If and when after the court case, we both decided, if we want to go out again, then we'd wait and see. I did, however, have Anne and her two children over for dinner one night. She had a boy aged six and a girl eight years of age. This night Claire turned up. She stayed in the kitchen and demanded Oliver to go with her that night.

I said, "No, I have guests here. You can pick him up as planned in the morning." She stormed off and said out loud, "I see you have your girlfriend and her kids here." I said, "She is a friend, that is all."

Two things out of all this are that Claire and Fiona thought this was Jessica Phillips as they also told others it was. The second point was they claimed I had a sixteen-year-old looking after Oliver while I was at the ball when Oliver was at his grandparents' house that night.

## Car Chase

There were mentions made particularly by Craig Kelly in statements about me running his car off the road when Claire and Oliver were also in the car.

He stated, "There were occasions when we have been driving along the road with Oliver in the back seat, and his father has come out of nowhere, pulled alongside, and literally dragged Oliver from the car. Oliver is an extremely nervous little boy, and the turmoil which he has been forced through at present will have a detrimental effect on his later life."

Now there was one incident, not occasions, that Craig stated. His recollection of events were farther from the truth. His accounts of things were just like Claire along with her mother, so exaggerated. The conclusion I came to is this: telling people half-truths, and you exaggerate and lie, and you then start believing yourself that these things actually happened to then make out you are the innocent party. This was Craig's way, his plan to make me out as the villain. There was only one occasion that I pulled them over did take Oliver from them. What Craig did not say was this was to protect Claire. This is how it unfolded.

I have mentioned many times that Claire always came around later at night, usually not long after Jim had left to go out. This night it was a Wednesday, just after 8:00 p.m. I had not long put Oliver off to bed. There was a car that came up the driveway. Before I could find out who it was, the back door flew open.

I said, "Oh yeah, just barge in. You do not bother to knock. What are you doing here?" She seemed very upset and yelled at me, demanded that she have full rights to see Oliver. I said, "At this hour at night, no, you do not."

She said she had to see him because I had cut her off her access.

"Yes, we have, until you come to your senses." I explained to her, "It is through your actions. You often cause unnecessary trouble. Upsetting Oliver is the reason why I have prevented you from seeing Oliver." I raised my voice at her. "You even got him to run away for you to say he ran away because he does not want to be with me. You must be aware a letter was sent by my lawyer to your lawyer on this matter."

I tried to be very calm on this as Claire was visibly upset. I said to her, "It's late. Oliver is well asleep. Please do not disturb him. I do not want any trouble. Please just go."

What occurred to me was that it was very coincidental that Claire knows the movements in and out of the house as Jim had not long left the house. It was not the first time she arrived late at night when I was on my own. Again Jim had not long left the house. I said to her, "Are you watching this house? It's convenient, is it not, that when Jim leaves, you arrive. Is James your spy or someone else is? Now leave."

She got very angry with me. In fact, she was at a point to almost becoming violent. With that she was heading down the hallway toward Oliver's room. I was right behind her. At that point, the phone rang. I took call in my bedroom, and on the phone was Greg, a workmate. He had some issues with his workload for the next day. While I was speaking to him for only just a few minutes, I heard a car pull away from the driveway. The bright lights lit up the kitchen and the house. This alerted me that something was amiss. I told Greg that I would call him back, realizing that Claire had gone. I suspected trouble, so I quickly went to Oliver's room and discovered that he was not in his bed.

I quickly grabbed the car keys off the bench and left hurriedly without locking the house up and also leaving all the lights on. I jumped into the car, reversed out of the driveway at a haste. The tires screeched as I turned around the street corner. Claire would have had at least three to four minutes start on me. I assumed that Craig was at the wheel or Claire driving. Inasmuch as she would normally keep to the speed limit, Craig would drive at a higher speed. I increased my speed. I knew they would be heading toward Henderson. I glanced at the speedometer and noticed that I was doing well over 80 kilometers per hour as I went over the Mangere Bridge. Lucky for me, there were no other cars in front of me. I was hoping that there were no police patrolling the area.

I drove to the end of the bridge, and at the *T* intersection, I knew I had to turn left to head toward Henderson. I then headed up the steep hill. I noticed a car going over the top of the hill. I guessed it was them. I increased my speed to catch up. I sped up and went over the top of the hill well over 100 kilometers per hour. I spotted the car. Yes, I knew it was Craig's, and they were not far ahead.

Then suddenly, Craig must have spotted me. He turned down another roadway, this time heading toward New Lynn. My car screamed around the corner fast, heading down the road. I was sure they must have spotted me as their car sped up. After a long chase down this road, I soon caught up with them. I was right behind them, I kept flashing my lights to get them to pull over. The flashing lights had no effect. Craig kept driving, which made me drive on the wrong side of the road to eventually level my car alongside theirs. I waved my fist at Craig to pull over, and he would not. I had no other alternative, so I increased speed to cut in front of them. I then slowed my car down gradually to force Craig to slow his car down without causing an accident. As Oliver was in the car, I knew I had to do this very cautiously.

They finally stopped the car in front of a block of shops. Their car was on an angle nearly on the footpath. Oliver was on Claire's lap. I got out of my car quickly and opened the passenger side door. I yelled at her, "Claire, what the bloody hell are you doing?!"

She said, "You allowed me to take Oliver!"

"No, you took him without my permission!" I said. "I am taking Oliver back home."

With that, I grabbed Oliver from Claire's lap. He was still in his pajamas. He was crying. I said to Claire that she would hear about this issue. Quickly I put Oliver in the car in the back seat. I went over to Craig and said to him, "You're a bloody idiot. You do not change, do you. You try this stunt again, and I will have you both charged for kidnapping."

Claire screamed at me, "He is my boy too!"

I left her screaming. I could still hear her while I drove off. On the way back, Oliver was terribly upset. He said to me, "Why did Mummy take me out of my bed?"

I said, "Son, do not worry, I will have you home soon."

I drove back home, this time at a sensible speed. Even though I was shaken up, I calmed down. When I arrived back to the house, Jim was home, and he could not work out why all the lights were on, the house was open, and also my car gone. He figured something was up. I told him what happened. I put Oliver back to bed.

Not long after, I got an abusive phone call from Claire. I just hung up on her. She did this repeatedly for about two hours, and I did not bother to answer the phone. Jim finally did answer the phone as it was getting rather late. He told her in no certain terms to bugger off and hung up on her. I am sure this came about as I refused her access over many incidents along with the trouble  she caused, mainly when she brought back Oliver from his weekend access visits, her part in telling Oliver to run away, and his grandfather telling him I was a bastard, but this did not stop her as she never relented. Her continuous allegations and the many more incidents took place mainly mostly at my home. I think by now the police have a good idea who are the perpetrators as 111 calls are used for emergency when lives are in danger or a robbery. In Claire's case and her mother, this was a regular occurrence. When it was investigated they were non-life-threatening false allegations, this then makes one think that when you talk to Claire, one would think butter would not melt in her mouth, as well as her mother. I often felt Claire had a split personality or something as the stories she told and allegations that came to nothing makes one wonder. Was she on drugs? Even her mother at one stage thought she was.

The incident was noted by the lawyer. She said, "If they bring this up, we will defend it. It's your word against hers, and I am sure she won't as she was in the wrong to take Oliver."

## You Have My Car Keys

The following incident was mentioned in court. Claire's plan this night, I am sure, was to set me up. However, this time, I turned the tables on her. At this point, quite frankly, I was full of her tirades, coming around at all hours, constant phone calls and allegations.

The same old pattern emerged as Claire arrived within five minutes after Jim left the house. I suppose there is an old saying that desperate people take desperate measures. Claire was no exception. I am not sure what led to this as earlier in the day, Rose called. She said over the phone that she found out I did not have interim custody of Oliver.

I said, "I know that I have interim custody, not custody, as that will be decided soon." She said to me, "Claire is his mother. She has her rights, you know."

I said, "Get off it. You do not know what you're on about. Go and speak to Claire's lawyer." With that she hung the phone in my ear. Rose never accepted at all I had interim custody. This was not the first time this had been raised.

Back to this night. It was well past 8:00 p.m. As usual, Jim left to visit Jessica. This, however, enforced my view that the house was being watched as Claire arrived soon after. This night she pulled up out front, parked the car not in the driveway as she normally did, but on the roadside in front of the house. She walked up the driveway and came in from our back door that leads into the kitchen and hallway. She was rather angry and demanded to see Oliver.

I said, "Claire, there is a time and place for everything. You have to live by the rules." She screamed, "What rules?"

I said, "Like now as I have told you many times before, you have no right to come here. If you behaved yourself, then things would be different for you."

She said, "You and your bloody lawyer are plotting against me."

I said, "No, you're the one that is doing the plotting, coming up with this crap that we hassled you at the courthouse. You just leave right now. Claire, you know damn well Oliver is well in bed, so why do you come around these times at night?"

The allegations that I keep Oliver up all hours at night may be the reason why she comes around trying to catch me out. With that I told her to leave.

I said, "You pull this stunt time and time again."

She pushed past me as she tried to get to Oliver's room.

I said, "No, you are not going up there and disturbing him." I then grabbed her by the arm and escorted her back to her car. She then started abusing me, calling me all the names under the sun. I am not sure why I did this, but I snapped, I think because I just had enough. So I took her

car keys out of the car and threw them on the roof of the house. She screamed, "Why did you do this for?"

I said, "I am sick of you coming here! Now get!" "What about my car keys?" she creamed out.

I told her to get away from here. With that she took off on foot down the road, screaming, "You have my keys!" No doubt she went to James and Fiona's place.

I suppose there is a funny side to this as a short time later, the cavalry started arriving. First Fiona came, and by then I had gotten the keys down from the roof as I got a torch and also a ladder from next door. I placed the keys back in the car. This was unbeknown to Fiona and Claire.

Then in a few minutes, Claire's mother arrived on the scene. She came up the driveway and demanded to see Oliver and pushed me aside. I then grabbed her by the arm. I said, "Move yourself, just get off the property."

She said, "No, I am staying here." I again asked her to leave.

She screamed at me, "It's my daughter's home, and I can go in!"

"Like bloody hell you will. No, get away as this is not Claire's home anymore. If you have forgotten, I will remind you that she left us. Now beat it!"

She stayed put.

I said for the third time, "Remove yourself!" With that I grabbed her by the arm then shoved her onto the footpath.

She screamed at me, "You have assaulted me! I am calling the police!" I said, "Good luck to you, just go."

As Fiona and James lived just around the corner, she took off with Fiona, no doubt to call the police. In the meantime, I had to deal with Claire as she was screaming and swearing at me.

It was some thirty minutes later that the police arrived. I could see Fiona and Rose coming down the street toward our house. Oliver came out as the commotion woke him up.

I said, "Go back inside and go back to bed. Daddy will be in soon."

Oliver did not go to bed as I could see him looking through the lounge window. I thought to better sort this out quickly as this was getting out of hand. The police officer asked what was going on, and Claire said I had taken her car keys. "He threw them on the roof!"

I played the innocent card here as I just had it up to my neck with her constantly coming around, which I explained this to the police. Rose butted in, and she yelled out, "The boy is also my daughter's son!"

I said, "Yes, he is, but what justifies her coming around at all hours?"

Then Rose said to the police officer, "Danial assaulted me, now I want to lay charges." Claire start screaming again, "My keys are on the roof!"

I said to the police as I acted dumb, "I do not know what she is on about." I said to Claire, "You may have thought I threw the keys on the roof."

Then one of the cops went over to her car and opened the driver's door. He told her, "Your keys are in the ignition."

I said, "See, they were there all the time."

I said to the police, "I have interim custody of my son. They have no right to be here. I should be the one charging them as they came here uninvited. They continually cause disturbances."

The police said to Claire and also to Rose, "Leave the property, and we will speak to you later. If you want to lay charges, put in a report at the station."

Rose yelled, "Yes, I will!"

I said, "Good luck to you both as I too will lay a complaint also!" With that, Claire, Rose, and Fiona drove off in Claire's car.

The police officer said to me, "Come down in the morning to the station, and we will sort this out."

I said, "Yes, I will."

The police officer said, "I will be on again after 10:00 a.m." I said, "I will be there." I thanked them, and they left.

I did go down to the police station the next day just after 10:00 a.m., and I made a report. I said to the police officer, "This has been going on for months now, and there are plenty of police reports from this station as the police have been to the house on many occasions." I think it's about time someone stepped up and told them to stop making false allegations. Well, like all the rest of the police complaints, this was not different.

The police did investigate this, and I was informed that as I had interim custody and with the time they came around at night, I had my rights to order Rose off the property. As to the car keys being tossed onto the roof, it was another matter as they said when they were there, the keys were in her car. No further action was taken on this.

I admit, yes, I lost my cool, and I did throw the keys up on the roof, but I did retrieve them and place them back in the car. This was what I said earlier to give some of her own medicine back as I was fed up. I suppose two wrongs do not make it right. Did she learn anything from this? No. For a change, I had the last laugh on Claire and also her mother as they made absolute fools of themselves in front of the police. In fact, one of the cops I got to know very well, he told me, "They should be looking into her allegations against you as they are all frivolous and come to nothing."

I said, "It's very unfortunate that you the police have to deal with such matters, and in family disputes, things get out of control. In my case, my ex will try anything to discredit me to better her case when it goes to court."

The cop said, "Yes, we understand all that. We take all this into consideration if charges need to be laid, made on the type of complaints that are presented to us, and if the person making such complaints is a serial complainer, then we view this entirely different."

I said, "Surely my ex-wife must fit that category. What kind of call did you respond to?" They told me 000.

I said, "That is for emergencies. This incident was not an emergency." The police said, "We will deal with that."

## 111 Emergency Call: "He Is Going to Murder My Son"

If you think things so far are quite bizarre, then this incident is up there with the best desperate tactics, is what one has said. Now it's well documented that Claire left the family home on her own undertaking, despite my efforts to stop her in a loving and kind way. Looking back at it now, what a fool I was as I did plead with her not to go. Then after a while, it came out by her the allegations that I was a violent person, that I stopped her from taking Oliver, I threatened her, and the worst was portraying me as a potential murderer. This was a feature in the statements made along with various different accounts. This was, without any doubt, to discredit me. Did the court see through all this? Was this called out?

Claire's lawyer played along with these allegations. My lawyer did not as she in cross-examination relating to the allegations said by Claire and her witnesses were questioned at length. Claire stopped at nothing. In my opinion, she was allowed to do what she wanted to do as she had her mother Rose and Craig as allies. To date, I have been put through hell. I often said it's like being in a horror movie, and I am the victim.

This incident until today I cannot forget, and what was the real motive she had? I recall that I was home from work around four thirty that afternoon. It was not long after I picked up Oliver from Fiona's. Usually when I get home, I get Oliver settled, then start preparing the evening meal. Oliver was in the lounge watching his favorite cartoons. The phone rang, and you guessed it, yes, it was Claire. She as usual started ranting on as she said, "I am not happy Oliver is going to kindergarten."

I said, "Why not, for god's sake? He loves going to kindergarten."

Then she blurted out that Oliver was being bashed up at the kindergarten.

I said, "Who told you this rubbish? You ring me up, and you then make allegations about the kindergarten that he is being bashed up.

She then said that she would give up work and look after him during the week, then I can have him on weekends.

"You're bloody kidding, aren't you? That is the last thing I would do is hand over Oliver to you when you are with that piece of garbage. Anyway, are you that stupid I would agree to something like that? You look after Oliver during the week and take him out of kindergarten?" I said to her in a blunt voice, "No way you will have Oliver other than the weekend access that has now been agreed upon. As far as your partner Craig, I am telling you now, he is not going to be part of Oliver's life. In fact, you're a screwball yourself, also very unstable."

I did yell at her down the phone. I also called her a stupid bitch as I was so angry and said, "I have to put an end to all this." Then I hung up the phone on her.

Now I am not sure what way she took my comment saying "I must put an end to this." What I meant by that statement was I must put an end to this was with my lawyer as we must stop this continual harassment and the phone calls.

It was not long after, say within fifteen minutes, my barrister Mrs. Chamberlain called me on the phone. She said? "What's going on?"

I said, "What do you mean?"

She went on to say she had just received a call from Claire's solicitor and was told by Claire that I was going to kill Oliver and that also I am off my head. I told Mrs. Chamberlain the conversation I had with Claire as she wanted to take Oliver away from kindergarten as she was going on about him being bashed up at the center. "She was the abusive one. I did call her a stupid bitch. All I said was we should put an end to all this and hung up the phone. I meant by this that with your help, we have to stop her phoning all the time and also coming around all the time."

Mrs. Chamberlain said she will deal with that. "I will now call her solicitor and explain what you said." She again asked me several times, "Are you okay?"

I said, "Fine, but this harassment must stop." She said, "Call me if anything happens."

I said, "Yes, I will. Claire is the one that is driving this insane nonsense."

Shortly after I got off the phone from Mrs. Chamberlain, I heard a police siren coming down the street. They pulled up in the driveway, and out jumped two cops. They nearly broke the door down, and they were yelling loudly. They rushed in, pushing me aside. They said, "Where is the boy?"

I said, "Why?"

"Where's the boy?!" they shouted.

I replied, "He is in the lounge room watching cartoons. Also he is eating an ice block."

They went in, and I could see the look on their faces when they did see Oliver eating an ice block I had given him. Oliver was laughing at the cartoons he was watching.

The cop spoke to Oliver. He asked, "Are you alright? Did Daddy hurt you?" "No," he said, "but I heard Daddy yelling on the phone."

I knew one of the cops as he had been here before on other wild-goose chase. I said, "This has to stop. The harassment I am getting from his mother as well the police following up false alarms all the time is crazy."

The cop said, "Yes, I understand. In these matters, we take calls where children may be harmed very seriously. Your boy seems very happy here. When it comes out to be a false call, this is a very different matter. We do take a dim view of calls that turn out to be false alarms. We can assure you, we will be chatting with the mother. Don't you worry, this will be in our report."

They left, and I called back Mrs. Chamberlain and explained everything to her. Now I was branded a violet person and a potential murderer by the mother. I was now more than convinced I was dealing with a very vindictive person who will do anything to discredit me.

Next day, I told Ms. Tuohy at the kindergarten what Claire had said about Oliver being bashed up at the kindergarten. I can tell you she was not impressed at all. Also she said, "If anything like that happens, I would be the first to know. The boys do play rough at times in good fun, so nothing to worry here."

The other point was also being the president of the Parents Club, I would also have heard if anything like Claire claimed was going on. I was sure this will not be the end of the matter.

This gets even better as we found out later that Craig Kelly went to the Otahuhu police station. He made the complaint that I was going to harm Oliver. Now this was around the same time Claire called me at home, also when her solicitor called my solicitor. Read into this as you will. I am convinced this was well planned. Only Claire and Craig can tell if it was or not. The fact was the court hearing was getting closer, and she became a desperate person. It was quite chilling to think I would murder my own son whom I loved so dearly. This new allegation gets played out in court as now I am seen by Claire and her cronies as a potential murderer.

This has taken a lot out of me, including Oliver. He has been sick more than he should have. Then unbeknown to Claire, I had taken him back to Dr. Henderson. He said with all the trauma we had been going through, it has impacted us both, more so with Oliver. He has had a serious chest infection, which the doctor said the turmoil Oliver was going through has made his condition worse.

After a few visits, Oliver was back to normal. At one stage, I was going to the same doctor as Claire and her mother, but I changed that as somehow, they were told every time I had him there.

## A Good Friend Told Me

Confidence is better than perfection because perfection means doing the best, but confidence means knowing how to handle the worst. In your case, Danial, this fits you to a *T*.

## He's Playing with the Lawn Mower

People around me have known for a while the house was regularly watched, as many occasions occurred when Jim was not home, and Claire would turn up. Then we had the private detective on the main road. Jim had heard what he thought was someone creeping around outside during the night. My next-door neighbor has also said she has seen some snooping around at night. Then this happened. It was rather freaky in a way.

Oliver was playing outside with his dog Foxy. He had many toys he played outside with Peter, his young brother, and sister. They often came over, and they played happily together.

I could see out to the backyard through the kitchen window. They were all playing happily. Then the phone rang. Yes, it was Claire. She raved on that I was not looking after him properly. "You're not fit to have him!" And she got quite hysterical then said, "Oliver is outside playing with the lawn mower, and he may cut his hands off!"

I then instantly dropped the phone and flew outside. I found Oliver was playing with the lawn mower as he was pretending to mow the back lawn. I told him nicely, "Do not play with the mower as it might hurt you." With that I raced back inside, and the phone was dead. Then it dawned on me. *Where the hell is she?* This was spooky. She was up to her old tricks keeping an eye on me.

I guessed Claire would have been at the phone box on the main road, where she would have a direct view into the backyard. I quickly jumped over the back fence through the neighbor's backyard. I could not see anyone at all along the main road.

Mrs. Paki came out and said she did see a car earlier at the phone box. "It was not the same one that usually parks there, and the person has binoculars. This one was a dark green sedan, I think a Holden?"

I said, "Thank you for that as you now have identified the car as this belongs to Craig. If you see that car again at the phone box, can you get Peter to go along and get the registration number?"

She said, "Yes, I will do that for you."

Mrs. Paki was a lovely neighbor, and she did look out for me. She did on many occasions alert me if things did not look right. She also told me that at night, they had heard someone going through their property. When they got up, they were well gone.

This incident just shows me Claire was not going to stop, and this includes all her associates, I call them; this was typical of stalking me. If things were that I was doing this to her, then I would have an order to stop me doing this.

I brought Oliver inside, and the kids from out the back went home. Oliver could not understand why he came back inside as it was a lovely sunny day. I decided to go for a drive and get out for a while, so off we went. I drove over to the North Shore. We got some ice cream and sat at the beach for a while and came back home.

The next day, I took this latest incident up with my barrister. She said, "I can get a restraining order."

I did decline as I thought at this time, it will only make matters worse than they are. Mrs. Chamberlain kind of agreed, but she did say, "You're dealing with a very vindictive person."

Now I was trapped and at a loss. I was dealing with a woman who will stop at nothing, and her family goes along with this. I have many people I deal with during my line of work. These people are good businesspeople and also well respected.

I was in one of the supermarkets this particular day. One of my coworkers (I will call him Reg), he knew about my wife leaving me. I think that is why he poured this out to me. He was a father of two children, a boy of four and a girl aged six, and his wife ran away with another man. She did take the kids with her. He applied for custody and was totally rejected, and he was labelled a drunkard and a wife basher. This man did not drink. He was a well-to-do businessman. He never ever touched or abused his wife. What he told me was his ex-wife got people to lie and put in affidavits to the court that he was a wife basher and also a drunkard.

Despite his efforts to disprove these claims, these were not even taken into account. Then he said the child welfare believed her and her family and friends. He told me he was a broken man.

I said to him, "You must not give up on this and appeal this."

He looked at me straight in the eye, and he said, "I am not allowed to even see my kids."

This was heartbreaking to hear. We both went to a nearby café, and we had a coffee. I gave him my phone details for him to contact me if he needed someone to talk to. For some reason, he did not call. The last I heard was he left Auckland and went down south.

After hearing all this, this is what I am afraid of. Now as this is typical stories you hear, I now must face the same. With the Families Need Fathers group in Auckland, I did attend a few meetings, and the same stories are told. They do all they can to reconcile fathers with their children. Yes, I have no doubt the system is broken and does need change. My story is no different to lots of other fathers out there fighting for their rights to have custody or even access to their children. They just want to be heard and treated the same as the mother of the children.

After listening to Reg and what he told me gave me no reassurance what lay ahead. I do have a great barrister. Yes, we have won the right to interim custody, but that does not mean I will gain full custody. What Mrs. Chamberlain said to me many times was "You have a mountain to climb, and it is a long way to the top."

## Breakfast Down the Sink

I suppose reading this story makes you wonder where all this will end and the continuous incidents that I had encountered since Claire left. Yes, I want full custody as I want to raise my boy as I reject the person who could be the father figure in his life. As to Claire and her parents, I never ever intended for Oliver not seeing them. The issue is the continuous phone calls, coming around late at night, making allegations, and having a private detective watching me. The mother as well as the grandparents in this case have a right to see Oliver. My stopping access was for the purpose of settling things down, also making sure Oliver was not continually getting upset. This was in many ways why he had to go to the doctor's on many occasions as he had a cold, or he had a bronchial infection. This was put down to the stress and strain of what I describe as unnecessary confrontations, mainly when Oliver went with his mother or when he returned. For these reasons, at times, access visits were denied. These were done for short periods. I made sure these were done through my barrister, and a letter was sent to her solicitor to justify why.

I will stress that if—and a big *if*—I am successful in gaining custody of Oliver, then his mother has rights as well as his grandparents to have access rights. My recollections of events were miles apart from what Claire, her family, and Craig has said, and as it was also stated that in a case like this, you need to have "the wisdom of Solomon to work it out."

I was always at a loss what prompted by Claire to do stupid things. I was concerned about her mental state as she had done many bizarre things. She comes up with stupid unfounded allegations along with stories to the point I was going to harm my son, or in her words, murder him. The fact was people around her believed that, and this was a big concern.

What she did this particular morning, you figure it out. It was around 7:30 a.m. Jim had already left for work, and I was getting breakfast ready for both Oliver and I. Like every morning, I have a routine to get Oliver up, dressed, have breakfast, then take him to kindergarten. These mornings are planned, so I did not have to rush around.

I heard a car pull up in the driveway, and I looked outside the kitchen window that overlooks the driveway. Sure enough, Claire as usual stormed into the house and into the kitchen via the back door. Jim had left shortly before she arrived, and the back door was unlocked.

I had just finished making baked beans on toast for both Oliver and I as he loved baked beans. We did have these some days away from porridge and other cereals. I just buttered the toast and put the baked beans on the toast. Claire then for whatever reason grabbed the plates off the bench, then she tipped the lot in the sink. She quickly turned the tap on, and water poured all over the food.

I yelled at her, "What did you do that for?"

Claire said, "You cannot give that rubbish to Oliver."

I said, "Oliver loves his baked beans!" I tried not get too fired up as this, I know, was what she wanted me to do. I said to her quietly, "You must stop this nonsense just barging in here."

She looked pale and drawn, and she was shaking. She claimed I don't give him proper meals. "I know you don't. Baked beans to a child? That's not good food."

I said to her that baked beans are very nutritional. "Anyway, it's my concern what meals I provide Oliver."

Then she realized Oliver was not at the table. I said, "He is in the lounge watching his favorite cartoons as he does every morning after he is dressed. He waits for his breakfast. What the hell is wrong with you? Now you have destroyed our breakfast!" It was hard to keep calm. I tried my best, as the last thing I wanted was to have Oliver upset going to kindergarten. I said, "Go into the lounge, say hello to Oliver, then get your arse out of here. I have a routine every morning, and I do not want you coming here and upsetting things. We will be late as we leave here around 8:20 a.m. to have Oliver at kindergarten by 8:30 a.m."

I quickly grabbed some Weet-Bix out of the cupboard and warmed some milk and took this to Oliver. Claire followed me into the lounge.

Oliver said, "What are you doing here, Mummy? I am going to kindy soon. Daddy is taking me."

I put his breakfast on his own little table I set up for him. Claire spoke to Oliver while he was having his Weet-Bix. He asked me, "Where is my baked beans, Daddy?"

I said, "Daddy burnt them" as I could not tell him what his mother did to his breakfast. I then told her now to leave. She then said she wanted to go and get something out of Oliver's room. I said, "No, you don't, as you take things from this house. Please get out. You must leave, or we will be running late."

By this time it was well past eight o'clock. I had to have my own breakfast as well. I said to her, "No wonder Oliver is the way he is with you upsetting him all the time."

I then took her up to his room. Oliver followed, and he said, "Mummy, look what I have here!

It is my puppy Foxy."

Then she said to me, "You shouldn't have a puppy around Oliver. It's not good for his health." I finally lost my cool. "Now it's time you left the house." I then made sure she did not take anything and followed her out, and she left. In the future when Jim leaves in the morning, we keep the doors locked and also at night. The question of a restraining order was mentioned, but I felt this would create more problems. I felt she will stop at nothing despite many complaints sent to her lawyer by mine. I did, however, get Oliver to kindergarten on time, and I went off to work very upset with what happened that morning.

As mentioned earlier, Oliver was given a lovely puppy, which we called Foxy. It was what you call a sausage dog, and Oliver laughed at that. It was a dachshund. Oliver loved this dog, yet his mother continually told Oliver it's not good for him as he would get sick, which was nonsense, of course. I taught Oliver to wash his hands every time after he played with Foxy. Animals are good for kids—cats, dogs, horses, you name it, as this is part of growing up.

A few weeks later, we got home around four thirty in the afternoon, and Oliver would go straight to the garage where we kept Foxy during the day. Then Oliver would let him out and play with him in the backyard. We only had Foxy for a short time. Every time we left each day, we made sure Foxy had plenty of water as well as food to eat. We had him on a long lead just in case so he could move around. As he was locked up each day, it would be impossible for him to get out. He was not a noisy dog, very quiet in fact. If he did bark, it was not loud. Foxy was good for Oliver, and he loved his dog.

This night we came home around the usual time. Oliver went to the garage and opened it up. Daddy, Daddy, Foxy is not here."

Sure enough, he was gone, but his lead was there. Someone got in the locked garage, took the lead off Foxy, and took him. The garage, of course, was the home cinema, and strangely enough, nothing else was touched. How they got in, I am not sure.

My neighbor across the road was a police officer. I went over and told him. He came over and had a look around, he asked if I wanted to make a report.

I said, "I have my suspicions, but no, I won't bother."

Oliver was very upset. The odd thing was someone got in and just took the dog away, seeing nothing else was touched. Also, how did they did get in was the mystery. This garage was well secured, and there was no way Foxy could have gotten out.

I drew my own conclusions on this one. I could not prove it, but it smelt a bit fishy when Claire often said Oliver should not have a dog. We never found Foxy; the neighbors did not see any suspicious movements around my place. I did not bother getting another puppy for Oliver as I was afraid this may happen again. Oliver soon got over Foxy gone. The dog gave so much enjoyment for Oliver. Also, I may add, only a few people knew we had the puppy in the garage. It makes you wonder what may happen next.

## *Hit Me, You Always Hit Me*

I did have a lot of people I call loyal friends who gave me the love and support I needed and have them around for dinner. These are planned well in advance. This incident took place on a Saturday night, and this is how this unfolded and was mentioned in proceedings.

As I often, I had people over for dinner. It was good to mix with friends. I just loved cooking and entertaining. Oliver enjoyed me having people over as most of them had young children he could play with.

This night was a Saturday night. Oliver was not with his mother this particular weekend. I often planned these nights when he was with me as Claire had now alternate weekend access visits, which I was now hoping would settle things down. I was busy in the kitchen preparing the dinner. It was around 5:00 p.m. when Jasmine and Trevor along with their children arrived. As they arrived, the phone rang. It was

Claire, and she wanted to come over and pick up Oliver. I said, "No, I have people here for dinner tonight." She got very angry with me over the phone, and as usual, I had to hang up the phone. I had this feeling she thought I had Jessica at the house with her children.

While my guests were there, she rang a few times more. I had to just quickly hang up the phone. She did ask who was there, and I told her none of her business.

I said to Jasmine, "She keeps on calling, and I just get sick of it. She usually carries on about nothing or creates issues, so I just must hang up the phone on her." No doubt she was told that I had other people in the house, and this may have prompted her to do what she did.

We had a few drinks before dinner. We started the meal around six thirty. The early dinner was to make sure it was not a late night for the children. This night, I made a beef stir-fry with lots of vegetables along with fried rice. Then we finished off with a chocolate mousse for dessert. The children just loved the dessert. After dinner, we enjoyed a few glasses of wine, and the children had cordial. We chatted about work and the movie business. Soon, it was getting close to Oliver's bedtime. He said to me, "Daddy, I'm tired," so I put him into bed. I made sure he was tucked in, and he soon went off to sleep. This was around eight o'clock.

I then made coffee, and we all went into the lounge room to watch a bit of TV when suddenly Claire stormed in. She started yelling at me, "Where is Oliver?!"

I said, "He is already in bed, and please do not disturb him."

She yelled at me in a very loud aggressive voice, "I want to take him home with me!" I said, "No, you won't, not at this hour. Anyway, you had him last week."

"Yes, but he is my boy too. I am taking him." Then suddenly, to her shock and surprise, she saw Jasmine and her husband and their two children.

I am sure she thought I had a girlfriend around for dinner. It was obvious she was upset and did not even say hello to Jasmine, her longtime friend. I thought, *How I am going to sort this out?*

I said to Jasmine and Trevor, "I am sorry about this" as I got up from the table as Claire ran down the hallway. She stopped in the hallway heading toward Oliver's room, shouting at me that I do not keep him warm. I am sure she makes all this stuff up as she goes along.

I said to her, "Do not wake Oliver up as he is tired, he had a big day."

With that, she pushed me aside and entered his room. When I looked into his room, Oliver was not in bed. She screamed at me, "Where is he?"

I said, "I only put him to bed about a half hour ago." Then I looked under the bed. Sure enough, there he was. I said, "Oliver, what are you doing under the bed?"

He cried out, "I do not want to go with Mummy!"

I pulled him out from under the bed. He was crying and sobbed loudly.

I said, "Claire, see what you have done? Why do you come here all hours at night when you know damn well he would be in bed?"

She was screaming out loud, and she again accused me of not keeping him warm. She picked a cardigan out of the drawer next to his bed. Oliver then took off and ran into the lounge, where he then sat with the other children. Understandably, Oliver was very upset with all this. I had him in pajamas that were woolen and fleece-lined, and this kept him very warm as the nights get very cold. Claire was here this night just to cause trouble to make an issue out of nothing. This became very embarrassing to my guests I had over for dinner. Claire was making a terrible scene and was also very upsetting for the children. This did not seem to bother her. She insisted to put a cardigan on Oliver.

I said to her, "The house is very warm, I have the heating on. The house is very cozy."

Then she started shouting at me again and abusing me. She was out of control and was screaming and shouting at me, "Go on, hit me! You always want to hit me!"

I said, "You have worn out your welcome here. I think you better leave now." I tried very hard to calm the situation down, but the situation became very heated. With that, Jasmine and Trevor said they would go. They picked up their children.

As they were leaving, I said to them, "I am very sorry about this as it has spoilt a very good night."

Jasmine said to me, "I have never seen Claire ever like this. She did not even want to speak to me. Anyway, it is not your fault. Take care of Oliver, he is your main responsibility."

I was very emotionally upset over this incident. It was like I was dealing with a deranged woman, sad to say. This is not the quiet woman I married.

I turned to Claire and told her to get out of the house. I swore at her and said, "You have spoiled a bloody good night. You just come in when you feel like it. Now get out as now I want to put Oliver back to bed." I was so annoyed. "How dare you come here then accuse me of not looking after Oliver? You're just a stupid bitch, now get out!"

Oliver was in the lounge hearing all this. I said, "Please leave us alone."

With that she stormed out of the house. I then put Oliver back to bed, and he was very upset. He said to me, "Why did Mummy come here? Mummy was mad at you, wasn't she?"

I then said to reassure him, "Do not worry, Mummy just came to see if you are alright. Now you must go back to sleep." I gave him a big hug and kiss. He soon nodded off to sleep. I turned off his light and I said to myself, *This is a nightmare. The bitch spoilt a good night.*

See, throughout the lead up to the court hearing, the emphasis was on me that I was the one creating all the problems when it was the other way around. I was saddened by what happened this night, but also incredibly grateful that I had friends to see what goes on and be witnesses to Claire's behavior.

I went into the lounge and put on the Neil Diamond album. I poured myself a glass of wine, and I then called Jasmine. I said how sorry I was about what happened tonight as well as them having to witness this. It not only upset Oliver but their children as well.

She said, "I cannot believe how much Claire has changed. Claire did not want to speak to me or Trevor. It is very sad for you and Oliver. If I did not see this first-hand, I would have not believed it of Claire. Oliver is the one who gets hurt over all this. I'll speak to you soon, take care."

I said, "Thanks, yes, we'll speak soon."

I was fortunate this night that I had Jasmine here to witness this tirade, but it was also unfortunate they had to witness this. Jasmine was her bridesmaid at our wedding and was a longtime friend of Claire's from childhood, and Jasmine grew up with Claire's family.

This evening was quite bizarre. Claire with her ranting and raving was uncalled for. Oliver hiding under the bed as he must have heard her yelling at me told me that he was very unhappy going to his mother's place. I was starting to settle when Oliver came into the lounge room. He said, "I cannot sleep. Can I stay in your bed tonight?"

I said, "Of course you can."

What he said next just cracked me up. He said to me, "Daddy, I have a headache in my big toe." I said, "Really?"

"Yes," he said. Then he said, "A drink of Coke will fix it."

I am not sure where he got that from, but I did give him a small glass of Coke. He said, "I feel better now." With that, he said, "I want to go to bed now." I think he just wanted some security. I took him up to my room and put him into bed. I left the light on for him. It was obvious he was terribly upset over what happened this evening.

It is significant to note what happened this night was mentioned at the hearing and also the fact that Oliver at times was sleeping in my bed. This I think he did on occasions when there were storms and thunder and lightning, and he used to fly into my room for comfort, like what happened this night. He just wanted some comfort or security. I cannot see what the issue is when children for many reasons want to sleep with their parents.

The other point is that it's beyond me how she knows what goes in the home, like meals we have, coming around after Jim has left at night or mornings, that I buy fish and chips for Oliver, clothes not ironed or are dirty, and on it goes. It's beyond comprehension.

I checked on Oliver a few times this night, and he was fast asleep. I did stay up for a few hours. Jim came later that night as I was still up. I said, "You missed all the fireworks." Then I told him what took place, how Oliver was very upset, and I told him about his headache in his big toe and that Coke would fix it.

Just like me, he cracked up. Jim said, "How did he come up with that?"

I said, "I do not know, but it's a good one. He is a bright cookie. Anyway, I have put him into my bed for the night."

Jim then said, "Of what you told me, this woman is out of control."

I agreed, and with that, we then called it a night, and I trotted off to bed. Oliver looked so peaceful when I got into bed. I looked at him, then my thoughts were, *How does a mother of a child behave like she does? Oliver deserves better.*

This incident was reported to my solicitor. She said, "Just another episode to this drama. It's very unfortunate. However, this time you have witnesses that can corroborate your side of events." I agreed. I felt there was something amiss here that Claire was crying out for help. She is not getting the support I think she needs. Her neurotic behavior is out of control. Everyone on her side cannot see that, and that in my opinion is a huge concern. I am not married to her anymore, and

I really do not care; however, she is Oliver's mother. This cannot be denied.

## Allegations Against the Kindergarten

Allegations about me were many, but this time, she he has turned her attack on the kindergarten. There is no doubt all this was unfounded. To make allegations against institutions that are professionally and properly run just does not make sense at all.

Nothing stops Claire in making statements along with what she calls serious allegations, then get her solicitor to send my lawyer letters of her various claims. This time the discontent was toward the kindergarten. It makes you think what is going on? Her lawyer makes me wonder why she was allowed to make allegations without any proof.

This was in part what she said, "The other children in the area are pinching all his toys    and clothes, I do not know if Oliver is genuinely happy at kindergarten as I was told that other children bash him up. I also know the kindergarten staff tell him he has no mother, and this is very distressing for him."

After reading this letter, I was so disappointed as to her allegations against the kindergarten as he was well looked after. I dropped Oliver every day at the kindergarten. Also being president, I used to spend a few moments with Mrs. Tuohy as to what the committee was planning and up- and-coming meetings, trivia nights, movie nights in my home theater, along with bingo nights and cake stalls. All this was to raise funds for the kindergarten as all money raised went toward to buy or replace equipment, and also other things that were essential for the running of the kindergarten. These outrageous claims by Claire that Oliver was being bashed up at the kindergarten, I had to bring this up with the head teacher Mrs. Tuohy, as this was a trumped-up bit of nonsense. She ran a very strict control of the children as well as the teachers. The other point is Oliver never once said to me he was being bashed up. I am certain this was Claire's way of getting back at me by sending Oliver to kindergarten as she often would remark that she could look after him rather than go to kindergarten. I suppose making such allegations would strengthen her case or to make me take him out of kindergarten. As to the comments about Oliver not being neat and tidy and dirty when I send him to kindergarten, this is again just sheer, utter nonsense.

Then in the same letter sent by Claire's solicitor to mine was the remarks made by Craig Kelly that he goes past the kindergarten most days of the week and sees Oliver in the same clothes each day is also trumped up. He must have to be either spying on the kindergarten as most times they are inside, and there are only certain periods the children spend time outside playing.

Oliver is incredibly happy going to kindergarten. In the initial stages, he was very apprehensive, but this soon settled. He could not wait to go. In another letter there was the allegation about Mother's Day activities at the kindergarten. The children made cards for their mothers, and as far as I remember, he made three cards: one for Fiona, one for his grandmother, and one for his mother, and one I did receive. Despite what Claire said or claimed was I am sure was a figment of her imagination,; she made up a right damn lie. She further claimed that the teachers told Oliver that he has not got a mother. All these allegations were a smear on the kindergarten staff, which was not taken lightly.

Mrs. Tuohy, when I discussed this with her, said that she will be taking this matter further with my solicitor and also the authorities that control kindergartens to see what course of action could be taken to dispel these outrageous allegations. In fact, it was said that what Claire had done could lead to a defamation case against her.

## The Night 111 Call: "They Are Armed"

Well, if you thought when all this will end, then think again. This night, Claire just panicked or just created an incident that supports her narrative she is the one that is being harassed or that her life is in danger.

Claire called the police by dialing 111. She claimed there were four men with firearms. I was not there this night to witness this; however, I do believe Peter Benson and Dylan Watson and also what the police told them, and we did not believe Claire and Craig's account. This was a refreshing change when others were involved also on the receiving end as this just proves a point that Claire makes up stuff that involves other people like the kindergarten, my solicitor, and now Peter and Dylan. Also the police were being involved in many incidents along with the times that 111 emergency calls were made, surely it would raise concerns.

This incident was documented in various reports in relation to the up-and-coming custody hearing. Yes, surprisingly, there were different versions of this incident that was reported by Peter and Dylan as well as Claire and Craig's account of things.

This is also why it happened. I filed for divorce in December 1975 on the grounds of her adulterous relationship with Craig. Rather than pay a process server, my good friends Peter Benson and Dylan Watson offered to serve the papers to Claire and Craig. Now as I have said, I was not there, so I can only go on what both Peter and Dylan told me. They both went around to their house in New Lynn to serve the divorce papers. The drama unfolded that night when both of them came back and told me what happened. It just goes to the point I made many times before that they are either paranoid, deranged, and create situations to suit their own agenda.

So what did take place? Peter and Dylan arrived at their place, just the two of them. They parked their car on the side of the road. Lights were on in the house. It looked like they were home. They walked up the pathway to the front door and knocked on the door. There was no answer. Dylan knocked again, no answer. They then waited a few minutes, still no answer. They both went and looked into the garage. They could see through the gap alongside the sliding door. They did see the two cars parked in the garage. With that as there was no answer, they decided to go and park down the road as they planned to come back later. So they both sat in Dylan's car and waited.

They were hoping someone would come out from the house, and now where they parked was down the road also, and they had a clear view of the driveway of the house.

As they were waiting, they did see a police car drive along the street with its lights flashing. This was around fifteen minutes after they left their house. They then decided to go back. What happened next, you could not make this up, it is so damn ridiculous. They pulled up outside their house, and the police car was parked in the driveway. Claire and Craig we talking to the police, so they thought it was a great opportunity to serve the papers.

They walked up to where the police were talking to both Claire and Craig, and the policeman asked Dylan, "What are you guys doing here?"

He told the police, "We want to serve these paper to Mrs. Mason and Mr. Kelly." The police asked, "Were you both here before?"

Dylan said, "Yes, we were before, and we knocked on the door, and they did not answer. We waited a few minutes and knocked again, no answer. So we looked inside the garage, and we could see through the small gap alongside of the sliding door, so we knew they were home."

At this point, Craig took off into the bedroom. Dylan handed the police officer the divorce petition papers, and the officer said to Claire, "You must accept this." He then called out, "Mr. Kelly, you must also come out of the bedroom and accept these papers."

With that, the papers were duly served on them.

The policeman said to Dylan and Peter, "Please wait by the car as I need to speak to you both." They waited for a few minutes, then the two policemen came down. What they told Dylan and Peter was that they received a hysterical 111 call from Mrs. Mason. She said, "There are four men at the house, and they have firearms. They have knocked on our front door, rattled all the windows as well as the back door." She also claimed that she was here on her own.

Dylan said, "That is not true! We came here to serve the divorce papers, and also there is only two of us. There were two cars in the garage as we did see them in there."

The police officer said that Claire was on her own and Mr. Kelly was down at the shops. Dylan said this was rubbish. "After we left, we parked down the road. We had a clear view of

the house, and no one left the house or came in until you arrived." The police officer said, "Mrs. Mason said you had firearms."

Dylan said, "That is rubbish, she is paranoid. Where did she get that from? You can search our car if you like."

The police said, "No need to as I can see why you are here."

Dylan said, "Mr. Kelly, he was there for sure all the time. He is not telling you the truth. They both panicked when we turned up. Claire was not home alone."

The police said they would go back and talk to Mrs. Mason and advise her of the serious nature of making false calls, in particular about firearms.

With that, Dylan and Peter came back to my place and told me how this all unfolded. Dylan said, "Let's have a toast to a job well done as the papers were served courtesy of the Henderson Police. The look on their faces when it was discovered that we were not armed as we were there only to serve the papers, this told me what stupid people you're dealing with here."

The story they told to the police also calling 111 was a common occurrence throughout the whole dispute I had with Claire and Craig, along with the lies and false allegations as part of her ongoing agenda. Now independent people like Dylan and Peter have experienced this firsthand themselves, as well as my boarder Jim Baxter and others. This backs up what I have been saying all along, that they fabricate and exaggerate and make up stories, such as this incident involving Peter and Dylan having firearms and Claire calling 111. The same also applies to Claire's family, in particularly the mother as she has called 111 on a few occasions, and I just hope the justice system can see through all these false reports and exaggerations.

My lawyer Mrs. Chamberlain did receive a report from Claire's lawyer on this incident, and she then spoke to the police involved. It was established that a 111 call was made, as well Mrs. Mason said that there were four men, and also they were armed. She also said she was on her own, which was later proven she was not.

Dylan and Peter's account of this incident was the correct one. Claire was told by the police to stop making false allegations, and she was severely warned on this occasion.

Was this the end of Claire's outrageous and exaggerated claims? I do not think so.

# 25

# MEETING DEPARTMENT OF SOCIAL WELFARE

My lawyer told me at some point that the Welfare people will come to my place. She also warned me, "Be very careful of what you say as they do have a reputation of favoring the mothers. Maybe not in your case, however, be careful."

I thought these were wise words. The thought of the child welfare department coming to the house brought back memories when I lost my father. I was only seven years old, and I remember how they tried to take me and my brothers and sisters away from my mother. I always did not have too much faith in the system after that. Have things changed? Years later on in another country, I was soon to find out.

It was around 7:30 a.m. on a Monday, and as usual, I was getting Oliver ready for the day. There was a knock on the front door. There was a well-dressed lady with a man standing at the door. They introduced themselves that they were from the Department of Social Welfare and asked if they could come in. They were very nice and also polite. They said they were ordered from the court to speak to me and undertake a report. "This will be a brief visit. Also, we would like to see Oliver. We also would like to have a look around."

I said, "You're welcome to." I told them I was preparing breakfast for Oliver, so I walked back into the kitchen. One of them came in and said, "What are you preparing?"

I said, "Some porridge as Oliver loved porridge. That is a good starter for him."

They had a good look around. They did say hello to Oliver. They seemed satisfied and said, "We will call you later in the week to have an interview with you at our main headquarters in Otahuhu, at the Southern Region Head Office."

I said, "Okay, that's fine with me."

They left. In all, they did stay around about thirty minutes.

I was not prepared for the visit as they came, I suppose, to catch you off guard, As always I had the house spic and span. Oliver was well dressed, so I could not think of anything that they may have disliked.

Oliver said to me, "The lady asked me do I miss my mum."

I said to Oliver, "What did you say?" He said, "I don't remember."

I did not say any more to Oliver as I am not sure what they said to him or what Oliver said to them.

Later in the week, I had the phone call from the department of welfare. I had to front up at their headquarters in Otahuhu, South Auckland. Before the interview, I called my lawyer. She told me, "Be incredibly careful what you say. Keep your cool as the welfare department is well known for mothers to keep their children."

I said, "Don't fathers get a say too?"

"Yes, in your case, you will get your chance, but that does not mean they will agree with you. Just be careful," she said.

It was around 3:00 p.m. on Thursday when I arrived at the Department of Social Welfare and introduced myself. I was taken into a room where there were two ladies. One was the one who came to the house earlier in the week. Then another one came into the room. He was the South Auckland director of Child Welfare. *Gee,* I thought, *this may be an interrogation as three people to interview me.* The questions started off reasonably well, such as are you coping alright, is the boy happy, what do I do as far as work vs. time spent with Oliver. These types of questions went on for around an hour. Then the tone shifted.

"We have interviewed the mother of Oliver." They did not say my ex-wife. They also mentioned her new husband, Craig.

I said to them, "They are not married yet." "But they said they intend to."

I said, "Well, that is their business, not mine. What Claire does now is her business, not mine." They said to me, "They do not paint a particularly good picture of you."

"Why is that?" I asked. "Nothing would surprise me at all with what they say. You are doing the interview, so you tell me. It was Claire who left Oliver, not me."

They said, "Did you plan to kill Oliver?"

I said, "This is outrageous. What utter nonsense. That is rubbish! You honestly believe such accusations?" At that point, I got a bit hot under the collar. I said, "Do you honestly believe what they say? They concocted this story to benefit her own case. Do I look like a deranged person wanting to kill my son? Furthermore, I am not happy with your line of questioning. Did you ask the police? They were called that day. In fact, at the same time when Claire phoned the police, Mr. Kelly turned up at the same time at the police station. Don't you think that was odd, one calling triple 000 and the other arriving at the police station? More than a coincidence, wouldn't you think? I have no doubt Claire created this to better her chances at the custody hearing. I am telling you, these allegations have been investigated by the police. Did you discuss this with the police?"

They did not answer this. I was convinced they had not.

I added, "Oliver was well and safe, and in fact, Oliver was in the lounge eating an ice block and watching his favorite cartoon show when the police arrived." I thought to myself, *They are not taking my word for any of this.*

They were taking down many notes. Then they changed the subject to another matter. They then said to me, "You attacked her husband?"

I said again, "He is her lover. They are not married. You keep calling him Claire's husband. I am not going to deny that I had an altercation with Mr. Kelly. He got what he deserved as he was the one with Claire that broke up our marriage. Anyway, check with the police report as no charges were laid. Now if I was as bad as you claim what Claire and Craig have said about me, then why have I not been charged? You know why? Because what you hear is not the whole story. It's concocted hearsay."

At this point, I was more than convinced the welfare people got sucked in by Claire and Craig as they went to the brick incident. They said to me, "What about when you threw a brick right through Mr. Kelly's front car window?"

"I see. This is what they told you? Yes, I did, but did they tell you also that he tried to run me over as then his car mounted the footpath, and his car sped right at me? I bet they didn't. Was the police called? No, you know why? Because his car tire marks were right across the footpath." I got very agitated.

Then they said, "Mr. Kelly was robbed, and you were the main suspect."

I said, "This is getting ridiculous. This also was investigated by the police. It was established I was at work at the time the robbery took place. I am not happy with your one-sided view here. I feel you people are not doing your job." I got very defensive with them and said to them, "You better get some of your facts right. Everything you have said to me since I have been here is so inaccurate and also a one-sided view." I knew then this interview was not going well.

Then they asked, "Why should you have custody of your son?"

I quickly put it back to them, "Can you give me a good reason why not? I am the father of Oliver. I love him, he loves me. Also, he has been with me now for well over twelve months. In fact, when the case is heard in the Supreme Court, it will nearly be eighteen months. My objection is when the time comes when Claire remarries, in my opinion, Craig is not a fit person to be the father figure in Oliver's life.

"In your interview with Craig Kelly, did you ask why he left his first wife? He also had an affair with a young seventeen-year-old girl, whom he got pregnant. This is a well-known fact. Did you also find out Craig Kelly was involved in stock taken from a robbery where he worked and was also fired from his work?

"The problem I see with your interview is that there are many allegations about me, but nothing has been said about the harassment I have experienced with Claire, the phone calls, the calling around late at night, accusing me as having an affair. I suggest you talk to the people on my side who will be called in as witnesses. One in particular is the head of the kindergarten, Mrs. Tuohy. She can tell you how Oliver is getting along at the center."

I then handed them a list of people they should interview who are on my side. I said to them, "It is a known fact the welfare department favors the mother in custody matters. I understand fully what the law is, however, things must change, and you should not believe all you are told. There is always two sides to any story. Don't be taken in by Claire, Craig, and her family. Blood is thicker than water."

They just looked at each other. They did not respond. Then they said to me, "We will undertake a thorough investigation. We resent your remarks as we do not take sides. We do our work to the letter of the law."

I said, "Yes, you may, but it seems to me you have honed in on certain incidents. One in particular is that I was going to harm Oliver. If you seriously believe that, then I am wasting my time here and yours. As to what I can see here, you have already made your mind up as it is. The line of questioning sure shows that."

I tried hard to avoid in the interview not to speak ill of Claire as they would use that against me. I did not trust them. The allegations they grilled me on told me that they will not be supporting me. Most of the interview was all about what Claire and Craig and what her family told them. God knows who else they spoke to.

I said to them, "I do not think for a minute the mother of Oliver should have her son. She chose to have an affair, left our family home, left Oliver, her son, behind."

They fired back quickly, interrupting me, saying, "She did not take her son with her as you threatened her."

I then saw red. "You're just as bloody stupid as she is if you believe these allegations. Oh yeah? That is what she told you? I am sorry, she is a damn liar. She is a very vindictive person. You must then believe all that rubbish, or you would not have brought that up. I never ever once laid a hand on her, threatened her, never have spoken a bad word to Oliver about his mother. I provided well, gave them a new home. I bloody well worked hard to do all that. I did take on extra work to make sure I gave them a good home. I also did most of the cooking." At this point, I got very emotional and said, "I suppose all this accounts for nothing. It was months after she left that she applied for an interim custody order. the magistrate awarded that to me. Was that no coincidence? Oliver is my child, and as far as I am concerned, he stays with me. I will fight this all the way. I have looked after Oliver for nearly twelve months. I am the father figure in his life, and I intend it staying that way. I suggest you people do a bit more research on this. You then interview people on my list, and you will then get a more balanced view as to date, in my opinion, you have not done a good job as it's all on Claire's side. There is always two sides to any story. All the people that my barrister is bringing in as witnesses will tell you their account of many incidents. I do not tell any of my friends what to say or not to say. They tell the truth. Truth accounts for a lot. I know I am not totally innocent, but when you're under constant harassment, allegations made against you, police coming around, then Oliver is the one that suffers the most here. The fact of the matter is 'the welfare of the child is paramount.' If he goes with his mother, then he will be disadvantaged in many ways, as he has his friends at kindergarten, and a lot will go to school the following year from the kindergarten, he has a well-kept home, I provide well for him. These are the important things for the child."

With that, they concluded the interview, which went for over two hours. It was a grilling, no doubt, and when I left, I had a horrible feeling this was not looking good.

The next morning, I had an appointment to see my lawyer. I told her about the interview I had with the welfare department, including their visit to the house earlier that week.

She said, "I do not think you have the welfare on your side. They will have to also interview all your witnesses that will be at the hearing. Like I've told you many times, you have a huge mountain to climb. Then what you have now told me about this interview with the welfare really concerns me, as well as justifies my point of view."

It was now weeks away before the custody hearing, and we had our case prepared as there were statements and affidavits for our side we submitted along with answering affidavits from Claire's side. Claire's side made a range of damning claims against me as to my ability to have custody of my son, although there were many trumped-up claims. Some were legitimate to a point as they were, in my opinion, provoked or they were planned to make me the villain. It became obvious to us that Claire was very cunning and calculated in what she was doing. It came to the point that she was paranoid, and she would do anything to destroy me.

I often thought how someone you once loved and also cared for turns to such hatred. Claire was, in many ways, a convincing liar. She made situations worse than they really were. I think in her own mind, she believed it all to be true, as well as convincing others like her mother and father that it is all true.

The critical factor is that I was hoping to get a fair hearing, hoping the judge will see through what Claire and her cronies have conjured up. I do understand very well that the odds were not in my favor one bit. I am also sure Claire's lawyer has told her that the child under five goes with the mother, that she is in the prime position. This was also told to me by my lawyer.

My lawyer said, "Danial, as the law stands, it does not favor the fathers. Your faith and determination will go a long way."

Then I thought to myself, *I have a very astute, clever lawyer.* I looked back in what she did at the Magistrates' Court when I was awarded interim custody. I am not sure what she will do at the hearing. Also, I will go into the court the underdog, but I will put up a good fight for justice. Fathers are just as capable looking after their children as the mothers.

This night, I had Jonathon around for dinner. He brought his two lovely girls along. After dinner, we were in the lounge having a chat. The girls were down in Oliver's room playing with his train set. Then Jonathon told me this horrific story. What he told me made me sick, and this comes back to fathers having rights to have custody of their children. In this case, they got it 100 percent wrong. The welfare and also the courts got it so wrong.

Without going into the court case details, it's important to highlight that the father was applying for custody of two little girls. They were both under five. He told the court that he had evidence that the mother of the girls was mentally impaired, very unstable. He lost the case, and the tragedy of this was the night the mother was awarded custody, she killed the two girls and cut them up with a razor blade. The law should hold their heads in shame. This was a clear case the father should have had custody of his two little girls. He had evidence and witnesses to his claims but was dismissed. Hearing this alarmed me. Again put things into perspective as to what I am up against. I looked at Jonathon. "This is not right."

He replied, "Danial, I am afraid you are up against the law. You are among many who face the same problem. This poor man had all the evidence about his wife's mental state, but between the welfare and the judge, he was not allowed to have custody." Jonathon also told me that this man was a very good person as he knew him personally. He finished up a broken man as one would expect. The issue now that confronts me is knowing all this and also the circumstances of what the court decision was and also the welfare submitting to the court the mother is best to have custody, it does not give me much hope at all.

Therefore, groups like Families Need Fathers, they fight for the fathers' rights and support and counselling them in custody and access matters or have equal access to their children and the stories told by these groups such as FNF is heartbreaking.

## Letter from Claire's Legal Firm

This letter came to me in 1975. This was from her new lawyer. She changed solicitors after losing the case at the Magistrates' Court last December.

It said,

> We have been instructed to act for your wife, Ms. Claire Mason. She instructs us that she recently left home and that you refused to allow her to take her son, Oliver Kevin Mason, with her.
>
> After that, she has instructed us that you have refused her access to the boy. She also has instructed us you have been violent toward her.
>
> We also write to advise you that your wife is content to for the time being at least that you should retain custody of Oliver provided she is allowed regular and reasonable access to him.
>
> If you persist in denying access her access we are instructed forthwith to apply for custody of Oliver and failing custody being awarded o her then at least a court order for access.
>
> If you wish you can discuss this with your solicitor urgently and ask him to be in touch with the writer.

I did hand this to Ms. Chamberlain, and I said, "Claire has not told them about my solicitor. Also they assumed you were male."

*Decree Nisi*

It was June 1975 when the application for divorce was granted. It was also stated it would become absolute in twelve months. At this brief hearing, which was set down for divorce hearing, Claire tried to pull a stunt by adding custody of Oliver to her submission. This was denied. The presiding judge awarded her liberal access, which was every second weekend.

The access arrangement was that Claire pick up Oliver on Saturday morning every second week at 9:00 a.m., then return the boy on Sunday at 6:00 p.m.

This was the agreement. She claimed that she brought him back on Saturday nights or sometimes Sunday mornings, which was not correct.

Access was an issue all the time as she would turn up early to take him and to expect him to be ready, or she would bring him back late. Then there were the unannounced visits when he was well in bed asleep.

It was unfortunate that what she told her legal advisors on many incidents could not be substantiated, and they did not check her stories.

The allegations about me not allowing her to take Oliver and also I threatened her and later was going to murder my son were all fabricated. How does one prove who is telling the truth in these matters?

This was gearing up to be a hotly disputed custody case.

# 26

# STATEMENT FROM WITNESSES

There were many affidavits and testimonies put forward as these were an important part of the up- and-coming court case, and all these that I deemed as statement of facts. They were made by each person that provided an integral part of the up-and-coming court hearing. All will be questioned also cross-examined on what they have put in these statements. I am sure some did not look at this point of view being cross-examined. This applied to statements and evidence made by Claire, her mother, and other family members, not forgetting Craig Kelly.

You will find they were just repeating each other. On many points they were either hearsay or just outright lies. The statements were all submitted well before the custody hearing, bar one, which I was compelled to undertake another statement because of all the allegations that were put in statements by Claire and others. I just needed hopefully to set the record straight.

I had many people who would testify on my behalf, and each person was interviewed individually by my lawyer. I was not present at any of these interviews. I was not privy to any information until they were all lodged at the court when my lawyer had them served on Claire's lawyer. I then was allowed to read each one.

Ms. Chamberlain said, "You have some genuinely nice people that are prepared to support you. This looks incredibly positive."

Then the testimonies came pouring in from Claire's lawyer. I said to my lawyer, "There are so many things that are just not true, and that concerns me greatly. A lot of rubbish."

"Indeed," my lawyer said. "Yes, however, again they do not paint a good picture of you. These sworn statements will play a significant part in the court hearing, and you will find a lot of the evidence provided to the court will not be mentioned or contested or not even cross-examined. The judge, however, has all copies of sworn statements, so he will have a better understanding of what is put to the court. This also assists him with his final judgment. He may even ask witnesses questions, and this will include yourself and Claire. You have to be prepared."

I spent several hours at home preparing my statement, and once this has been gone through by my lawyer, she will amend and put this into a declaration of facts, which will be sworn at the court.

## My Statement

I said the usual requirements like my name, where I live. I stated I was seeking an order granting me custody of Oliver Kevin Mason, born in December 1971.

> My wife left the family home on May 18th, 1975. Since she had left my son Oliver has been with me.
>
> Since Claire left, I have tried to concentrate on what is best for Oliver. I passionately believe Oliver is better off with me. Oliver is happy with me contrary to what they say.
>
> In November 1975, my then wife filed proceedings in the Magistrates Court seeking custody of Oliver. At the same time, I filed proceedings seeking Interim Custody of Oliver. This was granted in my favor. Since then, Oliver has remained in my care. It is in the child's best interest that he does so. I have provided an amazingly comfortable

home than the respondent, Mr. Craig Kelly. Our home is fully equipped and carpeted and specially heated for Oliver's benefit. Oliver has his own room, his own toys. Our home is close to James and Fiona McDonald. His Aunty Fiona looks after Oliver during the afternoons when she picks him up from kindergarten.

It has been said that I do not devote enough time is just hearsay. The movie business I have people working for me, I organise my work around Oliver. I have the time to devote time spent with Oliver in the evenings also weekends. It's important that I organize his leisure so that he has a variety of interests and activities.

The difference I believe with Claire as to Oliver's upbringing that I fear will be neglected is his religious training, as I am a member of the local church also. He had been enrolled into the Sunday School, which he has been attending for some time now. I take him when I have him on alternate Sundays, also to my knowledge, Claire does not.

Our home is close to Oliver's grandparents, Mr. and Ms. Kevin McDonald. All his friends live by and play with him at our home or their respective homes. He attends kindergarten, which is close by, where he is happy and settled. He is happy with me, and I believe would prefer to be with me rather than his mother. Oliver is not yet five and at his age will at the age tries to please whichever parent he is with at the time. In saying that, I believe from what he says to me he would prefer to be with me. He has expressed many times dislike as to the co-respondent, Mr. Kelly. For lots of reason I feel he should not be the person involved with my son. He left his wife and daughter, also had a previous affair while with his wife. This resulted in a paternity suit with a young girl he supposedly got pregnant.

I have a great working relationship with the company I work for, Crest Foods. I can organize my work to fit in with Oliver's movements, and once he starts school this will become much easier. The school he will be attending is near to where we live, 5 minutes walking distance. As to my well-being, my life is a more stable one than Claire. I know what I want and where I am going. The same cannot be said for Claire. It is only natural Oliver is well cared for. I attend to all the usual tasks incidental to looking after him, such as cooking, washing, cleaning, ironing, as well all the housework. The house we live in is very modern, extremely easy to keep clean, it is well equipped with modern-day labor-saving devices.

Despite of what a lot has been said by his mother and others that I do not devote enough time is just hearsay. the movie business I have people working for me, I organise my work around Oliver, I have the time to devote time spent with him in the evenings also weekends, it's important that I organize his leisure so that he has a variety of interests and activities.

The company Crest Foods that I have worked for some six years now, I have a very sound future with the company. I earn a very good salary. This ensures that I have sufficient money to support us both comfortably. This is especially important as having a new home and a safe job, along with a part-time business that makes my life extremely comfortable.

My observation about all this is due to Oliver's mother and the conflict that has been placed upon my boy Oliver as he has been terribly upset by it all. This has resulted in the misbehaving more than usual and also being sick more than he should.

At this point, what I want now as I am very anxious that the matter of custody of Oliver be resolved to make sure he has certainty in his life that has been turned upside down. He has become more disturbed than he should be. The love of my son is what is what has made me seek custody of my son. The mother has rights to see her son, which I do not dispute. What I do dispute is that she left her son for someone else. She has made my life since she left a misery with her continuous outrages. This has made me want more than ever to fight in what I believe is right. I fully understand the law as it stands that a child under five goes with the mother. I know that I have one hell of a battle on my hands. I am prepared to fight for my rights as a father.

My affidavit was later submitted to Claire's lawyer as well as duly sworn in at the court. It was not surprising it triggered a chain reaction from Claire and her family, including Craig. It was obvious they all got together and submitted remarkably similar statements. The lawyer she obtained amused me as he allowed them to submit so many unfounded allegations, hearsay, all in a copycat nature. I am sure when you read their responses, you will agree. My lawyer said to me, "They all paint a very bad picture of you." She did not at this point agree or disagree what I said. I think she will somehow sort their allegations out to what is right or wrong. Then she said, "Let us go through what they have to say. Look at your wife's first as this is remarkably interesting indeed."

We both went through her declaration of facts she submitted. There were many things that we will challenge, I am sure.

## Claire Mason's Statement

He statements started with the usual, by stating her name, where she lived. She also said she is in an adulterous relationship with Craig Kelly, and also they plan to remarry after the divorce settlement.

She states that when she left the matrimonial home, Oliver stayed with her mother for the first six weeks after she had left.

Oliver had remained in the father's care by force since I left in May 1975, the respondent constantly called around where I lived, he abused myself and Mr. Kelly, Danial would create a most unpleasant scene. One time Danial came to our home in New Lynn when he kicked in the front door also smashed the lounge window.

Even though Oliver has been with his father he spends much of his time at either my parents or at my brother James his uncle and his Aunty Fiona.

In no way it is in Oliver's best interest that he stays with his father and his current situation is far from stable. Whilst Oliver may have his own room and toys with Danial the same is duplicated in the home unit which I now live in. The house is new also quite modern, Oliver has his own room with his own toys that we have brought for him,

I know that other children in the area are pinching all his toys and clothes.

I have concerns about the kindergarten where Oliver attends, I do not know  if Oliver is genuinely happy at kindergarten, I was told that other child bash him up. I also know the kindergarten staff told Oliver he has not a mother, this is very distressing for him.

Oliver is not happy being with his father as he expresses a desire to be with me. I also believe that when Oliver says he wants to be with his father it is said out of fear. Danial keeps asking Oliver who he wants to be with, but I do not ask this question. Oliver gets on well with Craig Kelly, and I have never known Danial to organize his work to fit in Oliver's movements, I am sure to the best of my knowledge this is the case.

Danial claims that he cooks meals for Oliver, however when I see Oliver, he usually has had takeaway meals or pre-cooked meals.

When I have access to Oliver his ironing never is done, he usually comes to me in unclean clothes. In fact, what I usually send him home wearing, she said the next time I see him still wearing the same clothes. I get so upset to see Oliver so dirty every time I have access to him. His body, hair and clothes need to be well washed. There was a time when I had to call the police because Danial threatened to murder Oliver and me, When I left the matrimonial home Danial threatened me

and would not let me take Oliver with me

Danial still shows movies, also he shows lots of movies in the home cinema he set up in the garage, a lot of these movies are classified as restricted or adults only, I know Danial allows Oliver to watch these movies.

I have not been able to take Oliver to Sunday School as after exercising week- end access, as I usually must have Oliver returned by me either Saturday night or early Sunday morning.

Daniel is very hostile toward her, his attitude makes Oliver extremely uncomfortable "I never like to see trouble to be shown in front of Oliver as he usually gets upset, Oliver does not misbehave with me" If Oliver is being naughty when he is with his Father surely this would show that he is rebelling against the Father,

I am upset to read that Oliver is being sick and I believe this must be as the result of the tension under which he is placed.

I have wanted for over a year now for this matter to be settled. There is no possibility of reconciliation between me and Danial, despite overtures to the effect, I was terribly upset when Danial received interim custody, I am now glad this matter is near conclusion.

Once the decree Absolute in divorce is obtained, I propose to marry Craig Kelly.

I said to Mrs. Chamberlain after going through the statement, "She comes across as very convincing. A lot she has stated is hearsay and fantasy in her mind. She has convinced herself in many things she states as true and believes these things did take place. For instance, she claims I was going to murderer Oliver. I stopped her from leaving and taking Oliver when he was not at home that day. He was with his mother, and on it goes. I think we should break for a coffee as this is really getting to me."

We did have a short break, then I said, "Let us go through what Mr. Kelly has to say."

*Statement by Craig Kelly.*

He stated his name and address, that he was the person behind the marriage breakup, and he left with Claire Mason in May1975.

> I left my own wife and daughter then at 13 Years of age.
>
> Danial Mason was given interim custody in December 1975 and leading up to this hearing and for several months he had indicated to Claire and other members of the family that he proposed to take Oliver back to Australia and neither Claire nor the members of her family would see them again.
>
> Oliver has remained in the father's purported care for some time now but seems to spend a considerable amount of his time either at his aunt and Uncles house, or at kindergarten or at his grandmother's house, sometimes with his father.
>
> I disagree that the home in which Oliver is living in is more comfortable than our home, as he has his own bedroom, has his own toys we brought for him, as to the

general home improvements that Danial referred to and the special heating by placing of "Batts" in the ceiling and this was done by way of general improvements rather than consideration for Oliver.

Daniel lives close to his brother and sister-in-law that is James and Fiona McDonald who do look after Oliver often, I do know his aunty Fiona does not look after him every day after he has been to kindergarten as Daniel often takes Oliver with him to his work and on his rounds.

Oliver has told him he does not have very many friends in the area where he lives, he also told us he is bashed up at Kindergarten, I am also aware that he has many of his toys and his clothing stolen by other children in the neighborhood.

I have been in Oliver's presence on many occasions when he has indicated to his mother that he would prefer to be with her and showed some contempt to his father, he has never showed a dislike to me in fact we get on well together, I have never known Daniel to organize his work to fit in with Oliver's movements.

Daniel states the school he refers to is not at the end of their street. The school where Oliver now lives is some five minutes away and he would have to cross a main road and would not be safe to walk back to his aunt's place. Where we live there are safe school crossings, and in walking distance from our house.

Claire and I have an extremely happy relationship and we have been together for over 12 Months now; this union has remained strong despite much criticism we have received and considerable abuse that has been forthcoming from Danial as he has created many situations, Oliver is not well cared for by his father and it was necessary for us to purchase clothes for Oliver, if we sent him away in those clothes, we never saw them again or when he came to us, he was wearing the same clothes but in a much dirtier condition. I never have known Danial to iron Oliver's clothes, if he washed them, he does this so quickly that no one would tell the difference.

I have on many occasions I have seen Oliver with either take-away or pre-packed food and not good home cooking which a young child should be receiving. Daniel shows a great deal of movies to his friends, some are which are in the restricted category and quite often he has parties where drink is consumed, and Oliver is present at these movies and parties.

About Oliver attending Sunday School has only been only a recent innovation by Daniel me, Claire has never been able to take Oliver to Church or Sunday School as the Petitioner always has him back in his custody either by Saturday night or early Sunday morning.

I am disturbed that Oliver is misbehaving with his father and that Oliver is rebelling against his him, I am also disturbed that Oliver is being sick more than he should be, this results from the nervous tension in which he is placed under, and his father has contributed to this.

I am further disturbed that over the past twelve months Daniels behaviour as he has been involved in several assaults, he came one Saturday afternoon Daniel came into my work, assaulted me, he ripped my shirt and later in June he came into the Sales Office where I worked and hit me in the face.

I am not if it was either July or August that Daniel grabbed me by the back of the neck, and he hit me against the back of a truck on which I was working. Then Danial threw a brick through my car window, one day he climbed into the cab of my truck and started beating me about the face, while we were staying at the flat in New Lynn he smashed into the front door and broke the lounge window, unfortunately Oliver witnessed this.

There were occasion's when we have been driving along the road with Oliver in the back seat and his father has come out of nowhere pulled alongside and dragged Oliver from the car.

My response is I will say repeatedly that yes, I did things wrong at times, but by God, I was provoked in many ways and harassed, and lucky for me, I had good people on my side.

After going through Craig's statement, my solicitor said that he will have his day in court, then he will have to justify his allegations against me. I said, "A lot is his word against mine. Over my dead body Craig will have my son. I swear to that as he is not the right person to bring up my son." However, in saying all that, Mrs. Chamberlain said to me, "He has made very serious allegations against you. Yes, I agree, but when you go through Claire's statement and now Craig's, what does

it tell you? They are nearly word for word."

"As far as the allegations, most of them are bloody lies and made-up stories as a number of them simply did not happen." I was really fired up about this and emotionally upset, and I said, "For example, how would he know what food I gave Oliver, even to the point about takeaway food? How would he know if Oliver goes to work with me or not? This all just hearsay and copycat stuff." I was really fired up as this guy Craig made my blood boil.

It is without any doubt Craig has repeated and again what Claire has told him to say. Yes, I am very angry over all this.

Mrs. Chamberlain listened to me explaining my side. I said, About Oliver not being clean, and the clothes he wears to kindergarten are stolen, and the toys issue is just bunkum. No children have taken his clothes or toys, where do they get all this from? The other point about Oliver being bashed up at kindergarten, how would he know this? It is a slant on the kindergarten and their integrity. It is simply not true. If it were, I would have heard about this by now, such behavior would not be tolerated at the kindergarten. Also me being president, no one mentioned that to me. Mrs. Tuohy, the head person, would be the first to tell me.

"As to Oliver going to Sunday school, this has been going on for over twelve months now, and if you recall, it was when I went to church, and Oliver went to Sunday school. By sheer luck and faith I found you. As to Claire not taking him to Sunday school, I think the roof of the church would cave in if she walked in.

"As to bringing him back Saturday night or early Sunday morning, again this is BS. When Claire has Oliver on weekends, it was standard that she pick him at around 9:00 a.m. on the Saturday and returned him on Sunday evening around 6:00 p.m.

"The assaults and incidents, there was only one at his workplace, and the police investigated this and no charges laid as there were no witnesses. The brick-throwing did take place, but it was Craig driving not his brother-in-law as he claims. The incidents with his truck are all fabricated and straight-out lies. I have never seen his truck he is talking about. I can assure you, Mrs. Chamberlain, I know I am not innocent in some incidents, but surely they must be able to substantiate their claims, and I just hope the judge can see through their consistent line of attack on me."

Mrs. Chamberlain said, "Just settle down, and Craig and all the others will have their day in court, and then this becomes far different from what they put in their statements and what they say or come out with when they are in court. The judge is no fool. He can see through people's evidence if it is fabricated or hearsay or the truth. You have to expect you're the prime target and must trust the court to decide on what evidence they present, if it is fabricated or not. I told you many times your ex-wife will stop at nothing."

Mrs. Chamberlain's words were right. It had to be left up to the court to decide what is the truth from the fiction. Nevertheless, it was very frustrating and concerning what they all conjured up between themselves.

Then we decided to go through Rose's statement. No guessing it was on the same old pattern with what Claire and Craig presented. It was well scripted.

I said to Mrs. Chamberlain that I had doubts about Claire's lawyer, Mr. Wadsworth, as he has allowed all the statements presented, which is just hearsay or fabricated or downright lies, and he has allowed them without question to make outrageous claims against me. No doubt all what has been said is to make Claire's evidence that much stronger. It's very strange indeed to allow so much hearsay, along with accounts of things that they were not present, like what food you give him or giving him takeaway food.

"These are some that will be contested among a lot of other remarks made," said Mrs. Chamberlain. "Now let us look at Rose's statement."

I said, "I bet this will be a good one just like the rest."

## Statement of Rose McDonald

My name is Rose McDonald and at the time I was to make this statement it has caused me a considerable amount of stress between me and Danial Mason, he threatened me at the time that if I were going to give evidence in support of my daughters that I would be deprived of any opportunity of seeing my grandson again, the petitioner Mr. Mason has deprived me from seeing my grandson at all.

Oliver remained in my care for at least the first six weeks. My Daughter Claire did not desert her son as when I had him his mother would see him at my home, the chores that Danial has indicated I have completed many of these. It is my belief that it is not in the child's best interest he remains with the father, Oliver's toys at their house have either been ruined or neglected and for example his bike has been left outside for so long is has been allowed to rust.

His Father takes him to work often, I also understand he sleeps with his Father and that he is being beaten up at kindergarten, also he does not have any friends if he has any friends, they would not be regarded as real friends.

When Oliver is in my presence or in the presence of any other person, he does not show considerable affection to his father, but when he is with his mother this is the only time, I see Oliver hug and kiss his mother and show any affection to any other person, we did everything for Oliver, he had most of his meals at our place, I did all the washing and ironing. Daniel does not s not even possess an iron.

I do understand Danial is a particularly good cook I also understand he has quite a few guests attending at his house and would cook good meals for them. During the daytime when Oliver is at kindergarten, my daughter-in-law gives him lunch and occasionally his father brings home fish and chips, which is an inappropriate meal for a child of this age.

Daniel on three to four nights of week he shows movies, on most occasions, he has Oliver up all hours of the night, I as well as my daughter-in-law Fiona, Danial in the past as a matter of convenience when he wanted to go to parties or things of this nature we had to look after Oliver. I have noticed that he is s drinking quite heavily when these parties are held, it also disturbs me Oliver is also allowed to attend such parties.

Danial on many occasions threatened to return to Australia and we do not see Oliver again, I know he does borrow money from everyone, I do not think he is in a particularly good financial position, also he has nothing in the bank as savings,   I have given him money at various times to buy meals and support him properly.

There was an incident that occurred at New Market Park on that day my husband and I together with my daughter-in-law and her child attended a soccer game where my son was playing, unfortunately, Danial came to the park and a disturbance occurred.

He punched my husband on the jaw and threatened and abused me and use all the foul language under the sun. When we were in the car park, Danial also tried to run us down with his car. Oliver punched his father to stop, I have never seen Oliver so upset. In the past we had taken a kindly attitude toward Danial, it has changed now. Since this incident, Danial has not allowed me to see Oliver at all, if I want to see him it is when I go to the daughters-in-law place when I know Oliver spends considerable time at her place.

As to Oliver being sick, he always was a sickly child, but he also becomes emotionally upset, I am aware that Daniel threatens my daughter all the time and he has caused considerable amount of uneasiness in our family. Sometimes Daniel can be the nicest of persons, but other times his mind goes, and he becomes completely irrational about his domestic affairs.

This is also coupled with his stubborn behavior; I am overly concerned for Oliver's welfare, and I wish only the best to be done for him.

After going through Rose's statement, I said to Mrs. Chamberlain, "She had said so many things, as did Claire and Craig, which was basically word for word. She stated about the toys at our house as she said they are either ruined or neglected, and for example, his bike has been left outside for so long, it has been allowed to rust. She said her son James and his wife Fiona, who live close by to the petitioner, look after him most days, and the petitioner also takes him to work often. Unless she is told, how does she know all this?"

The fish and chips incident, Craig also brought this up. I supposedly gave this to Oliver. I always thought fish was a nutritious item. If I have fish, I cook it myself anyway. I could go on.

Mrs. Chamberlain said to me, "Your mother-in-law has made some serious allegations against you."

I replied back, "Again, what does this tell you? Does it not surprise you she said nearly word for word what her daughter Claire and Craig has already said in their statements?"

I fully understand my lawyer was not happy at all with the submissions made against me, like the old saying "Throw enough mud, and it will stick." I felt very uneasy. No doubt to this point, you can see there is so much they have stated, there is no way in the world they would know that. For example, the comments relating to Oliver going to Sunday school, his mother could not take him to the kindergarten, also Oliver being bashed up, the movie nights and parties along with the food I give him, also the drinking.

I said, "Come on, surely I am much better than that."

Mrs. Chamberlain said, "Calm down. I have taken notes of all this as they will have their day in court. You wait and see as they have said on oath many allegations and many things about you, which they have to justify. However, I stress to you, Danial, they do paint a bad picture of you. There are many serious issues they have brought up, and we must take these head-on. You just have to trust me as they all will be cross-examined on the evidence they give in court. Same as the people on your side. I will be interviewing your witnesses later in the week. They can undertake their affidavits for you and Oliver."

We broke off for lunch. I went for a walk and tried to cool my heels as this session with my lawyer was particularly challenging indeed. I had something to eat, and about an hour later, I went back refreshed and a bit more relaxed.

If you have not been in such a situation like this, let me tell you, it does take a heck of a lot out of you mentally and physically.

When I got back, we convened in her office. I said to Mrs. Chamberlain, "A lot of what my mother-in-law has said is fabricated. She did not have Oliver all that time as she claims. Oliver spent most of the time with me. As to the incident at the soccer ground, that was just utter BS and exaggerated. Rose is a liar and has exaggerated many things. Her account of things she has now presented is no different to the others. I do agree that there was an altercation at the football park after the football game. I am sure this will be addressed in the court hearing."

Mrs. Chamberlain agreed with me, then said, "Now let us look at your sister-in-law's statement, Fiona McDonald.

## Statement of Fiona McDonald

This was noticeably short and said she lives in the same street as I do, and she is married to Claire's brother, James, and has been looking after Oliver every day of the week prior to Christmas 1975.

> I am happy to continue to look after him, and I enjoy having him at home.

I said to Ms. Chamberlain, "I wish they were all like that. Fiona and I did get along very well." Ms. Chamberlain said she wants nothing to do with this case.

I said, "Yes, it looks like it."

With that, Ms. Chamberlain arranged to see me later in the week after she has finished getting statements from the various people I have put forward. "I do hope what we present will counteract all the lies and damning evidence that Claire, Craig, and her family have concocted up between them all."

I went to Mrs. Chamberlains office on the Friday, and she said to me as I walked into her office, "You have a nice group of friends, and they speak so highly of you."

I said, "That's nice to hear for a change."

I do not know what was said and also what they put in their statements as I left that entirely up to them. I am not like Claire and her lot that made comments nearly word for word by each one. Mrs. Chamberlain said, "I agree. Let us spend some positive time and get started as to what each one has stated, and we go through them.

At this point, my lawyer's tone changed to a more positive one.

First, there was the statement from Peter Benson as he was a particularly good friend of mine, a well-respected businessperson in financial circles. Ms. Chamberlain said he has kept his statement quite simply put as he refers to the statements made by Claire, her mother, and of course Craig.

## Statement of Peter Charles Benson

He stated as to the allegations that Oliver is not properly fed, his clothes not washed properly or ironed, and that he is dirty:

> I can say that on many occasions I have seen him I have not found this to be so, I have been present at mealtimes and have seen what the family eat. It is nutritionally adequate and well cooked. Danial is an exceptionally good cook and creates incredibly good meals, he should have become a Chef he is that good. Far as Oliver is concerned every time when I have seen him at my work or at his home, he is always happy and obviously fond of his father, I have known Danial now for many years mainly through his work, in my opinion the allegations made by both Claire, and Craig I simply state that I believe these are deliberate attempts to blacken Danial's good character. My reason I am saying this is that I too have been on the receiving end of wild allegations which involved the police as last year I accompanied Dylan Watson to Claire's and Craig's address in New Lynn to serve the Divorce Proceedings Petition. We knocked at the door and there was no reply. The car they each drove was in the garage and so I concluded they would be at home. We then drove down the street to wait for them to appear. While we waited a squad car with two police officers came up the street, then we drove into their driveway of their house, I thought this was a terrific opportunity to serve

them the divorce petition both Dylan and I went to the door. The Police Officer in charge informed us they had come in answer to a 111 call in which it was stated we were in position of firearms also there were four men around the house, this was just utter nonsense of course and the Police quickly perceived this. The Divorce Petitions were served i.e., thanks to the local police.

After reading this, I said to Mrs. Chamberlain, "There is a pattern with Claire and Craig as how many times the police have been involved. They should have been charged for making such false allegations, and this time with Peter, they were caught out good and proper when Peter and Dylan were at their place. Also like when Claire called 111 when she phoned the police that I was going to kill Oliver."

"Yes," she said, "I agree with what you say. Peter comes across as a very sincere and honest man." Next, we looked at Dylan Watson's statement as he was a particularly good friend and neighbor, as well as he worked at the various clubs for me as a projectionist. This was to give me nights off so I could spend more time with Oliver.

## Statement of Dylan Watson

He stated his name Dylan Watson.

I like to refer to the statements made by Claire, her mother, also Craig John Kelly. They have stated Danial is a violent person, I can say on oath that he is not a violent person, the only time I have seen him involved in a fight was one evening he had to pull Claire's mother of Claire. This incident took place prior to Claire leaving home.

I was with Danial the day Claire left. On this day Oliver was at her parent's place, in fact Danial took Oliver to the grandparents place on the Saturday as they were going that day to a wedding, now if she wanted to take Oliver with her on the day she left, then she would have all day to do so, This day Danial and I were working we were screening a movie at the local leagues club for the kids, as to Claire's allegations in my view as to when she left Danial threatened her this is entirely not true, it is an attempt to justify her own actions in leaving Oliver behind.

I have heard Oliver say on a number of occasions he did not like Craig both before and after Claire left home, Craig did see movies before Claire left home at their home also one time at my place when we held a drive-in night in my back yard, this night Claire sat in the car with Craig, his young daughter, Oliver was reluctant to go and sit with them, instead he stayed with his father for a while, It was not a late night also my wife looked after Oliver with my girls.

I disagree with Claire that she more stable than Danial and I can state that since she became involved with Craig her behaviour has been most unstable. I know from my own observations she left Oliver at her parents when Danial was working so that she could go out with Craig, I used to see them when Craig brought her back home when Danial was still at work, I lived only two doors down from there place at the time when Claire started going out with Craig. Then there was the night she had taken an overdose of Valium. This night Danial and I were at one of the leagues club showing a movie, we go back around say 11.15 or so Danial tried his key in the lock at the front door and it did not work so we both went to the back door of the house, all the windows were closed we then looked into the main bedroom window and there was Claire lying across the bed, Danial called out and no response, I thought she was sick or something, we had to break in through the back door once we got inside I then went into the bedroom with Danial where Claire was sprawled across the bed, Danial tried to wake her up and on the floor I noticed there was   a small bottle on the floor, when I picked this up I said Danial said she has taken some Valium tablets, I then got my wife to come up as she was a nurse and we got her out of bed, in the meantime Claire came around but drowsy my wife did call the Hospital, as she was aroused the hospital said keep an eye on her if she worsens bring here in. I found that Claire now is not the Claire we all knew and liked.

Ms. Chamberlain said to me, "You did not mention this before about Claire taking Valium." "I honestly forgot this as so many other things had taken place."

She said, "Claire is an extremely sick person and needs help."

With that I agreed.

"I have spoken to Jasmine as she was a longtime friend of Claire's, in fact from early childhood, and I found her a very impressive person, one I think the judge would like."

I said, "Yes, she is a loving and sincere person, really likes Oliver."

*Statement of Jasmine Egan.*

My name is Jasmine Egan and I have known Claire most of her life and Danial about seven years. I did consider myself her closest friend, with that I was surprised and shocked when she left Danial, particularly when I saw what she had left him for, I believe Claire is acting completely out of character. Her standards were extremely high, I have read the statements which she has presented and her allegations about Daniel's care of Oliver are not true. Oliver is always well looked after, I with my husband and children, been present for meals at the Mason household and I consider the meals given were exceptionally good, may I say it is like he was a qualified chef as to the meals he creates.

One Saturday night we were having dinner at Danial's home, this night Claire came in and created an ugly scene, she keep saying to Danial, "Hit me go on hit me you always hit me," and with my husband we left with our Children she accused Danial of hitting her, she did not even speak to me that night which was upsetting.

Ms. Chamberlain said to me that Jasmine was such a sweet person, and she was disappointed in Claire as Jasmine said she was bridesmaid at our wedding.

"Yes," I said. "Jasmine and Claire were exceptionally good friends well before Craig came into the picture as we often went to their place as well as they came to our place. It's a shame how things change."

She said, "I must say the people you associate with are genuinely nice people and incredibly supportive of you and Oliver."

Ms. Chamberlain then said to me she had the privilege of meeting Merle Dubbeld as she was such a sweet and gentle person who spoke highly of me.

*Statement of Merle Dubbeld*

My name is Merle Dubbeld, I and my husband have known Daniel for many years and commend him for what he has achieved, I make particular reference to Claire's comments that Danial held a party because he was awarded interim custody and the reference to his son Oliver being at that party, I and my husband Max were guests at Danial's home that night along with many other people he had invited, as to what Claire Mason referred to, we had been asked there for dinner several weeks before, we came early so that Oliver could eat with us which he did. I remember he ate the fondue, and the main course was a roast. He did not want any pudding and was well in bed by eight 'clock. During the evening Danial mentioned he had interim custody of Oliver and we did have a drink to that, it is exaggeration to state Daniel was rushing around and that our quite dinner where all of us together drank two bottles of wine and was not a drunken party.

It is quite untrue that our dinner party was a spur of a moment thing as this was planned well in advance as Daniel always does, as he is a particularly good planner and exceptionally good cook and creates lovely meals and it is equally untrue that Oliver was up too late. Me and my Husband have been to the Mason household many times and you would not think he was a single parent as the house was always so neat and tidy, Oliver is so well mannered and always well dressed. He is such a lovely child.

Ms. Chamberlain said, "I had the head teacher of the kindergarten, Ms. Tuohy, where Oliver attends. She makes some interesting observations."

*Statement of Ms. Dawn Tuohy - Kindergarten Head Teacher*

I am Ms Dawn Tuohy, and I am head teacher at the local Free Kindergarten in Mangere Auckland and have been authorized to make a statement on behalf of myself and the staff there. I have been the head teacher for the past five years, have reared three children myself, I have been teaching for many years. I have under my control three qualified teachers; I have read the statements of Ms Claire Mason along with her mother, the allegations made relating to the kindergarten is disturbing to say the least.

I quote: "His mother states she does not know if Oliver is genuinely happy at kindergarten but I am told other children bash him up. I know that the Kindergarten staff tell him he has no mother, and this is very distressing for him. His Mother said:

…. he told us that he is bashed up at kindergarten…."

"…. but I understand that he has indicated that he has often been beaten up at kindergarten by some of the children…"

To make these statements by the respondent are not true, so say my staff would tell Oliver that he did not have a mother, to make such a statement would be irresponsible at best. In fact, we watch all children from broken homes very carefully and the last thing we would do is make such a shocking statement. It is also untrue that Oliver has been beaten up or bashed at the kindergarten. There are forty children on the roll for the morning sessions, on Monday, three other teachers assist Wednesday and Friday I. The staff pupil ratio on these days, assuming all the children attend, is one to ten.

All the children are carefully supervised, and it would not happen that a child was beaten up let alone regularly. In addition, Oliver is well liked by the other children in the kindergarten.

Oliver arrives at the kindergarten with his father punctually every morning and he is not just neat and tidy, he is immaculately dressed. He is a genuinely nice 4-year-old, and the staff consider he is a very well-adjusted one. Both his father and his aunt who collects him are fond of him and he of them.

I said to Mrs. Chamberlain, After reading this from what the head teacher stated and as to the allegations that Claire had made against the kindergarten begs belief, and for what purpose or reason Claire would do this?"

Mrs. Chamberlain said, "I told you earlier on she will stop at nothing, and any way she can to bring you down, she will."

I said, "I hope the judge can see through all this and sort out all these allegations Claire and her family are saying. I find this really disturbing."

Ms. Chamberlain was now seeing a different side of me, and the statements made by people on my side was more believable honest and not repetitive.

The next statement we went through was by David Thomas, who I worked with. He was one of the sales reps with Crest Foods, and he made a short statement:

*Statement of David Thomas*

>I have known Danial and Claire and their son Oliver for many years since Danial started at Crest Foods, I have been a frequent visitor at Danial's home since Claire left and have seen Danial caring for Oliver. I have read the affidavits filed by Claire and Craig Kelly and their statements that Oliver was wearing clothes that were not ironed and dirty. I find this hard to believe as when I see Oliver, he has always been appropriately dressed for whatever he was doing and his clothes sure did not seem to me, need ironing. They certainly appeared to me to have been ironed.

>I took notice of Claire's comments in her statement that Oliver tells her of his own free will that he wished to be with her and that he never has expressed a dislike for Craig Kelly, as I have been a visitor to Danial's home when Claire has called to collect Oliver. Oliver has been reluctant to go. Claire thereupon said that if he went, she would give him some presents. I can also remember Oliver returning home upset. When asked what was wrong, he said Craig had told him he was going to be his father. Oliver said to Danial "You're my daddy and I love you," he then said I hate Craig and he will never be my father.

The hearing was set down around four weeks' time, and Ms. Chamberlain said I should make a further statement due to the serious allegations made against me. "These statements made by Claire and her family and Craig will no doubt set the course, I believe, on how the court case will pan out."

Then it was decided we fight fire with fire as the allegations made were way off the planet, and I had to respond. This was all agreed upon. So I then got to work on my response, and this is my  response.

# 27

# MY FINAL SUBMISSION

I would like to respond to the affidavits made by Claire Mason, Craig Kelly, and Claire's Mother Rose McDonald, I simply state that in all applications which I have submitted, I have endeavoured to concentrate what is best for Oliver, also to weigh up what I can do best for him, against what Claire can do. Since Claire has left it's been a very difficult and emotional time, the various incidents that have taken place where Claire has been the main contributor, now having read their statements along with outright lies they have told as they have contrived between themselves, then made statements that are copycat by all, Claire, Craig, and her Mother, this gives me firm belief Oliver is better that he remains with me, despite what they say I firmly believe Oliver is happy with me.

I also agree with the fact it is a hotly disputed custody application, I also firmly believe also realise that regardless of who is successful in this dispute, I will still  see Claire and her mother, then I do not think it helps matters any if I submit long statements listing the problems I have had with Claire and her family since Claire left me and Oliver, The allegations about me not caring for Oliver adequately when investigated by Child Welfare also verified by trained persons independent of this dispute such as the kindergarten and their staff this include the list of people we have as witnesses, this is important as it will also enlighten the welfare department people who have interviewed me along with the information they obtained from Claire, her family along with Craig Kelly is very one sided view and many allegations made by them will be shown to be without foundation.

The Welfare in their capacity have examined our living conditions and my only comment here is that I have remained in the same house for over a year now whereas as Claire and Craig have moved three times and if Craig Kelly's statement is to be believed, they contemplate a further move in the future.

It is important that I respond to two allegations and those relating to the movie business along with alleged assaults, since my young days I have always been interested in the movies in fact when I was 12 years old, I was the lolly boy two years at the local cinema in Australia, I watched lots of movies for free, now I have a complete library of Walt Disney movies including Winnie the Pooh which is one of Oliver's favorites. I have had erected on the property an exceptionally large garage I converted this into a home cinema, which is contrary to what Rose my mother- in-law deposes, it is 100% paid for. It has an area of six hundred square feet, it is fully lined inside and has seating for forty people, it is like a small theater, has a projection box that contains all my projection equipment including the sound system all which is state of the art. When Oliver is here sometimes on a Saturday afternoon, we go around the neighborhood, gather up the children, we have a movie show. The children in the neighborhood love it and so does

Oliver. I have access to all the movies which are shown in town, and I order in advance from the major distributors. Thirdly, I enjoy a good night's rest and I have no wish to have it disturbed by getting up to a child with nightmares from scary movies, these comments apply to parties I allegedly have that Oliver attends. There is a time and place for everything. Lastly the movie business is highly profitable and well paid for and the extra income earned helped in purchase of the new home. Despite what is said that I have financial issues is far from the truth as the movie business has created extra income and after wages and income tax it shows an exceptionally good profit.

Far as Assaults referred to since Claire left home, I have been visited regularly by the police investigating allegations of assault brought to their attention by Claire, Craig, and Rose We found out there is a file in the New Market police station containing complaints which have been vigorously investigated and no prosecutions have followed. I have been a very trying time because it usually been a case of Craig, Claire's, and her mother Rose's word against mine. Initially it was exceedingly difficult to try and explain to a police officer, e.g., that I did not try to run Kelly of the road. However now I have three incidents which have been checked out by the Police independently all found to be without foundation.

I can now explain to the Police that the next complaint is another attempt to blacken my character and therefore cast doubt on my fitness to have Oliver. One of these incidents are the incident referred to in Peter Bensons statement, when they went to their house, and they called 000 and said four men had guns and the second incident was on the 20th of March after Claire endeavoured unsuccessfully to obtain an ex parte application for a non-molestation order.

Then as told to me by my Solicitor that Craig Kelly was at the at the Otahuhu Police Station making a complaint that I was about to kill Oliver and at the same time Claire called 111 emergency number to the Police was the coincidence or planned as this resulted that I was visited by the police who was called out to attend this so-called emergency as Claire told them I was about to kill Oliver. The Police when they walked in could not believe their eyes when they found Oliver in the living room watching cartoons and eating an ice block, I was in the kitchen cooking dinner. It is important to note here that Claire and her mother calls frequently the emergency services number 000 and connects to the police.

This incident I now refer to took place only a few weeks before the hearing as I was confronted by Claire's mother Rose who said I punched Claire in the face. I was then confronted by Claire's brother John, as usual this allegation was not true and once again, I was put into the difficult situation and position of having to explain to people who just did not believe me that I did not do such thing, again I had the inevitable visit from the police, in this case it was the constable that lived across the road from me, he was accompanied by a fellow officer, I insisted that Claire and her mother tell the police what I supposed to have done. In the presence of the police both agreed I had not assaulted Claire. However, Claire refused to say who had. I hope all this will stop once custody has been decided. I do not want my son brought up to believe that if you tell a big enough lie and no one else but the victim can disprove it, that you get away with it.

I make some points on Claire's Mother Statement that most of what she has stated it is hearsay or sheer speculation and making statements about things where she was not present as she had no way in knowing what took place in the home, I think she is frightened to losing Oliver in her head she thinks this is more likely to happen.

If I rather than Claire has custody of Oliver. Rose has said this to me, I do not think she is deliberately telling lies but rather than convincing herself that what Claire tells, and she wants to believe is true, is in fact true.

I do state there was an ugly scene at New Market Park as she has told, and it was by no means one sided or was it as she has stated.

I refer to Craig's statement as I doubt his sincerity. My belief is that his statements he submitted are in the same category as his various 111 calls to the Police- he thinks they are the right comments to achieve a particular result. I do think the Police are now awake to his false statements to them, saying he was not at home when he was, proven beyond doubt.

I refer to Claire's statement, I know she wants Oliver and like her mother she is trying to convince herself that Oliver is not happy with me, and he is not well cared for. I think the rationalising the fact that she left Oliver may become her downfall, I know there are procedures to keep people as violent and murderous as I am supposed to be away from temptation. I know there are procedures for separation and custody. Claire has had legal advice all the time and did not avail herself to any of the procedures. when she first left. It is a fair question to ask Why not?" Claire has made many allegations and how I threatened her not to take Oliver with her was believed by few, her downfall may be her unrelenting lies, un- proven allegations and the personal attacks on me, no doubt this all will be played out at the court hearing, on the downside for me is that the Court may decide on the fact that Oliver is under five years of age and the Judge may stick to the latter of the law and rule that he goes with the Mother.

What I put in this statement was from the heart and how I felt. I do know I made mistakes and honestly do own up. We are all not perfect as we do not live in a perfect world.

My solicitor has prepared me for the worst-case scenario. I just hope and pray by the grace of God that Oliver stays with me.

## Jessica Phillips

This is especially important to clarify about Jessica Philips as she was named in various statements and I was accused of having an adulterous relationship with her and that she was my girlfriend needs some clarification. I knew that Claire was not remarried. I already had the divorce papers served on her by my good friends Dylan and Peter, and for some reason, Jessica was an interest to Claire. This included Craig as it turned out he was friends with Jessica's ex-husband, Sam Phillips. Then Claire and Craig teamed up with Sam Phillips. It was later found out Craig paid for the private detective to investigate Jessica and me. Ironically, the week before the custody case, in fact, the Friday before I was served with the divorce petition to accuse me of adultery with having an affair with Jessica and named me as the co-respondent.

This was ironic as it was Claire who left Oliver and me for a married man, and it was her who broke up the family unit. Then she and Craig teamed up with Sam Phillips to try and put dirt on me. I knew damn well this was their plan and now to be part of the court hearing.

I phoned Mrs. Chamberlain what I was served with. She told me ages ago no girlfriends as they can come and bite me later on as Claire will stop at nothing to get back at me.

Mrs. Chamberlain said, "And now you have been named in a divorce proceeding. No doubt this has been well planned by Claire and Craig along with this Sam Philips. Have you met this guy Philips?"

"No," I replied. "I have never met Sam, but what I have been told, he is a big and aggressive guy and would make two of me. Now as far as Claire and Craig goes, particularly Claire, her fried brain justifies their wrongdoing. She is out to show I am no better than them. The timing three days out before the case really shits me off, and now I have to deal with that on top of what I have to deal with next week. They are calculated sons of bitches. I hope next week I get custody, and this may put them back in their place."

Mrs. Chamberlain said to me, "Next week, it's going to be a tough one for you and me, and you have less than a fifty-fifty chance of succeeding."

For what it was worth, I then explained to Mrs. Chamberlain how Jessica came into the picture. I did meet Jessica some time back. Claire stated she was planning to remarry soon as the divorce was finalized. I then classed myself now as a free agent as the decree nisi will be done midyear. I thought that at least I could meet new friends. I met Jessica at a party held by my friends from the corner store, Simon and Pat, his wife. It was Pat's birthday, and this night, Simon introduced me to Jessica, who had been separated from her abusive partner for well over eight months. She had two children, a boy aged four and a girl two years of age. The boy was the same age as Oliver, but he was twice the size, a very chubby little boy. By the way, both the children had jet-black hair.

I told Jessica about our movie nights, and she said she would love to come along. Jessica was a very attractive girl. She was twenty-two years of age. I invited her around to dinner one evening. I introduced Jim Baxter to Jessica, and Jim pulled me aside and said, "Is she your girlfriend?"

"No," I said, "just a friend. You can take her out if you like."

So we had showed a movie. It was *Kelly's Heroes*. By the way, Oliver was with his mother this night.

Jim and Jessica hit it off, and she did stay a few nights, and she did bring her children around as well. Claire came in one night and did see Jessica there, and I am sure she felt Jessica was my girlfriend.

So after explaining this to Mrs. Chamberlain, I said, "Jessica and I will contest the divorce proceedings as Jessica is not my girlfriend. I did not have an affair with her, and furthermore, she was well separated when I met her and not living with her husband. Also, she had a restraining order on her husband. I am sure this will come up in the court case as this, I am sure, is Claire's little plan."

Claire no doubt concluded I was going out with Jessica, and added to that, they seem to have proof she stayed at my place as they hired a private detective. I know Jim said a few times he thought he had heard someone outside. Also the other boarder at my place, Donald Monroe, said he had heard as well. He stayed for a short period while he got his own home in Auckland. We all called him Don, and we all spent evenings out as a group.

Jessica told us that Sam, her ex-husband, said to her, "You're being watched as we have a private detective on your trail." With that we assumed that it was Claire and Craig behind it.

As it was only three days out from the hearing, it gave us no time to respond, so we decided we will deal with that when it comes up in court as we were 100 percent sure it would.

# 28

# REPORT BY DEPARTMENT OF CHILD WELFARE

Ms, Chamberlain called me the week before the court hearing and told me, "You need to come to my office. I have a report sent to me by the Department of Social Welfare, and there are several things we must address and prepare ourselves for next week."

I went the next day to her office, and we then started going through the assistant director of social work's report by Mr. Noel Taylor.

The report and reference he made was about my son Oliver and his welfare, so we started going through the report. He stated he had interviewed me, Claire, Kevin and Rose McDonald, Claire's parents, James and Fiona McDonald. He also stated he spoke to the doctor who looked after Oliver when he was sick, and then he spoke to Mrs. Tuohy at the kindergarten.

I said, "What the bloody hell, he interviewed all on Claire's side, and what about all the people you and I gave him the list to speak to? This was to clarify some of the allegations made by Claire and others as many of the people that should be interviewed were witness to various incidents." I was angry and said, "This is so typical of child welfare. It looks like it will be a one-sided view."

Mrs. Chamberlain said, "Danial, let us not jump to conclusions just yet as we may see a different side to this report."

I then read this report given to me by my Solicitor.

I visited Mr. Mason and his place, this was very brief, we did see Oliver, but I did not speak to Oliver, the lady who came with me did, I went around to the flat where Claire Mason lived, as they were not home but I did see inside the flat through the window, at this point I had not met Craig Kelly.

I may add this is an extremely difficult case and I am unsure how he I would deal with this as it involves to a very great degree questions of feelings and emotions, rather than objective factual material; I have accordingly been uncertain as to how far I should involve myself in the sensitive issues, as to the welfare of the child is concerned. I have thought it better not to take my investigation beyond their present stage, I would be extremely happy in resuming the report if that were required.

There is no significant difference of on the general fitness of Danial Mason and Claire Mason to be satisfactory sole parents of their child. I may add that both parents impress as intelligent, caring people and are both willing and anxious- to carry out our parental duties and it does appear they can both provide more than adequate care for Oliver, I could not see any significant deficiencies in the standard of care provided following the making of an order. Any conflict of views on this issue would be concentrated on the question of the fairness or otherwise of Claire Masons wish to remove her son from Danial Mason's his Father's care and take him to the home of the man for whom she chose to leave him and desert the child.

Danial Mason is in an unusually strong position against most of solo fathers of pre-school children, Danial holds a position which enables him to do a great deal of his work at, or from, his home; he is away from his home for a relatively short business day, being able to take Oliver to Kindergarten on his way to work and returning around 4 p.m. or sometimes earlier to prepare the evening meal, collecting Oliver on his way home. His employer (Crest Food NZ Pty Ltd) is aware of his domestic situation and have been most considerate in permitting departures from their normal requirements. This is to be expected of a man in his position (he is a regional supervisor of sales promotion campaigns for major retail outlets). Danial comes across as an articulate, persuasive, competent person, and I believe a very good manager, I have no doubt he keeps his home to a high standard and from a cursory inspection one would hardly know that he was a solo father and of course I am sure there is help from others he has been successful in looking after Oliver for the past 15 Months.

I visited the kindergarten where Oliver attended and he spoke to Ms Tuohy as she has of course highly experienced in dealing with children who are the victims of matrimonial breakdown, Mrs. Tuohy was taken completely by surprise when she learned that Oliver was deserted by his mother and that he now the center of a custody dispute. Even now, Mrs. Tuohy told me, despite close observation, she said she has been unable to identify any emotional or other problems with Oliver which she could attribute to his unhappy circumstances, Mrs. Tuohy went on to say she sees Oliver as a normal, bright, well-adjusted 4-year-old, and he is a very regular attender and has hardly missed a day and is notably well dressed and cared for, she said I may add although on occasions he had been upset on arrival, presumably by tensions arising from difficulties between his parents concerning access arrangements, Oliver nevertheless quickly settled down and joined in the kindergarten activities.

I went to see Dr. Mathews said that he had been favorably impressed by Danial Masons competence as a sole father and had observed an excellent relationship between father and son, Dr. Mathews did express strong feeling about the unfairness of any suggestion that the child should be allowed to go to the mother who had deserted a functional marriage. Some six weeks after moving into a new matrimonial home, to go away with another man.

I then interviewed Claire's Brother James and Fiona McDonald.

"I believe the very most important single factor in Danial Mason's evident success seems to be the very unusual no-partisan attitude taken by Mr and Mrs James Mc. Donald, brother and sister - in law of Mrs. Mason,"

Mr and Ms James Mc. Donald, live in the same short street as Danial Mason and look after the boy each weekday afternoon. Fiona Mc. Donald collects him from kindergarten, and provided him lunch, and cares for him until Danial Mason gets home in the late afternoon. I am impressed and admired the attitude of Mr. Mrs James Mc. Donald very much.

Mr. Ms James Mc. Donald are not only prepared to subordinate their own mixed feelings about the dissolution of the Danial Mason's marriage, what they have done every day is in the most helpful and practical way. I have no doubt their co-operation has made possible such rational discussion and practical accommodation on the matter of access as has occurred. They have daily contact with Oliver and the time he spends in their home every day have been especially crucial factors in the high standard. of physical care noted by the kindergarten director Ms Tuohy and Dr. Henderson and whether other people, less competent than his uncle and aunt, would be able to match this high standard on a long-term basis, open to doubt.

I say the latter point seems to be highly significant because the attitude of Mr. Mrs. James McDonald seems to be changing, especially over the last few weeks, and I do hope very much, for Oliver's sake, that they will remain acceptable intermediaries and confidants for both his Father and his Mother, I suspect that their progressive disenchantment with Danial Mason may cause some difficulties and I am uncertain how long the present daily care arrangements will persist if the strain now becoming evident is not dissipated.

Then Mr. Ms James McDonald was upset by an incident which occurred the day before I met them. They had found that Oliver had been missing from his home for something in the order of around half an hour, without Danial knowing about this as quickly as they felt he should have been. When found, Oliver was in the company not approved by James and Fiona and had been taken across busy streets in conditions of some physical danger. This can occur despite the vigilance of the most conscientious parents, and may well have had a satisfactory explanation, clearly James and Fiona McDonald were shaken not by the incident but more particularly by what they felt to be insufficient concern by Danial Mason. Then this incident coming on top other incidents, of an unprovoked assault on Mr. Kevin McDonald (father of Ms Mason and Mr. James Mc. Donald at a senior soccer game, has inevitably damaged their earlier attitude to Danial Mason.

Prior to Claire Mason leaving the matrimonial home Danial Mason had taken secondary employment on his own account, showing movies at various clubs and he also equipped the garage as a small cinema and frequently invites neighbors and others to film screenings, he says disagreement about this work was one of the earliest indicators of strain in the marriage, but the significance for me was that Danial is away from home more often than he let me think and, on these occasions, he has to make arrangements for other people to look after Oliver and he did not seek the assistance of Mr. and Mrs. James Mc. Donald on these occasions.

I was impressed by Claire Mason as competent, intelligent, well brought up young women, Claire is bewildered to find that she could be capable leaving Danial her husband and Oliver to live with another man, no doubt Claire has developed highly developed guilt feelings about having betrayed the standard she has been brought up with to respect and this I believe underlines and in part explains what looks like uncaring neglect of her maternal responsibilities.

Claire has felt so much in the wrong that she was unable to attempt to exercise her natural rights to custody of Oliver by just picking the child up from her mother or sister in-law, when immediately following her desertion. Claire is still this feeling of guilt, and to emphasise that she has done, and will do, nothing to denigrate Danial Oliver's father in the child's mind, If I am awarded custody, I would not impede. reasonable access to the father, or in any way set up Craig Kelly as a replacement for Oliver's own father. Ms Mason has been advised by her doctor that a further pregnancy cloud be serious and could have serious, fatal, consequences, then she goes on to say that it is unlikely that can have further children.

From my observation of Claire Mason where she lives and what I can see of the flat through the windows, in my opinion she is clearly a very competent housewife and mother, which Danial did agree on, I see no reason why the flat now occupied by Craig Kelly and Claire Mason should not be suitable; The other point I make is Claire Mason is working full time, I believe as an accounting machine operator and pending the outcome of the present proceedings, it would not be surprising to me if her home were ever it was, not well kept.

In Claire Masons efforts to convince me of her lack of malice toward Danial Mason, along with the fact that she would ensure that Craig Kelly did not supplement him as his father in Oliver's mind, I do feel that Claire Mason was being unrealistic in her assessment of Craig Kelly in his role as stepfather.

Then Mr. Ms James McDonald was upset by an incident which occurred the day before I met them. They had found that Oliver had been missing from his home for something in the order of around half an hour, without Danial knowing about this as quickly as they felt he should have been. When found, Oliver was in the company not approved by James and Fiona and had been taken across busy streets in conditions of some physical danger. This can occur despite the vigilance of the most conscientious parents, and may well have had a satisfactory explanation, clearly James and Fiona McDonald were shaken not by the incident but more particularly by what they felt to be insufficient concern by Danial Mason. Then this incident coming on top other incidents, of an unprovoked assault on Mr. Kevin McDonald (father of Ms Mason and Mr. James Mc. Donald at a senior soccer game, has inevitably damaged their earlier attitude to Danial Mason.

Prior to Claire Mason leaving the matrimonial home Danial Mason had taken secondary employment on his own account, showing movies at various clubs and he also equipped the garage as a small cinema and frequently invites neighbors and others to film screenings, he says disagreement about this work was one of the earliest indicators of strain in the marriage, but the significance for me was that Danial is away from home more often than he let me think and, on these occasions, he has to make arrangements for other people to look after Oliver and he did not seek the assistance of Mr. and Mrs. James Mc. Donald on these occasions.

I was impressed by Claire Mason as competent, intelligent, well brought up young women, Claire is bewildered to find that she could be capable leaving Danial her husband and Oliver to live with another man, no doubt Claire has developed highly developed guilt feelings about having betrayed the standard she has been brought up with to respect and this I believe underlines and in part explains what looks like uncaring neglect of her maternal responsibilities.

Claire has felt so much in the wrong that she was unable to attempt to exercise her natural rights to custody of Oliver by just picking the child up from her mother or sister in-law, when immediately following her desertion. Claire is still this feeling of guilt, and to emphasise that she has done, and will do, nothing to denigrate Danial Oliver's father in the child's mind, If I am awarded custody, I would not impede. reasonable access to the father, or in any way set up Craig Kelly as a replacement for Oliver's own father. Ms Mason has been advised by her doctor that a further pregnancy cloud be serious and could have serious, fatal, consequences, then she goes on to say that it is unlikely that can have further children.

From my observation of Claire Mason where she lives and what I can see of the flat through the windows, in my opinion she is clearly a very competent housewife and mother, which Danial did agree on, I see no reason why the flat now occupied by Craig Kelly and Claire Mason should not be suitable; The other point I make is Claire Mason is working full time, I believe as an accounting machine operator and pending the outcome of the present proceedings, it would not be surprising to me if her home were ever it was, not well kept.

In Claire Masons efforts to convince me of her lack of malice toward Danial Mason, along with the fact that she would ensure that Craig Kelly did not supplement him as his father in Oliver's mind, I do feel that Claire Mason was being unrealistic in her assessment of Craig Kelly in his role as stepfather.

What seems to me is whether the parties want it or not, Craig Kelly, as stepfather of an incredibly young child Oliver, will need to accept a great deal of the day-to-day responsibility for the boy Oliver. Craig Kelly could hardly dissociate himself from involvement with Oliver.

Craig Kelly could hardly dissociate himself from involvement with Oliver. The inevitable erosion of Danial Mason being the father of the child the relationship combined with Danial Mason's natural resentment of whom a man he clearly despises would lead to tension which could hardly avoid damage to Oliver.

This brings me to what I find the most difficult, and one of the most important elements in this situation, Danial Mason as one would expect – impresses in an interview and would no doubt in court setting as very articulate, fair, restrained, and mostly sensitive, it does appear to me Daniels reactions in the presence of Oliver to what he sees as provocation by Craig Kelly and Claire Mason, or members of the McDonald family belie this impression.

Then I add the discrepancies in the parties versions of some upsetting incidents can hardly be resolved outside a judicial setting, however, there seems on the surface for the provocation in a general sense experienced by Daniel Mason, he has repeatedly lost control of himself to a degree and in circumstances which raises some doubts as to whether he is, after all, the more suitable of the two parents to have continuous custody of Oliver. Then on the other hand most certainly, Claire Mason is genuine when she said that physical fear of the violence has been an important influence in her failure to assert her claims to Oliver's custody long before she did. She is still apprehensive.

The final part of his report stated,

I request that some amicable arrangement should be made on the days of access and on Oliver's return, I trust that the parties and their counsel will be able to negotiate some acceptable standing arrangements themselves; the respect of both parties for the Rev. W.D Anderson suggests that he might be able to nominate a suitable person, if some friend or relation is not acceptable.

In conclusion I do regret that I do not feel able to make a clear recommendation in this case at the present stage.

*Response to the Social Welfare Report*

After reading this report, it really disturbed me, and my solicitor agreed with me that this report was very one-sided. We also agree that this should not be allowed to be part of the evidence in the up-and-coming custody hearing. Our reasons are that this report by the social welfare officer touched on incidents wherein they took the word of James and Fiona McDonald, particularly in two incidents. Then he did not fully inspect Claire's place where she was living, only just peeked through a window. He did not interview Craig Kelly. These are valid questions, in particular Craig Kelly, as he played a major part in the marriage breakup.

This is an especially important observation that I was terribly upset about as his report did not provide an accurate or balanced view as the welfare did not interview anyone that provided affidavits in relation to this court case on my side except the kindergarten head, Mrs. Tuohy. If they took the time by interviewing others on my side, then I am sure it would have provided a more balanced view. For this reason, this report should be challenged.

There were many incidents they did not look at, but he did refer to a couple, which does not disclose the true account of such incidents.

I have mentioned many times Oliver plays with the Māori children who live at the house behind ours. This day, it was when Oliver was seen by James and Fiona when he was going to the shop with the Māori children. To me, by the comments made, they felt Oliver was in the company of people that they would not approve of. This in my opinion is a racist slur on the Māori people and indeed a very racist comment. This should have been challenged. The Māori in New Zealand are loving and outstanding people. The children referred to do come from an outstanding family, and Oliver and I have a great deal of respect and time with this family.

There are always two sides of any incident. The incident with the Māori children was no different, and the welfare officer should have followed this up with me and also others to get this clarified, but he did not.

This is what actually took place.

*Oliver Going to the Shops with the Māori Children*

It was a Sunday afternoon, and Oliver was out playing with the children in our backyard. Their mother always made sure Oliver was well cared for, and she watched over them and Oliver when he played at their place. They are a lovely family, and often they would invite Oliver and myself over when they have a Māori *hangi*. The children would come over when we have the Saturday afternoon movies.

Peter, the elder boy, who was twelve years of age, this day came to me, and he asked me if I would allow Oliver to go to the shops with him and his younger brother and sister.

Oliver yelled, "Please, Dad, can I go?"

I said, "Yes, but be careful crossing the main road. Use the school crossing as this would be safer," knowing this would not be staffed on the weekend. I gave Oliver some money, and off they went.

Now this is what Oliver told me later. "Dad, we were walking along the street close to the shops when Uncle James and Aunty Fiona grabbed me and put me in the car and asked me where I was going, and I told them I am going to buy lollies. Uncle James took me into the shops, I brought my lollies, and they brought me back to Uncle James's place."

I did get a call from James and said he found Oliver, and James said, "He was with some Māori kids, and they did not have permission to take him as I asked the elder boy, and he did not answer me. Anyway, they had to cross the main road. They are not the type of kids I would let my kids be with."

I said to James and Fiona, "You both are overreacting. I gave the elder boy permission to take Oliver to the shops."

James said again very sternly, "They are not suitable kids to be with Oliver."

I said, "You're kidding. Are you against Māori kids? These kids are well looked after, and the elder boy is a responsible boy. He is twelve years old and old enough to be responsible. I took Oliver on leaving. James, this whole thing has been blown out of proportion, and you're making a big issue out of it. You're just against Māori people. You should be ashamed of yourselves as they are an integral part of New Zealand culture and history."

When I got back home with Oliver, I spoke to Peter, and he said, "That man did not ask me anything, he just scooped Oliver up and took him away in his car." Peter was very upset as he ran home and told his mother that some people took Oliver.

I know there are two sides to any story. I was very angry when I was told what James and Fiona told the welfare department, and to say I did not know where he was and the children he was with were not desirable children for Oliver to be with, I found this very offensive. The welfare officer took their side of this incident and classed them as responsible and worthy people.

## Incident at the Football Park

Now this next incident. I may add that James was not present on this this day when there was an incident after the football game. As I said, James was not there, but he stated I hit his father. This was so far from the truth. This highlights the issue I have with the welfare report. It was very one-sided and, in my opinion, very biased. The officer failed in his duty by not investigating the facts and making assertions and taking on board one person's point of view. It is not the right way to handle any investigation. If this was so big of an issue, why not come and speak to me about this and not take someone's word recalling an incident when they were not there? This really astounds me. In short, this incident required further investigation.

On the incident after the football game, it was claimed that it was an unprovoked attack on Kevin McDonald. Now this stemmed from early in the day as I decided to take Oliver to see his uncle James play at the local park. I then called Rose and Kevin to tell his grandparents that I was taking him to the football game today. The reason why I called around was because they phoned earlier as they wanted to take Oliver with them.

On arrival at their place, Kevin confronted me and was all fired up and very agitated and shaking. This was because I decided to take Oliver with me rather than them. Then he abused me and shouted at me that I did not have interim custody. Then as he was yelling at me, he said I threatened Claire and did not allow her to take him when she left.

I said, "That is not true."

He continued yelling at me and called me a liar and that I was a lousy bastard. I said to Kevin, "I do have interim custody, so what you are saying is not true."

Then Rose, my do-gooder of a mother-in-law and an interfering old bitch she is, she called me a bloody liar.

I said, "How come I am a liar when you were at the interim custody case?"

Then she blurted out, "Claire called me on the phone last night, and she told me you did not have custody."

I said, "You people are very confused. I have had interim custody nearly six months now. Claire did call me this morning, and she asked could she have Oliver for the day. I told her I had made arrangements to go to the football match today with Oliver so he can watch his uncle James play." Rose continued ranting and raving and screamed at me and called me a rotten liar again. Then Oliver started crying and got terribly upset. I picked him up and took him to the car. Rose was screaming and abusing me, and she was like a deranged person.

I said to her as I was backing out of their driveway, "It is only natural you are going to believe your daughter, but I am telling you the truth."

She tried to stop me, and I then drove off in such a hurry, I nearly knocked her over.

This spilled over to the end of the football game. Oliver at the football game did wander over to his grandparents, I think more for what he can get from them like drinks and something to eat.

The game was a great one. At full time, the scores were level, and it had to go into extra time. By the time the game finished, it was very late, and it was also getting dark and cold and wet, and I just wanted to get Oliver home.

I was in the car park heading for my car when Rose and Kevin confronted me, still no doubt very angry after the morning confrontation. Rose approached me and said if Oliver could go to his great-grandmother's place to see her.

I said to Rose, "It's late, it's wet and cold, and I just want to take Oliver home, get his dinner, bathe him, and put him to bed." It was drizzling slight rain, and we were all getting wet, and I said I just wanted to get out before it got to heavy.

Well, Kevin could not hold back as he abused me, clenched his fist to my face, and said, "You are the rottenest so-and-so," whatever than means, along with calling me a bastard.

I brushed his hand aside and said, "The trouble is with you, Kevin. You cannot accept the truth, and after this morning, you know what you both can do? Get lost. I am just sick and tired with the abuse and crap from you all. I am taking Oliver home, and that is that."

I started again walking to the car, then Rose chased after me. I arrived at my car. I then put Oliver in the back seat, and I jumped into the driver's seat. By this time, Oliver was getting terribly upset with all the yelling and screaming going on. As I had my window down, Rose started screaming at me through the driver's window. I then quickly wound the window up. Rose started bashing on the driver's side window at me, then Kevin joined in and was hitting the car, swearing at me and calling me all the names you can think of.

I started the car up and put this in reverse as they stepped in front of the car to try and stop me going forward. I then fast-forwarded the car and kept going, and they had to jump clear of the car. I did notice while this commotion was going on, a woman who I did not know stepped in, and I heard her having a go at Rose and Kevin, saying, "What are you playing at? Leave these people alone." Also as I was driving out of the park, I noticed Fiona came up to them.

As you recall, James alleged that I hit his father in the face. He was wrong. It did not happen. Fiona was not there at the time the altercation took place. James was not there either; he could only have gotten this from his parents.

As I was driving back home and terribly upset, I said to Oliver, "Sorry about Nanna and Grandpa."

He said to me, "Daddy, they are angry at you?"

I said, "Yes, son, they are, but it is not all your dad's fault." I am sure Oliver did not understand what it was all about.

The point I make on this incident is that it not only affected me but also Oliver, and this incident like many others was not thoroughly investigated by the welfare, and I was made out to be the aggressor. I know I was warned many times about the Department of Child Welfare. It has now become very apparent they were right.

## *The Movie Business*

This was a contentious issue about my movie business showing movies to the clubs as well as my home cinema that was brought up by many and in the welfare report.

It was stated,

> Mr. Danial Mason had undertaken secondary employment on his own account, that of screening movies at various city clubs; he also has equipped his garage as a small cinema and frequently invited neighbors and others to film screenings. The further comment made that there was a disagreement about this work was one of the earliest indicators of strain in the marriage.

This again emphasizes the fact that you believe what you hear and are told without this again to be further investigated. It was further from the truth. The movie business brought in extra income and provided extra funds to buy the new house. Claire had an affair well over six months before she left, and it was also found out Claire knew Craig Kelly at least twelve months before she left. Claire also worked at nights, but conveniently, the report did not mention any of this. Also, it was through her part-time job she met Craig and started having an affair right under my nose. So then she used the movie business as an excuse for her reasoning as to her insecurity. I considered we had a very good relationship until Craig came on the scene. That is what Claire never mentioned. When Claire worked part-time, I stayed home looking after

Oliver, and I had people like Dylan Watson and others who worked for me to do the movies at the various clubs. Funny that Claire did not mention this as to me being home when movies were being shown at the clubs, and who I employed like Dylan Watson and John, Claire's younger brother. Now to say this was for my sole benefit was not correct as it brought in a very good weekly income from that business. I did the "1/3 × 1/3 × 1/3 rule"—33% covered the wages and operational expenses, 1/3 was for the hire of the movies, and 1/3 was the gross profit before tax. I could make more money in one week than I brought home from Crest Foods. I paid a substantial deposit for the house, but that was irrelevant. I felt the welfare officer did not do his investigation properly, and the conclusion by the officer was that the standards of care fall below those the child is accustomed to. His view is far from the truth as again he never bothered to find out how many shows I did work at nights to the nights I was at home looking after Oliver.

My criticism of the welfare department was backed up by my solicitor, who did file a complaint to the court to have the report not taken into evidence as the supposedly trained officer of the welfare department, for reasons he only knows best, did not undertake a full investigation as so many issues were left. It was my concern this report could have a detrimental effect to the outcome of the custody hearing, who knows? It also pointed out the failure to interview my witnesses is a bloody disgrace. His final comment was "This is an aspect I would be looking into more closely if I were asked to pursue my enquiries further. I would do so."

Mrs. Chamberlain agreed with me that the report was very one-sided as the officer did not interview any of my witnesses such as my next-door neighbor, Mrs. Sue Ingram, Mr. and Mrs. Greg Doherty, Dylan and Emily Watson, Peter Benson, Mr. David Thomas, Donald Monroe, and Mrs. Marlene Dubbeld. All these people had all put together statements, and not one of these people were interviewed as my lawyer gave the officer details of each person. Instead, he interviewed Claire's family and took the evidence of Claire's brother and his wife

Fiona, and of course, Claire's lover, and that is why he came to the conclusions he had as they were not independent witnesses; they were family and not contested.

Like Ms Chamberlain has said, "Blood is thicker than water."

One final point on dealing with the welfare people, it has brought back memories and reminded me of when my father died when I was seven years of age, and what the welfare tried to do for us children was take us away from our mother and home we grew up in. I just hope the judge, in his wisdom, will sort the truth out in this hotly disputed matter.

It is now a few weeks away from the Supreme Court hearing that has been set down for one week. We have got what we believe a very strong case. I am prepared for the worst-case scenario. I have the backing of my boss at Crest Foods as they have given me ample time off to prepare for the upcoming hearing.

Looking back, I married a very loving girl. She was younger than me, I was four years older than her. We got married and were very happy. Yes, we had issues like any other couple has. Then came along Oliver. This was the blessing that made us both so happy. We nearly lost him at birth, but he survived, and as far as I was concerned, we were a very happy couple. We shifted into a new home, and six weeks later, my wife was gone. For whatever reason, Claire had an affair with Craig Kelly.

## What My Friend Jonathon Told Me

Taking a thing apart is always faster than putting it together. This is true except marriage. Then he said, "After a breakup, the loyal one stays single and deals with the children and the

damages caused until healed. The other one is already in a relationship and leaves behind the damage."

I had to think about this. I know I was blindsided in many ways, and also, what he said made more sense to me as this fitted me perfectly.

One would think as the hearing is close, you do not want any more incidents. I was wrong.

# 29

# INCIDENT TWO WEEKS BEFORE THE HEARING

For the life of me, I could not find the motive for this. This was well orchestrated by Claire.

It was Saturday morning around ten to eight. It was Claire's weekend to have him. She would pick up Oliver usually around 9:00 a.m. This day for some reason only she could explain, she came around early. We were all at the breakfast table. Oliver, Jim, and myself were enjoying our breakfast. The back door suddenly flew open, and it was Claire. She stormed into the dining area where we were eating, and she straight away demanded Oliver's clothes. She yelled, "I am taking him now!" I already had Oliver's clothes ready for his weekend in his room. Claire demanded to get his clothes from his room. I could see for some reason she was not a happy person. I asked, "Why are

you here so early?"

She did not reply. She then started heading up to Oliver's bedroom.

I called out, "Stop there! You have no right to come here like this, then demand things to me. You're supposed to come at 9:00 a.m., not nearly 8:00 a.m. I already have his clothes for you when you come at nine as you usually do. Now I will get them."

"No!" she screamed at me. "No, you will not! I will get them!"

For peace sake, I let her go into Oliver's room. With that, she went up to Oliver's room, then a few minutes later, she came down the hallway into the dining room, screaming at me. She accused me of giving away Oliver's clothes.

I said, "This is crazy. Why would I give away Oliver's clothes? This is not true."

Claire then said I gave Oliver's clothes to a Jessica Phillips, who had a young boy John. He was a bit smaller than Oliver but the same age.

I said to Claire, "This is utter nonsense. This boy is twice the size of Oliver. Why would he need Oliver's clothes? This does not make sense at all. You come her early in the morning when you're supposed to pick Oliver up at nine o'clock, not eight o'clock. You come here all irate, then accuse me of giving Oliver's clothes away when I paid good money for them. Why would I give them away? You're talking a lot of shit. I am sick of you coming here and accusing me all the time. Now we have to finish our breakfast, just leave us be."

Oliver was watching all this. I could see that he was getting upset with this outrage from his mother.

She started yelling at me again. I said, "Please quiet down as you're upsetting Oliver." Well, that sure did not make any difference. She was here for an argument as this was quite often her usual procedure, yet I get the tag as the villain. Claire yelled and screamed at me again and said she had seen Mrs. Phillips and the children the night before, and her boy had Oliver's clothes on.

I said again, "This is utter nonsense. You're just making this up."

With that, Jim got up from the table, and he said to Claire he will call Jessica Phillips as he had her phone number. Jim calling Jessica did not go down well at all with Claire as she went hysterical. Then while Jim was dialling the number, Claire pulled the phone away from Jim and became uncontrollable. Then a scuffle took place in the hallway.

Oliver started crying and became terribly upset. I then took hold of Oliver to calm him down. Claire rushed into the lounge and tried to pull Oliver off me. I held on to Oliver. Jim was then dialling Jessica's number, and that is when she flew back into the hallway. I then took Oliver out of the house to my next-door neighbor Susan and asked her to mind Oliver as Claire was at our place, and she had gone crazy.

While I went across to my neighbors with Oliver, I left Claire and Jim in the hallway. When I returned, they were still arguing. I noticed Claire's mouth was bleeding. I was not sure at that point why her lip was bleeding. She was in a hysterical state, still in a rage. She had uprooted the telephone from the wall and had smashed this into pieces on the floor.

It was at that point I told Claire to get out of the house. I said to her, "Look what you have done, and your son, you have upset him! Just get out of here."

Claire then stormed out of the house and took off in her car at high speed down the road.

I asked Jim how she got blood in her mouth, and he said, "It could have been two things. When she yanked the phone from the wall, it did fly back and hit her. I did try to grab the phone from her. Or in her rage, she bit her lip. Either way, I did not hit her."

I am sure Jim was telling me the truth as he is a very quiet person. He was visibly shaken by this. He also said he has never experienced this type of violence before.

Well, if we thought that is the end of it, we were mistaken. About an hour later, I was next door with my good neighbor Susan. She told me that Oliver soiled his pants, and she put him in the bath tub and cleaned him up. She said Oliver was still very upset. I ran back home, got a new set of clothes for him, and when I was coming back, Claire with her mother Rose pulled up into the driveway of my neighbor Susan. I quickly gave Susan Oliver's clothes, then went out to speak to them. I noticed Claire's mother was still in her night attire. Then suddenly, Rose jumped out of the car. She came running toward me, screaming and using some bad language, calling me a rotten bastard. Then she hit me fairly in the face.

Susan was standing at her doorway and did see all this. She told Claire and her mother to bugger off and to get off her property. After a lot of abuse, they then drove out of Susan's driveway, their tires screeching, then sped down the street. A number of neighbors did come out and witness the commotion. It was an embarrassment to say the least. Then shortly after, the cavalry arrived, the local police. They pulled up in my driveway. Then Claire and Rose came back. The police officer said they had a 111 emergency call and that Jim hit Claire in the face.

We explained the whole incident to the police, and it was her word against Jim's. He told the police that she had done a lot of damage and how aggressive she was. Susan also told police that Rose, Claire's mother, hit me in the face, and they used a lot of foul language, which was also witnessed by other neighbors. Then later we heard that Rose made a complaint against me to the police as she said I hit her. When the police spoke to my neighbor, they learnt it was the other way around, and after the police investigated this at length, they took no further action.

This was no doubt planned by Claire to make further claims as to the pending custody case in a few weeks. After this incident, Oliver was not well. He often suffered with a bronchial condition, and the doctor told me that Oliver was a very upset child, and he needs stability. It seems the trauma surrounding him was not helping his condition.

I then took his advice on board and contacted Mrs. Chamberlain, and she sent a letter to her solicitor and explained the situation and to have access visits stopped until after the hearing.

*Grandparents Get Their Way*

This incident took place at James and Fiona's place just a week out from the hearing. I was not there. It was what Fiona told me over the phone as she was terribly upset. I have no doubt what she told me took place. This changed her course of direction and also support for me. She told me that Rose and Kevin came around to their house last night. "Because I supported you and Oliver in my statement, they demanded for me to give back the pram they loaned me as they wanted it back because they already arranged to sell it. They also asked for the money we owe."

I asked, "How much?"

"It was $100. James wrote them out a check, but I did not think it will go through the bank as the account is short on funds. They also asked for the trailer and also all the garden tools back."

After Fiona told all this, I said, "Okay, I will see you in the morning. I will give you a check for the $100, then you can put that in your bank to cover the check that James has given to his parents."

She said, "Thanks for that."

I went down the next morning. Fiona was still terribly upset. I gave her the check for $100, and she also told me she rang her mum in Christchurch and told her what happened.

Fiona told me she was torn between James her husband and also Rose and Kevin, his parents, then me and Oliver. She said, "I love Oliver. I dearly love looking after him as he is such a lovely little boy. I do also respect your rights to have him with you."

If Fiona was now put in a position where she cannot look after Oliver, then that changes a lot of things. No doubt this was Rose and Kevin's way to make sure my position as to looking after Oliver was diminished.

This adds to the drama yet to unfold. This has been a very bitter dispute, and it does not stop here. I feel sorry for Fiona as she has been so wonderful looking after Oliver. She has been put between a rock and a hard place. Fiona was now not going to testify now for my support, so I asked my lawyer to subpoena her. Ms. Chamberlain was not happy about that as she said this may go against me.

## My Final Briefing

The Friday before the court case, I had a final briefing with Mrs. Chamberlain. While I was waiting to go in, since her office overlooked Auckland, I gazed out. It was a great view. I was pondering over what Mrs. Chamberlain was planning when her receptionist said, "You can go in now."

I walked in, and she said, "We are due in court on Monday at 10:00 a.m., and we have to be 100 percent ready. I am sure, Daniel, you fully understand you do have a battle on your hands. Your ex-wife with all her submissions, that also includes her partner, Craig Kelly, her mother, brother, and some of her friends as they all paint a very bad picture of you. I just hope we get a good judge that will sort out the true facts in this matter rather than the fictional stories being told by Claire and her people."

Mrs. Chamberlain said, "You must keep calm and pay attention. Do notes if you like, and pass that on to me. If you may like to add in any cross-examination of witnesses, please do so. This case could go two to five days, so be prepared for this. You will take the stand first, and after that your witnesses, and then it will be Claire and her witnesses later on in the week. You will need to follow my every direction."

I knew I was well cared for as Ms. Chamberlain was a very smart barrister, and she had really studied this case. Like she said to me many times, "You have a mountain to climb as the odds are against you, knowing very well Claire to this point has the law on her side."

I am not sure what Ms. Chamberlain has up her sleeve, and if she did, she kept this close to her chest.

The court case was now three days away on Monday morning. On the Friday before, I was served with a divorce petition, and I was named as the co-respondent. This was very convenient for Claire as this came part of the custody hearing. She claimed that Jessica Phillips was my girlfriend, and I committed adultery with her. This will be denied as I along with Jessica have obtained legal advice and will have this dealt with in court and have this struck out.

I recall this quote, and I thought to myself it was so meaningful.

There comes a time in your life when you walk away from all the drama and people who create it. You surround yourself with people who make you laugh. Forget the bad and focus on the good. Love the people who treat you right, pray for the ones who do not. Life is too short to be anything but happy. Falling is a part of life, getting back up is living.

(José N. Harris)

# 30

# THE CUSTODY HEARING DAY 1

The day has finally come, and I would have my time in court to put my case to have full custody of my son Oliver. Over the past seventeen months, it's been a very trying time for both Oliver and I. He will be five soon, and I have no doubts in my mind that he wants to be with me. I know this is going to be a hard-fought battle for Oliver to stay with me. Yes, I have done things that will go against me, yet on the other hand, Claire has, in my opinion, done more damage than I.

I was now portrayed going into this court case as the wife basher, potential murderer, and do not care adequately for my son and the scathing attacks on my character. Yes, I fully understand the law as it now stands in favor of the mother. I go into the court to fight for what I believe is right, and now it's up to the courts to decide who Oliver goes with.

It's worth mentioning here that last Friday, I had a call from my solicitor, and she said while the case is on, child welfare will look after Oliver while the case is on. My reply was, "Not over my dead body they will have him." This request came from—guess who—Claire, his mother. I had made arrangements that Oliver stay with my good friends, Greg and Allison, Oliver likes them very much as he has been to their place many times and loves playing with their children.

Because of the law in New Zealand, the actual court transcript cannot be used, and because of this, my barrister Mrs. Chamberlain made notes, and this will provide details of the case and outcome along with what I can recall. All names of all persons and places have been changed.

It was Monday, October 19, 1976, the first day of the custody hearing. I arrived at the court around 9:30 a.m. I met up with Mrs. Chamberlain. We went into the court room, and we sat directly opposite where the judge will be. I was very nervous, to say the least. I had dropped off Oliver early to Greg and Allison's place in Panmure, and I would pick him up after each daily adjournment, take him home, then bring him back again the next day.

As I sat waiting for the judge to appear, my mind flashed to when my dad died as this was a traumatic experience in my life, and now having Oliver being exposed to so much trauma since Claire left. This is why I firmly put my foot down and said, "No way I would agree to have strangers take Oliver for that week."

Yet his mother, the loving, caring person she says she is, requested he should go with the welfare people. What a joke. This woman does not let up.

I am hoping and praying by the grace of god that Oliver is allowed to stay with me, but it is unknown how this will turn out. I then glanced over and spotted Claire coming into the courtroom with her mother Rose and Craig. Then I noticed the clerk of courts speak to them, then Rose and Craig left the courtroom.

Mrs. Chamberlain said to me that it was a closed hearing. All others must stay out until called upon.

"Oh," I said, "that is why our witnesses have been told to be available Wednesday." I glanced over again and said Claire was not looking too good. She just gave me one almighty glare. If looks could kill, I would be a dead man. I just smiled back at her.

The usual formalities took place, and the clerk of courts read out the case details. Claire's lawyer, Mr. Wadsworth, stated he was acting for the respondent and the co-respondent, and Mrs. Chamberlain addressed the court and said she was the barrister for the petitioner.

## Evidence of Danial Kenneth Mason

I was asked by Mrs. Chamberlain to take the stand.

I raised myself out of the chair and walked over to the witness box, and I was duly sworn in. Mrs. Chamberlain asked where I resided and asked if I was the petitioner.

I answered yes and said, "I am seeking custody of my son, Oliver Kevin Mason."

Then Claire's lawyer Mr. Wadsworth gingerly got out of his chair. He ruffled many papers together and came across to where I was standing in the witness box. He wiped his brow and looked at me straight in the eye. To me he looked extremely nervous.

Again, I had to state my name and address, which I was obliged to do so. I answered questions like when was I married and how long we were married. Then I was asked, "Mr. Mason, I understand from your wife that before separating from you, there were some differences?"

I then looked at him straight in the eye and said in a stern voice, "Well, that all depends on what you call or define as differences. I see the only differences I would say between my wife and myself is what Mr. Craig Kelly has caused by coming into our lives."

The I was asked told, "However, Mr. Kelly came on to the scene a considerable time later. Was that not the case?"

"Sir, again, this also depends on what you define or mean by *later*. If you are referring to when my wife left in May 1974, I would say my answer is absolutely no. You see, as I have recently found out, Craig Kelly and my wife had been seeing each other for well over twelve months before she left. The twelve months prior to her leaving was not the happiest time of our marriage. This is because my wife was having an affair, with that I have no doubt, and it was Craig Kelly that coerced my wife to leave. We were a very happy couple until he came into our lives as we had a lovely son and a new home."

Then I was told, "There are many reports that you have likewise caused Craig Kelly and your ex-wife Claire Mason a considerable amount of trouble. Also, can you recall the incident at the football ground where you struck your father?"

This really amused me as I said out loudly, "You've got to be kidding me, telling me that I caused trouble to my ex-wife and Craig Kelly. What about all the trouble they have caused me? So you dismiss all that?"

At this point, I felt this was going to get rough. I intended to answer Mr. Wadsworth's questions but not letting him get away with anything with his line of questioning.

"Sir, with due respect, both Claire and Craig Kelly have made my life difficult in many ways, and as this hearing continues, you will find out by others this was not one-sided, but the other way around. Now as to your reference to the football game, yes, I certainly do remember this, and I like to put it to you straight. My father died when I was seven. I think you mean my father-in-law, Kevin McDonald, and regarding this day you refer to, I would like to start off saying this started not at the football ground but early in the day when I went to the McDonalds' house. This is where it all started from and did finish at the football park later in the day.

"Sir, I would like mention back to the Sunday morning when I did take Oliver around to tell his grandparents that I was taking him to the football game. However, when I got there, Kevin McDonald confronted me, yelling and screaming at the top of his voice. He kept yelling, saying that I did not have interim custody of Oliver or the decree nisi. He yelled I have no rights to have him. At this point, I am sure and have no doubts and also believe that my ex-wife, their daughter, has told him this. When I tried to explain to Kevin, he then yelled at me again, raised his fist, and he called me a bloody liar. I said to Kevin this is not true. Then Rose, Claire's mother, stepped in, and she too started on me and also called me a bloody liar. Now in due respect, I ask you if I did not have interim custody, then who did? As well I am sure they did not tell you this side of the story that took place that day."

"Mr. Mason, I ask you that Rose McDonald said that Claire called you on the phone the night before?"

"Yes, Rose McDonald did make reference to that. She assumed Claire called, but I can assure you 100 percent, Claire did not call. However, I will say that Claire did call me in the morning around 8:00 a.m. In fact, she asked could she have Oliver for the day. I then explained to her that I had already decided to go to the football match at the park.

"Now I go back to the McDonald household when Rose was yelling at me that I was a bloody liar, the fiery Mr. McDonald yelling at me I did not get the decree nisi and I should not have Oliver, his mother should have him. It was at this point Oliver started crying, and he was visibly terribly upset. I then picked up Oliver and took him to the car when Rose was still screaming at me. She was calling me a rotten so-and-so, whatever that means. I then put Oliver in the back seat and then got into the car and wound down my window. I said to Rose, 'It is only natural you are going to believe your daughter, but you are blindsided by Claire.' I said to her to hell with all this. I felt it was no point arguing with them as I was telling them both the truth, and if they want to believe their daughter, so be it. As I drove off, Rose grabbed hold of the left-hand side mirror, yelling for me to stop. With that she fell to the ground. I then I drove off and headed to the football park. The accusation by Rose that I nearly ran her over is unfounded as well."

"Mr. Mason, this is when you then assaulted your father at the park?"

"Sir, with due respect, I already told you he is not my father and never will be."

"I will rephrase my question. It is when you assaulted your father-in-law at the park?"

"Sir, my response to you is simple. I did not hit anyone at the park, and at the end of the game when I was leaving the ground and heading back to my car with Oliver, only Rose and Kevin were there, and just as I was ready to leave, Fiona McDonald showed up, and if you did not know who Fiona McDonald is, she is my sister-in-law."

"Mr. Mason, I put this to you. There was Fiona McDonald and Rose and Kevin McDonald, all were witnesses. They all say this was without provocation that you struck Kevin McDonald. What do you say about that?"

"Sir, I can assure you as to what you are implying is totally inaccurate, and in due respect, if you want to believe all they tell you, that is your prerogative. You say witnesses, were there any other witnesses to this? I do not think so. My recollection after the game is Rose and Kevin McDonald came up to me and asked could they take Oliver to see his great-grandmother. I said no to them as it was a very cold and wet day, and also the game finished late as this game went into extra time, extra fifteen minutes each way as the scores were level at full time. This is why it finished later than normal. With that they then abused me and chased me to the car. They then started banging on the car window. Your assertion as to the provocation you have referred to and the other witness being Fiona McDonald as she turned up just before I drove off with Oliver, so she witnessed nothing. Fiona McDonald was simply not there until I was ready to drive off in my car. So who are the witnesses you say you have, or do you count the McDonalds as your witnesses?"

Claire's lawyer was not getting anywhere with this, so he changed to another topic.

"Mr. Mason, is it not true you made a great deal of noise on the fact that your wife was living in an adulterous association?"

"Sir, I give you credit as you could not say it any better as you are right. Yes, that if it came up in conversation, I was just stating a fact as it cannot be denied my wife was with Craig Kelly for at least twelve months before shifting in with him. To make matters worse, she carried on with him while being married to me. Surely that is stating the bleeding obvious, is it not?"

"Mr. Mason, can you now tell the court what took place last Friday when there was a divorce petition served on you, and you were named as the co-respondent?"

"Sir, this had been well planned and orchestrated, no doubt by your advice as well to bring this up in the court today. Do you honestly think for a moment I am so stupid why I question this being served Friday before this hearing that I was served with a divorce petition? It is very obvious to me and surely others this was my ex-wife's plan so she can discredit me, then she can claim I committed adultery just like her. Please, can you let me explain a few things?"

Counsel said to go ahead.

"I can say to you and the court, this is like many other claims against me by my ex-wife as she has very conveniently had this petition served on me so you can stand here today, and you want me to confess to this outrageous claim. I am sure you, your client Claire Mason, along with Craig Kelly this is a 'gotcha moment.' Well, I am very sorry to disappoint you all as this is another attempt by you and your client to now say I am now no better than she is. You have made already today accusations against me, which are totally unfounded and not true. I challenge you in this court to prove this or retract this allegation. You as a lawyer must have given my wife directions on this. One must think for a moment how convenient this is to serve papers on me the Friday before this hearing. You of all people mention this today.

"I will add this has also been organized by Craig Kelly, as he knows the petitioner. Also you will find when it all comes out that Craig Kelly and Claire Mason paid a private detective to get evidence, which did not exist, and then have a divorce petition served on me."

This sure got me all fired up, and I got very agitated. Mrs. Chamberlain looked at me and nodded her head to calm me down, and the judge for some reason had a slight grin on his face.

Her lawyer then said, "Mr. Mason, the divorce petition has now been served on you, and you have been named the co-respondent."

At this point again, I looked across to Ms. Chamberlain and the judge as I was getting terribly upset with this line of questioning. I was hoping for an objection by Ms. Chamberlain or the judge, but they just let me proceed.

I then raised my voice quite loudly, "Do I have to repeat what I have just told you? In due respect, I have explained this to you, so why should you ask me again and again this question? Back to your line of questioning, and I am not stupid as this was very convenient by them, and you present this at the court today. I had already known about the petition and also who hired the private detective. It was the co-respondent Craig Kelly. Why do I know this? As the woman you are claiming committed adultery with me told me it was her ex-husband and Craig Kelly that paid for the private detective. I have no doubt when we defend this, it will be struck out of court. I may add, the woman in the petition does not go with me, she goes with someone else, who is a friend of mine. I will leave this to the court to sort that out."

The lawyer did not let up as he again stated, "The divorce petition has been served on you, and you have been named the co-respondent. Again, Mr. Mason, I put it to you, you have been named as co-respondent?"

I then looked straight at the judge and my barrister. I shrugged my shoulders and replied, "What more do you want me to say, as you keep asking me the same question over and over? Okay, yes, I was served with papers. I will not, in this court, agree to your suggestion that I committed adultery as that is what you're implying just to make your client's case that much better. Sorry to disappoint you, you can ask me as many times as you like. You have come into this court today, so you can say you have got me on this one. I just simply deny it, so will the respondent in the petition, and we will jointly deny it. It is a simple case they have accused me wrongly. This is typical of Craig Kelly and Claire Mason as they will stop at nothing to get one back on me.

"The only way you got hold of this information was by Claire Mason and Craig Kelly, and again I repeat, it was my wife and Craig Kelly who committed adultery, not me. Is this not the real issue here, is it not? Can you here today prove this? The issue is me wanting custody of my son, and that is all that matters to me, and his mother committed adultery, not me. These are the factual issues here."

I was terribly upset, and at this point again, I looked at my barrister and the judge and said aloud, "This pigheaded lawyer is just badgering me."

This is when the judge intervened. The judge kindly asked, "Mr. Mason, are you the other party named in the petition served on you last Friday, and is it your intention to apply to the court to have it struck out?"

I replied in a terribly upset voice, "That is correct, Your Honor. I also have not seen the woman in question for a while now as Mr. Bailey decided not to have her at my place due to the private detective that was snooping around, I confronted the private detective that was spying on the house with binoculars. He was also seen at night by neighbors, snooping around my house. With that they have simply got the wrong information and the wrong person. Your Honor, I may add the woman in question, she has been at my home, but not with me as a girlfriend. I may add, Your Honor, is that what constitutes adultery, and surely then one can have friends and not be cited as having an adulterous affair.

"Then in my case, I have served a divorce petition on my ex-wife as she has admitted to an adulterous affair with Craig Kelly. What has been presented to the court today on this matter should be dismissed."

The judge asked, "Mr. Mason, on this matter before instructing your solicitor, did you also instruct other solicitors?"

"I can assure you, Your Honor, that is certainly correct, as this is being dealt with by the woman in question along with her solicitor, and I think it is only fair her name be supressed as she has nothing at all to do with this court hearing. I may add the fact is my ex-wife and her solicitor have made an excessively big issue of out of this, very conveniently, one would say. Now as to the divorce court and after hearing the evidence that we will jointly present, we have been advised that the petition will have to be struck out. The woman in question wants a divorce, but not on the terms of adultery.

"I felt this is especially important to raise my objection to this barrage of questioning by the wife's counsel as it seems very convenient to raise this at this hearing, also that I get served with a divorce petition

Friday prior to this hearing. This is very strange indeed to give way to demeanor me, without any foundation at all. I am sorry if I got upset."

The Judge replied to me, "I have taken your point—no further questions." The court clerk ordered a recess for fifteen minutes.

At the recess, I sat down with my barrister, and she asked me if I was doing well.

I said to her, "All the questions of Claire's solicitor, he is badgering me a lot, hoping I slip up. He is also giving me a free rein on answering a lot of questions. I know that I got very upset, but wouldn't anyone? I cannot see the purpose of this of trying to pin this adultery thing on me as I am not going with that person at all. It is Jim Baxter whom you have already met. It was Jim she was going out with, not me. Anyway, it was Claire and Craig that committed adultery, not me."

Ms. Chamberlain said, "They are trying to get at you in any way they can. Your answers were exceptionally good, and her lawyer did not get the answer he was looking for."

I said, "You did not raise any objections to his line of questioning."

She said, "No, as you have responded very well, and, Daniel, you are in the hot seat. Just think about what you say. The judge has noted your last comments."

I said to her, "The solicitor seems a bit frazzled."

She did not answer that but said to me, "Get ready, the court is being reconvened." The court resumed at 11:15 a.m.

I was not sure what was coming next as I went back in the witness box. I gave Claire an almighty glare as she looked at me across the courtroom. I did give her a filthy look as I just wanted to let her know I was not happy with the divorce petition as she was involved in this right up to her neck, no doubt. If she thought she got me on this one, well, she will be disappointed as Jessica Phillips was not my girlfriend.

Counsel Mr. Wadsworth continued his questioning. "I ask you, Mr. Mason, did you enter into a separation agreement as this was done with Ms. Mason's previous lawyers and had occasion to write to your solicitor around July 1975 and when you entered in a separation agreement?"

"Sir, no, I do not recall anything like that."

"Mr. Mason, that firm drew up the agreement in July 1975." "Well, if you say so, as I cannot recall the exact time."

"Mr. Mason, then even at the early stage, you were quite prepared to live separate lives being apart from your wife?"

"Sir, the fact is and the truth of the matter is that she left for someone else in 1974. I did try most of last year to get her back, it's on record. I tried right up until the beginning of this year. I was hoping she may come to her senses to come back, even for Oliver's sake, but this was not to be." "Mr. Mason, your minister, Rev. John Anderson, indicated he was unable to affect a reconciliation?"

"To answer your question to the best of my knowledge, he may have done so earlier on. I was unaware of Rev. Anderson speaking to Claire. I can say now after all that has happened and what she has done to my life, who would want her back anyway?"

"Mr. Mason, was that last year?"

"I am fairly sure it was not last year, but this year. Now far as the agreement goes, this was made up by Claire and her mother by her previous solicitor as they got together. With that they both wanted me to sign over my son Oliver to her parents. I bitterly objected and would not agree to their demands. I made it very clear to them and told them no way I would give up my son or sign him over to his grandparents. What mother would even think of this? In my opinion, this is where it all went off the rails because I would not sign the agreement or agree to any terms with what they had planned, the lies told as to the claims I abused my wife. Sir, I may like to add another exceptionally good reason. Claire's father, the grandfather of Oliver, does drink a lot. This is a known fact. So the last answer I decided on was one big no. One thing you failed to mention that Claire was willing to sign Oliver over to her parents, what mother would do that, I may ask?"

"Mr. Mason, did your lawyers draw up the agreement on your instructions?"

"Well, I can say this was partly correct. However, unknown to me at the time, as mentioned they got in touch with the grandparents. This was Claire's and her previous lawyer's idea. They discussed the plan between them, then they shifted the goal posts on me. This is when I found out in the agreement it had dramatically changed as they wanted me to sign over Oliver to her parents. I said no way that I was prepared to do that. This is why I refused to sign. A very good reason, don't you think? Again, I stress to you, and surely it is worth noting once more, that Claire was prepared then to give up her son, like when she left the home I provided. The question is what mother would do this to their child?"

"Mr. Mason, let us now go back to last year, and how many times did you go to see a marriage guidance counselor?"

"Good question you ask, as the answer is no. In the early stages when she left, I wanted to, but Claire refused as she did not want to go, no doubt influenced by Craig Kelly."

"Mr. Mason, you engaged in an incident when you went to your ex-wife's flat in Henderson and where she was living with Mr. Kelly, and you kicked in the front door and broke the plate glass window. Do you recall this incident?"

"Sir, again, my account of this incident is poles apart as to what she and others have stated. To start with and to set the record straight, I never kicked in the front door. I do agree the side panel of the door was broken, also I was pushed into the plate glass window."

"Mr. Mason, on this night, there were many witnesses as your ex-wife and her parents and Mr. Kelly, and they did witness all this, and they all said you were uncontrollable. Is this not the case?" "Sir, if I may in my defense, I will try and explain this the best way I can so you may be able to understand this much better and also hopefully make a better judgment of this situation. Now there were witness as you said, then I question how reliable these witnesses are. All families say the same thing, so when you are telling just one side of the story, also when you quote something, you must tell the whole story rather than the bits and pieces that make it look more dramatic than it really is. I would like to explain to the court how this all came about. First this was all over Oliver, and what you have conveniently omitted that Claire's parents were involved in this up to their necks, but you did not tell this side of the incident. Her parents, particularly Rose her mother, you will find is very conniving and stretches the truth to fit their own agenda.

"Sir, If I may, can you let me start from the beginning? Also how it did come to the altercation at Claire's place. Rose and Kevin, the grandparents, they came to my place early in the afternoon as they wanted to take Oliver to a football match, in which I did agree, very happy to do so. As far as I know, they did take him to the game, I assumed that.

"Now as I was told, the match finished just after 4:00 p.m. I did ask the grandparents to bring Oliver straight back after the game. This was to get him fed and bathed before bedtime. This night it came well after 6:00 p.m. I did get quite concerned as they had not brought Oliver back. I went down to James and Fiona's place. They were Oliver's uncle and aunt. When I went in, James was well home as he played in the game this day. I asked, 'Do you know where Oliver is as he is with Rose and Kevin? They were to bring Oliver back home after the game.'

"With that, Fiona said, 'They are at Claire's place in Henderson.'

"So I was very angry, not happy about this, and I went over to Claire's place in Henderson to get Oliver.

"I arrived there well after 6:00 p.m., and it was quite dark. I parked out front. There was the grandparents' car. I knocked on the door, and someone inside said, 'Who is it?'

"I called out, 'It is me, Danial.' I called out again, and they would not open or come to the door, so I knocked harder on the side glass panel that was beside the front door, and my hand went through this. It was stated in their statements that glass flew everywhere. That was not true as a small piece did fall out, but it did not shatter as it was thick glass. The other point that I smashed the door open was farther from the truth. This was to make the situation more dramatic than it was. Craig Kelly said he was shattered with glass, which again was exaggerated."

"Mr. Mason, surely, you must have really banged hard to break the glass."

"Yes, I did knock on the glass panel quite vigorously and had no intention of breaking the glass, but the panel fell out. If they were not so bloody minded and opened the door to speak to me, this would not have happened. All this could have been avoided. Her parents were the ones that deceived me in the first place. The door was not kicked in at all.

"The door finally opened, and out came Craig, Claire, and her father Kevin. It was Kevin who knocked me to the ground. Also as it was cold night, and I had a cardigan on. As I was getting up, the cardigan slipped up over my head. That is when Craig and Kevin pushed me around, and Kevin pushed me so hard that I went into the plate glass window. You also must understand, this was not entirely my fault as the grandparents should have brought Oliver home on time as I requested. I was worried that something may have happened to them. I think that is a fair point.

The grandparents have to share some blame on this as well as I trusted them to bring him back after the game, and they did not.

"I am sure they never told you the whole story as to what actually happened, what was said about this. I also paid the cost of the damage of $100. Another point to make, you say there were many witnesses to this. Were they independent witnesses? I do not think so. Of course they will say things to suit their course and make me out as the villain."

"Mr. Mason, was it correct they said they would proceed against you for the damage?"

"Sir, in due respect, in case you did not hear what I said, I will repeat to make sure you are up to date on this as you asked me that they would proceed against me for damages. Now as I told you that I already paid them the next day, so what is your point of the question?"

The court adjourned for fifteen minutes at 11:30 a.m.

At the recess, Ms. Chamberlain said to me, "They are trying to badger you and ruffle you up, and you must keep your composure. The responses you are giving are particularly good. The judge I am sure will see this is not entirely your fault as there are faults on both sides. They will make you out all the time as the guilty party. As I have told you on many occasions, this is going to be difficult as Claire and in particular the grandparents are well on her side and will make you look like the aggressor."

I said, "The questions about this incident would not have happened if the grandparents brought Oliver back on time and having been away for so long, I was terribly upset."

Ms. Chamberlain said to me, "Danial, a lot is against you on many fronts, and they will have their turn, just wait and see. I have also noticed the judge is taking a lot of notice of the questioning, and I feel he sees it not all one-sided."

I said, "I just hope so. Is her solicitor for real as he asks the same question after I have given him the answer. Surely, he is not that stupid."

Ms. Chamberlain just smiled at me, and that was enough answer for me. I have no doubt my barrister is right up with this and cannot wait until Claire and her side give evidence.

Court resumed 11.45 a.m.

I walked back to the witness box, and I glanced over to Claire where she was sitting. Again she just glared at me. I smiled at her, then I got back into the witness box, not knowing what next was in store for me as to the point of the proceedings it's been full on.

The questioning continued.

Mr. Mason does Oliver attend kindergarten every day?
Yes of course, he does.

Mr. Mason, are you sure about that? As I ask you has he been going to the kindergarten over the past 10 days?

Of course, he has been attending but not every day.

Mr. Mason, I put this to you and ask has he been living at his home? At this point not now.

So, I ask you where he has been, would it be staying with friends in Pakuranga?

Sir, I am glad you ask this question as this week he is staying with friends while this case is being heard. This has come about as it was suggested he goes with the welfare people requested by his mother, so I did not want him with strangers. It was my decision that I decided to keep him out of harm's way. Also that is my reason he is my responsibility until this court decides otherwise. The point here is the mother of Oliver requested this, and I am not sure why?

Mr. Mason, there seems to be a big issue as to access with your ex-wife, the mother of the child Oliver. I ask has she had access to him in the last ten days? On the tenth day, the Saturday, the weekend before, in fact I believe she has had no access at all. And you denied her access?

Sir, my concern is Oliver's welfare and until it is decided I am his custodial parent, I would not put it as a matter of denial. I am sure you would have received a letter from my lawyer on this very matter why access was stopped, this was due to a very ugly scene at my place that occurred, you were duly notified on this. Far as I am concerned this is my right as I have the responsibility and must do what is right for the child. If she comes to her senses then access would not be an issue.

Mr. Mason, I ask you who was present on that occasion?

Now, I know you were aware that an incident took place when there was Jim Baxter who boards at my place, also my neighbor Susan, then there was Claire, her mother, as well Fiona McDonald. Because of this incident, that is why access was stopped.

Mr. Mason, can you explain what happened that day?

Yes, I certainly can. It was a Saturday morning around ten to eight. Claire normally starts her access around nine a.m. She came early this day, I am not sure why she came early. I am not a mind reader either, as one does not know from one day to the next when Claire comes around, so I simply do not know, you will have to ask her. That is what I would like to know. This particular morning we were all having breakfast. I had Oliver's clothes already for when his mother would come at nine a.m., so on the morning in question, Claire arrived around ten to eight.

Did she indicate why she arrived early?

I did get a phone call around seven a.m. that morning. She did not mention coming early except she said have him ready as we are going away for the weekend and make sure he has plenty of clothes.

Ms. Mason claims you received a phone call on Thursday night, saying why she would be there early?

Well, that is her account to justify her coming early, and if she rang me and asked, then I would remember, so I tell you she did not. As I said, we were having breakfast. Soon as Claire walked in, Oliver stopped immediately eating when he seen his mother. Claire said where is his clothes. I said in his room. She said she would go and get them, I said no, I will get them myself. She said do not bother, I will, and she went up to the room. She came back a few minutes later, screaming at me, and she accused me of giving away Oliver's clothes. I said this is this absurd, this is not true. She implied and said I gave my clothes to a Mrs. Jessica Phillips who hasa young boy John, a bit younger than Oliver in age but twice the size. I said to Claire that is not correct, this boy was twice the size of Oliver. Why would he need Oliver's clothes? It did not make sense as they would not fit him. With that Claire said she had seen Mrs. Phillips and the children the night before with Oliver's clothes on. This is when Jim Baxter got up from the table. He called Ms. Phillips as Jim has her phone number, then Claire went hysterical, pulled the phone away from Jim, and Claire became uncontrollable in the hallway. Oliver started crying and became terribly upset. It was then when I took hold of Oliver to calm him down, I took him into the lounge. Claire run in, she then tried to pull Oliver away from me. I then decided I will take him out of the house. I then went through the side door and took Oliver to my neighbor Susan, who lives next door, and asked her to mind Oliver as I told her that Claire is at our place, and she has gone crazy. When I left Claire and Jim, they were arguing in the hallway.

Mr. Mason, I then put it to you that you and Mr. Baxter assaulted Ms. Mason, and she was bleeding by the mouth?

Sir, that is your version and hers as she did claim this took place. Claire Mason is a serial liar, and she creates things to suit her own agenda, and what you suggest to me that I assaulted my ex-wife is utter rubbish. If you go through all the incidents and in particular this one you refer to, that is what she wants you and others to believe.

I may add this whole incident and alleged assault were orchestrated by Claire. I am sorry to say that the assault did not happen, and what she claims is not true. Claire creates issues all the time. She has a history of many claims she has made, this is what she wants you to believe. That morning Claire was in such a hysterical state, I am sure she would not even known what happened. She grits her teeth and was shaking all over, and she was in such a rage, Oliver did not even want to go near her, so that is why I took him next door, and when I came back to the house, I entered the hallway. Claire had uprooted the phone from the wall. I am sure she did not mention that the unit was smashed to pieces and the contents strewn across the floor. I could have charged her for the damage she caused. The other very valid point I would like to make is when Claire attacked Mr. Baxter, I did see this with my own eyes. I have been attacked by Claire before. In this incident, I told her to get out of the house on no certain terms. With that she did leave, then about an hour later, Claire came back. She drove down the road this time with her mother. I then went back in next door to see if Oliver was okay. As you recall, this was my neighbor's place. When Claire and her mother pulled into her driveway, I then went out to speak to them. I did notice Claire's mother was still in her nightgown. In an instance, Claire's mother flew out of the car. She came running fast at me, screaming and waving her fists at me. She was swearing and frothing at the mouth. With that she then came at me, hit me in the face. That is when Susan next door witnessed this, told them to get off her property.

Mr. Mason, I ask why did then Rose McDonald complain to the police that you assaulted her?

Sir, you do ask an exceptionally good question. This was the theatrics by Rose McDonald as she always puts on an act. She comes across as a very convincing person, exaggerates incidents to suit her daughter's efforts to better her cause in this custody hearing at this court today. I can assure you I did not assault her. It is the other way around as she hit me in the face. Like I said, this was well planned, just another blatant attempt to discredit me. You being her lawyer should be aware of that. I may add I have spoken to the police at length about this, as Claire and her mother had made a several complaints, the police said they would take no further action. One other point I would like to make, for a moment don't you think this all not too coincidental just a few weeks out from this hearing? Surely I would not be so damn stupid to even contemplate such actions knowing very well it could affect the outcome of this hearing, This along with last Friday getting served with papers for a divorce proceeding, all this is very coincidental, don't you think? Also this makes you wonder why because of her actions from that Saturday resulted in her access temporarily stopped, surely I am in my rights to do so after such turmoil she caused. For a moment, it's all about her and her mother, what I was supposed to have done along with Mr. Baxter and no mention of what the effect it has on Oliver.

Her lawyer now changed the subject as I am sure he realized this was no one-sided incident, and then he asked,

Mr. Mason, do you know the police at Otahuhu Station very well?

Sir, I know what you are implying. In no way does the police take sides. All I can say on this that the police are regular visitors to my home due to various 111 calls by Claire and her mother also Craig Kelly as they make numerous ridiculous also unfounded allegations. In fact, I would say around twelve times at least over the past year.

Mr. Mason, what about the police officer, your neighbor, that lives across the road from you and works out of Otahuhu Police?

So I asked, "What is the issue here as there is a police officer that lives across the road from me? I do see him now and then, but has come only once when on duty when police have been called by Claire or her mother."

Well, what Claire's solicitor came out with next got me all fired up as he referenced to and insinuated that I was in cahoots with the police at Otahuhu Police Station in South Auckland. I was questioned as to one of my statements I referred to, I quote, "There now is a file" in Otahuhu Police Station. I was then asked then how an ordinary layman like me can find out such information like that.

My explanation on this was quite simple, and I said, "You see, I have an exceptionally good lawyer. This was found through my solicitor, Mrs. Chamberlain. I am not entitled to ask about what inquiries were made."

Then I was challenged, "How was your barrister, Mrs. Chamberlain, being able to get into the file?"

"Well the answer is a simple one," I said, "as this came about because we were intending to subpoena the police that were involved in many incidents."

So then I was asked, "So where did you get the file number from?"

Now this line of questioning went on for some time, and I said, "As I told you previously, my solicitor got this information."

Then I was asked, "Are you sure the police did not give this to you?"

This questioning was getting rather ridiculous. I raised my voice and said out very loudly, "It seems you cannot, in due respect, like my answer. I think I already have answered your questions properly, so I will say it again. The answer to your question is no, the police did not give me the file, and furthermore, if you think Constable Donald gave it to me, you're dead wrong. He did call at my house on one occasion when Claire and her mother were involved in another incident. He was with another constable, but I hardly see him from week to week. Police told me they prefer to keep out of domestic matters, especially this one. I think you should tread carefully if you think I am conspiring with the police as the police would not take this accusation lightly either."

It was very obvious Claire's lawyer was not getting anywhere, so he changed the subject. I had no intention to let him walk over me with his line of questioning, particularly when he tries to get me to admit to his line of questions. He seemed to me to get flustered. I did have a valid point as he was suggesting I was conspiring with police. He then changed the subject. It was like I was in a boxing ring and getting punched, but nothing collected me. Then he talked about Fiona McDonald.

Claire's lawyer at this point was not happy with my responses. It was obvious he was not getting anywhere by me not admitting to his submissions. I did glance at the judge. I noticed he had a slight grin on his face. The strange thing was on all this that I was allowed so much latitude, also being able to put my view across without any objection.

The he started on Fiona McDonald, my sister-in-law.

Mr. Mason, in one of your statements you said that Fiona McDonald your sister-in-law can look after Oliver during the day.

Yes, to a point this has been the case. However now there is change to her looking after Oliver. I have no doubt she has been pressured by Claire, along with her mother-in-law also her husband James, to stop her looking after Oliver and change her support for me. I may add here that Fiona is very nice person, and I know why she changed her mind, as the other point I would make is that Fiona was being hounded by Mr. and Mrs. McDonald as they were around at her place last Thursday week. They caused a commotion. They virtually told Fiona to keep right out of it and stop looking after Oliver. I know this for a fact as she told me.

Mr. Mason, is this why she was subpoenaed yesterday?

Sir, all I want to say in this matter that I do really feel sorry for Fiona as she is in a very awkward position like me. She is also an in-law, and I have no doubt she is being forced to side with them, I fully understand that. I really like Fiona. She has been put under an enormous amount of pressure, and again I may add it was Fiona who told me what happened. She loves Oliver, and she said to me, "I am sorry." I also think her husband James is behind this as well. The reason why she was subpoenaed was to allow her to tell her side of the story.

Mr. Wadsworth, Claire's lawyer, was all over the place. He then changed the topic by saying, "When Mrs. Mason left you and Oliver, Mrs. McDonald Senior was on your side. Was that not the case? Then now why the sudden change in her attitude?"

I responded and said to him, "Surely you know the old saying 'Blood is thicker than water.' If you do, then you do not have to be Einstein to work this out. Yes, I am sure, and no doubt Rose McDonald has changed her mind. This is very obvious, is it not, as she wants to back up her daughter. When Claire left, her mother was against her. Then as time went on, Claire told her so many lies about me, then you start believing in such untruths and was told about incidents that never happened and coming involved in many incidents. In my opinion, she should have not get herself involved. The sad fact is Mrs. Rose McDonald got caught up in it all."

At this point, I was not sure what was coming next. I do not think he liked my comment about blood is thicker than water, as this, in my opinion, sums up the family. Her lawyer then honed in about my work, and also about me having a company car. He first said, "Mr. Mason, reading your original statement, you mentioned you organized your work?"

My answer to this was, "Yes, I do, as I am a supervisor and have to pre-plan work ahead of schedule."

Then he asked, "Is it correct that you also indicated you can work from home?" "Yes, I do, lots of times."

Then he asked this stupid question, and I mean stupid. He said, "If you're able to work from home, then why do you have a firm's car?"

Well, this got me all fired up. I said, "I certainly object to your line of questioning and do not think it is any business of yours or of the court or anyone else that I have a company car. This is part of my condition of employment, and furthermore, I am not sure what you are driving at. I may ask what has this got to do with this case? It is like if I asked you does your legal firm supply you with a car. I am sure you would say mind my own business, and as to your point, working from home, as I have reports also planning to do at times, it's more convenient to do this at home rather than at the office. As long as this work gets done, it is irrelevant."

At this point I got very annoyed with this line of questioning.

I said, "Surely, I do not have to answer this line of questioning?"

Then my lawyer did see that this was getting to me, and she quickly got out of her chair and jumped to her feet. "Objection, Your Honor. Mr. Wadsworth is badgering my client, Mr. Mason." The judge responded and said, "Mr. Wadsworth, yes, I do agree with counsel for Mr. Mason, and please contain your questioning. Objection is in order."

Mr. Wadsworth, her lawyer, changed tactics, and the look on his face showed he was not happy. He wiped his brow, and he knew he was not getting his way. He said in a stern voice, "Very well then, I will change my question. I ask you, therefore, you travel around?"

No doubt at this point, I thought this solicitor was not going to stop, so I thought he was not going to get the better of me, and I responded by saying, "I work around Auckland only, and I work for Crest Foods Pty Ltd. Also I am not a traveller, I am a promotions supervisor."

"Mr. Mason, your line of work is setting up displays in shops, is that what you do?" Then he asked, "Is it correct that you also indicated you can work from home?"

"Yes, I do, lots of times."

Then he asked this stupid question and I mean stupid, he said If your able to work from home then why do you have a firm's car? Well, this got me all fired up, I said I certainly object to your line of questioning and do not think it is any business of yours or of the court or anyone else that I have a company car, this is part of my condition of employment and furthermore I am not sure what you are driving at, I may ask what this got to do with this case, it is like if I asked you does your legal firm supply you with a car, I am sure you would say mind my own business, and as to your point working from home as I have reports also planning to do at times its more convenient to do this at home rather than at the Office, as long as this work gets done it is irrelevant, at this point I got very annoyed with this line of questioning, I said surely, I do not have to answer this line of questioning then my lawyer did see that this was getting to me, she quickly got out of her chair and jumped to her feet, said Objection, your honor Mr: Wadsworth is badgering my client Mr. Mason The Judge responded and said Mr. Wadsworth, Yes, I do agree with counsel for Mr. Mason and please contain your questioning, objection is in order." at that point he again changed tactics and the look on his face as he was not getting his way he said in stern voice, very well then, I will change my question I ask you, therefore you travel around? No doubt at this point I thought this solicitor is not going to stop so I thought he was not going to get the better of me, I responded by saying I work around Auckland only, I work for Crest Foods Pty Ltd, also I am not a traveller as you say, I am a Promotions supervisor, he then went on to say, Mr. Mason your line of work is setting up displays in shops is that what you do?

> Sir, I am not sure of what you are driving at as I find your line of questioning about my work, also if I did display work, I am very confused at this point as to what, for the life of me, it has to do with this case. Now to answer your question, I don't actually do the displays. I have been a supervisor for some eighteen months now. I organize the

merchandising team within the company to undertake the displays in the stores I delegate them to do.

At this point, I was still wondering where all this was heading, and now here comes the punch line.

Mr. Mason, I take it you travel around frequently? And how often would you take Oliver to these calls?

Now I see what you are driving at as to your line of questioning and where you are coming from. I certainly do not take him into my visits to the stores I call on, as you seem to imply.

Mr. Mason, are you quite sure of that?

This went on for some time.

Yes, I am quite sure, in fact positive. It would not be hard to guess who gave you this information. I would often pick Oliver up when he finishes kindergarten and take him for a drive. He may play on the beach, for example, and as I would do my paperwork, being a supervisor. Like I said earlier, I have to do weekly reports on each person on my team, that is what I do.

If it is said you take Oliver on your rounds?

Sir, I cannot follow you as I do not understand that I take Oliver on my rounds, what is rounds as I do not have rounds. If you are referring to my territory, as this is the whole of Auckland. I would like to make this point to you that I get spied on in my own home. Oliver is spied on at his kindergarten, now you tell me my work is also. I ask when does all this harassment stop? As to where I go within my work capacity, only myself and the company, my Manager

I work for, do know my movements, of course unless I am being followed or just sheer guess work, which seems to be the case here, that is the situation.

There was one time I took Oliver to the Food Town supermarket after hours where he met Cookie Bear and was given a Cookie Bear for his birthday. I prearranged that. Now if that constitutes Oliver taken to my work, God forbid me.

It's hard to believe all this was played out in court as a lot was so trivial. Claire's lawyer I am not sure was getting anywhere. What he came up with next was all about who did Oliver's washing and ironing. This did, however, go on for a considerable time. Then he asked, "Mr. Mason, who  did Oliver's washing and ironing up until November 1975?"

I replied in a smug way by saying, "As to your question you put to me, and seeing Oliver was in my care, why do you ask who did Oliver's washing and ironing?"

He got a bit annoyed, then said loudly again, "Mr. Mason, I ask you, who has done his washing and ironing since November 1975 to June this year?"

I responded, No one else. I have looked after Oliver's washing and ironing all the way through from when Claire left, so November last year was when I got interim custody, so why mention from then to June this year? This did not make sense at all as she left in May last year, and I have been looking after Oliver's washing and ironing, contrary to what Claire and her family want you to believe. They may have done some from time to time. This is when he has been with them."

Then the issue came up about if I owned an iron or not.

Mr. Mason, when did you buy yourself an iron?

Sir, I will try and answer this the best way I can. Firstly, there was one iron in the house. The iron also like a lot of other chattels, these were taken or what I deem as stolen by Claire. When she came to the house, she did take a lot of possessions, including some of my private stuff like documents. I allowed her to take her own things. I found out later a lot of other chattels which belonged to the family home were taken, this included the iron.

Mr. Mason, Mrs. Mason said it was given to her as a birthday present?

Yes, of course she would say that. Also I can say that about a lot of things as well Claire always tries to justify a reason for everything she does.

Mr. Mason, I ask you again, was this given to her as a birthday present?

I cannot remember if it was a birthday present or not. Who cares as she has  it now? Maybe she got it for her birthday, so therefore, the iron can very well be owned by her. So what is the point here if she owned the iron or not? I will repeat what I said earlier, the possessions in the house should remain in the house until it is decided upon. That's the law, isn't it? You do not come in, take things away without the other person's knowledge.

Mr. Mason, when did you get yourself an iron?

I cannot recall exactly when, but most likely about six to eight months ago. This was just after Claire took the iron from the house, and up to when she took the iron, I did all the ironing. If that is what you seem to be driving at.

This again went on for a considerable time; he would not relent. I had a fair idea at this time what he was driving at. Then he asked, "Mr. Mason, I think it would it be fair to say you got the iron when you read the affidavit stating you did not have one?"

I replied, "I am sure that you would come to this, what you're leading up to. Again, I am not sure what is your point here, you sure seem to be very concerned if I owned an iron or not. Would it not stand to reason if the iron were taken from the house and I needed one, then I would go out and buy one? This would be the most logical thing to do."

I was at a loss at this point where her lawyer was getting at and making an issue over if I had an iron or not.

Then he continued this "if I owned an iron or not" issue. He said, "Mr. Mason, this would take us up to April this year then?"

I said, "That would be quite possible."

Then I was asked, "Before you got the iron, then who did the child's ironing?"

To answer your question, I did most of it. This was until I purchased another iron. This was for a brief period. I did borrow one from my next-door neighbor Susan, and sometimes Fiona would offer to do some for me at various times. This was until I purchased a new one. After that, I did all the washing and ironing.

Mr. Mason then would it be fair to say that Mrs. McDonald, the grandmother, had at no time do the ironing and washing?

I can certainly say you have made a big issue over one iron. I am no fool, I know what you are driving at. I have read all their affidavits on this topic. I find this rather offensive on your part and others to suggest I did not wash or iron clothes for Oliver, including myself. On occasions when Oliver stayed at the grandparents, yes, the grandmother did some washing and ironing, but not to the extent she has said she has done. What you're suggesting is that I do not care for my son. I may add also that the grandmother of Oliver went hostile toward me when I refused to sign Oliver over to her and Claire. That is the time when it all happened. This drawn-out saga of ironing and washing by Claire and her mother are simply to say I neglected him is utter nonsense as I always made sure Oliver had clean and ironed clothes. This is contrary to what Claire and her Mother say. You ask people who Oliver and I associated with, and you will get a different story. This includes people who live at my place or where he goes like the kindergarten. You will find that I look after Oliver like any responsible parent would.

Claire's lawyer, I will give him his dues as he tried in many ways to get at me. Yes, I was annoyed, and the strange thing was that he allowed me in many ways to elaborate on the many questions he asked me.

Now the topic changed again as he was not letting up with his insinuations that I did not take loving care of Oliver. This case is all about one little boy, Oliver, and on Claire's side to be true and prove I am unfit to have him.

The tone now shifted to how much time I spent with Oliver in relation to the movie business along with movies I show in my home theater.

Mr. Mason, in your affidavits, you said that you devote your time on weekends to Oliver. What do you do on Saturday nights?

That is a very broad question you ask. Well, I am not sure why you chose Saturday nights. Do you refer to when I have Oliver home with me every second weekend? I will try and answer your question the best way I can. As to Oliver when he is with me, I do the usual things like playtime, may go to the beach or go to the zoo, having dinner. Oliver would have a bath, then in bed between seven and eight p.m. That is usually my Saturdays. Now back to Saturday nights you refer to, Oliver will have dinner, and as I said, I get him ready for bed. He is usually well in bed by eight p.m.

Mr. Mason, can you recall sixteenth October?

Yes, I can. I showed a movie in my home cinema that night. I can assure you Oliver was in the house if that is what you are driving at.

Mr. Mason, are you sure he was not at the movie? Yes, I am sure 100 percent.

Then how often would you show these films? Possibly now on average, one a week.

On a Saturday night?

Most times on Saturday nights, other times on Sunday afternoon or middle of the week.

Please, can you tell the court what type of movies you show?

Yes, I can as I have a list of them, and recently, I showed *Tora! Tora! Tora!* That a is general classification. *Kelly's Heroes.* And for the kids, Bruce Lee's *Enter the Dragon.*

Can you tell us what other films? Including *Barry McKenzie Holds His Own*? Yes, I did show these movies as they were great Australian movies like *Barry McKenzie* as well as *Alvin Purple.* Also *The Sting* was another, and these films were also recently screened at the city cinemas. I screened these movies at the various clubs. I then screened them in my own home theater.

Then, Mr. Mason, with that, I take it you indulge extensively in showing movies for your friends?

Yes, but that is part of it as I have been involved in movies for many years now and operate a business, and my plan with my home theater was that I was going to form a movie club.

What type of club?

This was to get around the license to show movies as the clubs were by membership, and under the hire arrangements, this was in order. When I spoke about a club, this was to be set up to show the movies and be able to charge people to see them again under the license agreement. My plans that I was hoping to form such a club similar to the classic cinema in Queen Street, Auckland, in essence, a private cinema club.

You said you were going to set up a club? Yes, that is what I just explained to you.

I have this document, and it appears that you have formed a club?

Well, that is not entirely correct as this document you refer to is not entirely accurate, as when I put out the flyer at the time, trying to get people interested in establishing a private movie club. I did get around twenty people. My aim was to get, say, around fifty to make it pay. At the time the film distributors MGM and Fox said you cannot have people coming along paying for movies, so the only way to do this legally was to form a club and provide the movie free. That is what took place.

Do you provide refreshments?

Coca-Cola. They can also buy peanuts and other things like chips. Your document said free drinks?

Yes, that was the plan as this would be covered on the opening night if it went ahead. You are now talking about something that did not happen.

Mr. Mason, reading the document you sent out, it sure does not say you serve Fanta and cola?

It was a flyer I sent out to my friends, and Fanta and Coca-Cola are drinks. However, if the club was going ahead, this was for the opening night, and because of the poor response I got, the club did not get off the ground. So again I tell you, no club was formed.

Mr. Mason, then on these movie nights, you cannot devote your time to Oliver?

In due respect, as I am sorry to say, you are getting the incorrect information as you are stating and insinuating I am neglecting my son, that is not true. These Saturday nights you are referring to when Oliver is at home with me are the alternative fortnights with me, and his mother has him the other Saturday nights. Do you ask her what she does with Oliver when she has him on these nights? Does she devote her time to him? That's a fair question.

Claire's lawyer raised his voice at me and shouted, "Mr. Mason, please answer the question! Do you devote your time to Oliver on these nights?"

"Of course I do. My sole responsibility is my son, and again, you are making a big issue out of this. Please let me explain, and stop jumping out of your seat, and I am sure this will provide you what you do not want to know. Oliver is with me all day Saturday. This is of course when he is with me on these alternate weekends. On these nights if I show a movie, we would have dinner around six p.m., then I would give Oliver his bath, I then would dress him for bed.

"When the other parents arrive around, say, seven thirty, and many of these would bring their children, and Oliver would play with them until he went to bed around, say, around eight p.m. Generally the movie would start around eight fifteen, and most nights anyway, Dylan Watson would be there. He would start the movie. I guarantee the children are well supervised, including Oliver. He is often checked on during the night. Now if you think for one moment that Oliver is neglected or I do not devote time for him, you're horribly mistaken when these movies are on. You seem to be very concerned, or there is an issue relating to my movie business. When I show movies at my home and on it goes, let me say a few facts here. For one, is Claire present when I show these movies? No, she is not. Is Craig Kelly or her parents or James and Fiona? A big no. So what I say to you in all due respect, you have your facts totally wrong, like many of the issues you raised today and tackled me on. Whoever gave this information, I am sure, was not at these movie nights. I most certainly don't think so."

The court adjourned for lunch and would reconvene at 2:00 p.m.

At the recess, I said to my lawyer, "I got no interjection from the judge or any comment from you as Claire's solicitor was trying to show the court that I was neglecting Oliver. The badgering about the iron and the clothes not being ironed, I am sure all this was to make me look like I was neglecting my son."

Mrs. Chamberlain said, "Danial, I am letting him go on as he is saying a lot, which is hearsay. Also he has no proof of a lot he is bringing up, or he would submit that. The other point, your questions along with answers you're giving back to him is good. I am telling you again, the judge is taking down a lot of notes, you are doing well. I know it's hard on you, but by letting you go without my direction is good. I am sure the judge is also allowing you to give your full side of the issues being put to you. Rather unusual, I admit, as he has given you a lot of latitude. This just shows the judge you are no fool. In many cases, the judge would intervene, so that is a good sign. Now go have some lunch, and be back at 2:00 p.m."

I went off to the local café down the road from the court, and when I walked in, there was Claire along with her mother and Craig. Craig called out to me, and I was not sure what he said. I just ignored this and sat way down at the end of the café.

While I was walking out after I finished having coffee and something to eat, Claire spoke to me and said, "How is Oliver?"

I said, "Fine, he is being well cared for." I then went back to the courtroom. The court convened back at 2:00 p.m. from the luncheon adjournment.

It was just after 2:00 p.m., and I went back to the witness box. I always glanced over at times to see the look on Clair's face. I am sure she thinks that her lawyer has the better of me.

Then the questions that were put to me next was about me taking Oliver to Sunday school.

Mr. Mason, how many times you have taken Oliver to Sunday School in the last month?

At least three times.

What church do you take him?

Presbyterian Church in Auckland. How long has this been going on for?

Oliver started kindergarten at the beginning of this year. That is when he started Sunday school. Before that when I went to church, he played in the children's crèche.

Her lawyer skipped any more questions on Sunday school, and he changed the topic that I denied Claire access visits.

Mr. Mason, I put it to you why you did not allow your former wife access?

I am not sure, seeing you have asked the question, you have to tell me when. Were you allowing your wife to have access to Oliver in July and August this year?

I cannot specifically recall which month it was, however, there was one time, although I am not sure what you're driving at or referring to as Claire was denied access for a couple of weeks. Again this was over a dispute at my place.

Mr. Mason, you were in court when the decree nisi was made? Of course I was. I was the one who filed for the divorce.

Then, Mr. Mason, did you not hear the judge say the mother would have reasonable access?

Sir, yes, I am aware of all this. The judge did give her reasonable access. This did not change from when I was awarded interim custody in December last year. I am glad you asked this as it is a fair question. A letter was sent by my lawyer as per my instructions to her solicitor, now I assume it was you. This was to advise that access was stopped. I know she had her rights to have access. The decision I made, I can assure you, this was not taken lightly. Stopping of her access did arise from various incidents, that is when I decided to deny her access. Now you should have been fully aware of all this. Oliver is my son, and having the interim custody, then I have the full responsibility to take care of him. If I think it is not in the child's best interest when Claire creates issues at the home, I would deny her access and do it again.

Mr. Mason, there was an incident over car keys, and you denied her access.

Yes, there was this one incident on this Sunday night you mention. Claire dropped Oliver late around eight p.m., he usually comes back around six p.m. This was much later than normal. Most times Claire would just drop him off then go, but not this night as on this occasion, she just wanted to argue with me. She brought up things like his clothes stolen, getting bashed up at kindergarten, all this to cause an argument. Oliver watched all this play out from the lounge window. It was by no way a coincidence the police that night was also called. We learnt later it was her mother who called the police. Not long after they arrived, her mother turned up also. Claire alleges I threw her car keys on the roof. I did not. The police found the keys were in the ignition, and they told Claire and her mother to go.

Her lawyer quickly changed topic as he did not get any admission out of me as I clearly showed why I stopped access to Claire. Then he started on my financial position. This went on for some time as he tried to claim I was not in a very good financial position.

He first said, "I refer now to your affidavit that you have stated, 'I have sufficient money.'" And then he asked, "Do you have any debts?"

I replied by saying, "I think everyone has debts if you're paying off a house or running a business. Yes of course, I do, as I do have the house loan to pay. I am also paying off the color TV. I may add as to the house loan, even the deposit, Claire did not contribute, or she has paid anything toward the home loan. The loan payments came out of my business operating account."

You say you have a color television, so what is the TV worth? This is worth around $800.

The TV then, is that on high purchase?

Yes, I pay $33 a month. There is around $400 left to pay off. Claire was with me when we purchased this for the new home.

Then do you owe money to the taxation department?

No, I do not, as when I do my annual returns, they will owe me. Do you owe money to AMP insurance?

My answer is no.

Are you in arrears?

No, this is impossible to be in arrears as the payment automatically comes out of my wages from Crest Foods.

Then, Mr. Mason, there would be no reason for you to have a lengthy list of debts. I ask you, please look at this document. Is it your handwriting?

Of course it is. Yes, it is my scribble, and what about it? Read it out.

This is getting rather ridiculous. I now know where you are coming from. This is an old piece of scrap paper. I wrote all this down some time back. Claire stole that piece of paper from the house amongst other things. Now as you can see, I paid Mrs. Chamberlain $296. My TV payment and other payments for the house, as you should be aware of in business, you do a P&L profit-and-loss sheet, and if you had seen, this would show a different picture. So what you're showing me is stolen property. It is meaningless as this is outdated information. Now what about Claire taking this out of the house? She had no right to, and you bring this up in court today. That is my personal business. Surely it shows how shifty she is.

What about Burns, Lowe, and Clarke? What about them?

What does it show owing?

You are worried about $150 that it shows?

Did you happen to find out if this was paid or not? This was.

The next item that you owed, the taxation department $160.

Everyone does tax returns each year, and on my annual return, I received a payment back from them $360, and they had deducted the $160, so now, in fact, I did not owe them anything. You see that in fact, all you have asked has come to nothing.

The next item shows you owe James and Fiona $30.

Yes, that is paid also. Sir, I will say this to you that I am possibly more financially sound than Claire and her partner. I operate a very lucrative business, have a full- time job, and am well paid, so if you see my bank statement, it would verify this. So I think you're barking up the wrong tree here, and again, I stress to you, the document you are referring to is just a scrap of paper, and it was taken from the house by my ex-wife. This was well over six months ago. I get exceptionally good money from my work being a supervisor, around $9,000 per annum, and I have regular money coming in from the movie business. This can be up to $200 clear profit or more most weeks, so the information you have with due respect is irrelevant as it's not current. I am reasonably well off, also have accumulated many assets.You offered Claire $2,000 in settlement. When did you do this?

I am not sure exactly when, possibly beginning of the year. It was Claire who asked for this.

Was this conveyed to her then solicitor, and do you know when?

Sir, I am not a mind reader. I do not have a clue. Also, how would I know what she tells her solicitor? I think you should ask her that question. Also you being her solicitor, you should know, so why ask me?

Regarding your offer to your ex-wife, Ms. Mason, I now put it to you, simultaneously with you making that offer of settlement, this is when you drew up the lists of debts?

I would often scribble out stuff relating to payments before I do a budget in my books, like a profit-and-loss statement, as I told you before and again. I often use pieces of paper, and they may have different calculations. Doing budgets is what I call properly running a household or a business, which is what people do, would you not think so?

Your wages you earn at Crest Foods Company, is this before tax? Yes, that is my gross amount before Tax.

This hearing was getting to me as a lot was what I called trivial stuff as Claire's lawyer dealt with issues that, in my opinion, were irrelevant. The affidavits provided by Claire and her family made an issue about the movie business and that I also operated the home cinema. I was well prepared when this came up, and now this was her lawyer's next line of attack.

Mr. Mason, your movie business, what is it you undertake to screen films?

I have an agent as well as a contract with the film distributors in Auckland. I hire the movies, then I screen them privately to clubs. Members only. What we do is screen these feature movies, and I charge the club $250 per screening, and I employ the projector operators.

Does the movie business undertake screenings when you are not present?

Yes, as I employ another projectionist, and we rotate the nights. This frees me up to look after Oliver.

What is the name of the company? Auckland Movie Hire Services Pty Ltd.

I ask you, were you at the Auckland Workingman's Club a week ago, on a Thursday night?

No, I was not there a week ago. The last time was well over a month ago. This was the only show I have done recently as Claire's young brother, John, was going to work that night. I have trained him to be a projectionist as a backup for both Dylan and I. However, I was told this night, his mother and father put pressure on him and stopped him working for me.

Was this Claire's brother?

Yes, I did tell you this. It is Claire's youngest brother, John. Also he was going to do the Saturday afternoon show at the rugby leagues club for the children as he was stopped by his parents. I then had to make other arrangements.

When did you cease employing John?

I never ceased employing John. He stopped doing the movies after I was told his father hit him, and he was told not to go to my place again and do the work for me. John then stayed with James and Fiona for a while. I did not cease his employment, his parents did.

Was the real reason his mother, Rose McDonald, and his father told John not to go because you are consuming alcohol at these clubs? Was this not the reason?

Well, the reason was not clear to me as John had been doing this for a length of time, and the alcohol never were questioned as one would know that these clubs serve alcohol, so that was not the position here. Also he was employed by me, not the clubs. He is a good guy and a good worker.

How old is John?

He is seventeen years old, and as a matter of interest, he borrowed the use of the home cinema one night when I attended a ball, and he had a party there with his friends. He arranged this. I did not, and his friends came along to see a movie.

Do you show X-rated movies, what they class as blue movies?

No, I do not. I know this has come up in various affidavits. The police did raid my property and found nothing at all. You see, all this was to try and discredit me, allegations that I show blue movies, to having Oliver up all hours watching movies, also suggesting that I have him to watch movies like *Barry McKenzie* and others is just sheer nonsense. Where is their proof? If they are not there at the movies or at my home, how would they know what goes on in my house?

I also operate Friday night movies at the local hall opposite the shopping town center as this is a community service sanctioned by council, shopping center, and police. And due to this, the crime rate on Friday nights has dropped, and up top two hundred kids turn up each week. I also do charity shows to raise money for the kindergarten.

I am sure none of this is mentioned regarding my movie business.

Then the questioning turned to when Oliver goes to school, and the line of questions was, in my opinion, way over the top as you will see.

Mr. Mason, when Oliver reaches the age of five, what do you propose to do for schooling?

This of course highly depends on the outcome of this hearing. If I was awarded custody, I would propose. he goes to the school in Buckland Road in Mangere.

This next lot of questions like "How far this from your home?", this is where he just lost the plot in my opinion.

Mr. Mason, can you tell me how far the school from your home is? Not far as it is less than five minutes' walk.

Mr. Mason, did you say in your affidavit that the school is at the end of your street?

Technically, the school is not. It was just a figure of speech.

Mr. Mason, you said it was, but now you say it is not at the end of the street?

Sir, you're splitting hairs. This is really annoying me to no end. I just told you this was just a figure of speech. I am sorry, but you are messing with words. End of the street or around the corner, down the road, all the same thing. If you go down to the bottom of the street, you look to the left, the school is in sight, just over the main road. Few hundred meters away. So what is the big deal you're getting at?

But it is some distance from where you live, is that not the case?

Sir, I am not quite sure what is your point here, as I have just told you it is at the end of the street, and again I say it was just a matter of figure of speech. So the point I ask is if Oliver will be going to the local school, what is the issue then how far it is? The important thing is he will be attending a school close by, only a few minutes' walk at best. You and Claire and Craig and others have made a big issue of this in their affidavits like you have shown today. The school is only less than four minutes maximum from my home. I may add Oliver will have at least ten children he has grown up within the neighborhood that will be attending the school, as well as there will be at least six children who go to the same kindergarten as him. They are all his mates. Some might be older than him, but they have grown up together, that is a good thing. I cannot see for the life of me the issue you are trying to make here as to how far is the school from our house. If you try to say is it safe for him, yes, there is a designated manned crossing over the main road that the school takes care of. I can assure you he will be well looked after going to school and after school.

I am not happy with your constant line of questioning when you do not get your facts right. Also you try to nipper late things to suit your own agenda.

The judge looked at me, and he kind off smiled. I took that as he agreed with what I was saying. This next line of questioning made me terribly angry, and it just showed what lengths they will try and discredit me.

The topic changed to that I do not take proper care of my son. I was asked, "Mr. Mason, Oliver, the child in your care and custody, do you constantly keep an eye on him?

Yes, of course, I always do.

I put to you, does Oliver run or wander around and you not knowing about it?

Of course not, as I always know where he is. He certainly does not wander around as you suggest.

You sure now? Not even for a half hour?

Here we go again. I do know exactly what you are referring to. I just wish people will get their facts straight, including the welfare officer report. As to the matter you are referring was on a Sunday afternoon, the Māori boy Peter, who lives in the house at the back of us, came over and asked could he and his little brother and sister take Oliver down to the shops. He is a very sensible boy, he is twelve years old.

I did know the family very well, they are a very respected Māori family, so I let Oliver go with them, and I gave him some money to spend at the shop. The older boy Peter, I trusted him with Oliver. On the way there, his uncle James and his aunty Fiona were going along in their van. They spotted Oliver with the other children, and they brought Oliver back to their house, then they called me.

I understand they crossed a main intersection on his journey? Yes, they had to cross the road, it was a main road.

So they crossed the main intersection on that journey, and the school is across the main intersection with patrols and flags and teachers at the crossing? And on that day, the patrols, were they there?

Mr. Wadsworth, in due respect with your line of questioning, I may say it is getting rather ridiculous. This was on a Sunday afternoon. Also anyone would know this crossing would not be staffed or have flags on a Sunday, only on schooldays patrols would be at the crossing. I may add, the sad part of all this is I cannot put a foot right, and the whole scenario about how far the school is from our house, the school crossings, and you are implying that I am not a responsible father. I object to that line of questioning as I do take care of Oliver and his safety, and the eldest boy, he was with his younger brother and sister, and he did ask me for permission, and I said yes. I said use the school crossing for safety. This is despite what his uncle James has said. He also has made a very racist slur on the Māori people as he did not like the children Oliver was with as they were Māori. This is very racist in my view, and you say nothing about that, do you? I know you are acting in good faith for my ex-wife. There are many allegations you have made so far today, which does not have a bearing on what is best for my son. Please get your facts right.

I looked at Mrs. Chamberlain, and she gave me a nod of approval I think she will agree with me he has made some terrible errors and has not done his homework on what he is presenting. Does this help Claire? I am not sure at this point. The racist remarks about the Māori children, in my opinion, are not acceptable.

Mr. Mason, you said that Oliver is not present when any movies are shown?

I have already told you, I do not have Oliver at the movies at night when he is with me on the weekend, and I show a movie to the local kids, he would be there as these are usually on Saturday afternoons. At nights when I have movies, Oliver, he is in the house. I can assure you he is not at the movies. He might occasionally wander into the projector room, but I would take him back inside. The other point I make is that other parents with children are there also, and one parent stays in the house to supervise the children. It is well organised as I previously explained.

Mr. Mason, I take it you show many moves, including Saturday, how many movies you run each week?

I presume you are referring to my home theater as this depends as usually on what movies I screen at the clubs on a given week, and I then show them in my home theater on average one per week. Sunday may show a special screening, for instance the church youth group as I ran a special night for them that was on a Sunday night, but again this is not frequent on Sundays. Also on odd occasions, I would have a midweek screening to raise money for the kindergarten. Now as far as the clubs go, usually twice a week, and I have others now to run this for me. I also do a Friday night show at the town center as community service, and Dylan runs this night. You now seem to be focusing on my movies I have at home, despite what you say or others, I can assure you Oliver is well cared for when the movies are shown when he is not at his mother's. One other point I will make is this. Claire and her family are not present at these movie nights, so they cannot know what goes on and particularly where Oliver is concerned.

I was asked about what doctor I take Oliver to.

Mr. Mason do you take Oliver to a Dr. McGrath from November last year? Who was your doctor at the time?

Dr. Henderson.

Then why did you change doctors?

I felt extraordinarily strong about this as Claire's mother was saying things to the doctor regarding Oliver as we all were going to the same doctor. He was not doing the right thing for Oliver, and I changed Doctors. I cannot see what the issue is here also what you are applying. If I think Oliver can get better medical treatment elsewhere, then surely that is my prerogative.

Then he asked the ridiculous.

Has your wife ever been to him?

That is her business what doctor she goes to, that is private. The same applies to me, that is my business what doctor I go to. I do the best for Oliver, that is my concern and priority.

Mr. Mason, would it be fair to say when you see this doctor, you tell him things, he is not able to know if they are true or not?

Well, I suppose that is your learned opinion. I am not sure what you are driving at here. If it is about Oliver's sickness, he would know all about it. That is also patient confidentiality.

The doctor thing with Claire's lawyer did not relent, and he went on to say,

As you have Oliver in your custody all the time, I am talking about when Oliver comes back from his mother's that you have taken Oliver every week to the doctors.

Again, Mr. Wadsworth, I am not sure where you get this information from, it's simply not true as I do not.

Tell me then, how often would you take him to the doctors?

On average, I would be about once a month, however, lately, it has been once  a fortnight, not weekly as you suggest. He has been taken to the doctors mainly because he has a bronchial condition that has been over the past six to eight weeks. Recently he had tests done at the Middlemore Hospital, and they came back okay, and they said there was nothing wrong. The doctor treated him for a viral infection.

Then I was asked another ridiculous question.

Can you tell me how did he contracted the viral infection?

Sir, in all due respects, I am not a doctor, and the question you ask me, how does one contact a viral infection, it is the same as you or I do. Also seeing I am not a doctor, you should ask a medical person that one.

Then I ask you, is Oliver properly clothed and dressed?

What a question this is. It is like going up to someone in the street and asking, "Is your child properly clothed and dressed?" I am quite sure I know what this is leading up to. Oliver gets sick, and his mother then says I do not dress him properly or make out he is not warm. All children get sick at some stage. Oliver is no different than any other child. Sometimes they pick up various illnesses mainly from others. This could be at his kindergarten or elsewhere,who knows. I do spend a lot on his clothes. I may add I have never been given one cent from Claire to buy clothes, or she has given me any, contrary to what she says. Oliver is well cared for, I can assure you of that. I take offense if you suggest otherwise.

Then her Lawyer embarked on who gave him what as to his toys.

Mr. Mason, Oliver has a slide. Can you tell me who gave him the slide he owns?

His grandparents gave the slide to Oliver. What about the tricycle?
Again, his grandparents.

Does Oliver have a rocking horse?

Yes, he did have one as a child. He has grown out of that now. Of course, it is only natural grandparents will give him toys.

What about the electric train set?

Yes, I bought that for him. It's a full electric train set in which I purchased and is still operating, and a lot was spent on that. It was around $300 for the complete set. I also brought a lot of extra accessories for it. Oliver has his own books, many toys for a child of that age. You see, Claire and the grandparents are always trying to outdo each other on presents to encourage affection for Oliver. I do not go along with this as this is not my way. One good example, I bought Oliver a bicycle, so his mother bought a better one, then the grandparents did the same. These are just material things. What Oliver needs most is stability in his life.

Then the topic changed about me taking Oliver to Australia.

Mr. Mason, I understand you have taken Oliver to Australia twice now?

Yes, I have. Oliver loves the airplane ride. He is quite a different boy, I must say, away from all the upsets he experiences here.

Do you plan to take Oliver this Christmas to Australia?

It all depends on this hearing and who gets custody, so I would love to.

Then, Mr. Mason, I would say to you is this very unfair that you have had Oliver for two Christmases, running and taken him to Australia?

Sir, my answer to you is quite simple as my mother in Australia, his grandmother, has not seen him for now over twelve months, whereas his mother and grandparents here in New Zealand see him often. So I see no issue here. They also have time with him before he goes away and when he returns.

The grandmother of Oliver and his great-grandmother here in New Zealand would not be able to see him at Christmas?

Well, like I have just said, they can see him before he goes if that is what happens. Mr. Mason, the grandmother here that is Claire's mother is forty-five, her mother has just turned eighty. They will be deprived some two Christmases running.

Sir, you are making a big issue out of this. Then why cannot they arrange a pre- Christmas dinner and exchange presents as do a lot of families undertake? I do not think that me going back with Oliver for Christmas as they all see him throughout the year.

Mr. Mason, why is that not so?

On the surface, technically, yes. However, with the way Mrs. Rose McDonald is carrying on as she does, also Mr. Kevin McDonald along with Claire and the rest, it will do

Oliver a lot of good to get away from it all for a while. It's a breath of fresh air for us both, and Oliver can see cousins along with his grandmother and his uncle and aunts, which there are many.

I have no further questions at this time.

I still found the line of questioning by Clair's lawyer in lots of ways quite bizarre. This was over several hours and also was quite exhausting. I know in a lot of my answers I was allowed plenty of latitude. I did question him on many of his questions. I did notice the judge making plenty of notes. I also looked at him many times when I answered questions put to me. The issue is now how much was said and went against me.

*Re-XD Mrs. Chamberlain*

Mrs. Chamberlain raised herself out of her chair, and I did notice she had taken down many notes and was ready to readdress me. I felt the line of questioning by Claire's lawyer was way over the top as he was just clutching at straws. I also understand that it is his job. He was trying for me to confess or say things that suited him. He just wanted to make some key points stick, but I just did not allow him to get away with a lot he said that could not be substantiated.

I know a lot was hotly disputed, and now this may be my chance to now set the record straight as Mrs. Chamberlain is I am sure more experienced and astute than Claire's lawyer.

Ms. Chamberlain commenced her re-XD. She always spoke in an incredibly quiet but a very authoritarian voice.

Mr. Mason, for the duration of your marriage, did you form an adulterous relationship with anyone?"

No, not at all.

Craig Kelly, was he living with his wife when he formed the adulterous relationship with your wife?

Yes, I do understand both people left their respective family homes at the same time on the same weekend.

How do you know that about Craig Kelly?

It was just after Claire left, Craig's wife called me. She said, "Claire your wife is with my husband" She was terribly upset about her young daughter as I was told she took this very bad. I arranged to meet up with Craig's wife, and she did tell me a lot about Craig and his past.

Prior to Mr. Kelly coming on the scene, were you happily married? Most definitely. I loved my wife dearly.

Today you told the court that you take Oliver regularly to the doctors?

This I found usually was the case when he comes home from his weekend stay with his mother, and often, he would come home and start crying, and often he would start vomiting. The things he would come out with like "I hate going around to Mummy." When I take him to the doctor, we do not question him at all. He has recently come out with saying Craig is belting him. I think this may be made up as I am sure in the mother's presence, she would not allow that to take place. For some reason he says he does not want to go back there, he comes out with that quite a bit. Maybe Oliver is seeking attention.

Mr. Mason, we have discussed many and various incidents which have taken place over the last month or so. I refer to the last incident when Mr. Baxter was present when Fiona McDonald arrived, was Oliver present?

Yes, Oliver was present, and then he became emotionally upset. He also messed and wet his pants. He wanted to be sick. He was just up in the air filled with emotion.

Who caused that?

His mother Claire did.

You also refer to another incident as a result access was withheld. Was Oliver present then?

Yes, again he was terribly upset. He had difficulty sleeping at night. Has Mrs. Mason collected the child without any incident?

On a few rare occasions, not many though.

Mr. Mason, in your view, would it assist Oliver if someone else was to collect him and bring him back home?

Many times, I have suggested this, but she always refuses, and she still wants to pick him and bring him back home to my place.

So you have made suggestions?

Most certainly on several occasions, I have suggested the town center or somewhere, rather than at my place to avoid having a scene or confrontation as this seems to be the crux of the whole problem. Like I said to the police officers on many occasions, only if she would come and take Oliver away without any problem. I feel it would be better and right for both me and Oliver, but Claire always seems to pick on something. When Oliver is returned, she hangs around for far too long rather than leave. Then Oliver gets into a terrible state.

What contact, if any, do you have with Mrs. Mason during the week?

I just try and avoid her. None I suppose. Occasionally she comes around during the week without notice.

Does Mrs. Mason telephone you?

Yes, she does. Most days all the time. Also this can be up to four times day.

When does she call you?"

When I am at my home, I usually hang up anyway. She seems to know when I arrive home later in the day and usually when I am ready to leave in the mornings.

Were there any other witnesses to the last incident in which Mrs. Mason and Mrs. McDonald claim to be assaulted?

There were several. When Fiona McDonald arrived on the scene, there was Mr. Jim Baxter at the window looking out, my next-door neighbor, and there were two other neighbors also watching on.

What was the language like?

Absolutely foul. I sat half the time on the front steps of the house laughing my head off as they made such a fool of themselves. Getting back to the incident that took place that day as they claimed to police, they were assaulted. I was never charged by the police.

As I understand, the police have investigated their complaints? Yes, they certainly did.

And you have never been charged?

That is correct. Of all the complaints, I have never been charged.

I now refer to the paper in which you claim Mrs. Mason had taken this from the house showing debts. Can you say whether you owe the amounts of $500?

I am glad you have mentioned this. That is the paper Claire stole that you are referring to, and the $500, that amount that you also refer to is not owing. The plan now is it will now go into a new company. I along with others will form a new movie business. The $500 originally borrowed from them to purchase extra equipment, as all the equipment is worth a lot of money fully paid for worth several thousand dollars. I am using that as collateral and contribution asset. We decided to do this because of Claire. It is a shame we have to fold the original Movie Hire Company.

Mr. Mason, I now ask you, in your affidavit, you stated that you could write a lengthy epistle about your problems?

Yes, I could, and I will say this. Oliver will always have his mother, also his grandparents, and no one can deny them the rights to see the child. With all the trouble I have had, I have stopped taking him down to the grandparents as in my opinion, they are not acting responsibly. On many occasions, I have been thrown out of their house. It is unfortunate that Claire goes down there to her parents as she tells them things that are not true. I have tried not to get into any arguments as to what she is telling them. I try and speak the truth to them what is going on, but that falls on deaf ears, but Claire's father, if he has too much to drink, he will attack me.

Would you make Oliver available to Mr. and Mrs. McDonald Sr.? Yes, most definitely.

The judge then asked.

Mr. Mason, you said that you would permit the grandparents to have access? Yes, Your Honor, that is correct.

What about your wife? Yes, definitely.

How much access do you think your wife should have?

I would say on a reasonable basis. I would give her access each weekend. The whole weekend?

I suppose some weekends as I would like also to spend time over weekends and take the boy away for the day, but I would not object if she took him Saturday morning and through to Sunday night.

Some weekends?

Yes, in all honesty, I have not denied her that right. The only time it was done was when she abused that right or when she had caused trouble at my home.

Do you know of anyone who would act as a go-between for the purpose of handling the boy over to your wife?

Yes, I could think of several people who would do it. There is a couple in Pakuranga, a Mr. and Mrs. Doherty. They have young children of their own, and they have also suggested to me they would. I think also if all settles down, Fiona his aunty would be quite happy to do so as she always says she really loves Oliver. I think even Mr. Peter Charles would also do it for me. I could possibly think of a lot of people that would be only too happy to do this to defuse any future issues.

Suppose I was to say that your wife should have custody? How much access would you expect to have?

Well, Your Honor, then again, I suppose it would have to be on the same basis, would it not? Can I please make this point that Oliver has been with me now for eighteen months, and to uproot him now will set the child back. The affair has been going on for now two years. Twelve months prior to her leaving, she was associated in an affair with Mr. Kelly. It has been difficult for Oliver as well as me. Over the time she has left, I have talked to Oliver and told him he must go with his mother as he was anti his mother. I have persuaded Oliver and encouraged him to see his mother.

Judge said, "No further questions." He then said to Mrs. Chamberlain she can continue, and she replied, "I have no further questions."

I sat down next to my lawyer. I said to her, "There is a lot you could have asked me regarding what Claire's lawyer went on about on many issues."

"Danial," she said, "what you responded to her lawyer was very good. Now settle down and let your witnesses tell the court the other side of many arguments put forward today."

The court was adjourned at 3:05 p.m. The court resumed at 3:20 p.m.

*Evidence by Mrs. Dawn Tuohy*

Mrs. Chamberlain called her first witness. "I now call on Mrs. Tuohy."

This has come about that Claire Mason had made serious allegations about the kindergarten and its staff as well as the way I dressed Oliver.

Maria Dawn Tuohy was sworn in, and Mrs. Chamberlain asked, "Can you tell the court your occupation and that you submitted an affidavit in reply to the allegations made regarding the kindergarten?"

Yes, I am head teacher of Kings Lake Kindergarten. I confirm my submission as being true and correct.

Mr. Wadsworth opened by asking,

Can you recall when did Oliver Mason first start at Kings Lake?

She answered,

To the best of my knowledge, February this year.

Then he asked,

In your capacity as head teacher, do you take care of him? Yes, I do.

You are a regular teacher of him? Yes, I am.

I put it to you if the suggestion was made to members of your staff that they had indicated to Oliver, he had not a mother?

Mrs. Tuohy replied,

This is outrageous. I could not imagine any of my staff say such a thing, let alone to a young child. I would most definitely say this is incorrect and a slur on the kindergarten.

Mrs. Touhy, do you recall the activity you had the children perform for Mother's Day?

Yes, we had various luncheons mothers can attend. They can also attend our programs every day. Quite often the children like to paint for their mothers.

For Mother's Day, were the children asked to prepare a card for their mother? Yes, this would have been done.

Did you remember seeing a card made by Oliver Mason?

I cannot recall, but possibly it would be the same as everyone else.

Who often collects Oliver from kindergarten? Normally his aunt, I think she is.

Ever spoke to her?

Just said hello or goodbye.

How often would Mr. Mason collect the child?

Well, I would say once or twice, on average some weeks three times. I see more of him in one week, not the following. He always brings the child in every morning.

You said the child started in February this year? Yes, that is correct.

Did Mr. Mason arrange this and introduce himself at this stage? Yes, he registered Oliver late last year.

From June, has there been any difference?

The same standard as before, however, a bit quieter than normal for a four-year-old. Has he been upset?

Yes, some mornings. I would not say upset, I would say incredibly quiet as he would not answer me when I spoke to him.

When would this occur?

Usually the beginning of the week, Mondays.

The questions changed to the allegation made by Claire Mason that Oliver was bashed up at kindergarten.
Mr. Wadsworth asked,

It would be usual for children at school to have a fight with another child? Yes, very normal.

When he says he has been bashed up at kindergarten, this would be the type of thing?

Yes, when boys play tag, they push against trolleys, which is normal. Quite often, they would act out a TV program they have seen the night before.

Have any children been injured as a result? No, they are very well supervised.

No further questions, Your Honor.

*RE-XD Mrs. Chamberlain*

Mrs. Tuohy, if you were asked what Oliver's clothing was like, would you say his clothes were clean?

Oliver came every day neatly dressed, in fact, well dressed, and always clean and tidy hair. It's a credit to his father.

The judge then interrupted the questioning and asked,

Mrs. Tuohy, where precisely is this kindergarten?

100 Kinglake Drive, Mangere. This is right next to the shopping center.

What are the hours?

Quarter to nine in the morning until twelve noon.

What time do the children usually arrive?

Usually between eight thirty to eight forty-five. I am always there at eight a.m. each day. The children leave around twelve middays. It just depends, but I am always there as we have a double session.

If a child were not picked up, there is somebody there to look after them?

Yes, always.

The judge said, "No further questions. You may stay down."

*Evidence of Dylan Watson*

Mrs. Chamberlain called her next witness, Mr. Dylan Watson.

Dylan was my neighbor where I previously lived in Buckland Road, and he also was my projectionist running the screenings for me at the various clubs.

He was duly sworn in and stated he was a plumber by trade, and he knows both the petitioner and the respondent. "I have sworn an affidavit, and I confirm that as true and correct."

Mr. Wadsworth asked Mr. Watson,

How long have you known the parties before they separated in May last year?

Around eighteen months. Danial was a neighbor, and after a while, we became associated through the movie business that Danial set up. I was friendly with both. Also my wife knew Mrs. Mason.

Mr. Watson, I now refer you to your affidavit when you stated that Mrs. Mason had taken an overdose of sleeping pills, and you stated Valium. How did you know that?

Sir, Danial and I were out this night showing a movie at the workingman's club in Onehunga, and we arrived back around 11:30 p.m. Daniel took out his house key and could not open the door, so we went around the back of the house to the back door. We could not open the door either. All the windows were closed. We looked into the main bedroom through the venetian blinds. We could see Claire in the bed. We could hear slight moaning. We knocked on the window loudly, and she did not reply.

This went on for some time, I then said to Danial, "Looks like she is sick." Danial again was knocking on the window, yelling out, "It is me!" and no response. I said to Danial, "The only thing we can do now is break down the back door" as this was the only way we could get inside of the house. We did that with a jemmy I had at my place. On entering the house, the only light on was the hall one, which filtered into the bedroom where Claire was. Then we both entered the bedroom, and Danial tried to wake her up. I noticed on the floor by the bed was a small bottle containing tablets. Danial picked the bottle up, and I said, "What is in it?" He replied, "Far as I know, it's Valium tablets." I asked how many were in the bottle, and he said quite a few. I said, "Has she taken many?" "It seems she has," Danial replied, not sure how many as by the state she was in, it looked like a few.

I then left the house and got my wife Addison out of bed. I brought her to the house as she was a registered nurse. At that stage, we all panicked as we could not arouse her. My wife said we need to ring the hospital, so in the meantime, after some constant shaking and calling out to her, she started to come around. The hospital asked my wife, "Is she conscious?" My wife answered, "Yes, but drowsy, very drowsy." Also she could not speak to us. They advised to let her sleep it off, and if there was any change, we had to bring her in and call 111 for an ambulance.

Mr. Watson, I then suppose Mrs. Mason told you she took an overdose?

How could she as she was so drowsy? To answer your question, no, she did  not tell me. I said the evidence was on the bottle found on the floor. She was very unresponsive, and my wife being a trained nurse as well confirmed that.

Look, we all knew what she had done. Claire had been a sensible woman, but now she has become very emotional.

Then how did you see through the windows?

I said before, through the venetian blinds as they were not fully closed. Is it your opinion Mrs. Mason has never been violent?

Not to my knowledge.

If allegations are made against her that she has a violent propensity, that would be correct?

Yes, but with Mr. and Mrs. McDonald, her parents, behind you, who would not be violent?

How often did you do into the Masons' house? Very often, at least four times a week.

Judge: When you were neighbors, where did you live? 150 Buckland Road, Otahuhu.

How far from where Mr. Mason lived?

Two houses away.

Judge: Back to counsel, Mr. Wadsworth.

How often did you visit them when they lived at their new home in Clee Crescent?

Quite often to help Danial around the section as it was a new home, and I offered my services the best way I could.

How often would you go?

Most times two or three days a week. How many weeks altogether?

I would say about every week.

For how many weeks did you see both at Buckland Road?

I have been there nearly every day of the week virtually apart from when I do overtime, the reason being I am Daniel's backup projectionist.

It was said that you have never been in the house when Mrs. Mason was there once, is this correct?

Yes, definitely, this is since she has left. Ever been to Mr. Mason's picture shows?

Yes, sir. I just explained to you that I work for Danial, so of course, I have been to them as I said that I work for Danial as his projectionist and run movie nights for him.

Was this being the reason the house at Clee Crescent had the home cinema setup?

Daniels's love of cinema. He told me that is why he wanted his home cinema, and yes, I go often to the movies there. It's a great setup.

I ask you, does Mr. Mason do long hours?

No, it was me who did the long hours. This was the reason Danial employed me to make sure he spent nights at home with Oliver.

Was alcohol provided at the movies?

No, unless they bring their own. I have a wife and kids to keep, and I cannot afford to buy alcohol.

Mr. Watson, you did not like wandering the streets when you were slightly intoxicated?

I take exception to this. For heaven's sake, I do not know where you got that from. This is totally incorrect and very unfair to say at all. I am now wondering if this is now the plan to discredit people who support Danial or to suit their own agenda, and what has this defamatory remark about me to do with the case at hand? I think you should retract this remark.

Mrs. Mason left Oliver at her parents' place on occasions? Yes.

The judge then asked Mr. Watson,

Mr. Watson, you spoke of the time Mrs. Mason was on the bed asleep, did you go into the room with Mr. Mason.?

Yes, I did.

Did you see the bottle? Did you see the label?

Yes, I did and told my wife.

What was on the label?

It said Valium tablets.

Yes, and I gave it to my wife when she rang the hospital as they wanted to know what the tablets were.

The judge said, "Back to counsel."

Can you recall if when Mrs. Mason left the child at her mother's place?

If you refer to the weekend she left, she did on the Saturday.

Was Oliver there at the house on the Friday?

Yes, and he was taken to the grandmother early Saturday morning.

Mrs. Mason has stated her mother received the child Friday night, is that correct?

Sir, far as I know, I could not say that as I was not there Friday night at their place. However, I assumed he was at his home Friday night because went I went around on Saturday morning, and Oliver was there.

Mr. Watson, you said he was taken Saturday.

Yes, that is right as I was there that Saturday morning. Was Oliver taken to the mother-in-law's?

That is right, to his grandparents' house by Claire around ten a.m.

Wadsworth: No more questions, Your Honor.

Mrs. Chamberlain then readdressed Dylan Watson.

Mr. Watson, you said if you had known what Mr. and Mrs. McDonald were like, what did you mean by that?

I found they are very unstable people. I have met them on several occasions, and when there is an argument, they're always being there, and they were the cause of it when we came home from doing a movie screening at the club. They were there this night. They knew very well that there was something between Claire and Craig then. There was an argument, and it ended up in the street. Mr. McDonald had too much to drink that night. The argument was about Claire going out with Craig Kelly. Claire denied this to her mother, and Mrs. McDonald belted Claire right across the face with an open hand.

Have you seen Mr. or Mrs. McDonald Senior since the separation?

Yes, on several occasions. There has always been more harassment lately. Once they got it into their minds there was nothing wrong with Claire, they switched sides, but Mrs. McDonald always twists the truth. Mrs. McDonald on one occasion, I was there at the new house, and she was asked to get off the property as she was abusive to Danial, and she had been asked to go several times, but she refused, saying it was her daughter's home.

What was her language like?

I would not like my wife to use that language in public.

Mr. Watson, were you present at Oliver's fourth birthday party and the movie *The Sting* shown?

Yes, I was there with my wife and children, and I operated the projector that night.

Where was Oliver?

He was inside with the other children, and my wife minded them while the movie was on.

Did the McDonalds stay for the movie?

Yes, they were all there.

No more questions, Your Honor.

*Evidence by Peter Charles Benson*

Peter was a particularly good friend of the family, and he also knew and worked at some point with Craig Kelly and Claire. He is a single father himself with two lovely daughters. His wife hada breakdown and was placed into an institution, and he was given custodian rights for his two girls. His situation was totally different from mine.

Mrs. Chamberlain called Peter Benson to the stand as her next witness, and he was sworn in, and he stated that he knew both the petitioner and respondent and co-respondent. "I have sworn an affidavit, and I confirm it as true and correct."

The line of questioning to Peter Benson by Mr. Wadsworth was all about when he served a divorce petition on Mrs. Mason as well as Craig Kelly. He also stated that he was with Mr. Watson, and jointly they served the petition.

> Mr. Benson, can you tell the court where the garage is situated in relation to the premises?

> Sir, there are two units, and the garage separates the two units.

> Can you then tell the court does the garage door go up or down?

> Down.

This became quite interesting as he was asked where the car was, and he answered there were two cars inside the garage. Then he was asked this.

> If the car was inside the garage, how can you say the car they each drove was inside the garage?

> No, sir, I do not think I said that at all as I said two cars.

Mr. Benson, I refer to your affidavit, you said the car was in the garage and the doors down, and if that was the case, how did you know the car was there?

Sir, I could see there was a chink like a space at the side of the sliding door, and you can see clearly inside there were two cars inside the garage, not one car as you claim.

Both you and Mr. Watson went around trying all the doors?

If you are referring to Ms. Mason's affidavit that I read, this is not at all true. We only, however, knocked on the front door and called out.

Mr. Benson, I ask you as you stated they dialled 111. How do you know that?

Sir, I would like to explain to the court how it all unfolded that night, as we both knew they were the two was home. As no one answered the door, so we waited down the street in my car. We would have been out of sight, say ten to fifteen minutes, we noticed a police car drive past. Then we decided to go back to the house, and we did see the police car in their driveway. With that we thought this was a suitable time now to serve the petition. The police asked what we were doing there. We explained that we are here to serve the divorce papers. We also said we came around earlier. Then the police constable told us they got a 111 call, and there were at least four men outside armed with guns.

Mr. Benson, at best, that would be pure hearsay then?

No way at all as both I and Mr. Watson can verify that. I will say on oath. Also I would believe the police before I would believe Claire Mason and Craig Kelly.

It was obvious that Mr. Wadsworth was not getting the answers from Mr. Benson as it was made very clear that what Claire Mason has stated in her affidavits was sheer fancible. He then said no more questions.

Ms. Chamberlain dealt into this further as she asked,

> Mr. Benson, were you told by a member of the police that they came to the house in response to a 111 call?

> 100 percent yes, from what I can recall on the night, the senior constable told us it was alleged at the time by both Claire and Craig Kelly that either Mr. Watson or I or both were armed, in fact, stated four people were outside their unit, hence, why this was the reason for their visit.

> Did you have any reason to disbelieve the police?

> If you cannot trust the police, who can you? Also, he was a senior officer.

> Mr. Benson, no doubt you were closely questioned about the firearms you were alleged to have?

> Oh yes, the Police did, but they soon could see it was a ridiculous allegation they made, and they said they will talk to them about it after we leave.

> Mr. Benson, can you tell us, when you were at their house, what was Mr. Kelly like and Mrs. Mason?

> Mrs. Mason did all the talking to Mr. Watson. Mr. Kelly for some reason disappeared to one of the bedrooms. Then one of the police officers convinced him it would be best if he came out to the front door and accept what Mr. Watson had in his hand. It was the police who served the papers on them. One other point I would like to make,

which was obvious that Craig Kelly stated that he was down the shops when this started, this was a downright lie as he was there all the time as the two cars were in the garage.

Where we were parked, no one left or came in, except when the police arrived. The line that Mrs. Mason said she was on her own is not true. Mr. Kelly was there all the time.

Thank you, you may step down.

Mr. Benson's testimony just highlights the facts that Claire Mason and Craig Kelly do not tell the truth, and with his evidence along with the police involved, this must put doubt on their credibility.

*Evidence by David Thomas*

The next witness was David Thomas. He worked for Crest Foods, and I was his supervisor for some time. He came to our place on many occasions to visit and also to see movies. He did stay at our place for around six weeks until he got his own place. He was privy to a lot that went on in the household.

He was duly sworn in, then Mr. Wadsworth started the questioning.

How long have you known the parties?

At least eighteen months, in fact, around March 1974. I am a friend of Mr. Mason, initially both.

So you worked at Crest Foods working with Mr. Mason?

Yes, that's correct. He was my supervisor for a period.

Remember early on, Mr. Wadsworth made a big issue about if I had an iron or not. Well, he did not let up as he asked David Thomas if I had an iron in the house.

The answer he gave to Mr. Wadsworth was simply, "I cannot believe I have been asked such a question, and how would I know that?"

Then the questions changed to when Oliver was in my care. This is how it went.

> Mr. Thomas, at the time you have known Mr. Mason, has he always had Oliver in his custody?

> I believe so.

> Between May and December last year?

> Yes, he did.

> All the time?

This line of questioning has come about because Ms. McDonald Senior, the grandmother, claimed she had him for that period, some six months. Mr. Wadsworth was trying to establish Oliver was not in my care in that period.

David Thomas answered,

> Yes, every time I was there, Oliver was always there, and he always said hello to me.

> Then how often would you visit the home?

> Very frequently as we often met up his home to work out our work schedule.

> Up to December last year, can you estimate the number of times you went to the home?

> Maybe three to four times a week, apart from when I stayed there for some six weeks.

> Mr. Thomas, although you lived with him for six weeks, you are unable to say whether he kept an iron in the house?

You could see on David Thomas's face that this line of questioning was just bizarre. He answered, "Sir, this is a very hypothetical question.

All I know for a fact is he must be ironing clothes as his clothes and Oliver's always appeared ironed and neat and clean. I was not there during the day and at nighttime as I did see my fiancée regularly, so I would not be there all the time to see what he was doing.

Mr. Wadsworth said, "No further questions, Your Honor."

Mrs. Chamberlain said, "No questions. Mr. Thomas can stand down."

*Evidence by Mrs. Marlene Dubbeld*

Marlene and her husband became exceptionally good friends, and I met Marlene before she got married when I was doing the cleaning work in the city offices. Marlene is what you would call prim and proper, well-spoken, and a loving person, and she just loved Oliver. Both Oliver and I spent many times at their place and them likewise at our home for dinner. Both Claire and I went to their wedding.

Mrs. Chamberlain called her to the stand and was sworn in, and she stated, "I know Mr. Mrs. Mason, and I have sworn a declaration of facts, and I confirm the contents as being true and correct."

Mr. Wadsworth asked,

> You are a friend of Mr. and Ms. Mason?

> That is correct as I knew them both.

> Out of the two, who are you more strongly associated with?

> To Mr. Mason.

As you recall, when I was awarded interim custody of Oliver, I had a dinner party, and many assertions were made by Claire and her mother in relation to this night. This like many other matters, like if I had an iron or not, trying to prove I was not taking good care of Oliver, and you can judge by the relentless effort by Mr. Wadsworth to get a clear answer, but he was not getting any.

Ms. Dubbeld, you have stated you were invited to dinner one evening. This is when Mr. Mason mentioned he had obtained interim custody on this day. Is that correct?

Sir, that is not correct as my husband and I we were invited to dinner about  a fortnight before. At that time the case had not been set down or heard. Danial asked us if we might like to come to dinner on the Thursday evening, and we just left the date free on the calendar. As it turned out, it coincided with Danial gaining interim custody.

I ask then, how often have you been at his place?

For the last month often, and quite often we invited them both to dine with us.

How much advance notice would you get?

Quite a few days, sometime a week or two in advance as my husband and I are remarkably busy people.

This get-together on the night of when Mr. Mason was granted interim custody, how many people were there?

It was around a dozen guests.

Any members of the McDonald family there?

I do not know the McDonald family. There might have been there, I cannot say.

Can you recall when Oliver went to bed?

Yes, he went after the main meal, and he did not want dessert, and Danial took him to his room around eight o'clock. Also I did see Danial go down and check on him.

Was alcohol served that night?

Yes, between us, we had one or two bottles of wine. As it was a working week, we did not consume much at all between us.

Mr. Wadsworth: No more questions, Your Honor.

Mrs. Chamberlain: No questions.

This was the end of day 1 proceedings, and court was adjourned to 10:00 a.m. Tuesday.

At the end of the day's proceedings, the clerk of courts came up to both myself and Ms. Chamberlain and said, "The judge wants to speak to Oliver tomorrow. Can you have him here at 1:00 p.m.?"

"Yes," I replied, "he will be here."

Mrs. Chamberlain asked, "Who can bring him here?"

I said, "My good friends in Panmure can, Greg and Allison Doherty, as he is staying there all week during the day, and I pick him up each night and drop him off on the way here."

"Great," she said, "as the welfare has offered." I said, "No way, it will be arranged."

For some reason, my barrister was not happy with the day's proceedings as she said, "The allegations made against you by her lawyer is not looking good, I can tell you."

"I also requested to have Fiona McDonald to take the stand."

Mrs. Chamberlain said, "I think it may be a bad mistake on your part wanting to have Fiona McDonald to take the stand." Mrs. Chamberlain was concerned how things were going, and she said, "Let's hope tomorrow will be better."

I then left the courtroom. I felt a bit dejected. I went and picked up Oliver from Greg and Allison Doherty's place. I explained to them that the judge wants to see Oliver tomorrow at 1:00 p.m., and can they bring him to the Supreme Court for me where they will be met by the clerk of courts, who would take Oliver to see the judge.

The reason I have Oliver with Greg and Allison is to keep him out of harm's way while the case was on as they also know Oliver very well. It was better to make these arrangements than, say, the welfare take him for the week, which he would be with strangers, and I felt that he has already been through enough and it was not a wise choice. I would pick him up each night and bring him back each day.

I am not sure why my barrister said today was not looking good as I felt that some of the line of questioning by her solicitor Mr. Wadsworth was very unusual indeed. He did not get the response on many issues and the evidence so far by the kindergarten, and others did not give Mr. Wadsworth what he was aiming for, in my opinion. However, Mrs. Chamberlain was not happy with the day's evidence as she said for whatever reason, I am not sure.

On the way back from Greg and Allison's place, it was around seven o'clock, and I went past James and Fiona's place. There was Claire and Craig's car along with Rose and Kevin's and two other cars, which I was not sure who owned them. It was obvious to me that they were at James and Fiona's place to discuss the court case.

It was on day 2 of the court case. I discussed this with my lawyer when I arrived at the court. She said, "This is not good on Claire's part, I can assure you."

I said, "You were not happy with yesterday as I thought many things by her lawyer was very odd indeed."

"Let's put yesterday aside," she said. "Let's hope things go better for us today."

# 31

# THE CUSTODY HEARING DAY 2

I am not sure what today will bring. Fiona McDonald is the first one called to give evidence. Fiona, as we all know, was the sister-in-law to both Claire and I. She was married to Claire's brother James. She was a great supporter of me and loved Oliver as she looked after him after he attended kindergarten. Then things did change. I do not blame Fiona at all. She is such a lovely person, and now I have learned she was now pressured into changing her mind looking after Oliver.

Mrs. Chamberlain was not happy on my request to subpoena Fiona as she said this could be damaging to my case.

*Evidence of Ms. Fiona McDonald*

Mrs. Chamberlain called Fiona McDonald to the stand, and she was duly sworn in. She stated that she is Mrs. Claire Mason's sister-in-law, and we live in the same street at Clee Crescent.

> Is it correct you are happy to continue to look after Oliver?

> No, I have changed my mind since swearing the affidavit.

> Do you not wish to become involved in this dispute?

How do you mean?

Do you want to keep out of it? Not particularly.

Why then?

I feel that the mother, Mrs. Mason, would be far better if she got custody to have him and in the circumstances in my home, which have now changed.

Is it not the case that Mrs. Mason has asked you if she got custody of Oliver, would you look after him?

No. She certainly did not.

Have you been approached by Mr. and Mrs. McDonald Senior about your affidavit and looking after Oliver?

No. I have not.

Have you never had discussions with them about your affidavit? Mainly about what I had written, and that is as far as it went.

I ask you, have you discussed the case at all with the family? Not to any great extent, no.

Have you discussed this with your husband, whether you are willing to look after Oliver?

Yes, it was he who suggested I do not carry on looking after him. No more questions at this point, Your Honor.

*Mr. Wadsworth's Redress*

Mr. Wadsworth asked Fiona,

Is this correct you said that you are now not prepared to look after Oliver if Mr. Mason has custody?

Yes. That is what I said.

What has changed and brought that about? How do you mean?

Have you seen some unfortunate incident?

Mrs. Chamberlain objected. "Mr. Wadsworth is leading the witness."

Then I draw your attention to the time you were with Mrs. McDonald just after the football game.

I was with my mother-in-law, and we were at a football game, and somehow Oliver found us, and Oliver sat with us most of the day.

At any stage during that time Oliver was with you, did his father approach you?

No, I did not know where he was sitting. After the game, Oliver said he would like to go home with the grandparents, and Mrs. McDonald said only if his father agreed. Then we found Danial, and Danial said no, then Danial started to get a bit wild and said something to Mr. McDonald, "You better get your facts straight." Mr. McDonald said, "Why cannot we have the child?" Danial went berserk. He threw a fist at Mr. McDonald. He then grabbed Oliver and went to the car.

What kind of language did he use? Quite strong language.

Did Mr. McDonald use abusive language?

I do not think so because his son was playing, and he did not want to make things look bad for James. Mrs.

McDonald went up to the window of his car, and she tried to tell him to keep calm. Danial revved up the car and took off.

I understand you were at the home one night when Mrs. Mason returned Oliver to his father's custody where she said and complained that her keys were taken?

Yes, that is right.

What had happened that night?

Claire went to pick up Oliver, and they got into an argument, and Danial picked her keys up and threw them onto the roof of the house. Claire then went to the phone box on the main road and called her mother.

Did you see the keys being thrown?

No, I was not there, but I went around to see Danial on my own, and I saw him get up onto the roof, and he was looking for them, and he eventually got them down.

Did he say who owned the keys? He said they were Claire's keys.

Did the keys get returned to Mrs. Mason?

No, we did not know then that the keys had been put back in the car. We found this out when the police were called. I kept asking for the keys, not to cause any trouble. After a while, Danial said he did not have the keys, they were in Claire's car in the ignition.

She had to come to pick the boy up? Yes.

The judge asked,

She must have left without the car then.

She walked to the phone box.

And rang who?

Her mother.

What was the first time you knew of the key incident?

I really cannot remember, somehow they rang me, or I was at Mrs. McDonald's, my mother-in-law's, place.

You went around there?

On my own, yes, the purpose being to do something about the keys as Claire was upset.

Where were you when she came back again?

I drove her back in my car to pick up the keys.

Who asked for the keys?

I think Claire and I did.

What did Mr. Mason say?

He kept on saying he did not have them.

Which was right, being it not, as they were in the car?

But he did not say that.

Were the police called?

Yes, when Claire rang her mother, I think they were called then.

The clerk of courts announced a court adjournment from 12:45 p.m. to 2:15 p.m.

*Incident at Court House Day 2 of Hearing*

Oliver came out from having a chat with the judge. It was around 1:35 p.m. He came out with a smile, and he ran up to me and gave me a big hug. I said, "Are you okay?"

He said, "Yes, Dad." Then we were heading outside the court, and we were blocked by his grandmother and Craig, and I am not sure who the other person or persons were, and they were shouting at Greg and Addison. The grandmother tried to grab Oliver. I said, "Back off, will you, and let us through."

With that the clerk of courts was standing by, and he said to us, "Come with me," and he took us downstairs by a stairwell, and it had a door that opened at the side of the Supreme Court. We all stepped out and were heading up the hill to where they parked their car. I decided then to go back to the court house.

When I was walking back, I spotted Rose McDonald and Craig were chasing after Greg and Addison. Later I was told by Addison that they caught up with them as they reached their car as Greg had Oliver in his arms. Craig lunged at him, and he then pushed Craig away. Addison told them on uncertain terms to leave them alone. If she swore at them, I am not sure, but the whole episode was unnecessary.

This was noted by the clerk of courts, and I think this behavior will not end well as the Courts frown upon disturbances at the Court.

Then there was the other issue. At the end of the first day of the hearing, the McDonalds, Claire, and Kelly all met up at James's place. Mrs Chamberlain said she passed this on to the clerk of courts, and rest assured the presiding judge will be informed of the incident at the court today as well as last night's meeting at James and Fiona's place.

To this point, so much emphasis has been on me, it's time a few things turned my way, despite my lawyer's concern over many allegations made against me. Then the issue of the sleeping tablets, the kindergarten evidence, and issue of the 111 calls when the divorce papers were being served must account for something.

It's a long way to go, and now we are well into day 2, and Fiona McDonald after recess took the stand.

The case recommenced at 2:00 p.m.

*Ms. Fiona McDonald Continues Her Evidence*

Mr. Wadsworth asked,

> More recently, there was another incident at the Mason household?

> Yes, that is right.

> Tell us what happened then?

> It was on a Saturday morning early. There was a knock on my door. I was only in my nightie, and I put my dressing gown on, and there was Claire's mother, and she said, "Quick, call the police. She said she had been assaulted by Mr. Baxter." I then started up my car, and Claire's mother took off on foot down the road, and I picked her up around the corner and took her to Daniel's place. When I got there, I went inside, and Mr. Baxter said that Claire had thrown the telephone at him. I then asked where Oliver was, and he said, "I do not know where he is." I was worried about this as the child was upset. Before the police came, Danial came out and pulled Claire by the arm and told her to get off his property. The police came after that, and Claire was upset, and the police said to Danial, "Let me go, and I can see Oliver," as apparently, he was in the house next door. I knocked on the door, and the girl said she did not know where Oliver was, and she did not want to get involved. The police said to Claire, "Get the child and go." The child was

there apparently. He was next door. The police did nothing about the assault on Claire by Mr. Baxter and Danial as Danial had grabbed Claire by the arm hard. She had bruises all around her arm, her left arm, I think. After that I had to take her to the doctor.

On that occasion and other occasions when Mrs. McDonald Senior has come to the assistance of her daughter, has she used abusive language?

No, not what I know of.

Has Mrs. Mason used abusive language?

No.

You have been looking after Oliver for some time?

Yes, I have done so.

Do you recall last May last year when the parties separated who had custody of the child?

Did not Danial have him?

Yes, he did all the time.

No, his grandmother did have him a few nights and has given him meals.

Who did Oliver's washing and ironing?

At first, I know his grandmother did a fair bit of it.

Would it be the case she did this up until November last year?

Yes, I think so.

Has she done it since November?

Occasionally, as she has not been seeing Oliver as she was before.

Do you know why?

There has been a bit of strife between the McDonalds and Mr. Mason naturally.

How often would you yourself have done the washing for Oliver?

It was very rarely, but one day I had him for the night, and I did them that night because once he was sick in my car. I took his clothes off and washed them, but he did not have any other clothes to put on, so he stayed in bed.

Recently, Mr. Mason has had boarders in his house?

Yes.

How many?

At one stage there were two.

Where did they sleep?

Presumably, I think one in the spare room and the other one in Oliver's room.

Where did Oliver sleep?

With his father.

In Mr. Watson's affidavit, he said he was present one night when Claire's mother slapped her across the face with her open hand, and she caused a big scene. Were you present when this took place?

Yes, I was there that night.

Did Mrs. McDonald attack her daughter?

She tried, but I intervened. She may have hit her, but I doubt if she would have hurt her.

Did Mr. Watson have to pull Mrs. McDonald away from Claire? No, I am not sure, but he was there that night.

Can you tell me if Mr. McDonald had been drinking all night?

I do not know about that.

May I ask did Mr. Mason try to separate them?

I am not sure, he may have done, but I tried myself to stop Mrs. McDonald and pull Claire away.

Was there a match with one hitting the other?

No.

Can you recall when Mr. Mason got interim custody?

Yes.

What did Mr. Mason say?

He said he got interim custody and that he was having a dinner party that night at his home and invited me and my husband to go.

Did he mention Mrs. McDonald at all?

I think he may have mentioned it.

I understand on the Friday following, you looked after Oliver.

Yes, I did, and he was extremely tired and fell asleep on the couch between 6:30 and 7:00 p.m. I carried him into the bedroom, and he slept to ten the next morning, and I had to wake him up by shaking him.

Did he wake up during the night?

No, he did not.

What does he usually do?

Lies on the couch or the floor.

Have you seen him in this state before?

Yes, often it is fine. I make him go outside and play.

Do you put this down this time that it was due to extreme tiredness?

I am sure it was.

How often have you been present when Mrs. Mason has attempted to exercise access?

I do not think I have ever been there, not that I can recall.

Can you recall if there have been other instances where access has been exercised, and there has been emotion?

No, I cannot really think of any.

Was Oliver ever reluctant to go with his mother?

No, I do not think so.

Ever known Mrs. Mason to entice Oliver from his father by offering gifts?

No, not that I can recall.

I understand you look after him most afternoons of the week?

Yes, I did.

Is this most afternoons?

Yes, it was most afternoons.

Does Mr. Mason take Oliver on his rounds?

Yes, Mr. Mason would take him on his rounds and give him lunch, or else he was having a short afternoon nap, and he would take him out.

Would these be called his rounds?

Yes.

Would these not be special outings for Oliver?

No.

Does Oliver also show considerable affection to his father.?

Yes, I think so.

Did Mrs. Mason entice Oliver at any stage?

No, I do not think so.

Was Oliver always well dressed?

Yes, always.

Oliver, he has suffered for some time with a bronchial condition?

Yes.

Would you say this was attributed to in no small way by the nervous tension?

The last time Oliver was taken to the doctor, the doctor thought it was emotional.

Mr. and Mrs. Mason have either taken Oliver to the doctors?

I cannot answer that as I am not sure if they had or not. I would assume they did as he is often sick, but I have taken Oliver myself to the doctor.

Why have you taken him to the doctor?

One Monday morning, Danial dropped him off and said Oliver was not well, he got sick and was vomiting. I rang Mrs. McDonald, and she said rush him to the doctors, in which I did, and the doctor gave him two injections to stop him being sick.

Did the doctor say what the problem was?

The doctor said it was something to bronchial infection.

Do you remember early this year in connection with a Mother's Day card?

Yes, all the children made these for their mothers. When Oliver came home, Oliver gave one to me. I said to Danial, "Should he not give this card to his mother?" and Danial said, "Oliver did this for you."

Has Oliver complained to you about being punched at kindergarten? He used to joke about it as he said it was all in play.

However, to your knowledge, he occasionally has hurt himself?

Yes, he does come home and says so and so did this, but it is soon forgotten, and there have been no injuries at the kindergarten.

Mr. Mason was served with a divorce petition naming him the co-respondent, has he ever been out with a lady?

Yes.

How often?

I could not really say, I think he had a girlfriend last summer, but that which lasted a wee while, then there was another one, but that is off I heard.

Have you ever seen him take a lady friend out?

I was at Mrs. McDonald's place once, and one of his girlfriends was in the car, and I had met this girl and another at his home.

Do you know how often Mr. Mason has movie shows?

I have been to one of his movies a long time ago, but I do understand he has them once or twice a week. He does show kiddie ones.

What movie did you see?

*The Sting.*

What time did it stop?

I am not sure as it would have been late as it was at night.

Did Oliver remain throughout the performance? Yes, there were other children there as well. Were your own children there as well?

My own child is a baby in arms. How old is she now?

Eight months old."

Do you think Mrs. Mason is a good mother?"

She looks after Oliver extremely well, and she always knows where the child is, and she feeds him well. I think they could have a particularly good relationship.

Can you recall some months ago, Oliver was away from his father? Yes, he was up on the main road near Ash Avenue shops.

Was he with two older children, not old enough to be in charge? Was one a Māori child?

Yes, I think so.

Did they say why they had Oliver with them?

They were going to the shop to buy lollies, Oliver told me.

Did either Māori boy indicate they asked Mr. Mason if the child could go with them?

No, we did not ask.

What was Mr. Mason's reaction to this?

Well, we took him to the shops to buy lollies and then took him to our place, and I rang Danial up. He said he wondered where he got to. He said to leave him at our place for a while.

Did Oliver often do this?

He may have done, but I do not know of any other occasions. Has he ever wandered away from you?

No, never.

Are there any other small children who play with Oliver?

There was one boy over the back he has started playing with recently, and he is a bit younger than Oliver, and recently Oliver had gone outside and started playing with him again, with this child and my child as I only have the one.

Does Oliver attend kindergarten most mornings? Yes, he does.

So apart from the afternoons he spends with you, and apart from his attendance at kindergarten, there are few other children with whom he could play?

That is correct.

Oliver is at present suffering from bronchial trouble?

Yes, he seems to have had this upset for a while now, and I do not know how it was caused, but seeing he has not been getting rid of it, the doctor has put this down to emotional problems.

Oliver is well behaved, and you mentioned earlier on that you would like Mrs. Mason to have custody of the child?

Yes. Why?

Well, bringing up my own child now and having Oliver in the afternoon, when he comes from kindy and has a lot to tell me, and it is extremely hard to have him when I have my own child running around now.

Do you talk to him?

Yes, his mother sits down and teaches him the alphabet, which I have not got time.

Mr. Mason also listens?

I do not think so, he has not got the time.

Have they played at your place?

Yes, they have the odd punch-up games.

How often does Oliver go to Sunday school?

I do not think that often.

Has he gone three times in the last month?

I doubt it.

Have you come here with anyone today?

Yes, my mother-in-law, Mrs. McDonald.

A short adjournment was called.

*Judge Addressed Fiona McDonald*

The judge said,

I take it you would prefer not to talk to either Mr. or Mrs. Mason over this short adjournment.

Yes.

I also propose to make an order that neither Mr. nor Mrs. McDonald should speak to you?

Fiona replied. Yes.

And I ask you not to discuss this case with Mrs. Rose McDonald?

Yes, I understand.

*Afternoon Adjournment 3:47 p.m.*
*Resumed at 4:05 p.m.*
*Fiona McDonald Resumes Her Evidence*

Mr. Wadsworth asked,

I understand that you are not able to look after Oliver now.

Yes, that is correct.

Are you yourself going out to work?

Yes, if I can find the right type of work.

What will you do with your own child?

If possible, a day nursery or something like that.

Would you be prepared to leave your daughter with your mother-in-law?

I do not really know as I have not asked her to.

Would Mrs. Mason be a fit-enough person to look after your child?

Yes, I would love her to go to Claire, whether she would accept the responsibility, I do not know. She is quite capable of looking after her.

No further questions.

*Re-XD Mrs. Chamberlain*

The questioning started on the incident at the football park, and the answers that Fiona gave were rather peculiar to say the least. It was obvious she was not answering the full facts rather than saying she does not know.

Ms. McDonald, now, I want to start with this incident at the football oval. Can you tell me what time did the match finish?

Matches always finish at around 4:15 p.m.

On this day, did it finish late?

I cannot really remember, I do not think so. I cannot remember if the game ended late or not.

Ms. McDonald, I ask you, did the game not go into extra time?

I do not remember.

Mrs. McDonald, I put this to you, that your husband played in the game and you cannot remember?

I am not sure.

Can you then tell what the weather was like that day?

It was fine day.

In Mr. Mason's evidence, he said it was getting dark, and it was a cold and wet winter's day, and it was the reason why he wanted to take Oliver home.

No, I do not think so.

Surely, Mrs. McDonald, you cannot remember what sort of weather it was and if the game finished on time or into extra time?

Fiona got very agitated.

Quite honestly, no, and I know what you are getting at. I go to many football games, every weekend I go to football in the wintertime.

It seems to me you have a good memory on what Mr. McDonald Senior does, and if Mr. Mason said it was extremely late, cold, and wet and wanted to take Oliver home, you cannot remember?

Look, he may have. I do not think Mr. McDonald started abusing Mr. Mason. Mr. Mason started first.

In evidence, it was stated by Mr. Mason that Mr. McDonald, your father-in-law, said, "You are the rottenest so-and-so" to him.

Well, he may have had reason to say that because of what Mr. Mason said. Ms. McDonald, was it because Mr. Mason said the trouble that he could not accept the truth?

He did say something like that.

Then did not Mr. Mason then walk to the car park with Mrs. McDonald hot in pursuit?

Yes, that is what it was. Danial was in the car then with Oliver when Mrs. McDonald wanted to talk to him.

I ask you, Mrs. McDonald was also yelling, was she not, in the car park and banging on the window?

She just only wanted to speak to him to calm him down.

Then if Mr. Mason was leaving, why didn't she leave him alone? Why ask me? I do not know, you should ask Mrs. McDonald that. What was Mr. McDonald Senior doing?

I cannot recall.

I put it to you was he not bashing at the other window? No, he was not.

I ask you which way Mr. Mason left the car park, in reverse or straight ahead?

Danial reversed fast and then took off, missing Mr. and Mrs. McDonald by inches. Mrs. McDonald was right beside the car.

How would you describe Mr. and Mrs. McDonald? Mild people? Oppose to what?

Argumentative people?

I would not say they were argumentative. How long have you known them?

Ever since I have been going out with their son James and now my husband about eight years.

The questioning now shifted to domestic violence matters relating to her and her husband James. You will see by the answers given that she was not prepared to give anything away as she was afraid of what reaction the McDonalds may have.

Ms. McDonald, did not you stay at Mr. and Mrs. McDonald's home prior to you getting married?

Yes, I did.

Can you recall when James and his father were fighting, and James ended up in hospital?

No, I cannot remember that at all.

Mrs. McDonald, you are telling me that you cannot remember when your now husband finished up in hospital?

No, I cannot remember.

You were living at their house then? Yes, I was.

How old is James now?

The same age as me, twenty-four, and James is my husband. What has this got to do with Claire, Danial, getting Oliver?

Ms. McDonald, I am simply asking if Mr. McDonald Senior assaulted James, and James ended up in hospital, and you cannot recall?

I already told you no.

You were at the house this night? Yes, I was.

Then you cannot recall why, as you say James your husband fell. Sorry, I do not remember.

Yet you went to the hospital in the ambulance with Danial Mason and Claire Mason.

I do not remember.

Did you not stay with Mr. and Ms. Mason?

I did for a brief time before I got married. I had a row, and Claire asked me to stay there to keep out of it for a while, but it was not exceptionally long.

Was this not long before Oliver was about to be born? And was not it suggested you did not stay with Claire as she went into hospital and therefore you decided to go back?

Yes.

Would you say that Mr. McDonald Senior drinks too much?

No.

Does your husband see a lot of Mr. and Mrs. McDonald now? Yes, we live close.

When did you last see them? Friday night, I think.

Friday just past?

Yes.

Ever had John McDonald to stay with you? Not recently, not this year.

About August?

I would not have a clue. It does not seem important to me.

I remind you, was not it the reason he stayed because he had a fight with his father?

No, he had a fight with both of his parents. I was not there at the time.

Can you cast you mind back to last week where Mr. and Mrs. McDonald visited you, on the Thursday night?

You mean the Friday night they called around?

No, I am referring to the Thursday. Did they ask you to do anything on that night?

No.

Ms. McDonald, please answer this as you have very selective memory and evading many questions. So I ask, did they ask you to return the pram, the money, and the trailer?

Yes, but I cannot see what this has to do with this custody case. Surely I am not on trial here for something of which I am not sure.

She paused. Then she replied,

What happened at my house has nothing to do with this case.

Ms. McDonald, I am not sure of that. Then is it not true they asked you for the return of assorted items, also when Mr. Mason came around next morning, you talked to your own mother in Christchurch?

Yes.

Then you said you're fed up? That's right.

Now let us now go back to the incident when the police were called. Yes.

Once the police were called, was there a discussion started by Mr. Mason saying to Claire, "Now you tell the police that I did not hit you, and I will give the car keys back," isn't that what happened? And what was said by the police?

They got the keys out of the ignition and asked Claire to take the boy and go, nothing was done at all.

You told us Mr. Mason raised with the police the alleged assault on Claire. What did he say to the police?

I cannot really recall what he said, but I think he was quite violent, shaking his fist at her, "Will you tell them I did not hit you?" She was so frightened. She said, "He did not hit me" to the police. I think he had. He made out Claire had caused all the trouble and everything. She was only to get the boy as it was the right to take him, and there was a fight between Claire and Danial, and he threw the car keys onto the roof, and that is when it started.

Would you say the police was on Mr. Mason's side?

Yes.

Do you think the police are objective? Not at all.

Just in this case?

Yes, the way I saw it.

Mr. Mason said that Claire brought Oliver back late around eight a.m. from her access, and you say she was picking him up?

She may have, but I thought she was picking him up.

Ms. McDonald, either way, don't you think it's an odd time to bring him home or pick up Oliver?

Yes, I think so.

You told us about the movie *The Sting*. Can you recall the occasion? Was it not a birthday party?

No, as I have said, it was quite a while ago. It was last summer, I think. Was the time about December?

I honestly could not say that. Was there a barbecue that night? If there was, I did not go to it.

Do mean to say you cannot remember about the barbecue, the movie *The Sting*, and what occasion it was?

No, I already told you, I was not there.

Ms. McDonald, there is evidence put to this court that you were there at the barbecue, and you along with the other members of the family stayed and watched the movie *The Sting*.

I do not know where they got that from as I do not recall being there. Have you heard Oliver talk about Mr. Kelly.?

No.

No more questions. You may stand down.

Mrs. Chamberlain was not happy with me asking to subpoena Fiona. I said to Mrs. Chamberlain, "Surely with Fiona's account of things, it is no doubt she was got at by Claire's parents and to dismiss the fact of Oliver's fourth birthday and the barbecue and the showing of the move *The Sting*, and the incident with James and his father and when he was taken to hospital, and Fiona was there when the incident happened, in the ambulance, and James when he was in hospital. I am sure the judge did see through all this."

The next witness was a longtime friend of Claire Mason and was her bridesmaid at our wedding. She always wanted to stay mutual and be friends with us both. As this turned out, it was not to be.

*Evidence by Jasmine Egan*

Jasmine Egan was sworn in, and Mr. Wadsworth asked the following.

Ms. Egan, how long have you known Mrs. Mason?

Most of my life.

Do you know the parties separated?

Yes, of course I do.

How many times have you spoken to Mrs. Mason since she has left?

Only a few times.

Has she ever told you why she left her husband?

No.

Has Mr. Mason told you?

No. Danial does not know himself.

Do you still say the standard is high?

Yes.

Any reason to your knowledge why they should not be high?

No.

How many times have you been to dinner to Mr. Mason's place?

I would say several.

Did you go to Mr. Mason's house when he and Mrs. Mason lived together?

Yes, and I was usually invited a few weeks beforehand.

No more questions, Your Honor.

Then Ms. Chamberlain asked,

Mrs. Egan, you said you had been for dinner at the Masons. Have you been there since the separation?

Yes, a few times with my husband and children.

Has Ms. Mason been present?

Yes, only on one occasion. She came in, and Oliver was well in bed asleep, and she accused Danial of not keeping him warm. She seemed a little bit upset. She had a few words with Danial. She went down to the bedroom to get something, with that Oliver must have heard his mother, and he hid under the bed as he did not want to go with her. Danial then went down and got Oliver out from under the bed as he was emotionally stressed.

She had phoned a few times in the afternoon, and Danial did not want to talk to her. Danial came back to the lounge, and Claire put a cardigan on Oliver. He was crying and visibly upset, and Claire started arguing with Danial. Claire said, "Go on, hit me, that is all you want to do all the time." That is when me and my husband decided to leave as we had small children with us, and Claire was very distressed and shaking. I could not believe what I was witnessing as Claire was always an exceptionally good friend of mine. Oliver did not go, by the way. It was getting very late, and Oliver was so upset that Danial said, "He is staying here and not going with you." This is when we all left and went back home.

You have said Ms. Mason's standards are extremely high.

Yes, and I have never known Claire to swear, but she certainly did that night. She was always quietly spoken and reserved.

Can you say whether she has changed?

Yes, she has, as she always has been a very friendly person. I tried to keep contact with her, but she did not seem to want to be friendly anymore at all or have contact with me. I did think she thought I was on Daniel's side, but I was not. I thought a lot of Claire as well as Danial, but I think at this point, that it is Oliver's life that matters. Danial, he is a better housekeeper than I and has the house immaculate and is an exceptionally good cook.

What about the McDonalds?

Mrs. McDonald would ring me up a lot, more or less, for somebody to talk to, as I was at that time the only one who knew something about it. She was terribly upset and said she looked after Oliver for Danial, and Fiona looked after him as well when she had to go to work. She was also concerned that Claire may have been on drugs at the time, and she was concerned that Claire would come and take Oliver, and Claire used to come and call out, "Oliver, Oliver." Claire was terribly upset at the time.

Does Mr. McDonald Senior drink too much? Yes, he does. It is a known fact.

Has he ever assaulted people? Yes, he has.

Did James finish in hospital?

Yes, he did. I was not there. Claire had a lot to say about this to me, and I do know that Fiona stayed at the Masons' house over this incident just before she got married as Mr. McDonald took to her as well, so Claire and Danial put Fiona up. Fiona lived with the McDonalds as her family lived in the South Island.

Ms Chamberlain said, "No more further questions, Your Honor." The judge then asked a few questions.

How long have you known Claire Mason?

All my life. We grew up together.

How long have you known Mr. and Ms. McDonald?

All my life.

How old are you now?

I am twenty-seven.

Thank you, you may stand down.

*Evidence by John Paul McDonald*

Next person to take the stand was Claire's youngest brother John. He was a very nice young fellow, and he also worked with me as a projectionist. He fully understood what his father was like as he said on many occasions how scared he was of his father. He was in my opinion a very likeable guy and was misguided by his parents. Unfortunately, he was caught up in this dispute.

John was sworn in. He stated his name was John Paul McDonald, and he lived with his parents.

Ms. Chamberlain commenced asking.

During this hearing, it has been suggested you lived with James and Fiona McDonald for a while as your father had hit you, is that true?

This is very untrue. I did have an argument with my parents about the alcohol being drunk down at Daniel's place, and my parents were getting annoyed with me, so I went down to Daniels's place and told him I could not work for him anymore.

Isn't it true you told Mr. Mason that your father had hit you? No, I did not.

The judge asked,

How old are you?

Sixteen, sir.

What school do you go to?

Auckland College.

Do you operate a movie projector for Mr. Mason?

Yes, I do. Danial trained me as one of his projectionists.

Did you do this more than once?

Yes, sir. I have many times.

So you worked for him in a way?

Yes, that is correct.

Did you get paid?

Yes, on most occasions.

Were you asked to stop working for him?

Yes, my parents asked me to stop.

No more questions. Over to counsel.

Mr. Wadsworth then asked,

On the evenings showing movies, was Oliver present?

Yes. Most times.

How many times would they have been shown?

It is hard to say, once or twice a week. When I was there, Oliver was there for every showing except one.

What time of night did they stop?

This depended on what time they started.

Did Oliver stay for the ones that finished at, say, 11:00 p.m.?

Sometimes.

Was alcohol consumed? Yes, it was.

About a week ago, did you answer the phone early last Sunday morning?

Yes, I did, as Mr. Mason was on the line.

What did he say to you?

I honestly cannot remember.

Can you recall the day your mother spoke to Mrs. Mason?

Yes, I answered the phone. My sister Claire was screaming, "Quick, get the police!" I was yelling back, "Why, what is wrong? Where are you?" And I heard her scream, "I am at Daniel's place!" With that my mother grabbed the phone from me.

Does your mother or father swear a lot?

No, definitely not.

Do you know if Claire has been on drugs?

No, definitely not.

Has she ever been on medication from a chemist such as Valium tablets?

Not to my knowledge. I did not take an interest in that.

Do you know what Valium is?

No.

When you're asked about drugs, what do you think it means?

Pills in bottles.

Does your father drink to excess?

Not at all. He may consume two bottles a night watching TV, but that would be about his limit unless it was a special occasion.

Have you been present when Mr. Mason has come around to your house?

Yes, on many occasions.

What was his behavior?

This I suppose all depends. A couple of years ago, everyone was friendly, it was a good family. Then everything deteriorated. I do not know why, as I did not take too much notice at the time, but I have noticed now the situation has changed considerably.

With the situation changing, what have you noticed? Does Danial swear and carry on?

Yes, Danial has done on occasions, but usually his behavior is very good. There are some occasions when he has acted stupidly.

For example, what stupid things has he done?

There was one incident when Danial hit my mother across the face and jumped into his car and drove off. My brother John stopped him on that occasion.

Did your mother provoke him at all? I do not think so.

Does your sister swear? No, not at all.

Are you quite sure of that? No, none of our family swear.

Why are you able to say none of your family swear?

Well, the language in our house, we just do not swear. My mother and father would get angry with me if I did swear.

Ever seen Oliver with his mother?

Yes, I have, as she brings him over often.

Over the last couple of months, does he like being with his mother? Yes.

Does Oliver like being with your parents? Yes, definitely.

How often does your mother and father see Oliver?

We used to see him a lot, but more lately we have not seen Oliver, unless my sister Claire brings him around.

How often would she bring him around? On all occasions Claire has access to him.

When Mr. and Ms. Mason separated, did Oliver stay with you for a while? Yes, that is correct.

Do you remember the day of week he arrived? No. Danial brought him around.

How long did Oliver stay with you?

That is extremely hard to say.

Did your mother do the washing and ironing?

Yes, a lot.

Has your mother bought clothes for Oliver?

Recently Mum bought him a shirt. Lately he has not stayed, but he used to stay one night a week.

Have you known your sister to offer him presents to go with her?

No.

What is Oliver like when his mother says she is going to take him home?

It varies. Sometimes he does not mind, and other times he kicks up a performance and does not want to go.

Any reason one week he minds and another he does not?

Well, it is hard to say. If he had an enjoyable time with my sister, sometimes he does not want to go back, and other times he does.

No more questions, Your Honor.

Mrs. Chamberlain replied, "No questions."

I think you can now start seeing the pattern emerging here as Claire's family have difficulty recalling many incidents or events whereas witnesses on my side are telling a different side to many incidents or events that have taken place.

*Evidence by Jim Baxter*

The next witness was Jim Baxter, and he has been boarding with me for some time leading up to the court case. He has witnessed many incidents that have taken place at my home. He stayed at my place as it served several purposes, and he was a witness to Claire's many tirades and phone calls. Jim was also going out with the person I was named having an adulterous affair with, Jessica Philips. His evidence is important as a crucial witness to many incidents.

Jim Baxter was duly sworn in, and he stated that he is a bachelor of science and bachelor of administration, and he was at present living at Danial Mason's home.

Mrs. Chamberlain commenced her questioning.

Mr. Baxter, a complaint alleging assault by you on Mrs. Mason has been laid? Can you please tell the court what happened?

Yes, most certainly I can. Mrs. Mason arrived one Saturday morning to pick Oliver up. She arrived an hour earlier than expected. She stormed straight into the house without knocking on the door and demanded why Oliver was not dressed. Danial went down to the boy's bedroom to pick the child's clothing up, then Claire went down to the bedroom. She then starts screaming that Danial had given Oliver's clothing to some other woman, and she stated she had seen the children wearing his clothing. I knew very well this was not the case. When I asked her where she was last night seeing children wearing Oliver's clothes, she soon realized her bluff had been called out. She then became very hysterical. I then went to the phone and said to her, "I will call the woman myself to verify what you are saying." She became more hysterical. She then started knocking over things we had in the hallway. She then pulled the phone out of the wall socket. This was a result of that she claims I assaulted her. In fact, as the phone was pulled out, this flew back and hit her in the face. Also she was too hysterical to say anything or make sense at all.

Can you tell the court who was the woman you called?

Yes, that is my girlfriend, Jessica Phillips.

Have you had any previous convictions for assault?

I have no convictions of any sort.

Have you told your boss about this incident?

They are not particularly impressed. I have just changed jobs in the same company, as I applied for work in Auckland, and they gave me an allowance to live in a hotel for a month. As I worked with Mr. Mason, he said I can stay at his place. I now work for a cosmetics company that produces various cosmetic products.

Have you seen Ms. Mason much?

I have been there when she has arrived on occasions when she came to pick up Oliver. The last time she was most hysterical as I said earlier, and other times, she has been reasonable. Now she has become uncontrollable. Oliver is just a little boy, and his bottom lip trembles with fear. This day he was very frightened. He just sat there at the table. I have seen Oliver with his mother. Oliver has told us that he wants to stay with us, but that is because he has been promised he will get something if he goes with his mother. A brief time ago we were looking through the newspaper adverts, and there were some toy cranes or something like that, and Oliver said to his father, "If you do not buy that for me, Mummy will."

You were present on one occasion when Mrs. Mason said she was going to return Oliver?

This was a weeknight when I had come home later than normal. Danial and Oliver were having their evening meal at the table. Claire was there, and she wanted to take Oliver away that night, and Danial told her that she cannot as Oliver had been sick. Danial said he would be better off going to bed. But she bundled him up, and because of the previous assault, Mr. Mason was reluctant to take the child from her. Danial was afraid that she might take the boy and not bring him back.

During the time you have been with Mr. Mason, has he shown movies at his house?

Yes, he has. It is an impressive setup, like a small theater. How often? On a weekly basis?

All depends on what movies are shown at the time at the various clubs as Daniel shows them as the cost of hire has already been paid for. This can be sometimes twice a week, Wednesday and Saturday nights, and lately I have seen three only, and these are shown once a week.

Where was Oliver during this time?

As I can recall on two occasions, he has been with us, which was a Friday night, and Oliver can sleep in next day providing he was not going to his mother's. Then there were either Saturday or Sunday afternoons, he often put on a movie for the neighborhood children, and the number of kids who turned up was amazing as the word got around. Oliver loved sitting with the kids watching the movies. He was in his element and so happy.

Have you heard Oliver discussing Mr. Kelly?

Yes, on many occasions he has said several things. He also told us he did not want Craig Kelly to be his father.

The court adjourned to 10:00 a.m. tomorrow.

*Summary of Day Two*

The evidence given by Fiona surely must have shown the judge that something was not right here as she cannot remember so many things like the football game and what time it ended to what was the weather like, then when James's father hit him and finished in hospital when she did witness this, then Oliver's birthday and the movie shown, *The Sting*, and she blatantly lied as she was not there at Oliver's fourth birthday.

It was obvious that they got to her and to say what she did. How did the judge see this? I am not sure. Everything at this point at the court case is entirely against me.

# 32

# THE CUSTODY HEARING DAY 3

I arrived at the courthouse around 9:30 a.m. after dropping off Oliver at Greg and Allison's. On the way there, Oliver tells me about meeting the judge the previous day. He told me he asked him how he was, also about the kindergarten. Oliver said, "He was a nice man, Dad." I did not press him anymore.

Mrs. Chamberlain arrived a few minutes after I had arrived, and there was Claire and Craig, and they were muttering something to me, but I could not hear them. Mrs. Chamberlain said, "Ignore them as they just want to stir up trouble, and after yesterday's episode, I can assure you this has not gone unnoticed."

I asked how it was looking.

"Hard to say," she said. "At this point, a lot is against you. Let's see what today brings as there is a lot to give evidence for and against." She did say the judge was asking a lot of questions. "He is impressed with some of your people who gave evidence. There is one or two issues that has been brought to the judge's attention. Let us see how this pans out today, and it may be an interesting day indeed."

*Evidence by Jim Baxter*

The day started with Jim Baxter as he was recalled from yesterday giving evidence.

Ms. Chamberlain asked,

Mr. Baxter, have you heard Oliver discussing the relationship between his mother and Mr. Kelly?

Yes, I have. One occasion which is very firm in my mind, he came back from a day out with his mother, and he said, "Mummy and Mr. Kelly were throwing bread and cream buns at each other." He laughed and said, "One smashed on the ceiling."

What is Oliver's attitude as to going to his mother's?

He always seems very indifferent about it. He never really expresses a desire to go. *Reluctant* I suppose is the word I would use.

Then how does he behave when he returns?

Well, I have found him an objectionable child when he has come back as to any discipline he has had in the past. He would come in and say, "Hi, Jim," but lately when he comes back, he is like the American films. He has shown no respect to me or his father. At times he has come back home and vomit. A very mixed-up little boy.

Oliver being sick, how many times have you cleaned up after that?

Once was enough for me, as there have been numerous occasions when he has been sick on return from his mother, and that must account for something.

Mr. Baxter, has Ms. Mason displayed any violence?

Yes, I can say firsthand, as I have seen it toward Mr. Mason and myself. One incident described yesterday was when she attacked me when I was on the telephone to Jessica Phillips. She also showed no respect for the child.

What was she doing?

She was going to take the child for the day. This was when Oliver was in his pajamas when she arrived early one morning and created a scene.

Were you present when the mother-in-law came on the property?

Yes, I was. She carried on like a fish wife. She came in screaming and attacking Mr. Mason. The reason I stay with Mr. Mason is that he had many allegations made about him. I stayed in direct view this time purely as an independent person.

What was Mr. Mason's language like?

The only time he raised his voice was when he ordered his mother-in-law off the property. She got pretty irritated and worked up about this, so he told her in no uncertain terms to move herself from the property.

You were present when the police were called that day? Yes.

And present when discussion with police about which party had custody as Mrs. Mason claimed he did not?

Yes.

Can you tell the Court what Mrs. Mason did say to the police?

Well, in her hysterical way, she told the police that her husband did not have custody. Then Mr. Mason said he had interim custody, and she is not telling the police the truth. I think she did this thinking the police will hand over Oliver to her. I think she did this because Danial could not locate the papers at the time while the police officers were there, and he again told them he has interim custody of the boy. They did believe him as he was telling the truth. This was on the occasion the last time Ms. Mason came on the property, and the police were called not by Danial but by someone on Claire's side.

The police again arrived later that same morning after Ms. Mason's mother turned up along with the sister-in-law.

Notice any physical change in Ms. Mason?

There is no change in her physical appearance or control of emotions. She was very hysterical right through. When she came into the place, she wet her pants. She obviously had no control over her emotions whatever. She was just raving on madly.

Mr. Mason said Ms. Mason telephoned during the day?

We get constant calls every day. It can be at mornings at breakfast time after seven a.m. onwards, and at night it would vary between five thirty and six thirty, usually around mealtime. Virtually she rings every night and morning of the week. She also comes around later at night around, say, eight p.m., and Oliver is well in bed by then.

You told us you have been in the house for some time. You were present when Mr. Monroe stayed there?

Yes. I was.

Do you recall when Mr. Monroe stayed there?

I was present. I did not actually answer the door. She does not normally knock anyway.

What did you see?

I heard her screaming and struggling. Why was she struggling?

I cannot recall why she was struggling. I cannot say.

You told the Court that Mr. Mason has shown movies at his house? Yes, on an average one per week.

Where was Oliver during this time?

He was with his grandparents as he stayed there overnight.

And other times, say Sunday or Saturday afternoons, he stayed with us. The movies started on Saturday afternoons around 2:00 p.m. and Sundays about 5:00 p.m.

Can you recall Oliver's fourth birthday and the movie *The Sting*?

Yes, I can, as after the barbecue and the clown finished, I helped to set up the cinema with others.

What time did it start and finish?

It was around seven thirty and finished around nine thirty. Was Oliver present for the movie?

No, he was well in bed by eight o'clock.

Do you recall if the McDonald family stayed for the movie?

Yes, they were all there. His grandparents, James and Fiona, also John McDonald.

Judge intervened and asked,

How long have you stayed with Mr. Mason?

I arrived in Auckland on fourteenth June. I moved in three weeks later. I stayed there until eleventh July. When I went into hospital for three weeks, then about August, three weeks after the seventeenth of July, I returned and am still there.

Mr. Baxter, you mentioned an incident when Mr. Monroe stayed the night. Can you put a date to that?

I am quite sure it was after I came out of hospital. Mr. Monroe has been away for a suitable time now, so I cannot provide an accurate date.

Thank you, no further questions. Back to counsel.

Ms. Chamberlain said, "No more questions."
Mr. Wadsworth then did the cross-examination.

Mr. Baxter, Mrs. Mason called at the home of Mr. Mason a week ago. What type of shirt were you wearing?

A red T-shirt.

What did the T-shirt have on it? Pommy Bastard.

Is it not true you tried to get Ms. Mason to say those words to you? No, those words were across my T-shirt.

What was Ms. Mason's mouth like?

Nothing was wrong when she left. She may have been sore after the phone flew back and hit her after she pulled this out of the socket.

Was it bleeding because you punched her?

This is her side of the story. I did not hit her. I am sure it was from biting her lip or the phone hit her. I have never ever punched a woman in my life and not likely to start now.

Because of such incidents, this is precisely why I stayed with Mr. Mason with all the allegations made. Ms. Mason makes up stories and creates situations to suit her cause.

On previous occasions she arrived at the house, you mentioned once when you did not answer the door.

Yes.

Who else was with her that day? She was by herself in the car.

If evidence is given on that day, she arrived with her own landlord. He was assaulted by Mr. Mason for no apparent reason?

This was another occasion. They arrived at the front door. My room looks straight out. The house is a boomerang shape, and I watched the whole incident unfold. Mr. Mason ordered the man off the property, and when he would not go, Mr. Mason took his arm and led him off the property, and I can assure you, sir, he did not assault him.

Can you remember the date?

It was before the occasion when Ms. Mason turned up when Mr. Monroe was there.

Before the time when you assaulted her?

Sir, you like the word *assault*. Yes, allegedly, glad you mentioned that. While Mr. Monroe stayed in the house, where did you sleep?

We were not sleeping together if that is what you are suggesting. Which bed did you sleep in?

I just explained where my bedroom is as it is on the east side of the house, and Mr. Monroe slept on the couch. He had his own bedding that he brought with him.

No further questions.

I quickly said to Ms. Chamberlain, "Well that makes a few things put more into perspective as he verified the showing of the movie *The Sting* and other things."

She replied to me, "Danial, don't get ahead of yourself."

*Evidence by Sue Ingram*

Sue Ingram was my next-door neighbour, and she shifted into the house next door shortly after Claire and I moved into our new home. Oliver would often play with her two young children, and Sue and the children would come over often to have a meal or see a movie. She was a great neighbor. It was her and the Māori family that alerted me that I was being watched and that someone was snooping around the house late at night.

She was sworn in and stated her name as Sue Ingram, and she was a next-door neighbor of Mr. Mason. She stated, "I have been a witness on several occasions when Mrs. Mason has turned up to the matrimonial home."

Ms. Chamberlain started the questioning.

Do you know Ms. Fiona McDonald?

Yes, I have met her a few times. She used to come into the pharmacy where I worked.

Is it the case Oliver was taken to your home the weekend before last?

Yes, and he was terribly upset.

Ms. McDonald came to ask where Oliver was?

Yes, she did and was very irate.

You said he was not there?

Yes, that is correct.

Ms. Ingram, you have been brought here today under subpoena to tell us what you saw that day.

Yes, I do fully understand as I love Oliver and am good friends with Danial, and I did not want to get involved.

Did you hear shouting prior to Oliver coming to your house?

Extraordinarily little as I just got up, at about quarter to eight or around about that time, and there was a knock at the door, and Danial brought Oliver over as he was nervous, terribly upset, and wet his pants. Danial said quickly, "Claire is over at my place, and she has gone off the rails." He then took off. I then put Oliver in the bath, and Danial went and got some clothes for him. My children had not had breakfast as we all just got up. There was no sign of Ms. Mason. After I bathed Oliver and dressed him, I gave him something to eat and drink and took him to the bedroom to play with my children, they are five and two. Oliver settled down and seemed very happy.

Does Oliver play with them quite frequently?

Yes, every time he is home, he comes over to play with them.

Are there other children in the street?

Yes, there are, my girlfriends have two children, and she lives just round the corner. Then just two to three houses down there is another boy plus two girls, are about five, and the little boy down the road is four and a half, so there are plenty of children in this street. Also the Māori family at the back of Danial's as they are lovely children, and they all play together.

Do your children go to the kindergarten?

Yes, the government one, right opposite the town center. What school does the five-year-old go to?

The school in Badger Drive. I will be enrolling my girl there next week. It is the same school Oliver would be going to next year.

How far is this from your place?

It's just a few minutes, I would say four to five minutes' walk.

Can you tell me what happened when Ms. McDonald arrived at your house?

Oliver was in the bedroom playing with my children, and I had gone back to the kitchen to start my dishes. I could see the car at the corner. The next minute it came back, and it drove into my driveway and parked near the bottom of my driveway. Mrs. Mason and her mother, Ms. McDonald, and I may add she was still in her nightwear. I have seen Mrs. McDonald, her mother, when she came to the pharmacy, also when she has been at the Mason household. They then both got out of the car and went up the driveway, and then Danial came over from his place and headed down the driveway toward them. There was lots of yelling and shouting, along with abusive language. Then Ms. McDonald raised her hand to Danial, and it connected.

What part of Mr. Mason was hit?

It must have hit his hand or his face as he went to stop it. I could hear Danial saying, "Come on, get off this property" or words to that effect. I shut the window as I did not want Oliver to hear all the language as he was happy playing. Not long after that, the police arrived.

Is this the only incident you have witnessed?

I have witnessed a couple of others. One night I asked Danial and Oliver over for tea, and Mrs. Mason arrived wanting Oliver. He did not get a chance to eat his tea. There was a lot of shouting and abusive words.

That happened in front of Daniel's property, I am sure it was a Saturday, they mostly been Saturday or Sundays.

How has Oliver reacted?

He is such a beautiful little boy, and for a child of his age, he has taken this well. On many occasions he has been terribly upset and has got sick over it, I have noticed that.

You told us you witnessed another incident?

There was another weekend Ms. Mason arrived to get Oliver, and there was the usual shouting and language.

Who does the shouting?

Ms. Mason. Danial does say things back, not that the street can hear. Can you recall what Ms. Mason says?

She uses swear words, which I will not repeat, lying, that sort of thing, different words that are nasty.

Is this in front of the child? Yes, it has been often.

You are aware Mr. Mason shows movies?

Of course, he has a great setup, and yes, I have been to many of his movies he shows.

How often does he show them?

Usually around one per week, but he has not shown any for quite a long time. Then for a while it was once a week, and then it stopped, then mostly it was Saturday afternoons for children.

Did your children go?

Yes, it is to keep the children off the street. He sometimes would have fifty or more from all around the neighborhood. The kids just love it.

Have you been present at the shows?

Not at the children's shows, but I have been over to see how it is going. It is usually packed. Like I said, it does keep the children off the street as it is a busy street, and the parents love it what Danial is doing.

When you're present at the movie shows, was Oliver present?

No, he was usually in bed as Danial always made sure he was in bed by eight o'clock, and there always was an adult in the house. When I have been to the toilet, he has always been there in bed and again with someone checking on the house.

He is always well supervised, Danial always makes sure the children are well taken care of as many adults bring their children to the movie shows.

How does Oliver get on with the other children?

Kids have their own arguments and that, but they get on very well. He is a well-liked boy.

No more further questions.

Mr. Wadsworth also said, "No questions."

This concluded the evidence for the petitioner, Danial Mason.

The judge then addressed Mrs. Chamberlain, "I have drawn counsel's attention to two matters which are not adequately put to Mr. Mason. One related to an incident involving the throwing of Ms. Mason's car keys upon the roof. Ms. Fiona McDonald went into detail as far as this incident is concerned. This arose out of her cross-examination by Mr. Wadsworth. Mr. Wadsworth did not cross-examine Mr. Mason on the incident, although in answer to another question, Mr. Mason made some scant difference to the matter.

"Another matter is evidence which was obtained in cross-examination about Mr. Mason having boarders in his home giving rise to the necessity for Oliver to sleep in his bed.

"Now, Ms. Chamberlain has sought leave to have Mr. Mason recalled in respect of these two matters."

Then Mr. Wadsworth loudly raised an objection and asked the judge that Mr. Mason not to be heard.

The judge then said, "I rule that he will be recalled on these two matters. Now there is a third matter, and in respect of this, Mr. Wadsworth consents to Mr. Mason being recalled, and this relates to arguments to be made by him for day care of Oliver in view of Mrs. Fiona McDonald's decision not to care for him in the future. So I ask counsel for Mr. Mason to be recalled and to deal with these matters."

*Danial Mason Recalled Giving More Evidence*

Ms. Chamberlain started the questions.

First, regarding your boarders, how long did Mr. Monroe stay with you?

Donald Monroe was working at Crest Foods with me. He left Auckland and shifted to Wellington, and then he applied for work back in Auckland with another company as New Zealand sales manager. When he came back to Auckland, he had no accommodation. He asked me if he could stay for a few weeks, two to three in fact, until his family could come up from Wellington as he was in the process of buying a house, in which that was done. Donald has a lovely wife and two beautiful little girls.

Mr. Baxter stayed with you?

Yes, he is still living at my home. Jim is also buying his own home here in Auckland, and the reason he is staying on at this point is the continuous hassle and problems at my place. For the past eighteen months, I have had no way whatsoever to prove that these allegations made against me by Claire and her family. I have been up against a family of vicious people. They have done some very lousy things to me. That is how it goes. I have Mr. Baxter there as an independent witness. He was reluctant to do it in the beginning. In view of the circumstances, he said  he would do it for me.

That was also you as my lawyer's advice to have someone independent to stay at the house.

The incident about the car keys, in your statement in reply, you stated you had not thrown the car keys on to the roof?

That is correct.

Is this part of the key incident?

That is correct.

It has been suggested you threw Claire's keys on the roof.

No, that is not correct. I had them on my person. I took the keys from her, yes.

Would you like to elaborate on that?

Claire brought Oliver back, not like Ms. McDonald said yesterday that she came to pick him up. This was 8:00 p.m. at night. She was extremely late bringing him back. I then took Oliver inside, and I said to Claire, "I was down at the garage this morning and was confronted by your brother John, and he was about to hit me in the face." He said, "I do not care what you say to my sister, but do not hit her." I said, "What do you mean?" He said last Saturday I had punched her in the face. I said, "John, this is not true." He told me his mother told him. So I confronted Ms. McDonald with it, and she said, "You rotten bastard." I thought this was a setup.

Now when Claire brought Oliver back that night very late, in fact some two hours late, I did ask her, I said, "Claire, what is this story I hit you in the face?" She then took off in the middle of the road and started screaming, "You are always hitting me."

Well, this made me very angry, and that is when I then took the keys out of the ignition and went inside. I did say to her, "I am not giving the keys back until you tell the truth. All these allegations have been your word against mine, and I am fed up with all this crap." With that Claire took off.

It was not long after Fiona came down and asked where the keys were.

I said I have them. I said where's Claire, and Fiona said on the main road. I said I will give back the keys if Claire comes down. Soon after Claire and Fiona arrived back and said where the keys are. I said, "I am not giving back the keys until you tell Fiona what happened." She still claimed I did hit her. A few minutes later, up comes her mother as usual screaming her head off and calling me all the names under the sun. A few minutes later a patrol car pulls up, and two constables arrive on the scene. They asked what the trouble was. I said that I have been accused of assaulting my wife. She claims I smacked her in the face the Saturday before. Her mother says she witnessed this from the window, then someone said I had Claire's car keys. I said, "Yes, I have the keys, but I will not let them go until Claire tells the truth."

I then first asked, "Ms. McDonald, did you witness me hit Claire in the face Sunday night?" She did not reply. Then I turned to Claire and asked her if I had hit her, and she said no. Then the police said to them they had to go. They said they have been called out on numerous occasions to this house. The keys were in the car when the police did investigate the car before they left. Claire then drove off, and shortly after she came back when the police was asking me questions. She said to the police, "I want to see Oliver," and the police told her leave Oliver alone as she has done enough damage for the night.

The following day John came down to my place and said he was sorry what had happened. His mother had told him that I hit his sister and what had happened, and he believed her. He said, "I know now you did not hit her." I said to him, "Do not believe everything they tell you."

What are you going to do if given custody of Oliver?

The company I work for has given me extended leave of absence until February next year when Oliver starts at school. In the meantime, I can be a full-time father to Oliver day or night. I have holiday pay and superannuation due to me, and I am selling up completely the movie business.

Has your employer put this in writing for the agreement for your leave of absence?

That is right.

Can you produce this to the court? Yes, I can produce this to the court.

What do you propose to do when Oliver is at school?

There is a friend four houses from the school, Mrs. Watson, Dylan's wife, and she will pick up Oliver when they pick up their son, same age as Oliver, from the school, and they will hold him at their place until I come to pick him up around four thirty, so he would only be with Emily for a brief period anyway. The company I work for said I can drop him off in the mornings at school. This arrangement spells out any concerns that his mother has to Oliver crossing a busy road going to and coming from school.

Do you know of any other people who you may like to help?

Yes, I have had many offers from people in the street whose children go to the kindergarten where Oliver goes now, and they have children starting school the same time as him, and he knows them, so I cannot see any issue here.

What if Oliver gets sick?

This is well taken care of, as the time I have had off this year, the firm I work for, Crest Foods, has been more than fantastic. There is no problem at all. Being a supervisor, I do a lot of paperwork and planning, and they said on these occasions I can work from home. Therefore, I do go home during the daytime. If Oliver gets sick, I can take sick leave.

The judge asked,

It has been suggested that Oliver has had to sleep in your bed on occasions.

Well, occasionally, he has, yes. I also think any normal child does now and again sleep with their parents. Oliver is no different. A good example is on a stormy night, if there was loud thunder or lightning, he would come running in for comfort and hop into my bed.

How many bedrooms in the house?

Three.

So you can have one boarder without disturbing Oliver?

That is precisely what I have been trying to do. Oliver has his own room, toys, and everything.

Has there been one or more than one occasion when, because of boarders or people staying over, you had Oliver in your bedroom?

It all depends really, as when Mr. Monroe was staying for that short while, he spent most of the time in the lounge, as the double bed I had was in two halves, and we put one half in the lounge for Donald, and he slept on this quite comfortably, and this did not interfere with Oliver. Also, Donald did work strange hours, and it was more convenient to have this bed rolled out in the lounge. Also, he was not there most weekends as he flew back to Wellington to be with his family, and he only stayed for three weeks. I did this to help him out as I am sure most people would do the same for their friends.

Then what about Mr. Baxter?

He is there until he gets his own place, and occasionally when he has gone away mostly weekends, I make myself scarce to make sure Claire does not come around as I would not be home.

Over the past six months, how often Oliver would sleep in your bed?

At the most eight or nine times, and sometimes when he was not well, he came into my room and hopped in, which again is normal for any child as they want that security. What bothers me is how Claire or her family knows what goes on in the house when they are not there. Also Mr. Monroe brought his own bedding with him, such as pillows, sheets, and blankets.

Said no more questions.

*Cross-Examination by Mr. Wadsworth*

Names of the constable at the key incident?

One was Constable Smith, who lived across the road from me. The other I do not know.

No further questions. You may stand down.

The court case now turns into another direction where all the following people giving evidence on Ms. Claire Mason's side, the evidence they provided were very one-sided a lot, without any proof or was seen as sheer hearsay.

I am sure reading this will enlighten you how Claire's side helped her case…or did they?

*Evidence of James McDonald*

James was the older brother of Claire, and I always found him to be a reasonable. He did for most of the time keep out of the breakup between Claire and I. Things did change for obvious reasons, as you will see.

James McDonald was sworn in and stated, "I live in Mangere. I am the brother of Ms. Mason. I have known Mr. Mason about ten years."

Mr. Wadsworth started his line of questioning.

How often have you visited them in their own home?

Many times.

How often have you visited the home since they had separated?

About half a dozen times.

About a week ago, an incident occurred at the Mason household in Mascot Avenue in which your mother was involved. Can you recall that?

Yes.

Did you actually see that incident?

No, I did not.

What was the state of your mother when you saw her?

I was not home, but I did come in later. She was distressed, and she could not move very well, and she had a fair sort of bruise on her collarbone and her arm. I thought she broke her collarbone, but I knew she had not as I had broken mine before playing sport, so I knew it was not broken. I also did see Mrs. Mason, my sister, as she was very distressed and had a cut on her lip. She said the chap who lives with Danial, a Mr. Baxter, had struck her.

I understand that some time ago, you witnessed an incident one night involving some bricks?

Yes.

Can you explain that?

I was in bed, it was fairly late, about ten or eleven o'clock, and there was a knock at the door, and I answered that, and it was my sister Claire. She was very distressed, and she said Danial has gone berserk. I got dressed and went outside, and there was Danial with a couple of bricks in his hand. I found that Craig Kelly was in his car around the block. Our street is circular and has one entrance in and one out, one entrance just past our place. Craig had gone to pick Claire up as she was dropping Oliver off, and Danial then took off and chased the car. The car came around the corner and went past our place, and Danial threw a brick, and it hit the bonnet of the car, then he threw another brick at the windows. By this stage Claire chased the car herself, jumped in, and took off. Danial was swearing. I stood there being woken up, and I did not know what was going on.

Does your sister swear a lot?

Well, in all honesty, I can hardly remember her ever swearing.

Does your mother swear?

No, she does not at all.

Evidence was given your father consumed a lot of alcohol.

I heard about this last night and was quite shocked. Although he enjoys a beer, he does not drink to excess. To suggest he is a drunkard is incredible to me.

Does your father go to the pubs? Yes, he has a beer.

I ask how often would he go to the pub?

A few times a week.

Does he drink in excess at home?

I would say he has one or two bottles a night watching TV.

Do you know Mr. Mason going out with girls during separation?

I know he has gone out with one girl, and I cannot remember her name.

When was that?

A couple of months after Claire left.

Was this about July, August 1975?

If that were around the time Claire left, that would be around the time.

Did you know the circumstances when Claire left?

Well, I would only be giving my opinion on this, but obviously they were not getting along, and she left to live with someone else.

Do you know Mr. Mason ran a movie business?

Yes.

How long has he been running it?

I would be only guessing around two years or so.

How many times a week he shows the movies?

I would estimate two nights a week, maybe three.

Does he show movies to the children on Saturday or Sunday afternoons?

I am afraid I cannot comment on that as I am away most weekends playing football.

Ever been to his movie shows? Yes, once.

When was that?

I would say six months ago perhaps, or four months ago. Was alcohol consumed at the show?

Yes, it was.

Who supplied the drink?

Mr. Mason did as he had a bar at this movie show with liquor, spirits, and beer. You buy the tickets, and with those you obtain the liquor.

How many nights a week would Mr. Mason go out? He goes out regularly, I would say.

The judge asked,

How do you know this?

I would say two nights a week.

The question I ask is how do you know that?

He must go past our place to get out of the street. Our place is on the only exit out.

The questioning then went back to counsel. He comes home at what time?

He has said to my wife that he has come home late after some function. Who does he leave Oliver with?

Occasionally with us, but sometimes with his next-door neighbor or Mr. Baxter, and sometimes with a friend's sister, but I do not know who.

Now turning to the affidavit of Mr. Watson, what comments do you make?

The second statement he makes, that Danial is not a violent person, well, every time that anytime he has seen fighting or perhaps not fist-fighting but certainly when arguments occur, this Watson chap is there. After an incident when my father was teaching my younger brother John to drive, Danial and this Watson fellow did run my brother off the road. They swerved in front of him in such a way they forced him off the road.

The judge asked,

Did you see this? No.

Then how do you know?

They rang me up after the incident happened and told me about it. Back to counsel, Mr. Wadsworth.

Mr. Wadsworth continued asking.

So you were not present?

No, I was not. Can I make another point? After they phoned me about it, my mother came around, and Danial also this bloke Watson turned up and were swearing something terrible. I had to tell them to get off my property, which they did. They then drove past my property and swore and waved fists. That is what

I mean by "not being a violent person." Not being involved in a fight is true, but only a minor degree. It does depend on what you call a fight. If you have an intense argument with no fists being thrown, do you call that a fight or argument?

Have you seen Danial engaged in a fight? Yes.

The judge asked,

What do you mean by a fight?

In that case a fistfight.

*Back to Counsel*

How often have you seen him involved in a fight?

Twice that I can recollect.

Any other comments about the statement of facts you submitted?

No, that one, that was the comment I wished to make.

The other statement of facts that Danial made, dated sixth August, about the movies. I know one here is a complete lie. It says "At night Oliver is not present"?

The movie I went to, which was at night, and Oliver was there watching the movie with us, and the movie was *The Sting*.

How late did the movie end?

It started around nine p.m. and finished around eleven or eleven thirty, I suppose.

Any other comments?

There was a mention of blue movies. My wife went down there this night, and she was going into the house, and it was all dark, and Danial said blue movies were being shown so, she did not go in. This is the only occasion I know of the mention of blue movies. I was not there myself, my wife told me. Danial had also asked me if I could get hold of any blue movies, and he will show them.

Mr. McDonald, you have made a list of comments?

Yes, I have, and made these this morning. One I like to make is this drinking thing, as I have seen Danial drunk many times.

How many times would you estimate that to be?

I would say fifteen to twenty times, and I would say of those twenty times, perhaps half he has been rolling drunk. One time Claire and Danial went out, and we looked after Oliver, and when they came back, Danial was so drunk, he broke the cot. Another night Danial spewed into the toilet and lost his teeth down the toilet.

Does your sister drink in that manner as well?

No.

Ever seen you sister drunk?

I have seen her when she has had a drink, but certainly not drunk.

Has she ever been sick?

Not that I know of.

The judge asked,

How long have you been in the same house as your sister?

It would have been since she got married. Also I heard that Jasmine made comments yesterday that she has never seen my father sober. She would have seen my father perhaps twice in ten years, so how would she know if he drinks too much? That is sheer speculation. Also, she would have seen our family a couple of times. And she also goes to Daniel's movies.

She also said she knew your parents all her life.

Yes, but what she meant was she lived in the same street as my mother and her mother, but certainly had no contact except the occasional meeting in the street, but certainly not that she knows all about a person for that length of time. Another point, I see in the affidavits they talk of stability. I know Danial has had several traffic offenses, including dangerous driving. Danial has come and told me.

Now discussing about my family's stability, there is no one in my family who has had a traffic offense at all. Also, the incident with the Māori boy we found up the road, my wife and I were travelling along the road, and we saw Oliver with this Māori boy, and we stopped. I said to Oliver, "What are you doing?" He said, "To the shops to buy some lollies." I said to the Māori boy, "Has his father given you permission to take Oliver to the shops?" He was very evasive and did not say too much at all. I gathered from that he did not have permission. I did not know what the story was. We then took Oliver to the shops, got his lollies, and then took him home to our place, and then rang Danial. Danial said, "I wondered where he was." That is a busy road, and they had to cross the highway to the shops. I did not think the Māori boy was particularly responsible.

*Back to Counsel*

When Oliver is with you is, he allowed out?

No, we keep an extremely strict eye on him.

*Morning Adjournment at 11:30 a.m.*
*Resumed 11:45 a.m.*
*James McDonald Evidence Resumed*

There was another incident at my mother's, in answer to the violence, I did  see Danial strike my mother, then later he leapt into his car. Oliver was in the car with him. Claire ran after them, and she was yelling at Danial to stop.

Claire then grabbed the handle of the car door, and Danial kept accelerating, and Claire went smash on the road, and her face went onto the ground, and she was lucky the back wheels did not run over her.

On that occasion, did your mother provoke the assault?

No, I do not think so. From what I remember whenever Danial came around, he was saying very antagonistic remarks toward my parents.

Did your parents do anything to make him antagonistic?

I would say no. Danial used to bowl in and make comments both before Claire left and after, but especially after, he would make comments about what Claire was doing to him, and this caused ill feeling in the family. He would start off with reasonable language, but as it went on, the language went out of control, quite serious swearing, and this was one of the incidents when he came around and it developed. It got heated and he swore, and he struck my mother. I chased him when he struck her, and he leapt into his car, and this is when the incident occurred.

Have you had a fight with Mr. Mason?

No. There is also a comment, when the welfare officer came around, explained that he could see a lot of problems with the dropping off and picking up Oliver. He suggested that when Claire wanted Danial to drop Oliver at our place, and we agreed with that, and we heard that Danial made a statement we would not do that, that is not true. We agreed to do that with the welfare officer, and we are still prepared to do that.

Your wife said she would not look after Oliver now?

No, as one of the reasons, when Danial goes to anyone's place, he goes back to this case, and then he starts provoking trouble. We have taken this for a long time. I am getting tired of the situation. He often would cause trouble also stirring up my wife, when I came home at night, well, I was not interested. Another reason my wife might go out to work is that my mother or Claire would like to look after our child. Since my sister left, I have hardly seen her at all.

Why doesn't she talk about it?

I told her it was her life, and I did not want to interfere or hear the ins and outs of the case, but somehow, we have landed in the middle of it, and there is no way we can keep out of it.

Is your sister the type who tells everyone her problems?

I would say not. In fact, she tries to hide things. I have since found out she covered up incidents. She has told me of incidents, and she has not pressed me.

Dylan Watson said he did concrete with Danial and his lawns. Is that true?

Well, far as concreting goes, my brother John and myself and a mate did most of the concreting of the garage and paths to the garage. Also this business about he keeps the outside tidy, he does not mow the lawns often. At one stage I borrowed a tractor from work and cut his lawns as they were overgrown. That was a few months after Claire had left.

How many times have you been to his house since your sister separated? I might say about half a dozen times.

Can you recall why you went there?

We were trying to help him. One time I helped him line his garage for his home theater, and then on occasion just went there to see Oliver.

Mention was made yesterday there was an occasion when a violent argument or a fight with your father took place when you went to hospital.

This is another incident blown right out of proportion. Yes, I had an argument with my father, slipped, and banged my head, and I got concussion. Certainly my father did not strike me.

Do you recall when your young brother came to stay with you because of an argument?

Yes, he stayed overnight and went back next morning. I think he could have an argument with my parents. He left and came to my place. He stayed the night.

Any idea what he said?

No, I would be only guessing. He told my mother that he was at our place. Would you say you are a heavy drinker?

No.

Why do you say that?

Because I do not drink heavily. How often do you drink?

I have a couple of beers after football, that is about it. A few times a week. Do you know how many small children are in the neighborhood?

What I have seen is a couple of small kids down the road. There is a group of Māori kids that live over the back of Daniel's place. They are a bit older, and I have seen Oliver playing with them. I do not like Oliver playing with them. They live some ten houses away from us. We have seen them often down the road playing. That worries us a bit. He has sometimes walked to our place, he will have to cross two roads to get to our place. People speed down past our place and do a whirly around the *S* bend. We are not keen on him coming down to us like that.

Have you seen Oliver with his mother?

Yes.

Since the separation?

Yes.

Ever seen an occasion where she has enticed him with gifts?

No.

Ever seen when he was violently objected?

No, he always seemed happy to go with her.

Seen him when his father has him?

Sometimes, but not all the time, when Danial would take him home from our place.

Do you know why he does not like leaving?

Oliver is at the age where he likes to play, and I gather the impression that Danial does not spend enough time with Oliver.

Has he played with your child?

Yes.

Has Mr. Kelly played with him?

I do not know.

Does he violently object to Mr. Kelly?

I never talk to Mr. Kelly, and I have hardly had anything to do with him. As far as Oliver is concerned, he possibly does not know I know Mr. Kelly.

No further questions, Your Honor.

Ms. Chamberlain then started her readdress.

Mr. McDonald, you told us that Mr. Mason goes out at least twice a week?

Yes, I did.

And that the car passed your house?

Yes.

What time would he go out?

Obviously, he does not go out the same time as me. He would go between six o'clock or eight o'clock or various times.

Whereabouts are you?

In my house, you can see the road clearly.

If sitting at the table?

Yes, you can see the road clearly, and if in the lounge, you also can see the road clearly.

During the winter months, it would be dark?

Yes.

So, Mr. McDonald, you would have your blinds down?

Yes, but you can still see Danial go. We can tell his car as he drives it amazingly fast, and the wife and I say, "That's Danial," and we open the blinds, and that is Danial.

Do you have the TV on?

Yes, but you can still hear the car clearly.

What kind of car is it?

It is a Holden. You can hear any car that goes past.

But you can tell it's Daniel's car going past?

Yes.

You also told us he shows movies once or twice a week or three times?

Yes.

If Danial is out maybe two to three times a week, probably more, and shows movies, how do you know he is showing movies when you do not hear the car?

The cars are all lined up along the road. You cannot help but notice.

Mr. Baxter stated he was in the home since July there and has been movie nights three times. Is he wrong?

He must be then.

How far is your house from Mr. Mason's?

Perhaps some seventy yards.

What is the contour of the road like?

If you mean we cannot see his place from our place, that is correct, but at the top of the road, you can see Danial's place. Our road comes down and runs into a circle, and on top of the road, you can see Danial's place.

Once inside with your blinds down, you cannot see his place?

That is correct, but the movies are often at weekends, and I can see the cars when it is around eight o'clock.

One night a week?

I can see the cars, I know the movies are on. I recognize some of the cars. There is also cars in the driveway.

Can you see the driveway from your place?

No, but from the top of the road, I can.

How often is this?

As often he has the movies.

How often have you noticed?

Many times.

Over the past two to three months have you noticed?

Three or four times.

That is a bit different from two to three times a week you have stated.

Maybe.

You told us your mother does not swear along with Claire?

Yes.

Danial's next-door neighbor, Ms. Egan, and Mr. Baxter, they all have said they have heard them both swearing. Are they all lying?

They must be. When have they heard it? Have they mentioned the fact that Danial swears?

You told us that you were in hospital because of concussion during an argument with your father?

Yes, but I struck my head.

What caused that? You were having an argument with your father at the time you slipped?

Yes, I argued with my father, and then I slipped.

What was the explanation you gave at the hospital?

I do not know what explanation was given to the hospital.

What injuries did you sustain?

No injuries, just concussion, and I was out of hospital next day.

Has your mother to your knowledge ever hit Claire?

No.

Would you say such an action would be completely out of character?

Yes.

Ms. Fiona McDonald, your wife, has told the court she has seen Mrs. McDonald Senior, your mother, hitting Claire?

Well, if she has, I do not follow my wife all the time.

Would you not have discussed this?

You asked me if I had seen my mother strike my sister, which I have not.

Would your wife not discuss this matter with you?

Yes.

Mr. McDonald, I put this to you that your wife discussed this.

Yes, we discussed the incident.

You told us Mr. Mason had several driving offenses?

Yes.

Would you elaborate?

I could not comment any further.

What did he say to you about the dangerous driving?

The incident I was referring to is when he crossed a railway line, and he did not change down, and he got a ticket for that, and for speeding, he got a ticket for that.

Was this dangerous driving?

Perhaps I was wrong with that, but I understand it was dangerous driving. Yes, I was wrong, it did not go to court.

Mr. McDonald, how many things are you wrong in your evidence to this court?

No other things.

Have you and your family discussed these proceedings which was given yesterday?

No.

Did you say that you have not discussed the evidence which was given yesterday?

No. I have not.

If this is the case, how do you know what Mr. Watson has said?

I discussed this with my wife.

What did you talk about?

Football as I had been to a meeting.

You told us that your wife Fiona told you what Mr. Watson said? Yes.

But Fiona was not in court when Mr. Watson gave evidence and could not possibly know what was said.

Someone must have told her.

Mr. McDonald, I put it to you that you and your wife and family discussed this case last night so Mrs. Mason can be granted custody?

No.

How long was the family there at your place last evening?

Perhaps an hour or so.

Once you ceased discussing football, what then?

We discussed my work.

Do you want me to believe you discussed football and your work with your family? Would it be fair to say the family gathering last night was to discuss the court case? So I ask again, who was it that discussed Mr. Watson's evidence?

Like I said, my wife told me.

I will tell you again, your wife was not in court.

Then someone must have told her.

You told us you were a witness to an incident when Mr. Mason threw a brick. Who was driving the car?

I could not see.

Who do you think was driving?

Craig Kelly.

Was it one or two incidents?

I would say two.

Where was Mr. Mason standing?

In the middle of the road.

Did Mr. Kelly come straight toward him?

No, he swerved to avoid him as he was picking up Claire.

Then why should he drive down the street to pick her up? Did Mr. Kelly know that Mr. Mason was there?

He must have done as Claire was dropping Oliver off.

Said it was 10:00 p.m. to, say, 11:00 p.m. That is an odd time to bring Oliver back as he should have been well in bed by then?

It may have been earlier, but I am not sure.

What speed was Mr. Kelly driving at?

He was travelling very slowly, 15-20 mph.

You told us Fiona is considering going back to work?

Yes.

Will Claire or her mother will look after your child?

Yes..

I put it to you this arrangement is the reason for Fiona McDonald's change of heart not to have Oliver? She has got herself a babysitter?

She has one anyway.

Your wife, Mrs. McDonald, said she had a visit from your parents last week. What was discussed?

That was when they came around, we were going to lend the pram we had, and they wanted it because they already arranged to sell the pram.

Did they also ask for a refund of the legal fees they had helped you with?

They mentioned the fact we owe them money, and we wrote them a check.

Who assisted you to write the check?

No one.

Did Mr. Mason give you a loan next day?

Apparently, he did. I have since found out it was $100, but the check has never been cashed.

Did your parents also ask for the return of the trailer and gardening tools?

Yes, they wanted to use them.

Was Fiona upset when they left?

Mildly upset.

Did Fiona ring her mother in Christchurch next day?

She often does.

Did you know she rang her on Friday morning?

No, I was at work.

Did she tell you?

She did later.

Do you know the meaning of "Blood is thicker than water"?

Yes.

What does it mean?

I would say it means you are more inclined to stick up for your own than someone you do not know.

Mr. McDonald, would you not agree, the true meaning of "Blood is thicker than water" that it means that someone's loyalty to their family is greater than their loyalty to anyone else?

Yes, if you say it like that.

Prior to the breakup of the marriage, were you and Danial on good terms?

Yes.

Your wife stayed with them prior to the marriage?

Yes.

Why did she stay?

They offered to take her in, so she went.

Why?

I cannot remember.

Could it be she fell out with your parents, and she was hit by them?

In no way.

How long did she stay with them?

Until we got married. I cannot remember the time, it was a few months.

To buy his house Mr. Mason is now in worked extremely hard?

They both worked hard.

At one stage he worked at three jobs? Would you also agree your family hoped she would go back?

Yes, I think so.

Would your family agree that they do not like Mr. Kelly?

I do not know.

Do you like him?

I do not know him.

Is he not a visitor to your place?

He is not a visitor at all, regardless.

The judge asked,

Ever seen him at all?

No, I have hardly seen him at all, just since this courtroom as he is downstairs.

Counsel resumed questioning.

Would you agree Oliver is happy with his father?

He is happy some of the time, not other times.

Would you agree he is happier than not?

He is not going to be sad all the time.

No more questions, Your Honor.

*Re-XD by Mr. Wadsworth*

Mr. McDonald, you said that you had not heard your sister swear?

That is right.

Did you say Mr. Mason uses abusive language?

Very much.

Ms. Chamberlain put it to you that several people have said Mr. Mason does not use foul language.

That is incorrect, he does use foul language.

Who told you about the driving incidents and charges against Mr. Mason?

Danial told me about some of them.

Did he also tell you about the dangerous driving charge?

I thought he did, but I could be wrong.

How often would you see these cars parked outside Mr. Mason's place at night?

Like I said before, not so much lately, but certainly before two to three times.

You mentioned that you were able to distinguish Mr. Mason's car as it came down the road?

Yes.

How?

Like I said, Danial drives extremely fast, and you come around an *S* bend past our house, and you can hear him before he gets to the *S* bend. We just know it is him.

You were asked at length in cross-examination about your family having discussed yesterday's evidence?

That is right.

As a reasonable man, would it not be reasonable to expect Mr. Mason to discuss his evidence?

The judge then asked,

> Did you discuss the evidence at length with your parents last night?

> No.

> Did you wife discuss it?

> Yes, with me, but not at length.

> Have you ever known your mother to hit your sister at all?

> No.

> An incident has been referred to in Mr. Watson's evidence where he says one night at the McDonald house, Mr. Mason pulled your mother off Claire. Do you recall that?

> I was not there.

> Did your wife discuss this with you?

> Yes.

> What did she say about the incident?

> It was a long time ago.

> This was well before she left Mr. Mason, was it not?

> Yes, that is right.

*Back to Counsel*

> Would you say your parents are very argumentative people?

No.

No more questions, Your Honor.

*Evidence by Ian Jim Cole*

Ian Cole was sworn in, and he stated his name. "I live in Manurewa. I am an accountant, and I have known Mrs. Mason and Mr. Kelly since February this year."
Mr. Wadsworth asked,

Do they live near you?

Yes, in a flat at the rear of my house.

How big is this flat?

It is about 650 square feet, it has two bedrooms, and carpeted throughout.

Who furnished this flat?

Mr. Kelly and Ms. Mason.

Would you say the flat is well kept?

Yes, very well kept.

Why would you say that?

Mr. Kelly cleans the deck once a week, cleans windows, and been in the flat on odd occasions, quite frankly it's 100 percent.

Recall the first occasion when you met Mrs. Mason?

Yes, I cannot remember the exact date, but one evening when I came home from work around 5:30 p.m., I chatted to Ms. Mason and Mr. Kelly in my driveway, and all sudden Mrs. Mason became upset.

What was her reaction?

She sort of jumped and said, "Oh quick, quick," she became emotionally upset. With that Mr. Kelly said can we come inside, I said sure. We went inside, and I looked through the lounge window on to the driveway. With that a Holden station wagon came up the driveway fast. At that stage I did not know who it was. The person tried to get out of the car, and there was a scuffle by the car. He forcibly hit Ms. Mason. With that I ran outside my front door, and I said, "What is going on?" The comment made by the person in the car, whom I understand was Mr. Mason, and he said to me, "Keep out of this."

Is this the gentleman here today?

Yes. I went out to the car, he told me to mind my own business in bad language.

In fact, he swore?

Yes, and he said to me that he would have me on adultery as well. This was foreign to me, as I did not know what the relationship with Mrs. Mason and Mr. Kelly. I said, "Hang on, let us go inside and sort this out." He pushed me aside and went inside. I explained that Ms. Mason was in a flat behind my house, and it was not my house. I took Mr. Mason through my house to the flat outside and showed this to him. He then pushed me to one side and went back to his car. He started the vehicle up then sped backwards fast, and to my amazement, he put the car in forward gear as if to run us down. Mrs. Mason was beside me and holding me back rather hysterically, and she said, "He is going to run us down." He came toward us and stopped. He made a statement if she was not home in half an hour, there will be big trouble, then he left the premises.

At any time whilst he was there, did Ms. Mason use foul language?

No, sir. I have never heard Ms. Mason use foul language.

How often during the week do you see Ms. Mason?

It would be difficult to come to a definite figure. Quite often I would be in the garage, and they would arrive home. On weekends we may come across each other on one or two occasions.

You met Mr. Mason on a second occasion?

Ms. Mason wanted an independent to accompany her on Saturday morning to collect her son, which I understand at the time she was quite legally entitle to. The idea was to go there, to the door, to see that she could pick up her son, and we would drive home again. I was driving my own car at that stage. I preferred as I did not want to anticipate any problems. We walked up the driveway, which I thought was the front door, but it was not. It went up the balcony to a ranch slider. WhereI stood, I could see right through to the dining room, but I stayed at the front door. The radio was quite loud, and Mr. Mason could not be seen.

Have you been invited on to the property by Mrs. Mason?

Yes, I made it clear that I would accompany her if I were within my rights, which I understood she has spoken to her solicitor previously, and it was okay. So we went up to the ranch slider, the radio was loud, no answer to the knock. Mrs. Mason went in and found Mr. Mason.

What time was this?

It was midmorning, more nine than ten. I could be an hour out. With that she made the comment that Justice Barker had given her access to Oliver, and Mr. Mason seemed to accept this.

When she said that, did she say that in an antagonistic way?

I am sure not in an antagonistic way. With that, Mr. Mason stood back, and he was not sure how to take it, so she repeated it. At that point, Mr. Mason saw me at the door, and he came to me aggressively. He told me in extremely foul language to remove myself from the property. I said to him, "I am going, I have no intentions of staying." I explained to him I came with Claire to pick up Oliver. With that he tried to forcibly to remove me. He thumped me a few times.

Ms. Mason tried to take him off me, and I went off the property, and we then drove her back to her place.

The judge asked,

What was the extremely foul language?

The four-letter word. He told me to f——off, sir.

*Back to Counsel*

Did Ms. Mason take Oliver that morning?

No.

Did you see Oliver at the house that day?

No, not that day.

When did you see Oliver the first time?

When did you see Oliver the first time?

Yes, he was in the vehicle when he came around that night.

How did Oliver behave when this went on?

He was crying, very emotional. Mrs. Mason was extremely upset to think that her son should have to go through this.

Mrs. Mason has mentioned to you that she had trouble in access?

She has mentioned this a couple of occasions, yes.

Do you believe her when she said that?

Yes.

What was her reaction when you saw what went on the second time?

He was quite unstable from the time he spotted me at the premises.

What opinion did you form of Mr. Mason because of that?

I think really, I probably formed my conclusion the first time I saw Mr. Mason, but I am always prepared to give someone a second chance, and my feeling did not change at all. He was the same person to me the second time as the first.

Seen Oliver with his mother?

Yes, he is happy with her.

Is he well looked after?

The time he is with his mother, I would say yes.

How can you say that?

On the odd occasion I had my sister's kiddies at our place, they are the same age as Oliver, and they have played together.

Do you make decision on that basis?

Yes.

No further questions, Your Honor.

*Re-XD by Ms. Chamberlain*

She asked,

How much does Ms. Mason and Mr. Kelly pay?

$38 per week.

When they rented, you thought they were married?

The question never came up.

Did they give that impression?

I do not think so. My wife and I interviewed lots of people that morning. The question never came up were they married.

On the first occasion Mr. Mason came around to their unit, do you recall him telling his wife that Oliver was sick?

He may have told her that before I came out from my lounge, this is possible. Was there a phone in the flat at the time?

No.

Did you see the beginning of the conversation?

I did not hear it as I went to my back door, into my lounge, and I could not hear anything.

The only thing I saw was Mr. Mason attempting to hit Ms. Mason. I do not recall that she did anything prior to that. She was standing beside the vehicle.

You stated that Oliver was in the car that night and upset? I thought he was in the car that night.

Mr. Mason states he went there to tell his wife that Oliver was sick?

If that was what was said, I did not hear.

When he is with his mother, does Oliver appear to be a happy, well-adjusted child?

From the times I have seen Oliver, which is not often, he appears to be a normal child.

No further questions, Your Honor.

*Re-XD by Mr. Wadsworth*

Do you see Oliver as a happy child with his mother or father?

I have not seen Oliver with his father, so I cannot comment on that.

No further questions, Your Honor.

It was now my ex-wife, Claire Mason's, turn to give her evidence. You can make your own mind up as to her testimony. In my opinion, this was like a drama queen and gave many accounts of incidents, and she came across as the one that was hard done by. Will the judge see through this and take her side? This was the part that concerned me and my lawyer.

I looked across to Claire as she was called up, and I gave her a dirty look. I noticed she was very pale and shaken. I did not feel sorry for her one bit as a lot of what has been said so far in the court case was her doing along with her family.

Claire Mason was sworn in, and she stated that she was the respondent and the mother of Oliver Kevin Mason. "I have confirmed my affidavits sworn is true and correct."

*Evidence by Ms. Claire Anne Mason*

Mr. Wadsworth opened the questioning.

Ms. Mason, I understand you attempted to exercise access to Oliver about a week ago?

Yes. That is correct.

Can you tell the court what happened?

It was a Saturday.

What time did you arrive?

Around eight o'clock.

Did your husband know?

I told him the Thursday night, I told him we were taking him to Rotorua for the day and may call around early to pick him up.

What happened?

I walked into the house, and everything was okay. I said hello, Oliver said hello, Danial said hello. Oliver was still in his pajamas, and I said I would go to his bedroom and get his clothing. I went to the bedroom. There was not a jumper in the drawer to put on him. He should have had a fair few, he used to have. A lot I believe was given away. Oliver has told me that a lot has been given to his father's girlfriend.

It has been said that you said you had seen another boy wearing Oliver's clothes.

No, that is not true. Danial was still calm. With that, Mr. Baxter got up and went to the telephone and dialled a number, said, "Good day, how are you?" Then he came and pulled me to the telephone. I still have a red mark where he pulled me to the phone. He said, "Talk to Jessica, as she will tell you she has not got the jumpers." I said, "Look, Jim, I am only making a statement as to whether he gave her the jumpers for her boy."

What happened then?

Jim then started pulling me and pushing me and telling me to talk, so I put my finger on the button. Oliver was frightened and said, "Mummy, mummy." I am sure he was scared they were going to hurt me.

It is said Oliver's lip started to tremble when you first came in. That is quite untrue as both Oliver and Danial spoke to me.

*Court Adjourned at 5:15 p.m.*

I stayed in the courtroom after everyone left and spoke to Ms. Chamberlain and asked how things were looking.

"Your people who gave evidence was excellent, and I am sure the judge was impressed. Now on the other side, there are a few things I am sure the judge will deal with, and one discussing the evidence is a sure no. Not the amount of evidence given by witnesses on your ex-wife's side is very damning indeed. However, a lot of evidence changed in cross-examination by your ex-wife's witnesses. A lot of different account of many issues is interesting, such as Oliver either being picked up or dropped off later at night, the amount of movie nights you have, the birthday party for Oliver's fourth birthday, the different accounts of who was there or not there, and of the course the movie *The Sting*, the time it started to also Oliver being up late watching movies. All this I am sure will unravel.

"Now as you know, the courts favor the mother, so let's hope she does not convince the court that she should have custody. While I am not happy with a lot so far said, I think it's a 50/50 at this point where no one at this point I can say has a clear advantage.

"This is a hard-fought-out battle, and let's see what transpires tomorrow and the decision handed down." She put her hand on my shoulder and said, "Hang in there, Danial. It's not over yet. There is a long way to go."

# 33

# THE CUSTODY HEARING DAY 4

*Court Reconvened at 10:00 a.m.*
*Claire Mason Continues Her Evidence*

Mr. Wadsworth continued with his questioning. Claire commenced with a very emotional speech, and this was not asked by her lawyer.

> I would like to tell the court just how much I do love my little boy. He is the world to me. He is my life. I love him.

> Now going back to when this assault took place, it was said Oliver's lip started to tremble. You said this was quite untrue.

> Yes, as they both spoke to me.

> Mr. Baxter pulled you by the arm?

> Yes, he wanted me to talk to the girl on the telephone. I did put my finger on the button to cut her off.

> What if anything did Mr. Baxter have on?

> He had that shirt on with those words he said yesterday. Were the words "Pommy bastard"?

Yes, they were. He kept putting his chest out to me, saying, "Come on, tell me what this shirt says." I said I was not interested. Oliver was frightened at what was going to happen to me.

What did your husband do?

I do not know. He took Oliver to the woman next door, Mrs. Ingram. Whilst Oliver was in the house, what happened?

Danial sort of picked up Oliver and shook him and said, "Come on, pull yourself," and took off with Oliver.

Did Mr. Baxter make you say those words on his T-shirt?

No, I would not say that. He said, "Come on, say what it says," and I would not, and he said, "I will tell you what they say," and he spoke to them, which made me think that Mr. Kelly was English, but the interesting part is the shirt did not mean anything to me. It did not make any difference to me if he likes wearing such a shirt. He was still pulling my arm, and I was trying to pick up the phone and dial my mother's place. That is when he got his fist and tried to punch me, and as he did, I turned, and it caught me on the top of my lip. All inside of my mouth was cut as well as it was bleeding inside my mouth.

This was Mr. Baxter that did this as Danial and Oliver left the house by this time?

I did not know where they had gone to, and I did scream.

Who did you try to ring up?

I did not know the police number and would not have time to ring up anyway, but I rang home, and my young brother answered. Mr. Baxter went to the bedroom and picked up the phone there and kept trying to dial, but I would not go through, so I ran to the bedroom and put the phone back on its hook there. As I was coming back, there was like a home-made cigarette box packed together with hardboard, and he pushed that at me and hit me on the side of my arm. I screamed. It landed on the ground, and the cigarettes were all scattered on the floor. There were a lot of several types in there.

No. Jim cut me off, I think. He pushed the button on me, I think, so I got out of the house and drove to my parents' place. My mother got a bit upset when she saw the blood around my mouth. She gave me a glass of water, and I rinsed my mouth out.

How was your mother dressed?

In her nightwear.

Dressing gown?

Yes.

Where did you go?

We went or stopped outside Fiona's house and sat there for about five minutes.

Why?

There was only one exit to the street, and we thought it would be better to wait there for the police to come. Waited there for some time, and Mum said, "We better go over to Fiona's and ring the police again," which we did, which we did when we went over there, in which Mum did when she went over there. She phoned up and was standing at the door talking to Fiona, so I waved and said I was going to Damien's place. I went on down. I parked the car across the driveway and sat in the car. Then Fiona arrived with my mum in Fiona's car, both in their nightwear. They got out and stood on the grass verge. Mr. Baxter was at the window looking out, and Danial came running out. At that stage, we were on the grass verge. He took one look at Mum, and he goes crazy. I cannot say what, but he started yelling and screaming. Mum walked up past the letter box, then he started shaking her by the shoulders and said, "Get off my property." He was not punching her off, just shaking her.

I tried to get between them as I did not want to see my mother hurt. He tackled her again, and then she kind of came off and stood on the footpath, and Danial kept yelling at her, and the police arrived.

Mention has been made that he pulled her arm and caused some bruising?

She was black and blue under the arm, across the chest, her fingers were swollen up. She could not move her hand. It was completely black and blue.

The left arm or both arms?

It was the left arm. She had to keep it up sort of thing.

Did your mother provoke Mr. Mason at all?

No, we do not have to provoke Danial. He just must see you, and he goes crazy.

Did your mother swear at Danial?

No.

What happened when the police arrived?

The police said, "Let us go inside and discuss this situation." Danial said, "I am not going inside with her," pointing at my mother. Danial said, "It is bad enough if she comes inside," referring to me, but he would not definitely go in if my mother went in. We went in, and the constable asked me what happened. I said I walked in the front door. There was Danial and Jim Baxter. I told the constable what happened, not about my mother, about myself. Jim said he would like me removed from the house so that he could get or give his description, but the interesting part is that before the constable came, he put a jumper over his T-shirt. He had seemed to provoke me.

Was it cold enough to wear a jumper?

No, it was sunny and fine, but he did not have this on when we had arrived. It was a gray jumper.

Did you say you would be easily provoked?

Would hide things to cause no trouble, to keep out of it.

Did the constable take the opportunity to speak to both Mr. Mason and Mr. Baxter?

Yes, he did, but I could not hear what was said.

What happened then?

The constable said both Mr. Mason and Mr. Baxter were against me, and I didn't have a witness, and he didn't see any significance in taking them down to charge them.

Did you show the constable your cut lip?

He said, "I will do all the typing tomorrow, and by that time, there will be nothing wrong with your lip, you all will have made up. It is a domestic dispute." He said people forget about these things so quickly, they are sorry next day.

Did you then all leave?

Yes, I left in my car by myself, and Mum and Fiona went in another car. They took Oliver too. He came from Sue Ingram's place next door. Sue did deny having him, but the constable went over, and he was inside the house.

Do you know Mrs. Ingram at all?

She shifted in some six or eight months after Daniel and I moved in.

Have you spoken to her?

Not a word. I do not know her.

How many children does she have?

She said this morning two. I do not know them. I would not know them if I saw them.

Mention was also made of the incident involving car keys.

Yes, I recall that.

What happened on that occasion?

It was not what Fiona said I was picking up Oliver, but it was when I was taking him home.

What time of day was this?

It was dark, but it was wintertime. It could have been about seven o'clock.

What happened?

What I usually do when I take Oliver back home, I let Oliver out and watch him go inside, and he goes to the window, and he waves to me and I drive away, but this very night before I had a chance to pull up, Danial ran out the driveway to me. He wanted me to say he did not hit me the week before. He pulled me out of the car, and he grabbed the keys and said I could stay there till I said he had not hit me.

Then what happened?

I stood there, and Damian went inside with the car keys with Oliver. I stood there for a little while, so I locked the car up. It locks automatically without the keys. I checked the car completely. It was locked. I then walked to the telephone box on the main road. This took about ten to twelve minutes, I suppose.

I called the police, I dialled the ordinary number. The only time I dialled 111 when Daniel told me he would kill Oliver, and I had no cents, and I panicked and asked them to go and check to see if Oliver was okay. After dialling I stood by the telephone box and waited an hour. I omitted to say before Danial went inside and put the keys on the roof of the house. I swear on the Bible I did see Danial throw the keys on the roof of the house.

Then after waiting an hour, lots of Island people stopped and asked did I want a ride. I started to get a bit nervous, so I rang my parents, and my father answered. "I am waiting by the phone box in Bucks Road, can someone stay with me until the police arrive?" Then Fiona and my mother arrived. When Fiona got there, she said she would go there to Damián's place and get the car keys and can go home.

She went down there and asked Damian for the keys. He refused to give them to her. He got a torch, and they were up on the roof. Fiona did see them on the roof, I did not, but I certainly saw him throw them off. He got a torch, and I am sure he borrowed a ladder. He got up on the roof anyway. Fiona came back and said, "He will not hand over the keys until you say he did not hit you."

So I went back to the house with Fiona, and Damian still had the torch in his hand. He was waving this in front of my face and saying, "You tell her," meaning Fiona, "you tell everybody I did not hit you." I still did not answer him at this stage, then the police arrived.

Mum was at Buck's Road, and she walked around to Danial's place. He shook the torch again and said to me, "Tell the police I did not hit you." It was Daniel's friend across the road and said, "What is the trouble?" That was Constable Dokeris. At that stage, I had not ever met him. He said to me, "Do you want to make an assault charge?" I said, "No, forget it, all I want is my keys back." The other chap who came with him did not come across the road. That was the other police officer. I could not tell what he looked like, he did not say a word. He never spoke to me or come near us. He may have gone inside with Danial after we had gone.

You mentioned that Mr. Mason did not want you to tell the police about his having hit you. What happened?

It was at my mother's place, and they did not know about it. I was with Oliver, and Damian pulled up behind with his girlfriend. They were going to a ball.

What time of the year was this?

About July this year.

How do you know it was Mr. Mason's girlfriend?

I had met her at Damian's place one night when I took Oliver. I was a bit worried about Oliver's medicine, so I took it in myself.

Let us go back to the incident at you mother's place.

Danial parked behind my car, and I was ready to go. I asked Daniel several times to remove his car, and he would not move his car, he refused. The he eventually came out. Everybody else was inside, and they thought he was going to let me go. He walked around my car about three times, took the car number, and started yelling abusive questions about where I got the car from and calling me names. He flung his hand at me and said, "You are just a such and such," and he got in his car and zoomed off with his girlfriend.

Do you know why he came around to your mother's place that night?

It was to bring pajamas for Oliver as Danial was going to a ball.

You mentioned when talking of this incident and going to your husband's house with the medicine, and his girlfriend was there?

Yes, she was in the lounge. This would have been about two weeks before the car keys incident. I walked in and knocked on the door. Oliver went in and handed Danial the medicine, and a little blond boy came out with stained orange around his face. I said to Oliver, "Who is your little friend?" Oliver said to me, "Come and see Jessica." I did not know who he was talking about. We went into the lounge, and she was sitting on the floor watching TV with a baby about eight months old. I just said hello and walked out. I said goodbye to Danial and goodbye to Oliver, and out I went. The next time I saw Daniel, he said, "What did you think of my girlfriend?" He sort of said, "Better than you are, is she not?" I said, "Well, if you think so. If you want to start a new life, fair enough."

Was this Jessica a married woman?

That is right, yes.

Did you know her surname?

Ms. Phillips.

Who told you her surname?

Well, I saw it written down on Danial's phone pad, Jessica Phillips.

Do you like going to your husband's house to pick up Oliver?

I definitely do not. I spoke to the welfare officer about it and asked could I arrange something. He said he would try and do what he could. I said I would like to pick up Oliver from somewhere neutral, I did not like going near the house.

Have you experienced some difficulties when exercising access?

Yes.

What does this entail?

Danial just does not want me to take Oliver. He always finds excuses. I have to say where I am going, what I am doing, I must drop him off at a certain time.

I understand there was an occasion on Sunday when he parked his car outside your address at Manurewa.

That is right, Craig's daughter and I were hanging out the washing. We both happened to look up at the same time. Oliver was digging with his bucket and spade a couple of yards from us, and we looked up, and we saw Danial's car. When I see Danial, I always get frightened and upset as I fear trouble in front of Oliver. Oliver ran into the house, and he hid behind the lounge chair. He got really frightened. I said, "Look, love, you come with me and see what Daddy wants." So I when I got to his car, he was sitting with a pair of binoculars staring into our place. I asked him what he was doing, he said he was making sure Oliver was okay. I said, "Oliver is due back at four o'clock, and he is fine. He will be back then." Oliver did not express any desire to go to his father. He just came back with me, and we had lunch and played around the rest of the afternoon, and I took Oliver back around four o'clock as arranged.

When did this happen?

It would not have been exceptionally long ago, six weeks ago at the longest.

Could you relate to the incident at New Market Park?

No, I was not there. I was not at the New Market incident at all.

Did you abandon your child in the first instance?

I certainly did not. I love my little boy more than anything in the world.

Did you experience some difficulty in your marriage?

Yes, we had violence in the house. The incident that Dylan Watson was talking about that he saw from the window, that was completely untrue. That was the night Danial and Dylan went out. They took off, and I got upset and locked the doors so that he could not get back in. They arrived back about two a.m. They banged on the door. They banged on the door again, and I did not answer it. Danial said, "I would smash the door down if you don't open the door." So I undid the door, but not the chain, and they pushed in the door, and it cracked all the way down the beam of the front door. Danial tried to attack me, but Dylan held him away from me. I wished I could work out where they go the incident of the Valium.

Ever taken Valium tablets?

No, I have not. I do have medication from my doctor I have with me. I also have blood pressure pills, which I take every day, also migraine pills. They are Dystopian, that is a mild tranquilizer. Connected with my blood pressure, they work together. I have high blood pressure. It has got worse. I have had this since Oliver was born.

Was it first diagnosed when you had Oliver?

Yes, I never had a test before. The fact is I had a terrible time having Oliver, I nearly died having him. There was a 50-50 chance of me pulling through, and the doctor said it would be detrimental to my health to have any more children, so Oliver is really all I have.

If that is the case, the circumstances under which you left seem most odd?

Yes.

Why did you leave in those circumstances?

Danial and I hadn't been getting on for months. I didn't agree with the movie business at all.

How many nights a week was he showing films?

Just about seven nights a week when living with me. He showed them at clubs, football functions.

How long have you known Mr. Kelly?

Probably this was about twelve months before I left, when I started working part-time.

How long before you separated from your husband were you going out with Mr. Kelly?

About five months. When you say going out, we used to deliver cars together. We used to take two out and bring one back. I worked at a Holden dealership. I used to pump petrol at their service station to get money for the house. I must point out, Danial did this movie work so he can buy projectors, and this extra money was spent on buying projectors for his movies. I was trying to live on my money.

How long before you separated did you go out with Mr. Kelly on a social occasion?

We never went out socially. I saw him at work and places like that.

Why did you decide to go with Mr. Kelly?

Perhaps we had a lot in common. I could sit down and talk to Craig a lot. Danial never had time, he would not be in for dinner, and I would be home on my own. Danial was so preoccupied with his movie business, he did not seem interested in the house at all. It was always rush, rush, rush.

What day of the week did you leave?

A Sunday, eighteenth of May. Before that night, the day before, Danial and I went to a wedding of a friend of his from work who got married. He was out all day on the Saturday and came home just in time to get ready to go to the wedding that Saturday afternoon. When we got to the wedding, it was all okay, then Danial started telling everyone at the wedding about the situation, then he took off and left me at the wedding on my own.

Was Oliver at home?

No, he was with my parents' place from the Friday night previously. I did see him on the Saturday.

When you left your home on the Sunday, why did you not take Oliver with you?

Danial threatened he would murder me and Oliver. I wasn't concerned enough about myself, but I was about Oliver, as he was only nearly four, and he has a life to lead.

How long was he with your mother?

He was there an awful long time. Danial went to Australia in July for a week, and Oliver was still there at my mother's. The night I left, I did not go to four thirty, and I was back at the house at seven o'clock, and Oliver was not there. I went back to see if I could talk Danial in letting me take Oliver with me.

Did you see your husband then?

Yes, I cannot recall what he said, but I did ask if he would let me take Oliver, and he said no. What I said still stands and that he would get both of us.

Where did you and Mr. Kelly first go to live?

A flat in Henderson.

How long did you stay there?

Not long, it was only temporary. We were looking for something clean and better. We were there some six weeks.

During that six weeks, did you see Oliver at all?

Not ever. I went around every single night. I was told he would be there, and when I got there, I was told he was out. I went around a couple of times to my mother's house, but there again, to be honest, they were against me, but I am reserved. I don't think or talk about things. It is between Danial and myself. It is little Oliver I am concerned about, and he should be our main concern.

When did you first see Oliver?

I really cannot say, it could be a month or six weeks after I left. I used to ring my mother up, and she said Oliver is not interested, and that is all she would say, but I never told her what Danial had threatened to do. Craig's daughter visited us most weekends.

When did you first told your mother what Mr. Mason had said?

She was shocked about it. She questioned Danial on it, but he just looked at her and laughed and said something.

I cannot tell you what was said. She can tell you better than me.

After that, did you see Oliver again?

Yes, Oliver used to come over for the day or weekend. I would pick him up and drop him off again.

Although you did not see him for some six weeks, what was his attitude to you when you first met him?

He did not seem any different. I was still his mum. He still seemed the same little boy.

You have been seeing him ever since?

Not regularly, but I have been seeing him.

What do you consider is regularly?

Well, I was awarded to see him with reasonable access, but I do not feel I am getting reasonable access. I go one weekend, and I might get him, and there is no problem at all. He is at the window waving at me. I would stop outside. The boy would not leave the window. I asked him one day, I said, "Why don't you come out to Mummy?" He said, "I am not allowed to go until Daddy says I can go." He says, "I am scared you might drive away, and I will miss you." He is so happy bright and cheerful when he is in the car. He has so much to tell me, he bubbles over. We could spend the whole of Saturday telling me what he has done at kindergarten for the week.

Does he like kindergarten?

Yes, I think he does. Yes, he expresses dislike at times for it, but I suppose he has had a fight with someone, and he just says that, but all children are like that.

Does he like being with his Aunt Fiona?

Yes, he loves her. He has grown up with their little girl. She says, "Oliver, Oliver," but she cannot understand where Oliver has gone.

You have not seen him for ten days?

No, I have not.

Why not?

Danial shifted Oliver to Panmure to a friend of his, and he said I was not to see Oliver. I was parked at the dairy on Monday night at Panmure, and Danial was going down in his car. He spun around and came back, and he pulled up alongside me. He had been drinking very heavily. He got out of the car and stood with his hands on the car and started on about today. "How you think you will cope with it, wait until we pull you down, wait till Mrs. Chamberlain questions you." I said, "Do not go on, Danial." I said, "Can I have Oliver for the weekend?" and he said no. I said, "I will ring Fiona tomorrow, and you ring her and let me know," and when I rang Fiona, she said Danial said I was not to have him.

Something made you upset at the luncheon adjournment yesterday.

I was coming out of the coffee bar up the street, and we saw Oliver and Danial and his two friends walking down the road. As soon as they saw us, they then went into the Hotel Intercontinental. They did not come back, then I saw Oliver later down the road, and he waved to me. Why shouldn't I be able to say hello to my little boy?

Have you made accusations of assault against your husband to the police?

Yes, I have.

When?

One time we had Oliver with us, and he came to Craig's work as I was dropping Craig off. He waited for us, and there are two entrances there. He came in one, and we went in the other, and he blocked our way. Soon as Oliver saw his dad, he wet his pants, and Danial came over and pulled Craig out of the car.

I got out of the car to try and get them to stop. People were out of the factory next door and his factory, and he yelled and screamed and called me horrible names and said I walked out on Oliver and left him and what sort of mother I was.

Any other occasions?

There was a time when he smashed the windows at Henderson. This was told to me by the Henderson police, and they asked me if charges were to be laid. I said I did not want Danial to go to prison. Danial said he would not do it again. Over the incident at Craig's work and the smashing of the windows, I took him to the doctor's.

What happened at Henderson?

Mum and Dad were going to drop him off. They were not coming in, but Oliver wanted them to come in. So they came in with him, and they would have been in only five minutes, as they just brought him back from a football match to my place. I looked up and saw Danial walking across the lawn. I got quite upset, and Danial started banging on the door. He said, "Open the door, or I will smash it down," and he smashed through with his hand. I felt a person in his right mind would not have used his hand but his boot. He just did not seem to know what he was doing. His hand got cut, and he said, "I am looking for Kelly, I am looking for Kelly," and the glass damaged the furniture inside.

I do not know who called the police, it could have been a neighbor, but then he got outside, and the lounge window broke, and there was glass everywhere. I was frightened the police would come and take him away. It would be awful for Oliver to see something like that happen. Oliver had come to spend the weekend with me.

After Oliver witnessed this incident, did he like returning to that address?

No, after I took Danial to the hospital and got him fixed up, I took him to a friend to sleep the night as I was worried about him as I did not know what to do. He may have done anything in that frame of mind he was in. The doctor gave him an injection to calm him down. We had to pay for the window straight away, or I do not know what the landlord would have said. I was embarrassed about it. But Danial did give the money back we paid and reimbursed us.

After that incident, how did Oliver behave when he came back?

When we pulled up outside, he just screamed. He was frightened. He said, "My daddy might be back, my daddy might be back."

How long after that incident did you move to your new address?

Not awfully long after as I knew Oliver was frightened.

Can you recall the separation agreement drawn up by Burns, Lowe, and Hart?

Yes.

Did your former solicitor, Mr. Bartel, draw up the agreement or a Mr. Lowe?

Mr. Lowe felt it was right, it was the best thing for Oliver. He was a genuinely nice chap, and he tried to think of what was best for Oliver. I never met him but spoke to him on the phone. It was given to my solicitor, and Mr. Lowe put it to me and said it is in Oliver's best interest till he knew what he wanted to do. I would have him one week and Danial the other, and things would work out fine. He said it was in Oliver's best for me to sign it. I did sign it on the condition I had him on alternate weekends and Danial has the other. I felt this would work out fine. Perhaps when Oliver is seven or eight, then he can make his own mind up. It was not custody of Oliver to my parents. Danial did not agree and did not sign.

I show you a piece of paper with a list of items, in total $2,036 and $4,036. Do you know when you got this?

It was around two and a half months ago.

Where did you get it from?

It was on Daniel's telephone table. There were two actually, and I took this one as I thought it might help me. I am not interested in the $2,000 settlement, all I am interested in is Oliver.

When was the first time the matrimonial property settlement was mentioned to you?

About two or three months ago. Have not discussed it. Said I do not want to discuss it. All I want to settle is Oliver. Danial can have the house. All I want is Oliver.

A letter was read out yesterday dated sixth of August 1976, the paragraph of which reads, "My client has discussed Matrimonial property of all claims"? Is this the first time you heard about this?

Danial has mentioned this, and I said I am not interested. He just said, "What do you want from the property?" I may add all I have taken from the property was a painting given to me for Christmas, also the iron I got for my birthday, and that is all.

Did you take your glory box?

No, I did not.

Will you produce this document to the court?

Yes.

What happened to your glory box?

Called Danial up and asked him about it as it was a present from my grandmother. She is now seventy-six. It had sentimental value to me. Asked Danial can I come over and collect it, he said not with Craig's car, so I asked my brother James to go and pick it up for me. He then said to me no, they cannot, I had to collect it. In the meantime he phoned me and said I was not getting my glory box, and he said he would smash it. He kept the phone off the hook. I do not know what he used, but he smashed that in front of me on the telephone.

You heard that?

Called my brother James and Fiona and asked them to go around and see if it was my glory box. When they got there, Danial was with Oliver in the backyard, burning my glory box. It was on fire, completely burnt to a cinder.

So you have not seen your glory box since?

No, I have not.

*Afternoon Adjournment at 3:45 p.m.*
*Resumed at 4:00 p.m.*
*Interposed by Leave*

*Evidence by Graham David Sanders*

Mr. Wadsworth called on Graham David Sanders and was duly sworn in, and he stated, "I live in 29 Farm Crescent, Manurewa, and I am a sales supervisor."
Mr. Wadsworth commenced his questioning.

Can you please tell the court an incident which you witnessed where several bricks were involved? I cannot bring dates to mind. The incident went as follows. Mr. Kelly and Mrs. Mason came to my place this evening, and he was going around with Mrs. Mason, I am not sure of the reason. I believe to pick up the child. He felt there could be trouble and wanted me to go with them. At that time, I understood there has been violence with Mrs. Mason and Mr. Kelly. I accompanied them. Sat in the back of the car, Mrs. Mason went into the house, was confronted by Mr. Mason, she felt for her safety and came back to the car and asked Mr. Kelly to go away as Mr. Mason was going to get him. Mr. Kelly proceeded to drive away. I told him to stop, and we would talk to this man. Mr. Kelly said he was violent, and he elected to drive away. As we drove away, we were chased by Mr. Mason. The road is a cul-de-sac, one entrance and one exit. We drove till we came back to where we started from. Halfway round we did see Ms Mason somewhat distressed, quite distressed.

We asked her to get in the car, she would not. All she could do was scream, "Go away, he will kill you!" I said to Craig stop the car, we will confront this man, it is best. Craig also feared for his safety as he had seen the man in action before. Mr. Kelly then proceeded to vacate the street via this one way in, one way out, and on doing so accelerated. Mr. Mason was in headlights then threw a brick, and it connected with the windscreen but fell off. On going past, he threw another brick, which entered the left rear window of the car and hit me on the head. The window was shattered. I was covered with glass. I asked Mr. Kelly to stop the car, and we picked up Claire, and we went back to my house in Manurewa.

From the incident, I cannot remember what Mr. Kelly did, if he went to the police or not. He reported it, I am not sure, but that is that incident.

Did Mr. Kelly attempt to run Mr. Mason down on the road?

No, I think it's fair to say that he tried to avoid him, but in doing so, the swerving nature of the car, I think it's fair to say Mr. Mason tried to maintain his position as we swerved. He swerved in the same direction, and it made it very hard to avoid him.

Apart from that incident, have you had any other contact with Mr. Mason?

Yes, the first contact I did have with him by assumption mainly. Received a telephone call one night, prior to that, the previous evening, and asked If I was Graham Smith who worked for General Foods and is Mr. Kelly available. "No, he is not, I will take your name and ask him to get back to you." The caller said do not worry, it was not necessary. We both looked at each other and thought this was strange and thought no more of it. The following evening, the phone rang again, and I answered it, and this pleasant voice said, "Good evening, is Mr. Kelly there?" I said no. I will not quote the language, it was not good. I did not like this too much and said, "Mr. Mason, I would appreciate if you did not talk to me in this manner." He said, "How do you know who it is?" I said, "It is a calculated guess." I have never met the man. He continued to abuse me and told me I was lying, and Mr. Kelly was there, and he was coming around. Invited him to come around and see he was not there. That's one incident when I had voice contact with Mr. Mason.

Did the police visit you on one occasion?

Yes, I was visited by a detective from Auckland Police Station and was asked was I in receipt of any stolen radios. I assured the police I knew nothing of what he talked about, and he explained that Mr. Mason to investigate this as he said I was in receipt of stolen radios. We talked at length over different things. I invited him to go to the garage and check my radio in the car and my wife's car, and he found the car radios we had was not what he was looking for, and I heard no more of this.

Had any other contact with Mr. Mason?

Yes, I then had the displeasure to meet him personally. I was at a Crest Foods ball a few months ago. I was with a particularly good friend of mine who also knows Mr. Mason. He got my attention, and he said, "There is a gentleman you might know over there, Mr. Mason." I then went up to the bar and bought a drink, and I was introduced to him. I questioned him about him ringing me up and abusing me. He replied that is nothing to worry about, forget it. I do not like it and still do not like it. We had little words, and I told him if he were to carry on his doings and goings on to me in the same way as Mr. Kelly and Mrs. Mason, he would be dealing with a different type of person.

How are you related if all to Mr. Kelly?

Mr. Kelly is my ex-brother-in-law. He was married to my sister.

Have you any other contact with Mr. Mason apart from those occasions?

Fortunately, no.

The man sitting in court now, is he the same person who threw the brick through the car window?

Yes, he is the same person.

No more questions, Your Honor.

Mrs. Chamberlain then asked under cross-examination,

Mr. Sanders, how would you feel if your wife left you for another man?

I am sure I would be most distressed for a certain amount of time until I got myself into a situation where

I could adapt to it, which I would say a matter of a few months.

If you were frightened of a violent person, would you move into contact with such a person?

I think I would keep far away.

Would you ring every day to that person you are frightened of?

If I were very frightened with a person, I would have as little contact as I possibly could.

You would not ring twice a day and speak to that person?

No, I do not think I would.

You would not ring twice a day?

Possibly if I was concerned about something which that person had which was of mutual interest to me, yes. I said when I made my statement, I am not sure of the nature of the visit that night. I do know Mr. Kelly asked me to accompany him. He had to visit the Mason household and feared for his safety and Mrs. Mason.

Did he say he had to visit?

No, I must be honest, I cannot remember.

What time of night it was?

It was dark, it would have been eight and nine o'clock."

Was it a weekday?

A weeknight.

Would you in the same situation have gone to visit somebody at night without assistance from police?

I do believe Mr. Kelly has tried to get police protection and failed.

In the same situation, would have you gone around?

Yes, I think I would as I am a different nature to Mr. Kelly.

If you were the other man who is living with a married woman, would you go around and see the irate husband?

Possibly if I was in protection of his wife at the time, and if I had mutual reason to, the child.

What would you expect in a situation like that?

I would possibly expect to strike some sort of anger, but not absolute violence.

But would you expect to strike some trouble?

Yes.

Normally you would keep away.

Right away yes, but if there is a mutual and reasonable excuse for this case, which is the child.

What time did you say it was?

Between eight and nine at night.

The child would be in bed at this hour?

Yes, it could have been a bit earlier.

Mr. Sanders, I put it to you that Mr. Kelly went around to stir up Mr. Mason so that he could justify Mrs. Mason leaving her husband.

My answer is that is not the case. Mr. Kelly accompanied Mrs. Mason to go around there. Mr. Kelly stayed in the car while Mrs. Mason was in the house. I cannot remember, but this could be brought to light why she went in.

Would it be reasonable for Mr. Kelly to assume he was violent and then try to run him down?

No, but Mr. Mason was making himself an obvious target.

Mr. Kelly, he could have stopped?

I agree, but he explained to me this man was violent. I asked him to stop on many occasions, the reason he continued was because he could not be sensible to this man. This man in his own words is a violent man.

Mr. Kelly in fact need not have gone to this place?

He must take Mrs. Mason to the home.

No further questions, Your Honor.

Mr. Wadsworth then said, "No re-examination."
The judge asked, "How big were the bricks?"
"A common house brick, full size. I still have the brick at home."
The judge said, "You may stand down."
The clerk of courts then announced, "Court adjourned to 10:00 a.m."

# 34

# THE CUSTODY HEARING DAY 5

The final day of the hearing, and Claire Mason was recalled to the stand. Mr. Wadsworth continued.

We finished yesterday when talking about your glory box. Have you ever seen it since, and you said you have not?

No, I have not.

Apart from items of property which you said you took, did you take anything else?

No, I did not. I only took the painting some six weeks ago and the iron. I have taken nothing else. I have none of Oliver's possessions at all. I bought him a new set of clothes, which I keep at my place.

Did you take any of Oliver's toys?

No! Definitely not. I have brought numerous clothes for Oliver and sent them over but have not seen them again. When he started kindergarten, I bought four pairs of corduroy boxer pants for him, a couple of pairs of pajamas, slippers, long pants, singlets, underpants, jumpers, shirts.

Where the clothes have gone, I do not know. Admittedly Danial buys clothes, I definitely do not deny that.

Have you bought him any shoes?

Yes, I have, about four pairs. My mother just recently bought two pairs. She sent one pair to Danial's, and one is at my place.

Have you given any maintenance to Mr. Mason for Oliver?

Danial collects the family benefit. I have brought food, I have brought meat and dropped this over to them, I have brought drinks, and in no way would I see Oliver without any proper food. I have brought clothing for Danial as I worked for a clothing company. I never took any money from Danial. I would have brought around $60 of shirts for him. I have dockets to prove that, you think I am a fool? But we should not have this fight, it is upsetting, and everyone can see it.

Before the separation, what was Mr. Mason's attitude to you and Oliver?

He really did not have much time for us. He was so occupied with the movie business, he would not come home for tea, and then rush out again with this movie business. They had permanent bookings, one at a food company and various rugby and working men's clubs. It was sort of in and out continually.

Did Mr. Mason ever babysit for you?

No, I would not leave Oliver with a babysitter. I have and never would. I do not trust a babysitter. Oliver is only a little boy, you do not know how I worry about Oliver at night, where he is. The only time I have left Oliver was with my mother, when we went to a social function at Daniel's work, that is the only time I went out. Otherwise, I was home all the time.

You went to Australia with your husband?

Yes, when Oliver was twelve months old.

How long for?

Three weeks.

What did you do?

James my brother and his wife Fiona came with us. They stayed at one of Daniel's brothers while we stayed at Daniel's mother's place. Her house was unequipped, the washing machine did not go, she did not have hot water, but Danial was out with his mates, and James said Claire is in holiday too. I was left at Daniel's mother's place. Even on Christmas day Danial went to a barbecue, and I was sitting with Oliver. I have spent three nights in a row when Oliver had been sick at night.

Does Danial sit up when Oliver is sick?

Yes, he has done so. My parents also when Oliver has been extremely ill, we sponge him down and do what we can for him.

How often is Oliver sick?

Over the past year it has been a lot, it worries me terribly. He has bronchial problems for months. He just keeps coughing bronchial all the time. I asked Danial to take him to the doctor in Panmure, which is my doctor, but he insists he takes him to his doctor. He is not being taught to blow his nose either, in which I have been trying to teach him.

Have you seen Oliver wet his pants?

Yes, I have. he does that when he is terribly upset and frightened.

In Mr. Baxter's evidence mention, was made that you enticed Oliver away with presents?

That is quite untrue. In no way have I.

Has Oliver been reluctant to go with you?

He runs to the door, he stays at the window, and when allowed to run out, and when he is in the car, he is bubbling over with excitement. He has so much to tell me. It has been insinuated we seem to look for Daniel, but Danial drives around looking for us when Oliver is with us, and when he sees an orange station wagon and is scared. He has pulled us over and demanded to take Oliver out of the car. So we usually take Oliver to Helensville or Rotorua, away where he has no show of seeing his father for the day.

When do you have Oliver, and Mr. Mason tries to run you off the road, is Oliver with you?

Yes! Definitely.

Has there ever been an occasion when you have taken Oliver from Mr. Mason without him knowing before?

No, there is no occasion when I have taken Oliver without Danial knowing. I did not want to do anything wrong as I am frightened for Oliver.

Mr. Mason told you take Oliver back by six o'clock Saturday night, would you?

Yes, I certainly would, as I am always there. He could not say he has a problem with me returning Oliver when he says so, never I have done what I thought has been right the way through.

If custody is awarded to Mr. Mason, what would you say?

I would be terribly heartbroken. There is nothing I can do, I know, but do not you think it is the welfare of the child? Who is going to make his lunch for school, and when he comes home, and there is no one there. I am his mother, Danial his father. Danial may remarry, and there will be another woman taking my place. She will not treat him like her own. There is always that difference. If I had Oliver, Danial could have Oliver at weekends, If he were married to someone else, he would be with her. Danial does not want Oliver near Craig, he does not like Craig, but the fact is I would be with Oliver all the time. Craig will be at work during the day if that is concerning to Danial.

The thing is everybody in town knows of the situation, and my boy is going to be victimized at school. Children are very cruel. They will say you are the boy whose mummy ran away.

One of the people who made affidavits came to me and said, "Give me your side of the story, and then I will make a statement of facts." The only ones who know the true story is Fiona McDonald and my mother. If I were making a statement of facts, I would like to know both sides of the story before I put my signature to it.

If this court gives you custody, what arrangements for access would you make?

I would promise Danial If I got custody of Oliver, he would get access every weekend. He could have him from Saturday morning or Friday night. I would let his solicitor draw this up. I just want to see Oliver settle down.

You mentioned that the child should be brought up by its own parents?

Yes.

Would it be best to serve your husband's position if Oliver were in your care?

Yes, but Craig is not Oliver's father, Danial is his father, in no way is Craig his father. Craig would be his stepfather, yes, Oliver knows that. He knows he has a natural father and mother. The same if Danial remarries, his wife would be Oliver's stepmother, not his mother. No one can take the place of your natural parents.

How long have you known Mr. Watson?

Have not seen Mr. Watson. The night he brought the affidavit, till I left, only once, I do not participate in the coffee mornings by his wife. I keep to myself. I keep Oliver in his own backyard to play, and if her boy wanted to come and play, he did, but I would not let Oliver go to their place as there was no fence. Also, when she came to my place, all she could do was run Dylan down and how he drank. I did not want to hear about this. I never ran Danial down, and I did not want to know about Dylan. These coffee mornings are just a hate session. I never participated in anything like this at all.

Mr. Watson mentions in his statement of facts an evening where it is alleged that you were involved in a fight with your mother, and Mr. Mason had to pull your mother off?

That is not true. There was an argument, yes, we had an argument, and Mum and I was arguing. This was over my relationship with Craig, but they or here, and I cannot honestly remember how it all started, in no way did Dylan have to. I don't think he was there. There was Danial along with Fiona, and she was pregnant at the time, and my mother and myself.

Did your mother hit you at all?

No, not that I can recall.

Did anyone pull your mother off you?

No, that is stupid.

Did anyone have to do that?

No, I said before, not that I can recall at all.

Is that when you lived at Roberts Road?

I think she may have slapped my face, which is all. I did not touch her, I would not touch anyone, but in no way was it a fight at all.

When living at Roberts Road, how often did Mr. Watson visit?

He did not visit me, but he came down every night about the movies. He would go to the spare room to pick up the movie equipment and take off.

How long did you live at your new residence?

Three weeks.

During that three-week period, how often did Mr. Watson come down there?

I never saw him. Danial was quite upset as he had not helped him with his grounds, and Dylan did not offer to help. If he came after I left, I do not know.

In relation to that fight, Mr. Baxter said there was an argument on the front porch. Danial tried to separate them and ended up in the side street, where your mother Mrs. McDonald was trying to belt Claire across the face with an open hand?

No way did it go on outside, it was in the passageway.

Have you ever used abusive language?

No, I do not use abusive language.

Ever used it in Mr. Watson presence?

In no way, no, that is what Mr. Baxter, Jim, was trying to make me do, to try and say the word the other Saturday. There was an incident Danial told me where a neighbor asked if he could quiet it down a bit and not have so many movies. I cannot say how many movies, they were annoyed about the commotion going on. The neighbor apparently went over about three weeks ago when I went to pick up Oliver, and Danial told me about this.

Have you ever met the kindergarten teacher Mrs. Tuohy?

No, I have not. I enrolled Oliver some three years ago, and it was a Mrs. Kent there then.

Do you recall an incident around Mother's Day this year?

But I did not make one for you as they told him he did not have a mum. I said, "But you know you have me, you know I am your mummy."

He said, "They told me to make the cards for Auntie Fiona and Nana." Tears came to my eyes, and I said, "Never mind, love, it's good you made a card for Nana and Aunty Fiona," and we forgot the incident. But I am not alleging Mrs. Touhy said that to Oliver, there is more than one teacher there, but why it was said, I do not know as it just does not make sense to me. I am not saying Mrs. Tuohy is a liar. She is probably a good teacher, it's just that it was said at the kindergarten.

Ever been at the kindergarten when Oliver has been there?

No, Danial has told me never to go there. I have asked Daniel if I can go there, and he said, "You put one foot in there, and look out." I have asked, "Can I take Oliver there one morning?" and he said no, so I do not know what activities they do or how they go about their work.

Has Oliver told you he has been bashed up at kindergarten?

Yes, he told me they do fight, he has had scratches and bruises. This was something I would have liked to discuss with the teachers. Mrs. Touhy said it was in play, boys do have rough and tumble and what not. I would have liked to have the opportunity to meet the teachers and introduce myself to show them that Oliver did have a mother.

Could you not go to the Kindergarten without Danial knowing?

Danial said they would kick me off the premises, he said they have heard the story and did not want to know me.

Does Oliver like kindergarten?

He does not seem to mind, he has said he does not want to go, but I said to him, "It's good for you, and you meet other children."

Do you teach him things at home?

Yes, I have taught him the alphabet, to write his name. I asked Danial if he is doing this, and he said, "I have not got the time." I have been teaching him how to write *dog* and *cat*. We have bought him things that we can do together. June is Craig's daughter, she spends a lot of time with Oliver too.

Who potty-trained him?

I did.

Who taught him to feed himself?

I would have.

During the formative years, what responsibilities did Mr. Mason undertake?

He was not interested. Oliver clung to me, you could not leave him with Danial. I know he was his father, but they never played together or do things together.

Did you stop his father doing these things?

No, I must be honest, my brother James has played with him more than his father has. James has spent more hours on the floor with Oliver. I remembered I brought Oliver a soccer set, and I remember my brother James spent hours on the floor for hours playing this game, but it really amused the child. My father and him, he takes Oliver to the garage, and Dad makes things. He makes pouches for his gun, and Oliver helps. It is just getting the child involved in your activity, thinking he is helping too.

He helps me with the dishes, and he helps me bake, he likes to do it, and I let him help in anyway, so he gets to smell and touch everything. It is just getting the child involved in your activity, thinking he is helping too.

Do you tend to spoil him?

Not really, I was overprotective, but I do not think I spoiled him. I watched everywhere he went and what he did. I never let him out of my sight.

Did you smack him?

When he was naughty, I did, but not often. Does Mr. Kelly ever smack him?

No, never. Oliver is never naughty when he comes for the day, he is always bubbling over, and in no way is he ever naughty for the day.

You heard the evidence on Tuesday of Mr. Peter Benson?

Yes, I did.

Do you recall when the petition for the divorce was served?

Yes, I do. I cannot tell the time they had arrived. It was last year. They arrived at the flat, four of them in the car. They all got out of the car, and somebody went to the front door.

Where were you?

I was sitting in the lounge watching TV. I was there on my own. Somebody went to the front door, some to the back door, some to the garage, which was between the units with the rolling doors coming down. I did not answer the door, I do not think they knocked. Someone was rattling the back door handle. The front door handle was a silver one, that you can shake. Another was shaking the garage roller door to try and open it. Four men arrived, three came to the house, and the fourth stayed on the footpath.

Did you know these people?

The first one was Charles Benson, and there was Dylan Watson, and another friend of Dylan I did know, the other I did not know at all.

What was your reaction when these people started trying the door?

I became frightened as to what they were doing. I had no idea they had the divorce papers. It was not long after Danial smashed the windows. The first thing I did was ring Fiona McDonald. I told her what they were doing and asked if she knew what they are doing at my house. She said that they had to come over to serve some papers on me, she said that a Mr. Charles Benson was coming to serve the papers on me, not the four of them.

After you spoke with Fiona, what did you do then?

I called the Henderson Police.

Did you dial 111?

No, I looked up the directory and called the number in the directory.

What did you tell the police?

I told them that that my husband and I are separated, and there are four people outside I believe to be delivering papers on me, and that they are at my door, and I am not answering the door as I am here on my own.

Did you tell the police at all if they were armed?

I certainly did not. I do not know where this business came from. In no way did I see any arms or no mention of arms. The police never mentioned it that night, they never said one word to us that night.

What else did you tell the police?

I told them I believed they were going to serve papers on me, when they came around as I was on my own, and I would not answer the door. In the meantime, the whole four drove away.

How long after your telephone call to the police station did the police arrive? About a half hour.

What happened when they arrived?

In the meantime, Craig had come back. He had to go down to the shops, and when he came back, there was no sign of Mr. Benson's Holden car anywhere. Craig put his car in the garage. Craig was back about ten minutes when the police arrived.

When the garage door is closed, are you able to see in it at all?

No, the doors pull down, and you cannot see through that all. There is an internal entry, but you cannot see through there anyway. We have a little dog that sleeps in the laundry, and we keep the garage shut, and we did not want the dog to wander in.

Are there any chinks which someone can see into the garage?

Most definitely not.

When the police car arrived, how long after when the others arrived?

Around ten minutes after the police arrived and came inside and were talking to us.

Did you accept service of the petition?

Yes, I did. I invited Benson and Watson to come inside and discuss the whole thing, but they refused.

Mr. Kelly accepted the service of the petition on him?

He did, we both accepted them. We never signed for them, they were handed to us.

Mr. Benson and Mr. Watson in evidence said, "Mrs. Mason did most of the talking"?

No, that is not true. I opened the door or Craig might have, I am not sure. We were in the lounge with the police when they arrived back. It was the police who handed us the papers. Mr. Watson handed them to the police, and they then handed them to us. It seemed strange why Mr. Watson and four of his friends should come around and deliver the papers, why not a person of the court or someone we did not know? Therefore I got so frightened that four chaps should come and deliver the papers.

Do you know David Thomas?

Yes, I do.

How long have you known him?

Well, David stated he knew Danial in March this year, I am not sure. That is when he started with Crest, but he went to work as a representative with Danial.

In total how long have you known him?

Only from March to May when I left. And never saw David again until one incident when I rang Fiona to see how Oliver was during the day. It was lunchtime, there was no answer, so I called Danial. Oliver answered the phone, he told me he answered the phone in the garage. I asked him who was minding him, and he said, "I cannot find anybody, Mummy, I cannot get into the house, I do not know where everybody is." I said, "Oliver, stay on the end of the phone. Sure no one is there?" He said, "David is here, but he will not answer the door," he said the music is very loud.

Oliver was talking to you on the phone, and Mr. Thomas would not answer the door. Where was the phone?

In the garage, there is an extension in the garage. I told Oliver to stay on the phone, and he will have to try and get David's attention and get inside, but Oliver hung up the phone. I called back again, and that is when Mr. Thomas answered the phone. I said, "David, it is Claire here, can you please tell me where Danial is?" He said to me, "It is none of your business, but he is at work." I said, "Who is minding Oliver then?" He said, "I do not know and do not care." I said, "David, would you mind Oliver until I get there? I will get a taxi and come over, and I will stay with him until Daniel comes home. He told me to mind my own business, he then said do not come over. I called again, and there was no reply, so I took a taxi straight to Daniels's place. I was terrified who had Oliver, where he might be, where he might wander to, but when I got there, no one was at the house.

Those are the only two times you have met David?

Yes.

Do you know if he stayed with your husband?

Yes, he did. Well, I never saw him, when I went to get Oliver, he was never there. He did stay there, but he was always with his girlfriend. He has a fiancée or something. He was never at home at all.

Do you know Mrs. Dubbeld?

Yes, only vaguely.

Ever met her before Tuesday?

Yes, I have.

Is she a friend of yours or your husband?

She is Daniel's friend, she seems a genuinely nice person. I have nothing against her at all. I have not had a chance of sitting down and talking to her.

Were you ever inviting Mrs. Dubbeld and her husband to come around to your house to dine?

No, never. I did go to her wedding, this was a long time ago, Danial was invited, and he said we were going to the wedding. I never got a chance to speak to her at the wedding. This was the last time I had spoken to her. She has with her husband been to Daniel's place for dinner, but I was not there. She is not an abusive person. She is a noticeably quiet person.

Do you know Mrs. Egan?

Yes, I do.

How long have you known her?

I have known her most of my life, not that we have been in contact all that time. She lived near my grandparents. She came from a big family, and my family tried to help them out a lot.

Had Mrs. Egan ever been invited to dinner to your place when you were with Mr. Mason?

No, not for dinner, no. She came to Oliver's third birthday party, maybe at Oliver's second birthday party, but we did not see each other over these times.

Ever spoke to her after you left?

No, I have not. I have not spoken to anyone about our situation. It is between Danial and me. It seems terrible that the whole of Mangere knows of our situation. It seems terrible that Oliver must grow up in that atmosphere.

In her re-examination, she mentioned an incident when you came around to the Mason household, Oliver was asleep, and you accused Mr. Mason?

I recall going around there. I most definitely know Oliver was not asleep. He had the ice block stain around his face like Jessica's boy had. It must have been an ice block.

Danial was cooking dinner for Jasmine and her husband and two children. I was supposed to pick up Oliver at nine a.m. that morning.

What time of day was this when you came to the house?

It was around four thirty or five p.m. I went in and asked Danial where he was all day as I was supposed to pick him up at nine a.m. in the morning. I went there, and he was not home. I went back at eleven a.m. Danial always said I do not turn up, but I do. I went back at two p.m., but he was not at home.

What happened?

I went in and asked Danial where he has been all day. He told me to mind my own business. I said, "Well, I may take Oliver now with me, I will give him dinner and bring him back tomorrow." He said, "No, you are not having him." Oliver wanted to come. I was astounded for Mrs. Egan to say that Oliver ran and hid under the bed. This is quite untrue. She did say incidentally that Oliver did not go with me, I cannot remember, I thought he came with me, but I cannot be honest about that as I am not certain. Danial kept telling me to get out of the house, "It is not your house, get out."

Mrs. Egan goes on to say, "Go on, hit me, that is all you want to do all the time"?

No, I never said that. I do not hit my husband, but he hits me. Danial, now I am frightened of him, and he comes to me when nobody is around. He comes on the streets waving his fists at me, and he knows I am scared.

Did you swear at him on that occasion?

No, I did not.

Did you swear at anyone?

No one. I did say hello to Jasmine and her husband, but otherwise, there was not another word between us.

Has Oliver ever run away from you and hid under the bed when you have come to exercise access?

Oliver is always so eager to come, he cannot wait. He keeps asking me, "Am I coming tomorrow morning, Mummy?" He keeps asking me to ring up his father to ask can I keep him. He says, "Ring Danial if I can stay, Mummy." I had to explain and sit down with Oliver why I should take him back.

Mr. Baxter in his evidence said at p. 34, "He has told us he wants to stay with us….if he goes." Did you ever entice your son away?

This is definitely not so. Oliver seems happy with us, we do activities with him, do things with him, we take him for barbecues, we take him to the beach. Only about three weeks ago, we went to the beach on a Saturday morning, it was around ten o'clock when I picked him up. It was a sunny day, not a summer's day, but we were the only people on the beach. We played there for a while, and Oliver was happy.

Mr. Baxter said that the morning when the alleged assault took place, you wet your pants?

When did he say I did that?

The morning when your mother was assaulted allegedly by Mr. Mason about a fortnight ago.

Did he say after I came back or outside?

Did you at all?

Yes, I did. He was belting me, and I got so frightened, just screamed. Nobody seemed to listen to my screams, maybe Sue on the other side may have. The lady on the other side, she had enough of the situation, she can hear the screaming. The only noise I make in the house is screaming when they hit me.

You wet your pants. Would not that be reasonable to infer you are a very emotional type?

I was frightened, terribly frightened, as Danial had gone.

Could it be said that you were emotionally unstable?

Most definitely not. Oliver seems so frightened for me, it worried me what they have done to Oliver. Danial has shaken him. Danial is frightened that I am going to get hurt. I found two razor blades in his pocket one day, not in a packet, just straight razor.

By his left collarbone?

That is right, just here right near his chest. He had a check shirt on with a pocket in it.

Did you investigate this?

I did and looked in his pocket, and most astounded, I found two razor blades in his pocket.

What did you do?

I took them straight out of his pocket. I asked Oliver where he got these from, he told me, "David gave them to me." I had to sit down to Oliver and explain the dangers of razor blades. He could have cut his chest open. These were not the normal razor blades as they were the cutthroat razor you see.

Do you know Mrs. Ingram?

Not really, I have only seen her in the courtroom. She may have known me, I may have been pointed out to her, but otherwise, I have never spoken to her.

Was she living in her house when you moved into your new house?

It would be months after we shifted into the new home, I do not know any of the children. I only knew her when she stood in the witness box.

When will Oliver be five?

On December 14, this year.

So will he stop going to kindergarten?

When it breaks up, yes.

If you have custody of Oliver, what school will he attend?

Fern Park School, which is about two minutes' walk from our house, at the end of the street, across the road.

Is the road a busy one?

It is very busy, yes.

How would you get him from one side of the road to the other?

There is a patrol crossing, but I would take Oliver every day and pick him up. I would not let him go on his own, and I would not trust anyone else. He knows three little boys who are going to that school. One will start in February when Oliver starts, the other two have already started.

Did you or your husband go to a marriage guidance?

Not referred to one.

Has your husband asked you to go?

No, only Reverend Anderson.

That is the Reverend Anderson?

Yes.

When did he mention that to you?

This year sometime, I cannot remember the exact month.

Were you aware that in May 1975, your then solicitor wrote to Mr. Mason requesting access?

Yes, I was. I even went to a solicitor even before I left Danial. I asked about advice first.

Ever asked your husband to enter into a separation agreement?

Yes, I may have done.

When?

I have not a clue.

Ever likely to be reconciled with your husband now?

I do not think there is any chance now, it is way past that.

Before you left your husband in May 1975, did you and Mr. Kelly have sexual intercourse?

Most definitely not, no.

It was in fact after the separation that it took place?

That is correct.

What doctor do you usually go to?

Dr. John Patten.

How long has he been your doctor?

It must be around six years now, would say. It was well before I had Oliver. Also when I was pregnant, I was referred to an obstetrician. I went to Dr. Patten well before that.

Did you ring Dr. Patten up recently and ask him to be in court on your behalf?

Yes, I did, but he said he cannot afford the time as he had a busy practice.

Has your husband ever been to or consulted by Dr. Patten?

Oh yes, he was our family doctor, until he started going to Dr. Henderson in November last year.

Do you know why he stopped?

I do not know, he just stopped. I do not know why.

You told the doctor about your difficulties?

I have not, no. Danial apparently had, I think this was discussed with my mother to him as well, but I never discussed this with the doctor. It is in the last three months or so, the doctor spoke to me about it. It is between two people I feel, I could have brought friends here, but this was between Danial and I, and who is going to be the best person to look after Oliver.

Did you know that your husband had boarders at his house?

Yes, I do know.

Did you know where those boarders slept?

At one stage he had two, Mr. Monroe and Mr. Baxter. Danial purchased modern furniture for Oliver's room. We only had one bed at that stage, not two, the double bed plus Oliver's bed. He brought more on HP at the department store, but that is what I have been told. Mr. Baxter has been sleeping in Oliver's original bed, which is now in the spare room. Mr. Monroe was sleeping in Oliver's bed.

How do you know that?

By the pajamas under Oliver's pillow. I have seen Mr. Baxter in bed, never Mr. Monroe, but under the pillow was his pajamas, also things in his drawer. Oliver's things were cleaned out, and there was men's clothing in there. I do not know whose it was, Mr. Baxter's or Mr. Monroe's.

Do you know how often he slept in his father's bed?

He sleeps quite often. Oliver tells me he sleeps often with his father. I suppose he enjoys being in bed with his father. I am not objecting either, but I think he should be in his own bed.

Where does Oliver sleep when he is with you?

He has his own bed in his own room.

You heard yesterday Mr. Cole, your landlord, give evidence yesterday about an incident the first time he met Mr. Mason when he came to his residence in Panmure?

That is correct.

What happened on that occasion?

We both arrived more or less the same time, which is Mr. and Mrs. Cole and Craig and me. Mrs. Cole went inside to start her dinner. Mr. Cole was talkingto us, and we were both standing there. Before I go on, I think Danial did not know where we lived at that stage. I found out he had a private detective to find out where I was living.

Anyway, as we were chatting, all of a sudden we saw Danial coming down the street. He sort of passed the driveway and then backed up, and the car was screaming down the driveway very quickly. I knew there was going to be trouble, and Craig said to Mr. Cole, "You should go inside," and Danial only has to see Craig and that is it, he is ready to have a fight. Oliver was standing up on the front seat, and I went to the car and said, "What do you want, Danial?" He was trying to get out of the car. He started using abusive language, and "I am going to tell all the neighbors about you." Oliver was crying and crying. He got out of the car and was pushing me around, swinging my arms, not actually punching me.

Did you try and punch him first?

Oh, definitely not, no. He stood there and started yelling, "These two are not married, they are living together, she just left her son, I want to tell your neighbors, I want to let them all know," then he started pushing me around again, and Mr. Cole came out as he gone around to his back door through the lounge and saw what was happening. He said to Danial, "Come on, what is happening here, calm yourself down." Danial shook his fist at him and said, "So you are the one committing adultery with my wife, right, I am going to have you up."

He then pushed his way into Mr. Cole's house, and he told Danial, "She does not live in here," and he said, "Show me where she lives." He took Danial through his house out the back door and showed Danial where I lived. This was a unit at the back of his house. Then Danial saw Craig and tried to have a scuffle with him by the kitchen door by the Cole house. He then went back to the front door and yelled more abuse. It cost him $50 to find my address, he said it was worth it. Mr. Cole ordered him off the property. Danial got in his car.

While Mr. Cole was with Danial, I was trying to console Oliver, who was in the front seat. He snatched Oliver off me, he reversed the car, and then Mr. Cole and I came toward them, then he took off.

Mr. Cole mentioned another incident the second time he saw your husband, at your home?

Yes, that is correct. What happened then?

I went over on the Friday as I was not getting access. I was granted access on when Danial got interim custody in December last, but I had not given access. When I went over on my own on the Friday, Danial said no, I cannot have him, so I left. So I was advised to take an independent witness with me. I did not want to take anyone from the family with me, so I asked Mr. Cole was he willing to come with me when I go over to collect Oliver. Mr. Cole said, "I will as long I am able to go on to the property." I did check this out with my solicitor, and he said yes, as it was a joint family home property.

We arrived around nine to nine thirty, I suppose, on the Saturday morning. We went up, knocked on the door. There was no reply. There was music going, it could have been the radio or cassette, it was very loud. I walked through to the kitchen cum dining room, and Danial was in there. He asked what I was doing here, I said I have come to pick up Oliver, he said I am not having him. I said well. We walked to the passageway, and Mr. Cole was standing there. I do not think Danial knew he was there. I said, "I have been awarded access to Oliver, reasonable access." I had not been exercising any and I had brought Mr. Cole along with me just in case he did not give me Oliver, as I had no proof, I had not been getting him.

He still did not seem to sink in, he just stared blankly. So I repeated it again, then he sort of looked at Mr. Cole and just went for him. He started punching on the chest. I tried to pull him away, and Mr. Cole said, "Look, I have not come here to make trouble or harm, just as a witness to see whether Mrs. Mason gets Oliver or not." So Danial kept pushing him over the rail of the balcony and then managed to get away. Danial yelled abuse all the way as we went to the car, and we drove off without Oliver. I do not know where Oliver was as he was not in the house.

Mr. Sanders mentioned a night when he accompanied you and Mr. Kelly to Mangere?

Yes.

Why did you go around that night?

Danial called me at work and told me Oliver was sick. He called me so many times at work, he just keeps calling me all day at work, and I got into trouble, but I could not help it. I told him not to, but he keeps on ringing me.

How long ago was that?

Right up until I left, this was May this year, which was when I worked at Deco Clothing Company. I worked in the office there as accountant machinist.

I would say about eight o'clock at night. I cannot honestly tell the exact time. This incident would have happened twelve months ago now, and I cannot be definite on the time now.

How many times does Mr. Kelly go to Mr. Mason's home?

He does not, but I was upset on this occasion, but he dropped me off, and he went. Oliver was not in the house then, that was when my mother was looking after him. I rang Mr. Kelly to get me, there was no reason for me being there. He drove around the street to pick me up. This is the only time Mr. Kelly was being in the street, otherwise, he has never come with me.

Where did you ring Mr. Kelly from?

I called from Greg Sanders's place, which is where he would wait for me. He said he would wait there till I rang to say what was going on with Oliver. I cannot remember which way we came. I think we had dinner that night, he may have dropped me off with Craig, but I know Craig went back to Greg's place to wait for me to ring.

You are at present working. If you had custody of Oliver, what would you do?

Cease to work. I do not want to go to work, but I am not going to get money from the government or social welfare. I just could not stay home and worry about Oliver. I do not know what he is doing in the day.

If you had custody, would you work part-time?

No, I want to be with Oliver. There is so much to tell me about kindergarten, what is it going to be like when he goes to school. He is going to be taught things, it's rather hard to go to work when a child is so young.

Do you and Mr. Kelly propose to get married?

Yes, soon as the divorce case becomes final.

After the luncheon adjournment yesterday, you said to the court, "I would like to tell the court just how much I love my boy." That almost seems rehearsed.

No way it is rehearsed, in no way. Oliver knows how much I love him. I just wanted made known, people say she does not want her little boy, and nobody knows how much I want him.

Even if your husband were given custody of Oliver, would you consider returning to him at all?

For Oliver, yes, I would.

No more questions, Your Honor.

Claire's testimony she gave was full of lies and exaggeration to many issues and events. Her portrayal of me as a father before she left is totally untrue; in fact, regardless if I worked at night doing the movies at clubs I was never home, I did at least one show a week at best as I had people employed to undertake this. I would most nights come home from work and prepare dinner. I was renowned for cooking good meals.

She tried to discredit me in many ways, that I did not take care of them. The movie business was a very profitable business, and it helped to secure the new house. Also a lot of the furniture and fittings in which Claire did not contribute.

Then there is the issue that I was going to murder my son and was abusive to her. I never ever laid one solitary hand on her; you do not hit people you love.

Claire made an issue of the marriage in trouble. We had a happy and loving relationship until Craig Kelly come on the scene.

Out of all this, I do understand whoever gets custody has to take care of one little boy, Oliver. That is what this court case is all about.

I think we are going to hear more from the judge about the discrepancies in her witnesses, mainly her mother, James her landlord, and not forgetting Craig Kelly.

The possibility is that I may lose this case, as my lawyer said there is many things that are against me. God willing I hope the judge sees through Claire's testimony.

Now my lawyer has her turn to cross-examine Claire. I think this will be an interesting session.

Mrs. Chamberlain commenced her cross-examination to Claire Mason.

You told us you love Oliver very much?

Yes.

Is it not also the case that Mr. Mason also loves Oliver very much?

Yes, I agree.

Is it not also the case that Oliver is the only one thing surviving from your marriage? Oliver is all he has got left?

Probably, but I am thinking of Oliver's welfare.

Oliver is all he has left?

It probably is, but what about his welfare? Who is going to do the best for his welfare?

Is it not the case that he pleaded with you not to go?

No, he asked me after I had left, would I come back.

How often did he ask?

Quite a few times in the first few months.

These telephone calls to your work, was he not trying to talk things over with you?

He used to ring me up and abuse me. I was in tears. One day he waited for me at lunchtime, and I went with him to the park, and he said he would kill me. When I got back to work, I was upset and in a state. My boss took me home. The minister Rev. Anderson came to see me, we had a cup of tea, and in no way Danial's name came up.

Who initiated that visit?

I do not know.

Was it your husband?

It could have been, yes.

You told us you associated with Mr. Kelly for some five months prior to you leaving?

Yes, that would be about right.

What was your husband doing during these five months?

He was working. At one stage he had glandular fever, he was at home, I did everything for him, but he was not put out in anyway.

How hard was he working?

He had two jobs.

Why?

To get his movie business off the ground.

What about the home?

That came from Danial's wages, I also worked part-time. I paid for the grocery bill. We did not have time payments. Danial said he would work for his movie business. The projectors were expensive. I told Danial from the start that I did not like the movie business.

What was the purpose of the movie business, to make money?

The movie business was for Daniels's enjoyment. I sat down one night and talked about it and said, "Please, Danial, why cannot we do things together?" Danial was also paying Dylan Watson to do some of the movies. I would say there would have been more money spent out than coming in.

Would that be the case in any business that you hire workers, and they are part of the business operation and costed into the fee paid by the clubs? And the records clearly show that the movie business was highly profitable one, and a lot of the profit went into buying the new home.

I would not know about that.

Since you left the home, the carpet was installed?

No, that was when I still living there. We paid a deposit on it.

Where did the money come from?

I was still working my part-time job.

After you left, it was Mr. Mason's responsibility?

I suppose it was, but I could have helped him out. He told me he borrowed $2,000, and he told me he did not want me to put any more money into the house after I left.

Since you left, driveways have been installed?

Before I left, the driveway to the house was there.

Who did the concreting?

Craig and his brother-in-law Greg Sanders and another couple of people.

Was Mr. Kelly paid or any of the others?

For the materials, I am not sure, but Danial paid for all materials.

The concrete in the garage and from the back steps, who done that?

My brother James, I believe, and others from Daniel's work did this. He did pay James's friend for the materials, I understand.

You told us you had been working for Mr. Kelly when he was in the car business?

Yes.

And the two of you go away on trips?

Only one trip, the others where within the region.

Where did you go on the trip you mentioned?

To Wellington. We took one car down and brought two back, and yes, we spent the night in a motel. Oliver was with us. I took Oliver everywhere I went.

All this took place while you were still married to Mr. Mason?

Yes, that is correct.

You told us you stayed in a motel on this trip, so I ask you, while you and Mr. Kelly were associated?

That is quite true.

Once you left, you went and lived with this man?

Yes.

And start sleeping with him?

Not straight away.

Eventually you did?

Yes.

You told us you took legal advice even before you split up?

Yes, that is correct.

Did you tell your then lawyer that you were terrified of your husband?

I told my lawyer he was of a violent nature.

Could you have not got a non-molestation order?

I have been asking for one. I cannot say exactly.

Was this the day after you left in terror of your own life?

Danial said if I get a non-molestation order to look out as it takes a week, and he said he would get me before the week is out.

You have phoned Mr. Mason frequently?

Yes, I call him at nights as I am worried about Oliver, not every morning. My little boy worries me sick, and if he is sick, I ring up and see if he is all right.

Mrs. Mason, I put it to you. If you were so worried about Oliver, you would have not left him, is this correct?

He was with my parents, and I knew he was well looked after.

If you loved him so much, why did you leave him with someone else?

My parents were quite capable.e.

Mrs. Mason, despite your great love for this child, you were prepared to leave him with your parents.

Yes, however, I knew he would be well looked after. It was not custody, it was a guardianship order. As Danial and I were to be legal guardians, my parents would look after Oliver during the week, and Danial and I would have alternate weekends. I was working on advice from my solicitor. I did not make that agreement.

This also must have been on your advice to your solicitor, and you were prepared to sign it?

Yes.

Mrs. Mason, would it be true that your lover then, Mr. Kelly, did not want Oliver with you?

No, that is not correct.

At one stage you were prepared to let your husband keep custody of Oliver?

No, I was not.

I have a photocopy of a letter to Mr. Mason dated 28th May 1975. "We write to you to advise that Mrs. Claire Mason will allow you to have custody of Oliver with provision I have access to him." Is that not correct?

I did not know that letter was written, but I never wanted to give custody up.

This was done by your solicitor and surely on your instructions.

I do not remember.

Mrs. Mason, I do not fully understand that you cannot remember such an important document, and you were prepared to sign him over to your parents?

That was the only way.

Mrs. Mason, I ask you, why did you not take Oliver, get yourself a non- molestation order, and get police protection?

He would have got me in some way.

Would not the police be capable of protecting you?

All he would have to do is get a gun and shoot through the window. I have a little boy whose life is at stake here, not my life.

How many wives in Auckland are killed over dispute on custody?

I do not know, but I know Danial would.

Then why have you not got a non-molestation order?

That is coming.

I put it to you, that you could have taken Oliver with you, had also non- molestation order if you were so concerned about your safety and Oliver's?

No, I did not, but I was concerned for Oliver's safety. I cannot stress enough how I fear for his safety. Danial has run the car off the street.

You could have done this some eighteen months ago?

I stopped the police from arresting him before. Why should I put Oliver through seeing his father in prison?

But a non-molestation order would keep him right away?

Do you think that would keep Danial away? I do not think it would make any difference.

Mrs. Mason, in your affidavits and in this court, you have portrayed your husband as a violent person and a potential murderer and make us believe all these allegations, and yet you have declined to avail yourself of this opportunity, and do you think a non- molestation order this year would be better than having one last year?

If I have custody, I will need such an order.

Once you left your husband, there was a period where he did not know where you lived?

He knew from the start, he knew I was in Henderson. I took him there as he said I did not know where I was. He came the next night with a chap yelling and screaming, and it was only temporary accommodation anyway.

By showing him where you live, he would make more trouble, would he not?

He would have found out anyway, also we did not have the phone on as well at that stage.

If you had a non-molestation order, he would have not been allowed to come near you?

He did come near me and still does. How do you ring police when you have no phone, and he smashes his way in?

Mrs. Mason, the point I am making to you is if you had an order, he would not be allowed near you, that is what the laws says.

But I do not think that would stop him.

You have not done that, and you had trouble after trouble?

I have tried to prevent it.

Yes, you have been ringing Danial twice a day.

When Oliver has been sick, yes.

You have done this for eighteen months now?

I cannot give up my little boy.

Mrs. Mason, you have done this for eighteen months.

I have rung him, and he also rings me regularly as well.

You have gone back to the house after you left?

Yes, I slept there for three nights on one occasion.

I put to you, Mrs. Mason, would Danial let you know when Oliver was sick?

Sometimes, and sometimes my parents would let me know.

*Adjournment for Fifteen Minutes*

At the break, I said to Mrs. Chamberlain, "All the lies she is saying, it is unbelievable. She never came back and stayed three nights. I think she is a drama queen and keeps saying I would murder her and my son, it is insane. I find this very distressing."

All Mrs. Chamberlain said was, "This is very odd indeed." And then the court resumed, and Mrs. Chamberlain continued with Claire Mason.

Mrs. Mason, let's continue. Now when you left Mr. Mason for Mr. Kelly, your parents were opposed to this?

Yes, that is right.

You had an argument with your mother, which Mrs. Fiona McDonald and Mr. Mason has referred to?

Yes, I never told them anything about it. It was Danial who told my parents about the situation.

Your mother liked Mr. Mason?

It is fair to say she liked me too.

But she liked Mr. Mason?

Yes, she did.

Your mother did not want you to leave?

I cannot say my mother did not want me to leave, she just mentioned my association with Mr. Kelly and did not like me leaving.

Would it be fair to say that your parents hope you get over this infatuation and return home?

I do not know about that either as I did not have very much contact with them over this at all. We have discussed it now, but we have not discussed back to the first month or so as I did not see Mum or Dad or anybody, other than telephone calls to see how Oliver was.

At any stage did you give your husband hope that you may come back?

Yes, he kept asking me, but I did not know. I do not think it was fair to tell Danial anything about it. He never asked if Mr. Kelly loved me.

Can you recall going to the household at Mr. Mason's request and discussing reconciliation?

I cannot recall that at all.

Can you recall seeing a tape recorder?

Mr. Mason often says, "I tape what you say." I have seen him do it, he cuts pieces out and joins them together.

He could have recorded something when you said you loved Mr. Kelly.

It is possible.

Did he say he hoped you would come back?

At the beginning yes.

What about the beginning of this year?

No.

Once you left your husband and Oliver, you were in a tricky situation as far as applying for custody went, and you left your husband for another man?

I do not feel I was in a tricky situation as far as applying for custody went.

But you left your husband and child for another man?

As soon as I went, I spoke to my solicitor. I already spoke about that.

Did you file any proceedings?

As I said earlier, I spoke to my solicitor, and he wrote a letter about proceedings for custody, and then he said, "Seeing that your husband is such a violent person that perhaps if we let it settle down for a while, then we would apply again."

Your solicitor never suggested to stop your husband coming around seeing he told you that your husband was such a violent person?

There was such trouble that he felt the non-molestation order would cause more trouble. This was at my solicitor's discretion.

Mrs. Mason, I find this very hard to believe as to your husband you portray as violent and potential murderer, and you were not prepared to take the risk?

Again, I tell you, I left this up to my solicitor's discretion.

Once Oliver is returned to the family home, would you agree Mr. Mason, his father, looked after him very well?

Yes, but when I had him, I washed his hair, cut his nails, I did a lot of things.

Would you not say Oliver is happy with his father?

Yes, with me too, he is happy with both of us.

Would you not also agree that to enable you to upset existing agreements, it is necessary for you to establish severe defects on Mr. Mason's part?

I do not know what you mean.

You have told the court that Oliver is well looked after and happy?

But Oliver is being put out at nighttime when Danial goes out. I know a sixteen- year-old girl who looked after Oliver one night as Danial went to the Crest Foods Ball when Mr. Sanders gave evidence. I am not denying this, Danial is most welcome to do this, but Oliver is put out because of this. I never went out except one a year to a social Christmas party.

How did you know that a sixteen-year-old girl looked after Oliver that night?

I was told, I cannot remember when, I can recall a telephone conversation with Mr. Mason and Mr. Benson. I was on the extension. Mr. Benson said to Danial, "You have to get Oliver to learn he must take second place, whether he likes it or not, he has to stay there, he must know you are in charge."

Mrs. Mason, you said you were on the extension on the house phone?

Yes.

Then what were you doing in the house?

I was in the garage, and it has a phone extension there. I went in there after dropping Oliver off.

Mrs. Mason, you keep telling us Mr. Mason is a violent person?

Yes.

Now let us look at some of the things in your statement of facts, p. 3 para. (d), you said, "The other children in the area his toys and clothes stolen." Is that correct?

Oliver has told me this, yes, and his toys disappeared, the toys when I lived there have vanished. There is not a lot of clothes at the house either.

So did you say the clothes have been stolen?

Well, I am not sure. I do not know if Danial has given them away.

Did you specifically say "pinching" in your declaration of facts?

I have, yes.

Then this leads to what Mr. Baxter has told us of such an incident that you marched in the house recently, and you did not say hello to anyone?

That is untrue.

It has been said you went up to Oliver's bedroom to get his clothes and came back and accused Mr. Mason giving them away. You have denied that?

Yes, I never accused Danial, we spoke nicely to each other.

At para. 56 of your evidence, you said, "A lot of jumpers were knitted by me."

"He dialled a number." Could you tell us in view of your denial how could have Mr. Baxter have dialled a number? He would not know who to ring?

He knew Danial's girlfriend. He also knew of the papers served on him.

Why did Mr. Baxter jump up? Unless you accused him, how would he know?

He did, he most certainly did it.

The judge then asked,

Did you say you did not mention a name but a girlfriend? Daniel's girlfriend?

I said to Danial, "Did you give Oliver's jumpers to your girlfriend's little boy?" Danial had no time to answer me. When Mr. Bailey jumped up to the phone and was calling someone, I assume it was Danial's girlfriend.

But you were not sure it was his girlfriend?

Like I said, I assumed it was.

Mr. Mason in this hearing has told the court it is not his girlfriend.

Again, I assumed it was.

*Back to Counsel*

Did you ask to whom he has given the clothes?

Yes, I said Oliver told me he had, but Danial did not answer.

Why didn't you say that before?

I went up to the bedroom to get a jumper to put on Oliver.

You were asked. It had been said that Danial gave away Oliver's clothes.

That is not true.

Let us look at your statement of facts, when you accused the kindergarten of saying to Oliver, as it states that Oliver has no mother. Mrs. Mason, how do you know that?

Oliver told me when he came with his Mother's Day cards. I am not saying it is all the staff, it could just be one person. Why did he make the card for Fiona and not me?

Have you seen the card?

Yes.

Mrs. Chamberlain handed a card over to Mrs. Mason.

Is this the card?

No.

Mrs. Mason, please look at this card. What does it say?

I never got that card.

It still says Happy Mother's Day.

I never got the card from Oliver.

This does say Happy Mother's Day. Who has had it then?

I never got that card.

Mrs. Mason, I put it to you that you are making that up along with other things you have told the court today.

I swear to God I am not.

Mr. Wadsworth jumped out of his chair and shouted that he objects to the line of questioning.

The judge declared, "Overruled. Continue, Mrs. Chamberlain."

I swear on the Bible I have never seen that card, I never got it.

You do not know that the kindergarten told him he had no mother?

Oliver told me that.

I put to you, Mrs. Mason, you have to persuade yourself that Oliver is unhappy, that he is badly looked after, and you are ill-treated to justify the steps you have taken?

I agree I left him for another man, I am not hiding that fact.

What evidence have you apart from Oliver saying he was told he had no mother as this is a serious allegation against the kindergarten?

I stated that Oliver told me.

Do you honestly believe the kindergarten staff would do that and be so irresponsible?

I do not know. I have asked if I can go there, and I am told I cannot go there. I would not expect it, no.

But you claim that they might or hoped that they might, you persuaded yourself they would do such a thing?

I did not persuade myself, no. Oliver told me that was what he was told. My younger brother made a card for me with Oliver.

You have said Oliver does not have any friends in the area, and the children are pinching his toys. What evidence do you have for that?

The Māori children in the back house are always in the garage. I have seen them walk off with his toys, and I have called out to them.

It seems you do not like Māoris?

I am not prejudiced. I have a Māori girlfriend. I say it is because others have said it is a Māori family at the back. The children have broken the back fence down.

Mr. Mason has brought to court several witnesses, Mrs. Egan, Mrs. Ingram, Mrs. Dubbeld, and others, all say you get hysterical, your language is shocking. Are all his witnesses telling the truth?

No, they are all liars, absolutely.

Does it matter to them who has custody?

I presume they wanted Danial to have custody. They are trying to help Danial.

Would you say that they would go to the extent of committing lying under oath?

No, I have said I would hear two sides of the story before making a statement of facts.

Mrs. Mason, you then say the evidence given by Mrs. Ingram, Mrs. McDonald, Mrs. Egan that is all lies?

If they say I use abusive language, yes, because I do not use abusive language.

What about Mr. Watson? Is he telling lies when he said you dialled 111?

Most definitely as I looked it up in the telephone book.

Are the police also not telling Mr. Watson the truth, and he made all this up?

Yes.

Is he also lying when he said there had been a call about people carrying firearms?

Most definitely, I never mentioned that at all.

And is he lying when he said Mr. Kelly was hiding in the bedroom?

No, that is not true, he was not hiding.

I direct you to the evidence of Mrs. Dubbeld. She has told the court that Oliver is clean and tidy. Is she not telling the truth?

No, she is not.

Mrs. Dubbeld also said that Oliver was in bed by eight p.m.?

I do not know, I cannot say what time he went to bed.

Mrs. Egan has told the court you said, "Danial, hit me, come on, hit me, that is what you always do." Is she lying too?

Yes.

Mrs. Mason, I put this to you, Mrs. Egan was telling the truth, and the reason you said that was you wanted to establish your husband as a violent person?

That is not true. I have tried to cover up a lot for Danial's violence. I have been hit before I left.

Have you any evidence of that?

I never went to a doctor when I had bruises on me. I am reserved to the fact that I do not tell people my troubles.

Prior to Mr. Baxter sharing the house with Mr. Mason, if there was a domestic incident, it was usually his word or your family's word against his?

It was usually mine against Danial as I went on my own.

All your family was there, and Danial was on his own?

No, that is not what I heard.

The incident of the keys, until the police came, it was Danial's word against yours.

Mum did not see the incident. I swear he got the keys and threw them on the roof.

What did he say to you when you came around that day? Did he say you are not going until you tell the truth?

It was in the evening, and we were talking when I came to the house.

Did Mr. Mason say, "You are not going until you tell the truth that I did not hit you"?

Yes, he did say something like that, but he did hit me.

Until the police came, you were prepared to say he hit you?

The policeman was a friend of Danial, and I just wanted my keys, and I wanted to go. I do not recall saying that I recall Danial having a torch and shaking this in my face and saying, "You tell them, you tell them," and he did hit me. I do not make these things up. I have covered for Danial for a long time, not only this but other things as well.

Now, let us return to the last incident to which Mr. Baxter refers, that he has no convictions, he was a reluctant visitor, but he stayed to help Mr. Mason. Mr. Baxter has now been charged with assault on you?

That is correct, he pulled me to the telephone.

Mrs. Mason, in all due respect, you make us want to believe your husband assaults you without reason, Mrs. Egan tells lies which Mrs. Egan says at page 32, "Go on, hit me, as you always want to hit me." So Mrs. Egan telling lies and along with Mr. Baxter, and he is hitting you as well?

Mrs. Egan did not say, "Hit me."

Mr. Baxter is also telling lies?

Mr. Baxter is absolutely telling lies.

I put this to you, Mrs. Mason, your family are all truthful as well?

I would hope so, yes. It is extremely hard to remember back over incidents eighteen months ago, exact times and dates.

Mrs. Mason, let's now look at as it was suggested that your father has assaulted your brother James, and James told us in a course of an argument, he slipped and suffered a concussion. What is your recollection?

I do not recall the incident at all, but I have seen James in hospital from football.

Mrs. Egan once again heard this, that Mr. McDonald hit James, and he ended up in hospital. Is she lying again?

Most definitely yes, how would she know when I do not even recall it? Somebody would have had to tell her.

Ms. Egan in this court that Claire had said about it, was that not true?

I do not see Jasmine from one year to the next, in no way would I say that.

Mrs. Egan said she has spoken to you over the phone, and she has gone and spoken to you at your place after the separation, as well as when the incident happened with your brother James. You told Ms. Egan that your father, and you say in your affidavit in response to Ms. Egan, you have stated she is lying. Is it now another lie?

Yes, I would say so.

Ms. Mason, I would now refer to another matter. Did Fiona come and live with you and Danial?

Fiona came to live with us, yes. Fiona and James could not live together and live in the same house when they were getting married. It was unfortunate that I had to go back into hospital, and she went and stayed at my aunt's place in Manurewa.

Ms. Mason, yes, it was said Fiona returned to the McDonald household when you went into hospital because this dispute got sorted out then? Not because of the reason you put?

Everybody has family disputes.

Mrs. Fiona McDonald agreed your mother did hit you? Is this an isolated incident?

Most definitely.

Your mother did hit you?

She did, yes, across my face.

Can you remember when you wanted to have a bath?

No, I cannot, that is six to seven years ago.

In your statement of facts, you mentioned Oliver going to church Sunday school, is a recent innovation. Do you approve?

Most definitely I approve, I would take him myself.

Mr. Mason enrolled Oliver at the age of two at Sunday school?

Not to my knowledge, I do not think he had to.

Quite sure about that?

No, Oliver used to get a card, he automatically went on the roll for Sunday school from the time being christened, and when he is four, he can attend Sunday school.

When you met Mr. Mason, were you a churchgoer?

I did go occasionally.

Was he a Sunday school teacher?

Yes, he always went to Sunday school.

Have you attended church since you left Mr. Mason?

No.

Does the co-respondent go to church?

He goes to the Salvation Army, I am a Presbyterian. I will not go now as it is my own feeling about it, I have done wrong. I certainly knew nothing about Oliver being enrolled at the age of two, I thought he was automatically on it.

Were you not interested when he was two to discuss it?

Danial was not going to church then. I was going on my own. I would like to speak to the minister Rev. Anderson about this as I know nothing about this.

What is this I have here? This is to certify that Oliver Mason is enrolled into Sunday school?

This is automatically done. I do not think you go and enrol them. I will speak to Rev. Anderson about this.

Then how did Mr. Mason get hold of this?

I was to get little cards from the church, I kept them in a drawer.

But do you have no recollection of Mr. Mason enrolling him, yet you did not enrol him?

It was done automatically. This may have been posted to me, and it was in my drawer altogether for Oliver. I do not know his christening certificate is there. I would like to speak to the minister to see if Danial went along personally. I am pleased it is done, and I want Oliver to go to Sunday school.

Ms. Mason, on page 4 of your affidavit, you have made many allegations saying Oliver's clothes are dirty, not ironed, and not well looked after.

That is right, singlet and underpants are dirty.

Mrs. Tuohy the kindergarten teacher in this court hearing has stated Oliver is immaculate. Is she lying too?

No, I completely strip Oliver down and bathe him, I wash his clothes, I keep clothes at my place to re-dress him.

How many mornings Oliver goes to kindergarten?

I assume every morning, but he has stayed with my mother for some time. I think that statement was made when Oliver was with my mother. Mum could have done the washing and ironing for Oliver, I do not know.

Is it then not the case that Oliver is always immaculately dressed?

Not immaculate, but he is clean and tidy at times.

He is clean and tidy?

I hope so.

But when Oliver goes to see you, he is not?

Well, very untidy, yes.

Mrs. Mason, I put this to you very strongly that you just want to convince yourself that Oliver comes to you dirty because it makes your case stronger?

That is not true, may I mention the shoes? I said to Danial these shoes are a bit dirty, can I have his new ones, and he said there is nothing wrong with his shoes, so I fixed them up and sent them back.

Ms. Mason, I strongly put this to you again, when Oliver comes and sees you, is he clean and tidy?

I wish you had asked my landlord about this. He sees Oliver when I bring him back to my place. I wash him and send him back in washed and ironed clothes. He is sent back in clean clothes.

Ms. Mason, you are avoiding the question, and it's no point asking your landlord if Oliver comes to you clean, and today, we would not know the answer to that. You have told us at least twice when Oliver comes to see you, he is bubbling over and has lots to tell you?

Yes.

Is his life during the week interesting and happy?

It is his kindergarten he is telling me about, what he does there, at times he is happy there, he tells me of the fights they have, the rough play.

You said, "I do not know if Oliver is true and happy."

Yes.

Ms. Mason, then surely if Oliver is bubbling over at kindergarten and he is happy, and this is another attempt to convince yourself he is not happy?

That is not true, even his kindergarten teacher Mrs. Tuohy said Oliver was quiet on some days. She did say at the beginning of the week, but could this suggest the child wanted to stay with me?

Ms. Mason, this I could also suggest he was not happy over the weekend? It could, but no, that is not true.

No further questions, Your Honor.

*Re-XD by Mr. Wadsworth*

Mrs. Mason, what happened when the application for non-molestation was filed this year?

We went to the court.

Can you recall what your husband did to you when he read your affidavit?

He really abused me about it, he really went mad. I cannot honestly recall, but I know he went violent toward me.

That non-molestation application was March 1976?

Yes.

The day the court was set down for the hearing?

That is correct.

Do you know why it was not proceeded with?

I was advised to let things lie for a while as there was so much trouble. I cannot explain it, but it would be better to not make things any worse, but do this after the custody hearing. I properly said it wrong. I cannot explain what I mean.

When you first went to see Mr. Jackman, did you tell him about the non- molestation order?

Yes, I mentioned this and Danial's violence. I did not understand it then, what he said to me.

Do you recall when you first saw me as your counsel?

Yes, I do.

When was that?

It would have been this year, the weekend or the time after Danial went to Mr. Cole's place, my landlord. I saw you the day after, about April this year or March, would that be right? I cannot quite recall when you started doing the case.

So it was early this year?

Yes.

Did Mrs. Chamberlain read a letter signed by Mr. Jackman dated 28th May 1975?

I believe so.

Is this a true copy of the letter?

Yes.

Mrs. Chamberlain has drawn your attention to the words "We write to advise that your wife is content for the time being at least that you should retain custody of Oliver," is that the entire letter?

No.

"We have been instructed to act for your wife," etc. Is that the letter I have shown you here?

Yes.

Is that the true copy of the letter?

Yes.

I would like to produce this to the court as when you signed the agreement giving custody of Oliver or guardianship of Oliver to your mother, on whose advice did you act?

Well, on Danial and his solicitor as they made it up, and they instructed me it was the best thing. Danial told his solicitor to draw up the papers, and they said it was the best thing to do, so I did.

You mentioned in cross-examination that when you first left Mr. Mason, you advised him as to where you were living?

That is correct.

Why did you advise him?

Because of Oliver as I did not have a telephone, and if anyone wanted to contact me about Oliver, but anything could happen with him, and he had to know, my parents had Oliver, but if Danial knew if Oliver was not well, he can contact me.

It was inferred that you abandoned your child.

I certainly did not abandon my child.

Who took the child from your home?

Danial took him to my mother's place.

What did he tell you if you got Oliver from your mother's place?

He would murder both me and Oliver.

If there was a non-molestation order in your favor, would your husband obey it?

Most definitely not.

When he comes to your house, does he come announced or unannounced?

Unannounced.

So he could arrive without the opportunity to ring the police?

Most definitely. There would be a knock on the door, and he could be there. He could be there during the day when the doors are open, and he could walk straight in. How does an order help you there?

He stops you in the street?

Most definitely. If he sees us driving, he swings around and comes back and cuts us off until we stop.

You have rung your husband regularly as has been suggested twice a day?

Yes, I have, but not always twice a day, but I do ring every day.

Why?

To make sure Oliver is all right.

Does your husband often ring you at work?

Not now he does not, but when I was working, he did. This meant I did not have to ring him, but he would ring me all the time. Sometimes in the evening I did ring him, but he was ringing all the time at my work.

You mentioned that you said that some of his toys and clothing had disappeared?

That is right.

What drew you to that conclusion?

There were many clothes in the drawers, and when I looked, they were completely empty, the odd jumper and trousers left there, not much else.

His toys?

Well, his little bike is rusted and broken, completely unrideable. I have seen the kids at the back with his toys, and Oliver said his father had given the toys to them.

Any other cupboards and drawers where the clothes may be kept?

In the hot water cupboard, I checked there too. He has not a lot. I know Danial has spent money on clothes, and so do I, but they do not seem to be there now.

Do you see Oliver with clothing you have provided?

No, the clothing he came with, I washed it and sent him back home in them.

Have you provided Oliver with clothing at your place?

Yes.

Mention has been made that you have said that Oliver has told you he has no mother?

That is right. Yes, he has. I have sat down with him and said, "You have a mummy and a daddy. You have a grandmother here and a grandmother in Australia, an auntie, and uncles. You are lucky, Oliver." Then he is happy, and he runs away to play.

The card produced, have you seen that before?

No, never seen it before.

Did Oliver write that card? His writing is not on it? Whose writing is on it?

I have not any idea. It really has broken me up seeing that.

In evidence, you said both Mr. Watson and Mr. Benson came around to our residence to serve the divorce petition?

Yes.

Did you at all during Mr. Watson's evidence mention of his visit?

He never mentioned in his evidence coming at all.

In his statement. does he mention the incident at all?

No, he has not.

You have contradicted Mr. Benson on that very point, have you not?

That is right, yes.

I refer now to the incident of Mrs. Egan, where she maintains that you said to Mr. Mason, "Go on, hit me, that's all you want to do all the time"?

Yes.

You heard the evidence of Mr. Mason? Yes.

Has he made mention of that incident? No, he has not.

Then Mr. Mason had the opportunity to mention that incident.

Mrs. Chamberlain raised an objection. "Counsel is leading the witness."

The judge said, "Overruled."

How many times before you left your husband had you gone to the doctor because of bruises?

Only once did I go to the doctor.

This was a result of beating you received from your husband?

It was from the incident with the car when I was knocked down. I was scraped alongside my whole side.

Mention has been made that your husband attempted to affect a reconciliation, is that true?

Last year he did, not long after I left. Not of late he has not mentioned it. What date is on the divorce petition?

18th November 1975.

Does it not seem strange to you he filed a divorce petition and when he wants a reconciliation?

It does, yes. He did not mention it much after the first few months after I left. When did the Reverend Anderson see you? This year or last year?

This year.

Did he come to talk about reconciliation?

No, he never mentioned Danial. He just talked about where we live and everyday normal things.

Mr. Baxter has not been charged with assault on you? Not yet.

The police are still carrying out inquiries? Yes.

When did they tell you that?

On the Monday, and they told me they had about forty-five cases to go through, and when it comes your turn, we will let you know.

Why have you not gone to church since you separated from your husband? Because I feel bad. I have committed adultery, and it states in the Ten

Commandments that you must not commit adultery. It seems so bad.

Is there a church close to you where Oliver could go?

Yes, I would prefer the church in Auckland as this was where he was christened. The doctor you speak of and been to see, a Dr. Patten, how well do you know him?

I know him very well as he has been a family doctor for many years. Dr. Patten is unable to appear in court because of his commitments? That is true.

Have you ever written, or has he written to the court? Yes, he has.

Mrs. Chamberlain raised objects to this line of questioning.

The judge said, "Proceed, Mr. Wadsworth, without leading your witness."

The house when Mr. Mason worked at several jobs, for what was his money used?

To buy movie projectors to get his movie business started. It started about two and a half to three years ago. It was expensive, terribly expensive equipment. Even if a part goes wrong, it is expensive.

You said he borrowed $2,000?

Mrs. Chamberlain objected.

*Luncheon Adjournment at 1:00 p.m.*
*Resumed at 2:15 p.m.*

You said before the adjournment, your husband borrowed $2,000, and you said he told you he borrowed $2,000. Was that $2,000 separated from or in addition to the $500 on the list?

That $200 would have come through later. He borrowed the $2,000 first. I cannot prove it, but he has told my parents and Fiona that he has not hidden it any way that he did borrow the money.

No further questions. You may stand down.

Claire's statements she made as to the witnesses on my side were liars, the continuous allegations that I was abusive and was going to murder her and my son were repeated many times.

If she felt her life was in danger, then a restraining order to be placed on me would be fitting if I had done what she said I did. These were all unfounded. It will be very interesting now what the judge will say about her testimony.

My lawyer Ms. Chamberlain handled Claire to account, and the point I see as critical is when you have created incidents and comments about the kindergarten and many other matters to suit your own agenda.

In many incidents that have taken place, the mother, Ms. Rose McDonald, has been involved, and now she takes the stand to give her side of events.

*Evidence by Mrs. Rose McDonald*

She was duly sworn in and stated, "I live at 22 Maine Crescent, Otahuhu. I am the mother of the respondent, Claire Anne Mason."
Mr. Wadsworth commenced his questioning.

You have sworn a statement of facts dated 22nd July 1976. Do you confirm this on oath?

Yes. I do.

I understand about two weeks ago, you were present at the Mason residence where an incident took place?

That is correct.

Can you tell the court what happened on that day?

It was around 8:20 a.m., and my son John answered the phone, and my daughter Claire was on the other end, and she was crying. My son said to her, "What in earth is the matter, Claire?" and there was silence. I grabbed the phone, and no response, and I dialled 111, and I got in my son's car. We were ready to leave, and Claire turned up at my house. Her mouth was covered in blood. We took her inside and washed it out, then dialled 111. We took her in the car.

Do you know where the blood came from? Inside her mouth.

Did you see any cuts?

Yes, inside her mouth, her top lip inside, she had a small gash there, nothing really to speak of. From then on, we drove down the street, and the police were not there. We drove down Mascot Close Avenue. We drove around again, and the police still were not there, so we went to Fiona's place, my daughter-in-law. I then went into her house and dialled 111 again to see if the police were coming or not, which they said would be coming, and with that, Claire got in her car, and I got into Fiona's car. I was still in my nightgown and dressing gown.

When we arrived, my daughter pulled up inside the gate, so we all got out and stood there. Next thing Danial came out and said, "Get off my property," and he used abusive language. With that I said, "I believe I am allowed on the property if my daughter allows me on the property." With that he asked me once to get off the property, and I answered him. With that he took to me. He first punched right here (pointing to her chest) and he got my left arm and wrenched it right around and threw me back. All I can remember is my daughter tried to pull him away from me.

What injuries did you have because of the incident?

Well, at first the doctor thought he had broken my collarbone, but he had not, but it was badly ricked. And he said I had extensive bruising and gave me a certificate to go to Otahuhu Police, which I did, and he said I had to go back the Monday. When he looked at me, the bruising was worse than he imagined it to be.

Turning back to the incident, what happened when you were pulled in this manner?

The police arrived and said, "Come inside." With that Mr. Mason in front of the police used abusive language and said, "I will not have that so-and-so inside my house," referring to myself. So the police officer said, or I said to him, "I thought I was allowed to as my daughter can allow me to enter her own home seeing it is jointly owned," but the police officer said, "You better not come in."

We went in, and within a few minutes, Claire was back outside, and the chap that attacked Claire, Mr. Baxter, so I believe, I do not know him, said he wanted to talk to the police alone.

I was sitting in the car upset and hurt. From there the police told us to get on our way as he was fully convinced the man inside was right. He accepted whatever he told him.

Have you laid complaint of assault to the constable of this incident?

Yes, I asked to do it immediately, but the constable who arrived refused to do one. He said he is sick of typing out things for people, and then the case is squashed. I said, "I will not squash this case, I have been knocked too many times." He would not listen and said, "Get in your car and get on your way." I cannot remember exactly.

When were you able to lay the charge?

Well, I went up to Fiona's place, and she made a cup of tea, which I could hardly drink, and we rang the doctor, and he said he would be there at ten o'clock. I went to the doctor immediately after that, and that is what he told me was wrong. He told me I had to go to bed until Monday as I was pretty battered about.

In the afternoon, Claire and Craig come over. My husband was working in the morning and was dreadfully upset, and Craig and Claire said they will go and see someone at the Magistrates' Court at Otahuhu and see if they can lay a charge. But I could not move my arm, and all my fingers were swollen up.

The Sunday morning, my husband said we must lay our own charges as we had another incident where I laid a charge for my husband so that he could not be off work, but they said he had to lay it.

You went to the police station on Sunday and laid the charge?

Yes, and I took a witness with me, Fiona McDonald, my daughter-in-law.

I understand there was another incident at the football park earlier this year which you witnessed?

That is correct. That is what I am referring to. My daughter-in-law, husband, and my granddaughter and my younger son John went to New Market Park to a soccer match where my son James was playing.

Was this a Saturday or Sunday?

It was a Sunday.

Had you had Oliver?

No.

Had you had Oliver during the Saturday night?

No, not…no.

Did Mr. Mason come around to your house Sunday morning?

Yes, I think so, you are correct, yes.

Remember if either your husband or you asked Mr. Mason if you could have Oliver for the day?

I would say we did, yes, because we were always asking him.

Did you take Oliver to the football park?

No, I did not.

How did you meet Oliver at the park?

We happened to look where we were sitting under the stand and looked over and saw Oliver playing with two boys I had not seen before, and he did not know them, and Oliver was climbing a fence. Mrs. Fiona McDonald said to me, "Where is Danial?" I said, "I do not know."

With that Oliver said, "My daddy Danial has a drink for me. I will get it," and he did. So he came back with a can of drink. Danial knew we had him, and he was okay, and he was playing around, so we kept an eye on him, Fiona and me. Then at halftime, Danial did not come near him at all. I said to Oliver, "Go and tell your dad where you are." He said, "I told Dad when I got the drink, Nanna."

When was the first time you saw Mr. Mason at the park?

Not until after the game, and my son's team won. We were happy about that, and we were in a group talking.

Was it a wet or fine day?

It was a fine day. We were standing out in the open.

Did the game finish late or on the usual time?

I would say the usual time. I think I am right. It was still daylight.

What happened when Mr. Mason came toward you?

First of all, Oliver was with us, and he said, "Nana, can I come home with you?" I said, "We are going to see Nana the Great," this is my mother, and she is seventy- seven years of age, and she thinks the world of Oliver and sees him very often. That is also for Oliver's benefit. He also calls her Nana the Great. From there I said to Oliver, "Well, you will have to go and ask Daddy Daniel to see if you're allowed to come with us." Then he came back crying and said, "Daddy said I cannot go." We were waiting for my son to come out after the game. The next thing I know, Danial came over and took a swipe at my husband.

Did your husband provoke him in any way?

I will put my hand back on the Bible, my husband said not one word other than to ask Oliver's father can we take Oliver to see Nana the Great.

What did your husband do then?

Well, Danial just hit him. There were dozens of spectators around, but my husband tried to get away from him because as my son plays soccer, and he was not going to disgrace my son for anything.

Did Mr. Mason take the boy away?

No, Oliver clutched to his father. I am sorry, I mean Oliver clutched his grandfather's hand, so we said, "Go with your daddy," and he started to cry and said, "I do not want to go." So we walked him toward the car to make the child happy. With that Oliver started screaming. Danial picked him up and threw him in the car and then jumped into the car himself, and before I knew what was happening, a lady came up and said, "Do not go near that man, he is an absolute lunatic."

When Mr. Mason was in the car, did you knock on the window?

Most definitely not, I did not knock on the window. Oliver was screaming and punching his father.

Seen Oliver in this state before?

No not in this state, never.

When Mr. Mason went away?

He headed the car straight for me. I had to jump instantly or he would have knocked me over. Fiona did see all this and dozens of other people.

You were friendly toward Mr. Mason when your daughter first separated from him?

Yes, we were friendly with him. Do you want to know the reason? My son-in-law told me my daughter did not want anything more with us. He told so many lies that we went on his side as we honestly believed what he was telling us.

On the Friday before Claire, my daughter, left home, Danial brought Oliver around and said, "Keep him here, and do not let Claire take him under any circumstances, and do not let Claire have him at any stage."

Did your daughter ring up and inquire about Oliver?

All the time, but I was against her at the start, and I am sorry to say that.

When you had Oliver, how long did you have him?

For the first three weeks, I had him all the time until Danial made other arrangements. I had him all the time except I worked three days a week. We had him sleeping the night, my husband would take me to work, and then Oliver went to my daughter-in-law Fiona. Danial came on odd occasions to see him.

What interest, if any, did Mrs. Mason show in the child?

Claire came to my place every night, but I was dead against her as what Danial told me. If there was an odd night, she did not come to see Oliver, she would phone up and begged me to let me give her Oliver.

When did you change your attitude and accept your daughter's version as to why she separated?

She rang one evening and pleaded with me to have Oliver. "Why is it now you are so interested having Oliver now, and according to Danial, you were not before?" She said, "Mum, I went to see a lawyer first and explained the situation, and he told me to leave Oliver for the time being." Within a month to six weeks, she would have Oliver. She said most men are agitated if their wives carry on like this, but they do get over it. Since then, there has been an upset in the family, and he has caused it all, and I put my hand on the Bible I am telling the dead truth. Claire explained to me Danial had threatened to murder her if she took Oliver with her and broke down completely, and she said that he said that if it was for us, which he was making out he was on our side, and he said if it were for us to get him, he would finish him too as if he went to jail, his grandparents would not get him either. He dearly loves my husband and me.

I understand that you had Oliver in your care virtually until November 1955. That is correct, except the days that Fiona had him while I was working the three days a week.

The judge then asked her some questions.

Mrs. McDonald, I thought you said you had Oliver for three weeks?

Yes.

Except when you were working for Fiona looked after him?

We took him to Fiona and collected him after work and took him home. After three weeks, Danial made other arrangements. Fiona had him three days a week, and I had him the other two when I was working.

Where did he stay the nights then? With his father?

No, the nights I had him, he stayed with me. The nights Fiona had him then went with his father.

How long did this arrangement go for?

This went on until around November 1975.

Why did that arrangement stop in November?

Well, there was a disagreement, but I cannot think to tell you correctly. The reason we found Danial to be a liar is because he had no telephone at his house and was using our telephone. Not always did I hear the conversation as I did not want to listen what was being said, but my husband heard it on several occasions, and my husband told me Danial is telling lies, so I spoke to Danial and said, "You are telling lies." He said, "I will lie my way in court and out again, and no one will catch up with me," and that is the exact words he said.

In Ms. Mason's evidence, she said she called Mr. Mason daily. In fact, other evidence suggested it was three to four times a day. So you say he had no phone at his house?

At the time, no, but may have later.

Who did Oliver's washing and ironing between May and November 1975?

Myself. I did everything for Oliver.

Have you done any more washing and ironing for Oliver since November 1975?

Yes, but I have no dates. Oliver went with his father to Australia for Christmas, and I never saw him much unless Claire brought him around, and I took Christmas presents to Claire's place. Then he came back, I would say it was around February or March of the next year. We palled up again only because of Oliver, not because of Danial.

You said you did all the washing and ironing up until November?

I certainly did. Danial did not have an iron.

After November, did you occasionally do the washing and ironing?

No, Fiona said he borrowed her iron, just before he left for Australia at Christmastime.

You did all the washing and ironing up until November. Who did it after?

I presume Danial did, as if you could see the jumpers and cardigans that I brought for the child were all matted up to nothing, I presume it was Danial. We came friendly again because Oliver was fretting for us, and the only way we could see Oliver and come around was to bring Danial around and allow Oliver to come to us.

Have you done much of the washing and ironing since June this year?

No, I do not think I have. I have on odd occasions, when I made the statement of facts, I did say Danial did not have an iron. Fiona told me he went straight down and bought one.

Do you remember the incident at New Lynn when your daughter was living in a flat when Mr. Mason arrived?

I honestly do, yes.

What happened?

We took Oliver to the football game at Victoria Park. After the game, James and Fiona was there, and I said, "Danial, can we have Oliver for the weekend?" So we went to Claire's flat, and this was the first time we had been there, so I said I would take him to his mother and go back home again. In the meantime, Danial turned up at Fiona's place, and he was drunk and said, "Where Oliver is? The McDonalds are not home." So Fiona told Danial that Oliver is over at Claire's place, as the grandparents have taken him there on their way home. When we got to Claire's and Craig's flat, they were cooking tea, and they asked us to stay for tea with them. Before we got a meal, there was a horrific smash at the front door. The whole lot of us were showered with glass, and then my husband and Claire ran out, and Danial took a swipe at my husband and up with his fist knocked the lounge window out. With that my husband picked up Oliver and got him into the car as he was screaming at the top of his voice. Claire being such a good girl took Daniel to the medical center. I do not know which doctor was on. They had to take glass out of his hand, and his hands are still scarred. She got a lady to look after Danial overnight as she was worried about him as he was in such a state, but he was also drunk.

Would you say you are an interfering mother?

Well, I try to be helpful, I do not think I am. To be honest with you, I am, I do not know. No one has ever told me, but I do not know.

What would you say that was?

All I try and do is help.

Do you swear?

Most definitely not, and neither does my husband.

Does your husband drink excessively?

My husband buys a dozen beer every Saturday, and I go with him to the wholesalers, each night sitting, watching TV. My husband would drink one to two bottles, unless someone comes in, he would open another.

Has your husband ever been so drunk he has caused injury to a member of your family?

Never, never. My husband works from seven thirty in the morning until seven at night. He is a supervisor at Dynan Engineering, and he works five days a week, and he is home approximately at around seven fifteen to seven thirty at night, when he locks the factory up.

Does he work Saturdays?

Yes, mornings only from seven thirty to eleven thirty a.m.

In the affidavit of Mr. Dylan Watson, he refers to an incident of a fight where Danial Mason pulled you away from your daughter?

Oh my god, never, never have I once. The night he was talking about was Danial came down and got my husband

and I as he had us so upset. When I saw her, I wanted to smack her face. Fiona said do not do that, and that is my only time. I swear on the Bible, I never ever hit her. Or if I did slap her face, I do not remember, but if I did, I honestly do not remember.

Do you remember an incident around Mother's Day this year involving a card?

I can. I do not know for sure if it was this year, I am sorry, I am sorry, I did not hear you. Yes, Oliver brought me a Mother's Day card, with double-knitting wool stuck on the front of it. Somebody had written on it as Oliver cannot write properly yet, he said, "To Nana from Oliver." When I showed this to Claire, she had tears in her eyes because there was not one for her, so I said to Oliver, "Is there one for Mummy?" as she was so upset. Oliver said, "No, the kindergarten teacher said I do not have a mummy, but I have a nana and an aunty Fiona." Fiona did get a card, and I received a card, but my daughter never got a card, and I can honestly say that.

Did Oliver ever say he got bashed up at kindergarten?

When I do bath him, he says, "Do not touch me there, this is where Jason bashed me up," and he also said, "Do not touch me here, so-and-so did that." Oliver was a premature child and a meek and mild little boy.

Do you know Mrs. Egan at all?

Yes, I do.

She said in evidence that when Mrs. Mason separated, you were terribly upset, and she was asked about the McDonalds? And Mrs. McDonald was upset. "She used to ring me up a lot" and said that you were worried about Claire as she may be on drugs or take drugs. Can you remember talking about that?

Never, but Jasmine rang me up on one occasion, but drugs were never mentioned.

What happened on that one occasion?

This was in the first three weeks, and maybe I was upset, but I never stated anything about drugs to Jasmine Egan at all.

Do you know how often Mr. Mason shows movies at his place?

Well, according to my daughter-in-law, he has stopped showing as many as he was in the past.

You handed this document to me on Tuesday, which you received from someone you knew.

Yes.

Will you produce this to the court? Most certainly.

Is this a club by the name Club 51, which says movies are held every Saturday night?

Yes.

Ever been to those movies?

No, because he sells drink, and my husband does not believe in that, and he has told Danial so, and we have stayed away. That is why we do not go down. We have never been to any movies in their new home.

Then have you been to any movies in his old home?

Only once when it was Oliver's birthday party, and he showed movies after the birthday party, which was the only time.

Was the move *The Sting* shown?

Yes, it was.

Is Oliver happy with his mother?

Incredibly happy. If Claire ever gets Oliver, she brings him straight around to see me, as my husband is working on Saturday, and he does not see him as much, and Oliver is always happy to go with Claire, but Oliver makes it noticeably clear that he comes back in the evening to see his grandfather, which Claire has been doing this up until a month or so ago. Oliver was getting upset and started to fret, and I asked Claire not to bring him around as he wanted to stay with his grandfather. On four occasions, Danial let him stay overnight, as Oliver was getting upset, so Danial did allow him to stay, and his grandfather would take Oliver back next morning.

Would you say Oliver loves his father?

I never heard him say so, but I have heard him say, "I love you, Mummy." I have heard Oliver say, "My daddy says I do not love Mummy or Craig." I said, "Mummy is a good mummy to you," and he then told me, "Daddy told me that Mummy and Craig are bad."

You witnessed an event outside the court Tuesday afternoon?

That is correct, unfortunately, maybe I should not have done it, but I thought we would be allowed to say hello to Oliver. They had him surrounded, Oliver. When he came into the foyer, he gave me a little wave to me, and when he went outside the court, I went up to both Greg and Allison Doherty. I do not know Mrs. Doherty, but Greg has been to my home. He is a very good friend of Daniel. Then Mrs. Doherty starts swearing and yelling at me. I never have met her before, I would not want to meet her again. She screamed and yelled in the street.

I did not want to let Oliver see anything, but at this time, I got upset, and Oliver got upset and started to cry, and Greg picked him up by the arm and then hit Craig Kelly. Craig then yelled at Greg, "Let his grandmother say hello to Oliver!" I love my grandson. He is the most beautiful boy on this earth. I have one granddaughter too, and I love her as well, but I have had more to do with Oliver as he was a very sickly child, and we have had more to do with him. When he was sick, both Claire and Danial came to us for help. Danial even came to us when we are not speaking as he knew it was to bring Oliver around.

If Mr. Mason gets custody of Oliver, would you still like to see Oliver often?

I really would, but I know I never will as he stated this in the Magistrates' Court.

Were you there on this occasion?

No, I was not.

Mrs. Chamberlain said, "Objection, I would like this hearsay evidence not to be given."
The judge then noted counsel to proceed.

Sir, I did get this from my daughter, but I would say it was true as her lawyer, Mr. Jackman, told me as well. He said to Danial, "Be fair toward his grandparents as they love him too," but Daniel said, "They will never see him." I can say we have as he has come back to us.

Last year, a separation agreement was drawn up between Mr. and Mrs. Mason whereby you were to have custody of Oliver, and the parents to have exercise reasonable access between them, do you remember that?

Yes, that was done or drawn up. Danial suggested this to me, he tricked me, as he already told me he had signed it, and if I would ring Claire up and she can sign it, and he, that is Danial, would give us full custody of Oliver, but it was not Mrs. Chamberlain, it was his other lawyer. When Claire signed the agreement thinking they had agreed, she knew Oliver would be happy with us, and Claire would see a lot of him. Danial told us he would have as much access as Claire, and she signed it, and he did not. He told me he had signed it when Mr. Jackman drew that up.

In the past, there has been differences between you and Mr. Mason. What are you doing about that?

But we do not wish to fight, it is Danial who comes around and starts it and aggravates everyone. He starts not only with myself and my husband, but he also tells both James and Fiona a different story. This has been going on for about the past eighteen months. All I was to do was to have my grandson or see him, but unless there is illness or Danial will let us see Oliver, or when he starts fretting.

No more questions, Your Honor.

*Cross-Examination by Mrs. Chamberlain*

Mrs. McDonald, could we look at the time Mrs. Mason left the matrimonial home, did she tell you where she was?

Yes.

You told us she visited you every night for a start? That is correct, I told Danial.

What did you talk about?

Only her son, pleading with me to give her son to her.

In your statement, you told us that she rang every night, and Ms. Mason in her evidence also said she rang every night.

That is not correct. She (pauses) if she could not come, she rang, but she went to Danial's place every night, and when she was upset she came to my place.

So what you have said in your statement is wrong then?

No, it was not wrong.

Your statement sworn in the Magistrates' Court by you said, "In the days that followed, she phoned each night."

That was in the day, but Claire came around at night.

Your daughter said she telephoned you. Only was she mistaken? I would not know.

In your statement to the Supreme Court, you told us about a party at Mr. Mason's the night of the divorce petition.

That is correct, I was not present.

You said, "The petitioner rushed around telling everyone he had custody of the child."

That is correct.

Who did he rush around and tell?

He came straight from the court to Fiona's place, whom I was having lunch with. I take it she was looking after Oliver?

Yes, I was there, he most definitely told Fiona he had custody, and he asked her to a dinner party to follow. I said, "I am coming too, Danial" as a joke. He replied, "It would be embarrassing for you," and he said, "I will hold one for you much later," but I would not go anyway.

What time did Oliver go to bed that night after the party?

That I cannot tell you, but the following night Fiona had Oliver, and he fell asleep on her couch at 7:30 p.m. The following morning she rang and said, "I do not want to worry you, but Oliver, I cannot wake up." It took her about thirty minutes to wake him up. I could not say where the party was.

Mrs. Dubbeld said she was a visitor there that night, and Oliver was in bed by eight o'clock?

That is for you to believe one way or the other, but I say it is untrue. Oliver is allowed to go to the movies. When Danial has a party, he would normally put on a film.

Mrs. Dubbeld said it was not that sort of party, it was a dinner. Why do you say she is lying when you were not there?

No, I was not there, but Oliver was.

Mrs. McDonald, so you are prepared to assume a responsible woman is telling the truth or must be lying?

I am sorry if I said anything out of place, but I honestly believe Oliver as he told us he was at the dinner and the party afterwards.

Oliver was at the dinner and went to bed at eight o'clock. This was not a party as you claim.

I believe what Oliver told me.

Now let us look at the latest incident involving the police and Mr. Baxter. You told us that the police thought that Mr. Baxter and Mr. Mason was right?

I do not know about Mr. Mason as I have a charge against him pending, but the police did say Mr. Baxter and Mr. Mason were right, but we made charges after that.

Why did you go to the property when your daughter turned up?

Who else? I must protect her, she wanted to go down as I called 111, and I would not let her go on her own.

Why take your daughter down there? Was it so the police could see what a terrible life she had?

She was worried about her boy. Mr. Mason attacked my daughter. When the  police arrived, Fiona asked where Oliver was, Danial said he was with Mrs. Ingram next door. The police said, "You are allowed to get him." Fiona went in, and Mrs. Ingram said, "He is not here, and I do not want to get mixed up in all this and get off my property."

Why did you not take yourself and your daughter to the police station?

I already dialled 111, is not that the correct thing to do? Mr. Baxter had my daughter by the throat, my son could not get an answer from her, I took the phone. I just guessed where she was.

Knowing Mr. Baxter had her by the throat, you went back into the situation? I stood by the letter box.

Is that not Mr. Mason's property? You told us you went onto the property? Yes, well, is that Mr. Mason's property or the Council's?

Why would you go onto the property?

Yes, by the letter box. It is a short distance from the letter box to the road. There is no fence."

Mrs. Ingram said you struck Mr. Mason. Is that another lie?

That is a deliberate lie, and I hope God strikes her down dead to tell a lie like that.

Mrs. Ingram also said your language was very abusive?

That is another untruthful statement. The only thing I mentioned that my daughter left $300 in the bank, which belongs to my mother, who is a pensioner. I said to Danial, "Can you be as low as not to give my mother back her money?" which is the only thing I said.

Mr. Baxter in his evidence also said your language was shocking. Is that another lie too?

May God strike me down dead this minute.

Returning to the incident at the football park, you said Mr. Mason for no reason came and hit your husband?

I would say it was because we asked Oliver to go and ask his father to see if he can come with us to see Nana the Great.

There was no discussion about it?

It just came up, my husband was so unaware. I wish I could get the witnesses who saw this. Danial came up and grabbed my husband and then up with his fist. Oliver clung to my husband's trousers, so we followed Danial to his car. He got hold of Oliver and threw him in the car.

Was there no discussion that day as to whether or not Mr. Mason had interim custody of Oliver?

Not at all, not at the park.

What about in the morning? Recall a discussion with your husband and Mr. Mason in which Mr. Mason stated he had to get his facts tight and not his daughter's and that Danial Mason had the custody of Oliver?

I honestly cannot recall this, I must be truthful. I do not wish to tell lies. It seems you have selective memory on a lot of things.

I am only telling you the truth as I do not recall this discussion taking place.

The day the game was played, it was stated that the game finished in time, the weather was fine, and it was still daylight?

Yes, that is correct.

Mrs. McDonald, we have checked and found the game did go into extra time as Mr. Mason claimed. Also it was a wet and miserable day, and when the game finished, it was well after five p.m. and getting dark, so was Mr. Mason right?

No, he must have got his games and days mixed up.

Well, Mrs. McDonald, your daughter-in-law Fiona McDonald has told the court and agreed that Mr. Mason said to your husband something about getting his facts right at the park. What that might have referred to? Would this just be strange comment made for a reason?

To my honest belief, I do not know. I did not hear it said, but I am hard of hearing.

Do you have a selective hearing problem? No, not really.

You told us Mr. Mason has said he has lied his way in and out of court? Yes.

Did he also say he had instructed his witnesses to lie? No, he did not.

In your earlier evidence, you mentioned to Oliver about his father as you referred to him "my daddy Danial."

Yes, I also said, "My mummy, Claire."

I ask you, Ms. McDonald, is Oliver very fond of his father?

I would not say he is any fonder of his father than he is with his mother. Whenever I see him with his mother, he is incredibly happy with her. He hugs and kisses. But when he is with Danial, he does not show any affection to me whatsoever.

Prior to the separation, Danial worked extremely hard?

Mr. Mason used to go out showing movies and come home at all hours of night. Claire had rung around two a.m. and to say, "He is not home yet, and what should I do? He has arrived home drunk with Mr. Watson."

What evidence you have of that? I was told by my daughter.

So do you believe everything your daughter tells you? Yes. I do.

Can you recall Oliver's fourth birthday? Yes, I can.

Was this held at Daniel's home, and he had a barbecue and had a movie later that night, *The Sting*. I ask were you there that night?

I do not recall.

Several people have testified that you were at Oliver's fourth birthday party with your husband as well as James and Fiona as well as your youngest son John. And after the barbecue, *The Sting* movie was shown. So an important date such as Oliver's fourth birthday, and you cannot remember?

I am not sure as I thought it was at their old place. You were there at his fourth birthday?

Yes, I was.

At the beginning, you were against your daughter leaving?

Yes, that is correct as I did not want her to go was for Oliver's sake.

Mr. Mason was not prepared to sign an agreement giving Mrs. Mason custody. He wanted custody himself?

Yes, that is correct. I have been particularly good to Danial. He has come to my place and said he has no money. I have handed him money in cash, and he never has offered to pay me back. I do not want the money back. I love my grandson, I would give him all I have.

Would it be fair to say the relationship between you and Mr. Mason started to break down about October, when Claire put in application for custody when Mr. Mason filed his?

Honestly, I cannot remember. It would be wrong for me to state.

Have you had Oliver recently, apart from when he is sick and when fretting?

Yes, on four Saturday nights, Claire would ring from her place and say Oliver is fretting and would not go home, and there was an agreement to take him home, and Danial had agreed to let him come back to me because he vomited all over the place. As soon as he came back, he was the happiest child.

You said that Danial under no circumstances let you see the child if he had custody?

I cannot say he would, but I do not feel he would as he turns violent. You do not know how he carries on.

Have you seen Oliver in the past despite these incidents? Yes, I have.

*Adjournment for Fifteen Minutes*
*Resumed*

Mrs. Chamberlain continued.

Mrs. McDonald, I want you to consider the evidence and about the incident that took place Tuesday with Oliver and Mr. Greg Doherty and his wife Addison. You told us Mrs. Doherty, when she saw you, she started swearing and yelling. Was this outside the front door here?

No, it was up the road and across on the opposite side. The Dohertys crossed the road, and I was not up to Mrs. Doherty. It was Mr. Craig Kelly she swore at. I cannot tell you the language she used.

Sure this did not take place outside the court?

No, across the road. We got out, there is the front gate, they crossed the road, and then over the road between the cars to the other side of the road, and that is where it happened.

Mrs. Doherty started screaming and swearing?

At Mr. Kelly, yes.

And Mr. Doherty picked up Oliver?

Yes, Oliver started to cry, and Mr. Doherty picked him up with one hand and then hit Mr. Kelly with the other.

Is this another one of Mr. Mason's violent friends?

I do not think so. Mr. Doherty believes in what Mr. Mason has told him. He just believes what Danial has said. I tried to speak nicely to him, I said, "Greg, let me speak to my grandson," but he did not  seem to want to, unless he was given orders not to.

No more questions.

*Re-XD by Mr. Wadsworth*

You mentioned in evidence about a party after the court hearing earlier this year. Who told you there was going to be a party?

Mr. Mason told me and Fiona. We were having lunch, and he came in and said he had custody of Oliver and said there will be a dinner and party this evening. He also stated that to me that Mrs. Chamberlain had suggested that I withdraw my affidavit with Claire, and I said, "I am not going to do that." In the end he turned very nasty to me.

Who else told you there was a party that night?

Oh, I am sorry, Oliver told me there was a party that night, and he said his father brought all the stuff for the party the day before, and Oliver was excited as he thought it was going to be a birthday party.

Ever met Mrs. Dubbeld? No, never.

Mr. Watson?

Never.

It would be quite true when Mrs. Dubbeld said Oliver went to bed at eight o'clock?

Well, yes, it could be, but I cannot see it when he slept from seven thirty till ten o'clock the following morning at Fiona's place.

Was that the Saturday morning?

The party was supposedly on Thursday night, the Friday night Fiona had him, and it was Saturday morning she could not wake him up, and we had him on the Saturday night.

You speak very loudly, why is that?

I am sorry if I do, but I speak loud for one reason as I expect people to speak loud to me as I am deaf in one ear. I do not realize what I am doing, and I am not aware of it.

No more questions.

I could not believe Ms. McDonald Senior to say so much hearsay, and her accounts on many things such as Oliver's fourth birthday party for one good example, and to say I do not remember when this was only late the previous year, and of course the movie *The Sting*. One could not make this stuff up. The other point is when Claire left the matrimonial home, she did not come back to the home for many weeks, and she did not even phone. It was when I allowed her grandparents to have Oliver over, and they did look after him for some three weeks on and off, as did Fiona. This was where Claire was seeing Oliver as this was told to me by Fiona.

Finally, for both Ms. McDonald Senior and Claire saying all the witnesses on my side are liars, in fact through cross-examination, they have been caught out.

My evidence was backed up by reliable people. Let's now wait to see what the judge has to say about all this.

Finally, Craig Kelly, the final witness for Claire, was up next.

*Evidence by Mr. Craig Kelly*

Mr. Wadsworth called his last witness, Mr. Craig Kelly, and he is sworn in, and he stated that he lives in 50 Lorne Avenue, Panmure, and he is a sales representative.

How many times have you gone to the Masons' residence in Mangere?

I think only once, that was the time I had a brick thrown into my car window.

Been there at any other time?

Only before Claire left when I helped to concrete the driveway.

How long did you know Mrs. Mason before she separated from her husband?

About two years. At the time I worked at the car dealership.

Did you ever have sexual intercourse with Mrs. Mason before she separated?

Never.

Did you have it straight away on her separation?

No, not straight away, no.

Where did you first live?

In Henderson.

You used to live in New Lynn?

Yes, that is correct.

An incident happened at that residence. What happened?

It was a Saturday afternoon, round about teatime. Claire and I were cooking tea, and Oliver saw Danial screaming across the lawn. Mr. and Mrs. McDonald were there also. From that Oliver became hysterical. There was a crash and banging on the door, the front glass panel was broken, the glass went across the lounge and marked the stereo, which is still marked. He was halfway in, and Mr. McDonald went outside, and he told Mr. McDonald to take his jacket off and fight, and then he went through the front window. That cost $80. I rang the glass company, and they mended this on the spot. Claire's parents lent us the money to pay for it, and the police were called. Mr. Mason has the scars still on his hand.

Ever provoked Mr. Mason in any way?

Never at all. I could be driving along the street in my truck when he runs me off the road. He has cut me off the road with my truck, he has belted me up in shops, he has lurked around my car. One night he lurked in the streets, and there was a chase. Another time he lurked in the driveway, by the way he also reversed out of the driveway at the police station and hit a police car. I have experienced violence from this guy than is necessary. Nine times out of ten when Claire has gone over, she has not done the provoking. The welfare officer I spoke to asked for a neutral place for picking up Oliver, but it was not agreed to. Also she asked for a neutral place for the court hearing, which was not agreed to.

You have been to see the welfare officer and discussed the matter with him? Yes, it was a Mr. Lovell from Otahuhu. He is the superintendent there. Remember another incident at your address in Lake Avenue Panmure when one afternoon Mr. Mason called?

Claire and I returned home from work about five p.m. Mr. Cole, our landlord, arrived about the same time. Within about five minutes, there was a screaming up the driveway, and Danial was in his station wagon, and with Oliver standing on the front seat of the car. Danial came in making a big scene. He pushed his way into Mr. Eddy's house, there was a schemozzle outside, he was going to take to Claire. Oliver was in the car screaming. I might add every time there is violence, the boy is always present, the child is so scared.

Another time at my work, Claire was home sick for some reason, and we went to where my truck was in our car, and Danial screamed down on the private property at the Buckland Industries, and he came, he came nose to tail with my car. He laid punches at me, and the boy was so frightened, Oliver messed his pants. The police were phoned, but it was an hour before they came, and it was all over. All the charges we have made have gone to the police at Otahuhu as they have all gone to this area because this is where this guy lives, and all have been dropped.

Ever known Mrs. Mason to swear?

Never. She does not drink either. I have not seen her drunk. Does her mother swear?

No.

Does her father swear?

Not really, no. If he is in a temper, he might say the odd word, but he is not a violent man. He does not swear nor rave on all the time.

Ever seen him drunk?

Never, these people have said Mr. McDonald gets drunk, they are telling lies. I have never seen him drunk.

He may have a bottle of beer watching TV and ask do I want one with him. He only drinks at home watching TV.

How long have you known Mr. McDonald?

I have known the McDonalds ever since I worked at the car dealership, and that is going back around two years.

Do you have any children of your own?

Two. I have one girl, thirteen and a half, and one little boy who died from an accident when he was three years old.

If Mrs. Mason gets custody of Oliver, do you feel that you will be placed in his father's shoes?

Well, partly yes, but I will not be his full father, would I? I would be his stepfather.

Does Oliver dislike you?

Never. I have been to Fiona's place when Oliver is there, and he has come out with me to various places, in my car or in the boat. He has nothing against me as far as I know.

Before the separation, did you get on well with Mr. Mason? Yes, I suppose yes.

Ever been to any of Mr. Mason's picture shows?

Yes, I have, at Mascot Avenue when they lived there. Been to any at the new house in Mangere?

No, never.

Would you say you are a drinking man? I never go to a hotel.

What nationality are you?

English. I have been here since 1963. Why did you and your wife part?

It was a mutual agreement, we did not get on. She went her way, and I went my way. It probably emerged when my little boy died at three years of age, then I was not at home as I was away some twenty-one days at a time working for the car dealership.

What did your little boy die of?

Well, this happened at Christmas, when my wife put him to bed. I was away driving. He got out of his cot at around six thirty, and he had a pair of sandals in a plastic bag in his drawer, he then placed the plastic bag over his head and suffocated.

You are now living in temporary accommodation? Yes.

Would it not cause some upset that you have shifted around unnecessarily?

The reason I have shifted around is that Mr. Mason has been abusive. At New Lynn, we were on the phone, and he used to ring and abuse Claire all times of the night. We had the phone number changed, but he found out, and he used to ring Claire all hours of the night.

Do you know Mrs. Egan at all?

I have only seen the girl once, and that was at Oliver's birthday party when he was three years of age apart from yesterday.

Ever seen Mrs. Tuohy before? Never heard of her at all. Ever met Mr. Dylan Watson?

I have met him alright. There was an incident outside the leagues club in Ponsonby, oh, I am sorry Parnell. Claire received a message from Mr. Mason for some reason. This was quite a long time ago. He was inside showing a movie, and Mr. Watson came out and tried to give me a raspberry. I was sitting in my car. Then also when I was not home in the house in Panmure, he came to the home and shook all the doors around the house.

Was that the night the divorce petition was served on you? That is right, this was in December sometime.

Were you at the house when they first arrived? No, not the first time, no.

Who had the car? I did.

Where had you gone?

I went to the local shops. Why?

I was gone around thirty minutes, and I went to buy some shampoo for Claire, and when I came back, I drove straight into the garage, and Claire told me what happened, and the police arrived.

Did you run to the front bedroom? No, I was in the lounge.

Who served the petition on you? I cannot remember now.

You mentioned you did some concreting at Mr. Mason's. Yes.

Did Mr. Watson come and help as well? Not at first, but he did come around later. But he did come around?

Not while I was there. There was a chap named Cole doing the concreting with me, and a chap named Monroe, I think.

Ever met Mrs. Dubbeld? I do not know her.

Ever met Mr. Thomas?

Yes, I have. He is the guy from Crest Foods.

I understand that you were at one stage accused of being a father of a child not your own?

Yes, that is right.

You were going out with a girl at the time? Yes, and this goes back a few years.

Were you still living with your wife then? No, I left her for some six weeks.

Did she subsequently accuse you being the father of the child? Yes, she did, that is correct.

What year would that have been?

I am not sure, I do not know if it was five or seven years ago, quite a long time. Did you then take a blood test?

Yes, I did, and I acted on this. I paid for it where I had the tests done. It was at the blood transfusion center in Auckland.

The document I produce to you is a copy of that test? Yes, definitely.

Mrs. Chamberlain raised an objection.

Is Oliver happy when he is with his mother? Most definitely, he does not want to go home. Has he ever been sick at your home?

No.

Does he have his own room? Yes.

Have you bought him clothes?

Yes, we have clothes for him. We cannot take him out in the clothes he comes in. We put our own clothes on him, our landlord Mr. Cole can confirm that.

Mrs. Tuohy, his kindergarten head, says he arrives neat and tidy at the kindergarten?

I have seen him at kindergarten, and he has the same clothes on three days in a row.

Do you make a point of going to the kindergarten? No, but it's on my run.

Are you going to marry Mrs. Mason? Yes, soon as Claire gets the divorce, yes.

What type of home are you able to offer the boy?

We have now a brand-new unit we are renting, and it is fully furnished by us, everything is brand-new.

What religion are you?

Well, in England, I was in the Salvation Army and in the band, but since coming to New Zealand, I was never around on Sundays. When my little boy died, the Salvation Army minister came and officiated. They wanted me to go in the band here, but my work commitments made it impossible.

Do you still see your daughter?

Yes, whenever she wants to come over, she rings and says when she wants to come over, and she does.

Would you think you would supplement yourself in Oliver's eyes?

I do my best to be good in his eyes. I cannot say if I am the same as his father or not. Now he gets on well with me.

No more questions.

*Cross-Examination by Mrs. Chamberlain*

Mr. Kelly, in your statement filed in the Magistrates' Court, you told us your earnings average about $95 per week clear. Is that still the situation?

$6,800 a year, commission as well.

Have you evidence to prove that?

My wage slips.

Do you pay $8 a week for maintenance for the child?

Yes.

If you have $95 clear, and you pay $8 in maintenance, what you pay for rent,

that does not leave much, does it?

We do quite well.

You told us you went to the movies at Dylan Watson's home?

Yes.

Did you have your daughter with you then?

No.

Are you sure?

Mrs. Chamberlain turned and spoke to the judge. "Your Honor, why does this man laugh when he answers questions? Is this so funny?" The judge replied, "Noted, please proceed."

Mr. Kelly, this is a serious matter as it involves your partner Ms. Mason, Mr. Mason, and one small child, Oliver Mason, and you are not taking this seriously.

Yes, I do understand the gravity of the situation. When did you see the welfare officer?

I did see him twice. I received a letter from Mr. Jackman, Claire's lawyer at the time, saying the report is completed. Then he came to see me, which disturbed me a bit, so I decided one Friday to go and see the welfare officer. Then I also saw him again on a Monday of this week. He said he had heard nothing from the court or from either lawyer regarding access.

Did he tell you that? He did.

Regarding the incident at New Lynn, you said Mr. McDonald went outside.

Yes, Mr. Mason told Mr. McDonald to take his jacket off. Mr. Mason came over causing trouble, which he has done in the past. I have had my face bashed in and my shirt ripped off.

Did Mr. McDonald assist Mr. Mason to remove his jacket?

No, he did not.

After that, Mr. Mason went through your plate glass window?

Yes.

Mr. Mason said Mr. McDonald pushed him.

That is an utter lie.

Have you been to church yourself lately?

No.

You are not working at weekends?

No.

This is not the first time you and your wife have been parted, is it?

No.

No further questions.

Mr. Wadsworth then added, "No re-address, Your Honor." Evidence for the respondent concluded.

The clerk of courts announced, "The court is adjourned until 4:00 p.m. when the Honorable Justice Alfred Murray will deliver his judgment. Please rise."

# 35

# THE JUDGMENT

This has been a hotly contested court case for the custody of Oliver Kevin Mason. This case ran over five days, and the mother of the child, she claimed the father was an extremely dangerous person and a potential murderer.

The movie business was also a contentious issue throughout the trial. The movie *The Sting* shown at Oliver's fourth birthday was another issue. Also it was claimed that Danial Mason showed blue and adult movies when Oliver was present and up late. Another evidence by Claire Mason and her family claiming that Oliver was not cared for and did not love his father was another contentious issue.

The fact is this case was Danial Mason vs. them.

Now it is up to the judge to sort out who the boy will remain with, the father who has had him for now eighteen months, or the mother who walked out and left him.

The judge may stick to the letter of the law in custody matters as it simply states a child under five remains with the mother.

This judgment is as recalled by Mrs. Chamberlain, the lawyer for Danial Mason.

The judge came into the courtroom and said he is now going to deliver his verdict.

He started off by saying,

This case is all about one little boy, Oliver Kevin Mason. He has now been in the actual custody of his father, for a period now of some seventeen months.

This case has run now for five days. I have presided over evidence by both sides. I am sufficiently acquainted with all the facts to form what will be the proper judgment. I am very conscious of what Mr. Wadsworth has said, that one needs the wisdom of Solomon in a case like this.

Today, the fact which I am fully aware of one of the parties will leave this court greatly upset, this will not please me, but it will happen.

This has been a hotly disputed applications for custody. It relates to one child, Oliver Kevin Mason, born on 10th December 1971. He will be five years of age this December, and since the first of May 1975, he has been in the actual custody of his father, which is a period of some seventeen months.

The background of the parties are as follows. They were married on 7th February 1970, then on May 1, 1975, Mrs. Mason decided to leave the matrimonial home, when she only lived in the new house for some six weeks. She decided then to live with the co-respondent, Mr. Kelly, in which she has known the co-respondent for some two years now. He also was an acquaintance of Mr. Mason. He also came to their home, at some stage did some work around the new home. Mrs. Mason has clearly stated she met Mr. Kelly at where she worked, and this is where their friendship flourished.

Mr. Mason said on his evidence, and I am satisfied he was most upset and very hurt when his wife left him. He did try to get her back, as he has stated in evidence, but to no avail.

I am also not sure from the evidence as to how long attempts at reconciliation were made, however, it seems to me that at least around about October and November 1975, Mr. Mason was still trying to get his wife back. He also says that he continued to do so until early this year. I found this was a bit difficult to reconcile. The fact was he filed his petition for divorce on 12th November 1975. The petition was, of course, based on the grounds of adultery, then a decree nisi was made in June 1976. Now from the affidavits filed was that Mrs. Mason applied to the Magistrates' Court on 17th October 1975 for custody of Oliver Mason, her son, then her husband Mr. Mason filed a cross-examination on the 13th of November 1975 for interim custody to be. In December 1975, interim custody was awarded to Mr. Mason.

I find this is not clear whether or not the application for custody was responsible for him deciding to file his petition for divorce, this I do not know; however, it was certainly filed very quickly after his application for interim custody.

I have read from court documents it shows that the parties did have a meeting in the Magistrates' Court when the question for custody came up for hearing, and because of that, an amicable arrangement was come to whereby Mr. Mason was able to take the child to Australia for the Christmas holiday, and then temporary arrangements were made what was termed as staying access. I fully understand that access has been a problem throughout. I also say Mr. Mason not totally denied access. In fact, Mrs. Mason has had a considerable amount of access. I also understand there have been times when due to differences between Ms. Mason with Mr. Mason, arrangements had to be cancelled.

As to when Mrs. Mason left home, it is very clear her parents took an extremely hard line about it. They took the view, as did her brother James McDonald and his wife Fiona

McDonald, that she was quite wrong to leave home. I am also satisfied by the evidence they thought very highly of Mr. Mason at the time, prior to the separation.

I have no doubt they have been a significant help to him, because until more recently, the grandparents and Mr. James McDonald and his wife Fiona have rendered a tremendous amount of assistance to Mr. Mason. I shall deal more on this in a moment. It is unfortunate or more regrettably, they have changed their attitude toward him, as now they clearly support Mrs. Mason's application in this court being also for custody.

I have found it is not totally clear Oliver stayed with the grandparents for some three months after the separation, then later when he started at kindergarten in 1976, then a pattern developed where Mr. Mason took Oliver to kindergarten each morning, and Mrs. Fiona McDonald would pick him up around midday. She looked after him for three afternoons a week, indeed she inclined to the view that she had him most afternoons. Anyhow as far as she was unable during afternoons to look after Oliver, Mrs. McDonald Senior, the grandmother, did so. Mr. Mason's employment with Crest Foods Pty Ltd has enabled him to be picked up usually by 4:00 p.m.

This also meant that Mr. and Mrs. McDonald Senior and Mrs. Fiona McDonald have not had to have the child until a late hour, except on occasions when they babysat for Mr. Mason if he went out at night. There were many occasions that Mr. Mason picked up the child from kindergarten, then take the child with him as was termed his rounds. I understand he is a form of supervisor in public relations capacity for Crest Foods Pty Ltd. It was also in evidence criticism was made of that in the affidavits. The evidence presented and I think criticism is not justified. In the end, nothing really turned on that point.

It is also obvious and very plain that there were occasions when Mr. Mason thought Oliver would like to be with him on his rounds, and that is not an unusual position for a working man.

Then we found out in the last week Mrs. Fiona McDonald has come out and said she will no longer look after Oliver, then now Mr. Wadsworth told me today that she is now prepared to do so. Whatever may be the situation today, the reasons given by her for change in attitude were threefold.

Firstly, she stated and wanted to devote more time for her child, who is now eighteen months old.

The second point, secondly, she then said she wanted to start working part-time.

The third part and more importantly, her husband James suggested to her that the time had come to keep out of the problems which had been developing between Mr. and Mrs. Mason.

It is my judgment and have concluded what has happened was this: Mrs. McDonald and Mr. McDonald Senior had placed enormous pressure upon Fiona McDonald and also their son James. This pressure put on them has become perfectly plain to me that Mrs. McDonald now has a hatred for Mr. Mason. This in my opinion will be very hard to reconcile as to her earlier attitude toward him. I have no doubt and draw the inference that pressure was brought to bear upon Mr. James McDonald and Mrs. Fiona McDonald from their cross-examination.

Now the effect of it was this. It was that about a week ago when Mr. and Mrs. McDonald appeared at the house then demanded the return of several chattels, this included the repayment of a debt. Then it became perfectly clear that Mrs. Fiona McDonald was mostly upset about this so much, she telephoned her family in Christchurch, and James McDonald confirmed that his wife was upset by it all. I draw attention to the inference that it was made pretty plain to them that if they continued to support Mr. Mason, that things would be made difficult for them, as indeed they were because Mr. James McDonald found himself having to apply a loan that, unknown to him, Mr. Mason provided the money, which he, Mr. McDonald, ultimately tore up when he realized that Mr. Mason had provided him with a check to replace the money that he had to repay his parents.

Mr. Mason has now obtained leave of absence from his employment until Oliver commences school, which will be in in February 1977. He has arranged with a friend, a Mrs. Watson, who is a near neighbor and is close to the school, which will collect him from school and keep him there for one hour between three and four p.m. So the position is this: that up until the time when the lad is ready to go to school, Mr. Mason will be able to look after him full-time, and when he goes to school, arrangements have been made with this friend to look after him for a brief period, and there are other friends willing to help.

Mrs. Chamberlain said to me this came as no surprise as the judge did see through Rose McDonald, as he remarked on the rather obvious dramatic change in attitude of the grandparents toward Mr. Mason. He also said as he has seen it, regarding their decisions to blame Mr. Mason for allegedly telling them lies about the circumstances surrounding Mrs. Mason leaving the home also leaving the child.

Now they have made this decision to withdraw their support for Mr. Mason. This unfortunately has led them being committed, becoming involved in certain incidents, usually when Mrs. Mason has got herself involved in arguments with Mr. Mason.

The judge then continued saying,

At this point, I do not propose to go into the precise details of the evidence given by Mrs. McDonald Senior for changing her mind except to say I found them quite convincing. She knew very well what the position was when her daughter left home. I have no doubt she thoroughly disapproved of her leaving. The only possible lie which Mr. Mason could have told her is that her daughter may have expressed some wish to abandon her child, but this could have been easily checked by Mrs. McDonald. After all, the girl was her daughter, and it appears that was what crystalized. Her attitude changed because Mrs. Mason came out and said and told her she left the child because her husband threatened to murder her and the child. This I will have more to say about this matter later.

The emphasis was now on Rose McDonald as the judge said,

Surely one would have thought that the message would have got home to Mrs. Mason's mother long, long before she changed her mind, then Mrs. McDonald changed her mind because of pressure brought to bear on her by Mrs. Mason, her daughter. The result was that Mrs. McDonald filed an affidavit in the Magistrates' Court, sworn on the 28th of November 1975, supporting Mrs. Mason's application for custody. She later filed a similar affidavit in this court in which she made some serious allegations against Mr. Mason. This along with other matters I will be referring to in a moment.

The judge then said about the interview he had with Oliver. He went on to say,

> Tuesday of this week, I had an interview with Oliver Mason. It was not easy to interview a four-and-a-half-year-old child. I must say I was very impressed with this little boy. He is a real credit to somebody. I found he was well dressed, well groomed, very well behaved, very polite. He appeared to me to be a happy outgoing child. In short, I suppose I could say he is a particularly nice little boy and an intelligent little boy. I may say in a moment to whom this credit is due. It is obviously due to both parents and to the care and attention with the grandparents and the aunt and uncle have been able to give. I say this here and now that I have no doubt that Mr. Mason and Mrs. Mason can each provide adequately for the material needs and comforts of the boy. I say this here and now that each parent, in my opinion, is in his and her own way a good parent. Indeed.
>
> This is endorsed by the social worker who said in the report, which I think is worth reading. I do not know whether the parents have read this, they probably have not, but the report says:
>
> "I do not think that there is any significant difference of opinion on the general fitness of both parties to be satisfactory solo parents of their child. Both parents impress as intelligent, sensitive, responsible, competent, articulate, caring people. both are willing—indeed anxious—to carry out their parental duties and appear able at present, and for

the foreseeable future, to provide more than nearly adequate care for Oliver; It would be surprising if the unsuccessful party in these proceedings were later able to point to any significant deficiencies in the standard of care provided following making of an order."

Mrs. Fiona McDonald described Mrs. Mason as a particularly good mother, I have no doubt she is, and I have no doubt Mr. Mason is also a particularly good father. Mr. Mason's competence as a housekeeper and a father was the subject of attack.

I will have more to say about the welfare report later.

Mrs. Chamberlain said, "This next part is very significant to your case." The judge now turned his attention to the many attacks I received on my ability to be a father and how I dressed and fed Oliver.

The judge went on to say,

Mr. Mason's competence as a housekeeper and a father was the subject of many attacks as to Mr. Mason's competence as a housekeeper and a father.

However, Mr. Mason received generous references in this respect from several witnesses. For example, a Mr. Benson said in his affidavit:

"As to the allegations that Oliver is not properly fed, his clothes not washed properly or ironed and that he is dirty. I can state that on many occasions I have seen him I have found this not to be so. I have been present at mealtime and seen what the family eat. In my opinion it is nutritionally adequate and well cooked."

The Mrs. Egan, who has been a close friend of Mrs. Mason during the whole of her life, said this in her affidavit:

"Mrs. Mason's allegation's about Daniels care of Oliver are not true. Oliver is always well looked after." Then in this court in her evidence, she said that the standards in the home were extremely high and volunteered, I will recollect this remark: "He is a better housekeeper than I and a good cook."

We also heard evidence from Mr. Thomas, who also said in his affidavit:

"When I see him, he has always been appropriately dressed for whatever he was doing, and his clothes did not seem to me need ironing. they seemed to have been well ironed."

Also in his evidence, he told us he lived at the house for six weeks. He said that he saw Mr. Mason ironing the clothes for the boy, and he said that they appeared to him to be neat and tidy.

The fact was a big issue and large references made as to if Mr. Mason had an iron or Oliver was adequately dressed, his clothes ironed.

Then even Mrs. McDonald Senior, the grandmother, admitted that Mr. Mason was quite a good cook.

Even Mrs. Fiona McDonald, the aunt, said that the boy is always well clothed. She further said, "Oliver is really very well behaved."

Then Mrs. Mason herself in evidence said Mr. Mason looked after him very well. To the best of his ability, yes.

Now that evidence is supported by the social welfare officer's report, which reads: "He keeps his home to a high standard—from a cursory inspection one would hardly know that he is also a solo father, there is little doubt that with help from

others he has been very successful in looking after Oliver for the last 15 months."

Then the judge had a few things to say about the welfare report. I thought to myself when this was going to be mentioned or left out.

There is a qualification about Mr. Mason's fatherhood in the report where the welfare officer says he was a little disturbed to ascertain that he is away quite a bit in connection with his movie business, which means that he is away at nights.

With due respect to the welfare officer who did the report as I am satisfied on the evidence on the balance of probabilities that, that statement is quite incorrect.

This next part regarding the welfare officer, I am glad the judge did see this as Mrs. Chamberlain did lay a complaint that the report was one-sided. This is what the Judge said,

There is one major factor being critical with the welfare officer putting aside the delays in his report and finding. He had a duty, and he failed dismally to interview Mr. Mason's witnesses and then obtained a very one-sided view of Mr. Mason. Statements given by Mrs. Mason, Mr. Kelly Mrs. Mason's brother James, and Mrs. McDonald Senior, where a lot of their evidence again is quite incorrect. There were many witnesses for Mr. Mason in which the welfare officer could have interviewed like Mr. Benson, Mrs. Ingram, Mrs. Dubbeld, and Mrs. Mason's long-term friend,

Mrs. Egan. For whatever reason, this was not done, and in my opinion, he may have had a different view on some of his statements as this again was very one-sided.

Then the judge turned to the kindergarten and the evidence given by Mrs. Tuohy, in which he said,

Her character is unimpeachable and who was quite properly and fairly pressed by Mr. Wadsworth, she stated in evidence she is the headmistress of the kindergarten and has been in that position for five years.

Mrs. Tuohy stated, "Oliver arrives at the kindergarten with his father punctually every morning, and he is not just neat and tidy, he is immaculately dressed. He is a genuinely nice four-year-old, and the staff consider that he is a very adjusted one. Both his father and his aunt who collects him are fond of him and he of them."

There is no doubt in my mind that the child has great affection for his father. I mention this for the reason as there was an attempt made to establish the contrary. I think probably the most reliable testimony on this aspect of the matter comes from Mrs. Fiona McDonald, who was asked this question: "Does Oliver also show considerable affection to Mr. Mason? Yes, I think so."

Mr. James McDonald in his evidence replied to this question: "Would you agree Oliver is happy with his father? He is happy some of the time, not other times. Then would you agree he is happier than not? Obviously, he is not going to be sad all the time."

I noticed that he said this with a bit of a smile on his face. I did take that he intended to mean that he was happy with his father most of the time.

Then even was the comment from Mrs. Mason's landlord, Mr. Cole, in his evidence.

"Does Oliver appear to you to be a happy well-adjusted child? From the times I have seen Oliver, which is not often, he appears to be a normal child."

And then in re-examination, Mrs. Chamberlain asked, "Do you see him as a happy child with his mother or father? I have not seen Oliver with his father, so I cannot comment on it."

Then Mrs. Mason is recorded as saying in answer to a question: "Is he not happy with Mr. Mason? Yes, with me too, he is happy with both of us."

Mrs. McDonald Senior, on the other hand, was inclined to take the view that she had never heard the little boy say that he loved his father.

Although she did make it perfectly plain that Oliver loved his mother, but later as she was asked this question: "Is Oliver very fond of his father?" I would not say he is fond of his father than he is with his mother."

Far as I find quite conclusively that he is particularly happy with his mother, also I take the view that he is equally as happy with his father.

Over the past five days, this has been a very lengthy and bitterly contested hearing with evidence exploring collateral material to the point where the genuine issues have tended to become obscure. Despite Mrs. Mason's protestations in evidence that she could not see a real need for all this evidence which was traversed, and she could not see no real need for this evidence should not be confined to the parties and the interview with the boy, whether she understands the position this case developed. It has developed into a personal attack on Mr. Mason's character, his character as allegedly an extremely violent, irrational, vindictive person, and indeed as a potential murderer. These allegations are damning indeed.

There is also reference to another side of his character when he exhibited blue movies with some regularity to neighbors, also that they had drunken parties regularly.

Mrs. Chamberlain said, "This judge is very good at pointing out detailed allegations which were the ones I was mainly concerned of she said. Now let's see how now the judge now deals with the allegations about you, also the way it also developed the personal attacks on you." She also said, "At this point, the case is looking a bit better for you as he has taken the view of what her mother and others have said."

This I found it is to Mr. Mason's credit that he declined to enter this arena in his affidavits in reply, contenting himself by saying. This he said in his second affidavit. I will now read what he had to say in paragraphs 3 and 4.

3: "I realize that regardless of who is successful in the dispute I will still see Claire and her mother, and it does not help matters, if I swear a long affidavit listing all the problems I have had with Claire and her family since Claire had left me along with the faults of Claire and her family."

4: "I believe that the allegations about me not caring for Oliver adequately when investigated by the welfare and verified by trained persons independent of the dispute such as the kindergarten staff, will be shown without foundation."

The movie business was next as the judge then turned his attention to the movies and my movie business. After listening to what the judge has said in his deliberation that he has taken a lot into account, and either way, if I lost today, then I would say at least I did get a fair hearing.

Then the judge referred to the allegations about the blue movies:

Mr. Mason denied it, and I say categorically that there was no bit of evidence to support that allegation.

Then there were the numerous allegations of assault made against him. He maintains these allegations were either concocted or exaggerated for the purpose of getting the police involved, and indeed they have become involved on many occasions. May I ask what significance I should draw from the fact that he was never prosecuted, I am not quite sure.

Then a suggestion has been made that in some way, he is pally with a local police officer, and that in some way the police are not doing their duty. Also it was claimed because he is in league with them. Well, the probabilities are to the contrary. I fully believe Mr. Mason when he says that the police have now got to the stage where they know how to treat complaints against him with due caution. Also I am satisfied that our police force would not hesitate to prosecute him if he has done the things alleged and if he was to continue to do them. I also think the police would not take too kindly to the fact that they were not doing their job and is in league with them—no evidence at all to back this up.

The movie business has been a large part of this hearing along with many allegations relating to the drunken parties. They were simply not proved. There was another aspect of the movies which was referred to that was out to discredit him. He apparently is a projectionist of some repute with a business running movies for clubs. He has a movie theater in his garage. I cannot really imagine a man providing the enjoyment and entertainment he does on Saturday afternoon for the local children as being the blaggard his wife would have made me believe.

In affidavits also within the hearing relating to Mr. Mason's movie business and the showing of movies in his home theater, the allegation was that he ran movie shows for several nights a week, that drink is available. It may be that alcohol is available. The allegation is also that there was an overconsumption of alcohol. Well, that is not true. The nub of this was to suggest that Oliver was allowed to stay up until 11:00 p.m. or late hour, the inference being, of course, that he was not getting enough sleep, and the type of conduct he was exposed to is not the sort of conduct which would be to his welfare.

Well, I simply say this, that I prefer the evidence of Mr. Baxter and Mrs. Ingram to that of John McDonald and his mother. It was not simply proven that there were movie nights several nights a week. On the other hand, when there were movies shown, Oliver was not present except on one or two occasions, and when he was not present, he was properly cared for. I accept Mrs. Chamberlain's submission that Oliver could not possibly be the well-adjusted boy Mrs. Tuohy sees every day at kindergarten if he is kept up until eleven o'clock at night most of the week.

One other aspect is on Oliver's fourth birthday and a barbecue was held, also a movie *The Sting* shown. There were conflicting evidence on this, despite many of the McDonald family not recalling such a significant event or being there. I have no doubt they were present, and Oliver was not as they say up late at night as he was well in bed by 8:00 p.m.

I do not intend to mention all the allegations made against Mr. Mason in affidavit form and in evidence in this court, that there were many matters he was not cross-examined on and merely mention one by way of example, the time he allegedly threw bricks at the co-respondent's car. This to my mind, it is without significance that several of Mrs. Mason's witnesses indulged in extensive hearsay which, to my mind, showed that they were and are anxious to believe anything that anybody has to say to the detriment of Mr. Mason. This placed these persons in my eyes in the position of advocates, meaning "one who pleads the cause of another."

In this category are Mr. James McDonald; Mr. Sanders, who is the co-respondent's former brother-in-law; Mrs. McDonald the grandmother of the little boy; and Mr. Kelly himself.

Then there is another serious issue I must now turn to that I was disturbed to learn that on the first evening of the hearing of this matter, the McDonalds had a gathering and discussed the day's evidence. Some of Mr. James

McDonald's evidence related to evidence given by witnesses when the only person in the court who could have imparted the information to him was Mrs. Mason. He volunteered comment on some of the previous day's evidence without being led upon it, and a good deal of what he had to say was hearsay in nature.

It is not difficult to find the reason for the attacks upon Mr. Mason and the vigor with which they were pressed in this court when one reads from the social welfare report.

It states this now brings me to what I find the most difficult, and one of the most crucial elements in the situation. Although Mr. Mason—as one would expect—impresses in an interview (and probably in court) setting as articulate and fair, restrained, and sensitive, and it does seem his actions in the presence of the child to what he sees as provocations by Mr. Kelly and Mrs. Mason, also members of the McDonald family believe this impression. Discrepancies in the party's versions of some upsetting incidents can hardly be resolved outside a judicial setting, but there seems on the surface, some reason to believe that, even making allowance for the provocation in a general sense experienced by Mr. Mason, he has repeatedly lost control of himself to a degree and in circumstances which raises some doubts as to whether he is, after all, the more suitable of the two parents to have continuous custody of Oliver. Certainly, Mrs. Mason is genuine when she says that physical fear of his violence has been an important influence in her failure to assert claims to Oliver's custody long before she did. I found her to be still apprehensive.

The judge then spoke more about the welfare report.

This summary by the social welfare officer seems to me to be one of the most important aspects in this case.

At this point, I think I should make the point that Mrs. Chamberlain made: if he was that terrible man that I am asked to accept that he is, then why did she not take proceedings in the Magistrates' Court either for separation order or a non-molestation order?

Then Mr. Watson said, "Danial is not a violent person, and the only time I have seen him involved in a fight was one evening he had to pull Claire's mother off Claire. This incident took place prior to Claire leaving home."

Then Mr. Baxter, who has been a boarder there since June or July of this year, was asked about this, and this is what was recorded.

Mrs. Mason in her affidavits said she is frightened of Mr. Mason's violence. "Have you seen any indication of this? No. Has she displayed any violence? Yes, she has toward Mr. Mason and me."

And I will return to that later,

Mrs. Ingram, who is a next-door neighbor, gave evidence. I say this candidly that she impressed me as being a witness of extremely high caliber. I was most impressed by her. She spoke of Mrs. Mason's arrival at Mr. Mason's home and the provocative language she used on more than one occasion, and she also spoke of Mrs. McDonald's attack on Mr. Mason. She was not cross-examined at all. The inference to be drawn from her evidence is that if anybody is provocative or violent, it is Mrs. Mason and Mrs. McDonald.

Then there was a Mrs. Egan. I think I have already mentioned her. She has known Mrs. Mason for the whole of her life, also Mr. and Mrs. McDonald Senior. She struck me as a witness of unimpeachable character. She impressed me as being completely unbiased, truthful, and reliable, and she in my view gave the lie as to who the aggressive party really is. I make no apology for reading a long extract from page 31 of the evidence. She was there on one occasion when Mrs. Mason arrived.

She said this:

"She came in, and Oliver was well in bed asleep, and she accused Danial of not keeping him warm. She seemed a little bit upset. She had a few words with Danial. She went down to the bedroom to get something, with that apparently, Oliver must have heard his mother, and he hid under the bed as he did not want to go with her. Danial then went down and got Oliver out from under the bed as he was emotionally stressed.

"Apparently, she had phoned a few times in the afternoon, and Danial did not want to talk to her. Danial came back to the lounge, and Claire put a cardigan on Oliver. Oliver was really upset, and Claire started arguing with Danial. Claire said, 'Go on, hit me, that is all you want to do all the time.' That is when me and my husband decided to leave as we had small children with us, and Claire was very distressed and shaking. I could not believe what I was witnessing as Claire was always a very good friend of mine. Oliver did not go by the way. He was so upset that Danial said, 'He is staying here,' and we left and went back home."

Mrs Egan said that Mrs. Mason's standards are extremely high.

"Yes, I have never known Claire to swear, but she certainly used swear words that night. She was always quietly spoken and reserved. Can you say whether she has changed? She used to be a friendly person. I tried to keep contact with her, but she did not seem to want to be friendly or have any contact with me anymore. She thought I was on Danial's side, but I was not."

As to the welfare officer, if he had interviewed Mr. Mason's witnesses who gave outstanding evidence in this case, it may have taken a different point of view. Again I say his report was very one-sided.

I have concluded on the whole of the evidence that while there is substance in the allegations that Mr. Mason, I have no doubt, at times lost his temper, however, the blame does not lie entirely with him. I have concluded that he has suffered provocation from Mrs. Mason and, to a lesser extent, from Mrs. McDonald. It is more obvious to me that when Mrs. Mason realized the position that she was in leaving home in the circumstances in which she did, she considered good tactics to create situations which would trigger off what I call the explosive side of Mr. Mason's nature. Then I just cannot believe that Mrs. Fiona McDonald would be prepared to help with the child's care up to within a week of this hearing if she really believed Mr. Mason was the violent potential murderer that other witnesses would have me to believe.

I also like to make this point as it is also significant that at first, Mrs. McDonald Senior was distressed by her daughter's conduct leaving home, and she was sympathetic, friendly, and extremely helpful toward Mr. Mason. As I said earlier in this judgment, I have concluded that her change in attitude is due to pressure from her daughter. As I have said, I do not accept her reason for what she considers now to be her wrongly held opinion of her daughter's conduct.

Mr. James McDonald in cross-examination was asked, "Do you know the meaning of *Blood is thicker than water*?" He replied yes.

Then he was asked, what does it mean? "I would say it means you are more inclined to stick up for your own than someone you do not know." Mrs. Chamberlain said, "Mr.

McDonald, would you not agree, the true meaning of *'Blood is thicker than water,'* that it means that someone's loyalty to their family is greater than their loyalty to anyone else?"

Mr. McDonald replied, "Yes, if you say it like that."

When the time came for Mrs. McDonald to change her attitude, in my judgment, she overreacted to the situation to the extent she exaggerated Mr. Mason's faults.

She adopted an aggressive role when called upon to come to her daughter's aid. She was prepared in evidence to label him as a liar, and any person who disagreed with her point of view, such as Mrs. Dubbeld, even though she was not present on the occasion Mrs. Dubbeld said Oliver was in bed by 8:00 p.m. The really significant and most damaging evidence concerning her is the pressure which I have found she and her husband brought to bear on Mrs. Fiona McDonald a week before this hearing, with the result that in the end, she, Mrs. Fiona McDonald, who had provided an affidavit for Mr. Mason, and she then turned against him.

Then there was the evidence of Mrs. Ingram about an incident which I will later refer to when Mrs. McDonald raised her hand to strike Mr. Mason, clearly in my judgment, adopting the role of an aggressor.

It will serve no purpose to review all the incidents referred to in this evidence. I have no doubt Mr. Mason is an aggressive person when he is challenged, and I have no doubt that he sometimes has been unnecessarily challenged by his wife. Despite his aggressive character, he is by no means the nasty individual portrayed by his wife and her witnesses.

I must say that I was impressed with the high caliber and demeanor of all those who gave evidence for Mr. Mason. I just cannot imagine these decent people having anything to do with him if his character is so bad as his wife would have me believe.

I said to my solicitor, "This judge is amazing as he has sorted out Claire and her family and the remark made, which is so true, *'Blood is thicker than water.'* Also calling them out as advocates."

The judge now stated he was going to refer to four incidents only.

*The First Incident*

"It was likened to waving a red flag to a bull."

This happened some twelve months ago. Mrs. Mason had no real reason for going to Mr. Mason at eight or nine p.m. at night. It was also more than stupid of her to take with her the co-respondent Mr. Kelly. It is very clear that Mr. Sanders, the co-respondent's former brother in-law, was invited to witness something because to use Mr. Sanders expression, "Mr. Kelly feared for his safety."

While it is impossible to condone Mr. Mason's conduct in throwing bricks at his car, I have concluded that the purpose of Mrs. Mason's visit was to provoke him so that Mr. Sanders could see it and be a witness in this court. What better provocation could there be than taking the co-respondent along. It was likened to waving a red flag to a bull.

It was only necessary to take Mr. Sanders if she wanted protection. She succeeded in provoking Mr. Mason. The co-respondent, though he did not enter the property, waited outside in the car. I am satisfied that Mr. Mason acted wrong-headedly, came out to have an argument with the co-respondent, but he drove off at high speed, and so Mr. Mason threw bricks at the car. I also agree with Mrs. Chamberlain when she said tire marks were on the pavement. This indicated to me that the co-respondent did try to run him over. It should be remembered that at this time, Mr. Mason was trying to get his wife to return.

*The Second Incident Is the New Lynn Incident*

This incident took place within a few months of Mrs. Mason leaving home. It is quite clear to me that Mr. Mason went to the flat at New Lynn to find his child, who was due back at 6:00 p.m. and was out with his grandparents. He ascertained by inquiry that they were all around Mrs. Kelly's flat he was living with Mrs. Mason. I do not accept Mr. Mason's explanation that the glass in the door broke because he knocked on the door loudly to attract attention. I have concluded that he deliberately broke the door. Then there was an altercation with Mr. McDonald and Mr. Mason, and as a result the lounge window broke. It is more probable than not that this further altercation was the result of Mr. McDonald's intervention. Mr. Mason's conduct in breaking the front door glass cannot be condoned. The

fact he knew the co-respondent was inside is a possible explanation. This was still a time when he had been trying to achieve a reconciliation with his wife, without success, and he was still bitter about her leaving home. This incident, though bad, again not so bad as the evidence suggests because Mr. and Mrs McDonald remained friendly with Mr. Mason after it. Also Mrs. Mason drove her husband to hospital to have his hand attended to, and Mr. Mason paid $100 for the damage he had done.

*The Third Incident Is the New Park Incident*

This occurred on the Sunday following the making of the decree nisi on 24th June 1976. I am satisfied that Mr. and Mrs. McDonald did not believe Mr. Mason when he told them earlier in the day that he had been awarded interim of the child.

At that conclusion of the football match, Mr. Mason wanted to take Oliver home. Mr. and Mrs McDonald wanted to take him to see his great-grandmother and to have him for the night. I have concluded that Mr. Mason regarded the attitude of Mr. and Mrs. McDonald as being defiant of his right to interim custody, which he had been granted. The truth emerged from the cross-examination of Mrs. Fiona McDonald where she agreed that Mr. McDonald called Mr. Mason "the rottenest so-and-so," whatever that might mean.

She also agreed that Mr. Mason had said to Mr. McDonald, "The trouble with you is you cannot accept the truth." In making that statement, he was referring to what he had told them that morning, that he got custody, and they did not and would not believe him and did in fact and in law have custody. If there was physical contact between Mr. McDonald and Mr. Mason, in my judgment, it was provoked. As far as Mrs. McDonald is concerned, there was no need for her to have followed Mr. Mason to his car and knocked on the window and screamed at him. The whole incident was as much to the detriment of Mr. and Mrs. McDonald as it is to Mr. Mason.

### The Fourth Incident Is One That Occurred Two Weeks Ago

It involved a Mr. Baxter, the boarder that I have referred to. Having seen and heard the relevant witnesses, I prefer the evidence of Mr. Baxter and Mrs. Ingram. The incident in Mr. Mason's house was, in my judgment, provoked by Mrs. Mason. She became hysterical, and I am satisfied that she took to Mr. Baxter. I have no doubt she received an injured lip, but that was due to her aggression. I am also satisfied Mrs. McDonald Senior went down for a fight. She had no need to go when she did. She had telephoned the police, and she should have waited their arrival. As I have said, Mrs. Ingram was a particularly impressive witness. She was not cross- examined. I accept her evidence that it was Mrs. McDonald who attacked Mr. Mason, and not the reverse.

In my judgment, the whole incident has been magnified out of all proportion, and I am satisfied that Mr. Mason and Mr. Baxter did nothing that was not justified. It is not without significance that this incident occurred so soon before this hearing. While there as some aspects of Mr. Mason's conduct which I have been very critical of, I am satisfied that he is not the violent, irrational, vindictive person, potential murderer, that is painted by his wife and her witnesses. The onus of proof of these serious allegations is upon her as she has failed to discharge it.

On the other hand, I have already said that I am satisfied that he is aggressive when roused. I am satisfied that there have been deliberate attempts to arouse him and to provoke him so that Mrs. Mason's case could be better advanced in court. It should not be overlooked that Mr. Mason has been under considerable pressure for over two years. Before she left, he was holding down two jobs, which kept him working day and night. He just had provided a new home with a mortgage to pay. The suggestion the movie business was not profitable, and in evidence, I agree with Mrs. Chamberlain that it has also contributed to many items for the new home.

I am not degenerating the services given by Mrs. Mason. She worked hard too, she provided money too. Probably this was the downfall of the marriage. Regrettably, young people today find themselves in a situation where they have to work hard to keep up certain standards, and this must be destructive in the end of marriage. However, looking at it from Mr. Mason's point of view, while he was busily engaged in his daily occupation, what was his wife doing? She was associating herself with Mr. Kelly.

She walked out on her husband for Mr. Kelly, then for some considerable time, and I would say up to October of last year, Mr. Mason tried unsuccessfully to the get her to return. With these pressures on him, he also had the obligation to look after his child. If he had got aggressive tendencies, the pressures he has under would assist. In my opinion, when this litigation is complete, Mrs. McDonald will find Mr. Mason to be the person she described in one of her affidavits to this effect: "Sometimes he can be the nicest of persons." I am also satisfied that when this litigation has been completed, Mr. and Mrs. Mason will take a more reasonable attitude to each other.

I am satisfied that Mr. Mason genuinely wants his son to have liberal access to his mother, to his grandparents, and to his aunt and uncle and his other relatives. I am also satisfied that with this rising tension of this litigation, there have been issues over the access, these giving rise to incidents which I believe will not occur after the heat generated by this litigation is removed.

# 37

# THE CONCLUSION

The judge was now going to deliver his final verdict.

I said to Ms. Chamberlain, "I just hope for mine and Oliver's sake, he grants me full custody." I was all alone in the courtroom beside my barrister when the clerk of courts allowed Claire's mother, Craig Kelly, along with others to hear the judgment.

The judge then entered the courtroom and proceeded with his final verdict.

He stated, "Regarding custody, I have concluded that each party is a satisfactory parent in every way. On the debit side, while Mr. Mason has exhibited aggressive tendencies, so also has Mrs. Mason. She has also been given to hysterical outbursts, which are unsatisfactory as to Mr. Mason's aggression.

"I have concluded that custody remains with Mr. Mason, who has had custody for seventeen months. On the other hand, Mr. Kelly contemplates purchasing a new home. Just when that takes place will depend upon when he can adjust matters with his former wife.

"If custody now given to Mrs. Mason, there would be a change now in Oliver's present home to the unit where Mrs. Mason is now living, and in a few months or longer, a further change to their permanent home wherever that may be.

"Oliver's friends—and there are several—live in and around the neighborhood where they currently live. If he goes with Mrs. Mason and Mr. Kelly, he will have to find new friends in Panmure, where they are currently living.

"If Oliver stays in Mangere, his kindergarten friends will join him in his new school next year, whereas the contrary will be the case if he shifts to Pakuranga. He will also be closer to his grandparents and his aunt and uncle, who have been an important part of his life up until now.

"Furthermore, little evidence has been given about Mr. Kelly's background, what he likes, what his hopes are, what his upbringing has been, what his professional training has been. His somewhat unknown quality is put forward as the person who, no matter what happens, would ultimately replace Mr. Mason as the father figure if custody were given to Mrs. Mason.

"Finally, it was Mrs. Mason who broke up the family unit, and she must take the consequences of that, and having regard to all the facts, I have concluded that the welfare of the child will be better advanced if he remains with his father.

"Access to his mother and other relatives should be very liberal. I would prefer counsel, after consultation with the parties, to tell me if agreement can be reached on access. I would suggest a full weekend twice a month for Mrs. Mason, plus half of all school holidays, plus the odd day. I suggest some intermediaries be nominated to receive the child for access purposes, thereby eliminating any cause of friction between Mr. and Mrs. Mason.

"I leave this to the parties to try and arrange such person. It would seem perhaps that Mrs. Fiona McDonald might be suitable. Alternatively, the suggestion has been put to me by the Presbyterian Welfare Service may well be able to find a person to do this.

"At this stage I make and order for custody in favor of Mr. Mason with very liberal access to Mrs. Mason.

"I am prepared to define the terms of access if required.

"In conclusion, I issue this warning, that custody and access orders are never permanent. If either party in the future resorts to conduct of the type that I have listened to, which involves this little boy in conflicts between his parents, that party, or if it is both, will incur the risk of reversal of the orders made or denial of access. Access is the right of the child, not the right of the parent. Custody can be taken from both parents if the circumstances warrant it."

I turned to my barrister, Ms. Chamberlain. "Oh my god, we have won this case!"

Then there was an uproar by Claire Mason and her party, and they screamed out in protest. Claire Mason burst out crying and was hysterical, then ran out of the courtroom.

The final outcome was a very emotional time, and I can understand Clair's emotional state as when I was leaving the court after the final judgment was delivered, there were Claire's family and her friends gathered outside. They created an awkward scene and called me a lot of rotten names and telling me that Oliver does not deserve me. Claire was in tears and very distressed, and I could imagine the same if I had lost the court case.

Claire had herself to blame along with her family and Craig as they concocted stories, told untruths, and fabricated evidence to suit themselves. It was the way they went about things that lost the case for Claire.

When I walked past them, I felt all alone as I had no one there to greet me, and the emotion of the occasion really got to me. I thought of my family back in Australia, and I wished they were here to support me. I did not ever discuss with them to this day what I went through. I did tell them the outcome of the case, that I been awarded custody of Oliver.

I went to Greg and Addison Doherty's place, where I had Oliver staying there all week while the custody case was on. I arrived and told them the good news. I unashamedly broke down and cried as the whole week was so stressful, and I was exhausted.

Oliver asked, "Why are you crying, Daddy?"

I said, "I am happy you are allowed to stay with me, but you can still see Mummy, okay?"

He gave me a big hug and kiss, and it was all well worth it. This little fellow, I am sure, knew what was going on. He has been put through so much, and I just hope and pray now things will settle down.

Was this the end of the matter? Time will tell, but knowing what Claire and her family feel, I somehow do not think so.

The Single Mother's Pension, as part of the custody ruling, I was committed to stay at home with Oliver until he starts school the following year. The company I worked for gave me three months unpaid leave, and I had holiday money that was due, so the following Monday morning, I went to the Department of Social Welfare in South Auckland to apply for what was then the Single Mother's Pension, which I was entitled to. On arriving there, the head of DSW was the one who did the report, and I was not impressed with some of the comments he made as I told him that he was wrong in his report as he interviewed all Claire's side and did not bother to interview any of my people who had made sworn statements, and the delays in his report did not help my cause.

In that he did congratulate me and said, "In hindsight, yes, I should have interviewed these people, but what you have done has made a difference to the law obtaining a child under five. This is to your credit."

I applied for the Single Mother's Pension and later found this was changed to Single Parent's Pension because of the judge overturning the law as to a mother having custody with a child under five created a precedent, and the law was changed.

*The Access Arrangement*

An agreement was reached as to access matters relating to Oliver Kevin Mason.

1.  The question of custody remains with the father, Danial Kenneth Mason.

2. Mrs. Mason agrees to Mr. Mason taking Oliver to Australia for three weeks commencing 20th December 1976 and returning around 14th January 1976.

3. Mr. Mason agrees to have access as follows.

   (a) Alternative weekends from 9:00 a.m. Saturday and returning 6:00 p.m. Sunday

   (b) Each Wednesday from 5:00 p.m. to 7:30 p.m.

This agreement was signed by both myself and Claire.

*This Was an End to a Legal Battle over One Small Boy, Oliver*

The judge made a precedent by awarding custody to the father, and the law was changed to allow fathers to have custody of the children under five. The Social Welfare System was changed

from a Single Mother's Pension to Single Parents' Pension. This case is now in the *New Zealand Law Journal*, where future custody can be reviewed.

Oliver and I went to Australia and spent Christmas and New Year with my family in Australia and returned to New Zealand in 1967. In February, Oliver started school. I then returned to my work at Crest Foods.

The court case, I believe, took its toll on Mrs. Chamberlain, despite winning a historical case. She gave up her practice shortly after the court case was finalized.

Was this the end of the custody? Is blood thicker than water? Time will tell going by what took place since the court case leaves this open-ended.

Did she appeal, or was Danial left to look after his son? Claire married Craig Kelly after the court hearing.

## The End

# ABOUT THE AUTHOR

Danial Mason was the second youngest of 13 Children, the loss of his father at an early age and the impact it had on his mother and his 9 brothers and three sisters

His upbringing by his mother and the close ties with the Baptist church set the foundation in his later life and the respect of all people despite colour, race or religion.

His early life growing up was tough going and coming from a relatively poor family he became a successful in business management and marketing, he worked for International Companies, in various countries outside of Australia.

After New Zealand he operated his own business for many years back in Australia He remarried in the later 80's and remain to this day.

The Book Custody – Danial spent several years putting it together and the purpose was to outline the trauma of divorce and custody matters and importantly the plight that fathers have  to go through to gain custody or access of their children. The effects it has on the children is also significant. Men are portrayed as the villains and the abuser in most domestic disputes and even pays a large part in divorce and custody matters.

It is hoped that Fathers who do the right thing fight for their rights to have access or custody of their children.

Danial. Kenneth. Mason

9 781958 381571